Thy Children's Children

A NOVEL

Based on the True Story of Five Generations
Of a New England Grassroots Dynasty

Diana Ross McCain

ISBN-13: 978-1523837007
ISBN-10: 1523837004

CreateSpace Independent Publishing Platform

Cover:
   Lyman orchard photograph by Jack A. McCain, Jr.
   Portraits of William Lyman and Alma Lyman used with the
      permission of The Lyman Farm, Inc.

Author's Note

Thy Children's Children is a work of fiction. It is based on research into five generations and one hundred and thirty years of history of the Lyman family of Middlefield, Connecticut. Some characters who appear in these pages were real people, and some events depicted here actually occurred. Others are entirely my own inventions.

I've been guided, as much as is practicable when writing a novel, by the surviving historical record. But ultimately the book is a product of my personal interpretation and re-creation of personalities and events, and of my imagination.

Diana Ross McCain
Durham, Connecticut
April, 2016

For Chloe Grace McCain

"Thou shalt see thy children's children."

Psalm 128

Chapter One

July, 1738
Middletown
Colony of Connecticut

"*I forbid it!*"

The Widow Hope Hawley addressed the young couple in a tone as hard as granite. Then she focused her fierce glare on the nineteen-year-old daughter who shared her name. "And *you* are a wicked, ungrateful child to defy me so!"

The younger Hope Hawley stared back, upset but undaunted, for mother and daughter possessed the same iron will. The older woman had drawn on the indomitable spirit they shared to sustain her when her husband Jehiel drowned in the Great River at Middletown in 1727, leaving her, just thirty-two, a widow with three children. It had given her the strength to resist pressure to remarry, as most widows did at the earliest respectable opportunity. A new husband would be undisputed master of the Hawley family, would take ownership of the Widow Hawley's house and farm – to sell, lease, or give away, without so much as telling her.

The appearance of Hope and John Lyman around the side of her unpainted clapboard house on this summer morning had taken the Widow Hawley by surprise. She studied them with narrowed eyes as they picked their way to where she stood in the kitchen garden of flowers and herbs.

At slightly over six feet, John Lyman stood a head taller than either Hawley woman. He was lean but not lanky. Years of working on his family's farm in Durham, the town immediately south of Middletown, had given him a well-muscled physique.

John was two years older than Hope. His clear, dark-brown eyes were set too close to the prominent Lyman nose for him to be considered handsome. But they shone with a warmth and openness that made his long face appealing. His chestnut hair was tied back in a plain queue. He wore close-fitting leather breeches, a white linen shirt with long, full sleeves, and a buttoned-up waistcoat, open frock coat, and hat, all of brown wool.

John was shortening his stride to keep from outpacing Hope, who trembled with suppressed anticipation. Hope had bright hazel eyes, flawless skin, and a pert nose set in a heart-shaped face. Her abundance of wavy light brown hair was mostly covered by a white cotton cap. She wore a full-length petticoat, and a blue-and-white striped short gown, both of linen. A wide blue kerchief draped around her shoulders and tied in front over the gown's low scoop neck modestly covered the swell of her breasts.

As they approached the Widow Hawley, Hope could tell her mother had perceived their purpose. The older woman offered no word of greeting when John and Hope reached her, but simply studied them in stony silence. She knew she was a formidable presence, and used that fact to her advantage.

John respectfully removed his hat. He blinked as his eyes adjusted to the bright sunlight. His manner was respectful, yet, Hope was proud to see, he showed no sign of being overawed by her mother.

They stood there awkwardly, surrounded by the sights, sounds, and smells of a Connecticut farm in mid-summer. Chickens clucked and scratched in the barnyard, milk cows lowed in the pasture, the stench of manure contested with the fragrance of the flowers, in the distance a churn pounded steadily, turning cream into butter.

At last John spoke. "Mistress Hawley, I ask your permission to court Hope." Hope's cheeks, already flushed by the July heat, turned even redder.

John didn't wait for a reply, but continued with the speech he'd carefully rehearsed. "I reached my majority of twenty-one three months ago. I've been admitted as a freeman in Durham. My family is well-regarded. My father was elected to represent Durham at the General Assembly."

John paused to give the Widow Hawley a chance to respond. She deliberately waited just long enough for John and Hope to feel the first faint twinges of uncertainty before replying.

"Hope's great-grandfather was a graduate of Harvard, and the first minister of Middletown more than four score years ago," the Widow Hawley said matter-of-factly. She paused a beat before adding pointedly, "That was a full fifty years before your Lymans set foot in Connecticut."

John and Hope had expected her mother to counter with these facts. It couldn't be disputed that the Lymans boasted no such illustrious ancestor as the Reverend Samuel Stow. And they were undeniably relative newcomers; John's father had moved from Massachusetts to Durham when John was a baby. But the Widow Hawley had made her points with a cutting condescension that increased the young people's uneasiness.

John glanced down and fidgeted with his hat, sliding the brim through his fingers. Abruptly he stopped, but kept his head bowed thoughtfully.

Hope could tell what was going through John's mind. His hat had been hand-crafted by Jehiel Hawley, making it silent yet solid evidence that Hope's own father had started life as a simple tradesman. Heartened by the thought, John raised his head to look the Widow Hawley square in the eye. He forged ahead with the case he'd prepared.

"As one of only two sons, I can expect to receive a share of my father's property," John said. "That land will serve as a foundation for my own farm."

The Widow Hawley arched a skeptical eyebrow. She knew John still lived under his father Ebenezer's roof and worked on Ebenezer's sixty acres.

"Your father is a hearty man not yet sixty," the Widow Hawley countered. "God willing it will be many years before you come into any portion of his estate. Whatever you do inherit will likely not be enough to support a family."

She paused for a heartbeat, then delivered her next words as if striking an anvil with a hammer. "When my grandfather the Reverend Samuel Stow died at the great age of eighty-two, he bequeathed me more than two hundred and fifty acres in Middletown."

To Hope's relief, her mother's revelation of just how great a financial gap separated their families failed to make a dent in John's determination. He responded with the argument he and Hope agreed represented their best chance of gaining the Widow Hawley's approval of their courtship.

"Residing as my wife in Durham, Hope – and our children – will never be far from you."

The Widow Hawley quickly looked down, but not before Hope saw a melancholy yearning flicker in her eyes at John's words. Her eldest daughter, Mary, lived with her husband in the town of Windsor thirty miles from Middletown. In good weather it was a two-day journey, including a crossing by ferry of the Great River. Hope's mother had been deeply disappointed when she couldn't attend the birth of Mary's first child – her first grandchild – because snow-clogged roads made the trip to Windsor impossible in December.

The Widow Hawley kept her head bowed. After what seemed like an eternity to Hope and John, she raised her head – and Hope's heart sank.

The flinty resolve on her mother's face told Hope she'd made her decision – and that she'd based it solely on the practical factors raised in her exchange with John: wealth, piety, education, longevity, public service, ecclesiastical office, and "dignity of descent" – the quality and accomplishments of a person and his forebears. These determined an individual's standing in a New England town. By this measure, John Lyman's status was indisputably inferior to Hope's. The Widow Hawley knew it, Hope knew it, and John knew it.

The Widow Hawley looked John straight in the eye as she delivered her verdict. "Hope must look to wed a man of background and fortune equal to her own," she said firmly. "You do not have my permission to court her."

"But I love her!" John exclaimed. It wasn't a plea, or an argument, but a simple fact that to him counted more than everything else combined.

"And I love John!" Hope echoed desperately.

There followed an uncomfortable silence. Honey bees buzzed industriously among spiky scarlet bergamot blossoms, their beating wings producing a high-pitched thrum that heightened the aura of tension to an almost unbearable level.

The Widow Hawley at last spoke, addressing herself only to John. "You have my answer," she said with finality.

"*No*, Mama!" Hope blurted out, her eyes ablaze. She surprised herself by actually taking an aggressive step toward her mother. "You *must* give your consent! You *will!*"

The Widow Hawley froze, as stunned as if her daughter had slapped her across the face. Hope had always been willful, but never disrespectfully defiant. It was this shocking challenge that had caused her temper to snap, had goaded her into calling her daughter wicked and ungrateful.

Her mother's cruel, unfair charge hurt Hope deeply, but she didn't flinch. She opened her mouth to make a sharp retort, but stopped when John touched her lightly on the elbow.

Hope looked up and saw in John's eyes reassurance that this was merely a setback, that they would find a way to gain her mother's approval. Trusting in his judgment, she closed her lips against the protest she'd been about to make.

That subtle, intimate exchange disturbed the Widow Hawley as much as Hope's outburst. She returned her piercing gaze to John. "You should leave now," she said coldly. She signaled the end of the discussion by turning away and striding down the garden path toward the barn. Hope Stow Hawley might be a homespun-clad widow managing a family farm on the fringe of the British Empire, but she bore herself with the pride and dignity of an elegantly gowned duchess in a London palace.

John took Hope's hands in his. "Don't lose heart," he said encouragingly. She gave him a brave smile in return.

At that moment the Widow Hawley reached the garden's edge. She glanced back to see the two young people looking lovingly into each other's eyes. "Don't forget, John," she called out menacingly, "a man can go to prison for drawing away a maid's affections without her parent's permission."

Startled, Hope and John turned their heads sharply toward her mother. The Widow Hawley stared at them until John at last walked around to the front of the house. He mounted his horse and rode off.

Hope watched until John was out of sight. Then she began running toward the rear of the house, desperate to reach it before the tears brimming in her eyes spilled over.

Hope yanked the plank door open by its iron latch. She stepped over the threshold of the lean-to kitchen, then pulled the door shut behind her. She swiped the tears from her cheeks, then leaned back and closed her eyes, struggling to gain control of her roiling emotions.

As Hope's breathing slowed, and the rush of her pounding pulse faded in her ears, she heard a faint clicking. Opening her eyes, she spied her sister Mary, eight years her elder, seated on a stool by a window that looked out onto the garden. The sash was raised to let in fresh air and sunlight by which Mary was deftly manipulating four steel needles to knit a stocking out of brown wool yarn.

Mary had arrived three days earlier to visit, bringing her eighteen-month-old daughter, still the Widow Hawley's only grandchild. The toddler was napping in a cradle in the hall, as the room in which most of the family's everyday living took place was called.

Hope hurried over and planted herself in front of Mary. "Mama won't allow John Lyman to court me!" she declared indignantly.

Mary hadn't been blessed with her younger sister's head-turning good looks – but she also hadn't been cursed with Hope's high-strung temperament. "So I heard," she said wryly, tilting her head toward the open window while keeping her eyes on her needlework. Hope realized that even if Mary hadn't heard all the conversation in the garden, she couldn't have missed their mother's final, heated words.

"She says John isn't a fit match for me!" Hope went on, waiting impatiently for Mary to look at her. When Mary finally did, she continued knitting, as if her hands had a mind of their own.

"Papa was a common hat maker with little to his name when he came to Middletown," Hope continued, stoking her own anger. "And Mama was an heiress who would come into a handsome inheritance upon her marriage. But no one scrupled over Papa's family or fortune being inferior to hers. Certainly Mama didn't! They wed when she was barely fourteen years old to his twenty-three!" She paused, overwhelmed by her mother's hypocrisy and unfairness.

"Maybe that's why Mama refused John's request," Mary said with a somber thoughtfulness

"What do you mean?" Hope demanded in surprise.

"When Mama and Papa wed, everything Mama owned, including the land she inherited, became Papa's to do with as he pleased," Mary began.

"Of course it did," Hope interrupted impatiently.

Mary let her sister's rudeness pass without comment. "You were too young to notice such things," she continued after a moment, "but I doubt Papa ever once talked to Mama when he did something with the land she brought to their marriage – except to show her where to make her mark on a document. I think it pained a woman as clever and proud as Mama to be ignored so."

Mary dropped her knitting into her lap. She clasped her hands together in front of her before continuing slowly, as if reluctantly sharing a sorrowful secret. "I think Mama may have come to wonder if Papa wed her more for her marriage portion than for her person."

Hope frowned as she pondered this new, unsettling perspective on their mother. She tried to envision the Widow Hawley as resentful at being ignored, uncertain about her husband's affection. But Hope couldn't imagine her mother as anything other than the confident, capable woman she'd been since their father's death when Hope was just eight.

"Do you think that's why she hasn't remarried?" Hope asked.

Mary shrugged, picking up the knitting and resuming work. "Mama adored Papa – of that I'm sure. Whether she's never found a man to rival Papa's place in her heart, or is unwilling to again subject herself to a husband's control, only she knows. She hasn't needed to remarry, for she's managed the farm as well as any man."

Hope considered Mary's observation for a long moment. Was it possible that her mother wasn't cruelly thwarting her wishes, but trying, even if misguidedly, to protect her? At last Hope shook her head. "Whatever passed between Mama and Papa, it's no reason to deny me a chance at happiness with John," she said resolutely. "I fear Mama will never see that," she added on a note of despair.

Mary nodded in agreement. After a long pause, she said with studied casualness, "There is a way to secure Mama's consent for you and John to marry."

After a moment of puzzlement, Hope's eyes grew wide as she grasped her sister's meaning. "You mean–," Hope dropped her voice to a whisper, "get myself with child?"

Mary glanced up to meet her sister's eyes with a cool, knowing stare, then looked back down at her needlework.

"But – fornication is a sin!" Hope hissed. "You know how zealously Mr. Chauncey ferrets it out. When Abigail and Nathaniel Griswold's baby came five months after they wed, he wouldn't baptize it until they confessed to fornication before the entire congregation! At least they weren't fined or whipped as the law allows," she said with a shudder.

Hope's mind reeled at the other perils of such a gamble. If she got with child, some evil might befall John before they could wed. Another risk – that John might *refuse* to marry her – couldn't be ignored.

"Why should John and I have to pay a price of sin and shame to wed?" Hope demanded indignantly. "If I did this, I would be as wicked as Mama said," she added unhappily. "But it doesn't matter," she went on dejectedly. "John would never do something so sinful and dishonorable."

Mary glanced up to cast her sister a look of blatant skepticism. Hope had little awareness of the power of her good looks. Any man she couldn't entice into lying with her would have to be a saint – which John Lyman, as good a man as he might be, most definitely was not.

Chapter Two

May, 1740
Durham
Colony of Connecticut

Hope woke with a start. Lying on her back beside her sleeping husband, she assumed she'd been awakened by a clap of thunder from the storm that had begun battering the countryside the previous evening. But then the baby stirred in her womb. Maybe, she thought contentedly, the child's vigorous movement had awakened her.

Hope snuggled down into the feather bed that had been part of her marriage portion. She pulled the linen sheet up over her shoulders, and tried to go back to sleep.

For a full year after rejecting John Lyman as a suitor for Hope, the Widow Hawley had proposed for her daughter's consideration a succession of men she counted as worthy candidates for marriage. Hope had adamantly rebuffed them all. Her mother might be able to stop her from marrying John, but she couldn't force her to wed another man.

Hope had finally convinced her mother that she sincerely preferred sterile spinsterhood to marrying anyone but John Lyman. John had proven himself steadfastly devoted to Hope, refusing to look elsewhere for a wife. And the birth of Mary's second child in distant Windsor made the idea of Hope marrying close to home even more appealing to their mother.

The Widow Hawley at last conceded defeat in the battle of wills. Hope and John had wed on September 13, 1739. Her mother provided a marriage portion of cash, household goods, and land.

Hope conceived John's child within days of their wedding. She considered it God's blessing for resisting the temptation to force her mother's hand through sin.

The baby would be born around the end of June, in the five-room clapboard house that John's father, Ebenezer Lyman, built when he came to Durham two decades earlier. Hope and John had lived here with his parents and two sisters since their marriage.

Hope was almost asleep when she was jerked awake by a sudden uncomfortable squeezing around her lower abdomen. The pain lasted several moments before receding.

Frightened, Hope rolled awkwardly onto her side. She shook John's shoulder, calling his name softly. He turned onto his back, half awake.

"What is it?" he asked drowsily.

"I just had a pain in my belly. I'm afraid it may be the babe. Would you fetch your mother?"

John's eyes flew open, as if someone had dowsed him with icy water. He threw back the sheet, sat up, and swung his bare feet onto the wooden floorboards. A faint brightening in the eastern sky filtered through the small leaded-glass panes of the casement windows.

John retrieved his leather breeches from a peg on the wall, and pulled them on. Into them he stuffed the long shirt of coarse cloth in which he slept.

As John finished buttoning his breeches, his dark brown eyes met Hope's hazel ones in a look of shared concern. He started down the stairs to the parlor, the best room in the house, where his parents slept.

"I think your travail has begun," Experience Lyman told Hope after making a quick examination of her daughter-in-law. Experience's reassuring smile concealed her concern over the fact that the baby wasn't due for nearly another two months. A stout, graying woman of fifty-five, Experience had herself borne eight children, and been present at the births of dozens more.

"You'd best fetch the midwife," Experience called to John, who was hovering outside the chamber. He opened the door a crack.

"And my mother, too – please!" Hope's plea was cut short by another labor pain.

John pulled the door closed, and turned to find his father on the landing. Ebenezer Lyman placed a restraining hand on John's arm.

"It's the Sabbath," said Ebenezer. A powerfully built man, he stood nearly eye-to-eye with his son. "Fetching the midwife is a necessary task, and thus no breach of the law against travel on the Lord's day. But some might not consider riding to Middletown to bring back the Widow Hawley in the same light."

"Hope wants her mother," John answered simply, sitting down on the step to pull on his stockings and boots. Ebenezer made no further protest as John stood, pulled on a waistcoat, put on his hat, and clattered down the steep, angled stairway.

The older man shook his grizzled head ruefully. Where Hope was concerned, little could sway John. Ebenezer only hoped his son didn't encounter a constable with no sympathy for a young husband's concern for his laboring wife's peace of mind.

John returned with the midwife in less than an hour. He waited anxiously outside the chamber door until the woman confirmed that Hope's travail had begun. Then he hurried out the kitchen door, and again threw himself on his horse. He headed north to Middletown along the rutted dirt road that the previous day's storm had turned into a quagmire.

The drumbeat summoning worshipers to the Durham meetinghouse had begun by the time John returned with the Widow Hawley. She went directly upstairs to be with Hope.

"You need to get ready to go to meeting," John's mother told him. Connecticut law, based on the Congregational faith, required attendance at Sunday worship services, in obedience to God's commandment to "Remember the Sabbath day, to keep it holy."

John glanced up toward the chamber where Hope lay. His face was clouded with uncertainty.

"The first ones are always slow in coming," Experience added in a reassuring tone. "And it's not as if you can stay in the room with her. Be sure to explain our absence to Mr. Chauncey," she said with a gentle pat on his shoulder.

Reluctantly, John got ready for the services. He washed his face and hands, then stripped off his muddy breeches and soiled waistcoat and shirt. He donned clothes his mother had retrieved for him from a chest in the chamber where Hope lay: white linen breeches and a white linen shirt with ruffles at the wrist. He slipped on a pale blue linen waistcoat, and then a longer matching coat.

"John, we'll be late!" Ebenezer called from outside. John put on a hat, and went out to meet his father, who was waiting impatiently with John's two unmarried sisters, Mindwell, twenty-five, and Hannah, sixteen.

The four Lymans picked their way carefully among the puddles as they walked the mile along the dirt main street to the Durham meetinghouse. Other families emerged from their houses to join the procession to worship.

They crossed a narrow plank bridge spanning the ravine through which flowed Allyn Brook. The previous day's rains had swollen the usually placid stream into a rushing torrent that cascaded over a grist mill dam.

Finally the Lymans rounded the corner of the rectangular, clapboard meetinghouse erected two years earlier on the town green. They hurried inside just as the Reverend Nathaniel Chauncey, Durham's pastor for more than thirty years, emerged from his house across the road.

John fretted about Hope throughout the morning service, catching little of the sermon. He was relieved when the mid-day break came. During that time worshipers could eat, reflect on the minister's preaching, and mingle with fellow parishioners.

John choked down a few bites of bread. He strayed away from the small clusters of people on the green, preoccupied by his worry for Hope.

"Cousin!" A voice called out from behind John. He turned to see a man his own age striding toward him, a broad grin on his face.

John blinked in disbelief. "Phineas?" he said uncertainly. Doubt gave way to delight as the other man greeted John with a hearty hug.

Phineas Lyman was John's first cousin, the son of Ebenezer's brother Noah, who had died when Phineas was barely ten years old. Ebenezer had taken his brother's son under his wing, arranging Phineas's apprenticeship to a weaver.

However, Phineas had too keen a mind and too much ambition to spend his life at a loom. He'd graduated from Yale College in New Haven two years ago. His superior academic record had earned him a scholarship for additional study at Yale, after which the school had hired him for his current position as a tutor.

"What are you doing here?" John asked, pleased but perplexed. He hadn't laid eyes on his cousin in nearly two years. With sandy hair and bright blue eyes, Phineas favored his mother's people, rather than the tall, dark Lymans. Years immersed in books hadn't diminished his crackling aura of barely contained energy.

"I'm on my way to Northampton," Phineas explained. "I decided to stop in Durham to visit my mother and my brothers – and you!"

Phineas's open affection warmed John's heart. Only two years apart in age, as boys they'd been like peas in a pod, each closer to the other than to his own brother. Together they'd listened in rapt fascination to their Lyman grandparents' blood-chilling stories of surviving a brutal Indian raid on Northampton, Massachusetts, in 1675. The cousins, using tree branches in place of swords and muskets, had spent hours pretending to be the brave defenders repulsing the savages and saving the town.

"I plan to study law," Phineas went on.

John was even more puzzled. Most Yale graduates became ministers. The law was an alternative career, but John couldn't recall Phineas ever expressing an interest in it. And Northampton was at least seventy miles north of Durham.

"Why so far?" John asked. "Can't you find a lawyer in Connecticut willing to take you as an apprentice?" he teased.

To John's surprise, Phineas blushed. "One of my students from Northampton has a sister whose acquaintance I made when she visited him at college," he said with a shy smile. "I've grown very fond of her. She's related by marriage to Jonathan Edwards, the minister who led the great revivals in Massachusetts a few years past. I hope being in Northampton will allow me to advance my friendship with her."

John studied his cousin with bemused admiration. Phineas had always set his goals high, then worked with fierce determination to achieve them. It made sense he would pursue a similar course in romance.

John had never had Phineas's driving ambition. He knew some in Durham were jealous of Phineas for rising so much higher than a fatherless weaver's apprentice had a right to expect. But John was genuinely pleased for his cousin, who had labored hard for everything he had, yet never lorded his achievements over others.

"Speaking of the fair ones, my mother tells me you're to be a father!" Phineas said. He was dismayed to see the light fade from John's eyes. Before Phineas could inquire further, a matronly woman approached them.

"Where are your wife and mother, John?" asked Elizabeth Lyman, Phineas's mother

"Hope's travail began around dawn, Aunt," John replied worriedly. Clearly, Phineas realized, this wasn't a good development.

Elizabeth flashed a sympathetic smile. "As soon as afternoon meeting is over, I'll join them, and bring some other women as well."

"That would be a great kindness," John said gratefully. Turning to Phineas, he summoned up a smile. "God's blessings on your journey," he said. "Let me know how you fare." Phineas nodded, and the cousins exchanged a firm handshake.

Phineas and his mother turned to walk back to the meetinghouse. As he started to follow them, John glimpsed a sly, knowing glance flash between two women who'd overheard their conversation. A moment's reflection made him flush with anger. He turned away abruptly, almost colliding with his sister Mindwell, whom he hadn't heard coming up behind him.

"What is it, John?" Mindwell asked in alarm.

John jerked his head toward the two eavesdroppers strolling toward the meetinghouse. "Mistress Parmalee and Mistress Fairchild heard me tell Aunt Elizabeth that Hope's travail had begun. I know what they're thinking, with the baby coming not even eight months after our wedding. But it's not true!"

Mindwell's heart ached at how the evil suspicions of local gossips wounded John. "Pay them no mind," she advised compassionately. "Those busybodies always think the worst."

"And they'll tell it to anyone who'll listen," John replied bitterly. He and Mindwell joined the stream of worshipers returning to the meetinghouse for the afternoon's services.

John paced the length of the hall as he had for three hours since returning home. The law prohibited any labor or leisure activities on the Sabbath, which lasted until sunset. As a result he couldn't try to distract himself by working in the fields, or even taking a walk. As he strode back and forth, he silently beseeched the Lord to make Hope the living mother of a living child.

Every so often, above the murmur of female voices in the chamber overhead, John could distinguish a grunt of pain, a groan of exertion, or a gasp of fatigue from Hope. The sounds grew more frequent as dusk began to fall.

When any of the dozen women who'd come to attend Hope bustled downstairs to fetch something, she'd answer John's anxious inquiries with a compassionate smile tinged with condescension, assuring him Hope's travail was progressing normally. It was the truth – so far as it went.

Upstairs Hope was seated in a chair. She'd been laboring for twelve hours. On either side knelt her mother and mother-in-law, keeping up a stream of comforting, encouraging words.

"Squeeze my hand!" the Widow Hawley commanded as her daughter's face and body contorted with the beginning of another contraction. Hope obeyed, gripping her mother's fingers so hard the tips turned bright red. To Hope it seemed her body had assumed a will of its own; all she could do was try to hold on while it carried out the process of birth.

"You're doing good," the Widow Hawley said soothingly as the contraction ebbed and Hope's body relaxed. Experience Lyman held up a cup of wine for Hope to drink to maintain her strength. But Hope took only a small sip before she gasped with the beginning of another contraction.

"When the pains come like this, one upon another, your work is almost finished," the midwife said brightly.

Hope barely heard the words. She was only dimly aware of what was being said and done around her, her mind totally occupied by her body's struggle. Then the midwife's sharp command to "Bear down hard!" got through to her. She tried, but her strength was running low. She fell back panting, shaking her head in defeat.

The midwife squatted in front of the chair. She reached under Hope's shift and applied butter to lubricate the birth canal. She'd barely finished before Hope's body started another contraction.

All the women in the chamber urged Hope on in her efforts. Each had once had been in her place, on that crest of pounding waves of pain and exertion that preceded the final stage of birth.

Hope managed to draw strength from their relentless encouragement. After several powerful pushes, the baby slithered into the world.

"John!"

His mother-in-law's urgent summons brought John racing to the foot of the stairs. The distress on the Widow Hawley's face struck him speechless. "Has the baby come?" he at last managed to ask.

"Yes," she said, glancing back into the chamber, then down at John. "We need Mr. Chauncey. Fetch him now."

"What–," John started to say, but the Widow Hawley cut him off. "Go! Hurry!" she commanded, hastening back into the chamber.

John took a couple of faltering steps, then dashed out of the house. He raced the mile to the parsonage on foot. Terrifying questions rattled around in his brain. If the child had been born, why had he heard no cry? Was it a boy or a girl? Why was the minister so urgently required? Was Hope dying? Was the baby? Or both of them?

A Negro slave ushered John into the room containing Mr. Chauncey's extensive library, filled with the pungent odor of leather bindings. Glancing up from a volume the minister's eyebrows rose as he took in his unexpected visitor's sweat-streaked face.

"You must come, sir," John gasped. He bent over to ease the stitch in his side.

"Of course," Mr. Chauncey replied, rising to his feet. "What has happened?" he asked as he slipped on his coat.

John shook his head as he straightened up, still struggling to catch his breath. "I don't know. Mistress Hawley just told me to fetch you at once."

Walking at the older man's slower pace, it took John and Mr. Chauncey half an hour to reach the Lyman house. The moment they crossed the threshold, they heard a chamber door close. Experience Lyman descended the stairs cradling a small, linen-wrapped bundle. When she reached the bottom, she cast John a look of sympathy, then turned to the minister.

"He's come too soon into the world, parson," she said. "We thought you'd best christen him without delay."

John stared at his mother, absorbing the terrible meaning of her words. Then he gently pulled back a fold of the cloth bundled in Experience's arms to reveal a baby – his son – perfectly formed, but so tiny John might have held him easily in one hand. The fragile-looking infant didn't cry or squirm vigorously as John remembered his sister Hannah doing when she was born, but lay quietly in his grandmother's arms, barely breathing.

"What name?" Mr. Chauncey asked. It took John several seconds to realize the question was directed to him.

"John," he answered in a choked whisper. "If it was a boy, Hope wanted him to have my name."

John's eyes filled with tears as he took the baby from his mother's arms. He held his son as Mr. Chauncey baptized him with water fetched by Mindwell.

"Thank you, sir," John said. He raised his eyes to his mother's face, and forced himself to ask the dreaded question. "What of Hope?"

"She came through the birth well enough," Experience answered.

John closed his eyes and stood silently for several heartbeats before opening them. Cradling his son, he made his way carefully, step by step, up the stairs. He nudged the chamber door open with his elbow. Hope lay pale and spent on the bed, her eyes closed.

The matrons who'd assisted at the birth cast looks of pity towards John as they filed silently out of the room. The Widow Hawley, carrying a large bundle of cloths stained with dried blood, was the last to leave, closing the door quietly behind her.

When John sat down on the bed, Hope opened eyes rimmed with circles of exhaustion and pain. She looked at him in mute grief. He tenderly placed the baby in her arms. "Mr. Chauncey baptized him John, as you wished."

Hope looked down at her son and nodded in acknowledgement, too drained to speak. John put his left arm tenderly around the infant in Hope's arms and encircled her shoulder with the other, pulling his little family together within his protective embrace.

That night, Nathaniel Chauncey opened the leather-bound ledger in which he'd recorded the births, marriages, and deaths among his flock for more than three decades. By candlelight he wrote, under the date of May 4, 1740, "I baptized John Lyman, son of John and Hope Lyman, who died immediately."

Chapter Three

July, 1740
Durham

John and Hope heaved sighs of relief as the Lyman home came in sight. It had been five days since Hope received an urgent message that her mother, brother Samuel, and sister Hannah all were sick with the summer complaint, a bloody diarrhea common during hot weather.

Hope and John had hastened on horseback to Middletown. Hope had nursed her ailing relatives, prepared food their weakened systems could tolerate, and laundered mounds of soiled clothing and bed linens. John had performed the daily chores necessary to keep the farm running – and kept a close eye on Hope. She was recovering well from the ordeal of giving birth, but he wanted to be sure she didn't wear herself down caring for her mother and siblings.

By the middle of the fifth day, all three Hawleys were sufficiently on the mend for Hope and John to take their leave. As their horse reached the Lyman house, John gratefully dismounted. He tied the animal's reins to a wooden post, then helped Hope down. They walked toward the hall door – which was unexpectedly thrown open wide just as they reached it.

John and Hope stopped dead in their tracks. They gaped in astonishment at the burly young man on the threshold. Ebenezer Lyman, Jr., was four years older, four inches taller, and forty pounds heavier than his brother.

Ebenezer, his wife Sarah, and their infant daughter had left Durham three years ago to become the pioneer settlers of a frontier community called Torrington in the wilds of the Connecticut Colony's northwestern corner. This was the first time Ebenezer had traveled the more than fifty miles of rough, hilly road, much of it through sparsely settled terrain, to return to Durham.

"Little brother!" Ebenezer, Jr., boomed, clapping John hard on the shoulder. "And my new sister," he added almost as an afterthought, with a brief nod at Hope. He ushered them into the hall with an expansive sweep of his arm, as if he were the host welcoming them to his own home. He guided them to a bench by a table around which the rest of the family was already assembled.

Ebenezer, Sr., stood at the head of the table. His eyes shone with excitement. Ebenezer, Jr., joined him there.

"I was afraid you wouldn't return before your brother had to leave," the older man said. He sorted through a sheaf of documents on the table.

The elder Ebenezer looked up from the papers spread before him and fixed his gaze on John. "I'm finishing plans to move with your mother and sisters to Torrington before the snow falls," he announced. The three women sat in glum silence. They were clearly unhappy with the impending move, about which they hadn't been consulted.

Hope was stunned into silence by this development, of which she'd had no warning. She felt a twinge of uneasiness when she saw in John's expression that the news wasn't a complete surprise to him. Ebenezer was looking at John expectantly.

"Why, Papa?" John asked in a steady voice, then quickly continued before his father recovered from the shock of having his decision questioned. "Here in Durham you have a comfortable home and a sizeable farm. You enjoy the respect of the entire town. What more do you hope to find in Torrington?"

"Productive acres, for a start," Ebenezer shot back, irritated by even this mild challenge. "The land here is wearing out. Each year we work harder, yet each year it yields less.

"And by selling my property in Durham and buying land in Torrington, I can provide marriage portions for your sisters," he went on, his face flushing with agitation. "Mindwell is twenty-six, should have wed long ago," he said, oblivious to the embarrassment his bluntness brought to the homely face of his tall, ungainly daughter. "And Hannah is seventeen, ripe for marrying."

Ebenezer went on, his voice growing louder with indignation. "If those reasons aren't enough for you, I believe it's God's will that we populate this entire land, that we carry His holy word to every corner."

Hope saw that Ebenezer, Jr., was relishing John's discomfort at being the target of their father's tirade. When John tried to answer, Ebenezer, Jr., cut him off.

"You're still planning on coming, aren't you, little brother?" he demanded brashly. "You can pick up a good many acres with the cash from Hope's marriage portion, far more than you'll ever be able to buy in Durham. When should we expect you in Torrington?"

Hope stared in outraged amazement at the two Ebenezers. John ignored his brother, and spoke directly to their father. "I'll think on it," he said tersely.

Hope inhaled sharply and looked at John as if he'd suddenly sprouted horns. Under the table he grasped her left hand with his right, and squeezed it in a signal to keep quiet.

"What's there to think about?" Ebenezer, Sr., demanded. "I did well by following my father from Northampton to Durham when you were just a babe."

"But Durham wasn't a wilderness like Torrington," John pointed out.

"Durham had been settled barely twenty years when we came," Ebenezer snapped, "and your grandfather was sixty when he moved here, older than I am now!"

"Do you tremble at a whiff of danger, little brother?" Ebenezer, Jr., sneered. "Other men from Durham have already moved to Torrington. Most have wives, for not every man's backbone is softened by marriage." He darted a quick scornful look at Hope. "And it's a fine place to bring up a family. My Sarah has just given me a *third* child," he said smugly.

John shot his brother a look of scorching contempt. He got abruptly to his feet. Still pointedly ignoring the younger Ebenezer, he said in a tight voice, "I'll pray on it. I'll give you my decision tomorrow."

"In your considerations, do not forget the Lord's commandment to 'Honor thy father and mother,'" Ebenezer, Sr., said angrily.

John nodded, then abruptly turned and left the hall, passing quickly through the kitchen, and out into the yard. He had to leave before his father's disappointment and his own resentment led one of them to say something that could never be taken back.

Hope, unprepared for John's abrupt exit, sat for a long, uncomfortable moment, unsure what she should do. She was angry and upset that John had apparently kept some ridiculous idea of moving to Torrington from her. And she was incensed at how the two Ebenezers had treated John like a little boy. They expected him to obediently go along with a plan John clearly hadn't agreed to.

Hope would never speak disrespectfully to her father-in-law. But she did consider telling Ebenezer, Jr., what she thought of his cruel, bullying ways. Realizing that only would be a waste of good breath, Hope got up, and followed John out of the hall.

John didn't stop until he reached the field of Indian corn that, he noted absently, hadn't been hoed while he'd been gone. He stared at the rows of tall green stalks, struggling to calm his churning emotions.

The buzzing of insects filled the warm evening. The sun was still above the horizon, but blue-black clouds were piling up over the hills to the west. From them echoed the low rumble of distant thunder.

The rustling of tall grass behind him alerted John to Hope's approach. He turned reluctantly to face her. Her cheeks were crimson, but not from the heat. Her pupils had contracted against the slanting rays of the lowering sun, giving her eyes a deep green color that contained a hard glint. She stopped five feet from John. Her body was rigid, her hands clenched tightly at her sides.

"When were you going to tell me of this folly?" she demanded.

John's frayed temper nearly snapped at her sharp tone. Then he caught the hurt beneath the anger in her words.

"No – you don't understand," John said hastily. "Going to Torrington was a scheme my father favored when Ebenezer settled there, before you and I fell in love. My father bought land there, and talked about moving our family. He took it for granted that I, being eighteen and unmarried, would go with them. But then my father deeded his Torrington acres to Ebenezer, and I assumed he'd forgotten about it.

"A few weeks ago my father spoke of receiving a letter from Ebenezer about land in Torrington," John went on. "With so much on my mind, I paid little attention."

Hope's expression softened slightly. It had been grief over their baby's death and worry over her own health that had preoccupied John.

"I didn't realize my father had revived the idea of moving until I saw my brother in the doorway. Papa probably didn't think he needed to discuss it with me – just assumed I would go along as if nothing had changed."

"But you said you'd think about it!" Hope said. "I tell you right now, I will never go to Torrington!"

"*Will* not, *Mistress* Lyman?" John shot back in a rare flash of anger. It was a rebuke, not a question.

"Well – cannot," Hope retreated momentarily, taken aback by John's tone.

"It is a horrid wilderness to which they're going," Hope blurted out. "I've heard that at Torrington men keep their muskets close by while in the fields for fear of wild beasts and savage Indians! And I couldn't abandon my mother, leave her here with only Samuel and Hannah to rely upon." Hope searched John's face desperately for some sign of understanding.

Before this past week, John might have been amused by the thought of the indomitable Widow Hawley in need of anyone's assistance. But their just-completed mission of mercy was a reminder that each day could bring misfortune. And he had held out the prospect of Hope living close to her as one of the reasons the Widow Hawley should agree to their marriage.

John took a deep breath to steady himself, then stepped forward to wrap his arms around his wife's stiff body. "You can save your arguments," he said tenderly. A breeze spawned by the approaching thunderstorm ruffled Hope's hair and skirt, and bent the tall grass around them.

"I will think and pray on the matter as I promised. I owe my father that much. But barring a divine revelation, I know what my decision will be. Whatever it is my brother and father seek on a distant frontier, I do not need."

John gently brushed his left hand back over Hope's brow, pushing the linen mobcap from her head. He ran his fingers over the softness of her hair, as he tilted her face up towards his. "I'm content to stay here with you. When my father quotes the commandments, he forgets that Scripture directs a man to leave his father and mother and cleave unto his wife."

John's gaze moved past Hope's head, toward the Lyman house. "I love my parents and sisters," he said. "I'll miss them terribly." He was, she realized, speaking as much to himself as to her.

"I suppose I even love Ebenezer," John added with a short, humorless laugh. "Although I almost gave in to the urge to plant my fist in the middle of his taunting face – even knowing from painful experience that I'd be the loser in the brawl that would follow."

He looked at Hope, serious again. "The perils of the wilderness don't frighten me. We're all in God's hands. What I do fear is that if we go to Torrington, we'll never build a life of our own. I would always be overshadowed by my brother. And my father would never come to respect me as a man, not the boy he still thinks I am. To stay is right for me – for us. As going is right for my father."

"Truly, John?" Hoped asked, searching his face for any trace of hesitation. She knew the price he'd pay for this decision. His father would feel betrayed. His brother would taunt him mercilessly about being nagged into staying by a shrewish wife.

"Truly," he said, with a reassuring smile that carried no trace of doubt.

At last John felt Hope's body relax in his embrace, and she put her arms around his neck. "My marriage portion should be sufficient to rent or even buy a homestead," she said, then continued with a suggestive smile, "Perhaps tonight we might begin working again on a family to fill it."

Elated at the prospect of resuming the marital relations that had been suspended while Hope recovered from childbirth, John hugged her tightly. "Now *that*," he said with a smile that widened into a grin, "is one project I will gladly embrace."

Chapter Four

October, 1740
Middletown

Hope's footsteps echoed off the kitchen walls as she trod back and forth on the oak floorboards, spinning wool on a tall great wheel. John's parents and sisters had left for Torrington right after the harvest, leaving Hope and John alone in the Lyman house.

A scene every bit as ugly as Hope anticipated had erupted when John told his father he and Hope wouldn't be going to Torrington. John had held firm against the onslaught of angry disappointment from his father and contempt from his brother with a tenacity that made Hope proud.

Ebenezer, Sr., had left John and Hope to tend the farm and house in Durham until he could sell them, giving John and Hope time to find a home of their own. For the past month, they'd had the Lyman house entirely to themselves. It was a rare and disturbing situation.

A house should be full of people sharing life, Hope thought longingly, with a husband and a wife and a clutch of children, with maybe a grandparent or a spinster aunt thrown in for good measure. With her in-laws gone, there was no comforting chaos of daily activity that had helped distract Hope from her sorrow over the baby's death.

Hope had turned to her religion for support following her loss. She'd conscientiously followed Mr. Chauncey's well-meaning pastoral advice to attend Sabbath meetings, pray regularly, and read the Bible.

But those pious activities provided Hope no more solace than kneading bread dough or making soap. Her heartache had actually been deepened by disappointment over her failure after four months of trying to conceive another child.

She felt cheated, Hope realized with a clarity so sharp she stopped abruptly in her tracks. She'd done everything the minister had prescribed, everything expected of her, but God hadn't kept His end of the bargain.

The crack of metal biting into wood broke through Hope's depressing train of thought. She left off the monotonous spinning and walked to the kitchen window. In the early morning sun, at the far end of the homelot, John was splitting logs. The firewood would be added to the pile – already huge, but not yet big enough – needed for the coming winter, which augured to be a hard one. Already October had been as cold as November usually was.

She watched as John set a three-foot-long log vertically on a stump, tapped a metal wedge into the sawn end, then gripped the maul with both hands. The powerful muscles of his back, arms, and thighs strained against the fabric of his coat and breeches as he swung the maul backward and up over his head, then brought it down onto the wedge with sufficient force to cleave the log in two.

Hope was returning to her spinning when the sound of hooves on the road drew her back to the window. A man she recognized from Middletown reined in his horse next to John. He leaned over to speak a few agitated words, then jerked his mount's head around and galloped off down the road.

Fearing the rider brought bad news about her mother or siblings, Hope hurried to the door. She stepped out in time to meet John, who was hurrying toward the house. "Mr. Whitefield is coming to Middletown this morning!" he exclaimed.

The news kindled a spark of cautious expectation in Hope. George Whitefield was a charismatic young English minister who'd been traveling the colonies, preaching a message of salvation that reports claimed was reigniting the faith of multitudes. So many people had flocked to hear him in Philadelphia, in New York, and in Boston that no house of worship had been large enough to hold them. Whitefield had resorted to the unheard-of practice of preaching out of doors to crowds numbering in the thousands.

"Can we get there in time to hear him?" Hope asked.

"Maybe, if we leave right now," John replied.

While John saddled their horse, Hope hurried inside to don her cardinal, a hooded cape of red homespun wool. Mounted behind John, her arms wrapped tightly around his waist, they set off for Middletown. Other riders headed for the same destination joined them along the way.

Suddenly John and Hope spied on the horizon a thick haze from which echoed a reverberating sound. It took a moment to realize the sight was a massive crush of people on horseback, enveloped in a cloud of dust thrown up by hundreds of hooves pounding the dry roadbed.

Within a few minutes Hope and John were absorbed into the tightly packed moving mass of humanity and horseflesh. Riders urged forward foam-flecked horses, the animals breathing out streams of vapor into the chill morning air. Mounts and riders alike were coated in powdery dirt that made their eyes water and set them to coughing.

At last they drew close to Middletown's meetinghouse. As the horses stopped and the dust settled, Hope and John were awestruck by what they saw.

A massive crowd thronged the meetinghouse in eerie, expectant silence. People were still arriving from all directions on foot and on horseback. Half a mile away, the ferry deposited a load of passengers at the landing on the Great River, then immediately shuttled back to the eastern bank where still more people waited to be carried across.

When they could proceed no deeper into the crowd, Hope and John dismounted. At his uncommon height John could see over most people's heads. But Hope had to stand on her toes and crane her neck to catch a glimpse of the special platform erected before the meetinghouse. She suspected with disappointment that she wouldn't be able to hear more than a few snatches of what Whitefield had to say. John wrapped an arm around her shoulders to keep from being separated in the mass of people.

A slight man who looked scarcely older than John mounted the platform. He faced the enormous crowd with an aura of holy purpose that left no doubt this was George Whitefield.

"What does God say unto Abraham?" Whitefield demanded in a voice so powerful that Hope and John could hear him clearly despite their distance from the platform. "Take now thine only son Isaac, whom thou lovest, and offer him for a burnt-offering.'" The crowd knew Whitefield was quoting the Old Testament account of God testing the Prophet Abraham's faith by commanding him to sacrifice his only son with his own hand.

"I see the tears trickle down the patriarch Abraham's cheeks," Whitefield went on. "He cries 'Adieu, adieu, my son the Lord gave thee to me and the Lord calls thee away; blessed be the name of the Lord.' Then Abraham put a knife to his dear son's throat."

Whitefield stunned his audience by breaking into heart-rending weeping, as if he himself were the ancient prophet. He struggled to regain his composure.

"But the angel of the Lord called to Abraham," Whitefield continued, "and said 'Lay not thine hand upon the lad, for now I know thou fearest God, seeing thou hast not withheld thine only son.'" Even though his listeners knew that last-minute reprieve would come, Whitefield allowed them a long moment to savor the sense of relief.

"Come, all ye tender-hearted parents, who know what it is to look over a dying child," Whitefield called out. "I see your hearts affected, I see your eyes weep."

A shiver of fear rippled along Hope's spine. Looking down, she could almost see her tiny son cradled in her arms, drawing his last breath only hours after his first. Tears cut tracks in the dust coating her cheeks. She looked up at John. The blood had drained from his face, and his eyes were riveted on the man on the platform.

"Now behold the blessed Jesus nailed on an accursed tree," Whitefield thundered. He swept an arm up dramatically, raised his eyes toward an imaginary cross. "Now where are all your tears?" he demanded harshly. "Look to Him whom *YOU* have pierced, and mourn, as a woman mourneth for her first born."

Whitefield threw his arm out in an accusatory sweep that embraced the entire crowd yet at the same time seemed to target each individual personally. "*OUR* sins brought the blessed Jesus to the cross. God suffered *HIS OWN* son to be slain – so that *WE* might live forever!" he cried, his voice trembling with a strange combination of rage and exultation

Hope's grief was compounded by crushing guilt at Whitefield's exposure of her selfishness. She uttered a choked sob as she clutched John for support. He reflexively tightened his grip on her shoulders, but never took his eyes from Whitefield.

Hope had never heard a minister speak with such passion and intensity. Mr. Chauncey and other pastors read carefully prepared, dry sermons from the pulpit with a solemnity befitting their Yale degrees. They would no more break into tears before their congregations than they would cluck like a chicken.

Whitefield had to raise his voice to be heard over the shouts and moans of the many in the crowd who'd been stricken as Hope had. When he resumed speaking, the harshness of a prosecutor had been replaced by the gentle concern of a loving parent.

"Salvation is God's free gift, and we are saved, not by any or all the works of righteousness we do, but only through the active and passive obedience of Jesus Christ His beloved Son," Whitefield said. "Good works have nothing to do with justification in His sight. We are justified by faith alone."

Hope stared transfixed. How had this stranger seen into her thoughts? How was he able to speak directly to her torment of the past six months? She had indeed believed her empty actions – Sabbath worship, Bible reading, daily prayer – justified her. She'd thought to barter with the Lord as though haggling with a shopkeeper over a length of ribbon. She'd held her dead child and her failure to conceive a new baby as grudges against the God who'd sacrificed *His* beloved only son for the eternal salvation of her, an unworthy, ungrateful sinner.

"Remember," Whitefield called out, his clarion voice suffused with a rapturous joy. "Abraham your father was tried so before you; think of the happiness he now enjoys, and how he is incessantly thanking God for tempting and trying him when here below. Remember, it will be but a little while and you shall sit with them also, and tell one another what God has done for your souls."

That simple offer of salvation through unquestioning faith and acceptance of God's will swept away Hope's guilt, sorrow, and shame. She was exhausted, but exalted by Whitefield's message of a God of infinite wisdom and love whom she could trust without reservation.

Whitefield stepped down from the platform, leaving utter chaos in his wake. Men and women were convulsed in fits of weeping; they groveled on the ground in terror of the loss of heaven, or knelt in gratitude for the blessing of hearing the Lord's servant, George Whitefield.

At last Hope looked up at John. He was still staring out across the crowd, at something only he could see. At the touch of Hope's hand on his cheek, he looked down, his eyes glistening with unshed tears. "How–," he began in a wondering whisper, then stopped to swallow the lump of emotion in his throat. "How did he know what was in my heart?"

Chapter Five

March, 1741
Middlefield Section
Middletown

Deep, ice-crusted snow covered the ground, even though the almanac calendar said spring had begun six days earlier. The past winter had been the harshest anyone could remember, and there were no signs its frigid grip would be relaxed any time soon.

Hope had kindled only a small fire in the kitchen hearth to thaw the ink that had frozen solid in its earthenware jar on a small table. John, his father, and a Middletown man named Ephraim Coe stood around the table, the only piece of furniture left in the house. Ebenezer Lyman had packed up everything belonging to him, as John and Hope had done with their possessions.

Hope silently watched Ebenezer, John, and Coe take turns using a goose quill to scratch their names onto two documents set out on the table. Ebenezer Lyman had braved snow-choked roads and flesh-freezing temperatures to return from Torrington to sign one of them, a deed selling his house and sixty-four acres to Ephraim Coe for £1,000.

The other document would finalize Ephraim Coe's sale to John Lyman for £620 pounds, of a house, a barn, and thirty-seven acres in the southwestern corner of Middletown known as Middlefield, near the Durham line. This purchase, combined with other acres John planned to buy, would be sufficient land to support a family.

Hope couldn't suppress a twinge of resentment. Their new homestead was being purchased in John's name alone, even though most of the funds had come from Hope's marriage portion.

The paperwork completed, Ebenezer immediately prepared to leave for Torrington, in a wagon loaded with the household furnishings that had been left behind for John and Hope's use. After an awkward moment of hesitation, he hugged Hope, then turned to John.

The uncertainty on their faces told Hope both father and son were thinking that, given the many miles that would separate them and the unpredictability of life, this might be the last time they'd see each other this side of the grave. Ebenezer took John's hand and shook it firmly. "God preserve you, my son," he said in a choked voice. "Obey Him in all things so that if we do not meet again in this life, we may do so in Heaven."

"God bless you, too, Papa," John replied, placing his left hand over their clasped ones. After a long moment Ebenezer gave John a solid clap on the shoulder with his free hand, and they released their grip. Ebenezer walked out of the kitchen to the waiting wagon and team. From the doorway Hope and John watched him head down the road.

Now it was their turn to leave. Hope watched John take a few purposeful strides out into the yard, then turn for a long look back at the only home he'd ever known. He inhaled a deep breath of shockingly icy air, then helped Hope up onto the seat of their own wagon. He climbed up beside her, then snapped the reins to begin the journey to Middlefield.

As the crow flew John and Hope's new home was about a mile and a half from the Lyman house. The trip was actually closer to two miles, for the road skirted a swamp, known by its Indian name of Coginchaug, that separated Middlefield from Durham.

The house faced east toward the swamp and the narrow West River that meandered through it about a quarter mile away. The clapboards, never painted in the three decades since its construction, had weathered to a dull gray. Ephraim Coe had applied a fresh coat of red paint to the frames of the sash windows.

It was a solid structure built around a massive central stone chimney, with two rooms on the first floor and two chambers above. A recently added lean-to kitchen ran across the back. The interior walls were sheathed with wide, dark brown boards placed horizontally.

The front door opened onto a steep, tightly angled narrow staircase. A second door on the side entered directly into the hall.

That night, with their goods unloaded but still scattered in various rooms, John settled wearily onto the edge of the bed he'd set up in the parlor. He gazed into the large blaze he'd built in the fireplace. What heat reached him was welcome; at times during this past ferociously cold winter it had seemed impossible to get completely warm no matter how huge the fire.

Hope sensed something beyond physical fatigue in John's quiet pensiveness. She left off putting away sheets in a chest and stepped over to her husband's side. He was so absorbed in his thoughts that he didn't notice her presence. After studying his face in the flickering firelight, she asked quietly, "What's troubling you?"

John looked up, startled, then smiled at how easily Hope had divined his thoughts. He took her hand and pulled her onto his lap. He resumed studying the flames, then at last spoke.

"I'm bedeviled by contrary feelings," he began slowly. "Being here with you in our own home is a dream come true. I can scarcely wait for the snow to melt so I can begin tilling my own acres. And yet," he hesitated, then continued in evident embarrassment, "I'm homesick for my parents' hearth, like a little child. Parting with my father was more painful than I'd expected."

Hope put an arm around his shoulder and leaned her head comfortingly against his. She had only to imagine herself in the same situation with her mother to understand his distress.

After a long moment, Hope straightened up and wrapped both arms around John's neck. "I know something that will raise your spirits," she whispered in his ear, then leaned back to give him an almost coquettish look. John raised his eyebrows inquiringly.

"I'm with child," Hope said.

John's eyes widened in surprise, then lit up with joy. "That's the best news you could give," he said, his voice husky with emotion. "When?"

"The end of summer, so the midwife thinks," Hope said.

"We'll harvest two fine crops this year," John said happily. Then he immediately grew sober at the memory of the previous May's sorrow. "If God wills it," he added.

Hope nodded in somber understanding. "We'll face whatever the future brings as Mr. Whitefield said. We will have faith in the Lord who crucified His son to atone for our sins, so we can be united forever in Heaven with those we love."

John pulled Hope's head down to nestle against his shoulder. They sat contentedly, savoring each other's warmth and closeness, and the shared anticipation of a bright future.

At last Hope broke the silence. "I would ask a favor, John." He squeezed her shoulder to signal she should continue.

"I know you plan to sell twenty-one of the acres in Middletown I inherited to Mr. Coe," she began. "I think it would be wise to use the money from that sale to buy his swamp pasture next to our land."

"*That's* your favor?" John asked in puzzled amusement. "If so, it's granted. In fact, that's what I had planned to do."

"Buying the land is not the favor," Hope said, sitting up straight. She looked John full in the face, striving to conceal her unease. "The favor is – I would like buy the swamp pasture in my name only."

John's bemused expression dissolved into an uncertain frown. Hope's unexpected request disturbed him.

"Only spinsters or widows buy land in their name," John reminded her.

"I know," Hope acknowledged quickly. An awkward silence fell between them.

"To own land in my name alone would be a . . ." Hope hesitated, struggling for words to explain to John a longing she didn't entirely understand herself. "It would be a tribute to my forebears whose legacy to me helped make our life possible. It would be a personal tie to them, more lasting than any furniture or household goods that have come to me."

John's dark brows drew together as he searched his wife's face. He saw there the same yearning for land he felt – natural for a man, eccentric for a woman. He glanced away in confusion.

His instinct was to deny Hope's request. He thought of the example set by his formidable mother-in-law. The Widow Hawley still lived in a state of independence most women would have gladly relinquished at the earliest opportunity. He recalled Hope's defiant outburst over the issue of moving to Torrington. And now she'd made this new unorthodox request.

John felt a creeping, uneasy suspicion that perhaps Hope didn't truly accept a wife's subservient role in a marriage. If he granted this request, what unwomanly thing might she do or ask for next?

"I can't fathom why you want this, Hope," John began sternly. He turned his gaze back to her, expecting to see petulant defiance on her face. But while Hope's eyes were clouded in anticipation of rejection, her gaze also conveyed her willingness to dutifully accept his decision.

Relieved by this evidence of proper wifely submission, John thought of how very much he owed this woman. The strength he derived from her steadfast love, along with the property she'd brought to their union, had given him the courage and the power to chart his own course in life, free of his father and brother's domination. Now once again there was the thrilling promise of a child.

John drew a deep breath, then said, "But if it matters so much to you, I will agree."

It took a moment for John's unexpected consent to sink in. Hope's face lit up with delight, and she threw her arms around his neck in a grateful hug.

On April 6, 1741, Hope and John Lyman sold twenty-one acres in Middletown. Both husband and wife signed the deed of sale, in compliance with a recent law requiring that land inherited by a wife be sold only with her consent.

Then Hope, and Hope alone, purchased from Ebenezer Coe, for £200, twenty-five acres of swamp pasture adjacent to their homelot on the west. However, it was duly noted on the deed that Hope had made the purchase "with the free Consent and good likeing" of her husband.

Chapter Six

April, 1746
Middlefield Society

After tossing restlessly for an hour, the three children had finally fallen asleep in the trundle bed next to that of their parents in the parlor. Hope tiptoed in to check on four-year-old Catharine; Hannah, nearly three; and John, a toddler of fifteen months named in memory of their first son. The unseasonable heat and humidity had made them all cranky. It was a relief to have them asleep at last.

Hope gingerly straightened the children's tangled shifts. She brushed the damp hair back from their sweaty foreheads before picking three-month-old David up from his cradle. She crept quietly into the kitchen where she sat down by the open window to nurse the baby a last time before putting him down for the night.

As the sun slipped behind Powder Hill, the long ridge a mile west of the Lyman house, a fresh breeze sprang up, carrying the delicate fragrance of apple blossoms from the orchard. The scent was both pleasant and troubling. Several weeks of above-normal temperatures had caused the fruit trees to blossom earlier than usual. A cold snap could kill the flowers, destroying the year's crop.

Hope looked down at David, a sturdy baby with an abundance of his father's straight brown hair. His eyes were turning dark like John's as well. All five chubby fingers on one of his tiny hands curled trustingly around his mother's little finger. The breathy little mews of contentment he made as he suckled filled Hope with gratitude to God for these four children. Each had helped fill the void gouged in their hearts by their first baby's death.

Hope was also thankful, from a purely practical standpoint, that two of their four were boys. Daughters were valuable in the short term, for their help running a household. But eventually the family would have to tap its resources to provide a daughter with a marriage portion of household goods to take with her when she went to live with her husband.

Sons, while they lived at home, were free labor for the farm. Even when they married their value wasn't necessarily lost. When a son wed, he and his wife might live for a time with his parents, as John and Hope had done, with the household benefiting from the work of both. If a father was prosperous he might present a son who wed with land to start his own home. But he could avoid losing some of the benefit of those acres and of the married son's cultivation of them by retaining legal title to the property until his own death.

It was also a son's duty to support his parents in their later years if it became necessary. And sons would ensure that a man's family name lived on for another generation.

Every man prayed he would sire many sons, for all these reasons – and one more. Many children died from disease or accidents or being born too early. A couple had to produce at least a couple sons to have favorable odds of even one reaching adulthood.

Thus their abundance of children filled Hope and John with contentment. But a niggling anxiety overshadowed it.

Hope had conceived David only three months after giving birth to John, disproving the conventional wisdom that nursing protected against a new pregnancy. Caring for two active little girls and nursing the infant John, while carrying a new baby in her womb, had drained Hope physically.

The specter of conceiving another baby only a few months after David's birth had led John and Hope to decide not to resume marital relations as soon as she'd healed from David's delivery. But Hope fretted over how long they'd be able to abstain. John had a man's natural need, and she enjoyed the intimacy of lying together even when she was too tired to be an energetic partner. And they wondered guiltily if refraining from intercourse showed a lack of faith in the wisdom of the Lord who had commanded men and women to "be fruitful and multiply."

As Hope was laying the sleeping David in his cradle, she heard horses approaching the rear of the house. The voices of several men, including John, floated through the window as she sat back down.

"The General Assembly granted permission to form our own Middlefield religious society more than a year ago," John was saying with frustration. "But we can't even agree on *where* to locate the meetinghouse! How will we ever be able to build one, or settle upon a minister?" He heaved an exasperated sigh. "My family still attends Sabbath services in Durham – when we can get there. By the time the road was clear enough of snow this year to travel, the swamp flooded it. My newest son still hasn't been baptized!"

"I had expected the congregation to defer to the wishes of one of Middlefield's oldest families," lamented a baritone voice. Hope recognized it as coming from the barrel-like physique of Benjamin Miller, who had arrived in Middlefield some fifty years ago as one of its first settlers.

"Every man thinks the meetinghouse should be as close as possible to his home," observed a voice Hope identified as belonging to Moses Parsons. "And a Connecticut man can be as difficult to budge as the boulders in our fields."

"I've seen this kind of contention before," Miller said sagely. "Once each man is satisfied his voice has been heard, a compromise will be reached. I'm confident it will be to our liking. After all," he observed dryly, "since we in the south end of Middlefield are among the society's biggest tax payers, we'll supply a larger portion of the cost of building the meetinghouse than any others."

Hope's lids had grown heavy with drowsiness, but she smiled with satisfaction at Miller's clear inclusion of John in that "we". John's energy and skill had brought in harvests so bountiful that in five years he'd doubled the number of acres they owned. Just turned twenty-nine, he was one of the largest land owners in Middlefield.

Hope wanted to hear more, but couldn't keep from nodding off. Finally she surrendered to her fatigue, and retired to bed in the parlor.

Hope awoke the next morning to be greeted by all four children vomiting. Feeling each little forehead, she realized the unusually warm weather had masked the fact that they were developing fevers. Soon came pains in their heads and limbs, and listlessness.

John and Hope so far had escaped whatever was ailing the children. John summoned Benjamin Miller's daughter-in-law and his cousin Thomas Lyman's wife to help Hope care for the four invalids. Any good housewife had the skill to treat most ailments. A doctor's services were sought only for the gravest emergencies.

The women suspected that miasma, or unhealthy vapors, rising from the nearby swamp might be causing the illness. They treated their patients with traditional remedies, feeding them only light liquids, bathing their feet and legs in warm water.

After four days, the fevers started to drop, and the aches and pains began to subside. Mistress Miller and Mistress Lyman helped Hope tuck the children into bed for what all expected would be their first night of uninterrupted sleep in nearly a week. The women bade a grateful John farewell, promising to return if necessary, then hurried home to families and duties neglected during their absence.

John was up the next morning before sunrise. He dressed quietly in the darkness so as not to disturb the rest of the family, who had thankfully passed the night in solid slumber. He headed for the barn to do the morning chores.

John was crouched on the milking stool beside one of their three cows when he heard Hope cry out his name. He shot to his feet, upsetting the stool, and raced for the house. What he saw when he reached the parlor made him stop in his tracks – and made his blood run cold.

Hope was clutching the wailing David in her arms. The baby's face and chest were covered with a flat red rash.

John had seen this rash before, when he was a boy of eight – on his own body. It was the first sign of smallpox, the most terrifying disease known to man. There was no treatment or cure.

John was still haunted by memories of what he'd witnessed while confined to the pest house, where people infected with smallpox were isolated until they either recovered or died. He knew with gruesome clarity what the coming weeks held for his children – for the other three undoubtedly had the ferociously contagious disease as well.

Within another day, the rash would spread over their bodies. A couple days more, and the lesions would become raised bumps, which would quickly fill with a cloudy, thick fluid. These would turn into pustules that would crust over and form scabs. The scabs would drop off over the next week, the final stage of the disease.

The severity of smallpox varied from person to person. No one knew why. John had seen the disease ravage some victims with lesions so numerous they ran into each other, forming grotesque bumps like warts on a toad. The lesions could invade the eyes, causing blindness. Patients' fevers could soar dangerously high. The disease could spread into the lungs.

Some of the most severely afflicted died after days of agony. They were usually buried in hastily dug graves near the pest house. Some survived, hideously disfigured by deep, pitted scars.

John's own case of smallpox had been blessedly mild. He instinctively touched the round, pale scars on his neck that testified to his bout with the disease – and the lifelong immunity it had conferred on him.

John felt he was reliving a nightmare as he urged his horse down Durham's main road, the spring sunshine warm on his shoulders. He reined in his mount in front of the minister's house, but stayed in the saddle.

"Mr. Chauncey!" he called, hoping no one else would come out from the house to greet him. While John was immune to smallpox, no one knew how the disease spread. It was best for him to stay as far away as possible from other people, for their protection.

The horse pranced nervously, sensing his rider's anxiety. John was gathering his breath for another shout, when Mr. Chauncey appeared from behind the house, brushing soil from his garden off his hands.

"The children have the smallpox," John blurted out. Mr. Chauncey's expression immediately became one of grim understanding. "How bad?" he asked, retrieving his waistcoat from the bush on which he'd hung it while working.

"They're all very sick," John choked out. "The baby – he hasn't been christened."

The minister nodded, slipping on the waistcoat. He disappeared through the hall door, reappearing a minute later wearing his frock coat and beaver hat, and carrying a well-worn Bible.

John hadn't doubted that the minister would heed his summons. On his nose and cheeks Mr. Chauncey carried several old but noticeable scars from his own encounter with smallpox.

The next weeks merged into an exhausting, endless nightmare. Neighbors and relatives hadn't rallied to help as they had when the children were sick with what was thought to be an unexceptional illness. Even if a person survived smallpox and thus was personally immune, there still existed the fearsome possibility that they might somehow carry it away to infect others.

The Widow Hawley had hastened to help. She'd had smallpox before she was married. Hope and her brother and sisters had had what their mother recalled was a very mild case all at the same time when they were little.

With the assistance of her mother, and of John when he could spare time from his farm chores, Hope cared for the children according to the doctor's detailed instructions. About three weeks after the first spots had appeared, Catharine, Hannah, and David's fevers had abated, and they began to show signs of recovering. But that wasn't the case with little John.

The disease had vented its fury on the toddler. It had invaded his lungs, making it difficult for him to breathe. John had made a frantic trip to again summon the doctor.

"He must be bled immediately," the physician said, busying himself with the contents of his traveling bag so he wouldn't have to meet the terrified parents' eyes. He removed a jar of leeches, for bleeding by cutting open a vein was too dangerous a procedure to perform on small children. He took two of the slimy black worm-like creates, and allowed each to attach itself to one of the boy's arms. After about fifteen minutes he removed the blood-engorged leeches and returned them to the jar.

Despite the bleeding and the careful following of the doctor's instructions, John lost more ground each day. His parents and grandmother took turns walking the floor with him, listening to the piteously hoarse wailing they were powerless to relieve.

Hope stood in the hall one warm May day, hugging the fading little boy tightly to her breast, as if she could somehow force vitality to flow from her body into his, as she had when she'd given birth to him. She heard her mother come into the room to relieve Hope for a spell. Hope didn't want to let her son go, but she was feeling exceedingly hot, and thought she might be about to vomit.

Hope turned to face her mother, who reached out to take John – then stopped with a look of horrified disbelief. "Your, your face . . . ," she stammered.

Hope's eyes widened in fright. She had no looking-glass to check her reflection, but a glance down at her bosom showed that the evil smallpox rash had appeared on her skin as well.

Terror coursed through Hope, not just for herself. Greater than her fear of suffering and scarring from smallpox was the possibility that she might die, leaving her little flock of children without a mother's love and protection. It was too awful a thought to bear.

Chapter Seven

November, 1755
Middlefield

"Time to get up, slug-a-bed," Catharine said cheerfully to the small form tightly cocooned in the sheet and blanket on the bed in which Catharine and Hannah also slept. The chamber was still in deep shadow, for the sun was barely up on this Monday morning, November 17.

When her wake-up call didn't get a reaction, Catharine pulled back the covers to reveal a head of dark brown hair. She reached down to tickle her sister Esther under the chin.

A giggle bubbled up from the six-year-old girl. She scrunched up her shoulders and thrust her jaw down to trap and immobilize Catharine's fingers. Finally Esther Lyman rolled over and sat up with a cavernous yawn and a broad-armed stretch.

"Get dressed – breakfast will be ready soon," Catharine said. She crossed the landing to the chamber where her brothers slept.

David was already up and gone. Elihu, almost five, was nearly finished dressing. Catharine watched silently as he struggled to fasten the buttons on the woolen breeches that, to his great pride, he'd just been given to replace the skirts little boys wore from infancy. She resisted the impulse to step in and do the job for him.

Elihu's face lit up in triumph as he slid the last button through its hole. He jumped in surprise when Catharine scooped him up in her arms for a congratulatory hug.

"What a big boy you are!" Catharine exclaimed to the child's delight. "Soon you'll be going to school with David and Esther." She set Elihu on his feet. "Go down to the kitchen. Hannah's already there. Tell Mama I'm still helping Esther get ready."

Returning to the sisters' chamber, Catharine found Esther struggling to pull a horn comb through her snarled hair. Catharine took the comb and gently teased out the tangles in the long, wavy tresses, then bundled them up under the little girl's mob cap. Hand-in-hand, the sisters walked carefully down the steep stairway.

John came in from completing his morning chores just as Esther and Catharine entered the kitchen. He removed the mittens Hope had knitted for him, but kept his coat on; it was only slightly warmer inside the house than out.

Hope was supervising Hannah as she slid a peel – a long-handed utensil resembling a flat shovel – under an earthenware dish in the oven at the back of the fireplace. Hannah carefully extracted the fresh-baked apple pie that would be part of their breakfast.

Hope smiled with approval at Hannah, who turned carefully to set the pie on a table. Hope took a moment to survey the youngsters bustling about getting ready for the day. She marveled, as always, that children born of the same parents and raised in the same household could be so very different in features and personality.

Catharine, now fourteen, had her Grandmother Lyman's short, solid build. In her dark eyes and straight hair, as well as her even temperament, she favored John. She had inherited her mother's determination, but without, Hope was thankful, her obstinance.

Hope couldn't deny that Catharine wasn't especially pretty. But her gift for efficient housekeeping, and her warm affinity for children evident in her bond with Elihu and Esther would make her a good catch for some fortunate man in a few years.

Hannah, twelve, was far prettier than her older sister – and knew it. Slim, with Hope's wavy brown hair and hazel eyes, Hannah was maturing into womanhood with none of the awkwardness that plagued Catharine during the same transformation.

Little Esther was an adorable slip of a child, with John's large, dark brown eyes. Her sunny personality made her the pet of the entire family.

A hard kick rattled the door John had just come through. He opened it to admit David, carrying a load of firewood in his outstretched arms.

Two months shy of his tenth birthday, David greatly resembled John in features and physique. He carried himself with a confidence that came from knowing he held a special place in his parents' hearts, as the cherished surviving eldest son.

Hope had once or twice noticed David's assurance take on a flash of arrogance that reminded her unpleasantly of John's brother Ebenezer. Bullying Ebenezer – dead two years past at only forty-two.

Ebenezer had been with a hunting party that built a campfire against a huge rock. While the men slept the fire's heat caused the rock to crack. A large chunk broke off and crushed Ebenezer.

John had accepted Ebenezer's freakish death as God's will. Hope, while she'd borne her brother-in-law no affection, had been filled with pity for his widow and their nine children, the oldest not yet eighteen.

Ebenezer's death devastated John's parents. There'd been renewed pressure from his father for John to move to Torrington, but John had had no difficulty refusing. Ebenezer and Experience Lyman had plenty of family nearby. In addition to his brother's brood, Mindwell and Hannah had secured the husbands their father despaired of finding in Durham. Each had her own growing family.

Hope's musings were interrupted by a warning from Catharine to Elihu. The hungry little fellow had edged too close to the massive seven-foot-wide stone fireplace, tempted by the aroma of bread turning golden brown in the toaster on the hearth.

It was so typical of Elihu, Hope thought, shaking her head. His curiosity and fearlessness often led him into mischief – sometimes even into danger. More than once the boy had slipped away to explore the nearby swamp and river, touching off a frantic search.

Finally there was the baby, Phineas, just two months old. He'd been named for John's dear cousin, who'd risen to astonishing heights in the fifteen years since he'd gone to Northampton.

Phineas had wed the well-connected woman whose affections he'd sought. He had a brood of sons – four or five now, Hope wasn't sure. Phineas always made it a point to call on John during his infrequent trips to Durham to see his mother and brothers. But it had been three years since Phineas's last visit, for he had a great many demands on his time.

Phineas had studied law, been admitted to the bar, then settled in the town of Suffield on the border with Massachusetts. He'd become one of Connecticut's most successful and prosperous attorneys.

The people of Suffield had elected Phineas their representative to the lower house of the Connecticut General Assembly.

Subsequently he'd been elected in a colony-wide vote to be one of just a dozen members of the Assembly's powerful upper house, the Governor's Council.

Earlier in the current year Phineas had assumed a new role in public service. The hostility that had been simmering for three score years between the French and British and their respective Indian allies in North America had again boiled over into war. The General Assembly had appointed Phineas major general and commander-in-chief of the Connecticut troops recruited to fight the enemy.

The newly minted General Lyman and his men had merged with troops from other colonies into an army of more than five thousand, under the overall control of Major General William Johnson, Indian agent for the colony of New York. In late summer this force had marched off to confront the enemy French and Indians in the wilds of northern New York.

The leaves had just begun to turn color when news filtered back to Connecticut that the colonists had defeated the enemy in battle – and that the lion's share of credit for the victory was owed to General Phineas Lyman. When Hope and John learned the battle had occurred on September 8, the very day Hope had given birth to their newest son, it seemed the infant's name had been preordained.

Hope caught John's eye, and they shared a smile of contentment before she moved on to her next task. How blessed he'd been in his wife, John reflected.

Hope had inherited the physical and mental stamina of her formidable mother – still hale at nearly sixty. Smallpox had left a few noticeable, but not disfiguring, scars on her face by her ear and on her forearms. The only explanation for how she'd contracted the disease was that the illness she'd had as a child had been the benign chickenpox, sometimes mistaken for smallpox.

Catharine, Hannah, and David had also survived the smallpox with minor scarring. But the toddler John had lost his fight for life. Although Hope and John mourned deeply, in their hearts they knew the child's death had been a mercy. The rash had spread with such virulence over his little body that, had he lived, he would have been, from head to toe, a mass of pits and scars from which people would look away in horror. He would also have been blind, and likely damaged in other ways that would have later become apparent.

Hope and John had found strength to accept this tragedy in Mr. Whitefield's message, still fresh in their hearts after fifteen years. They'd also been grateful to the Lord for sparing the lives of Hope and the three other children – as Isaac had been saved from his father Abraham's sacrificial knife. And in the years since that nightmarish spring, the Lord had blessed them with three more healthy babies.

John resolutely pulled his thoughts from the sad past and refocused on Hope. Although not as slender as when she was a bride – eight pregnancies in fifteen years had seen to that – she still had a supple, appealing figure. Maturity had sharpened her delicate features. Not a single strand of gray was visible in her brown hair, although John knew he had more than a few in his own.

John watched Hope issue crisp directions to the children as she coordinated preparations for breakfast and for the coming day's work. She dealt patiently and firmly with the usual small crises: a lost schoolbook, a squabble over which child's turn it was to collect the eggs laid overnight by their hens. At one point in the middle of the bustle she rolled her eyes at John in good-natured exasperation. He smiled back sympathetically, but he knew she thrived on activity, and never let the grind of life's routines dull her spirit.

Their material fortunes had flourished as well. John had great success cultivating the more than two hundred acres he now owned. With David big enough to help, the farm in the last year had produced more than the family needed to feed itself or to barter for what they couldn't grow or make. John had used the surplus to acquire a few luxuries, such as pewter plates and knives.

There was a sudden rapping on the hall door. Hope shot John a questioning glance. He shrugged and shook his head to indicate he wasn't expecting anyone. He threaded his way through the crowded kitchen and into the hall.   Through the window he saw an unfamiliar horse tied to the hitching post.

John opened the door to reveal a man of medium height and sturdy build with curly black hair and bright blue eyes. Although barely out of his teens, the visitor carried himself with assurance. He clutched a long, narrow, cloth-covered bundle under one arm.

"Mr. Hierlihy," John greeted the man. Timothy Hierlihy had arrived in Middletown two years ago, and immediately set about applying his education, energy, and considerable charm to making a place for himself. This past spring he'd married a daughter of the prominent Wetmore family. Not long after, Hierlihy had enlisted as a private in the troops marching north under General Phineas Lyman.

That last thought sent a shiver of apprehension down John's spine. "What brings you here on this cold morning?" he asked.

Hierlihy caught the anxiety in John's question. He shook his head with a reassuring smile. "I don't bring bad news," he said, to John's relief. The almost musical lilt of Hierlihy's voice, a sharp contrast to the flat, sometimes nasal speech of Connecticut natives, marked him as a recent arrival from Ireland.

"And it's Ensign Hierlihy now, these two months past," the young man corrected with pardonable pride. John acknowledged that news with a small smile and nod, then waited for the young Irishman to explain his visit.

"I saw General Lyman before I left New York on furlough," Hierlihy said. "When he learned I was coming to Middletown, he asked me to bring you this." He tilted his head to indicate the package under his arm.

"Come in," John said, remembering his manners. As Hierlihy stepped into the hall, John turned to find his family clustered around, unabashedly curious about the unexpected visitor.

Hierlihy laid the bundle on the large oak table, next to the pie, toast, butter, and pitcher of hard cider that would constitute the Lyman family's breakfast. He pulled away the folds of cloth one by one. He paused to heighten the sense of anticipation, before lifting the last fold to reveal a gleaming black leather scabbard with brass decorations. The brass handle of a sword protruded from one end.

Hierlihy lifted the weapon with both hands and presented it with an air of formality to an astonished John. Holding the leather scabbard in his left hand, John gripped the carefully crafted handle in his right and withdrew a thirty-inch blade of steel tapered to a deadly point. The silence was broken by gasps of admiration for the handsome weapon.

"It's called a short sword," Hierlihy offered helpfully. "Best suited for stabbing." He added dryly, "It formerly belonged to a French soldier." His meaning was clear; the blade was part of the spoils from Phineas's victory over the enemy.

John held the sword vertically in front of him, turning it so he could see both sides. Sunlight streaming through the window glinted off its surface. As he studied the blade, his lips turned up in a faint, nostalgic smile, and tears gathered in his eyes.

John saw from Hierlihy's expression that the young soldier was puzzled by his unexpectedly emotional reaction to a trophy of war. But the young Irishman couldn't know that to John this sword was far more than a souvenir of battle. It was a token of remembrance of the hours two young cousins had spent fighting imaginary Indians with makeshift weapons in the woods of Durham. It was Phineas's way of saying that no matter how grand his current station in life, he hadn't forgotten those who'd shared his simple childhood.

Both David and Elihu's eyes had grown wide as they stared at the weapon's wickedly sharp blade. "Was this really used in a battle?" David asked with a mixture of awe and excitement.

Hierlihy smiled indulgently. "It was," he confirmed. "And your cousin Phineas was the hero of it." The family's rapt attention was all the encouragement he needed to launch into an enthusiastic account of the engagement.

"Our troops were camped near Lake George," Hierlihy began. "From there a thousand of our men, and some of our Mohawk allies, marched out – right into an ambuscade prepared by the French and their Abenaki and Caughnawaga Indian allies."

Hierlihy paused. "Some of our soldiers fought bravely, and more than a few died. But many panicked, and fled back to the camp as if Satan was at their heels. Soon after the pursuing French force came into view of the camp, General Johnson took a musket ball to the leg. He left the field of battle, and didn't return," he said, with clear contempt for his superior officer's action.

"General Lyman assumed command," Hierlihy continued with enthusiasm. "We feared the men fleeing the ambush would spread their terror to the soldiers in camp, setting them to running as well. But General Lyman stiffened their spines with his words and his example," he said proudly.

"With General Lyman leading us, we defended the camp for five hours against a thousand French and half again as many Indians! When the enemy gave up the attack and started to withdraw, we boiled out of the camp to pursue them like lions!" Hierlihy's Irish accent had thickened with the excitement of remembering the fight.

"General Lyman was under enemy fire the entire time. His horse was hit, but he was unhurt," Hierlihy said with a touch of awe. "He thanks God for miraculously preserving him in the heat of battle."

John carefully slid the sword smoothly back into its scabbard. "I'm in your debt, Ensign," he said solemnly, "for bringing me this fine gift and word of my cousin's victory and safety. Will you break your fast with us?"

"I must decline," the young man replied. "My furlough is only long enough to spend a few days with my family."

John nodded understandingly. Hierlihy laid his hand on the hall door's iron latch, then hesitated. He clearly still had something on his mind. "I hope to purchase some property in a year or two," he said to John. "Might I call on you for advice about land in Middlefield?"

"Of course," John said. Hierlihy responded with a slight formal bow, then stepped out into the cold morning.

John joined Hope and the children seated in ladder-back chairs, eager to start breakfast. He accepted a pewter plate with a large slice of apple pie and two thick slices of rye toast. He buttered the toast, then cut a bite of pie with a spoon.

"Hierlihy seems the type to make a good neighbor," Hope observed to John. "He obviously stands high in Phineas's opinion."

John nodded in agreement. "It's too bad he's a Churchman, not a Congregationalist," he observed as Hope filled pewter mugs with hard cider.

"Why is that bad?" asked Hannah, as she passed the mugs down the table. "The Birdseys are Churchmen."

John pursed his lips sourly at Hannah's mention of their not-always-agreeable neighbors to the south. "Mr. Hierlihy's ecclesiastical taxes, like those the Birdseys pay, support the Church of England in Middletown where he worships, instead of the Middletown Congregational church," he explained. "It would be the same if he moves to Middlefield. He would provide no new blood for our small congregation, which needs all the funds and members it can get."

"So it's about money?" David asked between bites. His appetite sharpened by two hours of chores, he'd polished off his pie and was tackling his toast.

"Not just that," Hope answered. "Churchmen recognize the king of Great Britain as earthly head of their faith. They don't consider Holy Scripture the only true source of God's word as we Congregationalists do. They observe religious ceremonies left over from the corrupt Roman Papacy."

"Our forefathers in England purified their churches of such corruption," John picked up the explanation. "For this they were persecuted, so they fled to New England, where they could worship according to their conscience."

David nodded, satisfied by the explanation. But John's thoughts remained on Middlefield's Congregational church.

By the end of 1747 the congregation had built a meetinghouse at a site less than two miles from the Lyman home, and had hired the Reverend Ebenezer Gould as pastor. Mr. Gould's history of disagreeing with his previous congregations on spiritual matters helped explain his willingness to accept the pastorate of a small, fledgling church like Middlefield.

Unfortunately, Mr. Gould was proving as contentious in his new post as he had in his old ones. After eight years, consensus was growing that Mr. Gould should be dismissed, and a search begun for a new spiritual leader.

With breakfast finished, David and Esther set out to walk the two miles to the schoolhouse. Hope, Catharine, and Hannah commenced the detested chore of doing laundry – made even more trying by the need for constant vigilance to make sure Elihu, who scampered about like a kitten, didn't topple into scalding water.

John ruffled Elihu's hair as he passed the boy, and set off for a day of mending fences and gathering corn stalks for cattle fodder. He and David had already fetched water to fill the large wooden wash tub, and firewood to heat it in Hope's biggest iron pot.

"I loathe wash day!" Hannah declared passionately as she agitated a load of linen sheets with a long, broad wooden paddle. "It's hot, and it stinks, and it turns my hands red as a boiled lobster!" With her forearm she brushed away strands of hair that had escaped from beneath her mob cap and fallen onto her face.

"Thinking of how nice it looks when it's clean makes it less irksome," Catharine advised in complete sincerity. She added two of John's shirts to Hannah's load.

Hope saw Hannah shoot her sister a look questioning the sanity of someone who found satisfaction in such drudgery. But Hope was pleased to see that, despite her disgruntlement, Hannah didn't shirk her share of the work. She continued energetically agitating the laundry.

By the time David and Esther returned from school in the middle of the afternoon, the entire kitchen was festooned with lines from which hung damp sheets, shifts, shirts, petticoats, and stockings. Esther and Elihu began playing hide-and-seek among the hanging laundry. Their game ended abruptly when Elihu stumbled against the baby's cradle, setting little Phineas to wailing.

John snuffed out the candle, then pulled the blanket up under his chin and sank down into the feather bed. Hope had taken the icy chill off the sheets by rubbing them with a warming pan full of coals.

John wrapped his arms around Hope. She laid her cheek on his shoulder. His chin rested lightly on top of her head. Never did Hope feel more secure than when she lay like this, enveloped tightly in her husband's strong, protective embrace.

John yawned, then said, "I think it's time to shut off the chambers and parlor and move everyone into the kitchen and hall. I'd not like to be cutting firewood in February because we kept fires burning in all of the rooms too late in the year."

He felt Hope nod in agreement. They drifted off to sleep to urgent whispers from upstairs as the children tugged and argued over who was getting more than a fair share of covers.

Shafts of bright moonlight were streaming through the windows when John was jarred awake by a roaring, followed a few seconds later by a violent trembling that shook the entire house. He sat bolt upright, sensing that beside him Hope was also sitting up.

For what seemed an endless moment John's brain struggled to grasp what was happening. "I think it's an earthquake!" he shouted, his voice barely audible above the rumbling that filled his ears.

The timbers of the floors and walls groaned around them, as the earth twisted and undulated like waves on the water. The structure shook so violently it seemed the beams and boards might come crashing down on their heads. In the kitchen pots and pans fell to the floor with a clang, and the spinning wheels and butter churn toppled over with a crash. In the hall the table and chairs slid around, banging into each other and the wall.

Hope snatched Phineas from the cradle and held him tightly against her breast, leaning forward to shield him with her body. From upstairs, above the din, they could hear small terrified voices crying for "Mama!" and "Papa!"

John leapt from the bed and started for the stairs. The violent rocking of the floor threw him against a heavy wooden chest. His head struck a corner, which gouged a deep gash above his right eye. He sprawled to the floor.

"John!" Hope cried out. Relief flooded her when, after several heartbeats, she saw him struggle to his hands and knees. He shook his head to clear it of the blow's dazing effect. He wiped blood from his eye with the sleeve of his woolen shirt. He leaned on the chest for support to get to his feet, then grabbed wildly for the wall as the trembling earth sent the chest lurching from under his hand.

John groped to the foot of the stairs. He felt his way step by step with his hands to the upper floor. The house continued to shake. "David? Elihu?" he called into the boys' chamber.

"We're all right, Papa," David answered steadily, despite the fear in his voice.

"Stay in bed," John ordered, then felt his way to the girls' chamber.

"We're unharmed, Papa," Catharine called out. In the moonlight he could make out the silhouette of the three sisters huddled together in the middle of the bed.

Suddenly the tremor ceased, as abruptly as it had begun. An eerie silence reigned, broken only by the whimpering of little Esther, who clung like a burr to Catharine.

"Is it the end of the world, Papa?" Hannah shrieked. Esther began to sob.

"I don't think so," John answered with as much reassurance as he could muster. "It was an earthquake. We had one when I was a boy." He didn't say that the quake in 1727 hadn't been nearly as strong as this one.

"Is it over?" Esther asked. Her tearful voice was muffled by Catharine's shift, into which she'd buried her face.

"I hope so," John replied. "But we should go outside. Put on your coats and shoes and come downstairs."

After giving David and Elihu the same instructions, John went down to the parlor. Hope cried out in alarm when she got a good look at him. The sleeve of his nightshirt, which he'd used repeatedly to wipe the blood from his head wound, was soaked crimson.

"It's not as bad as it looks," John reassured her. "The children are safe. I think we should go outside. The earthquake when we were children was followed by lesser shocks."

Hope wrapped Phineas, who amazingly hadn't made a peep during the entire furor, in a blanket. She laid him on the bed, then went into the kitchen for a cloth to staunch John's bleeding.

The clean laundry was strewn across the kitchen floor, soiled with ashes thrown out of the fireplace. Hopes eyes welled with tears of irrational irritation at the thought of how it would all have to be rewashed. She grabbed the cleanest cloth she could find, then checked that none of the coals banked in the fireplace for the night had been tossed onto the wooden floor, where they could start a fire.

The entire family was soon huddled in front of the house. Standing in the still, cold night under a star-filled sky, with a full moon bathing the countryside in silver light, it didn't seem possible that just a few minutes earlier the solid earth had convulsed beneath their feet like a wild beast.

From the barn came fretful sounds from the skittish livestock. From across the swamp to the northeast drifted faint voices from the house of their neighbors, David and Elizabeth Miller.

John's instinct had been to get everyone outside, away from things that might fall on them – including the house itself. But the children were shivering uncontrollably, their teeth chattering with cold. He realized they couldn't stay out here all night.

"Let's go back in," John said. The children looked uncertain, and Hope doubtful. "We'll all sleep in the parlor," he said reassuringly. "We can get out quickly if we need to."

A few minutes later Hope and John were back in bed, with Esther snuggled between them. Phineas was in his cradle, Elihu in the trundle bed, and the three older children lay on the floor wrapped in coats and blankets.

Hope stared up into the darkness. She would sleep no more this night, nor she was sure would John.

The earthquake was doubtless a sign from God. In the coming months, ministers across New England would lead their congregations in determining what they'd done to incur the Lord's wrath.

Hope reflected that not twenty-four hours ago she'd stood in the kitchen contemplating with satisfaction their solid home, their healthy family, their prosperous farm. The earthquake's fearsome power could have destroyed it all in the blink of an eye, had that been God's will.

It was a sobering reminder that they were no safer snug in their beds than Phineas had been on the battlefield. Whatever happened was part of a divine plan that mere mortals could never understand, but only accept with faith in the Lord.

Chapter Eight

October, 1759
Middletown

The eastern sky blazed red and orange from the sun hovering just below the horizon as John stepped outside on a frosty autumn morning. In low-lying spots near the river and swamp, patches of dense fog nestled like rolls of fleece. John harnessed the horse to the two-wheeled cart that would carry the entire Lyman family to the center of Middletown.

The early morning chill and mists had dissipated by the time they reached Middletown's main street, which paralleled the Great River, now commonly called the Connecticut River. The sun shone brightly in a blue sky streaked with wisps of high-flying clouds.

John's checked shirt, brown woolen waistcoat and frock coat had seemed a sensible choice when dressing in the pre-dawn chill. But as often happened in Connecticut, the weather had changed abruptly, turning a crisp fall morning into a sweltering August-like day.

Sweat broke out on John's forehead and on his neck under his queue of hair as the family made their way along Middletown's crowded, dusty main street. He broke into a rough cough that lasted for nearly half a minute before subsiding.

The main street and the byways running off it were lined on both sides with clapboard buildings of one, two, or even three stories. These served as homes or workshops or stores or offices – sometimes more than one at the same time – for a wide assortment of businessmen and tradesmen.

Walking toward the town house at the crossroads, the Lyman family passed five merchants' stores, three taverns, two joiners' shops, two shoemakers, and the establishments of four shipmasters, a silversmith, a tanner, a saddler, an apothecary, a slave dealer, a physician, and a hatter. North of the crossroads were more businesses, including a ropewalk – a narrow structure a thousand feet long in which strands of hemp were laid out to be twisted into miles of rope. That rope was an essential supply for the sailing vessels docked at wharves extending out into the Connecticut River.

Those ships were the source of the prosperity that pulsed all around the Lymans on Middletown's streets. Country produce and livestock from central Connecticut farms like that of the Lymans flowed steadily into Middletown, to be loaded onto vessels bound for the West Indies, or for colonial ports like Boston or New York. At these destinations, the meat, grain, vegetables, cheese, and other goods were traded for products ranging from Jamaican rum to nutmegs to iron nails to imported British cloth. These were brought back to Middletown for sale.

The trade was a highly risky gamble. Many a ship went down at sea, carrying its crew, passengers, and cargo to the bottom. It wasn't uncommon for a vessel to sail down the Connecticut River, the sunlight glinting off its ripples making it resemble a fluid, sparkling blue carpet – never to be heard of again.

But those merchants, ship owners, sea captains, investors, and businessmen who were both shrewd and lucky could garner spectacular fortunes from the trade and from enterprises needed to sustain it, such as shipbuilding, sail making, and rope making. Some claimed Middletown rivaled Boston as New England's wealthiest town. The rich spent their money in Middletown's taverns, and kept its tradesmen and artisans busy building handsome homes and crafting fine furniture and elegant silver pieces to furnish them.

"You go to Mr. Alsop's," John said when they reached the town house, nodding toward the store that occupied that building's ground floor. "I'll call on Mr. Hamlin."

"And you'll see Dr. Dickinson?" Hope said. It was a statement, not a question.

John frowned in irritation. "There's no need," he said.

Hope shot her husband the same exasperated look she gave the children when they objected to taking a dose of foul-tasting castor oil to relieve costive bowels. She and John had been arguing about this since the trip to Middletown had been planned.

"You've had that cough for nearly five months," she snapped. "None of my treatments or my mother's have worked. It's time to consult a physician."

They stared at each other for a long moment. John was the first to look away, in a sign of surrender. "Doctors often do more harm than good," he grumbled, half to himself.

"We'll meet back here," Hope said, turning to enter the store.

"Don't buy all Mr. Alsop's fancy goods," John called with mock seriousness in an effort to lighten the tension between them. That drew a short, sardonic laugh from Hope, the sharpest and most practical of shoppers.

John walked the short distance to Jabez Hamlin's establishment on the corner of the crossroads. Inside, the long, low structure's rough wooden floorboards were crowded with barrels of beef and pork and heavy sacks of wheat, rye, and Indian corn.

Hamlin, who was leaning with one elbow on a tall barrel, was a giant of a man in his late forties. A graduate of Yale, he, like John's cousin Phineas, hadn't gone into the ministry. Hamlin instead had opted to become a lawyer and a merchant.

It was Hamlin's position as commissary to Connecticut's troops fighting the ongoing war with the French and Indians that brought John to his store today. The man would be looking to purchase as much country produce as possible to feed the soldiers. That demand, combined with the quality of what John could supply, would allow John to negotiate a good price.

Hamlin was talking with Philip Mortimer, a bony man of about the same age. Mortimer's ownership of the ropewalk had made him one of Middletown's richest men. He lived in a massive gambrel-roofed mansion with a magnificent view of the Connecticut River.

Like Timothy Hierlihy, Mortimer was a native of Ireland – although he'd been in the colonies far longer. He was a Churchman as well.

"Mr. Lyman," Hamlin greeted him, straightening up. "I expected you would be coming to see me with something for our troops."

"Mr. Hamlin," John replied with a polite, restrained nod. Hamlin was one of Middletown's most respected leaders, with a reputation for sterling integrity. But he was also a merchant who by nature would squeeze the maximum profit out of any deal. John intended to bargain sharply with the man.

"Your cousin General Lyman and our soldiers again made Connecticut proud by helping drive the French from the fort north of

Albany," Mortimer observed. His Irish accent was much diluted, but still detectable.

"That he did," Hamlin agreed, then snorted. "They're lucky General Lyman agreed to continue serving after being cheated of credit for his victory at Lake George. That slippery General Johnson claimed the day's glory for himself. He didn't even mention General Lyman's name in his official report about the battle to the Crown!" he exclaimed in disgust.

"Then Parliament granted Johnson a fortune – five thousand pounds! – and the king made him a baronet as reward for his 'victory,'" Mortimer said, shaking his head. "That's rubbing salt in the wound."

John nodded. There'd been much ill feeling in Connecticut over this outrageous slight of the colony's hero. But so far as John knew, Phineas hadn't contested this injustice. And he'd accepted command of Connecticut's forces in every campaign since.

"Phineas is a man of unwavering loyalty," John said, "to his men, to his colony – and to the king and Parliament, who were deceived by Johnson's self-serving lies."

Mortimer shook his head as if to clear it of distracting thoughts. "This isn't getting you that rope I promised," he said to Hamlin. "I'll go back to work and let you two get on with business."

As Mortimer passed John on his way to the door, he said in an aside intended to reach Hamlin's ears, "A word of advice. Mr. Hamlin has no mercy when he's haggling."

John turned back to Hamlin, who looked half-amused and half-exasperated at Mortimer's comment. He assumed a sober, business-like expression, and asked, "What do you have for me, Mr. Lyman?"

An hour later, after striking a bargain with Hamlin to purchase quantities of the Lymans' beef, wheat, and rye at a price that would leave John with a good profit, John turned down a side street to the home of Dr. John Dickinson. He knocked on the door to the little addition that served as the physician's office. "Enter!" a voice called.

John stepped into a sun-filled room. A young man sat behind a desk, a thick leather-bound book opened before him.

Dr. Dickinson was twenty-eight years old, a short man with thinning blond hair and bright blue eyes that radiated confidence. Like all but a handful of physicians in Connecticut, Dr. Dickinson had no formal medical training. He'd acquired his knowledge of healing through a four-year apprenticeship with a practicing physician. He sought to augment that training by reading any medical treatises he could find, like the volume in front of him.

The office walls were lined with shelves stocked with an assortment of boxes, crocks, jars, and bottles. They contained liquids, plant material such as herbs, and other ingredients. John recognized a couple of labels, but most were mysteries.

"Mr. Lyman!" the doctor greeted John. The explosive hacking that seized John when he drew breath to respond caused the physician to draw his eyebrows together in concern. "How long have you had that cough?" he asked.

"I had a summer cold in June that lasted a week," John choked out after catching his breath, "but the cough hung on."

"Has it always been a dry cough?" Dr. Dickinson asked. John nodded.

"Any fever?"

"No," John answered.

The doctor put his palm on John's forehead. "You feel a bit warm, even considering the weather," he said to John's surprise. He took John's wrist between two fingers and stood silent for a moment. "A hard, quick pulse," he said to himself. "Have you lost any flesh?"

"A few pounds, perhaps," John admitted uneasily.

"A blood-letting is the first order of treatment," Dr. Dickinson said with brisk assurance. "Sit down and bare your right arm."

John did as instructed. Dr. Dickinson retrieved two earthenware bowls, one with calibration marks on the inside. He poured hot water from a kettle hanging over the blaze in the office's small fireplace into the unmarked bowl. "Put your hand in that," he directed John.

From a desk drawer the physician retrieved a box. He opened it to reveal an array of lancets. He selected one, lifted John's hand from the water, and tied cotton tape tightly around his wrist.

"Open and close your hand to make the veins stand out," Dr. Dickinson said. After John complied, the doctor pulled his patient's fingers down with one hand. With the other hand he made a small lengthwise incision in a vein on the inside of John's wrist between his hand and the tape.

John winced at the sharp sting. The doctor submerged John's hand again in the hot water, loosened the tape, then lifted the hand and positioned it so that the blood flowed into the calibrated bowl.

When the blood reached the one-pint mark, Dr. Dickinson pressed a wad of lint against the incision. He secured it in place with cotton tape he'd untied from John's wrist.

John tried to stand, but a rush of light-headedness forced him back down, fumbling behind him for the chair with his left hand.

"I should have warned you not to get up right away," Dr. Dickinson said apologetically. "You'll be unsteady for a few minutes. Some wine will help restore you." He took a dark glass bottle from a shelf, twisted out a cork, filled a cup half full, and handed it to John.

John sipped some wine, laid back his head, and closed his eyes. He opened them a couple minutes later to see Dr. Dickinson pouring hot water over ingredients in an earthenware bowl.

"I'm preparing an infusion of wild poppy leaves and marshmallow root," the doctor explained. "Come back in an hour and it will be ready. You should take a cupful whenever you have a coughing spasm."

John drained the rest of the wine from the cup. He again tried to stand, this time successfully if still a bit unsteadily. "My thanks," he said, rolling his sleeve down over his bandaged wrist.

"The charge is three shillings – that includes the infusion," said Dr. Dickinson.

"Will two bushels of turnips be sufficient?" John asked, pulling on his frock coat.

The physician nodded. He dipped a quill into an inkwell, then recorded the amount due in a large, leather-bound ledger.

Practically anything a person might need or want, from saws to salt, beaver hats to buttons, snuff to chocolate, raisins to ribbons, could be found at Richard Alsop's store. Most of these goods had come to Middletown on ships owned by Alsop, a beefy man of thirty-three with cool gray eyes who had been one of the big winners in the West Indies trade.

"I'll have a pound of tea, half a pound of coffee, half a pound of chocolate, and a cone of sugar," Hope instructed Alsop's clerk. Alsop himself stood at a tall desk, with a massive vellum-bound account ledger open on its slanted top. As his clerk fetched each of the items, Alsop wrote it down with its price on a left-hand page under the heading "John Lyman." On the facing page he would record when and how John paid for the goods – whether with bushels of Indian corn, wheat, oats, or flaxseed; barrels of pork or beef; a quantity of beeswax; or even hard cash, so scarce in the colonies.

"Also, three ounces of ginger and half a dozen nutmegs," Hope added. She was thinking of the pies to be baked and stored in the unheated chambers of the house for consumption over the winter. "And half a bushel of salt." John would need that to preserve the beef and pork after the autumn slaughtering.

Catharine and Hannah were examining an array of fabrics imported from England: shalloon, bombazeen, oznaburg, taffeta, chintz, calico, velvet, silk, and damask. All were far finer than anything that came off Connecticut looms. Catharine was trying to decide between a calico with a cheerful print of small flowers, or a chintz with a larger, bolder floral design, for a new gown.

Catharine, now eighteen, had no serious suitors yet, but young men had started to pay her attention. Hope and John had begun to consider what her marriage portion might contain. It would unquestionably include bedclothes, napkins, and tablecloths for her new home. These would be sewn by Catharine with help from her sisters and Hope. With that looming workload in mind, Hope directed the clerk to add three sewing needles and four dozen pins to her growing pile of purchases.

"Could we buy this, Mama?" Hannah asked coaxingly, indicating a length of deep green damask woven in a sweeping floral pattern. "It would make the most beautiful gown."

"It is very handsome," Hope acknowledged noncommittally. "Put it on the counter, and we'll see."

Hannah clearly wasn't satisfied with the equivocal answer. Still she refrained from wheedling, a display of self-control that inclined Hope toward granting her request. Most of Hannah's clothes were ones Catharine had outgrown, reworked to fit the younger girl's figure. Although Hannah chafed at rarely getting something new, she wore the used garments without complaint.

When John entered the Alsop store, he spied Hope standing in front of a large accumulation of goods on the counter. She was intently studying her reflection in a looking-glass, tracing a finger over its carved frame. He approached quietly from behind, until his face appeared beside hers in the looking-glass.

Startled, Hope lost her grip on the looking-glass. Only John's quick reflexes saved it from smashing into splinters on the shop floor – to the enormous relief of Alsop's clerk.

Flustered, Hope took the looking-glass and put it on the shelf.

"Buy it if you like," John said. "It can't be very dear."

"We have no need of a looking-glass," Hope protested. "Although," she went on, "if it were hung on the parlor wall it would reflect candlelight and firelight, brightening the room at night."

"We'll take it," John said decisively, retrieving the looking-glass and placing it atop the pile of goods which included the damask Hannah coveted. "I got a very good price from Mr. Hamlin. We can spend a few shillings on something that's caught your fancy. Think of it as an anniversary token," he said; they had marked twenty years of marriage the previous month. "Small recompense for half a lifetime's worth of happiness," he added in a voice meant for Hope's ears only.

As the clerk wrapped up their purchases, John said, "I must stop at Dr. Dickinson's. He's preparing an infusion for my cough."

"Did he bleed you?" Hope asked.

"He did," John confirmed. Hope nodded her approval.

John grimaced in mock pain as Alsop announced the sum of Hope's purchases. He held his arms out to be loaded up with goods to carry out to the cart.

Chapter Nine

July, 1760
Middlefield

The sound sent shafts of fear through fourteen-year-old David. He was clearing rocks from a field under a late-morning July sun so intense it seemed to have scorched the sky to white ash. A trickle of sweat ran down between his shoulder blades as he straightened up and glanced back at his father. John was leaning on the handle of his shovel, pressing a white cloth against his mouth as he struggled through a paroxysm of coughing.

It had been nine months since John had consulted Dr. Dickinson about his nagging cough. Neither his treatments nor the expensive ministrations of three other physicians had helped.

The medical minds all agreed that John was suffering from consumption – a disease that slowly ravaged the lungs. Victims of consumption wasted away, as if being physically consumed; John had lost so much flesh, and his skin had become so pallid, that he looked much older than his forty-three years.

Once consumption took root, it was rarely cured. Only smallpox was more feared.

David waited until the awful hacking ceased. When John lowered the cloth from his mouth, David saw splotches of bright red blood on it.

"Maybe we should rest a bit, Papa," David suggested.

John shook his head as he straightened up. "No, we're not even half done clearing this field. Let's keep on a while longer."

David nodded obediently as he bent over to continue prying loose a stubbornly imbedded stone. He thought of how the changes brought about by his father's illness had entangled him in a web of conflicting emotions that he couldn't share with anyone.

David both pitied and admired John, who endured his torturous suffering without complaint. But he felt increasingly overwhelmed as more and more responsibilities were shifted onto his young shoulders. And he resented how his mother's increasing reliance on him to fill a man's role around the farm and house left him with no time to do anything else but eat and sleep.

And as illogical as he knew it to be, David was angry with John for falling ill, for no longer being the prop of their family – a situation he knew his father would give anything to change. His mouth twisted in guilty frustration, David channeled his shameful confusion into a series of fierce pushes on his pitchfork that at last dislodged the rock. The stone and thousands of others unearthed over the years would be made into walls that served many purposes, including keeping grazing livestock from trampling fields of crops.

"Papa! David!" Elihu called from the edge of the field. "Mama says dinner is ready." Now nine, Elihu was a tall boy who did a good share of chores around the farm. Even little Phineas at nearly five helped out. But it was to David, her cherished eldest surviving son, that Hope looked for strength as her husband weakened.

"Come, Son," John said, clearly relieved at the excuse to stop working. As David slowed his pace to match his father's near-shuffle, he knew he'd be returning alone to the field that afternoon.

Chapter Ten

January, 1763
Middlefield

As 1763 dawned, Hope Lyman was a far different woman from the one who faced the world three years earlier. Remorseless necessity had squeezed the last drop of self-deluding optimism out of her. What remained was a flinty determination to confront and conquer problems that multiplied like weeds in a neglected garden.

John's health had so deteriorated he couldn't perform any physical labor. David, assisted by Elihu and Phineas, at times joined by Catharine, Hannah, Esther, and Hope herself, were working the farm. There was no money to hire laborers to help.

John also could no longer manage the family's finances or legal affairs. Hope had taken them over, and was grappling with the need to replace income lost because the farm didn't produce as much as it had under John's capable stewardship. She also had to pay the physicians' bills and buy the medicines they prescribed – although nothing had stemmed the grim advance of John's consumption.

Hope had resorted to selling more than half their land, but even that desperate step hadn't brought in enough to meet the family's financial obligations. Hope had borrowed money from relatives and acquaintances. She'd run up debts with merchants who, however lenient they might be to a family in distress, would eventually have to be paid in full.

In these increasingly difficult years Hope had relied for guidance on her mother. The Widow Hawley had shared everything she'd learned in more than thirty years of single-handedly cultivating her own farm and conducting financial and legal activities.

But the Widow Hawley, approaching three score and ten years, had been stricken with apoplexy in late December. She was now at death's door. Hope was facing the loss not just of a loving – if sometimes overbearing – mother, but of her most valued adviser.

Hope had known for several weeks what she had to do. Still she'd shrunk from the step that would amount to surrendering any hope that God might answer their prayers with a miracle for John.

"I spoke to Abraham Camp," Hope said casually to John one day when the new year was barely a week old. Camp was a friend who'd lived in Middlefield longer than the Lymans had.

"About a new minister?" John asked listlessly. He rarely rose from bed anymore, and then only for a few minutes at a time.

"No," Hope replied regretfully. The Middlefield pulpit had been vacant since the congregation dismissed Ebenezer Gould in 1756. Finding a new minister whose personality and spiritual beliefs were in harmony with a congregation's could be a slow process. But it didn't normally drag on for seven years – a delay explained in part by the modest salary the small Middlefield congregation could afford.

Some Middlefield residents had taken to worshiping in other societies, like Durham. Occasionally clergymen from other congregations conducted Sabbath services in the Middlefield meetinghouse. But such erratic preaching was no substitute for a settled minister who could make regular pastoral visits to John.

"We talked about how to transfer the house and homelot into my name," Hope went on. "So the children will always be provided for." She sat on the edge of the feather bed and busied herself stirring a steaming bowl of broth to avoid meeting John's gaze.

"Hope," John said tenderly. He laid a frail hand on her wrist to stop her stirring. After a long moment she looked up into his brown eyes, once so bright and clear, now dull with pain and exhaustion.

"We both know my time on earth is short," John said gently. "Sometimes at night I lie awake thinking of death, and fear closes in until I think it will smother me." He paused for a moment. "Then I remind myself I'm far more blessed than those who die unexpectedly. God has given me precious time to prepare my heart to submit to His judgment."

John struggled to catch a breath, then said with a harsh edge to his weak voice, "But I can't accept that my legacy to you and our children will be poverty. And I become angry at the Lord! I know I should trust you to His care. But I can't," he whispered, his features twisted in anguished guilt.

Hope set the bowl on the floor, and leaned over to rest her cheek on John's sunken chest. His confession touched her – and frightened her. John needed to humble his spirit and accept God's will, finding comfort in His promise that they would be reunited for all eternity. Maybe what she had to tell him would help him do that.

They lay there for several quiet minutes. At last John asked, "What did you and Abraham talk about?"

Hope sat up and wiped away unshed tears. "Abraham agreed to buy the house and homelot from you and then sell them to me for the same price," Hope continued. "They will be in my name alone. That should shield them from claims on your estate."

Hope saw a flicker of relief in John's haunted eyes. This legal maneuvering would ensure his family could keep their home after his death. "Do it," he gasped, "as soon as you can."

The transfer was completed before the month was out, but not as quickly as John and Hope would have wanted. It was delayed by her mother's death on January 23.

Hope Stow Hawley had chosen to be buried in Middlefield's burying ground, rather than beside her long-dead husband, Jehiel, in the Middletown graveyard. When Hope learned of her wish, she thought of her sister Mary's speculation about whether their mother had doubted their father's love for her.

Hope took from Abraham Camp the deed selling her the house and homelot that Camp had purchased from John a few minutes earlier. She recalled their first night in this house, when she'd asked John's permission to buy a few acres in her own name. More than twenty years later here was her desire fulfilled on a much larger scale – but how gladly would she give it up if John could be well!

Chapter Eleven

March, 1763
Middlefield

Hope sat on a stump outside the kitchen, plucking feathers from the goose she would roast for supper. She added the feathers to those in a bag that she was saving to stuff a pillow. A few feathers from the goose's wings would be set aside to be made into quill pens.

Hope was enjoying the warmth of the March morning sun, feeble as it was. Catharine was sitting with John in the parlor. Hannah was baking bread. Esther was in the kitchen carding wool – combing small tufts of fleece between two pieces of wood with wire teeth to straighten out the fibers so they could be spun into yarn.

Phineas was feeding the chickens and geese. David and Elihu were collecting buckets of sap tapped from their maple trees. The sap would be boiled down into maple sugar, some for the family's use, some to sell or trade for goods they couldn't make themselves.

They were good sons and daughters, Hope reflected gratefully. They all did their best to help keep the farm and the family going.

As her three eldest children had matured, their futures were a source of increasing concern for Hope. Catharine was twenty-one now, and Hannah nineteen – both old enough to have wed and started families. Their marriage portions would be small, owing to the decline in the Lyman family's fortunes. That explained why only a few young men had so far shown interest in courting the sisters.

It was a worrisome situation. A woman who reached her mid-twenties without marrying had a good chance of ending up a spinster. And the older she was when she wed, the fewer years she would have to produce children.

David, now seventeen, had changed in the past year from a boy into a man with a healthy interest in girls. Hope was keeping a sharp eye out to make sure some pretty face didn't distract him from his family's interests. She depended heavily on David, and she and his siblings would need him even more in the years to come.

David understandably chafed under his mother's scrutiny, but Hope felt she had no choice. It wasn't as though the age at which a man wed was the same cause for concern as for a woman. Since most men could father children into their sixties, delaying marriage didn't have as great an impact on the size of their families.

Hope set the plucked goose on a wooden platter on the ground. It was then she spotted someone coming down the road from Middletown. She stood and with a hand shaded her eyes against the sunlight.

It was a man on horseback, but at this distance Hope couldn't recognize the rider. Anxiety suddenly burned like acid in her stomach. She hoped this wasn't one of the many people to whom they owed money come in an attempt to collect. They'd have as much success trying to squeeze blood from a stone.

As the rider drew closer, Hope saw something distinctly familiar in his features. But it wasn't until he dismounted that Hope thought she recognized him. "Phineas?" she said uncertainly. His face broke into a smile that told her this indeed was General Phineas Lyman.

Hope and John hadn't seen Phineas since the beginning of the war with the French and Indians. The fighting in that conflict had only recently ended in a victory for the British and their colonial comrades-in-arms. Phineas had commanded Connecticut troops throughout the war, in military campaigns from Montreal to Cuba.

When it had become clear John's time was running out, Hope had written Phineas of that melancholy fact. She'd asked him to come see his cousin if possible. She'd done so without telling John.

Hope had no idea if Phineas would be able to make such a trip, or when, where, or even whether her letter would reach him. The last she'd heard of him was the previous summer, when he'd led troops besieging the fortress of Havana, more than a thousand miles away. But she'd tried, and now, nearly miraculously, he was here.

Phineas's years in the army had left their mark. He was no longer stocky as in his youth, but sinewy. A scar ran from his hairline to his right temple. Although dressed in civilian clothes, his ramrod posture bespoke his military background.

Time had added a good amount of gray to Phineas's sandy hair. But he radiated the energy and vitality of a man much younger than his forty-eight years. And the eyes were still those of the youth who'd gone forth from Durham determined to forge a distinguished future – bright blue, with an unquenchable spark of enthusiasm.

"Cousin Hope," Phineas said, giving her a quick yet affectionate hug. Phineas had known Hope growing up, but they hadn't been anywhere near as close as he and John.

The boy Phineas had come running around from the barnyard at the sound of the horse. David and Elihu were approaching the house, lugging heavy wooden buckets of maple sap by rope handles. All three youths studied the stranger with unabashed curiosity.

"Am I in time?" Phineas asked, with a directness born of army life, in which straightforward questions and answers were critical.

Hope nodded, still recovering from her shock.

"Is he sensible?" Again Hope nodded, and Phineas's intense expression softened with relief.

"I received your letter only a week ago," he explained. "I didn't return from the expedition to Cuba until late last year."

Hope shook her head to indicate that Phineas's explanation was unnecessary. "John will be so happy to see you," she said with a trembling smile.

Hope picked up the plucked goose on its wooden platter and the half-full bag of feathers. As she and Phineas turned toward the house, Hope caught sight of the boys.

"Let me present our sons," Hope said proudly. "This is David, our eldest, and Elihu." Both youths bobbed their heads in acknowledgement, still holding the sap buckets. "And this," Hope turned, "is our youngest, Phineas."

The elder Phineas arched an inquiring brow at Hope. She nodded. "He was born the day of your great victory at Lake George."

"Meet your cousin, General Phineas Lyman," she told the boys.

"You're the one who sent Papa the fine sword!" Elihu cried out excitedly, summoning forth a smile from the soldier. "We hung it on pegs over the fireplace in the parlor for everyone to see."

Hope and Phineas stepped into the kitchen. "Our daughters Hannah and Esther," Hope told him, as she set the goose on the table and dropped the bag of feathers on the floor. "And our oldest, Catharine," she added as the young woman entered from the parlor. "This is your cousin, General Phineas Lyman," Hope said.

All three nodded, flustered, like their brothers, by this sudden appearance in the flesh of a man who was a living legend throughout New England and about whom they'd heard many stories from their father. Phineas gave a courteous nod of acknowledgement.

"Is your father awake?" Hope asked Catharine.

"He just woke up," she said.

Hope put a hand on the door to the parlor, but Phineas stopped her before she pushed it open. "How much longer does he have?" he asked solemnly.

Hope didn't flinch at the blunt question. "The doctors say he won't live out the spring," she said in a low voice. "It's harder for him to breathe with each passing day," she cautioned him, then led Phineas into the parlor.

John was lying on his back on the bed. His eyes were closed in a weariness that was bone deep. Hope was struck by how the scar left on John's forehead from striking it on a chest during the earthquake mirrored the one on Phineas's face.

Phineas concealed his distress at John's pitiful condition. He'd lost so much flesh his ribs stood out, and he was pale as a ghost.

"You have a visitor, John," Hope said. He half-raised his lids and looked at her with tepid interest. When he saw the man beside her, his eyes flew open. He stared in confused disbelief.

"It's me, John," Phineas said, answering the unspoken question with a warm smile.

"Is it – really?" John asked, looking to Hope for confirmation, as his mind struggled to grasp this unexpected development.

"Yes, John," she answered reassuringly.

Phineas sat down on the chair Catharine had vacated and hitched it closer to the bed. "I know it must be taxing for you to speak," he said, leaning forward to take one of John's hands in his. "You say what you can, and I'll do the rest of the talking."

John nodded, tears gathering in his eyes even as his emaciated face brightened with joy. Hope stepped back and quietly closed the parlor door to give the cousins time alone.

After half an hour Phineas called for Hope. John looked exhausted, but happy. Phineas rose from the chair.

"Can you – come back?" John asked.

Phineas shook his head regretfully. "Some of my fellow veterans are forming a Company of Military Adventurers to ask His Majesty for a grant of land as compensation for our services in the war. Considering how Sir William Johnson lied his way to a title and a fortune after the battle at Lake George, we think it wisest to send someone home to London to present the petition in person. I'm confident when the king learns the truth about how faithfully the provincial troops served him, he'll be most generous. If they ask me to go, I'll need to sail at the earliest opportunity. And I'll likely be gone for several years."

"Then this is the last time – we'll see each other," John managed to say, the light in his expression fading.

Phineas's eyes welled up with tears, but a faint smile came to his lips as he shook his head. "It is only the last time until we meet in Heaven, as our Lord has promised," he said with solid conviction.

Chapter Twelve

April, 1763
Middlefield

"I, John Lyman, of Middletown, being weak of body but of sound mind and memory–." John, lying flat on his back on the feather bed, stopped to gasp for air.   Simply breathing had become difficult; talking was an ordeal. Hope watched their neighbor David Coe write down the words John had dictated, then wait for him to continue.

"Commit my soul to God that gave it hoping in the mercy of the Redeemer." John squeezed out the last few syllables before stopping again. He panted, open-mouthed, as if he'd just run a long distance.

"As to those worldly goods it hath pleased the Lord to bestow upon me I depose in the following manner," John resumed after a pause. "I bequeath to each of my children, David, Elihu, Phineas, Catharine, Hannah, and Esther twenty shillings lawful apiece."

How pitiful an inheritance those sums were, John thought, especially compared to what he'd once hoped to leave his heirs. He was almost embarrassed to have Coe write it down, but he wanted to acknowledge each of his children in his will.

John inhaled, but erupted in a fit of choked coughing. Hope stepped forward with a cloth that he pressed to his mouth to catch the blood gushing from his lungs. After a few torturous moments the coughing stopped, and John gathered his breath again.

"I bequeath to my well-beloved wife Hope Lyman all the rest of my real and personal estate after my just debts and funeral charges are paid to be at her disposal forever."

David Coe stopped writing and cast John a questioning look. Law and tradition typically gave a widow one-third of her husband's real estate to use – but not sell or give away – until her death, after which it went to his children. A widow also received one-third of her husband's personal property, or "movables," to do with however she pleased, with the remaining two-thirds going to his children. John was breaking with this practice; save for the modest monetary bequests to his children, he was leaving everything he owned, and complete control over it, to Hope.

Coe glanced at the Lymans' neighbor, David Miller, there to serve as a witness. Miller gave a small shrug and raised his eyebrows in response, letting Coe know he was equally taken aback.

Coe was about to ask John if he'd heard correctly. But he saw the answer to his question in the absolute trust with which the dying man regarded his wife. Coe hastened to write down the words.

"And I do hereby appoint my wife sole executrix of this my last will and testament," John forced out the final syllables.

Hope had known what John intended to put in his will. Still, her eyes blurred with tears. In two sentences John had acknowledged all she'd brought to their marriage and declared his confidence in her.

Coe slid an arm behind John and helped him to a half-sitting position. John scrawled a shaky but legible signature at the bottom of the document, then Coe lowered him back down. Coe dated the document, April 2, 1763, then passed it to Miller for his signature.

John turned feverish eyes toward his eldest son – still nine months shy of his eighteenth birthday. David had watched in uncomfortable silence as the adults performed the legal proceeding.

"David, you must be the man of the family," John said in a raspy whisper. "You're a good son. I know I can trust you to care for your mother and your brothers and sisters."

John's heart ached for the obviously terrified teenager. "Put your faith in God," he continued. "And always be guided by your mother." He looked at Hope adoringly. "She is wise and strong," he finished almost inaudibly, his eyelids drooping in exhaustion.

"I will, Papa. I promise," David pledged with desperation, relieved his voice didn't crack with the fear and grief threatening to overwhelm him. He took two steps toward the bed, gripped John's emaciated hand in his own strong, calloused one. "Don't worry about anything," he said in what he hoped was a reassuring voice.

There was no reaction on John's face. But David felt his father's hand squeeze his, ever so weakly, and knew John had heard his pledge.

A spring shower spattered the clapboards of the Lyman house during the first dark hour of May 21, 1763. Hope, her brother Samuel, and Abraham Camp were at John's bedside, maintaining a death watch.

Hope sat on the feather bed, holding John's limp, skeletal hand. He labored to pull air into his failing lungs, but he was slowly strangling as if a noose were tightening around his neck. Watching him struggle in the flickering candlelight, Hope couldn't stop herself from instinctively taking a deep breath, guiltily savoring the sweet sensation of her lungs filling to the very bottom with moist, fresh air.

John was conscious, but couldn't speak. His eyes never left Hope's face. She understood the soundless words he mouthed between wheezes: prayers for himself, for her, for their children.

Suddenly John's bluish lips stopped moving. His hand stirred feebly in Hope's, and she gazed one last time into his brown eyes before the life drained from them. His body ceased to struggle, then settled into the stillness of death.

Hope stood in the front doorway, gazing out over the dawning glory of a spring morning. The rays of the rising sun sparkled off droplets of rain clinging to the lush green foliage visible in every direction. Nature glowed in the light that spread over the landscape as the sun cleared the horizon. A gentle breeze blew across tall grasses, sending waves of yellow and red color rippling through the fields. Wherever she looked, she was greeted by scenes of another season of vibrant new life unfolding.

Hope thought of another sunny May day, twenty-three years earlier – the day on which her first son had been born and had died. And of the second son named John taken by smallpox in May seventeen years past. Now, in a coffin in the parlor behind her, her husband lay dead as well, in the forty-seventh year of his age.

Family and friends had dressed John's body in special grave clothes, then placed it in the open coffin in the parlor to await the funeral that afternoon. They'd shrouded the looking-glass with a cloth to discourage the vanity that was inappropriate in a house freshly visited by death. Then they'd returned to their homes, to prepare food for the mourners who would come to the Lyman house after the funeral and burial in the Middlefield graveyard.

Hope had roused David and Catharine to tell them of John's death. She let the other children sleep a bit longer; they would awaken soon enough into a world darkened by the loss of their beloved father.

Samuel and David had gone to the barn; even on the most sorrowful of days the cows still needed to be milked and driven to pasture, the horse fed and watered. In the kitchen a teary Catharine was starting breakfast. For a rare moment, Hope was alone.

Hope believed John had been as ready to face his God as any man could expect to be. In his last weeks, he'd wrestled his stubborn spirit into submission to the Lord's decision to take him when his family still greatly needed him. He had achieved the unquestioning faith in God of which George Whitefield had spoken. That peace had allowed John to surrender to death, which Hope knew he welcomed as liberation from the private hell of physical and mental pain in which he'd been trapped for more than three years.

Hope desperately recalled Mr. Whitefield's promise that those who were justified by faith would be reunited in joy for eternity, to "sit and tell one another what God has done for your souls." But when she glanced from Nature's glory spread before her, back into the parlor at the coffin containing the wasted shell from which John's soul had flown, the realization that never again on this side of the grave would she hear his strong voice, feel his tender touch, see his warm smile, was suddenly too awful to bear.

Clinging to the doorpost, Hope slid to her knees as though crushed by a giant weight. She collapsed into a crumpled heap, and sobbed convulsively in the sunshine. In the instant before grief overwhelmed her, she managed to offer up a desperate appeal to God to forgive this failure to accept His will.

Chapter Thirteen

September, 1766
Middletown

Hope thought she'd suffered every imaginable affliction of mind and heart in the three years since John's death. But on this bright September day, under a sky as blue as a robin's egg, a fresh blow was being added to the gauntlet of sorrow, fear, anger, frustration, and despair she'd run: humiliation.

The recently completed probate process had confirmed what Hope had known all along. John died owing numerous debts that when totaled exceeded the value of everything in his estate.

Hope's shrewd foresight had shielded their house and sufficient acres to feed them from the probate proceedings. And the law wasn't heartless. Hope had been allotted her "widow's thirds" of John's personal possessions. This included an assortment of kitchen and household utensils, a horse and a cow, a plow and other farm tools, and the family's Bible.

They'd also had been allowed to pay for a decent funeral for John. But her husband lay in an unmarked grave. No money could be spared from an insolvent estate to purchase even a simple tombstone, let alone a handsome carved one like Hope's brother had paid to have erected over the Widow Hawley's final resting place.

Now the probate court had ordered Hope, as executrix of the estate, to auction off all John's remaining worldly possessions, save for her widow's thirds and the family's clothes. The proceeds would go towards paying John's creditors.

Items to be auctioned had been laid out for prospective buyers' inspection at the public signpost in the center of Middletown. Hope, as executrix, was required to be present. David, now twenty, had insisted on attending. The rest of the children had been spared the mortifying scene. Hannah, Esther, Elihu, and Phineas were staying with Catharine, who'd married the year following John's death, at her home in North Guilford, south of Durham.

Hope struggled to remain stoic as men and women pawed through items that had been fixtures of her life. Seeing acquaintances and strangers alike finger John's favorite coat and beaver hat made her feel queasy, as if she'd somehow been personally violated. Her cheeks flamed with indignation when a matron, after a cursory examination, turned away dismissively from sheets and tablecloths woven from yarn Hope and her daughters had spent tedious hours spinning.

Watching a woman study her reflection in the looking-glass that had graced the Lymans' parlor, while a man examined the musket with which John had taught his sons to hunt, caused Hope's façade of self-control begin to crack. When some stripling brandished the sword John had received from his cousin Phineas, and worn so proudly at every militia drill, Hope could bear no more. She hastily looked away.

Mercifully, the auctioneer called for the bidding to begin. Hope joined David at the back of the crowd.

David was proud of his mother's conduct since John's death. Hope had saved their family from destitution by managing complex legal and financial affairs as competently as any man. With David she'd planned and coordinated every aspect of the farm's operation. She'd labored in the fields beside her children to plant a few extra acres of turnips, to harvest every last ear of Indian corn.

But at the same time, Hope increasingly begrudged David giving time or attention to anything other than running the farm. He rarely had the chance anymore even to go fishing with Elihu and Phineas. When the family attended Sabbath services in Durham, Hope kept David occupied with various tasks during the mid-day break, giving him little opportunity to socialize with the other young men – and women. It was the same when female friends visited Hannah at their house. David was increasingly resentful of this curtailing of his life beyond the needs of family and farm – which led inevitably to a sense of guilt that he might fail to meet those needs.

But today David was worried about Hope, wondering how she would bear up watching possessions that held so many intimate memories awarded, one by one, to the highest bidder. He focused his attention on the auctioneer, but stole a glance at his mother when an item of special significance was sold.

Hope's face remained impassive, as though she were observing an event of no special importance to her. But when a young couple cheerfully loaded onto a cart their newly purchased prize, the feather bed that had been part of Hope's marriage portion, David heard her take a sharp breath. He turned in time to see his mother bite down on a trembling lower lip.

By the time the sale ended, golden shafts of late afternoon sunlight were slanting in from the west, turning patches of leaves newly turned red and yellow into glowing jewels. David heaved a sigh of relief that the ordeal was over.

Suddenly Hope clutched his arm. He turned to see Timothy Hierlihy approaching. Hierlihy had served throughout the war against the French and Indians, rising to the rank of major, by which title he was addressed in civilian life. With John's advice, he'd purchased land in Middlefield and settled down to farm and raise a family that now included seven children.

Major Hierlihy carried John's musket, powder horn, and cartridge box, and on his hip hung the scabbard containing John's sword, for all of which he'd been the winning bidder. He held out the firearm and the powder containers to David. "I thought you should have these," he said, his voice still laced with the lilt of his native Ireland.

David slung the cartridge box and powder horn over his shoulder by their straps, then took the musket. Major Hierlihy unfastened the sword and extended it to David, who tucked the barrel of the musket into the crook of his arm, butt resting on the ground, to free his hands to accept it.

David studied the sword for a long moment. At last he looked up at Major Hierlihy, hoping the older man could read in his glistening eyes the gratitude that the lump of emotion in his throat prevented him from voicing.

"Thank you, Major Hierlihy," Hope said. She reached out to touch his hand, her low spirits lifted by his loyalty and generosity.

Major Hierlihy gave a short, sharp nod, almost as if embarrassed to be caught performing so sentimental an act. Then without a word he turned and strode away.

Dusk was gathering when David and Hope finally set out for home, Hope seated behind him on the one horse remaining to them.

A breeze carrying the chill of approaching autumn sprang up, raising goosebumps on Hope's arms.

For a time they rode in exhausted silence. Suddenly David yanked the horse to a stop. He twisted in the saddle and looked down at his mother with eyes that were fiercely determined – and haunted. "My wife and children will never endure a day like this," he said in a harsh voice. "Never. I swear it!"

Chapter Fourteen

November, 1772
North Guilford, Connecticut

Hope watched Hannah and Esther run ahead of her up the steep slope to the house Catharine had called home since her marriage to Lot Benton eight years ago. She followed in the furrow they cut through the layers of dry curled leaves of faded brown, red, and yellow.

Catharine reached the hall door just in time to open it for her unexpected visitors. Hannah rushed in and flung her arms around her sister's neck in a tight hug. "Mr. Williston has asked to marry me!" Hannah announced joyously.

"That's wonderful," Catharine said as she hugged Hannah back, hoping her voice didn't betray her conflicting emotions. She released Hannah, then embraced Esther and Hope in turn as they stepped over the threshold.

"We're to wed before year's end," Hannah continued excitedly, as she threw off the hood and untied the strings of her cardinal. Hannah's cheeks were ruddy from the five-mile ride on horseback to North Guilford in the cold autumn air. Her hazel eyes glowed with excitement as she turned, with the grace of movement Catharine had always envied, to face the other three women.

"We'd like to have the wedding here in your house, Catharine," Hannah rushed on. "It would be most convenient, North Guilford being nearly midway between West Haven and Middlefield."

As often happened, Hannah's exuberant impetuousness rendered the stolidly deliberate Catharine momentarily speechless.

She at last managed to answer with enough enthusiasm to pass muster with the others, "Of course you can be married here."

"I knew you would agree!" Hannah replied with a warm smile. She handed her cardinal to Catharine to hang with Hope and Esther's cloaks on pegs on the wall.

"For so long I feared I'd never find a husband," Hannah confessed with the relief of someone who'd narrowly escaped a terrible calamity. "I know there was gossip that at twenty-nine I was condemned to spinsterhood."

"But you've had suitors," Catharine protested. Although she hadn't lived in Middlefield since her marriage, she knew from Hope and Esther of two young men who'd expressed interest in courting Hannah.

"Abel Miller and Tom Crowell?" Hannah asked, waving her hand in an airy gesture of dismissal. "I could never wed either of them. They're both so–." Hannah caught herself before finishing her sentence with the word "common," for she knew no man more common than Catharine's Lot.

"They're not special, like Noah," Hannah finished after a brief, awkward pause. "He's been West Haven's minister for twelve years!" she continued with rising enthusiasm. "And you should see the fine house he lives in – with a maid servant to do the cleaning!"

"And he's very handsome," chimed in Esther. "You'd think him a man of thirty rather than one near forty. And he dotes on Hannah," she added with a hint of romantic yearning.

"He does," Hannah said with undisguised satisfaction. "He declares the deepest affection for me. He asked for my hand before even determining what marriage portion Mama will provide."

Catharine couldn't dispute anything her sisters said about Noah Williston. The few times she'd met West Haven's widowed pastor, she'd found him to be well-dressed, well-mannered, pleasing in appearance, devout, and openly enamored of Hannah. Catharine also considered Williston profoundly dull, fond of esoteric discussions – or more accurately discourses – about theology and politics. Based on this observation, Catharine was disturbed that Hannah had omitted one item from the reasons for her elation over snaring Noah Williston: that she loved him.

"You must be half-frozen from your ride," Catharine said. "Hannah, why don't you and Esther thaw out in front of the fire? Mama, could you help me brew some tea?"

Hannah and Esther pulled two chairs close to the hearth and sat down, chatting excitedly about wedding plans. Hope followed Catharine into the kitchen.

As soon as they were out of earshot of the hall, Catharine turned to confront Hope. "Are you pleased with this marriage, Mama?" she asked.

"Of course!" Hope answered, the satisfied expression she'd worn since arriving fading into confusion. "I encouraged it from the first. What more could Hannah hope for in a husband?"

"A man she loves," Catharine said bluntly.

Hope's hazel eyes locked onto Catharine's brown ones, as she called upon the resolve with which she had confronted unpleasant but unavoidable problems during a decade of struggling to build a future on the ashes of her family's misfortune. "So many times the Lord has seen fit to visit sorrow on our family," she said in an implacable tone. "I've always sought to have faith in His wisdom, no matter how painful. If now He chooses to bless Hannah with a marriage to Mr. Williston, a well-educated, well-to-do minister, I'll accept that as well – gladly."

Hope's reply dismayed but didn't surprise Catharine. It was understandable that her mother would view Hannah's marriage as an act of divine benevolence.

"Noah Williston will make Hannah a godly, affectionate husband," Hope continued with no-nonsense practicality. "He'll provide her and their children with a comfortable life. If she doesn't love him now, she may come to in time. If that doesn't happen, she'll find contentment in their mutual regard, in their family, and in their service to the Lord."

Catharine insisted on pressing her point. "I admit there are good marriages between couples who do not love," she conceded. "But you and I know what marriage can be when a husband and wife cherish each other. I fear Hannah is so bedazzled by Mr. Williston's money and status that she's given no serious consideration to how she truly feels about him."

"Are you jealous of Hannah's good fortune?" Hope demanded abruptly, her eyes narrowing. She grasped the startled Catharine's chin firmly with one hand, and searched her eyes as one might a child caught in a fib.

Catharine jerked her head sharply from her mother's grasp. But Hope had seen that her innately honest daughter was indeed searching her heart to determine if she was guilty of the sin of envy.

When Catharine met Hope's gaze again, it was with defiant certainty. "No, Mama, I'm not. Lot may be a common farmer, like Papa–." Hope stiffened at Catharine's barbed reference to John. "But I wouldn't trade him for any man, no matter how rich or handsome or important."

Hope waited for the sting of Catharine's words to fade before speaking. "You forget that Hannah is a woman in her thirtieth year able to make her own decisions, not the little sister you must protect," she said in a tone of reason. Then her expression and voice hardened. "You'll say nothing to Hannah about this. I won't have you planting seeds of doubt in her mind."

"Yes, Mama," Catharine sighed, but not in obedience to Hope's command. The Lyman family's mortifying social fall after John's death had scarred Hannah as deeply as it had David. Marriage to Noah Williston would elevate her to the pinnacle of local society. Given that reality, Catharine doubted anyone could persuade Hannah to ask herself if she was enamored not so much with Noah Williston the man as with the Reverend Mr. Williston, the prominent, prosperous, and powerful pastor.

"Of course, I'll have my hands full with Noah's little ones," Hannah was telling Esther on a note of resignation as Hope and Catharine approached from behind, both balancing a dish of tea on a saucer in each hand. Catharine stopped so abruptly that a bit of the hot beverage sloshed out of one of the dishes.

Hope saw a tremor of pain flicker across Catharine's face at Hannah's lack of enthusiasm for becoming stepmother to Noah Williston's four children, the oldest only nine. Catharine and Lot had no children. So far as Hope knew, Catharine had never once even conceived.

That Catharine, who of all women would make such a good mother, had so far been denied the babies for which she yearned was terribly unfair, Hope thought. Although unquestionably God's will, Hope's heart ached all the same for her daughter's barrenness.

Hope watched admiringly as Catharine recovered her composure, then politely handed Hannah her tea. She showed no sign of resentment that her sister considered the children for whom she would fill the role of mother anything but a blessing.

Hannah took a careful sip of the steaming brew as Hope and Catharine settled onto chairs. "Would you make over my green damask gown for the wedding?" Hannah asked Catharine. "You're so much cleverer with a needle than anyone I know."

"Yes," Catharine said with a nod before taking her own taste of tea. A dress made of expensive cloth was worn for many years. It was often reworked to keep up with changes in style or in a woman's figure.

"As far as fashion goes, maybe it was for the best that you didn't marry until now," Esther teased Hannah. "Not long ago, you might not have dared to wear a gown of English cloth, even if it had been bought before the non-importation agreement. Your bridegroom would have insisted you dress in homespun for the wedding."

Hannah wrinkled her nose in distaste at the image conjured up by Esther's words, and the memory of the political unpleasantness that had made it even a remote possibility. Two years after John's death, Parliament had passed an act levying a tax, represented by a stamp, on paper goods sold in the colonies. The colonists, enraged at this tax imposed without their consent, responded with outrage and even violence. In Connecticut a mob of five hundred men calling themselves "Sons of Liberty" had terrorized the colony's stamp tax collector into resigning his position.

Parliament repealed the Stamp Act, but in 1767 it approved taxes on paper, paint, lead, glass, and tea imported into the colonies. The colonies retaliated by resolving not to purchase any goods imported from Great Britain until the offending taxes were withdrawn. Nearly everyone in the colonies had felt the effects. In particular, spurning fine imported cloth in favor of coarser fabric made from wool or linen grown, spun, and woven locally had become a gesture of support for colonists' rights.

Again Parliament relented, repealing the new taxes – except for the one on tea – in 1770. Despite that exception, this action was considered a victory for the non-importation agreement. Colonial ports re-opened to British goods, and homespun cloth gave way to high-quality British fabrics. Even the still-taxed tea was drunk without qualms – especially because much of it was purchased from smugglers who paid no tax at all.

"I hope all that political bother is settled." Hannah replied impatiently. "Going without anything imported from Britain may have been necessary – but it was dreadfully dreary."

Catharine's visitors were donning their cloaks in preparation for departing when a gust of cold air from the kitchen followed by a door slamming told them Lot Benton had returned from his chores.

"Mother Lyman. Hannah. Esther," Lot greeted them laconically as he stepped into the hall. Tall and broad of build, Lot had dark gray eyes set in a face of sharp, angular features. Although only thirty-three, his sandy hair was liberally sprinkled with silver. He personified the stone walls crisscrossing every Connecticut farm – sturdy, formed of irregular facets of subdued hues drawn from the earth, attractive for their simple, honest plainness.

"Hannah and Mr. Williston are to wed, Lot," Catharine told him, with a bit too much bright enthusiasm in her voice.

"Is that a fact?" Lot said, a hint of amusement playing at his lips as he studied his sister-in-law. "I suppose if anyone can get Noah Williston to put his pipe down long enough to speak marriage vows, it would be Hannah."

Hannah smiled uncertainly at Lot's reference to her betrothed's extreme fondness for tobacco. She was never sure how to respond to Lot's teasing – or completely certain if it was teasing.

"I told Hannah she can have the wedding here," Catharine went on.

Lot's forehead creased with a frown as he looked at his wife, then back at Hannah. "Why not at Mr. Williston's? His house is far grander than ours."

"Your house is midway between West Haven and Middlefield," Hannah explained nervously. "It would be convenient for guests from both towns."

"When will it be?" Lot asked after a long pause.

"Before year's end," Hannah said.

"So soon?" Lot pursed his lips and shook his head in a slow, musing manner. "Catharine has a lot to get done before winter sets in. And all those folks coming through the house will traipse in mud, most likely snow as well." Only Catharine detected the glint in Lot's eye.

"We'll help get everything ready and clean up after," Hope told her son-in-law with poorly concealed impatience. She glanced pleadingly at Catharine, who said nothing, looking as if she were enjoying a private joke.

"No, Mama," sighed the deeply disappointed Hannah. "Lot is master of his own house. He's within his right to refuse."

Hannah turned in discouragement toward the door. A dismayed Esther struggled to accept the sudden pall over their bright plans. Hope held her ground with an air of disapproval, intending to press the issue with Lot.

"Now, wait," Lot said hastily. "I didn't say no," he added in a tone of grudging surrender. "If nowhere else will do, you can have the wedding here."

Hannah whirled around, her eyes wide with perplexed surprise. She took a moment to be sure Lot wasn't toying with her, then seized his hand between hers. "Thank you, Brother," she said with a brilliant smile.

Embarrassed, Lot extricated his hand from Hannah's. "I'll go wash up for dinner," he said to Catharine, hastening into the kitchen.

Catharine had deliberately stayed out of the exchange. Lot's show of reluctance had entertained, rather than perturbed her, because she'd known all along he would give his consent. For under Lot Benton's cranky exterior lay a kind heart that, once Catharine had discovered it, had won her own.

Like many a young woman, Catharine had at first been put off by Lot's petulant demeanor. But unlike the others, she'd sensed something good encased within his prickly shell. Her patience and persistence had been rewarded, as Lot gradually revealed to her a truly affectionate and generous personality.

Catharine suspected that Lot, the youngest of six boys, had developed his balky attitude to defend against his brothers taking advantage of his good nature. In manhood he'd been unable to shed the demeanor – and had actually come to take a perverse pleasure in it. Anyone who asked a favor of Lot Benton could be certain of having it granted – but only after earning it, in the New England tradition, by engaging in a verbal tug-of-war such as the one Hannah had just experienced.

Catharine's wish to marry the taciturn Lot Benton had puzzled Hope. She'd given her consent because she thought it the best match Catharine could expect, especially considering how meager a marriage portion Hope could provide just a year after John's death.

Looking back, Catharine thanked God that Lot had come into her life at that low point in her family's fortunes. Had she still been single when the Lymans' financial situation had improved enough to allow for a more generous marriage portion, her mother might have tried to steer her toward a husband of higher social and financial status than Lot.

Hope had been relieved when it became clear Catharine was content in her marriage to Lot Benton. Her mother wasn't indifferent to her children's happiness, Catharine knew. But since

John's death Hope had made the goal of rebuilding the family's fortunes her first consideration in everything she did, including shaping the course of her children's lives.

"We'd best be off," said Hannah, eager to leave before the mercurial Lot could reappear and change his mind. "We must arrange for Mr. Bray to post the banns on the next three Sabbaths."

Catharine watched out the hall window as her mother and sisters stepped carefully down the path. She offered up a silent prayer that Hannah would find with her pretentious minister the same contentment Catharine had with so seemingly unpromising a matrimonial prospect as Lot Benton.

Chapter Fifteen

December, 1772
North Guilford

Hannah was radiant in a gown fashioned from the green damask purchased at Richard Alsop's store more than thirteen years ago. Catharine's talented fingers had made it over into the latest style. The scoop neck, trimmed with a narrow ruffle of white lace, dipped low enough to reveal Hannah's alabaster shoulders and the gentle swell of her breasts. The sleeves were close fitting from shoulder to elbow, where they bloomed into a cascade of folds lined with layers of delicate white lace.

Hannah's light brown hair was pulled back tightly from her forehead and temples, and tied with a broad bow of green ribbon at the nape of her neck. Her wavy tresses hung freely almost to her waist. A large matching bow accented the front of the gown.

Noah Williston was dressed no less smartly than his bride for their wedding this day, the ninth of December. The somber richness of his brown broadcloth suit was relieved by the bright white stock wound around his throat and the white ruffles that frothed out between the unfastened top buttons of his waistcoat His frock coat fell to his knees, where the bottoms of his breeches were fastened by oval buckles of glittering paste.

"Isn't Hannah a lovely bride?" Esther whispered to Hope as the couple exchanged vows before North Guilford's pastor, Thomas Bray, in the Benton house hall. Hope nodded, but she was thinking that the great beauty of the Lyman family was the slim and graceful Esther, now twenty-three. Esther had John's height, along with her father's dramatically dark coloring – although she had mercifully inherited Hope's pert nose rather than John's sharp, prominent one.

Esther was bright like Hannah and warm of heart like Catharine. But she had a sweetness, a sparkling optimism uniquely her own, that the family's trials and reversals had never dimmed. Hope felt a sense of triumph over Hannah's wedding. Now she prayed they would find a man worthy of Esther, who in company had often been overshadowed by her older sister.

The brief ceremony concluded, guests crowded forward to congratulate the newlyweds. Generous servings of cake and glasses of wine were distributed. Darb, the Negro slave of Lot Benton's friend Ben Rossiter, struck up his fiddle for dancing.

Circulating among the guests, Hope stopped to chat with Major Hierlihy and his wife, Elizabeth. The expected polite remarks were exchanged about the bridal couple: how attractive they were, the good fortune each had in finding the other.

"Were you at the Military Adventurers meeting in Hartford, Major Hierlihy?" Hope asked.

"I was" Major Hierlihy confirmed. "As was General Lyman."

Hope studied the man with sharp interest. "The only news we had of Phineas after he sailed for England were brief, conflicting notices in the papers. One said he secured a vast grant of land, another that his petition was rejected. Then in October we heard he was back in Connecticut. How did he fare on his mission?"

Major Hierlihy's expression darkened. "The royal officials didn't see fit to treat General Lyman with the honor and fairness due a soldier who risked death in battle for the Empire," he said sourly. "The General approached one ministerial administration after another, receiving encouragement and promises of preferment – only to be repeatedly disappointed as they all proved worthless knaves. To the politicians it was a game, but to General Lyman it was a sacred trust. He refused to return to America without securing some compensation for his fellow veterans who had put their faith in him, and invested their money in his mission."

The revelations shocked and saddened Hope. It was difficult to imagine the brave, energetic, loyal soldier reduced to a humble petitioner, duped and shunted aside by arrogant royal ministers. She was glad John wasn't alive to hear of it.

"But he did come back, so he must have met with some success?" Hope asked.

"That's correct," Major Hierlihy said, his expression brightening. "General Lyman didn't return empty-handed. At the Adventurers' meeting he reported that before he left England, His Most Gracious Majesty King George promised him a large grant of land in West Florida to compensate the disbanded provincial veterans of the late war. And the new ministry is said to be favorably disposed toward this action. The General was assured that documents confirming the grant would be sent directly to the governor of West Florida."

Major Hierlihy took a sip of wine. "The Adventurers voted to send a party to survey the area of the grant," he continued. "Once they return with their report, the Adventurers will begin sending settlers. General Lyman will be taking his family – and I'm thinking of doing the same." He wrapped an arm around his wife, who managed a wan smile. "I can't provide four sons with a sound start in life on the expensive yet unproductive acres of Connecticut."

Hope was struck silent, disturbed by the specter of family and friends like Phineas and the Hierlihys removing to West Florida. When John's father and brother went to Torrington, it had been a dangerous gamble – and they hadn't even left Connecticut! Major Hierlihy and the other Adventurers would be taking their families to a wilderness so far away it might as well be on the moon.

Hope's mind ran quickly over the arrangements she'd made for her sons that she hoped would keep them close to home. Surveying the room for them, she spotted David on the far side of the hall – and wasn't happy with what she saw.

Now almost twenty-seven, David still strongly resembled John, although he was a bit taller, not as lean, and his features were less sharp. David was deep in conversation with a young woman Hope had never seen before – a very pretty girl of about twenty, with long, rippling honey-colored hair and a curvaceous figure attired in a dress of yellow silk. She was blatantly flirting with David, her head tilted up coquettishly, her smile blossoming into a gay laugh at some remark he made.

Noticing Hope's sudden distraction, Major Hierlihy followed her gaze. He quickly sized up the situation.

"Do you know the woman with David?" Hope asked.

Major Hierlihy shook his head. "No. But whoever she is, David seems quite taken with her."

"If you'll excuse me," Hope said with an abruptness that although she knew it bordered on rudeness couldn't be helped. She set her half-full wine glass on a sideboard, then worked her way through the crowded hall toward David and the girl. Before she reached them, Darb struck up another tune, and Hope watched in helpless frustration as David led his pretty companion out to dance.

The moment the music ended, Hope made a bee-line to her son. "David," she said, slipping her arm possessively around his. "You haven't paid your respects to Mr. Bray."

Startled, David stared down. "I will, Mama."

"Now would be a good time," Hope persisted. She turned to the young woman in yellow. "You'll excuse us, won't you?" she said with a forced smile. It was a command, not a request.

"Of course," the girl answered politely. She cast a look of puzzled dismay at David, whose cheeks were red with humiliation. He avoided the girl's eyes as Hope tightened her grip, then firmly steered him toward North Guilford's pastor.

After exchanging bland pleasantries with Mr. Bray, David excused himself. He threaded his way through the bodies packed into the hall until he reached the exterior door. He slipped outside, unnoticed he hoped, then stalked toward the rear of the Benton homelot.

David welcomed the shock of the raw, damp air on his flushed face. When he reached the house's well, he smashed a fist through the crust of ice in the bucket. He splashed his face with water so frigid it made him gasp.

David shook his head to clear the water from his eyes, then gripped the edge of the waist-high stone wall surrounding the well. He stared sightlessly into its depths, his mind swirling with mortification and fury.

"You'll catch a chill without your coat."

Startled, David spun around to face Hope.

"You needn't spy on me out here," David said with resentful sarcasm. "All the females are inside."

Hope let the insolent reply pass. "You remind me of your father," she said evenly. "When he was angry he would leave the house until his temper cooled." David turned back to glare down into the well.

Hope sighed, then walked around so she could see David's face. "I make no apologies for what I did," she said. She pulled the cloak she'd grabbed on her way out of the house tightly around her to shield against the sharp wind raking the hilltop.

When David still refused to look at her, Hope's irritation rose. "Have you forgotten the promise you made to yourself the day we auctioned your father's estate?" she demanded. He winced at the reminder.

"With God's blessing, you and I have accomplished much in ten years," Hope continued. "We've enlarged the farm, increased our livestock, improved the house and barn.   I've arranged good marriages for Catharine and Hannah, and apprenticeships for Elihu and Phineas. But Esther still needs a marriage portion, and your brothers will require help setting up in their trades. For you to be lured into marriage now would be a disaster – for the family for which you're already responsible and for the new one you would create. You must wait."

David swung around to glare at her. "For how long, Mama?" he demanded. "For how long?" I'll be twenty-seven next month. Yet I can't even converse with a woman without you meddling."

"Meddling!" Hope cried, insulted and infuriated. When she spoke again, it was in an ominously low voice. "Is that what you think of all I've done these years to provide our family with comfort and security?!" Her voice grew more strident. "Would you turn your back on your brothers and sister when they need you? Would you abandon them to satisfy your own selfish wants?" she asked. "Would you abandon me – as your father did, and my father before him?" she cried, her voice quivering on the razor edge of hysteria.

Hope's irrational casting of the deaths of John Lyman and Jehiel Hawley as acts of desertion turned David's rising anger into alarm. He'd never suspected such anguished fear existed behind the formidable, commanding, competent face his mother presented to the world.

Hope stared at her son, breathing as hard as if she'd just run a mile, waiting for his answer. "I would never do that, Mama," David replied at last, with defensiveness tempered by compassion.   She seemed not to realize that her panicked outburst had revealed her inner demons.

David hunched his shoulders as a shiver, only partly a reaction to the cold, shook his body. "But I believe I can marry and still fulfill my duty to all who depend on me. Why can't you trust my judgment?" he demanded. His frustration rose again in spite of the shock he'd just experienced. "Why must you treat me like a stripling without wit enough to make his own decisions?"

Hope's breathing slowed, and she regained her composure. She fixed David with a look so intense it was almost hypnotic. "Do you remember your father's words the day he made his will?" It was a rhetorical question.

"He told me to take care of the family," David replied.

"And?" Hope pressed remorselessly.

"And to be guided by you," David answered with a sigh of resignation.

Hope nodded sternly. "Your father trusted my judgment enough to leave all his worldly affairs in my hands. I expect you to have no less confidence. And I tell you that to marry any time soon would bring down upon you more responsibility than you could hope to carry."

David's shoulders slumped in surrender. Their arguments on this subject – more than a few over the past several years, although none as bitter as this one – always ended this way, with David feeling guilty, trapped, and despondent.

Hope understood her son's weak points. She knew invoking the memory of John's deathbed charge and David's dread of poverty could smother any flare of defiance. David's own secret fear was that, even after all his obligations to his brothers and sisters had been met, his mother would still find an excuse to keep him under her thumb – that he would remain a lonely bachelor until she – or he – died.

Hope read the submission in David's posture with relief. The thought of a wife and children making demands on his energy and loyalty touched off in her a terrifying sensation of the bottom falling out of her world, like that she'd suffered in the days immediately following John's death.

Still, Hope wasn't unmindful of the sacrifice David was making. She touched his arm in a conciliatory gesture. "We must go back inside before the guests start to gossip about our absence," she coaxed.

David brushed her hand away. He turned without a word and walked back toward the Benton house, leaving Hope standing alone by the well.

"Mama's done it again?" Phineas said to Elihu in a low voice as he came up beside his brother by the fireplace in the Benton hall. It was more a statement than a question.

"I fear so," Elihu replied with what Phineas considered admirable empathy. A less-generous man might have taken spiteful pleasure in seeing a favored sibling in David's predicament.

Now twenty-one, Elihu was taller and thinner than David, but he shared his older brother's resemblance to their father. Elihu surveyed the parlor, and saw with relief that no one besides David's crestfallen female companion seemed to have noticed the tense exchange between mother and son or their sudden exit.

"There was a time I envied David," Elihu mused. "Mama has always held him as special, even before Papa got sick. One day the farm will be his. But he's paying a far higher price for it than I would be willing to.

"Mama has earned such a reputation for chasing off any woman who approaches David. I doubt there's an eligible female in Middletown or Durham brave enough to welcome him should he come courting," Elihu went on. "It's poor reward for all he's done for us. No, I wouldn't want to be in David's shoes for anything."

"I agree," Phineas said. He took a sip of wine before adding, "But you're at least content with the course Mama has charted for you."

An undercurrent of longing in Phineas's words prompted Elihu to look closely at his brother. At seventeen Phineas had reached physical manhood. The baby of the Lyman family bore little resemblance to his siblings. Medium of height and stocky in build, he was the only blond, blue-eyed child among John and Hope's six children. Hope had once remarked that Phineas favored her father in appearance. If that were true, Elihu thought, Jehiel Hawley had been a devilishly handsome man.

Within the past year Phineas had discovered the opposite sex, as well as the happy fact that girls found his good looks and roguish charm appealing. Elihu knew Hope and David fretted that the youth might get himself into the kind of trouble that would require a hasty wedding to remedy.

Uncomfortable under his brother's thoughtful scrutiny, Phineas changed the subject. "Tell me, do you truly enjoy learning how to purge and puke and bleed people?" He was half-teasing, half genuinely curious.

Hope had told her sons that the entire farm would go to David, since dividing it up among them would provide no one sufficient land to support a family. That made it necessary to find other livelihoods for Elihu and Phineas.

Elihu had been apprenticed to Dr. John Dickinson to learn the physician's trade. The work was much to his liking. Mastering quantities of information and developing the analytical skills to diagnose and treat diseases and injuries were challenges well suited to Elihu's bright, inquisitive mind. And the many hours a doctor spent on the road visiting patients would provide an outlet for his restless energy.

"I do," Elihu replied sincerely. "I'm gratified to see my work relieve pain and cure disease. Physicking should provide a good livelihood – not so grand as a lawyer or a merchant or even a tavern keeper – but enough, along with a bit of farming, to support a family. I just wish I didn't have two more years to go on my apprenticeship," he said dispiritedly.

"Is it only a zeal to heal that makes you impatient – or is there another reason?" Phineas asked, bobbing his eyebrows suggestively. That earned him a sudden jab in the rib from Elihu's elbow.

The other reason to which Phineas referred was Esther Camp, the seventeen-year-old Durham girl Elihu had been courting for several months – without Hope's knowledge. The thought of pretty, sweet-tempered, devoted Esther, whom Elihu had known for years but who had only recently blossomed into womanhood, brought a smile to his lips, even as his eyes clouded with anxiety.

For the past month, Elihu each Sabbath had ridden from Middletown, where he lived with Dr. Dickinson, to Esther's home in Durham. He typically arrived late into the cold evening. Sunday nights were a traditionally popular time for courting visits.

Esther's family had thoughtfully – and trustingly – followed another tradition by retiring to other rooms in order to provide the courting couple a few precious hours of privacy together in the hall. It wasn't long before, alone in the chilly room lit only by the blaze in the fireplace, Elihu and Esther were locked in an intimate embrace. They'd slowly and sensually explored the contours of each other's bodies as best they could through layers of woolen clothing. Esther's ardent response to Elihu's kisses and caresses told him she shared the lust her soft lips and firm breasts ignited in him.

This past Sabbath Elihu and Esther had crossed into a bewitched world where nothing existed but their intertwined bodies now with only a single layer of fabric separating them. Each pounding heartbeat had driven them closer to the carnal coupling that would consummate their love. With almost superhuman willpower they'd managed to stop short, leaving them both frightened by the power of their lust and frustrated by the failure to satisfy it.

As he rode the rutted, frozen road back to Middletown that night, Elihu both yearned for and dreaded his next visit to Esther.

That more than a few unmarried couples succumbed to temptation was evident from the number of first babies who arrived six, five, four, or even fewer months after the parents' wedding.

But if Elihu got Esther with child, marriage might not be a solution; he was bound by the terms of his indenture to Dr. Dickinson not to wed until his training was complete. While it was always possible Dr. Dickinson might grant him permission to marry, it was by no means a certainty. If Elihu couldn't wed a pregnant Esther, their baby would be born a bastard, a stigma neither the child nor Esther would ever live down.

Even if they were permitted to marry, Elihu – landless, his medical training incomplete – would have no means of taking care of a wife and child. His only alternative would be to ask Hope and David for help.

Although David would be angry, Elihu was sure his brother would extend a helping and ultimately forgiving hand. But Elihu shuddered at the thought of how furiously disappointed Hope would be with him for squandering the opportunity for a secure future she'd arranged. No, Elihu resolved, he and Esther must find a way to master their lust – for another two years at least.

"Elihu?" Phineas said hesitantly, fearing his brother's extended silence, his strained, detached expression meant Phineas's remark had offended him. "I was only jesting."

"What?" Elihu said. He refocused his thoughts on the present moment. "Oh, I know you meant no harm," he assured his brother. "What of your prospects?" he asked the relieved Phineas, eager to steer the conversation and his thoughts away from Esther.

"Mama has arranged an apprenticeship for me with Return Meigs, to start with the new year," Phineas said with the grim resignation of a man condemned to seven years of hard labor. Elihu raised an eyebrow in surprise.

"Mama gave me my choice among the trades," Phineas went on. "Since I didn't care for one over the others, she decided if hatmaking was good enough for her father, it would be good enough for me. At least I can see more of you when I'm living with Mr. Meigs in Middletown."

Phineas paused for a long moment, then continued. "I once asked Mama if I might have a few acres of the farm to till, and save what I earned until I had enough money to buy land of my own. She said no, of course. She was as horrified as if I'd suggested cutting off David's arms," he said bitterly.

Elihu had no comforting reply to the raw pain in Phineas's reaction to their mother's refusal. Just four when John fell ill, and seven when he died, Phineas's childhood had been fraught with uncertainty.

Hope had been so consumed by the responsibilities she'd assumed with John's sickness that she'd had little time for Phineas. David had been too overwhelmed by the duties that had fallen upon him to fill the void their father's death created in his littlest brother's world. Catharine had mothered Phineas for several years, but then she'd married and gone to North Guilford. Esther and Elihu had sensed their brother's need, but there was little they could do, being barely teenagers themselves.

Elihu feared Phineas felt like an outsider, with no rightful claim to a secure place in the family. Hope's relentless focus on making David the cornerstone of their material foundation only made the situation worse. Phineas had developed a cavalier attitude toward life that Elihu suspected was actually a shield against attachments that might bring fresh disappointment.

Elihu saw Phineas's defenses go back up, as a wickedly mischievous grin replaced his forlorn expression. He drained the wine from his glass, then handed it to Elihu. "That pretty thing Mama dragged David away from looks lonely. I think I'll go cheer her up."

Elihu watched in stunned disbelief as Phineas started to walk away. He reached out to grab his coat collar and yank him back sharply.

"Are you mad?" Elihu hissed, glancing around to see if anyone had noticed his rough retrieval of his brother. "I know you might get some childish pleasure out of annoying Mama by flirting with that girl. But think of David's feelings."

"You certainly know how to spoil a man's fun," Phineas replied testily, jerking his coat from Elihu's grasp. "But you're right," he conceded grudgingly. "I wouldn't want to cause David any more grief – he looks as if he's had more than his share for one day." Phineas nodded toward their brother, who had just re-entered the hall, his face a mask of bleak despair. A few steps behind him came Hope, her expression one of grim triumph.

Chapter Sixteen

July, 1775
Middlefield

"God has selected America from all the earth's nations to be the sanctuary of freedom," the Reverend Abner Benedict said with grim pride. "Like the Israelites in the Bible, we are His chosen people."

Rain drummed on the Lyman house roof on the late afternoon of Sunday, July 2. Middlefield's pastor for going on four years, Abner Benedict was a short, slight man. A prematurely receding hairline made him look older than his thirty-four years. He had a striking countenance, with a long, sharp nose and piercing black eyes that looked out from beneath bushy brows with unshakeable conviction.

Hope had invited Mr. Benedict and his wife Lois, a plain woman of twenty-six pregnant with the couple's second child, to join the Lyman family for refreshments after the afternoon worship services. David was there, along with Elihu, who'd just moved back home after completing his apprenticeship. Phineas had walked five miles from the center of Middletown to spend this Sabbath with his family.

Esther was present as well. On January 30 of the current year she'd made a very good marriage – if not as grand as Hannah's.

Esther had wed David Beecher, a prosperous blacksmith and farmer from New Haven. She'd met Beecher, who was eleven years her senior, at Hannah's wedding. After Beecher's second wife died in childbed in the summer of 1773, he'd come courting.

Esther had been won over by the handsome, brawny mechanic who enjoyed reading books and discussing politics – and whose tender affection for Esther was obvious to all. They had exchanged vows before Mr. Bray in Catharine and Lot's house.

Esther had conceived less than two months after her marriage. Hope was looking forward with touching eagerness to the birth in December of her first grandchild, neither Catharine nor Hannah having yet borne a baby.

Esther had come to Middlefield hoping the pure country air would clear up a cough she'd developed after moving to New Haven, where she and David and his three children by his first two wives lived with David's parents in a house near Yale College. The physicians believed Esther's cough was caused by the less-healthful atmosphere of the crowded seaport.

"And as Pharaoh kept the Israelites in slavery in Egypt, increasing their burdens, so King George and Parliament have endeavored for a decade to oppress Americans, developing new ways to strip us of our liberties," Mr. Benedict continued. "The war now upon us was the inevitable result of their deliberate campaign of attacks on our rights that only grew worse as we resisted."

"Trying to use our own greed against us was devilishly clever," said Hope. "They allowed the British East India Company to sell tea in the colonies so cheaply that, even including the tax levied without our consent, it still cost less than smugglers charged."

"But the Sons of Liberty scotched that scheme," Elihu said admiringly, "disguising themselves as Mohawk Indians and dumping three ships' cargoes of tea into Boston Harbor to keep the tax from being paid."

Mr. Benedict nodded somberly. "And Parliament responded with a death sentence! They closed Boston to the trade that is the heart of its economy until the tea thrown into the harbor was paid for. If that wasn't a severe enough penalty, they sent three thousand British soldiers to occupy the city." Mr. Benedict's face flushed with indignation. "They punished all of Massachusetts as well; putting the colony's government under the control of royal officials, and gutting towns' power to manage their civic affairs."

"These 'Intolerable Acts' are a dagger stained with the blood of Massachusetts. It can be used against any man, any town, any colony that defies London!" David exclaimed. "If the king and his ministers thought other colonies would sit idle while they crushed Massachusetts, the meeting of the Continental Congress in Philadelphia to prepare a united response to their tyranny should have shown them how wrong they were." David shook his head at the incomprehensible stupidity of the government in London.

"And still they didn't learn," said Mr. Benedict in frustration. "Not three months past, when hundreds of British troops marched from Boston to plunder and murder, they should have expected Massachusetts militia to rally and oppose them. Many brave patriots died that April day at Lexington and Concord," he said sorrowfully.

Mr. Benedict's expression became one of satisfaction. "But the militia forced the Redcoats to retreat from Lexington and Concord, tormenting them all the way with musket fire like a swarm of angry wasps. Simple mechanics and farmers drove the king's soldiers, men who make a profession of war, scurrying back to Boston like whipped curs with their tails between their legs! It was proof of God's support for His people in this war," he said confidently.

The minister's conviction that colonial resistance to British oppression was a holy cause heartened his listeners. He continued, eyes glowing with excitement. "The Lord again sustained our patriot brethren when they fought the king's men a second time just two weeks ago on Breed's and Bunker's hills outside Boston. They twice repulsed assaults by an enemy that greatly outnumbered them, retreating only when their ammunition ran out. The king's troops gained the contested field, but they paid so high a price – nearly a third of them killed or wounded – that it was a hollow triumph."

Mr. Benedict's expression again grew sober. "The Lord afflicted the Egyptians with ten plagues before Pharaoh released the Israelites from bondage," he reminded them. "I fear our troops will have to inflict death and destruction on the enemy again and again before the king will realize it is God's will that Americans be restored to the freedom that is their birthright."

The minister paused for a long, thoughtful moment. "Many men will be needed in this sacred fight," he said. "He who enlists to fight these latter-day Egyptians not only serves his country, he ensures his eternal salvation. If he survives the conflict, he will also reap the benefits of liberty and the gratitude of his fellows and of countless generations unborn. If he falls in battle, he dies not a slave but a free man, and his memory will be forever blessed."

Elihu and Phineas exchanged glances of delight. Circumstances were proving more favorable than they could have hoped for the success of the plan they'd discussed at length before Elihu's move back to Middlefield, and which they intended to launch this day.

"I received some good news this afternoon," Mr. Benedict went on. "The Congress has appointed George Washington to command our forces outside Boston." Everyone throughout the colonies knew the name George Washington from his gallant service as a young Virginia militia colonel during the war with the French and Indians.

"He proved himself a brave officer when the French and Indians ambushed General Braddock's army near the forks of the Ohio in Pennsylvania," Hope recalled. "The enemy slaughtered hundreds of regulars and provincials, and then General Braddock was mortally wounded. Colonel Washington assumed command, just as our cousin Phineas did at Lake George after General Johnson was 'wounded.'" Hope said the last word sarcastically. "Colonel Washington saved what was left of General Braddock's army from total destruction. It was the same year."

"Colonel Washington retired from the military before the war ended," noted Mr. Benedict. "He'd doubtless grown sick of the contempt of British regulars and the Crown for provincial soldiers."

Hope nodded. "Our cousin Phineas would have done well to follow Colonel Washington's example," she said bitterly. "He was too forgiving of slights by the king and his servants during the war – and after."

Hope continued in a scathing voice. "Phineas trusted the king's word when he sailed for West Florida two years past to settle the promised Military Adventurers' grant. I can't imagine how mortified he was to discover that the king never sent the governor confirmation of the grant. Still Phineas carried on with his plan – only to die of disease just weeks after reaching West Florida. His reward for his persistence was a lonely grave in the wilderness."

"Indeed, sorrow and death await those who place their trust in corrupt kings," said Mr. Benedict gravely. "We must pray the Lord strengthens all of us, Colonel Washington in particular, for the difficult work ahead."

Elihu had been listening nervously, trying not to fidget with anticipation. At last he couldn't stand it any longer. He looked at Phineas, who nodded for him to proceed.

"Phineas and I have news," Elihu announced, his voice betraying none of the nervousness he felt. "We're going to enlist."

Elihu glanced quickly from face to face to gauge each person's initial, unguarded reaction. Mr. Benedict looked enormously pleased. Esther looked at Elihu and Phineas with a sister's admiration. David was distressed, although Elihu couldn't tell if it was worry or envy on his brother's face.

Last of all, Elihu looked at Hope. Her expression was one of astonished outrage – as he'd expected.

Mr. Benedict stood and clasped first Elihu, then Phineas by the shoulders. He gave each a firm shake of approval. "Two more soldiers for the Lord," he said. "They're sons to be proud of, Mistress Lyman." The minister's support bolstered the brothers' confidence.

But not even her pastor's approval could diminish Hope's fury at this flouting of her authority. She sprang to her feet. "I can't believe you hatched such a plan behind my back!" she hissed. "How can you throw away all the preparations for your futures? What of your indenture?" she demanded, focusing her glare on Phineas.

"Mr. Meigs agreed to release me from it until I return from the army," Phineas answered. His blue eyes were bright with anticipation at the prospect of exchanging his dreary apprenticeship for a soldier's exciting life.

Stymied by this unexpected reasonable response to her objection, Hope turned to Elihu. "What of your medical practice?" she demanded. "You've barely begun to engage patients."

"I can use my doctor's skills in the army, and return to physicking after my enlistment is over," Elihu answered with calm reason. "Securing our liberty must come before everything else."

Hope was left momentarily speechless by this parrying of her objections. She took several rapid breaths, but before she could resume her tirade Mr. Benedict interceded.

"I know how very difficult this must be for a mother," the minister said to Hope. "But they'll be fighting God's battle. Don't let fear or love or lack of faith – or injured pride – blind you to the rightness of their choice, Mistress Lyman."

Hope was taken aback by her pastor's unexpected admonition. She stared for a long moment at Mr. Benedict, then closed her eyes and bowed her head. She placed the fingers of each hand firmly against her temples, as if trying to physically control her churning thoughts and emotions.

Hope stood like that for the better part of a minute. Everyone remained silent; Elihu and Phineas dared not breathe.

At last Hope opened her eyes and lifted her head. Her face that had been flushed red with anger was now chalk white. She didn't look directly at anyone. "Mr. Benedict is correct," she said with a composure so radically different from her outrage it was unsettling. "I must be willing to sacrifice everything I hold dear if that is what God requires."

"If Elihu and Phineas enlist, I should, too," David blurted out. He turned to brave the anticipated torrent of objections from his mother head-on.

Their gazes met, and David saw a maelstrom of pain in his mother's eyes. "Perhaps you should," was all she said.

Suddenly Hope's eyes filled with tears, astonishing all her children. None of them could recall seeing her cry since the day their father died. She turned abruptly and walked to the window, where she stood staring out at the drizzle. Esther hurried after her and placed a comforting hand on her shoulder. David, Elihu, and Phineas exchanged wide-eyed looks of disbelief.

Mr. Benedict broke the silence. "I commend you for wanting to join your brothers in uniform, David," he began. "But your place is here on the farm."

Ignoring David's expression of wounded dismay, the minister continued, "Phineas and Elihu leave no duties that can't wait until, God willing, they return. But if you go to war, weeds will choke the fields of Indian corn and rye and peas. You must remain in Middlefield to raise the crops and livestock to feed our fighting men, the flax and wool to clothe them. Your mother is a strong woman, but she can't work a farm alone."

"Mr. Benedict is right," Elihu said, flinching at the look of betrayal David cast his way. He understood David's desire to join them – while also slipping out from under their mother's thumb. But Elihu honestly believed David's duty lay at home, just as his and Phineas's lay in the army. And Elihu knew David could always be relied upon to do his duty, no matter how painful.

David glanced instinctively toward Hope for her opinion. But she kept her back to all of them. Shamed by her selfish opposition to her sons' desire to fight for their Lord and their country, shaken by the terror she felt at the prospect of losing them, she refused to involve herself in this decision. She would leave their fate in God's hands.

David felt like he was suffocating. He hung his head and stared down at his calloused palms. After a long moment, he said in a flat voice, "I'll stay here to manage the farm." Elihu and Phineas knew just how much those words cost him.

Hope turned from the window, having wrestled her emotions under control. "When will you leave?" she asked, studying Elihu and Phineas as if seeing them clearly for the first time.

"We plan to enlist in the regiment being formed by Colonel Jedidiah Huntington before month's end," Elihu answered. Out of the corner of his eye he looked worriedly at David, who hadn't raised his head.

"God will strengthen each of you in your course," Mr. Benedict said confidently. David continued to study his hands.

By sundown the rain had ceased, and the clouds had broken up. When three stars could be seen in the sky in a single glance, signaling the Sabbath's end, Mr. and Mrs. Benedict departed. Phineas put on his hat in preparation for the walk back to Middletown. David and Elihu accompanied him for a short distance.

"What does Esther think of your plan to enlist?" David asked Elihu.

"I don't know," Elihu said, trying to sound unconcerned – and failing miserably.

David stopped in his tracks, grabbed Elihu's arm, and peered into his face in the fading light. "You haven't told her?" he demanded incredulously.

"Not yet," Elihu said with a half-hearted attempt at defensiveness, then decided to open his heart to his brothers. "I'm afraid telling her will be even more difficult than breaking the news to Mama. Esther has waited patiently for me to complete my apprenticeship, and knows it will take more time for me to establish a practice large enough to support a wife. Now I must ask her to wait longer still. I only hope I can make her understand why I must do this," he said wretchedly.

It was David's turn to feel compassion for the sacrifice Elihu was making in the name of duty. He couldn't imagine finding a woman you loved, waiting years to make her your wife – and then deciding to delay that day even longer.

"Esther may weep a bit, but she'll stand by you," Phineas predicted with jaunty confidence as the brothers resumed walking. "I wager marching off to war will make you all that more appealing to her. I've seen how girls admire men who've joined the army. I'd like to enjoy some of that admiration before we leave."

When neither David nor Elihu responded, Phineas rattled on with mounting excitement. "In a month, or two at most, we'll be outside Boston helping drive the Redcoats into the sea. I only hope all the fighting isn't over before we get there," he added worriedly.

David shook his head disgustedly. "This is no lark, Phineas. There are great principles at stake, and much danger to be faced."

Phineas's voice turned sober as he replied hastily, "I know, I know. You may find this hard to believe, but I really do have the fight for liberty at heart."

"He's speaking the truth," said Elihu. He knew Phineas's motives from serious conversations the brothers had had before making their decision to enlist.

After a long silence, Phineas said, half-defensively, half-mischievously, "But you can't deny it's exciting."

Elihu was glad the fading twilight concealed the smile of rueful honesty Phineas's words brought to his lips. For it was true that, despite the pain of parting with Esther, the frustration of postponing his medical practice, and the unknown dangers that lay ahead, he felt an adventurous anticipation that had nothing to do with duty.

He would see sights he'd yearned for years to behold – the great city of Boston chief among them. There would likely be the chance to test himself in battle, and if he survived, the triumphant return home. Then surely Esther would feel her prolonged wait had been worthwhile. He would tell their children and their children's children about how he'd fought for liberty in America.

The brothers were no more than silhouettes against the fading light by the time they reached the point in the road at which Phineas would continue on to Middletown, and David and Elihu would go back to the Lyman house. David said in a thick voice meant for both of his brothers, "I want you to take Papa's sword and musket with you when you join the army."

Elihu and Phineas were speechless. Since the day Major Hierlihy had purchased and returned the weapons at John's estate auction, David had cherished them. This was a truly unselfish gesture that told Elihu and Phineas that David held no grudge for how the day's events had played out.

Before anything else could be said, David turned and began striding back toward the house. Elihu hastened to catch up, while Phineas continued down the road to Middletown.

Chapter Seventeen

October, 1775
New Haven, Connecticut

Worries swarmed around Esther Beecher's mind like annoying flies as she sat peeling apples on a bench in front of her New Haven home on the morning of October 12, 1775. No sooner did she brush one away than another took its place.

There was her mother. Word had come yesterday from David that Hope was confined to bed with the bloody flux. Esther couldn't remember her mother ever having anything more serious than a cold.

Then there were Elihu and Phineas with the patriot army outside Boston. While there'd been no reports of fighting, military camps were notorious breeding grounds for deadly diseases like smallpox and camp fever.

And there was Esther's own health – and that of the baby she carried. The July trip to Middlefield hadn't helped her cough. Her slim frame had grown increasingly thin, save for her belly, which the midwife assured her was as round as it should be for the beginning of her eighth month of pregnancy.

But Esther's energy steadily ebbed. At summer's end she'd begun coughing up blood, undeniable evidence that she was suffering from consumption. Although the disease had killed her father, Esther refused to surrender to despair. She remained steadfast in her hope that, with God's mercy, she and her baby would survive.

The clear ring of a hammer striking iron told Esther that David Beecher was hard at work at his smithy. Her spirits lifted at the thought of her husband of nearly nine months. David Beecher was smart and well-read in everything from astronomy to history to the current events reported in the New Haven newspaper – all of which he enjoyed sharing with his young wife.

But David Beecher was no humorless scholar like Hannah's Noah Williston; he enjoyed jokes, as did his bride. Since their marriage Esther had discovered David had a tendency to unpredictable moodiness. But a few gentle words from her could banish his darkest humor.

David was an attractive man – powerfully built, his arms and chest thickly muscled from more than a decade as a blacksmith. His ice-blue eyes contrasted dramatically with his black hair.

Esther turned her attention to Mary Beecher, David's nine-year-old daughter, sitting beside her industriously peeling her own pile of apples. Having lost her mother, and then a stepmother, Mary had been understandably cautious of becoming attached to her father's new wife. But Esther's patient affection had prevailed; just recently Mary had begun calling her "Mama."

On the ground in front of them, three-year-old Lydia Beecher played at gathering acorns in a wooden bowl. The youngest child, David, two years old, was inside napping.

Esther set the bowl of peeled apples on the bench so she could stand to stretch out a cramp in her back. When she got to her feet, she was shocked to feel a warm wetness suddenly running down the inside of her thighs.

Panic ripped through Esther. Her water had broken, which meant her baby would be born very soon. Immediately she thought of her mother, whose first-born had been a seven-months' baby who lived less than a day.

"Mary," Esther said unsteadily. "Fetch your father."

The girl looked up, confused by the quaver in her stepmother's voice.

"Go!" Esther ordered sharply.

Frightened by Esther's stricken expression and curt command, Mary jumped to her feet. The bowl of peeled apples slid off her lap, the contents spilling into the dirt. The little girl raced to the back of the house.

A minute later David Beecher appeared around the corner at a run, still carrying his hammer. His eyes in his sooty, sweat-streaked face were dark with concern that turned to alarm when he saw the wet spot spreading down the front of Esther's skirt.

David dropped his hammer with a thud. He swept Esther up in his powerful arms and carried her inside, calling urgently for his mother.

By late afternoon Esther's travail had reached the point at which she needed to push to bring forth the baby. But when the midwife exhorted her to bear down, she could manage only a feeble effort. When Esther tried to draw a deep breath, she exploded into a coughing fit that brought up blood, which now stained the top of her shift. She repeatedly fell into a semi-stupor from which the midwife had to rouse her.

At long last a puny baby boy, scarcely alive, emerged from Esther's womb. Seeing that Esther was insensible, the midwife shook her head at the pathetically small infant. This time, she thought, not without pity, it seemed David Beecher would lose not only a wife to childbirth, as he had twice before, but the newborn as well.

The midwife hastily wrapped the baby in a handy piece of tow cloth and set him aside on a chair. She turned her attention back to Esther.

Catharine Benton reached the Beecher home shortly after sunset. As soon as Esther's travail began, David had complied with her desperate pleas to summon her sisters.

The anguish on David Beecher's face when he met Catharine at the door confirmed her worst fears. Still, Catharine wasn't prepared for the sight that awaited her in the candlelit chamber where Esther lay.

Catharine's beautiful little sister was barely recognizable. Esther's dark hair was matted with sweat and dried blood. She lay still, her cheeks and closed eyes sunken in a face the color of cold ashes. Catharine had to fiercely blink back tears.

"I've summoned Mr. Whittlesey," David Beecher whispered to Catharine, who took grim solace in knowing the minister was on his way. Husband and sister knelt beside Esther's bed, one on each side.

"Esther," Catharine said softly, stroking her hand tenderly back over Esther's damp forehead.

Esther's eyes fluttered open. She turned her head slightly toward the sound of Catharine's voice.

I knew you'd come," Esther said faintly. "Mama can't – she's sick. But I knew you would." A slight frown crossed Esther's face, her brow creased as if she were struggling to remember something. "My baby!" she cried in feeble agitation, looking desperately from David to Catharine.

Catharine, shamed she hadn't given a thought to the child, looked helplessly at David, who knew only that a baby boy had been born barely alive. He glanced fearfully at the midwife, who turned to the chair on which she'd set the tiny bundle. Astonished to find the child still breathing, she handed him to David, who placed the baby on his wife's breast. He pulled back the tow cloth so Esther could see the tiny, wizened face. "It's a boy," he said.

"Our son," Esther said with profound sadness. Suddenly she erupted into a violent coughing spasm. David snatched the baby away in time to keep him from being spattered with the blood and spittle spewing from Esther's mouth. Catharine tenderly wiped Esther's face clean with a damp cloth.

Esther closed her eyes in exhaustion. She reopened them to fix Catharine with a look of desperate pleading. "Catharine, please take care of my baby. You've been like a mother to me. I know you'll love him as I would."

Stunned by the request, Catharine glanced at David, whose misery at losing Esther overshadowed any other concerns. Feeling Catharine's unspoken question, David took his eyes from his wife long enough to nod at her in mute pain.

"Of course I'll care for him, Esther, as if he were my own son," Catharine replied, the tears she could no longer hold back streaking her cheeks. She didn't offer Esther false hope that she might live to raise the baby herself. That would be cruel and misguided; Esther needed as much of the time she had left as possible to make her peace with God.

At that moment Hannah appeared at the chamber door, disheveled from her frantic ride from West Haven. The appalling scene left her momentarily paralyzed. Recovering, she said softly, "Mr. Whittlesey is here," then stood aside to let the minister into the room.

Catharine reached across the bed to take the infant from David. She held the little boy down to Esther, who painfully raised herself up to kiss the baby's forehead, then fell back heavily and closed her eyes.

Catharine wiped away tears with a corner of the baby's swaddling cloth. She carefully navigated the stairs to the first floor, with Hannah hovering a step behind.

In the hall Catharine handed the infant to the midwife. "Could you wash and dress him, please?" Catharine asked, struggling to keep grief from overwhelming her. "Esther must have clothes for him somewhere," she said distractedly.

The midwife studied the frail baby dispassionately. His chances of surviving, poor to begin with in her experienced judgment, would be reduced to nearly zero once his mother died, which would happen within a matter of days. Even if a wet nurse could be secured, it was doubtful he would have enough strength to suckle. It would be a waste of time, and no act of mercy, she thought, to mount a struggle to keep this doomed child alive. "It's a pity he won't die with his mother," she observed matter-of-factly to no one in particular.

"Don't say such an evil thing!" Catharine cried wildly. The midwife stared at her in shock. "He must live – for Esther!" Catharine's voice cracked and she broke into uncontrollable sobs as Hannah gathered her into her arms.

Hannah glared over Catharine's shoulder at the shame-faced midwife, who hastily brought the newborn closer to the warmth of the fire. She asked another of the neighbor women come to attend the birth to ask David's mother, who'd been caring for the other children, for something to dress him in.

Weak early morning light filtered through the hall windows when Mr. Whittlesey and David Beecher descended the stairs. David's eyes were swollen and red; the minister's were bloodshot with fatigue. Still, both men looked composed.

A haggard Catharine rose from the chair in which she'd sat sleepless throughout the night. She faced David and the pastor.

"She's insensible now," Mr. Whittlesey said wearily. "But I prayed with her for much of the night before she lost consciousness. I believe her soul is as well prepared for death as could be hoped."

The minister's assessment gave Catharine a small measure of comfort. David, she could tell, felt the same. Esther had had the blessing all Christians hoped for: the opportunity to spend her last hours preparing for final judgment. It gave those who loved Esther even greater reason to hope her soul would enter God's kingdom.

Hannah started up the stairs to sit with Esther. David sat down heavily in a chair and leaned forward, his elbows on his knees, his hands clasped in front of him, staring sightlessly at the floor. Mr. Whittlesey put his hat on and started for the door.

"Pastor," Catharine said hastily. The minister turned around. "Would you baptize the baby?"

"He still lives?" David asked apathetically, tilting his head to look at Catharine. The child hadn't made a sound since his birth.

"Yes," Catharine answered, but the news meant nothing to David. He lowered his head.

The midwife handed the now-clean baby to Catharine. A lump rose in her throat when she saw how he was almost lost in the folds of one of the gowns, much too large for his premature body, Esther had lovingly sewn while awaiting his birth. She imagined Hope's disappointment when she learned she'd missed the birth of her first grandchild, her anxiety over the perils portended by the baby's untimely arrival – and her anguish over the gentle Esther's death.

David's mother brought water from the kitchen. "What shall he be called?" Mr. Whittlesey asked, directing the question to David. The grief-stricken husband continued to stare at the floor, shaking his head slightly. "We hadn't yet talked of names," he said tonelessly. Then he raised his head and paused as if listening to an inner voice. "Name him Lyman Beecher," he said.

Mr. Whittlesey proceeded to baptize the infant. When the water trickled onto his head, little Lyman Beecher fidgeted slightly and screwed up his face in discomfort, but he made no sound.

After Mr. Whittlesey left, Catharine, holding the baby in the crook of her left arm, placed her right hand consolingly on David's shoulder.

"Brother," she said, "this is your son. It's your right to raise him in the bosom of your family. If you wish to do so, I'll understand." She held her breath in suspense.

"No," David said, shaking his head. He looked up at Catharine. "It was Esther's wish – her dying wish . . . ," he stopped as his voice cracked. He gulped to steady himself, "She told me of how you cared for her when she was little. If, God willing, the child lives, I know you and Lot will be good to him."

"Thank you," Catharine whispered, giving his shoulder a grateful squeeze. "You'll never be sorry. I swear it."

Catharine walked over to lay the infant in the cradle brought out in anticipation of his arrival. He was the tiniest baby she'd ever seen. But she took hope from the healthy, pink color of his skin, and from how he stirred slightly when she stroked his incredibly soft cheek.

Despite her tongue-lashing of the midwife, Catharine realized clearly that little Lyman Beecher, come into the world two months early and with no mother to nurse him, had only a slim chance of survival. Yet if he did live, Catharine would at last have what she'd prayed for every day for more than a decade: a child. Not a child of her body, but still a child of her blood.

But why, Catharine wondered in despair, had the Lord sent her a child in this manner? Why had He required not the pain and danger of childbirth she would gladly have suffered, but the anguish of losing the sister who'd been more like a beloved daughter? She had to somehow accept that this tragedy was part of His plan, and do the best she could for the baby who soon would be all that was left on earth of Esther.

Esther Lyman Beecher died on the morning of October 14, having never regained consciousness. She was twenty-six.

Lyman Beecher, two days old, surprised everyone by summoning sufficient energy to suckle at the breast of a wet nurse located by his Aunt Williston. Within a few weeks he was strong enough to go home to North Guilford with his Aunt Benton.

Chapter Eighteen

December, 1775
Durham

"How could you do that?" Esther Camp demanded in a quavering voice. She and Elihu were walking down the road in front of her house. Light snow was falling, decorating Esther's cloak and the cape of Elihu's heavy greatcoat with large, lacy flakes.

The stint of military service Phineas and Elihu had signed up for in July had expired in mid-December. They'd left the Continental Army outside Boston on foot, reaching the Lyman house the previous evening.

Hope had been overjoyed to welcome her sons home, healthy and whole. They'd been shocked by how the tragedy of Esther's death, and Hope's own bout with the bloody flux, had aged their mother. She was finding some solace in Esther's baby, who had astonished everyone by surviving, although he was still fragile.

At first light Elihu had hurried to Durham for a joyous reunion with Esther. It was about to take an unavoidably unpleasant turn.

"Phineas and I didn't make our decision to re-enlist lightly," Elihu began to explain. Esther stopped walking abruptly to turn and face him. Elihu had expected her to be angry, but that didn't make the wounded look in her sky-blue eyes any easier to endure.

"Did you think about us?" she demanded with rising anger.

"Of course I did," Elihu said, taking her cold hands in his. "I missed you more than I ever imagined. I ached for you! But the colonies face even greater danger than when we signed up in July."

Esther tried to pull away, but Elihu gripped her hands tightly. "The damned British are sending mercenaries against us!" he said, desperate for her to understand the monstrous threat that had led to his decision. "They're Hessians, professional soldiers, animals who will plunder and ravage and murder if we don't stop them!"

Esther stopped struggling. She looked up at Elihu in alarm.

"King George has purchased regiments of these barbarians to set on his American subjects like mad dogs. That is what convinced us we had to sign up for another year," Elihu said. "Until we drive the British and their savage hirelings back across the ocean for good, no one's liberty or property or person will be safe. I'm fighting to protect all I cherish. I'm fighting to protect you!"

Elihu hoped his revelation was frightening enough to overcome Esther's resistance. He didn't want to terrify her with details about the blood-chilling prospects this development raised. He and Phineas had had to do just that the night before when their mother objected with dismay to news of their re-enlistment.

Hope had argued that they'd fulfilled their duty to bear arms in support of American liberty. They'd answered by describing with grim candor the possibility of British warships bristling with cannon like ones they'd seen in Boston Harbor transporting hordes of Hessians to the vulnerable Connecticut coast. Enemy vessels could sail up the Connecticut River to Middletown. The mercenaries could be unleashed to lay waste to homes and fields, to loot and burn, to ravish defenseless women like Esther, their sisters, their mother.

Hope had listened to her sons recount that horrifying scenario with a new regard earned by their military service. Together with her faith in the holiness of the American cause, it had convinced her to accept their decision, however much it pained her.

When Elihu saw the color drain from Esther's face, he knew his words had had the desired effect. She nodded slightly and swallowed to tamp down the fear. Then her eyes began to well up with tears.

"It's been more than three years since we started courting, and now you want me to wait even longer!" she cried plaintively. "I'm beginning to wonder if I'm being played for a fool, if you'll always find some excuse to put off our wedding," she accused bitterly, knowing even as she said it that the charge was untrue and unfair.

"No!" Elihu protested, his voice rough with passion. "I love you. I would never betray you." He gently slid the hood back from Esther's head, then slipped his arms under her cloak and around her waist. He embraced her tightly, placing an ardent kiss on her chilled lips.

The closeness of their bodies after so many months apart reminded Elihu vividly of the night a week before he'd left in July.

Carnal urges and the prospect of a long separation had overpowered their resolve, and he and Esther had lain together. The hurried, clandestine intercourse had been an exquisite pleasure, followed immediately by shame – and for Esther a nerve-wracking wait for the arrival of her monthly flux as proof she hadn't gotten with child.

Their lips parted, but Elihu kept his face bent close to Esther's. "I swear to you, after this enlistment is over, we'll be wed. I won't let anything stand in our way."

"Why don't we get married now?" Esther demanded desperately. "I think my father would consent – I'm twenty, after all."

Elihu placed his fingers gently against Esther's mouth to silence her. He shook his head slowly.

"Once I might have agreed," he said. "But while treating wounds and diseases in the camp hospitals, I've watched fathers and husbands agonize in their dying hours over what would befall the families they'd left behind." A haunted look came into his eyes.

"I love you too much to marry you and go away, leaving you tethered to an absent husband who might come back a cripple – or never return at all," Elihu went on. "Or leave you carrying my baby, to bear it and maybe–." Elihu's voice caught. Esther knew he was thinking of the sister whose name she shared, dead in childbirth. "Or to raise a child without a father," Elihu concluded. His eyes beseeched her to understand.

Esther stepped back from Elihu's embrace. She wiped her eyes, and studied the teardrops on her fingertip. "I understand," she said on a shuddering exhale of breath. "I believe you love me, and that is why you speak as you do. I will wait for you."

Relieved by Esther's concession, Elihu reached for her. But she took two paces back as she pulled the hood of her cloak up over her hair. She lifted her face and looked sternly into Elihu's eyes.

"Make no mistake," Esther said in a hard voice, "this is the last delay to which I'll consent. We can't forever postpone our lives for fear of what events may bring. If we don't wed upon your return from the army, I'll be done with waiting."

The warning made Elihu's stomach roil with anxiety. But he couldn't fault Esther. He understood a woman's fear, however groundless he knew it to be, of being abandoned by the man to whom she'd surrendered her maidenhead, to whom she'd already given years of her life.

Elihu nodded solemnly in agreement. He gently pulled Esther back toward him and lay her cheek against his chest, over his heart.

Chapter Nineteen

July, 1776
New York City

Elihu took a swallow of rum from a pewter mug. He was seated at a square oak table next to a window in the ale room of the Queen's Head Tavern. The inn was just three blocks from the waterfront, defensive fort, and battery of artillery at the southern tip of Manhattan Island. It was late on the afternoon of July 2, 1776 – exactly one year to the day since that fateful Sabbath when he and Phineas had announced their intention to enlist in the patriot army.

Elihu's uniform – a butternut-colored coat with black lapels, collars, and cuffs, trimmed with pewter buttons stamped with the number "17," worn over a scarlet waistcoat and leather breeches – identified him as a soldier of the Seventeenth Regiment of the Continental Army. A cockade of green ribbon affixed to the left side of his black, silver-trimmed cocked hat marked him as an ensign. He'd been promoted to that rank, the lowest of commissioned officers, upon rejoining the army in January.

Phineas and Elihu had spent the first two months of 1776 back on the dreary duty of besieging Boston. In early March, the situation had changed with lightning speed.

In a feat that beggared belief, soldiers under Colonel Henry Knox had used oxen to drag fifty-nine cannon taken when the patriots captured Fort Ticonderoga from the British across three hundred mountainous, snow-covered miles to the Continental Army camp outside Boston. On the night of March 4, in a phenomenal display of energy, discipline, and stealth, the Continental Army had placed the cannon atop Dorchester Heights, from which they could bombard most of Boston as well as the British fleet in the harbor.

The thunderstruck Redcoats had panicked. They'd frantically loaded as much as they could onto their ships and less than two weeks later sailed away from Boston, taking a thousand despised Tories with them.

Elihu and Phineas hadn't been among the Continental troops sent to take possession of the hastily evacuated city. Smallpox was widespread throughout Boston, and only men immune to the disease – which they were not – were permitted to enter. But their disappointment was soon forgotten when the Seventeenth Regiment was dispatched to an even more exciting destination: New York City.

New York was the Redcoats' obvious next target. The city sat on the southern tip of Manhattan Island at the mouth of the Hudson River, which extended north all the way to Canada. The British fleet could sail into the deep waters of New York's harbor, formed by the convergence of the Hudson and East rivers. If the enemy captured New York, it would serve as a base from which they could proceed to seize control of the Hudson, which would sever New England from the rest of the colonies.

The Seventeenth Regiment had arrived in New York in the middle of April. The city had proven to be unlike anything Elihu could have imagined.

When he first walked New York's thoroughfares, Elihu had had to make an effort not to gawk like the country bumpkin he felt himself to be. He marveled at the large, stately homes, many constructed of brick; at the imposing public buildings of stone that included a prison, a college, and a new hospital; at the enormous, elegant churches with soaring steeples that contrasted with the plain, boxlike clapboard meetinghouses of Middletown's Congregational societies.

An even greater revelation had been the people. Elihu had encountered French, Dutch, Germans, Scots, and Irish, few of which were found in Connecticut. On a stroll through the city he might hear three or four different languages being spoken. There were many more Negroes in New York as well. Most startling had been the houses of worship for Jews, Roman Catholics, and Quakers. Members of these faiths would be considered infidels in Congregational Connecticut.

There were thought to be twenty thousand people in New York City – four times as many as Middletown. Many were Tories – some open, many more secret.

The Queen's Head Tavern, a three-and-a-half story building of brick, was owned by Samuel Fraunces, a known supporter of the patriot cause. This explained why the several dozen drinkers in the ale room around Elihu were mostly soldiers in the Continental Army. Some wore formal uniforms of varying distinctive color combinations like Elihu's, others the tan homespun hunting shirts of riflemen from the backwoods of Virginia or the trousers waterproofed with tar of Massachusetts mariners.

Afternoon sunlight streaming through the window's square panes of glass created a hatch-work pattern on the oak table's scarred surface. A shadow blotted out the patch of light, and Elihu glanced up to see Captain Elihu Hubbard, his superior officer. Elihu shot to attention, thrusting his Windsor chair back so abruptly the legs scraped on the floor planks.

Captain Hubbard casually waved Elihu back into his seat. "Might I join you?" he asked affably. A tall, lean man in his late thirties, he was a shoemaker and farmer back in Middletown.

"Of course, sir," Elihu replied, settling back into the chair. "I'm waiting for my brother."

Captain Hubbard pulled up a second chair. He set a mug on the table.

"Ah, Private Phineas Lyman," the captain said with an indulgent smile. "When he first appeared in camp he behaved like a schoolboy on a lark. But army discipline has settled him down – without breaking his spirit. He's fast becoming a fine soldier, for all that he's not yet twenty-one."

"I agree, sir," Elihu replied.

Captain Hubbard drank from his mug, then licked his upper lip thoughtfully. "I've noticed," he continued, with a grin, "that Private Lyman's dedication to duty hasn't stopped him from flirting with the ladies at every opportunity."

Elihu smiled wryly in agreement. "He's made his share of conquests. At least he's had the good sense to confine his attentions to respectable women, unlike our officers and soldiers who visit the diseased whores at the Holy Ground." Elihu shook his head at the foolishness of men who patronized the five hundred prostitutes housed in that dangerous neighborhood of notorious brothels. The ironic nickname came from its location on land owned by the Anglican Trinity Church.

"I've warned Phineas to steer clear of that vile place, to avoid polluting himself with such women or coming to a violent end," Elihu continued. "He's heeded my advice – so far as I know."

Elihu drained the last of the rum from his mug, thinking of how much had changed between the two brothers during the past year. They'd consoled each other through the surprisingly painful homesickness that afflicted nearly every recruit, most of whom, like Elihu and Phineas, had never before been more than twenty miles from home. They'd struggled together to submit to the discipline and hierarchy of the military, so alien to New Englanders accustomed to abiding by communal decisions made only after each man had his say.

Phineas had lent a sympathetic ear to Elihu's confidences about Esther Camp. Together they'd worried over their mother's health – and mourned their sister Esther's death. The gap that now existed between them as officer and private hadn't weakened the newly forged fraternal bond.

Elihu glimpsed Phineas hurrying past the window. When he entered the ale room, Elihu waved an arm to attract his attention.

Phineas impatiently worked his way through the crowded room to Elihu's table. Recognizing Elihu's companion, he snapped into a ramrod-straight posture and executed a proper military salute by removing his hat, sweeping it all the way down to his knee, then replacing it on his head. Captain Hubbard acknowledged the salute without standing up, then gestured to Phineas to sit.

Phineas turned around an armless chair and straddled it, leaning his crossed arms on the back. "I finished it last night," he said excitedly to Elihu. Phineas waived off a waiter who approached the table. "I feel as full of fire as if I'd guzzled a gallon of rum."

From the inside pocket of his coat Phineas pulled a thick pamphlet the size of a man's hand. The words "COMMON SENSE" were printed across the top. Stories of this inspiring work by an unknown author had been circulating for months among civilians and soldiers alike. It had been in such demand that Elihu had only recently been able to put his hands on a copy. Once he finished it, he'd passed it on to Phineas.

"I've never read anything like it!" Phineas continued, his blue eyes shining. "The writer puts forth an unanswerable case for why America should cast off British tyranny and effect a permanent separation. Listen to this," he said, riffling through the pamphlet until he found the page he sought. "'There is something very absurd, in supposing a continent to be perpetually governed by an island,'" he read aloud. He looked up at both men. "Is that not truly plain common sense?" he demanded rhetorically.

Elihu learned forward to take the pamphlet. Phineas was right; it had an almost intoxicating effect on the heart and mind. "My mother and brother have written that this little book has erased the doubts of many people back home about the rightness of our fight."

Elihu leafed through the pamphlet. "'The sun never shined on a cause of greater worth,'" he read aloud. "''Tis not the affair of a city, a county, a province, or a kingdom, but of a continent – of at least one eighth part of the habitable globe. 'Tis not the concern of a day, a year, or an age; posterity are virtually involved in the contest, and will be more or less affected, even to the end of time.'"

All three men considered the inspiring description of the majesty of their cause. "These words will give our soldiers strength and courage for the holy mission of driving the enemy from these shores," Elihu said.

"We'll find out soon enough," Captain Hubbard said soberly, slapping a palm hard on the table for emphasis as he stood. "Just three days past two score British vessels sailed into the bay beyond the Narrows between Staten Island and Long Island – not more than twelve miles from where we sit! More will follow. And some will bear regiments of blood-thirsty Hessians."

Chapter Twenty

July, 1776
New York City

The Seventeenth Regiment fell into formation with its brigade at six o'clock sharp on the pleasant evening of July 9, 1776. Each man had made himself as presentable as possible for what all knew was an historic occasion. They stood at solemn attention, muskets by their side.

A rumor that the Continental Congress in Philadelphia had proclaimed the colonies independent of Great Britain had begun circulating in New York on the previous Wednesday evening, July 4. Confirmation had arrived two days later. This morning General Washington had ordered that Congress's formal declaration justifying the colonies' permanent separation from Great Britain be read to the troops.

Many citizens had gathered on the fringes of the assembled soldiers to hear the document. All eyes followed an officer unknown to Elihu as he strode to the front of the crowd.

The man began to read in a clear, powerful voice from a large sheet of paper. After finishing the introductory passage, he launched into what from the timbre of his voice was clearly the heart of the document.

"We hold these truths to be self-evident, that all men are created equal, that they are endowed by their Creator with certain unalienable rights, that among these are life, liberty, and the pursuit of happiness. That to secure these rights, governments are instituted among men, deriving their just powers from the consent of the governed."

In just two sentences, Elihu thought with admiration, the document's unknown author had expressed the values and principles for which Americans were fighting.

The officer proceeded to read stinging indictments against King George III, his voice growing stronger with outrage as he recounted each of the monarch's abuses. "He has plundered our seas, ravaged our coasts, burnt our towns, and destroyed the lives of our people," he declared. "He is at this time transporting large armies of foreign mercenaries to complete the works of death, desolation, and tyranny, already begun with circumstances of cruelty and perfidy, scarcely paralleled in the most barbarous ages, and totally unworthy the head of a civilized nation."

Elihu shifted his eyes left and right to gauge his fellow soldiers' reaction. Their faces were flushed with fury at this litany of offenses – especially the last one, which for them was very personal. At this very moment thousands of those "foreign mercenaries" – Hessian soldiers – were aboard some of the more than one hundred enemy ships anchored off Long Island. Many soldiers hearing the document would soon face these barbarians in battle.

"We therefore," the officer continued, his voice ringing with defiant pride, "solemnly publish and declare, that these United Colonies are, and of right ought to be, free and independent states, that they are absolved from all allegiance to the British crown." A thrill of excitement coursed through the troops.

"And for the support of this declaration," the speaker continued, "with a firm reliance on the protection of divine Providence, we mutually pledge to each other our lives, our fortunes, and our sacred honor." Silence reigned; every soldier present was risking no less than the men who had issued this document.

For a moment the crowd seemed unsure what should come next. Then, as if on cue, soldiers and civilians alike erupted into a series of three full-throated cheers. When the echoes died away, the military units were dismissed. Civilians pressed forward to mingle with the soldiers.

Elihu searched for Phineas, wanting to share this powerful moment with his brother. He spotted him, but before he could reach him through the crush of people, Phineas and several other soldiers, accompanied by a throng of agitated civilians, took off sprinting south. Suspecting where they were headed, Elihu struggled harder to get free of the crowd and follow them.

Elihu trailed the group down to the intersection with Broadway, then past the tall spires of St. Paul's Chapel and Trinity Church. They had enough of a head start that Elihu didn't catch up until they'd covered the two miles to what he correctly suspected was their destination: the Bowling Green at the very tip of Manhattan Island.

The Bowling Green was a parklike grassy oval, about a quarter of an acre in size, surrounded by a ten-foot-high fence of elegant wrought iron. In the center of this verdant oasis stood a fifteen-foot-tall white marble pedestal supporting a larger-than-life statue of King George III. The monarch was dressed as a Roman emperor mounted on horseback. The statue, two tons of lead covered with glittering gold leaf, had become an obnoxious symbol of royal arrogance.

Elihu, breathing hard, bent over with his hands on his knees to catch his breath. When he straightened up he couldn't see Phineas, who'd been absorbed into the mob – for that was the only word to describe the hundreds of agitated New Yorkers and dozens of Continental soldiers milling angrily outside the iron fence. Shouts of "Down with the tyrant!" and "Off with his head!" were greeted by frenzied roars of approval.

Suddenly several men – including Phineas, Elihu was shocked to see – scaled the iron fence and raced to the statue. They clambered up ladders to the top of the pedestal. Men tossed up ropes to those on the pedestal, who looped them tightly around the statue. The men on the ground pulled mightily on the ropes, while those on the pedestal pried at the enormous statue's base with metal bars. The inflamed mob cheered them on.

After several minutes of intense exertion, the gigantic equestrian statue began to separate from the pedestal. As those pulling on the ropes redoubled their efforts, the statue listed, then teetered, then slowly toppled over. The men on the ground dropped their ropes and scampered away from the spot where a few seconds later the massive statue struck the grass with a mighty thud that caused the ground to shake.

The mob screamed its approval. More men swarmed over the fence and onto the Bowling Green. Some clambered up to stand atop the fallen statue, thrusting their fists skyward in gestures of triumph. Others spat on the royal effigy. Someone produced an ax, and furious hacking soon decapitated the leaden monarch. The severed head was raised aloft for all to see, touching off near-hysterical cries of approval.

Elihu watched aghast, jostled by the surging crowd. For weeks the city had been an emotional powder keg. The Declaration's powerful prose, in particular the recitation of the king's sins against America, had ignited it. But that was no excuse for this outrageous act of vandalism by an out-of-control mob. Certainly soldiers should not have disgraced the Continental Army by taking part in it.

Elihu intended to seriously reprimand Phineas when he caught up with him – brother or no brother. But he wasn't foolish enough to attempt to interfere with the mob as it gleefully went about its destructive work. To do so would be as futile – and as dangerous – as trying to stop a pack of ravening wolves from devouring a lamb.

"What do you have to say about your disorderly conduct this evening, Private Lyman?" Elihu demanded sternly the moment a disheveled Phineas stepped through the flap of his tent. Since Elihu clearly had either witnessed or heard about his participation in the night's doings, Phineas didn't even try to equivocate.

"I participated in a demonstration of patriotism by a free people," Phineas replied, belatedly remembering to add "'sir.'" His vivid blue eyes met Elihu's angry brown ones steadily. "We destroyed an offensive idol of the tyrant who seeks to enslave us."

"You took part in a riot!" Elihu snapped in disgust. "And dishonored your uniform!"

Phineas bit back the angry reply he would have made had Elihu been only his brother. A year of military discipline had instilled in him a respect for rank and sufficient self-control to keep from making an insubordinate remark that would force Elihu to punish him. Besides, as Phineas's ardor cooled, he began to grudgingly realize there might be some truth in what Elihu said.

Phineas straightened out his sweaty, rumpled uniform, swept strands of hair that had come free of his queue off his face, and pulled himself into something resembling the posture of a soldier at attention. "Perhaps it did get a bit out of control, sir," he conceded, still looking Elihu square in the eye. "But it was more than a destructive mob. The king's statue is to be melted down to make musket balls. Our soldiers soon will be firing melted majesty at the Redcoats and Hessians and Tories."

Phineas kept a straight face as he repeated the ironic quip that had circulated through the crowd, but there was a mischievous spark in his eyes. Elihu's mouth twitched slightly with suppressed amusement, but he maintained a stern expression. "That may be, but I'm putting you on notice that any further activity of this kind will be punished severely."

Satisfied he had fulfilled his duty as an officer, Elihu's expression became one of concern. "Be thankful that mob contented itself with destroying a statue, Phineas. They might just as easily have vented their fury on Tories, perhaps killing or injuring innocent people in the process – to the shame of our righteous cause. What happened tonight was anarchy, not liberty."

Phineas's blonde brows drew together as he pondered Elihu's warning. Elihu placed a hand on his shoulder. "Don't waste your energy on lifeless symbols, Brother," he advised. "Save it for fighting the flesh-and-blood enemy we'll face all too soon."

Chapter Twenty-One

August, 1776
Long Island, New York

The hellish din of hundreds of pistols, muskets, and rifles firing, along with the roar of cannon and the screams of wounded and dying men had terrified Elihu just a few hours earlier. Now the uproar barely registered in his brain, as he focused intently on loading John's musket as quickly as possible, something he'd done perhaps forty times this morning.

Elihu bit the top of a paper ammunition cartridge, ripped it off, and spat it out. He poured gunpowder from the cartridge into the musket's pan. The remaining powder went down the weapon's barrel, followed by the paper cartridge and the metal ball it held.

Elihu jammed the ramrod into the barrel to tamp down the powder, ball, and cartridge. He set the butt of the musket stock against his shoulder, thumbed back the cock, wrapped his finger around the trigger – then waited, nerves taut, for Captain Hubbard's command to fire.

Nearly every day of the seven weeks since the inflamed mob toppled King George's statue had brought fresh evidence of the British monarch's commitment to crushing rebels who dared offer such an insult to the royal honor. As July turned into August, a seemingly endless stream of ships carrying British regulars and Hessian mercenaries appeared in the waters around New York. Now more than four hundred vessels were anchored, carrying what rumor claimed to be as many as thirty thousand British and Hessian soldiers – the largest British invasion fleet ever.

The Continental Army commanders had watched anxiously, trying to predict where the enemy's massive force – several times larger than that of the patriots – would strike. Five days ago, on August 22, enemy ships had begun to land large numbers of troops on the southwestern shore of Long Island, across the East River from New York City.

The Seventeenth Regiment was among the patriot troops transported by boat to the American fortification on Brooklyn Heights on the western end of Long Island, in response to the enemy's action. After a couple nights in the woods on guard duty, Elihu and his men had been recalled to Brooklyn Heights.

They'd been roused well before dawn this day, August 27, and ordered to move out. After marching south about two miles under an overcast sky in unseasonably cool temperatures, the Seventeenth Regiment arrived around sunrise at a treeless hilltop.

They were positioned with other units all under the command of Brigadier General Samuel Holden Parsons of Connecticut. The sun was well up when Elihu and his comrades at last experienced what they'd yearned for – and feared – for so long: battle with the enemy.

Elihu's palms were sweaty and grimy, but his hands no longer shook with the terror that had clawed at him during the Seventeenth Regiment's baptism of fire. He stared hard with stinging, bloodshot eyes into the swirling, opaque fog created by the smoke of hundreds of muskets firing repeatedly. He caught a glimpse of scarlet at which to point his weapon. When at last Captain Hubbard's voice rang out with the order to fire, Elihu closed his eyes to protect them against the flash should his gun misfire, and squeezed off his shot.

When he opened his eyes, Elihu couldn't tell if his ball had hit any of the enemy. But a number of dimly visible red-clad forms freshly littering the hillside in front of the American lines proved some patriot shots had found their mark.

Elihu lowered his musket and cast a sharp eye around the field. After a suspenseful pause, he realized that musket balls were no longer whistling toward the American line. No enemy soldiers charged from the slowly dissipating smoke. When a gap opened in the shifting haze, he saw the British retreating down the hill.

Relief was quickly followed by a surge of pride that the Continental soldiers had held fast against the fearsome enemy. Twice they had defended their hilltop position against assaults by the finest professional army in the world.

Elihu rested the butt of his musket on the ground. A swallow of rum and water from the wooden canteen hanging from a strap around his shoulder refreshed his parched mouth and throat, but didn't wash away the acrid taste of gunpowder. With a sleeve he wiped his eyes, stinging from salty sweat trickling down his face.

Elihu replaced the canteen's stopper. He peered through the dissipating smoke to check on his compatriots who'd been standing side-by-side with him in a line across the hilltop. Captain Hubbard was unscathed, Elihu was thankful to see, as was Lieutenant Jabez Fitch, a barrel of a man from east of the Connecticut River whom Elihu had gotten to know over the past months.

Elihu searched anxiously among the enlisted men for Phineas. He spotted his brother swinging down from the branches of a tree on the hillside into which he'd climbed to get a better vantage point for firing on the enemy.

Phineas's powder-blackened face wore the same smile of tired satisfaction as the other men in the regiment. Spotting Elihu, he waved his arm enthusiastically to signal all was well. Elihu raised his hand in an answering salute, and offered up a silent prayer of thanks to the Lord for their safety.

But for how long? Elihu had to wonder. That had been his last cartridge. The petering out of musket fire told him other patriot soldiers were out of ammunition as well.

Elihu now had only his bayonet – a sixteen-inch-long triangular blade attached to the end of his musket's barrel – to fight with. Not all soldiers had bayonets, and those who did hadn't been trained to use them in combat. A few men like Phineas had swords, but also lacked instruction in their use in battle. If the British attacked a third time, the Americans would be powerless to stop them.

Elihu's pessimistic musings were interrupted by a cheer from behind. He turned to see the regiment's ammunition wagon arrive. Relieved, he gathered around with the other men to receive fresh powder, paper, and balls to fashion into a new supply of cartridges.

The Americans discovered they'd lost just one man dead and a couple wounded. More than fifty dead and dying British soldiers were scattered around the battlefield. A dozen wounded enemy soldiers had been taken prisoner and were being treated by Dr. John Waldo, the Seventeenth Regiment's surgeon.

Their ammunition replenished, the now battle-tested Americans were ready when the enemy once more attempted to take the hill. The British had been reinforced by the 42nd Royal Highlanders, known as the Black Watch, outfitted smartly in plaid kilts, argyle patterned stockings, and flat bonnets topped with feathers.

Again the chaos of battle engulfed the hillside. When Elihu was able to sneak a glance at the silver pocket watch Dr. Dickinson had given him when he completed his apprenticeship, he saw it was nearly noon; they'd been fending off this third assault for two hours

Elihu was about to get off another shot when the sudden crack of musket fire behind the American position made him turn sharply. At General Parsons's command, the Seventeenth Regiment wheeled and set off at a trot toward the sound. After a short distance they were stopped in their tracks by an impossible sight: a large force of enemy troops advancing straight at them!

Elihu gaped dumbfounded at these Redcoats who'd appeared behind the American lines as if dropped from the sky. He recovered sufficiently to raise his loaded musket and fire.

Other Continental soldiers were shooting as well, and the British fell back in disarray. But some American troops, panicked by this unnerving development, barreled through gaps in the ruptured enemy lines, and kept running for the safety of Brooklyn Heights.

The Seventeenth Regiment's drummer beat the signal for retreat. The men fell back raggedly, firing as they went. Elihu took shelter behind a tree to re-load his musket, when a searing pain in his upper left arm caused him to him drop the weapon. He looked down to see circles of blood spreading from holes ripped in his uniform sleeve by a musket ball that had passed through his arm.

Elihu dropped to his knees, pulled off his haversack, then shucked off his uniform frock coat. He fumbled in his haversack for a linen shirt. He tore off a sleeve, and used his right hand and teeth to tie it tightly around his arm to staunch the bleeding. He realized thankfully that he still had use of the wounded arm.

Elihu got unsteadily to his feet, just as a British soldier who hadn't seen him crouched behind the tree stumbled upon him. Elihu reacted instinctively, jabbing the bayonet affixed to his unloaded musket into the Redcoat's gut.

For one hideous moment their eyes met, the British soldier's wide with stunned agony, Elihu's filled with fear followed by horror as the physician in him envisioned the gruesome injury he'd inflicted on this man. Breaking eye contact, Elihu wrenched the bayonet free.

The mortally wounded man dropped his musket, clutched his belly with both hands, and fell face down with an anguished grunt.

Elihu backed haltingly away from the motionless figure, then grabbed his coat and haversack and continued his retreat.

Trapped between British troops advancing up the hillside and the ones who'd materialized at their rear, the men of the Seventeenth Regiment ran west – only to encounter more enemy soldiers. The Americans reversed direction again, and headed east, their only remaining option. Elihu and the other officers tried to pull together as many of the scattered men of the Seventeenth Regiment as they could, including an uninjured Phineas.

Phineas's face brightened at the sight of his brother, then darkened with concern at the blood-stained bandage on Elihu's arm. Elihu shook his head to indicate it wasn't serious. Then he gestured to Phineas to join the men moving east.

The Americans entered a dense wood, which offered some protection from pursuit. The ground became progressively wetter, until it was clear they were proceeding into a swamp.

Phineas held his musket, powder horn, ball pouch, and sword over his head to keep them dry as he waded through the waist-deep water of the gloomy morass. Each step was a struggle to free a foot from the sticky mud. Dense undergrowth scratched his face and hands as he pushed it aside with his raised elbows.

At last the trees began to thin out, the water got shallower, and the footing became firmer. Phineas emerged from the swamp onto a partly wooded plain. He hurried over to several muddy, dripping soldiers of the Seventeenth Regiment congregating in the center of the clearing. Several dozen more men, including Elihu, emerged one by one from the swamp and joined their bedraggled comrades.

The officers began trying to form the men into some semblance of order. Suddenly a volley of musket fire exploded on their right. A private next to Phineas toppled forward onto the ground, a red stain spreading from the hole where a musket ball had penetrated his back. Phineas saw a line of Hessians drawn up along the edge of the plain. A second salvo of musket fire sounded to their left, and Phineas spun to behold more Hessians firing from that direction. The Americans were caught in the crossfire of the two enemy units.

"Back to the swamp!" General Parsons shouted. The men stampeded toward the marsh from which they'd so gratefully emerged minutes earlier.

Phineas had nearly reached the protection of the swamp when he suddenly pitched forward in the tall grass. He let go of his musket and sword, freeing his hands to bring them up, palms down, in time to keep his face from slamming into the ground. The jolt knocked the breath out of him.

After a long moment Phineas got his wind back, then tried to get up. A spike of pain shot through the back of his right thigh, and he realized he'd been shot. He collapsed back onto the ground, but powerful hands gripped him under his arms. General Parsons hauled Phineas to his feet, threw Phineas's left arm over his shoulder, put his right arm around Phineas's waist, and helped the young private hobble painfully the last few feet to the swamp.

Phineas looked back at John's prized sword lying on the grass where he'd dropped it. Its connection to home and family, especially to the steadfast warrior for whom he was named, had made it a talisman for him. He was seized with a foolhardy urge to retrieve it, even as Hessian musket balls whizzed past his head. When he tried to stop to go back, General Parsons pulled him forward, growling, "Keep going or we're dead."

Elihu's lungs were heaving desperately for air, his legs felt like they were on fire, and sweat streamed down his face by the time he retraced his route through the swamp. But no sooner had the first of the Seventeenth Regiment's dwindling number of men reached the marsh's edge, than a small detachment of British regulars appeared and opened fire. Elihu managed to load and discharge his musket three times, and the enemy soldiers backed off.

Elihu re-loaded his musket, then looked around to assess their situation. Not all the men who'd taken refuge from the Hessians' crossfire in the swamp had yet emerged. Nowhere did he see Captain Hubbard, General Parsons, or, Elihu realized in alarm, Phineas.

"Ensign Lyman!" Captain Joseph Jewett was waving him to join a small group of officers. Elihu hurried over, trying frantically to remember when he'd last seen Phineas.

"I see no means of escape," Captain Jewett was saying grimly. "We're surrounded by the enemy. Much as I loathe the thought, I believe we have no choice but to surrender."

"I agree." Lieutenant Fitch spat out the words like something rancid. "We fought bravely and honorably today. Our deaths now would serve no purpose."

Elihu was appalled by the idea of willingly delivering themselves into the hands of an enemy from whom they couldn't expect the slightest mercy. "Surrender might be the same as death, sir," he said candidly to Captain Jewett. "We have no guarantee the British will treat us as prisoners of war. They might turn us over to the damned Hessians for their amusement. Or string us up as traitors."

"You may be right," Captain Jewett conceded. "But we're staggering around like a bear attacked by angry hornets, unable to escape being stung no matter which way he turns. If we don't lay down our arms, the enemy will pick us off one by one. If we surrender, we have a chance, however small, of surviving the day."

Elihu had no good argument against this ugly reality. "I think it best we break up into small parties to surrender separately," Lieutenant Fitch suggested. "We may seem less threatening as we approach the enemy."

Captain Jewett nodded. "Let's do it," he said, teeth clenched against the rage filling him. The officers broke away, and Elihu gathered together half a dozen terrified soldiers to explain the desperate plan.

"Jabez," Elihu said urgently, grabbing Lieutenant Fitch's arm as they prepared to set out. "Where did you last see my brother?

"On the other side of the swamp – I think," Fitch replied distractedly. Then he began shepherding away his flock of men.

Elihu and his own dispirited little band limped along in search of an enemy unit to which to surrender. They hoped fervently that their captors would be British soldiers, not barbarous Hessians.

As they reached the crest of a rise, Elihu saw with cold terror a large party of Hessians several hundred yards away. Before he could hustle his men back down out of sight, a Hessian spotted them and cried out to his comrades. About a dozen of the mercenaries stalked toward them, muskets at the ready. If the Americans tried to run, the Hessians would surely give chase and shoot them down.

"Turn your muskets upside down and hold them in front of you, so they can see we pose no threat," Elihu told the men. As he did so in demonstration, Elihu was stricken by the guilt-filled realization that he was going to lose John's musket, entrusted to him by David.

Elihu took a deep breath, then exhaled slowly to steady himself. He assumed a stoic expression and pulled his shoulders back so that his posture was ramrod straight, hoping his physical bearing would help him conceal his fear and perform the mortifying act of surrender with some shred of dignity. He began to walk toward the Hessians with a measured pace that almost perfectly matched the rhythm of his pounding heart.

Elihu stopped about twenty feet short of the Hessians. To the enemy soldier who approached him, he declared in a formal tone, "I am Ensign Elihu Lyman of the Seventeenth Regiment of the Continental Army. My men and I surrender ourselves to you as prisoners of war." He enunciated the last three words slowly and with a deliberate emphasis; although the Hessian undoubtedly didn't speak English, perhaps this was a phrase he'd picked up since arriving in America.

The Hessians surrounded the Americans, muskets trained on them menacingly at point-blank range. The soldier Elihu had addressed was a sinewy, hard-looking sergeant of about forty, with a thin, pointed, upturned mustache. His uncommon height was accentuated by his tall, cone-shaped headgear. The sergeant emitted a derisive snort, then without warning grabbed the up-ended musket from Elihu's hands.

Not expecting the action, Elihu didn't immediately let go of the musket, so that the sergeant's rough yank on the weapon sent a fresh wave of pain pulsing through his wounded arm. Elihu bit down on his lower lip to keep from crying out, but anger flared in his eyes.

The Hessian regarded Elihu with contempt. He righted the musket and noticed the freshly dried blood coating its bayonet – evidence that Elihu had maimed or killed an enemy soldier that day. The Hessian's eyes narrowed in naked hatred.

The Hessian growled what was clearly a threat in his guttural tongue. Elihu began to fear he'd been correct about the fate awaiting them in the enemy's clutches. But he held his tongue, and saw that the Hessian seemed disciplined enough not to act without cause on his blatant loathing for Americans.

The prick of a bayonet in his back prodded Elihu forward. He and his men were roughly herded toward the main body of Hessians, where a dozen or so American soldiers were under guard. Phineas wasn't among them.

The Hessian sergeant reached out to relieve Elihu of his cartridge box and canteen, then gestured at the haversack. Elihu shrugged it off and handed it to his captor.

Rummaging through the haversack, the Hessian pulled out a handful of Continental currency, which he tossed contemptuously on the ground. He reached in again, and a satisfied smile crossed his pock-marked face. He brought out five silver dollars, which he jingled in his palm before pocketing them.

Next the Hessian snatched Elihu's silver-trimmed hat from his head. Then he gestured at Elihu's shoes, barking out what was clearly a command.

Elihu stared at the soldier in indignant disbelief. He'd expected to lose his musket and ammunition, and hadn't been surprised when the greedy mercenary confiscated his haversack, canteen, money, and even his fine hat. But something as essential as shoes was another matter.

"I protest this theft," Elihu said firmly. His defiance seemed to please the Hessian. Smiling wickedly, the sergeant pressed the tip of his bayonet against Elihu's breastbone and repeated his order.

Afraid the Hessian was trying to goad him into resistance that would provide an excuse to kill him, Elihu made no further protest. Pushing the bayonet carefully aside with a finger, he leaned over, unbuckled the mud-caked shoes with sharp, angry jerks, pulled them off, and handed them to the grinning sergeant, who passed them to a fellow mercenary.

But the Hessian wasn't finished. Clearly relishing the situation, he flicked back the black lapels of Elihu's uniform coat with his bayonet, and barked another order in German.

Seething at his impotence, Elihu ripped off his coat, unbuttoned his waistcoat with fingers trembling with barely contained anger, and handed them to his captor.

Feeling a hard shape inside the waistcoat, the Hessian searched until he found Elihu's silver watch in the pocket. Delighted with this unexpected treasure, the Hessian tucked the timepiece into his own waistcoat pocket before giving the garments to a subordinate.

The Hessian turned back and stared at Elihu expectantly. After a long moment during which Elihu felt he might explode with rage, he untied the linen strip from around his wounded arm. He pulled his shirt over his head, gritting his teeth against the fresh pain of the bullet wounds being torn open when cloth stuck to them by dried blood was pulled away.

Elihu put his shirt into the mercenary's outstretched hand, but the Hessian kept his arm extended, still waiting. Elihu leaned over to pull off his muddy stockings, which he placed atop the shirt.

Now wearing only his breeches, Elihu shivered as a cool breeze raised goose flesh on his bare arms and chest. Still the Hessian stood with his arm outstretched. When Elihu made no further move, the Hessian snarled a command and snapped his fingers.

Elihu desperately searched the mercenary's hard blue eyes for any trace of humanity – and found none. Realizing his life still hung in the balance, Elihu, blushing with humiliation, unbuttoned his breeches, pulled them off, and laid them atop his stockings. He stood naked as the day he was born, blood trickling down his arm.

The Hessian laughed in sadistic triumph. He turned to hand the garments to another subordinate, then whirled back and without warning raised his musket and dealt Elihu a vicious blow to the left temple with the butt of the weapon.

Blinding pain exploded inside Elihu's skull. He staggered, then fell to his knees. The Hessian struck again, ramming the butt of his musket against Elihu's lower back, causing him to sprawl prone on the ground as he cried out in anguish.

The Hessian continued to beat Elihu with the musket butt, cursing furiously in German. He struck his defenseless captive on the naked legs, shoulders, back, and head. Despite the disorienting blow to his temple, Elihu had sufficient presence of mind to curl his body into a tight ball, head tucked inward and hands clasped over it, thereby protecting his genitals and face.

Just when Elihu was sure the Hessian intended to beat him to death, the man broke off his assault. He delivered a last vicious kick to Elihu's ribs, then yanked him to his feet by his wounded arm.

The sergeant shoved the dazed Elihu towards a small group of American prisoners that included the soldiers Elihu had led into surrender. All of them had been robbed of everything but their breeches, the humiliation of being stripped naked apparently having been inflicted on Elihu alone as punishment for his defiance. The men gathered protectively around him, but said nothing for fear of being subjected to the same kind of brutal beating.

After a brief wait the miserable prisoners were marched through dense woods, the sharp foliage viciously cutting and scratching their unprotected skin. They emerged onto a hilltop close to where they'd made their successful stand that morning against the British. It was overrun with Redcoats, who greeted the nearly naked Americans with jeers and curses.

"We ought to string you filthy traitors up!" a regular shouted furiously. The other British soldiers cheered in enthusiastic agreement, and Elihu feared they'd be seized and hanged on the spot. But the dangerous moment passed, and the Americans were allowed to continue on unmolested.

The Hessians marched them a mile to a barn by the shore. They were herded into a yard already crammed with so many prisoners it was obvious the Americans had sustained a devastating defeat.

His feet bleeding, his body an aching, stinging mass of scratches, lacerations, and bruises, his wounded arm feeling like it was on fire, Elihu collapsed onto the ground.

"Ensign Lyman?" a familiar voice called out. "Elihu?" the voice said more sharply. "It is you!" Elihu turned his throbbing head far enough to look up and see Lieutenant Jabez Fitch leaning over him.

"Damn it, man, what did those stinking Hessians do to you?" Lieutenant Fitch demanded, studying Elihu's injuries with horror. "Only beasts would take a man's last stitch of clothing and then beat him almost to death. Here, let me help you." Fitch bent down to slip his shoulder under Elihu's right arm, and lifted him unsteadily to his feet.

"I have some clothes you can put on," Lieutenant Fitch said. He opened his haversack and pulled out a linen shirt and buckskin breeches.

"No one ever gave me a greater gift," Elihu managed to mumble. Fitch helped him pull on the breeches, which on Elihu's taller, leaner frame were baggy and several inches too short. Elihu raised his arms painfully to pull the shirt over his head, then tucked it into the breeches before buttoning them.

Lieutenant Fitch was shaking his head. "I was lucky – if there can be any luck in being captured," he said ruefully. "I surrendered to some Redcoats of the 57th Regiment. They took my musket and ammunition, but that's all. They cursed me for a rebel and kept reminding me that a traitor's punishment was a noose at the end of a rope, but other than that treated me civilly. Certainly they didn't rob me of my personal belongings, or steal my clothes, or thrash me within an inch of my life," he said with contempt for the brutish Hessians.

Looking around, Elihu saw other prisoners who'd lost nearly everything being similarly assisted by comrades sharing precious clothing or a blanket if no garments were to be had. Grateful as Elihu was to have his own nakedness covered, nothing could wipe away the unnerving feeling of being totally defenseless, at the mercy of a foe that had none.

Why had God forsaken them? Elihu couldn't help but wonder in despair. Was this a test of their faith in Him?

Elihu's despondent thoughts turned again to Phineas. He began to search the faces of the prisoners one by one, praying he would locate his brother, and wondering if any of them would live to see the sun rise again.

Chapter Twenty-Two

August, 1776
Long Island

The Reverend Abner Benedict stared out bleakly over the ramparts of Brooklyn Heights. The rising sun illuminated a sight on the plain below unlike any he'd ever beheld: hundreds of white tents, pitched with enviable efficiency the previous evening by hordes of British and Hessian soldiers fresh from their complete route of American forces. The order and discipline evident in the enemy camp contrasted depressingly with the chaos and panic that had reigned inside the American fortification since the first terrified fugitives from the battle had begun streaming in yesterday.

By mid-summer reports filtering back to Middlefield had left no doubt that the first major engagement between the Continental Army and British forces would occur at New York. Mr. Benedict had taken a temporary leave from the pulpit to volunteer as a chaplain to the patriot troops.

The pastor had arrived not a moment too soon. Since the start of the battle there'd been a continuous need for his services. He'd labored unceasingly to comfort the wounded, and to prepare and solace the dying.

Hundreds of Continental Army soldiers were missing in action. No one had any idea whether they'd been killed, drowned in the treacherous swamps, taken prisoner, or were lying somewhere too badly injured to move.

Mr. Benedict knew both Elihu and Phineas Lyman were among those unaccounted for. The minister's mind quailed to think that he might have to write to Hope and David with tragic news about the young men.

A sudden commotion distracted the minister from his dark thoughts. The sight of eight more bedraggled survivors trudging into the fortifications brightened his mood a trifle. He rushed forward with several other soldiers to greet the new arrivals, all of them coated from head to foot in thick, slimy mud. Six of the men walked unassisted. But one soldier, apparently unable to use his right leg, was being half-carried, half-dragged by the eighth man.

Mr. Benedict slid his hands under the injured soldier's armpits. Relieved of his burden, the man who had been supporting him staggered away and slumped down onto a tree stump.

Mr. Benedict gently lowered the wounded trooper to the ground. The man's eyes were closed, his face caked with mud. Someone handed a wooden canteen to the minister, who knelt down, lifted the soldier's head, and put the canteen's opening to his mouth.

The soldier's parched lips twitched as the liquid touched them, then opened to desperately slurp the water. Some dribbled down his chin and over his cheeks, dissolving the mud into brown rivulets. Suddenly he began to cough and splutter, and his eyes flew open. Stunned, Mr. Benedict recognized their vivid blue color.

"Phineas?" the minister asked with a dawning joy. After a moment the eyes lost their vacant look, and with difficulty focused on the face hovering over him. "Mr. Benedict?" he whispered weakly, confused. "How–? Where–?"

Mr. Benedict shook his head reassuringly. "Don't try to talk. You're safe."

The minister stood up and stepped back to make way for two privates carrying a wide plank of wood which they set on the ground. They gripped Phineas by the shoulders and calves and hoisted him onto the plank. Phineas cried out in sharp pain.

"Be careful!" snapped the soldier who'd brought Phineas in, with an authority that marked him as an officer. "That man has a musket ball in his leg. Take him to a surgeon at once."

The privates hastened to obey. As they lifted Phineas, Mr. Benedict took the young man's filthy hand. "I'll come to see you when I can," he promised.

The privates started to carry Phineas away, but were forced to stop when Phineas held onto Mr. Benedict's hand. "Elihu?" he asked faintly.

Mr. Benedict gently disengaged Phineas's hand from his.   "I don't know anything about him," he said, shaking his head.

Phineas's eyes filled with despair, and he fell back heavily on the plank. The privates hurried off with their burden.

"We hid ourselves up to our noses in the muck of the swamp most of yesterday and last night," Mr. Benedict heard the officer explaining as he turned away from Phineas. The man had removed enough of the mud from his face to be recognizable as General Parsons.

"We watched those murdering British and Hessians run our men down like rabbits – and there was nothing we could do," he said with anguished regret. "When the enemy finally abandoned their search, we knew we had to chance reaching the Heights under cover of darkness. It was slow going, with Private Lyman barely able to walk – but I wasn't going to leave him for those damned butchers! When we hadn't reached the fort by the time the eastern sky began to brighten, I feared the enemy would spot us. But the Lord guided us to safety."

The young physician squatted on a trunk, resting his head in the palms of his cupped, blood-stained hands. He raised his haggard face as two privates bore Phineas into the medical tent.

"Another one?" Dr. Waldo asked in a voice drained of all feeling by twelve hours of nightmarish carnage. His five years practicing medicine as a civilian before signing on as surgeon with Connecticut's troops hadn't prepared him to treat the horrific combat injuries that had paraded before him: musket balls buried in flesh or brain, gaping belly or chest wounds inflicted by bayonets, sharp ends of bones splintered by cannon balls protruding sickeningly through the skin. He'd lost count of how many mangled bodies had been laid before him on the wooden table, its planks saturated, like his clothes, with blood, sweat, mud, urine, feces, and vomit. His ears still rang with the shrieks of the suffering.

Dr. Waldo rose heavily to his feet as the privates transferred the unconscious Phineas to the table. "He's plastered with mud," the doctor said in exhausted exasperation. "How can I tell where he's injured?"

"The officer who brought him in said he had a musket ball in the leg," one of the privates said helpfully. With a knife Dr. Waldo slit open each leg of the patient's breeches. He dipped a discolored rag into a bucket of water, then washed the mud from the front of

Phineas's legs. Finding no wound, he gestured to the privates to turn Phineas over. This time the washing revealed the hole where a musket ball had penetrated the back of Phineas's thigh.

Dr. Waldo picked up a long, round metal rod that tapered to a point at one end. Like all his surgical instruments, it was stained brown with the dried blood of previous patients.

Thanking God this patient was unconscious, and wouldn't need to be restrained during the agonizing procedure, the physician probed the wound until he found the musket ball about three inches into the leg. With a scalpel he enlarged the wound so he could insert a bullet extractor, an iron instrument that looked like an elongated pair of scissors with cupped ends.

When the end of the extractor hit the musket ball, Dr. Waldo carefully spread the handles of the instrument apart, pushed it deeper into the wound, then squeezed the handles together, seizing the ball between the concave ends. He removed the extractor carefully until the ball appeared along with bits of bloody cloth it had carried into the wound.

Dr. Waldo applied lint to the wound, then wrapped a bandage of linen around it. "Turn him over," he instructed the privates. When they'd done as he directed, the physician used a blood-spotted fleam to perform the bloodletting that was standard treatment for wounds.

"Take him to the hospital and tell the nurses to clean him off and find him a bed," Dr. Waldo told the privates as he pressed some lint against the cut on Phineas's wrist. "Tell them that when he regains his senses he should be given a purgative to clean his bowels. And he may need to be bled again."

The privates hefted Phineas back onto the plank. He'd done all in his power, Dr. Waldo thought numbly as they carried Phineas out of the tent. The young soldier's wound had been relatively minor compared to many of the horrifying injuries Dr. Waldo had treated since yesterday, giving him reason to hope this patient might survive. But ultimately the injured man's fate would be in God's hands.

Chapter Twenty-Three

September, 1776
Middlefield

"Hello! You there in the field!"

David straightened up from digging potatoes on the cloudy morning of September 7 and looked around for the source of the voice. He spotted a lad in his mid-teens on a horse at the edge of the field.

The youth stood up in the stirrups and waved his hat. David raised his arm in response, then picked his way across the uneven ground, annoyed at this interruption by what was likely a traveler seeking directions.

"Is this Middletown?" the pudgy, sandy-haired stranger asked when David came within earshot.

"It is – the Middlefield Society," David said shortly, removing his hat and wiping his sweaty forehead with a handkerchief.

"I'm looking for David Lyman," the boy said.

David glanced up at the youth in surprise as he put his hat back on. "You've found him." What business could this teenager have with him?

"At last!" the youth exclaimed in exaggerated relief. "I've had a devil of a time getting here," he rattled on in exasperation, as if that were somehow David's fault. "I've been three days on the road. My father doubted I could make the trip alone, thought me too young, but I told him I could do it by myself," he continued proudly. "Besides, there was no one else to send."

"Who are you?" David asked irritably when the garrulous teenager stopped to take a breath.

"I'm David Comstock, Junior, from Norwalk," the boy announced, enlightening David not at all. The Comstock name meant nothing special to him. He knew no one from Norwalk, a town he knew vaguely was in southwestern Connecticut – down towards New York, he realized with a sudden flicker of hope.

"Why are you looking for me?" David asked sharply.

"I was sent to tell you your brother is at our house," the teenager replied.

"My brother?!" David burst out, grabbing the reins of young Comstock's horse so abruptly the startled animal skittered. They'd heard nothing of Elihu or Phineas since the fighting on Long Island. They had hoped for some word from Mr. Benedict, but in vain. They passed each day in agonizing suspense. "Why didn't you say so straight off? Which one?"

"Phineas," the boy answered, unnerved by David's agitated reaction. "He's got a hurt leg. Some soldiers were bringing him home, but when they reached Norwalk he couldn't walk any more. Our family took him in. My father sent me to tell you so you could come fetch him."

Elated, David released the horse's reins, turned and started running toward the house. He stopped abruptly, wheeled around, and pointed his index finger at the boy. "Don't go anywhere!" he commanded, then resumed running, shouting for Hope.

David Lyman and David Comstock, Jr., reached Norwalk on September 10. David drove a cart to bring Phineas home, in case his injured leg prevented him from riding a horse.

The fifty miles to Norwalk was the farthest David had ever traveled from Middlefield. After stopping in West Haven to share with Hannah and Noah Williston the good news about Phineas, they'd followed the post road that paralleled the coast.

By the time they reached Norwalk on Long Island Sound – a port like Middletown, but more densely populated – David had heard more than he ever wanted to know about the Comstock family from his loquacious fifteen-year-old traveling companion.

David Comstock, Jr., was one of fifteen children of David Comstock, Sr., a farmer, and his wife, Rebekah. Nine of them, five daughters and four sons, ranging in age from twenty-five to four years old, were still living. All but one were unmarried and living under their parents' roof. The youth had described in detail the faults and virtues of each sibling.

The teenager himself was wild to join the Continental Army. That burning ambition had been stoked by stories with which the recuperating Phineas had been regaling the younger Comstocks. However, the boy's father refused to give him permission to enlist.

"Papa! Mama! I'm back!" David Comstock yelled as they pulled up in front of the Comstock homestead. It was a larger version of the Lyman house. The impetuous youth slid off his horse, flung open the hall door, and disappeared inside. David Lyman was left to climb down from the cart and stand uncertainly in awkward abandonment.

A moment later a frazzled-looking matron who, David knew from her son's description, was Rebekah Comstock appeared in the doorway. She held out her hand in greeting.

"You must be Phineas's brother," she said in weary welcome. "Come in. I ask forgiveness for my Davey," she continued apologetically. "As you've doubtless discovered, he can sometimes be heedless of others' feelings.

"I'm sorry you find my household in such a sad state," Mrs. Comstock went on distractedly. "But since we took Phineas in, my two oldest daughters have come down with the flux. Tending three invalids has left precious little time for anything else."

David surveyed the hall furnishings, which suggested the Comstocks enjoyed about the same level of prosperity as the Lymans. "I can't begin to thank you enough for your kindness in caring for Phineas."

Rebekah Comstock waved away his thanks. "Your brother fought the bloody-backs and the Hessian beasts. And we have the room," she added sorrowfully. "Davey probably told you our oldest boy died in June."

David nodded sympathetically. He was aware from his traveling companion's monologue of the death three months past of twenty-seven-year-old William Comstock.

"Phineas is in the right rear chamber," Mrs. Comstock said. "Go on up."

David mounted the steps, then approached the chamber door hesitantly. Eager as he was to see Phineas, he was apprehensive about witnessing his suffering – and ashamed to face the brother who'd confronted death in battle while David remained safely at home.

Mustering his resolve, David pushed the door open. He stopped in shock at the sight of Phineas propped up on pillows in bed, holding himself rigid as a young woman dressed his leg wound.

Always the stockiest member of the Lyman family, Phineas had dropped perhaps twenty pounds since David last saw him in December. The weight loss gave his handsome face a sharp leanness. He appeared older than the twenty-one years that, David realized, his brother had reached a few days ago.

But the broad grin Phineas flashed when he saw his brother was, David was relieved to see, his familiar jaunty one. "David!" Phineas exclaimed in delight. He turned instinctively toward David, an ill-considered movement that made him wince with pain. "You came!"

"Of course I came," David replied, concealing his sadness that Phineas should be surprised to see him. "I've brought the cart. As soon as you feel well enough, we'll head home," he said with cheerful optimism.

"David, this is Sarah Comstock," Phineas said, gesturing toward the young woman ministering to his injury. She straightened up and turned toward David. "The prettiest nurse a wounded man could ask for," Phineas added gallantly.

Sarah Comstock rolled her eyes in good-natured exasperation at Phineas's flirtatious blandishments. "I'm pleased to meet you, Mr. Lyman," she said with a warm smile.

Sarah was taller than the average woman, although still several inches shorter than David. He knew from her chatterbox of a brother that she was the same age as Phineas.

Sarah's figure bordered on buxom, and her face was square with a blunt chin and a nose a tad too large. She was dressed for housework, in a brown linen petticoat and a low-necked, shortgown of the same material. An apron of blue checked linen was fastened around her waist, and she wore a matching neckerchief around her shoulders and tied in the front over her full bosom.

In David's estimation Phineas's flattery was something of an exaggeration. Sarah Comstock was by no means plain, but she wasn't particularly pretty, either.

"I must look to my sisters," Sarah told Phineas. "I want your promise to call for me if your leg feels worse or if you want for anything," she said with a good-natured sternness that drew an obedient nod from Phineas. "I'll send Hannah up with some supper," she added with an enigmatic smile. She radiated competence and compassion, enhanced by a sense of humor.

Sarah considerately closed the door to give the brothers privacy. Sitting down in the chair she'd vacated, David turned a concerned face toward Phineas. "How are you – really?"

"Tired of waiting for this leg to heal," Phineas groused, shifting uncomfortably on the straw mattress. "I'm told the surgeon had no trouble getting the ball out. I was bled and purged in the army hospital, and again by the doctor here, but it hasn't gotten better. If anything, it hurts more. Do you know anything about Elihu?" he asked abruptly.

"No," David replied, shaking his head with disappointment. "I was hoping you did."

"The last time I saw Elihu," Phineas said slowly, "we were trapped between the fire of two bands of Hessians. We were running for cover in a swamp, when a ball caught me in the leg, knocked me flat."

Phineas paused, then continued as if confessing a shameful secret. "I dropped Papa's sword when I was shot. I wanted to go back for it, but I would have been captured or killed for sure if I'd tried. One of those bastard Hessians likely has it now," he said bitterly. "I'm sorry, David," he added penitently.

That Phineas felt he needed to apologize for losing the sword when he was shot by the enemy touched a chord of melancholy in David. He shook his head to dismiss the issue. "All that matters is that you're safe," he told Phineas firmly.

Visibly relieved at David's absolution, Phineas went on. "General Parsons picked me up and dragged me along with him, else I would have been run through with a bayonet like a chicken on a spit. No one could tell me if Elihu made it out of the swamp."

Neither spoke for a long moment, thinking of the brother they might never see again. "How's Mama?" Phineas asked at last.

"Holding up well," David replied. "Catharine and the baby are staying with her. She's prayed almost constantly for you and Elihu since we heard about the battle. She refused to give up hope that you both would turn up alive. It was all I could do to keep her from climbing into the cart and coming herself to Norwalk when we learned you were here. But someone had to stay with the farm."

"She was that excited?" Phineas asked on a note of eager surprise. David nodded, then posed the question he'd been desperate to ask. "What was the battle like?" He hitched his chair closer to the head of the bed.

"Do you want the tale I've been beguiling the Comstock girls with?" Phineas asked with a mischievous grin. "Or would you prefer the truth?"

"The truth, of course," David replied, amazed that, suffering as he was, Phineas still had the will and the energy to charm any female with whom he came in contact.

"At first it was everything I had expected," Phineas began. His voice gained strength and heat with the memory. "I'll confess it was terrifying to see hundreds of regulars advancing with order and timing so perfect they seemed like a monstrous millipede, to hear musket balls sing past your ears, to see men around you collapse in bloody agony, and know you might be next. But it was exciting, too – more exciting than you can imagine!"

Phineas was so caught up in his memories he didn't notice David pull back abruptly. Phineas's last words stung like a slap across the face, although David knew he hadn't meant them to.

"And it was glorious!" Phineas went on. "We stood our ground with courage, beat back two British attacks. We showed those arrogant spawn of Satan that Americans are men, soldiers to be respected and feared."

Then the triumphant glow faded from Phineas's face, leaving him looking gaunt. He continued gravely. "But in an instant it all turned to Hell. We were surrounded without warning by British and Hessians. God knows where they came from! At first we retreated in an orderly manner, then we ran to save our skins. But no matter which way we turned, the enemy was there waiting to slay us. Some of our men were shot down, some stabbed with bayonets. Others escaped the trap, only to drown in the swamp."

David realized Phineas wasn't speaking to him. He seemed unaware of his brother's presence, his vision focused inward, as he relived the horror of that day on Long Island.

Feeling like a callow boy at the knee of an aged veteran, David waited in respectful silence for Phineas to pull his thoughts back to the present. At last he looked at David. "A few of us escaped by burying ourselves in the mud like turtles," he finished in a tired voice. He sagged back onto the pillows and closed his eyes.

A light knock on the door was a welcome interruption. "Come in," Phineas called out, opening his eyes and sitting up with obvious effort.

The door opened and in walked a petite, beautiful bud of a woman whom David recognized instantly from her brother's description as thirteen-year-old Hannah Comstock. In one hand she held a pewter plate with the supper promised by her sister Sarah, in the other a pewter tankard. She handed both shyly to Phineas. Only belatedly did she notice David, whom she acknowledged with a perfunctory smile before turning her worshipful attention back to Phineas.

"Thank you, Hannah," Phineas responded with grave courtesy, then smiled broadly and winked at the girl, who with her willowy figure, delicately sculpted features, and shining crown of golden hair was as different physically from the Comstocks David had met as Phineas was from the rest of the Lyman family.

Hannah responded to Phineas's wink with a smile that was instinctively, yet unconsciously, sensual. She was clearly infatuated with Phineas – and why shouldn't she be, thought David with a pang of jealousy. Phineas was every female's romantic fantasy – a brave, handsome, charming young warrior wounded while fighting for freedom from a wicked king.

Hannah reluctantly turned from Phineas and addressed David. "Supper is ready in the hall, sir," she informed him politely. Casting a last yearning glance at Phineas, she left the room. David shook his head in wonderment. He shot an accusing glance at Phineas, who sketched an almost embarrassed shrug, as if to indicate that his attraction for women was a power beyond his control.

David got to his feet. "I'll be back after supper," he promised, then went out, pulling the chamber door closed behind him. As soon as he heard David's footsteps descending the stairs, Phineas set the plate and tankard on the floor and collapsed back onto the pillows, his features twisted with pain.

Chapter Twenty-Four

September, 1776
Norwalk, Connecticut

Sarah Comstock was collecting clean laundry from the bushes on which the items had been spread to dry when she spied David Lyman walking in from the field behind the Comstock house. He'd been sowing winter wheat with her father, her brothers Davey and nine-year-old Daniel, and their Negro slave Peter. David was helping out in gratitude for the family's care of Phineas. Two days after David's arrival, Phineas was still confined to bed, his leg showing no sign of improvement.

David stopped at the well to pull the bucket up from its depths. Several hours laboring in the afternoon sun had clearly left him parched. He filled his cupped hands with cold water and drank deeply.

David had intrigued Sarah since his arrival. Based on Phineas's wryly entertaining description of how David's relationship with their mother had kept him still single at thirty, she'd expected him to be a mouse of a man. But David Lyman was neither meek nor passive. He behaved with an earnest restraint that Sarah recognized as self-control and self-denial exerted for the benefit of others. It was something with which she herself had plenty of experience.

Although not nearly as handsome as Phineas, David was decidedly good-looking. Sarah found his mature reserve a refreshing contrast to Phineas's unabashed flirtatiousness.

As David approached the house the sight of so many sheets draped over every available surface to dry brought to his mind for the first time since his arrival the two Comstock daughters sick with dysentery. Neither one had emerged from the parlor-turned-sickroom to take even a single meal with the family. David was embarrassed to realize he'd been so consumed with worry over Phineas's health and about how long he could remain in Norwalk neglecting his own farm in Middlefield that he'd failed to inquire about the ailing Comstock sisters. He needed to correct that at once.

Sarah smiled warmly at David as he approached, while continuing to work.

"I've been meaning to ask about your sisters," David said. "Are they any better?"

He was dismayed to see Sarah's smile fade. "Rebekah seems to be on the mend," she replied slowly, "but Mary is still very sick."

"I'm sorry," David said sympathetically. He surprised himself by adding earnestly, "You must take care of yourself, so you won't get sick, too."

Two days in the Comstock house had confirmed David's initial impression that Sarah, although the middle of the children, was the family's keystone. Everyone, her parents included, depended heavily upon her for physical and emotional support. She performed a substantial share of the endless household chores, while supervising her three youngest siblings with a warmth that reminded David of Catharine's tending of Esther, Elihu, and Phineas.

Sarah had also been devoting as much time as possible to nursing her ailing sisters and Phineas. David admired how she did all this without losing her composure or complaining, although he definitely detected signs of fatigue.

As soon as the words left his mouth David realized how presumptuous his unsolicited advice might sound. To his relief, Sarah's smile returned.

"You're kind to be concerned," Sarah said, blushing slightly. "But this is the work God has set for me."

In response to David's sympathetic nod, Sarah expanded her explanation. "My mother isn't very strong. She bore fifteen children in twenty-five years, and has buried nearly half of them. Rebekah and Mary are often not well. My father has only David and Daniel and Peter to work the farm. Hannah and the little ones help out, but they can only do so much. That leaves me," she said with a slight shrug of acceptance. "I trust God will give me strength."

An awkward silence fell, as David cast about desperately for an excuse to continue the conversation. "Let me carry the basket," he offered at last. "It will be too heavy for you by the time you've collected all the sheets."

"Thank you," Sarah said quickly. Her mouth twitched with suppressed amusement, as she forbore pointing out that if she'd managed to carry the basket out when it was filled with heavy, wet laundry, she was certainly capable of carrying it back in when its contents were drier and lighter. David's flimsy, if gallant, pretext for continuing their talk confirmed Phineas's statement that his brother had little experience with women.

David picked up the basket and followed Sarah along the row of bushes as she collected the items one by one, careful not to snag them on twigs, then folded them. When she set the last item in the basket, she turned to face David.

"You of all people must understand why I do so much for my family," she said with a directness so unexpected that the startled David nearly dropped the basket. "Phineas told me your father died when you were but seventeen, leaving you the man of the house, upon whom your family has depended ever since."

After taking a moment to recover, David nodded cautiously. "I suppose I do understand," he said, wondering uneasily how much more Phineas had told Sarah about their family.

"Still, sometimes I resent having to carry this burden that I didn't choose," Sarah confessed. David was taken aback by her candor, so at odds with the serene acceptance she'd displayed. He'd never before met anyone who spoke without shame of harboring unworthy emotions like those hidden deep in his own heart.

"Aren't there times when you feel the same?" Sarah asked David, stunning him into confused silence. Her directness made David uncomfortable, but he could tell she wasn't being rudely nosy. Sarah was genuinely curious about this man who, based on the sketchy details she had, she had reason to think was a kindred spirit.

"Yes," David admitted finally, in a low, strangled voice. That was all he intended to say, but Sarah's openness gave him the courage to reveal his shameful selfishness to this young woman he'd known but two days.

"For years I've yearned for a wife and family of my own," David continued. "But I've denied myself out of duty to my brothers and sisters – and to my mother. A duty I've come to fear will never end this side of the grave!" he spat out bitterly.

Sarah impulsively placed a gentle hand on one of David's. "I, too, dream of leaving my parents' house, of having a husband and children," she confided. "When my mother was my age, she was already a wife with two babies. Like you, I sometimes chafe with frustration, fearing that time – that life – will pass me by.

"But God in His wisdom has given us these responsibilities. We must fulfill them before we satisfy our private desires. By serving those who depend on us, we serve the Lord."

What had started as a casual chat had assumed an intimacy neither David nor Sarah had anticipated. David recognized in Sarah a strength of body and character and faith much like his mother's. But Sarah had none of the desperate, domineering quality that had marked Hope since John had fallen ill.

The two studied each other in silence. David noticed that Sarah's eyes were the soft, luminous gray of the pussy willow in early spring, her hair the color of ripe wheat. He felt the stirring of a tender desire he'd never before experienced.

The mood was shattered when Hannah appeared at the kitchen door calling Sarah's name. With a quick smile of apology – and regret, David was sure of it – Sarah removed her hand from his. She took the basket heaped high with laundry from him without effort.

Thank you," Sarah said, then turned to walk toward the house. Unnerved, David watched her until she disappeared inside, wondering what she'd felt in those moments that had meant so much to him.

"David!"

David opened his eyes with a start at the sound of his name being called in a low voice, followed by a rapping on the chamber door. From the nearly total darkness he knew it was deep in the night between September 12 and 13. He heard his name again, this time spoken more urgently, by what he thought was Sarah's voice.

"I'm coming," he said, throwing off the sheet of the bed he'd shared with Davey and Daniel Comstock the past three nights. The two youths remained asleep.

David fumbled in the blackness for his breeches, pulled them on and buttoned them. He walked barefoot to the door, and opened it to reveal Sarah in a long linen shift that didn't entirely conceal the contours of her body. Her hair was in a loose braid down her back. The candle she carried cast an erratic light on her troubled features.

"Phineas is awake. He says the pain in his leg has gotten much worse."

David felt a sinking sensation in his stomach. He nodded, then followed Sarah as she lit the way to Phineas's chamber.

Phineas was indeed a worrisome sight in the flickering glow of two candles. He was lying in bed, his face pale, from pain or fear or both. He didn't speak, looking at David with blue eyes clouded with apprehension. David gave him a smile he hoped was reassuring.

Sarah's father was leaning over Phineas's unbandaged leg, clearly disturbed by what he saw. He beckoned David over. As David got closer, he detected a peculiar, repellently sweet odor emanating from the wound.

"I don't like the looks of this," Mr. Comstock observed, making no attempt to keep Phineas from hearing. "The area around the wound is swollen hard as a piece of wood. And this bloody stuff oozing out is odd. I've never smelled anything like it."

Straightening up, Comstock heaved a deep sigh. He glanced at David, then spoke to Phineas somberly. "I think we'd better send for Dr. Betts right away."

David looked at Phineas, who for the first time since David had arrived appeared truly frightened. "I agree, sir," he said to Comstock.

"Sarah, wake Peter and tell him to fetch the doctor," Comstock told his daughter. Sarah studied both Phineas's and David's faces with sympathy before leaving to do her father's bidding.

The sun was well above the horizon before David heard galloping hooves coming down the road to the Comstock house. Rushing to the chamber window, he caught a glimpse of Peter and another man before they disappeared around the front of the house.

David had spent the time since Peter left on his mission praying with Phineas when the pain wasn't too bad for the younger man to concentrate. Sarah had dressed right after dispatching Peter, and had slipped in and out repeatedly, to join them in prayer, to examine Phineas's wound, and to offer gentle comfort and encouragement.

David had mentally cursed the physician and the slave for taking so long to arrive, for in the intervening hours Phineas's condition had deteriorated. His foot and entire leg below the wound had become swollen and cold to the touch.

The trudging of weary footsteps up the stairs was followed by the entrance of a bleary-eyed older man who was clearly Dr. Betts. Sarah was behind him. "I got here as soon as I could," he said grumpily. "Richard Fitch on the other side of the river sent for me yesterday at dusk. His wife had a fit of apoplexy. When Peter found I wasn't home, he rode over to fetch me. We came straight here."

While he removed his frock coat and rolled up his sleeves, the doctor studied Phineas's leg. He wrinkled his nose at the smell, which he clearly recognized. He touched the wound, and Phineas's entire body quivered. He squeezed his eyes shut against the pain.

The physician pressed his fingers against the swollen leg. "Cold," he said simply. "I feel no pulse." He straightened up and turned to David. "You're his brother?" David nodded.

"I would speak with you," Dr. Betts said with a quiet urgency. He motioned for David to follow him out of the chamber – a belated consideration for his patient's feelings that served no purpose. Phineas obviously knew something was very wrong.

On the landing, with the chamber door closed, Dr. Betts told David bluntly, "Amputation is the only option."

David stared at the physician blankly for so long that Dr. Betts wondered if perhaps he didn't understand the word. "That means cutting off his leg," the doctor said with weary impatience.

"I know what amputation is," David replied, aghast. He struggled to envision Phineas, who relied so heavily upon his good looks and physical charm to carry him through life, reduced to a hobbling cripple. A terrible thought occurred to David. "Are you asking me to decide whether to amputate?" he asked fearfully.

"No." Dr. Betts shook his head. "His condition has made the decision for us. Your brother must lose his leg or lose his life. I just wanted you to know before I tell him."

The physician took a moment to collect his strength for the ordeal that lay ahead. "I'll ask Mistress Comstock to summon her husband and Peter," he said. "You'll need help holding him down."

When David looked uncomprehendingly at the physician, Dr. Betts went on. "I have no laudanum to give him for the pain," he explained. "All of it has gone to supply the army."

David waited numbly for the physician to return. When he and Dr. Betts re-entered the chamber, they found Sarah holding Phineas's hand, the two of them reciting Jesus' words in the Garden of Gethsemane, before his betrayal and crucifixion. "Father, if it be possible, let this cup pass from me: nevertheless, not as I will, but as Thou wilst.'" Sarah was helping Phineas prepare for the worst.

"Phineas, I must amputate your leg without delay," Dr. Betts said with gentle directness, at last displaying some compassion for his young patient's feelings.

Phineas's face registered distress, but not shock. "I feared it would come to this," he admitted. Then his resolve failed him, and he pleaded softly, "Is there nothing else that can be done?"

"Nothing," the physician replied, shaking his head. "It's the only hope of saving your life." The doctor hesitated before adding, "I have no drugs to give you for the pain."

Phineas's features contorted in raw terror at the prospect of going under the surgeon's saw and knife without anything to dull his senses. He looked from David to Sarah to Dr. Betts with the desperation of a condemned man, but in their faces he found no reprieve, only pity. He quickly buried his face in his pillow so they wouldn't see a soldier of the Continental Army weep in fear.

Peter and David carried Phineas down to the hall, where they laid him on the long wooden table. They put pillows under his head.

Davey Comstock was delegated to keep the younger Comstock children outside, away from the frightful scene about to unfold. Mrs. Comstock was in the parlor with her ailing daughters.

David stood behind Phineas's head, his hands clamped firmly on his brother's wrists. David Comstock stood at the other end of the table, a hand gripping each of Phineas's ankles. Peter was beside Dr. Betts, holding the upper part of the wounded leg. On the physician's other side stood Sarah, who would hand him the amputating instruments, which were kept out of Phineas's sight.

Dr. Betts used a stick to tighten tourniquets of worsted binding around the leg above and below the spot where the limb was to be removed. He gave Phineas a piece of wood to clench between his teeth, so he wouldn't bite his tongue in his agony. Finally the doctor packed lamb's wool into Phineas's ears so he couldn't hear the rasp of the amputating saw cutting through his leg bone.

David Lyman had seen his share of physical suffering in his thirty years. He'd watched his father's painful decay into little more than a skeleton for whom every breath was agony. He'd taken his turn sitting by the bedsides of relatives and neighbors ailing or dying from any number of injuries or diseases. But never had he witnessed anything like the concentrated torture now inflicted upon Phineas in the hope of saving his life.

As Dr. Betts sliced deeply into the leg, Phineas arched his back and writhed in anguish. He made a terrible, gurgling, gagging sound around the piece of wood in his mouth. Tears trickled from the corners of his tightly closed eyelids.

Dr. Betts worked as swiftly as he could through the spurting blood. He cut through the outer half of the leg, then the inner half. He slipped a leather strap around the now-exposed bone, using it to pull the upper leg muscles away from the point at which he would use the amputation saw.

During that brief pause, Phineas's body sagged. Suddenly he opened his eyes, and looked straight up into David's in a silent plea for rescue. He closed them just as quickly and resumed struggling as Dr. Betts went to work with the saw.

Phineas fought so powerfully against the hands restraining him that David had to lean down and forward to exert the weight of his upper body to keep him still. As a result, David's head was almost beside Phineas's. David's hands began to cramp as he listened to the grisly grating of the amputation saw cutting through bone.

Suddenly David felt Phineas go limp under his grip. Phineas's head lolled to one side as he lost consciousness.

Thanking God that Phineas was senseless to the agony of the amputation, David remained bent over in relief. He took three deep breaths before starting to straighten up – then stopped when he realized he heard no breathing from Phineas. He looked closely at his brother's pale face, his closed eyes, his slack mouth.

"Doctor!"

"What!" the physician snapped. He kept his eyes on the saw blade with which he'd finally succeeded in severing the bone.

"I don't think he's breathing!" David said frantically. Dr. Betts's head came up sharply. He placed two bloody fingers against the side of Phineas's neck to search for a pulse. Then he put a hand in front of Phineas's mouth to feel for any breath.

"He's dead," the physician said in a voice heavy with defeat.

"You lie!" David cried out his denial with a fury that alarmed everyone in the room. He glared at the physician, then stared down at Phineas, his angry protest collapsing into a low, broken sob. "He can't be dead."

Sarah quietly circled around behind Dr. Betts and Peter to reach David's side. "He's gone, David," she said softly, gently prying his fingers from Phineas's wrists. "His suffering is over. He's with God now."

David looked into Sarah's gray eyes, brimming with tears of grief for a man she'd known less than a fortnight. The sight of her frank sorrow breached the fragile dam of denial he'd thrown up against the truth. His face crumpled with grief, and he turned away. Blinded by tears, he stumbled until he reached the wall. He leaned his forehead against the wood, and his shoulders began to heave as he cried silently and uncontrollably.

They buried Phineas later that day in the Norwalk graveyard. All the Comstocks were sincerely grieved by Phineas's death. Hannah had been nearly hysterical at the passing of her idolized cavalier.

Following a somber supper, David returned to the burying ground. Mellow rays from the setting sun filtered between the headstones, casting uneven stripes of light on Phineas's fresh grave. David stared at the rectangle of disturbed dirt. He wondered grimly if Elihu, too, lay rotting somewhere in an unmarked hole.

Suddenly David sensed another presence. He looked over to see Sarah standing beside him. "I'll leave if you'd rather be alone," she offered quietly. David shook his head; she was a welcome counter to the emptiness he felt.

David shifted his gaze reluctantly back to the raw grave. "Phineas was my brother, but I didn't really know him," he said in a flat voice. "He was the youngest of us all, and I was always busy trying to fill my father's place. And now . . . ," his voice trailed off.

Sarah nodded in understanding. "My brother William was six years older, but there are so many in our family, and so much to be done, that I race through each day, all my thoughts on the needs of the little ones and my mother. Then four months past William was suddenly seized with a fever. In three days he was dead."

When David offered no response, Sarah went on. "We must take comfort in our belief that our brothers are in the Lord's presence, enjoying eternal bliss. Our grief isn't really for them but for ourselves, for the pain their passing causes us.

"We can never understand why God took our brothers. But I believe their deaths are meant to teach us a sacred truth. We must not put off loving one another. We must find solace in the living who remain with us. We can't count on tomorrow."

David nodded in a vague acknowledgement of Sarah's words. But his thoughts were clearly fixed on something else – and Sarah thought she knew what it was.

"But you can't accept this comfort," Sarah said very gently, "because you're plagued by guilt."

David took an involuntary step back from Sarah, as if she'd slapped him across the face. His heart raced with something close to panic at this woman's uncanny ability to know his darkest thoughts.

Sarah almost flinched at David's reaction, but forced herself to continue. "Phineas told me you wanted to enlist with your brothers, how difficult it was for you to accept that your duty was to stay on the farm. He believed you did what was right, and he respected you for it. You have no cause to feel guilty."

David's shock and unease began to give way to a fervent desire to believe Sarah. But he couldn't so easily accept absolution.

"I can't stop thinking," he said, faltering, then continuing, "that if I'd been there with them, on the battlefield, I might have been able to do – something – to save them." Suddenly tears started to course down his cheeks. "I promised my father I would take care of my brothers, and I failed!" he cried out in anguish.

"No, David," Sarah said with absolute conviction. She took his right hand soothingly between both of hers, and held his tormented brown eyes with her serene gray ones.

"Phineas and Elihu weren't children," Sarah said. "They were men, responsible for their own actions. What happened was God's will, however painful. Nothing you could have done would have changed it. If you'd been with them you might be wounded, or missing, or dead, and your mother would be bereft of all her sons."

David stared at Sarah, wanting with every fiber of his being to accept what she was saying. Hope had assured him he'd done the right thing by staying on the farm. But he'd always wondered if her words sprang from genuine belief that he was fulfilling his duty or from her own desperate need to keep him home at all costs.

Sarah Comstock had no such personal stake in David's behavior. And she'd shown herself to be so unsparingly honest that David didn't doubt she sincerely believed what she said.

At last David lay down the guilt that had weighed on him since Elihu and Phineas had enlisted, that had grown heavier after the battle on Long Island, and that had nearly crushed him this day with Phineas's death. He was flooded with a sense of relief so intense it left him momentarily light-headed.

When David felt himself again on steady footing, his face lit up in a smile of gratitude for Sarah. She smiled back – with relief that she'd been correct in her guess that helping David face his deepest pain would open a way for him to heal.

The sun by now had slipped below the horizon, and a chilly dusk was gathering. David removed his hand from Sarah's, wrapped his arm gently around her shoulder, and led her away from Phineas's grave toward the Comstock house – toward light and life.

Chapter Twenty-Five

September, 1776
Middlefield

Hope snapped a dusky red apple off the branch, and dropped it into a basket at her feet. She pushed a bunch of leaves aside so she could see to pluck another apple hanging deeper in the tree.

Picking apples required little thought, leaving her mind free to fret over David, gone ten days now with no word. The trip to Norwalk and back should have taken no more than eight days, she estimated, even if they'd had to travel slowly on the return to Middlefield because of Phineas's wound.

With the passage of the ninth and then the tenth days, fear had begun to worm its way into Hope's mind. Was Phineas too ill to travel? Then why didn't David send a message? Had some evil befallen David and the Comstock boy on the way to Norwalk? Then why hadn't the Comstock family come looking for their son, or written to ask after him?

Hope pushed these worries away to focus on her immediate cares. Every day David was gone was another day of work on the farm lost. She and Catharine, who'd agreed to stay with Hope until David and Phineas returned, did as much as they could in the fields, while caring for the baby, keeping up the household chores, and tending the livestock. But they lacked David's physical strength, and his experience and knowledge.

Hope studied the half-full basket of apples with a frown. Once she would have filled it to the top before carrying it down to the house. But while she remained generally healthy and energetic, she'd begun to suffer from the aching joints to be expected in a body approaching sixty years old. With a sigh of resignation she picked up the basket and started down out of the orchard.

It was a warm, sunny day, and Hope was flushed and sweating by the time she reached the back of the houselot. She set the basket down for a brief rest before carrying it the remainder of the way to the kitchen. It was then that she heard the creaking of wood and metal wheels, the clopping of a horse's hooves that told her a cart was coming down the road.

Lifting her long skirts with both hands, Hope hastened around the corner of the house. There she found Catharine stepping out of the hall door, having heard the same sounds.

Mother and daughter watched the cart draw near. Their spirits began to rise when they could see it was indeed David at the reins. But anxiety tainted Hope's anticipation when she saw the cart bed was empty. Had Phineas been too sick to make the trip home?

At last David was close enough for Hope to see his dusty, sweat-streaked face. It was wretched with the dread of one with bad news to deliver. Hope's mind suspected the truth, but her mother's heart rejected it.

David reined in the horse, set the cart's brake, then dropped heavily to the ground. He faced his mother, then placed his hands gently on her shoulders.

"Where's Phineas?" Hope asked, her voice quivering. David looked into her vulnerable hazel eyes.

"I'm sorry, Mama," David said. "Phineas is no more. His wound was worse than anyone realized. He died four days ago."

Hope averted her disbelieving gaze from David's. She stared down at the ground, shaking her head slowly as if trying to solve some perplexing puzzle.

Suddenly Hope's shoulders began to shake beneath David's palms. It was just enough warning for him to brace himself before his mother collapsed against his chest, sobbing. David held Hope awkwardly in his arms, casting an appeal for help over her head to Catharine, whose own face was running with tears.

Catharine placed a hand on David's shoulder. She lay her head next to her mother's, and soothingly stroked Hope's hair. The three clung to each other in the September sun, a chorus of buzzing insects and the occasional chirp or trill of a bird mingling with the women's weeping.

At last Hope straightened up and stepped out of David's embrace. She looked at him with swollen eyes.

"Were you with him – at the end?" Hope asked.

"I was," David replied. He saw a flicker of relief in her expression. But he knew she had more questions; his mother never shrank from the truth, however painful.

"Was his death hard?" Hope asked tremulously.

"Yes, Mama," David replied honestly. She would know if he were lying.

"How–," Hope began, then stopped when David shook his head in grim warning. The details of Phineas's last hours would only inflict more agony on Hope to no purpose. And David didn't trust himself to recount the horror of Phineas's dying moments without breaking down himself. He would never be able to purge his memory of his brother's final, heart-piercing look.

"Did he die in God's grace?" Hope asked. Her voice came close to breaking as she posed this most important question.

"Yes, Mama, I believe he did," David said. Hope searched his face for any hint that he was dissembling to spare her further pain. Finding none, she closed her eyes and murmured a prayer of thanks that Phineas had been afforded this blessing.

David was relieved to be able to honestly give Hope the solace of this assurance. For that he was indebted to Sarah Comstock, who'd offered steadfast, compassionate attention to Phineas's spiritual needs during his final hours.

Hope opened her eyes, once more in command of her emotions. "It's as Mr. Benedict said – Phineas was a martyr in the war against tyranny. The Lord will welcome him into His presence."

From the house came the babbling of little Lyman Beecher, awakened from his nap. Before Catharine could respond, Hope walked off quickly to answer the call of new life.

David watched her go, then turned to Catharine. She was looking at him with compassion – and new respect.

"Has there been any news of Elihu?" David asked. "Phineas knew nothing."

"No," Catharine said, snuffing out David's last hope that any ray of light would pierce the gloom of this day.

Chapter Twenty-Six

September, 1776
Middlefield

It had been three weeks since the battle on Long Island, David considered gloomily while shaving in his chamber on the morning after his return from Norwalk. Each day without word of Elihu made it more difficult to keep hoping he was alive.

David and Hope had seen Catharine and Lyman Beecher off for North Guilford earlier. It was raining steadily, but Catharine couldn't be persuaded to stay a day longer than necessary away from Lot.

A sudden pounding on the hall door startled David. His hand jerked, and he nicked his chin with the straight razor. Annoyed, he snapped the blade closed, wiped the shaving soap from his face with a towel, then dabbed a bit of lint on the cut to staunch the bleeding.

David hurried down the stairs into the hall. He barely missed colliding with Hope as she hastened in from the kitchen to investigate the knocking.

David yanked the hall door open. In stumbled David Miller, a man of his own age, the third generation of Millers to live in the house across the swamp.

Miller was flushed and panting from running through the rain. From inside his damp frock coat he pulled out a water-spotted copy of the weekly *Connecticut Courant* newspaper, published in Hartford.

"Just saw it," Miller gasped. He took a deep gulp of air before continuing. "Elihu," he said, thrusting the newspaper at David and pointing to an item.

David snatched the paper from Miller, and focused on the spot indicated. "'A list of the Names of such Officers as are Prisoners with the Enemy,'" he read. He skimmed down the column until he found "Ensign Lyman" under "Colonel Huntington's Regiment."

"Elihu's alive, Mama!" David exclaimed, looking up at Hope with fierce joy.

"Let me see," Hope insisted, taking the paper with trembling fingers. As she stared at the name, her eyes brightened, but only for a moment. "This notice is dated September 11, from New Haven – a week ago," she pointed out in a flat voice. She handed the paper back to David. "Who knows how long it took to reach there from New York? Anything could have happened to Elihu since then."

David understood his mother's skepticism. The grievous shock of Phineas's death, following the elation of learning he'd survived the battle on Long Island, had been a particularly cruel blow. She wasn't about to risk another heartbreaking plunge from hope to grief based on a few words in a week-old newspaper.

"Thank you for this," David said fervently to Miller, whose color was returning to normal. "I must tell Esther," he added; he didn't know if anyone in Durham subscribed to the *Courant.*

David looked back at the notice. "It reports that these officers 'have by flag of truce, sent for their baggage and cash,'" he read. "'Their friends are desired to send to the house next door to General Putnam their trunks, properly directed, and to leave their cash at the General's, that they may be sent by the first flag.'"

"Maybe we can get a letter to Elihu," David said. "And send food or clothes, or anything else he needs."

David made his decision. "I'll go to New York as soon as I can," he said, looking up at Hope. He frowned as he thought of the farm work, already seriously neglected during his absence in Norwalk.

"I'll spend a couple of days bringing in at least some of the cabbage and potatoes before I go," he said, thinking out loud. "Maybe I can hire a boy to finish what I don't get done, and to cut the corn stocks for fodder." A plan was coming together in his mind.

"I should be able to leave for New York in four or five days," David went on. That journey, he decided, would include a stop in Norwalk to learn how the Comstock family fared – especially Sarah.

Since David had left Norwalk on his melancholy return to Middlefield, Sarah Comstock had occupied his thoughts, and appeared in some of his more intense dreams. She inspired in him a mixture of emotions unlike any he'd felt before. What it meant he didn't know, but of one thing he was sure: he had to see Sarah again.

Chapter Twenty-Seven

September, 1776
Wallabout Bay, East River, New York

Even as Hope and David were reading his name in the newspaper, Elihu was lying on a hard, narrow plank of rough pine that served as his bunk below the decks of the British prison ship *Mentor*. The vessel was anchored in Wallabout Bay in the East River, about a mile north of the tip of Manhattan Island. A chill rain prevented him from going topside as he did at every opportunity to stroll on the deck, the only exercise available to the *Mentor's* captives.

The enforced idleness, boredom, and severely restricted physical activity were irksome to all sixteen American officers imprisoned on the *Mentor*. But to Elihu, with his restless physical and mental nature, they were particularly galling.

Elihu had been aboard the *Mentor* for twelve days, and had no way of knowing how much longer he'd be confined there. His left arm still hurt, but the bullet wounds were healing, thanks in part to the ministrations of a British surgeon who'd come twice to treat the prisoners' injuries. The bruises from his savage beating had faded from their original ugly purplish-black to a sickly yellow-green.

Elihu counted himself lucky among the wounded, for many were in far greater pain and peril. Staring up into the ship's dark interior, the back of his skull pillowed on his interlaced fingers, he thought of Captain Jewett, who'd proposed surrender as the only hope for the survivors of the Seventeenth Regiment.

Once in British custody, Captain Jewett had been savagely bayoneted in the chest and gut. He'd lingered in cruel agony for more than a day. Elihu could still hear his ghastly gasping, "It is hard work to die."

Captain Jewett had pleaded that news of how he'd met his end be conveyed in a letter to his wife, who, Elihu knew, had nine children, including a babe a few months old. This was exactly the desperate situation Elihu had been determined to spare Esther when he refused her suggestion that they wed before he left on his second enlistment.

At least he no longer had to fear Phineas suffering a fate like Captain Jewett's, Elihu thought gratefully. When Captain Timothy Percival of the Seventeenth Regiment had come aboard the *Mentor* a week earlier, he'd told Elihu of a report from a recently captured prisoner that General Parsons had made it back to Brooklyn Heights with several men, including Phineas. Elihu wondered morosely if Phineas knew he'd been captured, or if he assumed Elihu was dead.

Word of Phineas's survival had been the only bright spot in Elihu's otherwise dismal confinement. Fear was a constant of his existence – a queasy sense of total vulnerability. Every word the prisoners spoke, every movement they made, had to be done with careful calculation, so as not to antagonize the captors upon whom they depended for the necessities of life. Doing so, while striving to maintain their dignity as men and their honor as soldiers and officers, was a juggling act Elihu worried they wouldn't be able to carry on indefinitely.

Adding to their stress was the news that, as Elihu had feared, Britain refused to acknowledge them as prisoners of war. To do so would imply recognition of the United States as an independent nation. Instead, the British classified them as traitors, a point frequently reinforced by threats of hanging.

There was also the chronic problem of hunger, which was approaching a crisis level among the prisoners. Their rations were set at two-thirds of what ship's crewmen received – an amount insufficient to support life.

Officers who hadn't been robbed of their money had pooled their funds to buy bread and cheese that they shared with others to supplement the inadequate rations. But that provided only a temporary respite from the constant gnawing in their bellies. Elihu could tell he was losing weight by the way the already baggy breeches provided by Jabez Fitch after the battle were growing ever looser.

Word of the Continental Army's misfortunes added to the gloom. For more than a week the men on the prison ships had heard the sounds and seen the smoke of battle at different locations on Manhattan. Then yesterday the *Mentor's* prisoners learned that the Americans had abandoned New York City, which was immediately occupied by the British. The Continental Army was retreating north along Manhattan Island.

Most tormenting of all was the lack of contact with anyone back home. Two weeks earlier Elihu had written letters to Hope and David and to Esther Camp. He'd presented them to be carried to the American lines under a flag of truce, from there to be forwarded to Middletown and Durham. But five days ago, a delivery of baggage and mail for officers on the *Mentor* had included nothing for Elihu.

Elihu had written more letters yesterday, but he held out little hope they would reach home, or if they did that letters sent in return would get to him. As far as he knew, his loved ones were totally ignorant of his situation.

Elihu struggled each day with the demons of depression and despair. He sometimes borrowed from Jabez Fitch a Bible given to the man by a British sailor. Elihu read and re-read certain passages, hoping they would help him reconcile himself to his captivity as a manifestation of God's will and a test of Elihu's faith.

Lying in the clammy darkness, Elihu's eyelids grew heavy. Soon he would sleep, and he would dream – dreams in which he was free, back in Middlefield, many miles from the dank, fetid belly of this wretched ship.

Sometimes in his dreams he was on a hilltop on a glowing spring day, surveying the sun-splashed hills and fields on which he'd worked and played all his life. Other times he was sitting in the homestead's kitchen, with Hope, David, Phineas, Catharine, and their sister Esther, savoring a warm, hearty meal after a long day's work. Still other times he was embracing a rapturous Esther Camp, assuring her again and again, between passionate kisses, that he was home for good, that they would never again be parted.

These dreams provided Elihu no escape. In fact, he hated them, for they made the reality to which he awoke all the more unbearable.

Chapter Twenty-Eight

October, 1776
New York City

On a stormy afternoon in the second week of October, Elihu reluctantly made his way to the Dutch church on Manhattan. It was as close to Hell on earth as he ever expected to visit.

A few days previously Elihu and other commissioned American officers had been transferred from the *Mentor* to Manhattan. Elihu was one of several dozen lodged in a large former tavern, where they'd been treated with minimal decency.

The captive officers had signed paroles, promising on their honor that they wouldn't try to escape or say anything directly or indirectly against King George. In return, they were allowed to leave their quarters and move freely within certain geographical limits.

New York was drastically different from the city Elihu had entered six months earlier. On the night of September 20, a fire had broken out near the southern end of Manhattan. Hundreds of buildings – a large swathe of the city – had burned. Blackened ruins scarred the landscape, and the harsh smell of charred wood still permeated parts of the city.

Elihu and other officers had used their freedom of movement to visit American privates and non-commissioned officers captured at the battle on Long Island. These men were confined in more than half a dozen houses of worship, including the Dutch church, which the British had hastily converted into makeshift prisons.

British and Hessian guards alike glared with naked hostility as Elihu approached the church. A stomach-turning stench filled his nostrils well before he reached the door. Such a smell was to be expected from a building crammed so full of men that each had barely enough room to lie down. None of the prisoners had had a chance to wash his clothing or even his body for weeks. But this building reeked of more than filth – it reeked of evil.

Elihu stepped over the threshold, then grabbed clumsily for the door frame, as his shoe slipped on the indescribably foul, slimy mixture of dirt, feces, urine, blood, and vomit that coated most of the floor. Denied access to even basic sanitary facilities, the prisoners had no choice but to relieve themselves inside the building. Many who'd fallen ill with the flux lay in their own excrement. Elihu thanked God Phineas hadn't ended up in a house of horrors like this.

Breathing through his mouth, Elihu closed the door behind him. Emaciated faces – some so fleshless they resembled skeletal heads carved into gravestones in the Middlefield burying ground – turned toward the sound, which could just barely be heard over the constant hacking and sniffling, punctuated by an occasional sharp cry of pain or retch of vomiting.

When the prisoners saw Elihu was one of their own, a feeble chorus of desperate pleading went up from men who had somehow stayed alive for weeks on starvation rations of moldy, weevily bread and tainted meat supplied by their British captors. The weakest could only moan; others begged piteously, "Please, some food, a scrap of bread – anything, for God's sake, please!" Bony arms stretched out imploringly from cadaverous bodies, clothed in tattered uniforms or cast-off civilian rags, that shook uncontrollably from cold, for the British hadn't provided the prisoners with fuel for fires.

Desolation flooded the men's sunken eyes as Elihu regretfully held up his empty hands. On his previous visit, he'd brought whatever food he could scrounge to help alleviate, if only briefly, the misery of these wretched soldiers. But this time he had only words of encouragement and support.

Even commissioned officers like Elihu never knew from day to day if they would actually receive all or even part of the insufficient rations their captors allotted them. Most of the time hunger gnawed painfully at their stomachs – and sometimes at their principles.

Just the day before, a local man Elihu and Jabez Fitch had gotten to know in the months before the battle on Long Island had compassionately invited the two famished men to supper at his home. They'd gratefully accepted, and partaken of some palatable roast pork – while sitting across the dinner table from a Hessian soldier whom their host had also invited in a prudent display of political neutrality.

The sight of these starving men made Elihu ashamed of his willingness to dine, almost literally, with the Devil. But passing up an opportunity for food that would maintain his own strength would do nothing to help these suffering soldiers.

Shivering inside a thin jacket given to him by an officer from another Connecticut regiment, Elihu stepped carefully into the room, searching for the faces of men he knew. He didn't have to be a doctor to realize that by entering the prison he was risking his own health and perhaps life. Self-preservation dictated he avoid this breeding ground for disease. But he couldn't live with the guilt if he didn't come. Save for a single step in rank – ensign being the lowest commissioned officer – he would be one of the men in this death trap.

Elihu picked his way carefully among the sprawled forms. Some men stared silently at the ceiling in utter despair. Others, delirious from fever or driven to distraction by the ghastly conditions, babbled or mumbled incoherently, their bodies twitching spastically. Two men Elihu passed were clearly dead, but their companions hadn't had the energy to inform the guards so the corpses would be removed – or perhaps they hadn't yet even noticed.

At last Elihu spotted one of the men he'd come specifically to see – Sergeant Rufus Tracy of the Seventeenth Regiment. Sergeant Tracy was about Elihu's age, with a teenage wife and an infant daughter back home in Connecticut.

Having entered captivity with an abundance of flesh on his frame, Sergeant Tracy was not quite as emaciated as most of the other men. But his shirt was stained with spittle and vomit, and his long, scraggly hair and beard crawled with lice. Most worrisome, his body shook with more than cold under the threadbare, filthy blanket that covered less than half his body. His face was now brightly flushed with the fever Elihu had detected on his earlier visit.

Elihu crouched down next to Tracy, who was lying on damp, matted, dirty straw. The ailing man could do no more than lift his head.

"Ensign," Tracy acknowledged in a hoarse whisper with a nod that, while weak, nonetheless sketched the ghost of a respectful salute. Elihu studied the man with undisguised pity. "I'm sorry I could find no food to bring," he said, even as his own stomach growled with hunger. He hadn't eaten since yesterday's meal of pork.

Tracy shook his head feebly. "Lieutenant Fitch brought soup yesterday. It kept us alive until the guards threw us some putrid scraps of pork last night."

"The bloody-backs came again this morning, coaxing us, pressuring us to save ourselves by enlisting in the British army," said the painfully thin youth sitting cross-legged, shoulders slumped from weakness, next to Tracy. He was a teenage private, also of the Seventeenth Regiment, by the name of Samuel Boardman. Both Tracy and Boardman had been among the group who'd surrendered to the Hessians under Elihu's direction. "But wretched as we are, not a man among us was willing to accept their cursed offer, to betray our country and our Lord," Boardman proclaimed, defiant pride shining in his sunken eyes.

"I would have expected nothing else from such brave soldiers and true patriots," Elihu managed to say, humbled by the raw courage with which they refused rescue at the price of their honor. He choked back hot tears of anger at the cruelty being deliberately inflicted on these good men.

Elihu clapped a consoling hand on Sergeant Tracy's shoulder. He glanced over at Private Boardman. "The Lord knows of your suffering in His name and in the sacred cause of liberty," he said. "Find strength in Him. You're honored in the hearts and minds of all who know you, and generations to come will be grateful for your sacrifice." The words sounded hollow even to Elihu, but they were all he had to offer.

Sergeant Tracy nodded feebly, then closed his eyes. Private Boardman leaned over to tug the blanket up a bit farther on the officer's shivering form.

Elihu straightened up stiffly, and made his way slowly to the door. As he left, he informed the Redcoat guard about the two fresh corpses that needed to be removed.

The soldier stared at Elihu, then spat contemptuously on the ground. "Only two?" he said with malicious disappointment, before motioning to a pair of Hessian privates to come to the building.

Elihu walked a couple hundred feet from the Dutch church before stopping to collect himself. He knew the soldiers inside that building were living dead men.

Wrapping his arms tightly across his chest, he fought to control the shaking of his body that had nothing to do with the temperature.

He closed his eyes and lifted his face to the lowery sky, overcast with clouds of various shades of gray that raced swiftly by. He breathed deeply of the stiff, damp breeze, listened to the continuous growl of distant thunder, and tried to purge from his senses any vestige of the ghastly scene he had, with shame-faced gratitude, left behind.

After a long moment Elihu opened his eyes and turned to leave. The two Hessian privates were lugging out one of the American corpses. They dumped it into a cart into which the other body had already been deposited. As the cart lumbered off to the pit that served as a common mass grave for prisoners, several young Tories cheered the sight. "There goes another load of damned rebels!" one crowed with gleeful satisfaction.

Half an hour after leaving the Dutch church, Elihu was back at his lodgings. He trudged wearily up the stairs to the second floor where he slept with Jabez Fitch and a dozen other officers. He sat down heavily onto a stool, and removed his thin coat.

There came a short rapping on the front door of the building. "Ensign Lyman," Lieutenant Fitch called from below. "Someone's asking for you."

Elihu closed his eyes for a moment, inhaled deeply, then let his breath out in an effort to compose himself. He hoped his caller hadn't come to fetch him to tend to a sick soldier; without any medicine or instruments or supplies he could do little more than bleed a patient.

When Elihu reached the bottom of the stairs, he saw that Lieutenant Fitch had closed the door, apparently leaving Elihu's visitor outside. Puzzled, Elihu lifted the latch, pulled the door open – and was flabbergasted to find Major Hierlihy and his eldest son, his namesake Timothy, on the stone doorstep.

Joy flared in Elihu at the sight of familiar faces from home in this land of despair. But it flickered out an instant later, as he got a good look at his unexpected visitors.

Both Hierlihy men wore bright red woolen frock coats, with dark blue facings trimmed with broad, shiny, flat brass buttons. Realizing that their attire resembled British uniforms, Elihu felt anxiety begin gnawing at his gut.

Elihu saw pity in Major Hierlihy's eyes as the older man sized up Elihu's appearance. He still wore the garments Jabez Fitch had loaned him nearly two months ago, now bedraggled and inadequate for the cold weather and hanging loosely on his thin frame. But

Major Hierlihy addressed Elihu as genially as if he were stopping by the Lyman farmhouse. "We came to pay our respects as soon as we learned you were here."

The years had been kind to the Irishman, who Elihu calculated must be in his mid-forties. Although Major Hierlihy was leaner, and his features sharper, he still had a full head of thick, curly black hair, albeit frosted with gray. His son was a slight, almost painfully earnest young man who, Elihu recalled Phineas saying, considered his father's every word gospel.

"Why are you dressed like that?" Elihu at last blurted out.

"We've enlisted in His Majesty's service," Major Hierlihy said proudly.

"You're Tories?!" Elihu spluttered. He looked from one Hierlihy face to the other for a sign that this was some kind of demented practical joke.

"Loyalists," Major Hierlihy corrected calmly. "May we come in?"

"No," Elihu snapped rudely, stepping out onto the stone step and pulling the door shut behind him. By doing so he crowded the two Hierlihy men down onto the lower steps so that he loomed over them.

"I can imagine how great a shock this must be," Major Hierlihy began. "But Elihu–."

"It's Ensign Lyman," Elihu corrected him sharply, even though he knew a Tory wouldn't address him by his Continental Army rank. That would be admitting that there was a Continental Army, and by extension an independent country for which it fought

Major Hierlihy smiled patiently, as if dealing with a stubborn child. But Elihu caught a glint of irritation in the older man's vivid blue eyes.

"Allow me to explain," Major Hierlihy said firmly. "From the very start of this unnatural and unprovoked rebellion I resolved to remain loyal to the best of sovereigns and the British constitution. I sought out men who share my sense of duty to the Crown. For a year I traveled throughout Connecticut, contacting men of like mind – and there were many – willing to take up arms in support of their rightful king and to spend their own money on raising a force for that purpose."

Elihu listened with sick fascination and growing outrage to this account of cold-blooded treachery, carried out under the noses of trusting neighbors, by a man whose kindness in a dark time had meant much to the Lyman family. "Are they all Churchmen like you

– their souls yoked to the king as head of your Anglican faith?" Elihu demanded scornfully.

The question annoyed Major Hierlihy, but the older man didn't take the bait. "Not all of them," he said smugly.

"When the royal forces routed the provincial troops from Long Island, I realized it was time to set my plan in motion," Major Hierlihy continued smoothly. "I sent Tim ahead of me to New York, and in September I followed."

"Why are you here?" Elihu demanded, even though he was sure he knew the answer.

"You've seen for yourself these past weeks the awesome power of the British military," Major Hierlihy said, his eyes meeting Elihu's with candor. "It's only a matter of weeks before the Crown's troops crush this sham of an American army.

"I'm offering you the chance to save yourself from the dire consequences of this hopeless insurrection before it's too late. His Majesty is a forgiving father. If you swear allegiance to him, you can join us in fighting to end this wicked rebellion. You can help return the colonies to the happy state they enjoyed as part of the greatest empire on the face of the earth ruled by the best of kings."

Elihu didn't doubt Major Hierlihy believed every word he said. But as he listened to the man speak, a caustic mixture of contempt and anger welled up inside him.

A small voice of reason in Elihu's brain cautioned him to tread carefully with Major Hierlihy. The Tory's British cohorts would surely welcome any excuse to kill a prisoner. But everything Elihu had endured since the fateful battle on Long Island – the suffering and sacrifice he'd seen, the calculated cruelty he'd witnessed not an hour past, the noble courage with which the victims of that barbarity had spurned the very same deal with the Devil now being offered to him – pushed him past the boundaries of common sense.

"So, you propose I betray my country for the great privilege of becoming the lap dog of the 'best of kings,'" Elihu replied scornfully, putting a sharp twist of sarcasm on the last three words. "A king who hires brutal mercenaries to slaughter his own subjects, mercenaries who after I surrendered to them on the field of battle stole my possessions, stripped me naked, then beat me nearly to death," he snarled.

Anger flared in Major Hierlihy's eyes at Elihu's offensive reply, but his expression remained impassive. This ability to conceal his true thoughts and feelings had doubtless served the man well during the year he'd slithered around Connecticut soliciting support for the British tyrant, Elihu thought with contempt.

"A king whose soldiers keep prisoners of war in conditions filthier than a New England hog pen," Elihu raged on, "starving them, denying them clothing and medicine and firewood, and when they at last die, dumping their carcasses into a hole. All of this I witnessed this very morning!" Elihu's temper was burning white hot, his hands clenched and unclenched spasmodically, as if itching to wrap themselves around someone's throat.

Major Hierlihy eyed Elihu with caution, but made no effort to interrupt or silence him.

"But those men are not prisoners of war," the younger Hierlihy corrected, speaking for the first time. "They're traitors who took up arms against their rightful king. Pain and death are the punishment for treason. They had no reason to expect anything else."

Elihu's response was to Tim Hierlihy's remark, but his eyes never left Major Hierlihy. "Consider then how the 'best of kings' treated a subject of unwavering loyalty – my father's cousin Phineas," he said. "He sought compensation for himself and his fellow veterans who risked their lives fighting Britain's French and Indian enemies. But for ten years the British ministry shunted him aside like an annoying beggar, put him off with false promises as if he were a tavern keeper dunning them for an unpaid bar bill.

"When he returned to America with King George's promise of a land grant and sailed to West Florida to claim it, my cousin discovered that the royal word was as worthless as all the other promises made in London. This is how your 'best of kings' rewarded a faithful subject whose only failing was being a provincial!"

Tim Hierlihy took an involuntary step back, as if physically pushed by Elihu's furious rant. Glancing quickly around the street, realizing the confrontation was attracting the attention of passers-by, Elihu fought to rein in his rage. He fell silent, but his eyes still blazed with an unspoken challenge to Major Hierlihy.

The two men's gazes remained locked for what seemed an endless moment. Major Hierlihy's eyes narrowed thoughtfully and his jaw worked slightly as he considered his response.

"I was disappointed by the Crown's response to General Lyman and those he represented," Major Hierlihy acknowledged, "of whom I was one," he pointed out. "His Majesty is a great man, but he's not perfect."

That was all the concession Major Hierlihy intended to make to Elihu's diatribe. "But the British empire is more than one king or one set of ministers," he went on earnestly. "It's the greatest, most noble force for liberty and civilization in the history of the world. We must not break faith with it because its current leaders are flawed like all men. Those who seek to weaken it to satisfy their own misguided grievances must be stopped – by any means necessary." Major Hierlihy's voice was as hard as stone.

Elihu's entire body was trembling violently from fury and from the cold, in painful contrast to the Hierlihy men, warm in their heavy woolen coats. Elihu defiantly wrapped his arms tightly around himself to try to stop the shaking, and waited.

Major Hierlihy sighed. "I came here in friendship, Eli–," he stopped before he gave the younger man another opportunity to demand he be addressed by his sham rank. "I came out of respect for your family, in token of our many years as neighbors. This is your chance to join the faithful service of the Crown, to reclaim your honor as a British subject – maybe even to save your life. How say you?" Behind his father, Tim Hierlihy stared intently at Elihu, willing him to accept.

"'Get thee behind me, Satan,'" Elihu spat in a voice clogged with loathing, echoing what Holy Scripture said Jesus replied when the Devil offered him all the kingdoms of the world if only he would worship him. Elihu turned his back on the two Hierlihy men, wrenched open the door to the tavern, stepped across the threshold, and slammed the door behind him.

Chapter Twenty-Nine

October, 1776
Norwalk

David's mount plodded wearily along the post road headed south toward Norwalk on a clear, crisp day in the middle of October. His departure from Middlefield for New York had been delayed by the discovery of Major Hierlihy's treason.

David and Hope had been as stunned as if the moon had fallen from the sky. Hope's shock quickly transformed into fury at Major Hierlihy's betrayal of those who'd been his friends and neighbors for twenty years, and at his cold-blooded abandonment of his wife and children to face the ire of those he'd deceived.

The revelation that for months before he went to the British, Major Hierlihy had been covertly mustering support for the king throughout Connecticut had sent waves of fear and suspicion through the countryside. If Major Hierlihy could operate undetected in their midst, people wondered if others like him might still be in place. Secret traitors could set fire to houses or stores of military supplies, sabotage bridges, even commit murder – all the more easily with so many men away in the army.

Men and women eyed once-trusted acquaintances warily for signs of disloyalty. Churchmen like Philip Mortimer, the Alsops, and the Lymans' near neighbors the Birdseys had come under particular scrutiny.

Unwilling to leave Hope alone in such an unstable atmosphere, David had arranged for his sister Hannah and her two youngest stepchildren to come from West Haven to stay in Middlefield until he returned. After much searching he'd also found a local youth who would work on the farm while he was away. When David at last departed, carrying cash, supplies, and letters – including one reporting the doleful news of Phineas's death – for Elihu, he expected to be gone no more than a week.

On the first leg of his journey, David had tried to sort out his feelings for Sarah Comstock. He mentally ticked off her qualities; she was kind, compassionate, honest, and brave. She was down-to-earth, good-humored, warm and patient, capable and energetic. And there was her pleasingly wholesome face and enticing figure

But something more attracted him to Sarah, David mused. The way she'd detected the resentment and guilt he kept buried deep inside, and the frankness with which she'd spoken about these shameful feelings had at first unnerved him. But then he came to understand that she didn't do it to judge, as most people would, but to help. With Sarah, David felt as if, after sailing a turbulent sea, he had reached a safe harbor.

Was this love? David thought it might be, but had to admit he wasn't sure. He needed to see Sarah, to talk to her, to determine what exactly he felt for her.

And to discover what Sarah felt for him – if anything. David knew Sarah might have already forgotten him, a suffering stranger she'd treated with the kindness she would afford any hurting human being, whose presence in the household had been but a brief, tragic distraction from the hectic routine of her life.

A stone mile post on the side of the road caught David's eye. Squinting, he saw "Norwalk 2 miles" carved into it. His chance to get answers to his questions was fast approaching.

As the Comstock house came into view, David was struck by the unnatural silence. He heard no voices inside or outside the house, no sounds of the daily routine of farm work.

His senses on alert, David got off his horse and tethered it to the post in front of the house. He mounted the stone steps to the front door. As he raised his hand to knock, he glanced through the parlor window. What he saw made his blood run cold: a looking-glass shrouded with cloth, the sign of a death in the family.

David stood paralyzed with dread, for how long he didn't know. At last he found the will to knock on the door.

It was opened by the Negro slave Peter. "Mr. Lyman," Peter greeted him in surprise, then informed him soberly, "The family is down at the graveyard."

"Who–?" David managed to squeeze out. He felt like there was a boulder on his chest.

"It's Mary they're burying," Peter answered. "She got sicker with the flux after you left. She died yesterday. The family's coming back now. Mr. Comstock sent me ahead to get things ready."

Relief sent the blood rushing from David's head. His face turned deathly pale, and he was suddenly so light-headed he almost lost his balance. Alarmed, Peter extended a steadying hand

David's relief was followed immediately by shame. Mary Comstock was only a name to him; he'd never even laid eyes on her. But she'd been a human being, and Sarah's sister, and her death should evoke only sorrow.

Peter ushered David into the house just as the Comstocks and the other mourners began to arrive. The Comstocks greeted David like a returning relative. It wasn't until he finally set eyes on Sarah that the crushing weight lifted from his chest, allowing him to once more breathe normally. He told himself she seemed more than just politely pleased to see him.

The Comstocks shared David's excitement over the report that Elihu was alive, even if a prisoner. They commiserated over Major Hierlihy's betrayal, although they weren't particularly shocked. Tories were thick in the southwestern corner of Connecticut, which had more than its share of Church of England parishes.

Sarah was occupied most of the day with comforting her parents and siblings and acting as hostess to the mourners who filled the Comstock house. David was constantly on watch for a chance to speak privately with her.

David's opportunity came around sunset, when Sarah at last sat down for a few moments in a chair in the hall. As she reached for her psalm book, David asked if she would like to take an evening stroll. She accepted with what David desperately assured himself was enthusiasm.

They walked slowly past the barn and down toward the fields, their bodies close but not touching. It was a fine evening, the sky clear, the autumn air fresh but not cold.

Sarah spoke first, her eyes focused on the path ahead of them. "Scarcely a month ago, we walked together like this, returning from your brother's grave," she reflected sadly. "And now there's another grave. I told you I wasn't close to my brother William. But it was different with Mary. With just nineteen months between us we were like twins. I still can't believe when I return to the house she won't be there. I feel as if half of me died with her."

Sarah came to an abrupt halt. Her features tightened in a determined effort not to cry that wrenched David's heart.

"I have to be so strong for everyone else, that I dare not show how very deeply Mary's death grieves me," Sarah at last managed to say. "She was the seventh child my parents have lost. I don't know how they endure it."

Sarah smiled bravely up at David, her eyes glistening with unshed tears. "I'm so grateful you saw my need to leave the house, to have a chance to unburden my heart," she said. David felt a twinge of guilt that it had been his own need, not any sensitivity to Sarah's, that had prompted his invitation.

Taking a deep breath to steady himself, David stepped around to face Sarah. "You gave me advice on how to help heal the grief of losing a loved one," he began with a nervous smile. "You said we should never put off caring for the living who are left to us. Those words are part of what drew me back to Norwalk, to tell you," – David hesitated, feeling like he was about to leap off a cliff into water of unknown depth – "that I love you."

David watched Sarah's face intently for her first, unguarded – honest – reaction. He had tried to prepare himself for anything – embarrassment, anger, pity, laughter.

Sarah's eyes grew wide and her mouth opened slightly in astonishment at David's declaration. Then her soft gray eyes took on a warm glow, and her lips turned up in a dazzling smile. "I love you, too, David," she said with a sense of wonderment, as if a magnificent truth had suddenly been revealed to her.

At first David just stared, afraid to trust his ears. When her reply at last sank in, he couldn't find words to describe the feelings sweeping through him. Instead, he leaned over and pressed his lips to Sarah's in a kiss that, after a moment of surprise, she joined in.

David slipped one arm around Sarah's waist, the other behind her back. He pulled her against him in an urgent embrace that, given his lack of experience, he immediately feared was too tight – until he felt Sarah wrap her arms around his neck with equal ardor. As the sky where the sun had just slipped below the horizon turned a flaming orange, they stood suspended in a moment of bliss, their trials and troubles forgotten, aware only of each other.

Their lips parted at last, but they continued to hold each other close. David then astounded himself by whispering, "Will you marry me?" Ten minutes ago he'd hoped for nothing more than a few words of encouragement from Sarah. A proposal of marriage hadn't even entered his mind. But what had just passed between them made it seem to David the natural, the logical, the right thing to do.

To David's dismay, Sarah's expression changed to one of deep distress. She looked away, unwilling to meet his eyes. "We cannot marry now," she said unhappily.

"Why not?" David demanded, confused by Sarah's sudden change of mood. "We're both of age. I can provide for a wife and family. What is there to keep us apart?"

Sarah reluctantly released her embrace of David's neck, then reached behind her to gently remove his arms from her waist. She stepped back until their bodies no longer touched.

"We say we love each other, David," she began slowly, looking down at her feet. "But we met little more than a month ago. We've not spent even a week in each other's company."

Sarah raised her head sharply to look into David's face. Her eyes now were clouded with uncertainty. "How well do you really know me – or I you? How can we be certain that a connection formed so quickly is love strong enough to serve as the bond for a marriage that, once made, cannot be broken?"

It was agony for Sarah to speak so. In their short time in each other's company David had left an impression on her heart like no other man had. She understood he was entangled in a complex web of responsibilities not of his choosing and often in conflict with his own desires. But his discontent hadn't hardened his heart or warped his spirit into something mean. Sarah had seen with her own eyes the strength, the courage, the tenderness, and the devotion behind David's reserved manner. And now she had been shaken to her core by his words, his touch, his kiss.

David stared off into the distance as he thought about Sarah's question. He brought his gaze back to her face, then spoke with as much control as he could muster.

"We may not have passed much time together," David conceded, "but in those few days we saw each other tested by the kind of trials that reveal a person's true character. I think we know each far better than couples who have courted for years but have only passed pleasant hours in parlors together."

His calm started to crumble under the weight of his passion. "And everything I know and have seen of you makes me love you," he said in a hoarse whisper.

"I believe you mean that," Sarah said reassuringly. "But–." She stopped, afraid of David's reaction to what she'd been about to say.

"But what?" David demanded, drawing his eyebrows together in a puzzled frown.

"Phineas–," Sarah began, then glanced back down at the ground. She twisted her checked apron nervously with her fingers. Her next words would hurt David, but they had to be spoken, for both their futures hung in the balance. She raised her eyes again to David's, then continued with brutal candor.

"Phineas told me your mother has interfered every time you tried to become acquainted with a woman, that she prevented you from courting anyone. How can you be sure what you feel for me is truly love, when you've never spent time with any other woman?"

David flushed with humiliation at Sarah's challenge. The wounded look in his eyes told her how deeply her words had cut.

"You speak to me as if I were a willful little boy – just as my mother does," he said with bitter resentment. "How many women must I woo before you'll be satisfied I know my own mind?" he demanded sarcastically. "A dozen? A score? A hundred? Perhaps you would prefer a suitor like Phineas – one who has lost count of how many woman he's dallied with?"

"I love you, David – not Phineas," Sarah said desperately, upset that he'd misunderstood her caution as criticism. She couldn't bear for him to be jealous of his dead brother.

The redness on David's cheeks lessened slightly. But he watched Sarah warily, unsure if more hurtful words were about to be hurled at him.

"I've been courted by other men, but none touched my heart as you have," Sarah said. "Still I feel the need to wait to be certain my feelings for you are strong and lasting before we speak of marriage. If our love is true, it will withstand a test of time – and distance."

"But I'm afraid to wait," David confessed in an imploring whisper, his anger and bitterness draining away. "You said it yourself, we cannot count on tomorrow. I've lost family before – my grandmother, my father – and friends and neighbors, too, as you have. But it took the deaths of Phineas and our sister to make me truly appreciate how uncertain is our mortal existence."

Sarah opened her mouth to reply, but David continued talking. "And I can't stop thinking of Elihu. He delayed wedding the woman he loves for years – first until his apprenticeship was finished, then until his service in the army was completed. Now he's a prisoner of war, for God only knows how long. I told his Esther myself that he'd fallen into British hands." David winced at the memory of his brother's betrothed's distraught reaction to the news. "Elihu may die in captivity. He may already be dead, leaving Esther with only blasted dreams."

Again Sarah tried to speak, but David shook his head to stop her. "When I stood on your doorstep today and saw the shrouded looking-glass, I was paralyzed with fear that it was for you. The thought that I might never see you again was unbearable. It was then I knew for certain that I love you."

Sarah's resolve wavered under David's impassioned arguments. She was all too willing to be persuaded to abandon common sense and immediately wed this man who a month ago she hadn't even known existed and who she now believed held the key to her earthly happiness. But the level-headedness and self-control Sarah had cultivated since childhood won out.

"I know how much we risk by waiting; I laid my dearest sister to eternal rest today," she reminded David solemnly. "But if we wed now, we risk a lifetime of misery."

The despair on David's face tore at Sarah's heart, but she willed herself to resist relenting. "We'll write to each other. You'll visit Norwalk when you can. In the spring if, God willing, we live and we both still feel as we do now, then I will marry you."

David said nothing for what seemed to Sarah like an eternity. It was growing dark, with just enough light remaining for them to make out each other's features against a sky in which scattered stars were winking into view.

Sarah began to fear she'd made a fatal mistake, had turned David away from her for good with her insistence on following the prudent path. When at last he spoke, it was in a steady voice that, to her enormous relief, was still vibrant with love.

"When I came here today, all I hoped for was to learn that you cared for me in some small way, that my attentions would not be unwelcome," David said. "I never dreamed you'd say you love me. That you might consent to marry me was beyond imagining."

David reached out in the near darkness to trace a finger along the contour of Sarah's cheek with the gentle reverence one might use to stroke a beautiful butterfly's fragile wing. "If you are so certain that waiting to wed is wisest, I will master my impatience. If you are to be the reward for all my long, lonely years as a bachelor, I don't regret a single day of them."

Chapter Thirty

December, 1776
New York City

Elihu's shoes crunched on frozen snow as he hurried back to his lodgings on a bitterly cold night in late December. Tucked securely inside his jacket was a precious bundle: a letter from Hope, money and clothing from David, and a letter from Esther. They were the first communication of any kind that he'd received from home since being taken prisoner four months ago.

Elihu had taken every opportunity to send letters to Middlefield and Durham. He hadn't received a single response, or even known for sure that any of his letters had reached his loved ones.

Elihu knew the channels through which letters traveled to and from captives in New York were unreliable at best. He wasn't the only prisoner who hadn't heard from home. But as week after week had passed with no word from anyone in Middlefield, or from Esther, or from Phineas, wherever he was, it was hard not to feel forgotten. At last, tonight, he'd been told mail was waiting for him at Major Levi Wells's quarters.

As Elihu walked, collar turned up, shoulders hunched against the cold, he reflected on another pleasant surprise this day had brought. Two hundred enlisted men and non-commissioned officers who'd managed to survive brutal captivity under the British had suddenly and unaccountably been released. That afternoon they'd boarded a ship to take them home. Incredibly, Sergeant Rufus Tracy and Private Samuel Boardman were among their number.

Elihu tried, and failed, to find a glimmer of hope for himself in this unexpected release. He'd had his expectations raised too many times by rumors of prisoner exchanges that always turned out to be false.

Upon reaching his lodgings, Elihu opened the door just enough to slip inside, allowing as little of the precious heat to escape as possible. Passing unnoticed by a group of men gathered in the adjoining room, he climbed the stairs to the second floor, where he found himself alone.

Elihu kept his jacket on as he stirred the small fire flickering on the hearth. He fed the flames a few precious sticks of wood, then sat down on a stool as close to the blaze as was safe.

He pulled the letters, coins, and bundle of clothing from inside his jacket. He set the clothes and cash aside; welcome as they were for the physical comfort they would provide, the letters filled an even greater need. He was starved for communication with those he loved.

Elihu first unfolded the letter addressed in his mother's hand. The wax seal she'd applied to keep the pages closed was broken. British censors opened and read all mail received by or sent to prisoners, looking for sensitive information or inflammatory comments.

Leaning as close as he dared to the fire for light and warmth, Elihu began to read. The letter was dated December 10. "Dear Son," Hope began. "We've just received your letter of November 30, the first communication from your hand to reach us since you were taken prisoner."

Elihu was appalled; none of the four letters he'd written previous to November 30 had reached Middlefield! He read on, "You can imagine our joy at learning that you're alive and in good health and being treated well."

Elihu snorted derisively. Knowing that a letter truthfully describing his situation would never pass the censors, Elihu had described his circumstances in vague terms, while noting that he would "be gratified" to receive some warm clothing, and also hard money – Continental paper currency was, of course, of no value in British-occupied New York – for "sundry articles."

Hope's letter continued, "David has sent, as you requested, clothing suitable for winter, with as many coins as we could gather, in the hope that these will add to your comfort.

"We've written four times to you," Hope continued, "but judge from your letter just received that those earlier missives miscarried. I must assume therefore that you are not aware of the melancholy fact that your dear brother Phineas is no more."

Elihu stared in horror at the last six words. He glanced quickly away from the letter, hoping irrationally that when he looked back the writing would miraculously say something different. When he found the courage to re-read the dreaded words, he whispered them aloud, as if receiving the news through another of his senses might make it more believable.

It's not true, Elihu told himself desperately. With the confusion of battle, the disarray of the army, and the poor lines of communication, he knew soldiers were sometimes reported dead, only to appear later alive. Such a mistaken report must have made its way back to Middlefield, he assured himself. Phineas would turn up somewhere in the vast, disorganized lines of the reeling Continental Army.

Elihu was able to cling to that desperate logic only until he read the letter's next line. "David was with him when he died, on September 13, in Norwalk," Hope wrote. "Although he'd been ailing for many days, his death came suddenly. He made his peace with God before the end, for which blessing I'm sure you share our gratitude."

This news was more excruciating and disorienting to Elihu than the blow of the Hessian's rifle butt to his head. The longed-for letter slipped from his fingers and fluttered to the floor. He buried his face in his hands.

Elihu's stomach churned, sending bitter fluid rising into his mouth, at the thought of Phineas – the brother to whom he'd grown so close this past year, the aimless youth who had found purpose in the fight for liberty – a corpse like those he saw being dumped daily into mass graves. That Phineas had died from battle-related injuries, Elihu had no doubt. If his death had been from accident or disease, his mother would have included the details, to which a censor would have no objection.

Elihu couldn't begin to imagine the anguish that lay beneath his mother's carefully worded letter. That she'd been able to write it was an indication that grief hadn't overwhelmed her. He expected David's sorrow was a wound made more painful by the salt of guilt that he didn't deserve.

Elihu lifted his head from his hands. He should retrieve Hope's letter and finish it, but an immobilizing inertia had come over him. At last he remembered Esther's letter. With foreboding he forced himself to unfold the single sheet of thick paper, its wax seal broken like the one on Hope's letter, and started reading.

"My dearest love," the letter began. Relief rushed through Elihu at those three words, proof that Esther's affection remained steadfast, a beacon shining through the tempest of trial and tragedy his life had become.

"The arrival of your letter of November 30 after so many months of silence since the battle on Long Island gave me more joy than I can express." Elihu sighed deeply. Esther, too, had received none of the letters he'd dispatched to her before the beginning of December.

"A most merciful God be thanked for preserving your life and health," Esther continued. "You have been in my mind and heart every minute of every day and night since we parted. I long for you with each breath. There is in my existence a great void that only your presence can fill. I take some solace in the knowledge that–." The rest of the sentence had been blotted out with ink by the censor. Elihu surmised Esther had made some reference to the righteousness of the fight against British tyranny.

"We are all well here, save for our concern for you and our sorrow over the death of your brother Phineas. My constant prayer is that God, in His justice and compassion, will keep you safe and restore you to those who care for you as quickly as possible. I am, until death, your devoted Esther."

Elihu re-read the letter slowly, then folded it and tucked it inside his jacket near his heart. He had fresh reason to love and appreciate Esther Camp. She must have suspected her letter would pass by an unsympathetic British censor. But she hadn't allowed that likely violation of her privacy to keep her from telling Elihu what she knew he most needed to hear: that her love for him remained true, unaltered by the misfortune that had befallen him and the resulting uncertainty of their situation. Esther's willingness to expose, for his sake, her most intimate emotions to the prying eyes of the enemy heartened him – just as the thought of some nosy Redcoat sniggering over the rebel woman's passionate declaration infuriated him.

Elihu sat for a long time, staring into yellow daggers of flame. Just as hot was the hatred burning in his breast for the British, their Hessian hirelings, and the Tory traitors like the Hierlihys who had inflicted such pain and grief on him, his family, his country – and, most importantly, the woman he cherished.

Chapter Thirty-One

March, 1777
North Guilford

"I have important news to share," David said to the group eating dinner around the table in the Benton house on a late-winter afternoon. Lot, Catharine, Hannah and Noah Williston, and Hope all looked up at him. Hope was puzzled; she couldn't think of anything important that had happened or been heard of in Middlefield since the family had last been together.

"I'm going to be married," David announced, relieved that his voice was steady, despite his extreme nervousness.

Forks and spoons stopped abruptly in mid-air. Astonishment registered on each face – save Catharine's, for David had earlier taken his sister into his confidence. The pregnant silence was broken by bursts of chatter from toddler Lyman Beecher. Although David Beecher had taken a fourth wife in December, he'd left his son, now nearly eighteen months old, in Catharine and Lot's care.

"Married?" Hope repeated blankly. She stared at David as if he'd spoken gibberish. "That's impossible. Who would you marry?"

"Her name is Sarah Comstock – from the Norwalk family who cared for Phineas," David said.

The exchange of many letters, along with two brief visits to Norwalk over the past five months had left David and Sarah confident that what they felt for each other was more than the transient passion of two strangers thrown together by crisis. What they shared was love, genuine and lasting.

They'd agreed to marry, which meant David couldn't put off telling Hope any longer. He was determined to stand firm; however ugly the confrontation with his mother would be, losing Sarah had become unthinkable to him.

David had deliberately chosen the Benton home, with its emotional connections to the marriages of all three of his sisters, to make his announcement. He'd decided to break the news to Hope in front of his sisters and brothers-in-law in the expectation that their presence would bolster his resolve.

"Some woman you met briefly last year?" Hope asked skeptically. Obviously, she thought, some pretty young thing had caught David's attention while he was out from under his mother's eye, and he'd built himself a romantic castle in the air around her. "That's ridiculous," she said, shaking her head and resuming eating.

David flushed at his mother's brusque dismissal. His palms began to sweat, but he willed himself to remain calm.

"It's the truth, Mama," David said firmly. Hope raised her head in surprise at being contradicted. "Sarah and I are to be wed in May. She is twenty-one, and her father and I have agreed on a marriage portion. Everything is settled."

"Settled, is it?" Hope said in an ominous voice, placing her cutlery on her plate with deliberate care. She glowered at David as her annoyance escalated. How had he conducted a courtship that had proceeded so far without her even suspecting? There must have been clues. Her mind flashed back to his two trips to New York to arrange to get goods and money to Elihu, still a prisoner – trips that would have taken him through Norwalk.

Everyone else sat in frozen fascination, their meals forgotten. Even little Lyman fell quiet, sensing from the adults' expressions and the tension in the air that something important was happening.

"How dare you make a commitment like this without my permission!" Hope said, narrowing her eyes accusingly. Her chair scraped the floorboards as she pushed it back to get to her feet.

"I don't need anyone's permission to enter into an honorable marriage," David replied evenly, remaining in his seat. He'd given much thought to how he would respond to Hope's predictable wrath upon learning of his impending marriage. Never for a moment would he treat her with anything less than the respect and gratitude she deserved as his mother and for everything she'd done for him. But he would no longer let that debt dictate the course of his life.

David's unruffled response left Hope momentarily speechless. Before she could reply, he continued with quiet intensity. "I've spent half my thirty-one years living for others. But the need for that is over. Catharine and Hannah are wed. Esther and Phineas are gone. I'll do all I can for Elihu, but his fate is in God's hands. I'll always care for you and honor you. I've fulfilled my promise to Papa." He paused a moment, caught on the memory of the terrified teenager who'd made that commitment to a dying father.

"I've worked as hard as any man to establish – with your help and the Lord's blessing – a farm as fruitful and a home as comfortable as any in Middlefield," David went on. "I've earned the right to build my own family and happiness, with the woman I love."

Rock-solid conviction shone in the clear brown eyes that met and held Hope's. Something familiar about that look dampened the anger David's words had set roiling in Hope's mind. With a pang she remembered where she'd seen its like. It was the same adamant resolve with which John had informed Ebenezer Lyman that he and Hope weren't moving to Torrington.

Hope was nearly overcome by the memory of how John had drawn from their love the courage to defy his father, to chart their own path through life. Now their son had discovered his own wellspring of strength and independence in his affection for this woman Hope had never met.

With that realization, Hope saw David in a new light. He had done all he'd promised John for his brothers and sisters and for her. He did deserve to carve out a future as he saw fit. She would be unpardonably selfish to oppose his marriage out of fear of giving up the control she'd wielded for so long over the farm and family – or out of pique over his secret courtship.

Hope carefully sat back down. She folded her hands in her lap and studied them for a long moment, struggling to adjust to this new reality. Finally she looked up at David, who could barely breathe with suspense.

"You say her name is Sarah?" Hope asked. David nodded "I will welcome Sarah as your wife and as a daughter," she said solemnly.

David was thankful he'd stayed seated; he was so weak with relief he doubted his legs could have supported him. He was also surprised. His mother spoke not with resentful acceptance of a new unpleasantness, but rather determination to rise to a new challenge.

"That will make Sarah and me very happy," David said.

When it was clear Hope had no more to say, the others erupted into a torrent of eager questions about David's bride-to-be. He answered every one, all the while keeping a nervous eye on his mother.

Chapter Thirty-Two

May, 1777
Norwalk

The hoofbeats of a horse galloping down the road from Fairfield drew the attention of the Comstock family members gathered in front of the house. Fear rose in their throats. "I pray it's not news of another British landing." David Comstock spoke what was on all their minds.

"It's David!" Sarah cried out as the rider drew close enough to recognize. David Lyman reined in his horse and leaped from the saddle. He strode over to Sarah, like a magnet to iron. Not caring that he was dirty and sweaty from two days of hard riding, he seized her in a hug so powerful that for a moment she couldn't breathe.

David released her, then took her face in his hands, and studied her intently. "You're unharmed?" he said, half-question, half-statement.

She nodded. "Yes, David," she reassured him when she could catch a breath. "We all are."

At last David noticed the others present. Sarah's parents and her three brothers and three sisters were staring at him in amazement. He wrapped an arm protectively around Sarah.

"Two days ago I saw in the *Connecticut Courant* a report that thousands of the enemy had come ashore on Friday about six miles west of Fairfield," David began. That Phineas and Elihu had imagined an invasion much like this when they re-enlisted had made the news especially chilling for David.

Sarah's father nodded in understanding. From that general geographic description David knew the raiders had landed not far from the Comstock home. "They came ashore at Compo, about four miles east of here as the crow flies," he clarified.

"The *Courant* said they marched to Danbury, burned supplies for the Continental Army, and set the town on fire," David continued.

"I left for Norwalk that day. On the way here I heard rumors and reports of a battle. There were claims that many had been killed. Is it true?"

"Enough of it is," growled Sarah's father. "The Redcoats had to fight their way from Danbury back to the Sound through hundreds of militia who answered the alarm that went out when they landed. The British killed a score of our defenders. They wounded several score more, and took more than fifty prisoners with them when their fleet sailed back to New York on Monday. Thank God, we were never in immediate danger here."

"But we could hear the cannon and musket fire," Davey Comstock reported excitedly.

"There've been skirmishes and illegal trading all along the coast since the war started," said David Comstock. "But this time the Redcoats and the Judas Tories shoved the war right down our throats! The whole countryside is terrified. There's no telling if or when or where the British might show up again to slay and destroy."

"I'm enlisting in a ranger company to fight them if they return," Davey announced proudly.

"We were just seeing him off," his father confirmed.

David studied Sarah's brother; he looked like he'd grown two inches since David had last seen him a month ago. Now all of sixteen, Davey Comstock was at last getting his wish to join the fight. An image of Phineas heading off to war with the same enthusiasm flashed through David's mind.

David looked down at Sarah "I'm taking you with me back to Middlefield," he said. "Tomorrow," he added in a tone of command she'd never before heard from him. Sarah stared at David, stunned.

"We can be married there," David went on.

When she found her voice, Sarah tried to protest. "I – I can't leave my family now," she began, looking around desperately at the Comstocks in the front yard

"I won't let you stay here with British-infested Long Island in sight across the Sound," David insisted.

Before Sarah could object further, her father placed a gentle hand on her arm. "David is your family," he said. "'Whither thou goest, I will go,'" he quoted from the Bible's Book of Ruth. "'Thy people shall be my people.'"

David cast the older man a look of profound gratitude.

"Still, you aren't yet married, and so can't travel alone together," David Comstock continued. "I'm sure Sarah's mother will be happy to accompany you. She deserves to see her daughter married."

It wasn't the wedding she'd planned, Sarah thought as she and David stood together in the hall of the Lyman house on May 20. She had imagined being married in her parents' house, surrounded by her brothers and sisters, a handful of other relatives, and a few close friends.

This was a smaller and simpler ceremony, before witnesses who, save for her mother, were little more than strangers to Sarah. But she didn't care; all that mattered was David's hand holding hers, the love in his brown eyes, and the sacred vows they were about to exchange.

David, Sarah, and her mother had reached Middlefield late on Saturday, May 3. David had arranged to have the banns announced at the Middlefield Congregational Church's Sabbath services the next day, and on the subsequent two Sundays.

Now Abner Benedict, returned from his stint as a chaplain in the Continental Army, would conduct the ceremony uniting them as man and wife. There were barely half a dozen people present: Sarah's mother, Hope, Hannah and Noah Williston, Catharine and Lot Benton, and little Lyman Beecher.

Hope had welcomed her future daughter-in-law and Sarah's mother with grace and warmth that made David proud – and grateful. She'd accommodated them as houseguests, and helped arrange the elements of a wedding on short notice.

Sarah had brought her best dress to be married in. Several years old, it was a sky-blue silk that complimented her gray eyes and flaxen hair. The scoop neck was trimmed with broad lace, and the fitted elbow-length sleeves ended in ruffles.

At another time Sarah might have made an entirely new dress for her wedding. Or she would at least have refreshed this one with lace trimming or new ribbons on the sleeves. But the war had made fine cloth and such accessories scarce and, when available, extremely expensive. The wedding refreshments were modest for the same reason.

The Bentons and Willistons would spend the night at the Lyman house, and return home tomorrow. Sarah's mother would go to West Haven with the Willistons, and Mr. Williston would escort her the following day to Norwalk.

The house was more crowded than it had been for many a year. Sarah and David spent their wedding night in the best bed in the parlor.

The bride and groom were both tired and more than a little nervous by the time they found themselves alone together in bed. David initiated intimate contact gently, hesitantly, from which Sarah judged this was likely his first time, as it was hers. The joining had been awkward, a little bit painful for her. Her body had barely begun to respond before it was over.

They'd fallen into an exhausted sleep for several hours. Sarah awoke to the arousal of David tenderly fondling her breast. She turned to him. There was no more sense of urgency.

David ran his fingers through Sarah's long hair, as smooth and soft as corn silk. Sarah's hands traced his hard, muscular body from shoulders to waist and lower. They continued the slow and sensual explorations until both were burning with desire and need. At last they came together again in the velvet darkness of the May night.

Nothing in the lingering kisses or occasional caresses Sarah had exchanged with David or other suitors had prepared her for what came next: the rapture that could result when a man and a woman lay together. She was astonished when the rhythmic uniting of their bodies drove her to an intensely pleasurable, pulsating climax that stripped her of control, mind and body, then left her breathless, her heart pounding.

The realization that this time had given Sarah as much pleasure as it had him gratified David. He kissed his wife on the lips, not hungrily, but tenderly, then rolled onto his back. Sarah nestled against his side.

Sarah thought of the nights to come when they would learn more of the power of a man and woman to give and receive carnal pleasure. They would indulge in the delight of their two bodies becoming one flesh – and, she prayed, create the children they both yearned for.

Chapter Thirty-Three

September, 1777
Middlefield

The warmth of the Lyman kitchen was welcome on the cool, drizzly morning of September 12. Sarah removed the metal door to the bake oven in the back of the fireplace. She deftly slid a peel under a tin pudding pan, and pulled it to the mouth of the oven.

Sarah had made her mother's recipe for Indian pudding so many times she knew automatically how much cornmeal, milk, eggs, raisins, butter, spices, and sugar to use. She'd had the four months since her marriage to learn the peculiarities of the Lyman kitchen's oven, so she wasn't surprised that the hour and a half she'd estimated for baking had resulted in pudding of exactly the right light golden color.

Sarah turned to Hope, who was examining a piece of beef roasting on a spit on the hearth. "Mother Lyman, does this look like it's ready to come out?" she asked.

Hope stepped over to the oven. She studied the pudding, appreciatively inhaling its hot aroma. "It could use a few more minutes," she said judiciously, then returned to the meat. With a small nod of thanks for the advice, Sarah slid the pan back in and replaced the door.

Sarah gathered up pewter plates, forks, knives, and spoons, and carried them into the hall to set the table. She almost collided with a damp David. He'd just come in the hall door in anticipation of the mid-day meal. He studied his wife with amused appreciation, then leaned down to whisper in her ear.

"I wager you've baked more Indian pudding than you can remember. Yet you needed Mama's opinion?" David teased, then pulled back far enough to see Sarah's face.

Sarah flushed, like a child caught in a fib. "Sometimes it's wise to ask for advice before it's offered," she replied in a low voice. "I've learned that if you let people have their way in small things they're more likely to be agreeable on more important matters."

David affectionately tucked a few stray strands of hair behind Sarah's ear. He'd watched with admiration as Sarah, through many such small acts of deference, had helped Hope grow comfortable with her new, unknown, unexpected daughter-in-law.

At the same time, Sarah had demonstrated on a daily basis her competence in housewifery. She had also come to genuinely admire Hope's strength and ability. What had evolved, to David's enormous relief, was genuine respect between the two women.

As he did every morning, David awoke in the pre-dawn darkness on Saturday, September 13. He didn't need a cock's crow to rouse him from sleep. He seemed to have an internal clock that enabled him to awaken any time he wished – in contrast to Sarah, who usually slept soundly until roused by a firm shake of her shoulder.

David folded his arms behind his head and stared up into the darkness, recalling the previous night's pleasure of lying with the woman he was fortunate enough to have made his wife. Joining with her, feeling her flesh respond to his with equal passion and abandon, was intensely satisfying.

David began to mentally plan out the day's work – only to have a cloud of despair descend upon his thoughts. It took him but a moment to identify the source: it was a year ago today that Phineas had died.

The terrible memories David had succeeded in pushing into the dark recesses of his mind came rushing back. Adding to his anguish was the fact that, more than a year after his capture, Elihu was still a prisoner of the British, his release nowhere in sight.

David turned onto his side and wrapped his arm around Sarah below her breasts. He pulled himself close against her so that his chest touched her back. He lay his cheek on the softness of her hair, seeking from her simple presence the comfort she'd provided after Phineas's death.

The weight of David's arm and the feel of his body against hers woke Sarah. In his cuddling embrace, devoid of sexual tension, she sensed a need for consolation. She had anticipated it, and had made a special plan for this mournful anniversary.

Sarah reached up to take David's hand, then guided it downward over her linen shift. David was dismayed that she'd misinterpreted his need for comfort through physical contact as a desire for sex.

But Sarah didn't direct David's hand to her loins as he expected. Instead, she stopped at her abdomen, and whispered back over her shoulder in the darkness, "Your child is growing in there."

Sarah felt David start at her revelation. "Are you sure?" he asked uncertainly.

"Yes," Sarah replied reassuringly. She hadn't yet consulted a midwife, nor brought Hope into her confidence, for she'd wanted David to be the first to know. But she'd learned much from her mother's many pregnancies, and understood her own body well enough, to be certain of the meaning of the changes she'd recently experienced.

David tightened his embrace as he placed his palm gently against Sarah's abdomen, stroking it tenderly with his thumb. He struggled to absorb the astounding fact that he was to become a father.

"It should be born sometime in spring – probably May," Sarah said. "If it's a boy, we should name him Phineas. Your brother was a brave man and a faithful servant of the Lord. A nephew bearing his name would honor him."

Sarah felt David nod in agreement. He raised himself up on his elbow, leaned over and kissed her gently on the cheek. "Thank you," he said, his voice husky with love and gratitude.

Chapter Thirty-Four

May, 1778
Middlefield

Hope bent over to cut a firm stalk of green asparagus, then added it to the dozen spears already in her basket. After months of eating the last of the previous year's crop of potatoes and turnips, dried fruit, and other preserved foods, anything fresh-picked would be a treat. Asparagus was one of the earliest foods to emerge in spring, and this was the first of the season. Hope would boil the tasty stalks and serve them with the chicken she had roasting on the spit in the fireplace.

Hope was enjoying having the kitchen all to herself, which rarely happened since David and Sarah's marriage a year ago. Eight days earlier, on May 3, Sarah had given birth to her first child, a robust girl. Hope had suggested to David that they call the baby Esther in memory of the beloved daughter and sister. But they'd named her Mary for the sister Sarah had lost soon after Phineas died.

Hope had accepted the new parents' decision without comment. Sarah was amenable on so many issues that Hope was more than willing that she have her way on something so close to her heart.

As was common with first babies, the travail had been long, but fortunately not unusually difficult. Sarah, blessed with a sturdy constitution, had passed safely through the dangerous days immediately after birth, when illness, particularly child-bed fever, was most likely to set in. Sarah's milk had come in, and she was nursing the baby with ease.

As was the custom, Sarah would spend the month after the birth confined to her bed. For those few weeks Hope would once again be sole mistress of her hearth.

Although she hadn't said so to David, Hope thought he'd done well selecting a wife. Sarah was devout, capable, hard-working, respectful, and even-tempered. She'd brought what David assured Hope was a respectable marriage portion – although to his mother's annoyance he'd refused to provide her specifics. And Sarah had just passed a wife's most important test by bearing a healthy child.

Sarah and David still gave every indication of being very much in love. Their relationship had not been, as Hope had cynically suspected when David sprang the news of their engagement, an infatuation between a man callow in affairs of the heart and a woman desperate to snare a husband.

Hope still had twinges of resentment that Sarah had a claim on David's attention. But she felt no such jealousy for the baby. David had adored Mary from the moment of her birth, and Hope shared his feelings for this grandchild, her second, but the first member of the third generation of Lymans to live on this land.

"Mama."

That single word, spoken by a man behind her, sent a cold shiver racing up Hope's spine. The knife fell from her fingers.

The voice was Elihu's – but that was impossible. He was still a prisoner in New York, with no prospect of release.

Hope straightened up slowly, afraid to turn around. If no one was there, it would prove that more than a year of death, sorrow, worry, and uncertainty had at last overtaxed her brain, causing her to hallucinate what she so desperately longed for.

Then she felt a hand on her shoulder, applying gentle pressure to make her body turn, until she at last beheld Elihu. He looked haggard, and had aged more than the two and a half years that had passed since she'd last seen him. He was dressed in a motley outfit of worn and dusty civilian clothes. A large bundle lay at his feet.

Hope stared warily, still fearful her mind was playing tricks. Elihu read the disbelief in her eyes. His lips turned up in a poignant smile of understanding. "It's really me, Mama," he said gently.

Hope threw herself into Elihu's arms with a cry of gladness. She broke into tears of joy and nearly hysterical laughter, hugging her son with a fierceness born of prayer finally, unexpectedly, miraculously answered.

"No, I didn't escape," Elihu answered David with a shake of his head. David was still recovering from the shock of having his brother appear as if conjured up by a magician.

Elihu was perched on the edge of a chair in the kitchen, his knees bent, leaning forward. He absently rolled a mug of cider back and forth between his palms, then took a large gulp of the beverage Hope had fetched from a barrel in the cellar.

David sat across from Elihu. Hope stood by in silence, letting David ask the questions, while she simply reveled in the sight of the son who, in her darkest moments, she'd thought of as another sacrifice to the Lord.

"Not that I couldn't have escaped – just walked away – and was sorely tempted to at times," Elihu went on. "But doing so would have broken my parole, violated my solemn oath and my honor as an officer. It would have given the British an excuse to revoke the paroles of officers still held prisoner, confine them more closely, treat them more harshly," he said bitterly.

"Then how did you come to be here?" David asked.

Elihu stood abruptly, walked over to the fireplace and placed his mug upon the mantelpiece. "It came from out of the blue," he began. "We got word on May 3 that there was to be an exchange of officers. I put no stock in it, for prisoner exchanges are scarce as hen's teeth.

"Three days later we were ordered to pack and be ready to leave," Elihu continued. "Still I wouldn't let myself believe we might be going home. I expected it to be a repeat of the time when we were moved to prison ships to keep us out of reach of American raiders who crossed the Sound from Connecticut to try to rescue us."

Elihu wet his lips with a sip of cider, then began walking back and forth in front of David and Hope. "We New England officers were put aboard a sloop, and set sail. Only then did I let myself hope.

"The next day we came in sight of the Connecticut coast. Seeing the clapboard houses, the fields, the meetinghouses of home filled me with a happiness I can't describe. We were let off on the docks at New Haven, and I walked the rest of the way home.

"So you see why I couldn't let you know I was coming. There was no time to send a letter, and if there had been it likely wouldn't have gotten here before I did." He stopped, and looked a bit mischievously at both David and Hope. "And the expressions on your faces when you first beheld me I will treasure to the end of my days," he finished with a satisfied grin.

"Your comrade Lieutenant Fitch wrote us after his release in November," David said. "He told of your capture and abuse by the Hessians. Such savagery is unbelievable."

"Believe it," Elihu said flatly. He strode back to the fireplace for his mug, then over to the window. He gazed out for a moment before turning back to David. "It's only through God's mercy that I wasn't bludgeoned to death or crippled for life." Hope inhaled sharply.

"The British eventually treated the commissioned officers well enough," Elihu said for his mother's sake. Then he curled his lip and added with a dry, sardonic laugh, "They didn't do so out of humanity or honor. It was because they knew if we were mistreated their officers in American hands might suffer. And it was always possible they might want to use us as chits to trade."

Elihu sat down for a second in the chair he'd vacated, then got immediately to his feet and began to pace agitatedly. "It is true we weren't locked up once we signed our paroles. But we were no less prisoners for that," he said.

"It was humiliating – like being a small child again," Elihu went on bitterly. "We couldn't say certain things aloud, only whisper them to each other. We could write only what would meet with our captors' approval. We had to live where they told us–."

A quavering squall cut Elihu off. He stopped pacing.

"My granddaughter calls," Hope said with a grin of delight unlike any he'd ever seen on her face. She hurried off to the parlor.

Elihu looked at David, whose own smile was, if possible, even broader than their mother's. He radiated happiness and pride.

"I was stunned when I got your letter saying you were married," Elihu said, starting to walk again. "I couldn't imagine how you triumphed over Mama in your wish to wed," he went on, half-admiring, half-teasing. His expression grew somber. "And at times I despaired of ever hearing the story from your own lips."

Elihu came to an abrupt stop directly in front of David. He looked his brother squarely in the eye. "How did he die?" There was no question who "he" was.

David reluctantly resurrected the horrible memory of Phineas's death from the dark corner of his mind where he'd largely succeeded in burying it. As he told the story to Elihu in a low voice, he kept glancing toward the direction of the parlor. He didn't want Hope to return unexpectedly and overhear the gruesome details he'd never shared with her.

When David finished, Elihu's face was a taught white mask. "I suspected from the careful way Mama worded her letter that his death was connected to the battle. But I didn't expect it to be so horrible." He was silent for a long moment. "Still, it may have been a blessing. His fate could have been much worse as a British prisoner."

David stared incredulously at his brother, reeling at the degree of cruelty Elihu's remark implied. Elihu responded with a weary wave of his hand.

"Someday I'll describe to you the torments of the damned enlisted men endure in captivity. Then you'll understand why I speak as I do. But not now. I just hope to one day have a chance to repay the British and their stinking Hessian hirelings." He paused, then added in a voice laced with venom, "And Tory traitors."

Elihu's eyes glittered with hatred. "Major Hierlihy–," he began, spitting out the name like something vile, "sought me out about six weeks after I was captured. He urged me to join him and Tim in their treason. If I'd known then about Phineas's death, I don't think I could have kept myself from trying to kill them with my bare hands."

"He left his wife and children behind to pay the price for his treachery," David told Elihu with disgust. "They are scorned and shunned. The state confiscated all his property, leaving them without a roof over their heads or any means of support. Her family has helped them, else they would have starved."

"One more betrayal of innocents to add to his account," Elihu said bitterly. He abruptly strode over to the kitchen window and looked out, as if half-expecting – or hoping – that Major Hierlihy would materialize.

The months as a prisoner of war had changed Elihu in a fundamental way, David realized. The manner in which his brother had roamed – no, prowled – the kitchen while he told his story was more than his natural restlessness. It had a disturbing edginess, as if Elihu weren't comfortable remaining in one spot for too long, lest he find himself again confined, as he'd been for months on end.

Elihu drew a deep breath to steady himself. He swept the bitter memories from his mind and turned his thoughts toward satisfying the greatest of his longings. "I trust I can borrow a horse to ride to Durham," he said with a passion he knew David could now fully appreciate.

"Be my guest," David said genially.

With a quick nod, Elihu pushed open the kitchen door. He ran to the barn, quickly saddled a horse, then pounded down the road to Durham.

As he rode, fears and doubts Elihu had fought to keep at bay while a prisoner began to worm their way into his thoughts. Had

Esther really remained true to him? Or had she accepted the advances of men who wouldn't make her wait forever for the marriage, children, and home for which she yearned? Had she continued to send Elihu messages of love and devotion out of patriotic pity, to sustain the spirits of a soldier who would likely die in captivity? The thoughts tortured Elihu as he galloped toward Durham, to learn if his long-awaited homecoming would bring the joy of which he'd so often dreamed – or devastating disappointment.

Elihu knocked sharply on the door of the Camp house. The scrape of a metal latch being lifted was followed by the door swinging open to reveal Esther.

The color drained from Esther's face at the sight of Elihu. She stared in disbelief – and fear, for she thought she might well be looking at a ghost.

Esther looked so pale and shaky that Elihu thought she might faint. He stepped forward to gather her in his arms. He bent her backwards with a kiss into which he channeled twenty pent-up months of passion denied.

Esther wrapped her arms around Elihu's neck, savoring the longed-for embrace, the delicious urgency of his lips on hers, surrendering herself to the bliss of a moment she'd feared would never come. Elihu closed his eyes and pressed Esther more tightly against him, as if he might meld their bodies together into a single being that could never again be separated.

Elihu didn't know how long they remained locked in their rapturous embrace. He didn't want to open his eyes, didn't want to let Esther go, afraid this reunion would turn out to be a dream, as it had countless times, from which he would awaken to the bleak despair of captivity.

At last their lips parted, but Elihu continued to hold Esther. He drew his head back far enough to look into her blue eyes, glistening with tears, and to rejoice in the dazzled smile that eased his doubts.

"In my darkest moments as a prisoner, when even my faith in the Lord wavered, your love sustained me," Elihu said, his voice husky with passion. "The thought that I might never see you again frightened me more than the threat of death." He gave Esther another long and tender kiss before continuing.

"There will be no more waiting, no more delay. I'll have the banns posted as soon as possible. We'll wed within a month."

"The sooner the better," Esther said, then kissed Elihu with an ardor so fierce it burned the last lingering doubts from his mind.

With Sarah and the baby settled, Elihu off to be reunited with Esther Camp, and David back working in the barn, Hope sought some time alone to master her surging emotions. She walked up the long slope to the crest of Powder Ridge.

She faced eastward, the sun at her back just beginning to decline from its zenith. Spread out before her was the gentle grandeur of the Connecticut countryside, the panorama of rippling hills and shallow valleys that was the only world she'd ever known.

To the south houses along Durham's main street were set against the backdrop of a distant ridge that was a twin to the one on which she stood, forming the valley through which the Coginchaug River meandered. To the north she could glimpse the spire of Christ Church on Middletown's main street and sparkling blue patches of the Connecticut River. Farther in the distance she could make out the profiles of steep mountains in Massachusetts, including Mount Tom in John's birthplace of Northampton.

Immediately before her was a patchwork of fields, homelots, houses, barns, and woodlands. Fledgling foliage was emerging in shades of pale green, light red, and bronze, mixed with the gray of trunks and branches of some still-leafless trees. The orchard on the hillside below was afroth with white apple blossoms. Over all stretched a sky of robin's-egg blue, streaked with wispy clouds so high they cast no shadow on the earth.

For fifteen years Hope had dreaded the approach of May, for it was the month in which her first baby, then their second son, then John had died. Elihu's return this day, almost as if from the grave, following the birth of her granddaughter, had brought new joy sufficient to disperse the mournful shadows that for so long had darkened the month for her.

A fresh gust from the west sent Hope's skirt and hair wrapping around her, almost as if in an embrace. She closed her eyes, felt the warmth of the sun on her skin, breathed in the pleasantly pungent smell of nature renewing itself – and offered fervent thanks to God for giving her back the glorious promise of May.

Chapter Thirty-Five

November, 1778
West Haven, Connecticut

For the third time in three years, death had claimed one of Hope's children. She watched numbly as four men lowered the wooden coffin into the freshly dug grave in the West Haven burying ground. The pastor of the White Haven Church in New Haven prayed as the mortal remains of Hannah Lyman Williston, just thirty-five, were consigned to the earth.

Hannah had died the previous day – November 4. Ten days earlier she'd developed a fever, chills, a fearsome headache, and extreme fatigue.

Noah Williston had summoned Hope from the Benton home in North Guilford. She spent more and more time there now that Elihu and Esther, who'd wed as soon as possible after his return from captivity, had moved in with David and Sarah in Middlefield. Not long after Hope arrived in West Haven, Hannah's hands began to tremble with palsy, and her sight and hearing started to fail.

Hope had frantically sent for Elihu, who reached West Haven on the fifth day of Hannah's illness, just as she began to break out in a hectic purplish rash that he diagnosed all too easily. As a soldier and a prisoner, Elihu had seen countless cases of hospital fever. Although the disease was most commonly found in military encampments, it easily spread into civilian populations – how, no one knew.

Despite the ministrations of Elihu and several other physicians, Hannah had deteriorated with shocking speed – and in a most horrible manner. Her once-fair skin started to peel and her lovely hair fell out – almost as if the decay that would turn her flesh back into the dust from whence it came couldn't wait until she was dead to begin its gruesome work.

Noah Williston stood on the opposite side of the grave from Hope, flanked by his four children. How deeply Mr. Williston mourned his cherished wife of just six years was evident from the grooves grief had cut into his haggard face. Several prominent ministers had conducted the funeral services for Hannah, as was befitting the wife of such a well-regarded clergyman as Noah Williston.

Hope's gaze strayed to Catharine beside her, then dropped to little Lyman Beecher, pressed close against his aunt's skirts, holding tightly to her hand. The sorrowful graveside scene understandably frightened the boy, just turned three. But the grieving adults knew a child was never too young to learn that death could come for anyone at any time, making it imperative to make sure one's soul was always prepared for the Lord's judgment.

David Beecher still hadn't reclaimed his son from the Bentons. Lyman was a handsome boy, with Esther's thick, dark hair and deep brown eyes, and a nose that showed promise of developing into the long, sharp feature found on so many Lyman faces.

Hope shifted her gaze back to the coffin. Like Catharine, Hannah's womb had never quickened with a child; although she never ceased praying that she might bear Noah a baby. Hope knew Hannah's barrenness had for a time diminished her daughter's sense of triumph over her marriage. But Noah had never reproached Hannah for her childlessness.

Noah's unwavering devotion had affected Hannah deeply. Hope had been gladdened – and relieved – to see a warm mutual affection develop between the couple, as she had predicted might happen when Catharine had expressed doubts about the union that day in the Benton kitchen.

Hope had also admired the way Hannah committed herself to being a devoted parent to the four stepchildren she'd originally viewed as unavoidable inconveniences. How well she'd succeeded could be read in the pathetically sad expressions of Noah's children, the eldest not sixteen, grieving the loss of a beloved mother for the second time in their lives. Hannah had grown steadily in grace and love, Hope reflected, making her spirit far more beautiful than the physical charms of which she'd been so proud.

The services concluded, some of the mourners began to leave, but Hope remained at the grave's edge. She stared down at Hannah's coffin, already disappearing beneath the dirt the sexton was energetically shoveling back into the hole. Her family stood on either side of her, even as a light drizzle began to fall from the leaden November sky.

At last Hope lifted her head. She turned to fix her gaze on Elihu, the son once thought lost but miraculously restored to her just six months ago. "'The Lord giveth,'" she quoted from the Biblical Book of Job. Then she turned her eyes back to the grave, and said in a voice heavy with grief, "'And the Lord taketh away.'"

Hope stood for another long moment, seemingly oblivious to the rain that was now mixing with sleet. Finally she said in a choked voice, "'Blessed be the name of the Lord.'" She turned abruptly and walked away from the grave, her family hastening to catch up with her.

Chapter Thirty-Six

April, 1779
North Guilford

Hope glanced up from the nightshirt she was stitching for Lyman Beecher to watch two men pulling a cart of firewood to the woodpile behind Mr. Bray's barn. She was sitting with a dozen other women outside the minister's house, spinning, knitting, sewing, and enjoying the soft spring temperature. They occasionally looked up to watch the group of men felling trees on the pastor's woodlot, then cutting and splitting them into firewood. By day's end they would have enough to supply Mr. Bray's household for the coming year, as part of the North Guilford congregation's agreed-upon compensation to him.

After working strenuously much of the morning in the April warmth, most of the men had stripped off their shirts. Hope let her gaze rest on one of them, Theophilus Leete. He was a good-looking man in his late fifties, whose lifetime of labor on his farm had kept him trim and muscular. His full head of chestnut hair was shot through with just enough gray to hint at his true age.

Leete had buried his second wife the previous winter, a fact that not so long ago would have been of little interest to Hope. But living much of the past year in the same house with David and Sarah and Elihu and Esther, two sets of newlyweds deeply in love, had stirred in Hope emotions she'd thought long dead. She'd found herself yearning for the companionship, emotional and physical, missing from her life since John's passing.

A sharp sting made Hope's left hand jerk. She'd jabbed her sewing needle far enough into the tip of her index finger to draw a bright red drop of blood. She put the finger in her mouth to staunch the bleeding, and looked around to see if anyone had noticed. Rachel Fowler, seated to Hope's right, was looking at her with a knowing smile of affectionate amusement.

Hope responded to Rachel's expression with an embarrassed shrug. She removed her finger from her mouth, and once she was sure the bleeding had stopped, resumed sewing.

"Perhaps you shouldn't handle anything sharper than a spoon when Theophilus Leete is around," Rachel teased.

Hope smiled at the remark from this short, delicate, gray-haired woman of about sixty. Hope had seen much of Rachel and her husband Daniel of late, since their daughter was married to Lot Benton's brother.

Rachel Fowler had the sweetest nature of anyone Hope had ever known – save for her dear, departed daughter Esther. A few of the older North Guilford wives, feeling threatened by the attractive widow visiting the Benton home with increasing frequency, had treated Hope with frosty politeness. But Rachel Fowler wasn't one of them, and it was easy to understand why. Daniel Fowler was a good-looking, stocky man with unusually courtly manners for a farmer. He had befriended Hope as well. But one had to spend only a short time with the couple to see that Daniel had eyes only for his Rachel. After more than thirty-five years of marriage, his face still lit up when she came into a room. The affection and trust between them was evident.

"Theophilus Leete asked me to marry him last night," Hope confided in a low voice. Rachel's face flushed with excitement that faded when Hope shook her head.

"I don't intend to accept," Hope said.

"Why not?" Rachel asked. "You've been alone for so many years, Hope – it's not natural for a woman." There was no criticism, only concern, in her voice.

Hope shrugged. "Mr. Leete is smart and good-looking, and a decent man," she said, "and he proclaims affection for me. But he's not sensible to the feelings of others."

Hope struggled for a way to illustrate her impression. "He puts me in mind of an arm that's become numb after being slept on. He feels shallow prickles, but nothing deeply." She didn't add that she had the distinct impression that Leete viewed marriage to her as primarily a shrewd deal – like acquiring a healthy, handsome older mare with many good years of service left.

Marriage to Hope would be an even better bargain than Leete could imagine, she thought wryly. David had realized that so long as she lived his mother wouldn't give him the house and farm; they would come to him only upon Hope's death. In February he'd purchased the property from Hope, with funds that in part came from Sarah's marriage portion. The sum she'd received was enough to make Hope an attractive marital prize from a financial perspective. Realizing that, she hadn't told anyone, even Catharine and Lot, about the sale.

Rachel knew Hope well enough by now to realize it was futile to try to change her mind. "I don't know how you've endured being a widow for so long," was all she said.

"I didn't plan it so," Hope began haltingly. "It just turned out that way. At first there were no suitors – few men are eager to wed a widow with six children and an insolvent estate to settle," she said with a sharp, caustic laugh.

"When my circumstances improved, none who came courting were men into whose hands I could in good conscience entrust my future and that of my children. I took heart from my mother's example – she never married after my father died, but ran a farm and raised her children on her own. And, I confess, I took satisfaction in what I was able to do for my family. Most men would call that unseemly pride in a woman," she said. There wasn't a hint of regret in her voice.

"It took great love and courage to carry on alone because you thought it best for your family," Rachel said admiringly. "I never could have done so," she admitted honestly.

Hope suspected Rachel spoke the truth. Rachel was no stranger to personal affliction – she'd buried two children and lived with the anxiety of having a son in military service. But she'd had the support and comfort of her husband throughout these trials.

"Your situation is different now," Rachel went on. "Your children are as safely settled in this world as can be hoped for. You can do what you think best for yourself now."

Hope gave a slightly sardonic laugh. "You're correct about my children being settled – most of them in the same house with me." She grew serious before continuing.

"My sons have found good wives, who are dutiful, respectful daughters-in-law," Hope said sincerely. "But three women sharing one hearth is not a recipe for harmony. After thirty-five years, I'm no longer mistress of my own home," she admitted wistfully.

There was a long silence, as Hope resumed her stitching and Rachel her knitting. "I would consider marrying again – if the right man presented himself," Hope said. "Although I would feel guilty about leaving David with the burden of running the farm without me." Hope might no longer hold legal title to the Lyman land, but she would always consider it her responsibility.

"What would you seek in the 'right man'?" Rachel asked. She tactfully refrained from commenting on Hope's concern about David's ability to manage the farm alone.

Hope thought back to that day when she and Catharine had clashed over Hannah's feelings for Noah Williston. "John and I shared a powerful love," she said quietly, her features softening at the memory. "To be so blessed once is rare. I'm not so foolish as to expect to find it again. But I would require friendship, trust, and respect from a man I might think to wed.

"For fifteen years I refused to marry just any man for the sake of relieving myself of a heavy burden of responsibilities. I won't now marry the first man who offers just to escape a household where things are no longer to my liking," she concluded resolutely.

Rachel nodded sympathetically, concealing her concern for her friend. Most widows in their twilight years would gladly settle for security, command of their own hearth, and decent treatment from a husband. Rachel suspected few men would be willing to accord a wife the level of consideration and independence that the self-assured, strong-willed Hope would require.

Chapter Thirty-Seven

May, 1779
North Guilford

Hope measured out a large spoonful of salt then stirred it into a cup of sweet oil. She turned to speak to Daniel Fowler. He was bending over the foot of the bed in his parlor, to which his Rachel had been confined since an attack of apoplexy three weeks earlier.

It was the last week of May. Many neighbors had rallied to the Fowler family's aid after Rachel was stricken. Hope, with more free time than most, had spent as many hours as possible helping Daniel and his sickly twenty-three-year-old spinster daughter, Polly, care for Rachel.

Hope glanced sorrowfully at her ailing friend. Rachel had been left paralyzed on her right side by the seizure, which had struck her down without warning as she ironed clothes. Most victims of an apoplexy died quickly. Of those who survived the attack, few ever recovered fully.

Mixed with Hope's sadness was selfish disappointment. This past week she'd finally given Theophilus Leete her answer to his marriage proposal. Supremely certain of his desirability, Leete had been completely unprepared for Hope's polite refusal. He was more disbelieving than disappointed, and Hope sensed he'd be back to ask again. She desperately wished she could discuss the situation with the insightful Rachel.

Daniel finished applying a blistering plaster to Rachel's right calf, then carefully pulled the linen sheet over the limb. He straightened up stiffly. His craggy features were haggard, his usually bright blue eyes dulled by fatigue and worry.

Hope's regard for Daniel had grown, as she'd watched him tend to Rachel with patience and devotion. He'd neglected his spring chores and, Hope feared, endangered his own health in order to spend as much time as possible with his ailing wife. He assisted with administration of the unpleasant plasters and other treatments the physicians recommended. He helped keep Rachel clean and neat. He talked lovingly to Rachel, even as the awareness in her eyes faded. And he prayed

"Daniel, please get some rest," Hope urged. "Polly can help me administer this clyster." She indicated the mixture in the cup, which the physician had directed to be administrated rectally to evacuate the patient's bowels. "After that I'll sit with her until midnight, and then I'll wake you – I promise."

Daniel nodded his agreement. With a cloth he gently wiped away some saliva that had trickled from a corner of the unconscious Rachel's mouth. He tenderly kissed her on the lips. "Good night," he whispered, although he knew she couldn't hear him. "I won't be long away from your side."

Watching the poignant scene, Hope was unexpectedly overcome with an intense longing to be the recipient of Daniel Fowler's tender affection. She quickly averted her face so he wouldn't see her horrified shame.

"I'll send Polly in," Daniel said. Hope nodded, staring into the cup as she busied herself stirring the clyster. When he reached the doorway Daniel stopped to look back over his shoulder at Hope. "The Lord truly blessed me and Rachel when He brought you into our lives."

Mustering every last shred of self-control, Hope glanced up at Daniel only long enough to acknowledge his words with a quick, tight smile and a short nod. He walked out of the room, leaving Hope to stew frantically over her covetous desire – unbidden, unwelcome, and already gone – for her friend's husband.

Chapter Thirty-Eight

December, 1779
North Guilford

Lot Benton and Lyman Beecher came into the kitchen of the Benton house on a blast of cold air. Catharine helped the little boy out of his coat, hat, and mittens, then gave him a hug and rubbed his hands briskly to warm them up. She smiled as her thoughts flashed back to doing the same for Elihu when he'd been Lyman's age.

"I showed Lyman how to break flax," Lot told Catharine, stepping over to warm his own hands at the massive stone fireplace. Catharine shot him a worried look. Breaking flax, one of the steps required to turn the plant into linen fiber, involved placing stalks between two hinged sets of wooden blades and slamming the top set down hard to crush them – or a finger or hand if one was careless.

"I didn't let him use the flax break by himself," Lot reassured Catharine. Lyman had just turned four; too small still to handle such a chore himself, but old enough to start learning the process.

"It was fun, Aunt Benton," Lyman assured her. "I untied the bundles of flax and gave them to Uncle Lot to break."

Catharine smiled at the boy's enthusiasm for getting to work with Lot. She fretted over Lyman's well-being constantly, but Lot acted as a brake on the protectiveness that otherwise could turn Lyman into a sheltered, timid child.

Although rarely sick, Lyman was thin, and Catharine had somehow gotten it into her head that the boy was weakly. "Go on into the milk room and get a piece of cake," she told him. Lyman gladly scooted off to obey.

Lot saw that Catharine was almost trembling with suppressed excitement. "My mother says Daniel Fowler is coming to call on her this afternoon," she told him. "She thinks he may ask her to marry him."

"Imagine that," Lot said laconically. "Well, it's been six months since Rachel died," he observed philosophically. Rachel Fowler had lingered in her pitiable condition until late June, when God in His mercy took her to Him.

A note in Lot's voice that only Catharine would catch made her look sharply at him. "Do you know something?" she asked, narrowing her eyes in suspicion.

"What would I know about Daniel's intentions?" Lot said in a manner that suggested he did indeed have information of interest.

"Tell me," Catharine insisted.

"Well, Daniel asked me a few questions about Mother Lyman," Lot admitted, with a glint in his gray eyes. When he said nothing further Catharine demanded, "What questions?"

"He wanted to know what it's like to live with Mother Lyman, since she's been here at our house so much of late."

"What did you tell him?" Catharine asked anxiously.

"The truth," Lot answered, with a look of wide-eyed innocence, as if there could be no other answer.

"Lot!" Catharine cried in exasperation, stamping her foot like a temperamental child. Lot couldn't hold back his grin any longer. He rarely subjected Catharine to the obstinance with which he treated most of the world. But he hadn't been able to resist teasing her a bit in this case.

"I told him she was usually agreeable, although a woman of strong opinions and sometimes stubborn," Lot began. Catharine waited uncertainly for him to continue.

"I said her deep faith is a comfort to us all," Lot said in all seriousness. "And that I've never known a woman with a warmer heart, nor one more dedicated to her family."

Catharine relaxed, and studied her husband with affection. She kissed him quickly on the cheek, then mussed his hair mischievously in retaliation for making her drag the information out of him.

That afternoon, when they were alone in the Benton hall, Daniel Fowler took Hope's hand in his. His touch was by now familiar and comfortable to her.

The weeks after Rachel's death had been particularly difficult for Daniel, worn out from endless days of devoted care and adjusting to the void in his life created by her loss. Hope had applied the lessons from her own experience to helping him heal.

Thankfully, Hope had experienced no repeat of the shameful emotion she'd felt for Daniel in May. Her guilt over that episode had faded.

As autumn turned to winter, the relationship between Hope and Daniel had taken a romantic turn. Hope drew pleasure from Daniel's company, the respect with which he treated her whether they were alone or with others. They fit well together, was the best way Hope could describe the connection between them. And she had rediscovered the delightful sensation of being the object of not only a man's attentions but of his passion – and feeling them for him in return.

"You become dearer to me with each passing day," Daniel was saying. "You treated my wounded heart with the balm of understanding consolation that could have been provided only by someone who's lost a beloved partner, and who herself cherished my Rachel. And I've come to find much more than comfort in your company." Daniel looked at Hope like a man seeing shafts of sunlight break through black clouds he'd feared would darken his world forever.

Hope looked into Daniel's bright blue eyes, in an attractively craggy face into which Rachel's death had etched new lines. "But I still mourn for her," Daniel continued, "and so hesitated to ask for your hand – until now."

Hope held her breath at Daniel's words, the first mention he'd made of Rachel's effect on their relationship. "What changed your mind?" she asked at last. She studied his sharp profile under its shock of silver hair.

"It was something that, in a way, Rachel herself said," Daniel said, with a rueful smile. Hope cocked a quizzical eyebrow but waited for him to continue.

"I received a letter of condolence from a nephew in Vermont who only lately learned of her passing. When he was still living in Guilford, his wife died before the first anniversary of their wedding. A year later he was still grieving for her so bitterly he couldn't pick up the threads of his life."

Daniel hesitated briefly before going on. "He wrote that Rachel asked him if he believed his wife was enjoying the eternal happiness

God prepares for the faithful. When he said he did, Rachel pointed out that his wife in Paradise had no need of his immoderate grief, but that it was harming him here on earth. And she bade him remember that Scripture tells us it is not good for a man to be alone."

Daniel paused again, reflecting on his late wife's advice. "Her nephew wrote he has always been grateful for Rachel's words of wisdom that day. They started him on the path to spiritual recovery that led to him marrying his current wife, with whom he's been very happy for many years.

"This helped me accept," Daniel continued, the words clearly still difficult to say, "that the flesh-and-blood Rachel I loved is gone forever, transported to everlasting joy. But my earthly needs didn't die with her, and I should look elsewhere for someone to fill them."

Daniel tenderly cupped Hope's cheek in his hand, his touch sending a tingle down her spine. "And so, at last, I feel I can ask – will you become my wife?" he finished in a voice that carried affection, desire – and need.

Hope's heart was full with the knowledge that those feelings were for her solely as a woman. She'd deliberately said nothing to Daniel about the property and money she possessed, and he'd never raised the subject. So far as Daniel knew, he was proposing marriage to a woman who owned little more than her clothes and whatever movables she still had out of her widow's third of John's estate.

"It's true as well," Hope said carefully, "that it is not good for a woman to be alone. Rachel herself had encouraged me to end my solitary state."

Daniel's eyes lit up. "Does that mean your answer is 'yes'?"

"I don't know!" Hope cried out in confusion. "I'm nothing like Rachel. Are you sure you can be content with a wife so different from the one who made you happy for nigh onto forty years?"

A bittersweet smile came to Daniel's lips. "My precious Rachel made me think of a violet nestled in the grass," he said, his eyes shifting from Hope's to gaze into the crackling fire. "She was gentle, sweet, fragile, in need of protection lest she be trampled by the blows life dealt her. I took great pleasure in safeguarding such a treasure from as much of the world's harshness as I could, and in comforting her when I couldn't.

"But you," he looked back to study Hope with affectionate appraisal. "You remind me of the mountain laurel – handsome, hardy, flourishing in shade and on rocky hillsides where many other plants can't survive." His fingers tenderly traced the outline of Hope's jaw; she closed her eyes for a heartbeat to revel in the pleasure of his touch.

"Yet for all its strength," Daniel continued, "the mountain laurel produces delicate blossoms that delight the eye. A woman with those qualities would be a fine partner for the winter of my life."

Hope blushed at the sweetness of Daniel's poetic response. She allowed a moment for the spell of his charm to fade before she spoke.

"If I had only myself to consider, I would accept you this very moment," Hope said slowly. "But I can't answer until I talk to my family. I must be sure I can in good conscience leave the farm in David's hands."

Daniel nodded. By now he understood Hope's justifiable pride in having seen her family through so many difficulties with little more than her faith in God and her sense of duty to sustain her. To point out that it was unlikely she was still important to the success of the Lyman farm would injure that pride. She must come to that realization on her own.

Daniel stood, and taking both Hope's hands in his pulled her to her feet. "To the considerations you'll weigh in making your decision, add this to the balance in my favor." He enveloped the startled Hope in muscular arms and bestowed upon her a long kiss full of tender passion, more intimate than any they'd exchanged before. It refreshed Hope's heart like a soaking spring rain on a field parched by sixteen years of drought.

Their lips parted, but Daniel still held Hope tight, their faces only inches apart.

"You're taking unfair advantage of me," Hope whispered when she caught her breath, but her protest was half-hearted.

Daniel smiled with satisfaction, and Hope saw a glint of triumph in his eyes. "I most certainly am," he agreed, then kissed her again.

Chapter Thirty-Nine

December, 1779
Middlefield

David laid two logs atop the roaring blaze in the kitchen fireplace, then sat back in a chair pulled as close to the hearth as was safe. The rest of the family was clustered around the fire, the sole source of heat and light on this night a week shy of the dawn of the year 1780. Candles were too costly for everyday illumination.

On the other side of the semi-circle around the fireplace sat Elihu and Esther. Elihu was slowly but steadily building up his medical practice, while also helping David work the farm. Almost a year after their marriage, Esther had at last conceived their first baby, expected sometime in April. Esther had spent this evening contentedly sewing a gown for the infant until straining to make stitches by the erratic firelight left her eyes too tired to see clearly.

Sarah, seated next to David, was cuddling their two-month-old son, Phineas. Every so often she would go to the parlor to check on eighteen-month-old Polly, as Mary was called, sleeping bundled up in the trundle bed beneath the one in which David and Sarah slept.

Between the two couples sat Hope, returned just that afternoon from a ten-day visit to North Guilford. Lot Benton had brought his mother-in-law home in a sleigh that had glided swiftly over the foot of snow that had fallen a week earlier.

"I fear it's going to be a fierce winter," David observed, leafing through the copy of *Bickerstaff's New-England Almanack* for 1780 he'd purchased a few days earlier. Despite the fire, the air was cold enough to condense his breath into vapor. "There's been no break in this cold since the middle of October, and no sign of it letting up.

When I was at the freemen's meeting, I saw the Connecticut River is frozen solid. It's been like that since the beginning of November."

"The winter before your father and I moved into this house was one of the harshest in memory," Hope commented in a remote voice. She didn't look up from her knitting.

David glanced curiously at his mother. She'd seemed preoccupied since returning from North Guilford. He suspected it had something to do with Daniel Fowler, with whom Catharine said Hope had spent increasing amounts of time the past few months.

David knew Catharine and Lot had a high opinion of Fowler. During David's own infrequent encounters with Fowler, most recently at Noah Williston's wedding to his third wife, he'd struck him as solid, intelligent, and good-natured.

David wondered if things had soured between his mother and Fowler, but he knew better than to ask. Whatever the development, Hope would share it with her family at a time of her own choosing.

David returned to the almanac, straining to read its small print by the flickering firelight. Suddenly he snorted in amusement. "Listen to this," he said to the others, then read aloud,

"'A gentleman happening to turn up against a house to make water did not see two young ladies looking out of a window close by till he heard them giggling. Then looking toward them, he asked what made them merry? 'Oh! Sir,' said one of them, 'a very little thing will make us laugh.'"

Sarah, Esther, and Elihu chuckled at this joke poking fun at men's well-known sensitivity about the size of a certain part of their anatomy. Hope didn't react; she seemed not to have heard anything going on around her. She sighed in irritation upon discovering a mistake in her knitting, and began ripping out stitches.

Hope dropped the needlework into her lap in frustration. Staring into the fire, she said, "Daniel Fowler asked me to marry him!"

David's eyebrows shot up in surprise. A glance at Sarah told him that to her the announcement wasn't unexpected. He supposed he should have seen it coming, too. But his mother marrying again had always seemed as unlikely as the Connecticut River drying up.

There followed a long silence, broken only by the crackling of the fire. "What was your answer, Mama?" Elihu asked at last.

Hope shook her head. "I didn't give him one."

"Do you care for him, Mother Lyman?" Sarah asked. Hope didn't take offense at the personal question, knowing Sarah's inquiry was motivated by sincere concern for her mother-in-law's happiness.

"I do," Hope answered confidently. "And I know he cares for me."

Hope looked at David, then Elihu. "It's not the same as it was with your father," she told them. "I'll never love another man as I did him. But Daniel has become a very dear friend. I could happily spend my remaining days as his wife. I've prayed for guidance, and I believe the Lord would smile on this marriage."

"Then why hesitate?" Sarah asked. "We would miss your company, your helping hands, but we can make do," she said with complete sincerity. Both she and Esther had decided Hope's virtues as a mother-in-law outweighed her faults. "And North Guilford isn't far away – almost as close as Durham, not nearly as far as Norwalk."

Hope shifted her gaze back to the fire, her furrowed brow signifying an internal struggle. "How will David manage the farm without me?" she demanded suddenly of no one and everyone. "How will he know when to go to mill, if I go off?"

Elihu gaped at his mother for a moment, then quickly turned his face away. He bit his lower lip to keep from laughing at Hope's concern that David, thirty-five, a husband and father of two, still needed his mother to remind him of his chores. Esther stared at Hope in disbelief. Sarah cast David a look of deep commiseration.

David was thankful his face was already red from the fire's heat, for it concealed his flush of mortification at his mother's question. He should have anticipated this, too, he thought. Even after he'd purchased the house and land from her, Hope had continued offering advice – sometimes welcome, sometimes not – on everything from planting peas to slaughtering hogs

"I'll get along. Mama," David said, managing to keep any trace of resentment or sarcasm out of his voice. "You don't need to put off doing what your heart and your prayers tell you is best."

Elihu turned a now completely sober face towards his mother. "David is right, Mama," he said. "You've sacrificed enough for us. Wed Daniel Fowler if that's what you truly want."

Hope's taut expression relaxed into one of relief. She relished having held her family together through years of adversity. But she was ready to relinquish the responsibilities she'd borne for so long. Her sons' words freed her to join her life to Daniel Fowler's.

Hope nodded, then her face brightened with a smile that made her look younger than her sixty-one years. "Then I'll accept Daniel's offer of marriage with a glad heart," she said with a deep contentment the others had only rarely heard from her.

Chapter Forty

May, 1780
Middlefield

"When I woke to thunder, I feared we'd have to ride to Middlefield in a downpour – or maybe put off coming altogether," Daniel Fowler told the small cluster of people in the Lyman hall. "But when the rain ceased at sunrise, we decided to proceed, even though the skies remained lowery."

From where he sat warming himself before the fireplace on the unseasonably cool morning. Daniel glanced over his shoulder at Hope. "Thankfully, the rain held off. You might have had second thoughts about exchanging vows with a soggy suitor." He gave her a mischievous wink.

"It would take far more than a soaking from a spring shower to keep me from wedding you this day," Hope replied tartly. "If you hadn't appeared by noon, I would have set out for North Guilford to fetch you myself."

Hope stepped toward Daniel and put her lips so close to his ear only he could hear her. "The deep snows and terrible cold of this winter have forced us to wait far too long for this day," she said tenderly. Daniel smiled, basking in Hope's affection.

For her marriage Hope wasn't dressed in the silk gown she'd worn first at Hannah's wedding, then at Esther's, David's, and Elihu's. This day, this union, would mark the opening of a new chapter in her life, one she hoped would be simpler and calmer than the past two tumultuous decades. As a token of that change, Hope had chosen to wear a dress newly made from woolen cloth woven from yarn she'd spun.

It was a new-style round gown – so-called because the skirt was fashioned from a solid piece of fabric rather than being split open in the front to display a contrasting petticoat. It featured a simple bodice with an untrimmed scoop neck and long, tight, wrist-length sleeves. Its warm russet color brought out the star-like splashes of golden brown that radiated from the depths of Hope's hazel eyes.

"So the bridegroom is here at last," David greeted Daniel as he came into the hall. "All we need is the minister. I expect he'll be here any minute." Abner Benedict had agreed to preside over the marriage.

But it was another hour before Mr. Benedict arrived – an hour during which the mood in the house changed from pleasant anticipation to growing apprehension. An enormous, ominous black cloud had rolled in shortly after Daniel's arrival, and now blanketed the sky from horizon to horizon.

The cloud blotted out the sun so completely it was as if night had fallen. It became impossible to recognize the features of a person standing more than a foot or two away. Through the window David saw wild birds and barnyard fowl settling down to roost as they did at day's end.

But this was nothing like the natural darkness after sunset. Outside swirling vapors cast a shining, eerie pallor, sometimes greenish, sometimes yellow, over everything.

"I'll light candies until this gloom passes," Sarah said with a calm she didn't truly feel. She was grateful that both Polly and Phineas had gone down for their naps a short while ago, sparing her the need to soothe their fear of the mysterious darkness.

Sarah slid open the lid of the candle box and took out two tapers. She lit them from the flames in the fireplace, inserted each into a short pewter candlestick, then put one at each end of the long table along a wall of the hall. The additional light allowed Sarah to see the worry on Catharine's face, not for herself but for Lyman Beecher. She and Lot had left the four-year-old boy, who was recovering from chicken pox, with Lot's family in North Guilford.

"Could this be an eclipse?" Daniel's daughter Polly asked in a strained voice.

"I don't think so," said Lot. "The almanac didn't predict one. Any eclipse I've seen covers only the face of the sun or the moon – not the entire sky." The uneasy silence that followed was broken by the three notes of a whippoorwill's call – a distinctly nocturnal sound.

Elihu was about to say what everyone was thinking – that this was no natural occurrence – when the sound of a horse cantering up to the house, followed by Mr. Benedict's voice, sent a wave of relief through the gathering. "I apologize for my tardiness," the minister said, stepping briskly into the hall. Guiding the Middlefield congregation through five years of war had left Mr. Benedict with even less hair. What remained had begun to turn gray. But the pastor's faith remained fervent. "I was delayed by this strange darkness," he explained unnecessarily.

"What do you make of it, pastor?" Lot Benton asked directly. He could barely see Mr. Benedict in the gloom. "It seems something like the darkness the Bible says lay over the land while Our Lord Jesus was dying upon the cross."

Mr. Benedict looked uncertain. "This atmospheric phenomenon may indeed be a message from God. But I cannot say for sure."

"Could it be the end of the world?" Esther blurted out in a voice teetering on the edge of panic. Both Elihu and David's thoughts flashed back to the terrifying night when their sister Hannah had cried out the same question while an earthquake rocked this very house.

Elihu wrapped an arm reassuringly around his agitated wife's waist and pulled her tightly to him. Esther had borne their child, a son, in early April, but the baby had lived less than a week. Not only was their grief fresh, but Esther, slowly recovering from childbirth, was given to emotional outbursts.

"I doubt it," Mr. Benedict said with a confidence that helped settle Esther. "But if we are being warned to repent of our sins, or are about to be summoned to account for our lives, we can only wait, and watch, and pray."

Daniel spoke into the semi-darkness. "If you're agreeable, Mr. Benedict, I would like to proceed with the business for which you came today." The others were caught off guard. In their anxiety they'd almost forgotten why they were here in the first place.

In the darkness Daniel intertwined the fingers of his right hand with those of Hope's left. Straining to make out her features, he said solemnly, "If today does indeed bring the end of the world, I should like to have had the joy of calling you 'wife' before it comes."

The lump that rose in her throat left Hope unable to reply to Daniel's touching expression. She simply squeezed his hand in assent, and nodded.

"You speak wisely, Mr. Fowler," Mr. Benedict replied. "Uniting two of His faithful servants in marriage cannot help but please the Lord."

The minister conducted the service from memory. As they exchanged vows, Hope humbly thanked God for blessing her with this new husband, whom she loved and who loved her in return.

As the ceremony concluded, David was overwhelmed by an unexpected emotion – joy for his mother's sake. John had been dead far too long for him to feel jealous over another man taking a husband's place by Hope's side. But until this moment David had viewed his mother's impending remarriage only as the long-overdue completion of his independence. He shamefacedly admitted to himself that he'd not given a thought to the fact that this union might bring Hope a happiness that had been missing from her life for decades, and that she richly deserved as reward for all her sacrifices for others.

Expressions of congratulations to the newlyweds were followed by a modest celebratory meal prepared by Sarah. Everyone remained on edge as the weird darkness persisted.

Around noon the sky at last started to brighten in the west. At the same time the ominous sable cloud began to retreat toward the east. The realization that the world would continue to exist, at least for the time being, introduced a note of merriment to the gathering.

The disc of the sun could be clearly discerned through a thin veil of clouds by mid-afternoon, when the new Mr. and Mrs. Fowler prepared to depart for North Guilford. As David hugged his mother goodbye, the realization that she was truly leaving for a new home sent a surge of bittersweet longing through him.

David's resentment of Hope's years of domineering treatment had steadily faded as he'd become his own man – a successful farmer, husband, and father. Now it vanished completely, releasing his long-pent-up affection and gratitude for this remarkable woman whose inexhaustible faith and strength had kept the Lyman family from foundering. Hope's going would create in his life a unique void – not simply as his mother but as a partner in fighting for their family's survival – that no one else could ever fill.

Hope started to step away from their embrace. But David clung tightly to her for a second more – just long enough for a mother's heart to sense the powerful love of the man who was her son.

Chapter Forty-One

May, 1785
Middlefield

David leafed through the pages of his leather-bound book of financial accounts. When he found the right page, he recorded the purchase of three hundred clapboards from William Miller's sawmill, followed by the date – May 10, 1785.

David suddenly realized that the fifth anniversary was approaching of the Dark Day, as the date on which Hope and Daniel Fowler were wed had come to be called. They'd learned later that the mysterious, terrifying gloom had been observed across most of New England. The cause – apart from God's will – was still unknown.

David could scarcely believe it had been five years since that memorable day. He'd been so busy, so much had happened since, that the time had seemed to fly by. David settled back in his chair, twirling the goose quill pen thoughtfully between his fingers, to admire one of the symbols of that change: the handsome combination desk and bookcase on which the account ledger rested. It was a massive piece of elegantly carved furniture, nearly ten feet tall, crafted for David by Middletown joiner Timothy Boardman.

David ran his hand appreciatively over cherry wood the rich, deep red of a fine wine. The ornate brass handles on the drawers and on the glass doors of the bookshelves gleamed in the twilight. It was finer and more expensive than anything David's parents had ever owned. It reflected David's steadily rising prosperity – as would the planned new house for which he was stockpiling clapboards.

David shivered as a chill breeze blew in through the window. He stood to shut it, pausing to look out at the field he and his hired man had spent the day plowing. It was just part of the more than two hundred and fifty acres David now owned.

Returning to his chair, he dipped the nib of a quill into the inkwell. But he laid the quill down when he heard feet coming down the stairs. A smile of contentment lit up his face as he turned to see Sarah, and their four children: Polly, just turned seven; five-year-old Phineas; his namesake, David, three; and the youngest, nineteen-month-old William, christened for the brother Sarah had lost the year she and David met. Four babies in eight years of marriage, and Sarah was big with another, due in mid-summer.

David and Sarah had been – so far, thanks be to God – spared the tragedy of burying a child. For an anxious time they'd feared for the life of William, nicknamed Billy. He'd been so fragile a newborn that Sarah had called him her "cobweb baby."

But Sarah's skilled nurturing had worked wonders. Although Billy was still worrisomely thin, he was walking, learning new words each day, and appeared to be developing normally.

"The children want to say goodnight," Sarah said. Little Polly scrambled up onto David's lap, and hugged her father around the neck. He kissed her cheek and caressed the straight, dark hair she'd inherited from him before setting her down on the floor.

David then embraced the three boys, one after the other, with special affection. As dearly as he cherished Polly, David especially prized his sons – an understandable attitude which neither surprised nor troubled Sarah.

Sarah shepherded the children upstairs to their bed chambers. David let his mind roam. He would turn forty on his next birthday – just two years younger than his father had been when he first displayed symptoms of the consumption that would kill him.

David couldn't ignore the possibility that disease or accident could send him to an early grave as well, leaving Sarah with a brood of babies to raise. Fear of such a disaster drove him to work tirelessly on accumulating property.

David gladly turned away from these morbid reflections. He hitched his chair closer to the desk's drop leaf. Dipping the quill into the inkwell, he recorded more of his expenditures for the new house. These included brownstone blocks hewn from the quarry on Powder Hill and carted to his homelot, hand-forged nails, and the labor for digging a cellar hole on the gentle rise west of the Lyman house.

He heard Sarah picking her way carefully down the steep, narrow staircase – always tricky for a woman in long skirts to navigate, but particularly perilous when her balance was hampered by advanced pregnancy. She walked over to lay a hand on David's shoulder. He affectionately placed his left one over hers as he continued tallying up his figures. He wanted to finish before it grew too dark to see without lighting a candle.

Sarah waited patiently for David to be done. She used the time to study her husband. From their first meeting she'd sensed in him a suppressed energy. But she'd been astonished by the intensity of the ambition he'd shown since Hope's move to North Guilford five years ago had eliminated the last vestiges of her domination.

In addition to expanding the farm, David had become involved in local government. Before the war ended with the winning of American independence in 1783, he'd been quartermaster for a troop of militia. He'd taken on responsibility for supplying families of Middletown soldiers with the necessities of life while their providers were in the army. He'd been named to Middletown's Committee of Inspection, charged with ferreting out disloyal residents.

These were low-level positions for which, like all town offices, the holder received no pay. But by tapping David for such duties, his fellow citizens expressed confidence in his ability and integrity, and provided him an opportunity to demonstrate his worthiness for greater civic responsibilities. The respect he'd garnered had let to his election in 1780 as lieutenant of a mounted militia troop. By long-standing custom, he was usually addressed in daily life by his militia rank of "Lieutenant Lyman."

From his face and physique alone, David didn't look much older than his thirty-one-year-old wife. But the hair at his temples had begun to turn a pewter gray. Sarah thought it gave him a touch of dignified maturity.

"Will you have everything ready for the house-raising next week?" Sarah asked as David shot the quill into the inkwell and closed the account book. He nodded and turned to gaze at her.

"I believe so," he said with a satisfied air. "If all goes well – and the weather cooperates – it should be ready before the baby arrives."

"Will you be sorry to leave this house?" Sarah asked. David had long since ceased being surprised by his wife's ability to sense his innermost feelings. He thought for a moment, then shook his head.

"No," he said firmly. "I feel as if I've outgrown it, as a snake sheds the skin that has become too small."

Sarah nodded understandingly. The new, larger, more elaborate house David had planned was proof – to himself and to the community – that he'd become one of Middlefield's most prosperous residents, and was climbing the ladder of influence in the larger arena of Middletown.

"Besides, you're leaving me no choice but to erect a larger house, Sally," David said calling her by the nickname he used only when they were alone. "The way you turn out babies, we'll soon be crowded out of this one," he teased.

"I didn't make this happen by myself," Sarah reminded him good-humoredly, laying a hand on her swelling abdomen.

"I'll not deny my responsibility," David acknowledged. "But I was only doing my duty as a good husband." He turned Sarah's hand over, and kissed her palm. "It was also my pleasure," he said softly, glancing up, his eyebrows raised suggestively. "Yours, too, as I recall," he added, bringing a bright blush to his wife's cheeks.

"You remember rightly," Sarah admitted in a low voice. For a long moment each relived the delights of the night this newest baby had been conceived.

Remembering the many household tasks to be finished before she could retire for the night, Sarah reluctantly withdrew her hand from David's. She started for the kitchen, then stopped to look back over her shoulder. "Who have you invited to the house-raising?"

"The Millers, the Coes, the–," David began, as he got to his feet.

"All of them?" Sarah interrupted, in feigned alarm. In her eight years in Middlefield, she'd learned that the Millers and Coes accounted for more than a quarter of all the households in Middlefield – upwards of two hundred people.

"No!" David replied, turning around. When he saw Sarah's face he realized she was pulling his leg. "I'll get a count after Sabbath services, so you'll know how much food to prepare, and I can lay in a sufficient supply of rum." He turned to close up the desk.

"Will your mother be coming?" Sarah asked, now serious.

"No," David said as he set the ledger on a shelf and closed the bookcase's glass doors. "She agrees with my plan to tear down this house and use some of the wood in the new one," he continued, turning the brass key in the lock. "And Mama is rarely sentimental about worldly possessions." He turned to look at Sarah. "Yet I understand if she'd rather not witness the razing of the house that was her home for nearly forty years."

David and Sarah had been amazed – and grateful – that in the five years since her marriage to Daniel Fowler, his mother hadn't tried to involve herself in David's operation of the farm. Hope Lyman

Fowler was busy and contented in her new life and home, especially because she resided conveniently near Catharine and Lot.

Lyman Beecher, now nearly ten, still lived with the Bentons. Hope took great pleasure in David and Sarah's children. But she had a special fondness for Lyman Beecher, her first grandchild, son of her cherished Esther. Lyman was very fond of his Granny Fowler.

"Will Elihu and Esther be coming?" Sarah asked,

David nodded. "Elihu will. He sent word that unless he's called to a medical emergency he must attend to, he'll be here."

Sarah smiled. "I'm grateful that with all their disappointments, they don't begrudge us our blessings."

Sarah continued into the kitchen, leaving David alone in the fading light to ponder her words. While Sarah and David had enjoyed steady good fortune, Elihu and Esther had experienced repeated frustration and sorrow. During the year and a half they'd lived with David and Sarah after Hope's marriage, Esther had given birth to a second baby, but the child soon died. In the three years since Esther hadn't conceived, a source of great disappointment.

Elihu at last decided they should strike out on their own. He and Esther had first moved to the town of Cheshire. Then in 1782, Elihu purchased a house and twelve acres of land with an orchard in the town of Southington, about fifteen miles from Middlefield. They still lived in Southington, where Elihu had achieved respect and modest success as a country doctor and part-time farmer.

God's will doubtless played a role in the unequal balance of the brothers' fortunes. Still, David knew it couldn't be easy for Elihu. He'd killed and bled and suffered and spent nearly two years as a prisoner during the war for independence. Despite his sacrifices in the sacred cause of liberty, he so far he hadn't been blessed with the family and prosperity enjoyed by David, who'd remained at home. Sarah's counsel and his own modest services to the war effort had enabled David to largely lay to rest the ghost of guilt over this disparity.

More than once David had cautiously broached the possibility of helping Elihu with a loan or even the transfer of some of the Lyman farm's acres to him. But Elihu, possessed of the Lyman pride and stubbornness, had cut off any such discussion.

It was indeed a tribute to Elihu's generosity of spirit and brotherly love that he hadn't allowed envy or jealousy to come between them, David thought. It was one more blessing for which he had reason to thank the Lord.

Chapter Forty-Two

May, 1785
Middlefield

Sarah awkwardly swung the heavy hammer once, twice, then a third time. The final blow drove the pin David was holding in position deep enough into the timber for it to stand unsupported. A cheer went up from the several dozen men, women, and children surrounding her, bringing an embarrassed smile to her face. She gratefully handed the hammer to David. "Well done, Sarah!" he said with a proud grin.

It was the custom for the first pin of a house frame to be driven in by the woman who would be mistress of its hearth. Although Sarah wasn't comfortable being the center of attention, especially so far along in her pregnancy, she hadn't wanted to miss the once-in-a-lifetime chance to take part in this tradition.

The two score men in the crowd scattered. Some set about sawing, hammering, and hoisting the lumber David had stockpiled. Others began constructing a massive central chimneystack out of brownstone blocks.

The past week's fair weather had created excellent conditions for this house-raising. The wood was dry and the ground firm. The eighteenth day of May had dawned cool and cloudy, good weather for the tasks at hand. They should be able to make considerable progress toward erecting his new home, David predicted to himself.

The house would face northeast, as did the one in which David had lived his entire life – but it would be twice as big. It was to be two and a half stories, with the second floor extending out slightly over the first, and the third featuring a similar "overhang" over the second. There would be five windows across the front on the second floor. It was a style common in Connecticut going back generations.

There would be four rooms downstairs, four chambers upstairs, and a garret above that. So much more space meant Sarah and David could put their bed in an upstairs chamber, as was becoming the custom, instead of in the downstairs parlor. The other three chambers would provide plenty of room for their four children and the baby on the way – and others still to come, God willing.

Into the garret would go worn, out-of-style, or even damaged furniture and possessions. Frugal New Englanders rarely threw anything out. One could never tell when an item might come in handy sometime in the future.

David had hired skilled carpenters to carve wooden mouldings and mantels in a pattern that, while decorative, was not ornate. The front doorway would be carved in a finely detailed, yet not ostentatious style. The clapboards would be painted white, and the interior walls plastered.

"Lieutenant Lyman!" called the young schoolmaster Joshua Stow, who was standing at a corner of the house frame. David looked up from surveying the transfer of stones for the chimney. He still wasn't used to being addressed in daily life by his militia title – although he enjoyed it.

"We need the shoe," Stow shouted.

David nodded. He called to Phineas, who was playing with other children outside the old house. Inside the women were cooking food for the laboring men, who would be famished by dinner time.

Phineas eagerly responded to his father's summons, hoping he was to be allowed to join the men and older boys in hammering and sawing. But instead of being handed a tool, Phineas received perplexing instructions from his father. "Go get my old shoe from you mother and bring it to me," David told him.

"Don't you want two shoes?" Phineas asked, his curiosity outweighing his disappointment.

"Just one," David answered. The mystified Phineas scampered down the hill. A few minutes later he was back with a leather shoe that had been patched and mended until it was beyond repair.

"What's this for, Papa?" Phineas asked.

David smiled at his son's bewilderment. "They say if you put a shoe inside a wall of a new house, no matter how far you travel, your feet will always find their way back home," he explained. "Now take it over to Mr. Stow."

Phineas trotted over to Joshua Stow, holding the shoe carefully like a talisman. If his father thought it might possess such power, Phineas would believe as well. But the boy wondered why in this case the shoe was needed; he couldn't imagine anyone choosing to go far from the wonderful new house taking shape before his eyes.

After giving Phineas the old shoe she'd saved for this occasion, Sarah returned to putting two chickens on a spit on the hearth. The kitchen was crowded with half a dozen women at work. Some of the wives had contributed foods such as bread, cheese, and pies. But so many people had turned out for the house-raising that Sarah wanted to err on the side of having too much to eat rather than risk the embarrassment of running out.

Out of the corner of her eye Sarah watched with fond pride as Polly trailed after David and Billy, bossing her little brothers in a manner Phineas would no longer tolerate. It was gratifying to see her daughter's maternal instincts emerging so early. But Sarah's satisfaction curdled to uneasiness when she saw Polly abruptly abandon her brothers to excitedly greet a new arrival, Irene Miller, with her year-old son, Levi.

Irene was a dark-haired girl of medium height, with heavy-lidded eyes and a broad nose in an oval face. In October of 1783 she'd wed her second cousin, Isaac Miller, Jr.

The marriage of second cousins wasn't noteworthy. Marriage between even first cousins was legal as well as condoned socially and spiritually. Since few people regularly traveled more than ten miles from home, young men and women typically found a spouse among their neighbors or their congregation, or in a nearby town.

In small communities like Middlefield, where descendants of the original settlers had been intermarrying for four generations, it was almost inevitable that many newlyweds would be blood relations to some degree. Some fathers deliberately arranged unions between cousins to keep property within the family. Thus Ichabod Miller had agreed to have his daughter, Irene, marry the namesake son of Isaac Miller, Sr., who was Ichabod's first cousin.

What had raised eyebrows and set tongues wagging was the fact that on her wedding day Irene Miller was a week shy of her fifteenth birthday, and her bridegroom was just seventeen. The suspicions raised by the marriage of two such extremely young people were confirmed by the birth to Irene Miller of Levi Miller, six months to the day after the wedding.

As she set fresh-baked gingerbread on a table, Betsy Hoadley saw where Sarah's gaze had strayed. A tall, angular woman married to Dr. Jehiel Hoadley, Betsy watched Polly follow Irene and her baby outside. She sniffed disapprovingly. "With the hot blood Irene's shown, I wouldn't be surprised if she already has another baby on the way."

"Babies begotten before their parents wed are nothing new," said Sarah. "Many people no longer feel shame for lying together without marriage," she added, shaking her head in gentle dismay. "David told me that when Hezekiah Miller and Sarah Higgins were called before the justice of the peace court on a charge of fornication, they were more annoyed than embarrassed!" She stepped over to a large wooden bowl sitting on a table, and with a wooden spoon began creaming a pound of sugar into a pound of butter.

"Did Isaac and Ichabod never consider that this might happen?" mused Jerusha Coe, a matron of about forty. "Talking for years about their plans for Irene and Isaac to marry. Didn't they ever think that as those children matured they might feel themselves as good as wed, with little reason to resist the urge to lie together," she finished in exasperation.

David and Billy, freed of Polly's supervision, were chasing each other back and forth in the hall with hysterical giggling that Sarah knew would end in crying when one of them tripped and fell. "Polly!" she called out the window sharply. "Mind your brothers. Take them outside, and keep them away from where the men are working."

An obviously reluctant Polly appeared in the doorway. She obediently herded the rambunctious boys out the kitchen door – then hurried back to Irene Miller's side.

Sarah began cracking the first of ten eggs into the mixing bowl. "I pray God spares me to guide Polly toward honorable marriage to a good man – at the proper age," she said worriedly.

Every woman in the kitchen knew Sarah was thinking of her impending confinement. Having delivered four babies safely was no guarantee that Sarah's next birthing would go well. The grim reaper began a fresh watch each time a new soul fought its way into the world.

Sarah dropped the last egg into the bowl. Balancing the rim against her enlarged abdomen, she mixed the eggs in with large strokes.

"But you surely don't want Polly to become a spinster, or allow herself to be courted for years on end by only one man?" said

Jerusha as she checked the beans boiling in an iron pot. The women understood that her teasing comment was directed at Elizabeth Miller, a tall woman of twenty-one with deep blue eyes and thick chestnut hair.

Sarah began sifting a pound of flour into the batter. "You have a point," she said, smiling at Elizabeth. "What could make a young woman wait half a decade for a man?" She very much liked Elizabeth, a young woman of common sense leavened with wit.

Elizabeth Miller looked up from placing dried apple slices into a pie crust. Following a five-year courtship, she was at long last set to wed strapping, twenty-one-year-old Elisha Coe in June.

"In truth, five years wasn't long at all to wait for Elisha," Elizabeth said philosophically as she continued assembling the pie. "He is, after all, well endowed with what really matters in a man."

Sarah nearly lost her grip on the mixing bowl. Susannah Miller, Elizabeth's stepmother, glanced up from the skillet into which she was pouring a mixture of Indian corn, milk, and eggs to make slapjacks. "Daughter!" she gasped in dismay.

Unruffled, Elizabeth said, "I mean, a kind heart, sincere affection for me, and sufficient property to support a family. What else could you possibly think I was talking about?" she asked with an expression of wide-eyed innocence.

The women broke into laughter. Sarah measured out a gill of rosewater she'd made by steeping fragrant rose petals in brandy, grated in some nutmeg, then carefully stirred both into the batter of the pound cake, so-called because of the pound each of sugar, flour, and butter that went into it.

"It wasn't desperation or doubt that kept Elisha from proposing that we wed," Elizabeth said as she put the last layer of apples into the dish. "When we fell in love, we were both but sixteen – too young to marry. Two years ago we felt ready to wed, but as you know–," she paused ever so briefly for emphasis, "Elisha's father refused to give him the land he was promised."

Susannah Miller made a rough noise of disgust in her throat. "Joseph Coe had his eldest son and his daughter-in-law living with him," she said. "He didn't need to keep Elisha at home – he just wanted to benefit from his youngest son's unpaid labor as long as possible. Had the Lord not seen fit to take Joseph to Him last summer, Elizabeth and Elisha would still be waiting to set a wedding date." Susannah simmered with anger at the man who had selfishly delayed her cherished stepdaughter's marriage.

Sarah thought of Hope clinging so tenaciously to the land. To part with it – even to one's own flesh and blood – was no easy thing.

"It's water over the dam now," Elizabeth said contentedly. "Elisha has his share of the estate, he was accepted as a freeman, and on June 9 we'll be married. This summer we'll raise a house of our own. And this time next year, God willing, I'll be a new mother."

Sarah poured the batter into a pan and placed it into the oven. She hoped Polly would grow up to be wise like Elizabeth, not heedless of consequences like Irene Miller.

Sarah collected the egg shells into the empty bowl and stepped outside to the spot behind the kitchen where all household trash was disposed of. As she dumped the shells on top of apple peelings and shards of an earthenware plate little David had broken, she heard footsteps approaching from behind.

"Why do we cluck like hens about babies coming early to lustful teenagers when there's reason to suspect much blacker sins among us," demanded Betsy Hoadley in a low voice. Sarah knew what she was referring to, and the thought soured her stomach.

Sarah turned to face Betsy and Jerusha, who'd also followed her out of the house. "I've known Lois Benedict since I came to Middlefield eight years ago," Sarah said quietly. "She's a loving pastor's wife, an affectionate mother, a good friend, and a pious Christian. I can't believe the rumors that she is an adulteress. I can scarcely bring myself to say it."

"I agree," said Jerusha, with a troubled frown. "Yet I'm disturbed by what some people are saying. Lois bore Mr. Benedict four children during their first eleven years of marriage. But it's more than four years since the birth of Abner, Jr., and Lois hasn't conceived again, even though she can't be much past thirty-five. Some whisper that Lois denies Mr. Benedict his rights as a husband – or that he no longer cares to claim them."

"There could be many explanations for why Lois hasn't gotten with child again," Sarah protested. "She and Mr. Benedict always appear contented with each other."

"Do you expect them to parade their unhappiness in public?" Betsy Hoadley demanded with a slight sneer. "And Lois seems excessively fond of Jotham Martin since he came to live in their house to study for the ministry with Mr. Benedict. He's handsome, treats Lois politely, some say even gallantly."

"He's a youth fresh out of college, far from home, and likely lonely," Sarah pointed out. "Lois is a warm-hearted woman who's almost old enough to be Jotham Martin's mother! Any affection she displays toward him is doubtless meant to help him feel welcome within their family circle."

"But that doesn't explain tales I've heard of travelers passing the Benedict house at night when the pastor is abroad visiting the sick, and seeing candles burning in Jotham Martin's chamber – even in that of Lois and Mr. Benedict – far into the night, long after anyone else would be asleep," Jerusha said.

"Martha Cornwell told me that at the Election Day festivities last week she twice caught Mrs. Benedict and Mr. Martin gazing longingly at each other when they thought no one was watching," Betsy added. "And where are they all today?" she demanded. "Have Lois and Jotham chosen to avoid another public gathering, fearful they can't conceal their unclean passion? Is Mr. Benedict avoiding the humiliation of everyone knowing his wife has betrayed him?"

"That the Benedicts or Jotham Martin aren't here means nothing," Sarah snapped. "I'm worried by how easily innocent actions can be twisted into reasons for suspicion. A candle in a chamber after dark doesn't mean people are committing adultery!" she exclaimed.

"I've never observed anything improper between Lois and Jotham Martin," Sarah insisted. "If there were any truth to this gossip, I can't believe I wouldn't have seen some evidence."

Jerusha shook her head. "You're no wide-eyed innocent, Sarah," she conceded. "And you sense things many others don't. But you've had so much demanding your attention: four little ones to care for with another on the way, two servant girls to supervise, and a new house going up."

Sarah didn't think she could have missed the signs of shameful behavior others claimed to see, even as busy as she'd been. What she did know was that just taking part in this conservation made her feel dirty.

"None of us can say for sure what has passed between Lois and Jotham – if anything," Sarah said at last. "We'd do well to heed Jesus' counsel to 'Judge not lest ye be judged,' and the commandment not to bear false witness against our neighbors."

"But what if it's not false?" hissed Betsy Hoadley, out of patience with Sarah's attitude. She turned and stalked back to the house. Sarah and Jerusha exchanged an uneasy glance before following her.

Chapter Forty-Three

May, 1785
Middlefield

As the sun reached its zenith, threatening to burn through the thin cloud cover, several men left off working on the frame of the Lyman house to gather around a tall wooden barrel in the shade of an oak tree and refresh themselves with rum. Rum was the staple of any communal construction project; it not only slaked the thirst but was known to be essential for sustaining a laboring man's energy. Much of the food for such a gathering was brought by those taking part, but the host was expected to provide the rum – and plenty of it.

"I'm grateful so many came to help today," David said. "I'd like to have a roof on the house before Sarah is brought to bed with this next baby." He handed a mug to Elihu Stow, a miller.

"You were late starting a family, but you've made up for lost time," said Stow. He took a draught of rum, followed by a deep exhale of satisfaction. "And Sarah's served you well – three boys out of the first four babes."

"That's true," said Ebenezer Allen, a portly farmer. He lowered himself heavily onto a tree stump, then immediately jumped to his feet. Frowning, Allen looked down and brushed off a pointy acorn.

David hid a smile behind his mug as Allen carefully sat down again. Looking up, he spotted Elihu arriving. He waved to catch his brother's attention and motioned for him to join the group.

"You could be in poor Will Miller's shoes," Allen went on. "Four daughters before his first wife died birthing the last one, and five with his second. Not a single son to help him work his fields, to support him in old age, to pass his farm to when he dies – if there's anything left after he provides marriage portions for all those girls."

Having five sons himself, Allen could well afford to feel sorry for Will Miller. The other men nodded in shared sympathy for a man cursed with such bad luck.

"Time was a man couldn't sire too many sons," said Hezekiah Hale, sexton of the Middlefield church. "But these days it's hard for most farmers to provide two boys with enough land to make a life in Connecticut." He brushed away a bee hovering around his rum.

"It's no wonder so many of our young people have left Connecticut," scowled Aaron Parsons, an elderly grizzled farmer.

Joseph Coe nodded in grim confirmation of Parsons's observation. Elihu's arrival prompted a quick round of greetings. After Elihu was set with a mug of rum, Coe spoke.

"When my grandfather divided up his land among four sons, each received enough to stay in Durham and Middlefield. My father's portion was sufficient to support nine children, but it wasn't near enough land for him to set up six sons. He tried to purchase more acres, but we've all seen the growing number of young men coming of age looking to buy drive the price higher each year."

Coe held up nine calloused fingers. "My oldest brother left for Massachusetts before the war," he said, bending an index finger. "Father sent Curtis to Brown College in Rhode Island, and now he's a pastor in New Hampshire." He bent the next finger. "It's ten years now that Joel went to New York. Ebenezer survived a British prison ship, then settled in New Jersey." He bent two more fingers.

"Sister Anne died in 1781, and Abigail moved to Colchester when she wed Chandler Otis," Joseph went on. He bent the thumb and index finger on his other hand, then shook it emphatically. "That leaves just three of us in Middlefield – me, Elisha, and Hannah. The future looks the same for my children. How many of them will be forced to move away – scattered like leaves stripped from trees by a nor'easter?" he concluded on a melancholy note.

Joseph's demonstration troubled David. Building this house represented his commitment to Middlefield. He felt confident that what he owned now, and what, God willing, he would add as his sons grew into valuable helpers, would be enough to provide five children a foundation for a future in Connecticut.

But if Sarah continued to bear babies as she had, they might well end up with a dozen. In a flash of stark honesty, David admitted to himself that there was no way he could ever amass enough property to provide a foundation for twelve children in Connecticut.

Maybe, David thought, he should explore expanding his business beyond growing and selling crops. He might look into quarrying brownstone, or partnering in one of the small mills cropping up along the banks of Middlefield's waterways to manufacture snuff, grind grain, or saw wood. Or maybe invest in cheap, virgin acres in Vermont, New Hampshire, or western New York that he could sell for a profit once settlers began moving in.

David forced himself to refocus on the conversation. "It bodes ill for Connecticut," Hezekiah Hale was commenting on Joseph Coe's demonstration. "But many have no choice. A man must do whatever is necessary to provide for his family."

"If this talk gets any gloomier, I'm going to stay right here and guzzle David's rum until I'm drunk," said Ebenezer Allen, eliciting good-natured chuckles from the other men. Allen slapped his knees hard and got to his feet. The workers drained the last few drops from their mugs, then one by one headed back toward the house frame.

Elihu lingered, leaning one hip against the barrel. David picked up the jug to take it to be refilled.

This was as good a time as any, Elihu decided. "I'm considering leaving Connecticut myself," he said with studied casualness.

David wheeled around in astonishment so quickly that the jug slipped from his fingers and flew several feet through the air. It struck the ground, then rolled until it came to rest near Elihu's feet. The rum remaining inside began to trickle out into the grass.

"I know this is a surprise, but it's certainly not worth wasting good rum," Elihu said in an attempt at humor that fell flat. He picked up the jug and held it out to David, who stood with his arms hanging at his side, staring dumbfounded at his brother. When David made no move to take the jug, Elihu set it on the barrel, and waited for David to recover from his surprise.

"Why leave Connecticut now, when you and Esther are settled?" David asked in bewilderment.

Elihu shrugged slightly, striving to put a positive face on what had been an agonizing decision – even more so for Esther. "I've always yearned to see more of the world – you know that," he began.

"I would have thought your army service at Boston and New York scratched that itch for a lifetime," David interrupted. "After you came home, you said you wanted nothing more than to sink roots as deeply as possible here in Connecticut."

"That's what I thought – at first," Elihu admitted uncomfortably. "But over these past years I've come to find Connecticut–," he searched for the right word – "confining. During the war I met men from other states who made me realize that while our way of life in Connecticut is good, it's not the only way, and not always the best."

David could think of no sensible reply to that heretical idea. Still reeling, he managed to ask, "Where will you go?"

"I've applied for a grant of land in Georgia." Elihu said.

David gasped. His eyes widened as if he'd been punched in the stomach. Georgia was much farther away than any of the other places to which their neighbors had emigrated.

"Georgia has encouraged members of the Cincinnati to take up within her boundaries lands due them for their Continental Army service," Elihu went on quickly. He was immensely proud of his membership in the Society of the Cincinnati, a fellowship of Continental Army officers formed at the end of the war. George Washington was president of the society, named for the Roman hero Cincinnatus, who left his farm to defend his country, then relinquished the power he'd accumulated to return to his plow.

"The thought of making my fresh start in the company of those fellow veterans is very attractive," Elihu went on. "I would receive two hundred acres; more than I could ever hope to buy in Connecticut. Any new community will welcome a trained physician."

When David made no reply, Elihu continued defensively, "Georgia's not on the moon! Other men from Connecticut who've gone there have done well. Dr. Lyman Hall from Wallingford signed the Declaration of Independence for Georgia. Abraham Baldwin from North Guilford is planning a university there."

As the shock of the announcement began to wear off, David's mind started groping frantically for arguments to dissuade Elihu from this venture. Esther couldn't be happy about abandoning her home for some distant wilderness. But David knew she would follow her husband to the mouth of Hell if that was what he wanted.

"Perhaps of late we haven't seen as much of each other as brothers should, in our busyness haven't tended to our bonds of kinship as we ought – but that can be remedied," David said tentatively, a forlorn hope in his voice.

Elihu glanced away uncomfortably, focusing his gaze on the grass at his feet. David wasn't going to let him go without a struggle, which both touched and tormented him.

Elihu had hoped to avoid telling David the whole truth behind his decision, afraid it would hurt his brother. But David needed to hear it from him, just as Elihu had needed to hear from David the painful details of Phineas's death.

Elihu raised his head and looked into David's eyes. "Do you remember when Papa took us to Torrington to visit our grandparents, our aunts and uncles and cousins?"

"Yes," David answered impatiently. What could this event more than twenty-five years past have to do with the crisis at hand? he wondered. "It was the year before Papa sickened with consumption."

Elihu nodded. "I was only seven, but to me it was such a great adventure that I believe I can recall every minute." His lips twitched in a shade of a smile as he remembered that little boy's excitement.

"When we were returning home," Elihu continued, "you asked Papa why he and Mama didn't move to Torrington with his father and the rest of his family." He paused, clearly waiting for David to pick up the thread of the memory.

"He said it was because had he gone, he would always have dwelled in the shadow of his older brother," David finished, speaking the last words slowly as Elihu's meaning dawned on him.

"It's the same for me as it was for Papa," Elihu said, with somber certainty. "Except I'm the one who must go."

Guilt and regret overspread David's face. Elihu stepped away from the barrel to place a firm hand on David's shoulder. "It's not your fault, David," he said earnestly. "You're a good man, a good brother. You deserve all God has blessed you with. But Connecticut has proven to be a barren land for me and Esther. Perhaps it's God's way of telling us to seek our future elsewhere."

Tears began to well up in both brothers' eyes. Elihu blinked hard to clear his vision, and went on as steadily as he could.

"To move on, to settle new places, is in our blood," he said. "It's what our Grandfather Lyman did when he left Northampton for Durham, and then Durham for Torrington."

The brothers studied each other for a long moment. Both had regained their composure, but anguish was clear in their eyes.

"Please don't let this cast a shadow over your new home," Elihu entreated. "Never has a man had more reason to rejoice, to believe he's following the Lord's path. Papa would be so proud of you."

David seized Elihu by the shoulders. "Never has a man had more reason to be grateful for a brother's love," he said in choked voice.

Chapter Forty-Four

October, 1785
Middlefield

David glanced somberly at the eight men around the table in the parlor of his just-completed house. He thought ironically of how he'd envisioned this room as the site of joyous occasions – his daughters' weddings, Thanksgiving dinners. He could never have imagined that the first gathering here would be a desperate attempt to resolve the greatest spiritual crisis ever faced by Middlefield's congregation.

"A monstrous wrong has been done to me and mine!" Abner Benedict raged at the group. "How can anyone expect me to continue the connection between us?"

The men exchanged looks of startled dismay at Mr. Benedict's words. He had asked to be dismissed as pastor of Middlefield's Congregational church. This group of church members had appealed to him to withdraw that request.

"We know we don't deserve to have you continue as our pastor," Joseph Coe said with sincere humility. "We've all sinned against God. We cruelly and unjustly injured Mrs. Benedict and Mr. Martin and you, whether we passed on gossip with our own lips, listened to it, or did nothing to stop its spread. We're ashamed of ourselves. We repent our offense." It was clear Coe spoke for all of them.

"We've begged God's forgiveness," Coe went on, his voice growing in fervor. "We hope you can find it in your heart to forgive us as well, and to remain among us. That is why the congregation voted to deny your request for dismissal, and appointed this committee to consult with you on how this breach might be healed."

"I stayed away from Sabbath meetings this past month to pray and meditate undisturbed upon that very request," Mr. Benedict responded in a hard monotone. Coe's expression of contrition and penitent plea appeared not to have moved the minister.

"Your absence during that time impressed upon us even more how great a blow it would be to lose you as our pastor," Isaac Miller interjected. Mr. Benedict gave no indication he'd heard the words.

"It's my duty as a Christian to forgive those who wrong me," Mr. Benedict replied at last. "That I can do." Committee members shifted hopefully in their seats – then froze as the minister shot to his feet, upsetting his chair, which hit the floor with an explosive crack.

"Yes, I can forgive those who, despite knowing me for fifteen years, whispered behind my back that I was a cuckold, a self-deluded fool," Mr. Benedict snarled. He strode over to the fireplace, seized an iron poker and thrust it deep into the blaze that was helping ward off the October evening's chill. With it he forced two logs apart, sending an explosion of sparks swirling up the chimney.

"But try as I might, I can't forgive those who inflicted such shame and agony upon my dear wife!" Mr. Benedict struggled unsuccessfully to free the poker from the logs, then simply left it there. He placed his hands upon the mantel, his back to the others.

"For fifteen years Lois Benedict has maintained a spotless reputation in our community. She has been the best of wives and mothers, and an angel of mercy to all in need. She offered chaste friendship to a lonely young scholar far from home. Malicious minds twisted that kindness into a hideous sin, then spread their evil suspicions, blackening my wife's name, staining her reputation!"

Mr. Benedict sagged against the mantel for a moment, his head hanging dejectedly between his hands. "Even if some were wicked enough to believe my wife would betray our marital vows," he continued, raising his head sharply, "how could they believe she would commit such a sin with the children she cherishes more than life itself asleep under the same roof!"

The minister slammed his palm on the mantel and turned to confront the committee. With his hooked nose, hairline that by now had receded far beyond the crown of his head, and fiery eyes glistening with tears of anger and anguish, he reminded David of a wounded eagle – a noble creature, injured by stones flung by thoughtless fools, perhaps crippled too seriously ever to soar again.

An awkward silence fell, as Mr. Benedict's unanswerable question hung in the air. The room had grown increasingly dim with the setting of the sun. David lit two candles from the fireplace flames, inserted them into pewter candlesticks, and set them at opposite ends of the long table.

Abner Benedict closed his eyes, inhaled deeply, held the breath for several heartbeats, then expelled it slowly. When he opened his eyes, he appeared to again have his emotions under some control.

"Even if I could forgive the wrong done to my blameless wife, even if she and I could forgive and forget all that has taken place during these past months, there would always be people who wouldn't forget – who wouldn't want to forget!" the minister said with deep contempt. "Gossip is to a religious society as an intermittent fever is to the human body. The outward symptoms may disappear, but the sickness lies hidden to erupt at a later date. Just as Dr. Hoadley can never be sure he's cured such a disease, so my family would never be able to rest easy that the vile slanders wouldn't surface to titillate a new generation some ten or fifteen years hence."

The minister's shoulders slumped as the outrage drained from him. When he at last spoke, it was with a resolve that, even with all that had happened, still carried a note of regret.

"I'm forty-four years old, had hoped to spend the rest of my life serving God in Middlefield," Mr. Benedict began. "But I can't condemn my wife and children to a life haunted by this scandal. We can consult another time on the conditions of my dismissal."

Giving the committee members no chance to object, Mr. Benedict stepped to the table and picked up his hat. He retrieved his greatcoat from a wall peg, and strode toward the front doorway.

The minister stopped to pull on his coat, and to add, "I intend to ask for an ecclesiastical council to make a thorough investigation of the slanders. There can be no doubt I left Middlefield not because there was even a shred of truth in the malicious rumors, but because the love and trust that must exist between a minister and his people have been irreparably damaged." Then he yanked open the door, stepped out into the crisp October evening, and pulled the door shut behind him.

David closed his eyes and leaned his left elbow on the table. He pressed his thumb against his left temple and massaged his forehead with two fingers, trying to relieve the painful sensation of his head being squeezed in a vice.

"What more does that spiteful bag of wind expect us to do to salve his precious pride?" groused Dr. Hoadley. "Joseph all but groveled before him. The blessed Jesus forgave those who crucified Him, but Abner Benedict can't forgive those who splashed a little mud on his wife's reputation?" he said disgustedly.

David opened his eyes and sat bolt upright. "You're a fool," he informed Dr. Hoadley with a cold contempt that left the man speechless. "Abner Benedict is a minister of God, but a mortal man first of all – and one who truly loves his wife. I'd rather not think what I might do should someone so slander my Sarah."

Isaac Miller, seeing Dr. Hoadley was about to offer an angry reply, quickly intervened. "We know the congregation's wishes. Since obviously there is no hope of removing the embarrassments–." He stopped when Joseph Coe snorted disdainfully at the euphemism used to refer to the crisis in the congregation's meeting minutes.

"Embarrassments," Miller repeated, "that Mr. Benedict has mentioned, it appears his request for a dismissal should be granted, upon condition that he return to the congregation such part of his settlement as shall be agreed upon. We'll report the results of this conversation with Mr. Benedict to the next meeting of the Society."

After seeing the committee members on their way home, David trudged wearily up the stairs to the chamber in which he and Sarah slept. He found his wife sitting in bed, nursing the baby Esther, born the last day of July and named for David's sister.

Sarah didn't need to ask how the meeting had gone. Their chamber was above the parlor, so she'd been able to hear enough to know the outcome.

"Mr. Benedict won't stay – cannot stay – and I can't fault him," David said as he sat down heavily on the bed. "Women's wagging tongues have cut him as deeply as a sword!" he added in disgust.

"Don't blame this on all women," Sarah said sharply. "The gossip was spread mostly by a handful. Their husbands had to know about it, could have put a stop to it, but they didn't even try."

It was David's turn to take offense. "As if most wives pay heed to what their husbands say, let alone obey them," he shot back.

They stared at each other in anger that faded to regret that they'd allowed the upsetting situation to set them quarreling. "Gossip is a poison that continues to cause harm, long after the whispers have stopped," said David.

Cradling Esther in her left arm, Sarah kneaded David's tense shoulder with her right hand. At last he pulled off his coat, waistcoat, shoes and stockings, then stood to strip off his breeches.

"It will be hard to find any minister willing to accept the call from a congregation that has driven away its pastor with spiteful gossip," David said dispiritedly. He lay down next to Sarah and pulled the sheet and coverlet up over his shoulders. He waited until

Sarah shifted the baby from one breast to the other, then laid his arm carefully over her abdomen in a gentle embrace. Drained by the distressing evening, he fell asleep almost immediately, leaving Sarah to contemplate the wages of a community's folly.

David found the notice at last, on the third page of the June 12, 1786, issue of the *Middlesex Gazette,* the weekly newspaper that had begun publication in Middletown the previous year:

> Mrs. Benedict, wife of the Rev. ABNER BENEDICT, of Middlefield, has been publickly and falsely slandered and scandalized by the Tongue of Malice, by which her Character has greatly suffered. In Justice to the Injured, the Publick may be assured that an Ecclesiastical Council hath thoroughly examined these Matters of Scandal, and have declared that Mrs. Benedict is and ought to be esteemed innocent of any such Conduct, and the Church have unanimously concurred therewith as may be seen on the Records of the Church in said Middlefield.

David read the words with deep regret that they'd become necessary and anxiety as to what they portended. Mr. Benedict had continued preaching in Middlefield into the spring, when he'd secured a new position in Columbia County in New York State. He'd sold his house in early June, but delayed his departure for New York until he'd seen with his own eyes the Ecclesiastical Council's official exoneration of his wife published in the local newspaper. Satisfied he'd done everything in his power to cleanse his wife's reputation, the minister and his family had left immediately for New York.

Mr. Benedict's departure was proving to be as great a disaster for Middlefield as David had feared. The congregation was so splintered it had been impossible to mount a search for a new pastor. The most they'd been able to achieve had been appointing a committee to invite ministers from neighboring religious societies to come preach from time to time. The Middlefield congregation was a flock of sheep without a shepherd, and for so long as they remained thus they would be easy prey for the wolves of sin.

Chapter Forty-Five

May, 1791
Outside Savannah, Georgia

The vista through the glass panels flanking the brick mansion's double doors was loveliest at dawn. Esther Lyman watched the rising sun's long rays touch first the far-off islands along the Atlantic coast, then the South Carolina mainland, then glint off the surface of the Savannah River, which formed the Georgia boundary. Finally the morning light streamed through the windows into the house, situated but three hundred feet from the riverbank in a grove of mulberry trees.

Elihu had envisioned such an estate for them when they sailed for Georgia more than five years ago. But they were only guests of the mistress of this large rice plantation a dozen miles north of Savannah: the lovely and notoriously flirtatious Catherine Greene, thirty-seven-year-old widow of Revolutionary War hero General Nathanael Greene.

So far anything even close to this kind of prosperity had eluded the Lymans. More accurately, Esther thought, they had eluded it. Elihu had proven no more able or inclined to light anywhere for very long in Georgia than he had in Connecticut – to Esther's great frustration.

After arriving in Georgia early in 1786, they hadn't settled on the two hundred acres of pineland wilderness northwest of Savannah that the state had granted Elihu. Instead, they'd taken up residence farther to the south, in Liberty County. There Elihu had plunged into law and politics, being twice elected to the Georgia House of Representatives.

Early in 1790 they'd moved to Savannah. But before the year was out they pulled up stakes again to move to Elihu's original land grant.

They'd cleared enough space to build a simple house. Elihu had started practicing medicine and became involved in local government as a justice of the peace. How long they would remain at this new location Esther didn't hazard to guess. But so far she hadn't realized the stability she'd hoped would be her reward for accompanying Elihu into exile – for her there was no other word for it – from Connecticut.

Yet in this alien land God in His goodness had bestowed upon them blessings denied in Connecticut. In 1787, after nine years of marriage, Esther had at last borne Elihu a healthy child, little Esther Maria. Two years later she gave birth to a son, named Alfred.

Esther fretted constantly over her children's health in this feverish climate. Although still early May, it was already steamier and stickier here in the marshy, flat low country of coastal Georgia than on the hottest, most humid August day in Connecticut. But both Esther Maria and Alfred so far seemed to thrive.

"So you took my suggestion to catch the sunrise," a soft voice said from behind Esther. She turned to smile at the man who was, she thought, indeed proof that as the hymn said, God moves in a mysterious way. For what were the chances that Phineas Miller, son of Isaac Miller, born and raised in Middlefield less than a mile from the Lyman homestead, would turn up in Georgia within a day's ride of where Esther and Elihu lived?

Esther and Elihu had known Phineas Miller back in Connecticut as an intelligent, reserved, yet warm-hearted youth. After graduating from Yale College in 1785, Miller had become tutor to the children of General Nathanael Greene, who was moving from Rhode Island to take possession of a confiscated Tory plantation called Mulberry Grove.

When General Greene died unexpectedly the next year, Phineas had assumed management of Mulberry Grove for Mrs. Greene – and had fallen deeply in love with her. Whether Kitty Greene returned Phineas's affections was still unclear.

Esther cherished their rare visits to Mulberry Grove, during which she and Phineas reminisced about growing up in the hills and vales of Connecticut, so unlike this flat, swampy low country. They traded news about people and events back home that they'd received in letters. For Esther these chats were like refreshing New England autumn breezes blowing away the humid oppressiveness of Georgia.

"It's every bit as beautiful as you promised," Esther acknowledged. "And yet," she sighed, "I'd trade it in a minute for one snowfall, one sturdy stone wall from Connecticut."

Young Miller studied her profile with sympathetic understanding. From the first time they met in Georgia he'd sensed Esther Lyman's dissatisfaction with this country, her homesickness for Connecticut. He couldn't help but be amused that it was two of the harshest features of their native land – the frigid winter weather and the rocks the soil brought forth constantly in great numbers – that she recalled with such nostalgia.

Dr. Lyman, by contrast, had enthusiastically embraced everything about Georgia. As if the thought had conjured him up, Elihu appeared behind them. "There you are!" he exclaimed. Phineas saw Esther wipe the melancholy from her expression before she turned to greet her husband.

"Mrs. Greene says breakfast is ready," Elihu said. "And General Wayne is here with news about General St. Clair's progress on organizing the federal military expedition to end the Indian raids on the Ohio frontier." General Anthony Wayne, whose bold, even rash behavior in battle during the Revolution had earned him the nickname "Mad Anthony," lived in Georgia and had become one of Elihu's close political associates.

"I'll be eager to hear what he has to say," Phineas said. Georgia's far western border still suffered from raids by Indians who had connections with those responsible for attacks on the Ohio frontier.

"May I escort you into breakfast?" Elihu asked Esther with a jaunty formality. He bent his arm and offered his elbow, upon which Esther placed her hand and, with Phineas leading the way, they went into the dining room.

Chapter Forty-Six

January, 1793
Durham

"Have you heard anything of late from your brother?" Samuel Camp asked David. A stocky man nearing sixty, Camp was related by blood or marriage – David wasn't sure which – to Esther Lyman.

The two men were walking toward the house of Thomas Lyman with a briskness due to the harsh cold. The temperature hadn't risen above freezing all day, and was dropping fast with the sun having just set.

"A letter came last week," David said, his breath forming vapor that streamed from his mouth like smoke from a chimney. "Esther and the children were sick with one of the fevers that plague everyone in Georgia's unhealthful climate, but they're better now."

David let a long moment pass before continuing, "And Elihu has asked General Wayne to secure him an appointment in the medical line in the new Legion of the United States being formed."

"Why on earth would he do that?" Camp asked in surprise. David's reaction had been the same upon reading the news.

This would be the third expedition the federal government had sent to try to subdue the Indians on the Ohio frontier. The first two had ended in disaster. In the fall of 1790, nearly half of the five hundred men commanded by General Josiah Harmar had been killed or wounded. A year later an army of one thousand soldiers under command of the inept General Arthur St. Clair had been ambushed by Indians. More than six hundred Americans had been butchered and buried in a common grave, including two teenage volunteers from Durham, John Dunn and Benoni Camp. The latter youth was a relative of both Samuel Camp and Esther Lyman.

"Elihu says it's hoped defeating the Indians north of the Ohio will help end Indian raids on the Georgia frontier," David said. "It's strongly suspected that the Indians are being encouraged to continue hostilities against Americans by British troops who still occupy forts they agreed to leave under the terms of the treaty securing our independence." That last bit of information was most illuminating. Camp knew how much Elihu hated the British.

"Why would Elihu think this new Legion has any greater chance of succeeding than the first two?" Camp asked.

David shrugged. "He may have confidence that General Wayne can lead the expedition to victory. He's gotten to know the man well in Georgia. And General Wayne was a successful commander in battle during the Revolution."

The two men had reached the stone steps leading to the doorway of Thomas Lyman's house. David stopped, then blurted out in perplexed frustration, "I've long since given up trying to fathom what drives my brother. He seems incapable of settling down anywhere. He's lived in four places during seven years in Georgia. He's farmed little, has practiced some medicine, dabbled in politics – and now this–." David's voice trailed off. "Esther must be frantic," he added with a shake of his head.

"When you write to them, please include my regards," said Camp. They mounted the steps to the door. David's troubled expression changed to one of irritation when he caught sight of Joshua Stow approaching from the barn. "The skunk has arrived to our party," he said sourly.

Samuel Camp's bushy eyebrows drew together as he read the scrap of paper. With a sigh of irritated resignation he looked up at the dozen men gathered in the parlor of Thomas Lyman's house. Thomas was a second cousin to David.

"Mr. Stow has proposed the question for discussion at this evening's meeting of the Ethosian Society," Camp announced.

"The question: 'Is there such a being or spirit as the Devil'?" Camp, stared disapprovingly at Joshua Stow, who flashed back a broad grin.

It was a legitimate topic for consideration by the Ethosian Society, founded by Durham and Middlefield men to expand their knowledge and open their minds to new ideas. They read not only the Bible, but secular works from the organization's private library. They sharpened their wits by spirited debate on sometimes controversial subjects.

"Favor us with your thoughts, Mr. Goodrich," Stow said to Durham's minister with a transparently false geniality. Now thirty, Joshua Stow was no longer a lowly schoolmaster, but a farmer in Middlefield, with a wife and two daughters. He had a squared-off chin and a strong, slightly skewed nose. Heavy lids drooped over intense blue eyes that looked like small stones. Above these features rose a forehead so broad and high it suggested a brain too large to be contained within a normal-sized cranium.

"There can be no doubt that the Devil exists," replied Elizur Goodrich, pastor for the past thirty-eight years of Durham's Congregational church. At nearly sixty, Mr. Goodrich was renowned for his keen intellect and depth of knowledge. He spoke patiently; it wasn't the first time he'd been challenged by skeptics.

"The Devil is mentioned several times in the Bible," the minister continued. "Mark, Chapter 4, Verse 1, says that, 'Then was Jesus led up of the spirit into the wilderness to be tempted of the devil.'" Mr. Goodrich quoted effortlessly from memory.

"If you believe in the truth of the Holy Scriptures, then you must believe in the Devil," Samuel Camp said emphatically.

Joshua pushed out his broad lower lip and nodded in exaggerated, blatantly mocking contemplation of the men's responses. "Yet I don't believe in the Devil," he declared. "I base my opinion on evidence more credible than the scribblings of men who've been dead well over a thousand years." He smiled with satisfaction at the consternation his attack on the Bible's veracity stirred up among the members.

"What evidence could possibly carry more weight than divine revelation?" demanded Mr. Goodrich calmly.

"The exact opposite of revelation," Joshua answered. "Last month, late one moonless night, I went alone deep into the woods near my home. I knelt down upon the dead weeds and fallen leaves, bowed my head, and prayed that if there is such a being as the Devil, that he might appear to me then and there, so that I might know of his existence."

A sense of horror crawled through the room. "You – you conjured up Satan?" Noah Talcott, secretary of the Ethosian Society, choked out. "That's witchcraft!"

"Settle down, Noah," Joshua said, as if speaking to an excitable dog. "Let me finish before you make such an ignorant accusation. I prayed, as I said, for the Devil to show himself to me. I waited for a very long time in the woods on my knees, until my legs were cramped and I was so cold I would have welcomed a bit of hellfire. But neither the Devil – nor any other spirit – revealed himself to me. Thus I conclude from my own experience, my own senses, that there is no Devil."

For a long moment no one spoke. Several men shifted uncomfortably in their chairs.

"Perhaps Satan had more important souls than yours to attend to on that particular night, Josh," Elisha Coe observed jokingly.

"Or perhaps the Devil reasoned that not answering your summons would lead you to doubt his existence, and then by extension the truth of the Scriptures which proclaim his reality," said David. "That Satan didn't appear when you played Doubting Thomas might itself be proof that he does exist."

"That's possible," Joshua replied with a clear lack of conviction.

"Just because you didn't receive something at the very moment you asked for it doesn't mean it doesn't exist," pointed out Mr. Goodrich. "Perhaps Satan will answer your summons at a time and in a place of his own choosing – when your soul is least prepared to resist him. Beware, Mr. Stow!"

Joshua bridled at the presumptuous warning. But Thomas Lyman interjected, "At least no one can accuse you of playing Devil's advocate, Josh." The observation had the intended effect of reducing to some small degree the rising tension in the room.

David pulled his greatcoat more tightly around him as he contemplated with annoyance Joshua's smug satisfaction at having unsettled the gathering by blaspheming the Scriptures. In some contrary way Joshua Stow seemed less mature than when he'd assisted at David's house-raising seven years ago.

Joshua Stow's behavior tonight was, thought David, a symptom of the infidelity that had been on the increase since the end of the Revolution. Sabbath-breaking, drunkenness, lechery, fornication, and profanity were just some of the sins that had become more common. Rebellion against the king had had the unexpected consequence of inspiring many people to defy other traditional sources of authority, such as the Congregational church. It was a problem in Connecticut in general, and in particular in Middlefield, which had yet to secure a successor to Abner Benedict.

David knew some people considered the Ethosian Society itself a symptom of moral and religious degeneration. Its members' willingness, as "free inquirers after the truth," to open the Scriptures for debate disturbed many devoutly religious people.

For the first two or three years David had enjoyed the Ethosian Society's weekly meetings, with their spirited debates on religious, philosophical, practical, and moral questions. But the tenor of the gatherings had changed of late, thanks to incidents such as Joshua Stow had instigated. David believed Stow raised such topics not out of a sincere desire to hear them debated intelligently in an honest search for enlightenment, but to agitate and create an excuse to spout his heresy.

An awkward silence fell again. No one wanted to prolong the contentious debate. "I suggest we adjourn for the evening," Samuel Camp said at last.

David picked up his hat and stepped out into the biting cold. He retrieved his horse from his cousin's barn, mounted it, and was heading west on Crooked Lane at a trot when he heard his name called. Elisha Coe spurred his horse to catch up with him.

"Don't judge Joshua Stow too harshly, David," Coe said at last. "We've been friends since boyhood. His faith once was strong, thanks to Mr. Benedict's spiritual guidance. But Joshua was greatly upset by the manner of Mr. Benedict's leaving, by how that good man was abused by some members of his flock. The hypocrisy soured him on religion. For all that, I believe he is truly striving to determine the truth."

David peered at Coe in the moonlight. He was a strong, solid, no-nonsense young man who in seven years of marriage to Elizabeth Miller had fathered four children, including two sons, and was expanding his property through thrift and hard work. David wondered if Joshua Stow knew how lucky he was to have such an honorable and steadfast defender.

"Joshua's faith may be a casualty of the Middlefield congregation's sinful folly," David conceded. "But I think part of him delights in being notorious for his more outrageous actions. We have enough troubles without Joshua Stow stirring up hornets' nests for no other reason than irritating and inflicting pain on others," he finished contemptuously.

With that David slapped his heels against the horse's flanks to spur the animal homeward. Elisha Coe watched him go until he was swallowed up by the darkness.

Chapter Forty-Seven

August, 1794
Ohio Country

Elihu had been certain no sight could be more terrifying than the human killing machines called Hessians he'd faced on Long Island. But he'd been wrong, he discovered on this rain-drenched summer morning in the Ohio Country wilderness.

Through the swirling smoke from the battle that had begun around nine o'clock, Elihu could glimpse half-naked savages rising like demons out of Hell from behind trunks of huge trees felled by a recent tornado. Their faces and bodies were decorated with stripes of war paint that ran in the steady rain. They brandished tomahawks and scalping knives wildly. Their blood-curdling shrieks caused the hair on the nape of Elihu's neck to stand on end.

Elihu was crouched down, his hands under the armpits of a cavalry soldier who'd been knocked off his mount by an enemy musket ball. He was struggling to pull the dazed man to his feet.

Elihu had felt confident that this army had a much better chance of victory over the Indians than the previous two. This Legion was twice the size of the one General St. Clair had led to slaughter, and it was commanded by the far abler Anthony Wayne.

However, these first few minutes of fighting gave Elihu reason to fear another massacre of American troops. Wayne's clever strategy to draw the Indians onto open ground and then encircle them wasn't working as planned, in part because the persistent downpour interfered with communication.

A foreboding had come over Elihu the previous night, during a violent thunderstorm. He resolutely ignored it as he focused on getting the wounded cavalryman upright and to a relatively safe spot – where that might be he had no idea – and there tend to his wound.

"Sir!" the injured soldier suddenly gasped in terror. Elihu looked up to see an Indian charging toward them, his mouth twisted in a fiendish grin, a tomahawk in one upraised hand, a wooden war club in the other.

Elihu dropped the cavalryman, then spied the wounded soldier's musket on the ground. He picked it up intending to use the bayonet fixed to its end to fend off the Indian. But then he saw the weapon had been loaded but not fired. Praying the powder hadn't gotten too wet to ignite, Elihu lifted the musket to his shoulder and fired without even taking time to aim. The musket ball struck the Indian, less than ten feet away, square in the chest.

Blood spurted from the Indian's wound, mixing with the streaked war paint. Although dead on his feet, the man had been running so hard that his momentum carried him forward far enough to collapse directly on top of Elihu, who was knocked to the ground.

Elihu struggled to free himself from the corpse. But before he could get clear he saw emerging through the smoke from his musket shot a second Indian, who'd been only a short distance behind the first. He watched in horror as the Indian brought his war club down on the wounded cavalryman's skull, smashing it like an eggshell. Then he raised the weapon, covered with blood and hair and brain matter, and turned toward Elihu.

His legs still pinned under the dead Indian, Elihu twisted to the right, grabbing frantically for the musket, which had been knocked from his hands when he fell. But before his fingers could reach it, the Indian's war club came down on his head with such force it seemed to drive his head into his shoulders. Excruciating pain was followed by blackness.

Chapter Forty-Eight

October, 1794
Middlefield

"Tell your brothers to crush all the apples that are left," David told Phineas as he pushed with all the strength his tired muscles could muster against the long, thick sapling trunk that served as the lever to turn the heavy wooden screw on the cider press. The teenager obediently hurried out the door of the large shed that housed the press.

The squeal of the turning screw was followed by the sound of juice squeezed from the crushed apple pulp, called pomace, trickling through layers of straw that filtered out seeds and stems, then down a wooden trough into a broad wooden bucket. It would require several more powerful turns of the screw to extract the maximum amount of juice from this batch of pomace. A heady odor, at once sweet and tangy, redolent of both summer and autumn, filled the air.

Phineas at last came back into the shed carrying a bucket of pomace in each hand. David paused gratefully while the youth set the buckets down, then replaced the nearly full bucket of juice with an empty one.

Although it was cool inside the shed on this chilly autumn afternoon, David was sweating profusely from his exertion. He was, however, breathing only slightly faster than normal – testimony, he thought gratefully, to the fine physical condition he enjoyed now at forty-eight, the result of long days of farm labor, He was now two years older than his father had been when he died, David thought. It was a comparison he instinctively made whenever the subject of age came up.

Since shortly after dawn on this late October day, David and Phineas had been taking turns working the press. A couple of days past his fifteenth birthday, Phineas had grown tall and strong enough to be of real assistance with even the most physically demanding chores on the farm. David doubted that Phineas, who took after Sarah's side of the family in physique, would ever match his father's height. But he had a solid, muscular build.

Phineas's once-bright flaxen hair had dulled to the color of straw. Along with Sarah's fair coloring and soft gray eyes, he had inherited his mother's even temperament. The result was that he remained, even as he reached the middle of the often troublesome teenage years, an amiable fellow.

Phineas took true pleasure in working the land, especially by his father's side. David, however, had been considering whether this bright son might be a candidate for college and the careers it would open, such as the pulpit or the law. David couldn't help but reflect with satisfaction on how different Phineas's fortunes were from the crushing responsibilities that had been David's lot at the same age.

Outside the shed, David, Jr., thirteen; Billy, eleven; and their little brother Alanson, seven, were making the pomace. Fresh apples placed in a circular wooden trough were crushed by a heavy wooden wheel pulled by a horse.

When Phineas finished switching the buckets, David noticed that his mouth was twisted in annoyance. "I had to pull Billy and David apart," he told his father in exasperation. "I gather David tried to slip away when Billy wasn't looking, but Billy caught him and was about to give him a thrashing. Alanson was cheering Billy on. I promised all of them they would have trouble sitting down to supper tonight if I caught them shirking or fighting again."

David rolled his eyes as he prepared for another push against the lever. Squabbling was an old story between these two brothers, but it must have been nastier than usual to have so ruffled Phineas.

Maintaining discipline among a brood that now included four boys and four girls – with Sarah set to deliver another one at year's end – was a responsibility for which David looked more and more to Phineas for assistance as well. Unlike most households, the Lymans had no grandparents, aunts, or uncles living with them to help keep youngsters in line and correct them when they stepped out. Polly, now sixteen, could handle minor disagreements, with Phineas stepping in when a firmer, possibly physical, solution was required with his brothers. Sarah and David became involved on the rare occasions when disagreements threatened to spin out of control.

"We'll finish these apples for the Birdseys today, press Elisha Coe's tomorrow, and Isaac Miller's the day after that. Then we'll be done with cider-making for this year," David said. Investing in the cider press had proven to be a wise move. He could turn much of his own apple harvest into more cider than his family needed, leaving a surplus to sell.

Since David was one of the few farmers in Middlefield to own a press, many neighbors brought him their apple crops to turn into the cider that, sweet or hard, was drunk in every household morning, noon, and night, year-round. Even when he'd paid a hired man to help, he'd turned a profit. With Phineas now able to do part of the labor, and David and Billy coming on, the cider press was increasingly lucrative.

The rectangle of light cast on the shed floor by late afternoon sun streaming through the doorway was suddenly blotted out by the figure of a tall, broad-beamed man. When after a moment his vision adjusted to the sudden drop in light, David recognized Isaac Miller.

"If you've brought your apples for pressing, Isaac, give them to David and Billy to put away," David said agreeably before Miller could speak, continuing to work the press. "We won't get to them until day after tomorrow – first come, first served," he observed in a voice filled with cheer at the thought of how much extra income his shrewd investment was bringing in.

"I received a letter from Phineas–," Isaac began. David cut him short. "Already?" he said curiously. "He barely had time to get back to Georgia from his visit here. Did he write to say he's convinced the attractive Widow Greene to marry him? It took but one look to see he's in love with her, and she gave every indication of being quite fond of him."

Isaac tried to interrupt, but David rattled on, a bit breathless as he continued to push on the lever. "Wedding Catherine Greene would be another feather in Phineas's cap," David said good-naturedly. Phineas was Isaac's pride and joy, first graduating from Yale, then setting himself up in Georgia where he'd become friends with many famous and powerful people. They included the hero of the hour, General Anthony Wayne, who'd led the Legion of the United States to a crushing victory over the Indians in the Ohio Country in August.

"Elihu's dead," Isaac finally managed to say. David stopped pushing against the lever so abruptly that he nearly lost his balance. Phineas looked up sharply from pouring juice from a bucket into a barrel, spilling a large quantity into the straw-covered dirt.

David took a long moment to absorb the meaning of Isaac's words and the expression of profound sorrow on his face. "Elihu dead?" he said in disbelief when he at last found his voice. "When? How?"

"In the battle General Wayne fought against the Indians in August," Isaac said quietly.

"But we heard that was a great victory for our army," Phineas objected. "The Indians were soundly beaten."

"That's true," Isaac acknowledged. "But some members of the Legion were killed in the fighting." Isaac turned to address David again. "Esther received the news several weeks ago, but couldn't bring herself to write to you herself. She waited until Phineas returned to Georgia, and asked him to send word. Phineas wrote to me and asked that I tell you."

David's mouth hung half open in shock. He looked down at the ground, as if searching for something.

"Couldn't it be a mistake?" Phineas demanded urgently. "I've heard tales of how during the war men were reported dead, only to show up later alive."

Isaac shook his head sadly in response to Phineas's attempt to deny the awful truth. "Phineas said Esther learned of Elihu's death in a letter from General Wayne himself."

"*Damn him!*" David cried suddenly in a voice full of fury. He grabbed a bucket of pomace, then turned and hurled it with all his might against the back wall of the shed. With a crash the bucket splintered into a dozen pieces, and the contents splattered everywhere. The startled Isaac and Phineas both jumped involuntarily.

Billy and David appeared on either side of Isaac in the doorway, looking for the source of the ruckus. A second later Alanson squeezed in next to Billy. They took in the disturbing scene, then looked for an explanation to Phineas, who silenced them with a sharp glance and a shake of his head.

David's shoulders heaved as he drew a deep breath, then let it out on a long sob. "He had no business going off and getting himself killed!" His voice was harsh with anger, but when he turned to face the others they saw his eyes were brimming with tears. "If he couldn't be content here in Connecticut, why couldn't he at least stay put in Georgia? Why did he go to war again? He'd already done his duty to his country – and more!"

"Uncle Elihu?" Billy breathed. When Isaac nodded in confirmation, the three boys stared with uneasy sympathy at their father, who was trembling violently.

All of David's sons had been too young when Elihu left Connecticut to have any clear memory of him. But they'd heard many stories about him from their parents. They understood why David was grief-stricken, but his anger baffled them.

Phineas was also perplexed by an undertone of guilt he'd detected in his father's outburst. Isaac Miller had sensed it too, and from a lifetime of knowing the Lyman family he could make a good guess as to its source. It would make Elihu's death all the more excruciating a cross for David to bear.

"Didn't he think of his children, his wife?" David demanded suddenly of no one in particular. Tears trickled down his cheeks.

"My son Phineas will do what he can for them," was all Isaac could offer.

"Poor Esther," David went on, as if he hadn't heard Isaac. "Elihu was everything to her. I don't know if she can survive losing him – or if she'll want to."

"She's a strong woman who has her children to live for and friends who will offer every assistance within their power," Isaac said consolingly. "With God's help she'll survive this horrible loss – as will you," he said with compassionate certainty

"But will my mother?" David asked somberly. Isaac had no reply, simply stepped aside to let David pass by and prepare to tell Hope she'd outlived another of her children.

"When he sailed for Georgia, I didn't expect to see him again in this life," said Hope. Eyes cast down unseeingly at the wooden floorboards of the parlor in her North Guilford home, she was speaking as much to herself as to David or to Daniel, who continued to hold her hand as he had while David broke the terrible news of Elihu's death. After a long moment she looked up at David and said in a thick voice, "But I thought it would be me the Lord would call home."

David had brought Phineas, David, Billy, and Alanson with him on this mournful errand. Once his guilt-fueled fury had burned itself out, he'd found a measure of comfort in his children, these four fine sons in particular. He hoped their presence would have the same effect upon Hope, would remind her of how very much she still had left in this world, of the abundance of masculine strength she had to support her in this awful hour.

The boys were uneasy, unsure of how to act in a situation so highly charged with emotion. David had explained to his sons why he wanted them there, but Phineas had taken pains to impress upon his younger brothers the surprising fact that their father needed their emotional support as much as their Granny Fowler did. And so they stood their posts faithfully, albeit stiffly.

David had feared Elihu's death would prove too great a shock to his mother. It had been more than fifteen years since Hannah's death, and she had good reason to hope that, at seventy-five, she would not bury another child.

"Maybe this is why the Lord has kept me alive for so long, even as I chafe at the infirmities of age," Hope said in a small voice. "He's testing whether my trust in Him is strong enough to withstand the death of another of my children." There was a long silence as Hope waged an internal battle. "And I say, 'Thy will be done,'" she whispered at last.

David couldn't help but marvel at how decades of difficult living had wrinkled his mother's face, turned her hair the color of cold ashes, and slowed her step, but hadn't dimmed her faith in the least. Yet for all the power of her inspiring example, when David looked at his four sons he couldn't conceive of enduring the death of even one of his children, let alone six as his mother had.

"Still," Hope said, her features tightening as her body began to tremble, "I wish God had called me to Heaven, there to greet Elihu many years hence, not left me here on earth to mourn him."

Chapter Forty-Nine

September, 1797
New Haven

Catharine Benton called on every bit of self-control she had to try to maintain the decorum appropriate to this occasion in the brick meetinghouse on the New Haven green. But she couldn't hold back tears when a young man of medium height, with dramatically chiseled features and thick black hair, rose. Lyman Beecher stepped forward to accept from Yale College President Timothy Dwight the document awarding him a bachelor of arts degree.

Catharine paid no attention to the rest of the graduation, or to the music that followed. She was thinking of her sister, Esther Lyman Beecher, in her grave these twenty-one years, yet still living on in this fine son.

David Beecher, now married to his fifth wife, had never sought to bring Lyman back into his home. He'd left the boy with Catharine and Lot, visiting Lyman on occasion.

Why David Beecher had done so – whether he felt bound to fulfill Esther's dying request that Catharine raise their son, whether he found Lyman a disturbing reminder of the cherished wife he'd lost after less than a year of marriage, whether he'd taken pity upon Lot and Catharine's childlessness – Catharine didn't know and didn't care. She simply thanked God every day for giving her and Lot this boy, whom they'd raised as their own son in all but name.

Following the closing prayers, the spectators spilled out of the meetinghouse onto the green, to wait for the graduates to emerge. It was a splendid September day, the cloudless sky a pure blue.

A short time later, Lyman Beecher stepped out of the meetinghouse. He searched the crowd, then made his way to David Beecher. The young man bore a noticeable resemblance to his father, but his deep-set eyes under full arched brows and his long, angular nose were testimony to his Lyman blood.

David and Lyman Beecher exchanged a firm handshake. "Congratulations," was all the older man said, a bit formally. Lyman replied, "Thank you, Father," then kissed his stepmother on the cheek.

Lyman turned and walked directly over to Catharine, the only mother he'd ever known. He bent over to embrace her plump form lovingly, squeezing from Catharine's tightly closed eyes more tears of joy. She hugged Lyman fiercely in return, then patted him on the shoulder as he released her.

Catharine wiped away her tears, then resorted to fussing unnecessarily with her eight-inch-high white lace mob cap to give herself time to regain control of her emotions. "Now look what you've done, Lyman," she scolded gently, fingering the cap's pleated front ruffle and flat satin bow. "Your Uncle Lot let me buy this hat especially for today, and now you've mussed it up." Lyman smiled in amused understanding.

Lyman looked to Lot Benton, standing beside Catharine. The look of alarm on his uncle's craggy face took the young man aback for a moment, until he realized the old farmer feared Lyman was about to hug him as he had his aunt.

Lot relaxed visibly when Lyman simply extended his right hand. When Lot took it, Lyman placed his other hand upon it like a seal. "Good job," was all Lot said, but there was no need for him to say more. Lyman had long ago learned that two words of praise from Lot Benton counted for more than an entire speech from most other men. And he could read in Lot's gray eyes love and pride that warmed his heart.

Lyman's face lit up when he saw Hope. She was leaning on David's arm. At seventy-eight, her body was growing frailer by the day, but her spirit remained strong. She had the love and respect of David and Catharine and their families. And she had Daniel, whose affection and understanding had made the seventeen years since they'd wed among the happiest of her long life.

Lyman hurried over to his grandmother. "I was afraid you might not feel well enough to come today," he exclaimed, kissing her on the forehead and hugging her carefully as if she were made of glass.

Hope stroked the back of her hand along the side of Lyman's handsome brow. "I wouldn't let anything keep me from being with you on this blessed day," she said. Even more gratifying for Hope than Lyman's graduation from college was his plan to study to become a minister. It was as if she and John – gone from earth these thirty-four years but never far from her heart – were giving back to God through their first-born grandchild's dedication of his life to His service.

"I was a fool to doubt that you would be here," Lyman said with a grin.

Hope searched his face and said, with a hint of wonder, "I can still see you as clearly as if it were yesterday – a little boy, just a stick of a thing, running into the house as I made my way up the road for a visit, calling 'Granny Fowler's coming!' to your Aunt Benton with such glee."

Lyman smiled at his grandmother's recollection. He straightened up to exchange congratulatory handshakes with his Uncle David and with Daniel Fowler, and to embrace Sarah.

Lyman turned to eagerly make his way to a young woman who'd been waiting with shy patience. Roxana Foote of Guilford was a short woman of Lyman's age. She had a full oval face with light blue eyes. Her gown of loose white muslin with puffy elbow-length sleeves was gathered at the waist with a wide pink satin sash tied in a large bow at the back. Her short, light brown curls were held back by a pink headband.

"I always thought it a great kindness for David Beecher to let Lot and Catharine raise Lyman, even after he re-married," David observed to Hope. "But I never truly understood how enormous a sacrifice he made until I had children of my own."

"He was likely moved as much by the tightness of his pocketbook as by generosity of spirit," Hope said cynically. David stared at his mother in puzzled surprise; stubborn and contentious she'd always been, but never spiteful. And he'd never heard her speak a word of criticism of David Beecher.

Hope's expression turned sheepish under David's inquiring gaze. "I'll always be grateful to him for the tender love he bore Esther," she amended. Realizing she couldn't let her first remark go unexplained, she reluctantly continued.

"Catharine and Lot will be furious if they learn I've told anyone. They've taught Lyman to honor David Beecher as his father, wouldn't want him diminished in that role in the eyes of others."

David said nothing, simply tilted his head a bit to indicate she should continue.

"Lot wanted to leave Lyman his farm and house in North Guilford as he would have to a son of his own," Hope said. "But when it became clear Lyman wasn't cut out for farming, Lot gave up that dream. He arranged for Noah Williston to prepare Lyman for college, in token of the love Mr. Williston bore for your sister Hannah."

None of this was news to David. He nodded to encourage his mother to continue.

"When Lyman was admitted to Yale, David and Lot agreed that Catharine would sew all Lyman's clothes and David would pay all the college bills. But David is always complaining he's close to bankruptcy – whether with cause I don't know," Hope said in exasperation.

"Catharine confided to me that David claimed paying to keep Lyman at Yale would ruin him financially – even with Lyman working to help pay the bills," Hope went on. "Lot couldn't bear for Lyman to be cheated of an education. Lot sold the farm and house. He used part of the money to buy a home on the Guilford green, and from what was left paid most of the cost for Lyman to attend Yale."

David was taken aback. He'd assumed Lot sold the farm and moved into the village because at nearly sixty he was finding it increasingly difficult to farm, especially since he no longer had Lyman's help. He'd had no idea Lot was financing Lyman's education.

Moved by this revelation, David surveyed the green until he located his brother-in-law. Lot was standing, as always, a bit apart from the group. His gaze was fixed on Lyman, who was chatting with Roxana and Catharine. For the first time in the thirty-five years he'd known Lot Benton, David had an inkling of why Catharine was so happy in her marriage and why Lyman felt such affection for his crusty uncle.

David gently removed Hope's hand from his arm. He walked over to stand next to Lot, both of them looking out at a trio of cows grazing on the other side of the green.

"It seems you were right to suggest Lyman go to Yale," David observed after a minute.

"Well, he didn't have the makings of a good farmer," Lot replied matter-of-factly. "Many's the time I caught him building castles in the air while he was plowing a row. I'd have to shake him out of it and make him do the row over again. Once I found him in the barn reading a book while he was breaking flax! There wasn't much else to do but send him to school."

Lot's casting of his selfless act as an unavoidable practical solution was no less than David expected. Still, he couldn't allow the sacrifice he'd heard about from Hope go unrecognized.

David stepped around to stand face-to-face with Lot. He looked him straight in the eye and said sincerely, "Thank you for all you've done, for Lyman, for Catharine – and for Esther."

Lot's jaw tightened, the faintest blush tinged his cheeks, and he acknowledged David's words with a short, sharp nod. Lot then quickly glanced away, but not before David could see that his meaning had been understood, and appreciated.

"Mother Fowler says you've got one of the largest lists in Middlefield now," Lot said, eager to change the subject to anything other than himself. "You own upwards of five hundred acres, as well as that land you've been buying up in Vermont and New York."

David winced in embarrassment at Lot's mention of Hope's boasting about her son's prosperity. "I'm no poor-mouth," he said, resisting the urge to add "like David Beecher." "I won't pretend I haven't done better than most in business."

"You've served your community, too," Lot said. "You're a colonel in the militia," said Lot. "And you've been elected selectman for – what is it, three or four years running?"

David nodded in acknowledgement. "That's all true," he said, then hesitated, trying to decide whether to share something that Lot could tell was weighing on his mind.

"But I'm past fifty now, with six sons and four daughters," David at last continued. "Sarah is forty-two, and while we pray our Elihu born in March will be our last child, she may yet present me with another baby – or two. Even with what I've acquired, I still lie awake some nights worrying about how much it will cost to raise them and provide all of them with foundations for their futures.

"I've decided that I've been devoting time to my public duties that I should be spending on my private affairs," David went on. "I'll stand again for selectman, but I plan to resign from the militia."

Lot's eyes widened in surprise. He knew David cherished the respect and the title that came with his militia rank. To give that up meant he must truly be feeling great pressure in his personal life.

Both men turned their eyes toward Lyman, who'd raised his left hand to attract everyone's attention. "Only one thing was needed to make this as joyous a day as a man could hope for," Lyman said in a clear, pleasant voice that David thought would sound well issuing from a pulpit. "Now that lack has been filled, for Roxana and I have agreed to wed once I complete my ministerial studies."

Lyman slipped his arm affectionately around the fiercely blushing Roxana's shoulders. The announcement was hardly a surprise, but nonetheless was greeted with exclamations of joy and heartfelt congratulations.

"Lyman's made himself a fine catch," Lot observed. David wasn't acquainted with Roxana personally, but he knew she was the granddaughter of General Andrew Ward, a Revolutionary War veteran whose family ranked socially and financially above either the Bentons or the Beechers.

"I can't help but wonder how she'll do as a parson's wife, though," Lot went on. "She's so shy around people she makes me look downright chatty. But she's bright, reads everything she can lay her hands on, from books on science to foreign novels. She can even talk French! She's very devout, but her family are Anglicans – what they call Episcopalians now. I don't know how she'll square that with being the wife of a Congregational minister. But she knows how to fill a woman's proper role in the home and family."

David stared at Lot. His description of Roxana Foote constituted the largest number of words David had ever heard the man say at one time. He smiled at the realization that gentle Roxana Foote had charmed her way through the complicated maze into Lot Benton's heart. A young woman who could do that was indeed a fine catch.

Chapter Fifty

November, 1798
Middlefield

Phineas leancd against the rough-hewn desk, resting his weight on his right hip in order to favor – inconspicuously, he hoped – his left leg. The pain grew worse with each day, but he fought through it, determined not to let his father down.

The blaze in the fireplace a few feet behind Phineas was so hot that the nape of his neck was sweating. But except for the lucky few seated close enough to the fireplace, which was the building's only source of heat, the forty or so students in the Middlefield schoolhouse on this cold afternoon wore their coats and hats.

Chill drafts blew through gaps in the small, one-room structure's clapboard walls, causing many children to shiver. The students sat on rough, backless benches in front of unfinished planks that jutted out at something close to a right angle from the walls, or along the side of a long table in the middle of the ramshackle structure.

The crude building and furnishings of Middlefield's common, or public, school were typical of those in any Connecticut town. Penny-pinching taxpayers wanted their children to be taught the basics of reading, writing, and arithmetic, but saw no need to spend money on anything but the barest necessities to do so. The parents themselves had been educated under such conditions, and most believed what had been good enough for them was good enough for their sons and daughters.

The scholars ranged in age from tiny children of four to adolescents not much younger than their nineteen-year-old teacher.

The student body included a motley assortment of Coes, Millers, and Birdseys, with a sprinkling of students bearing surnames less common in Middlefield. There were five Lymans in attendance: Urania, six; Sally, nine; Alanson, twelve; Esther, thirteen; and Billy, fifteen. The two toddlers, Andrew and Elihu, were at home, along with David, Jr., seventeen, and Polly, twenty.

"I'll be testing this group on easy words of three syllables, accented on the first," Phineas announced to about a third of the students. He glanced down at the book in his hand. The small, slim volume bore the pretentious title *A Grammatical Institute of the English Language*, but was commonly called the "blue-backed speller," from the plain blue paper with which it was covered. It had been written fifteen years ago by Noah Webster, a young Yale graduate from Hartford. Since its publication it had replaced all other books, most by British authors, to become the standard text for teaching reading and spelling across Connecticut. The book was rapidly gaining popularity throughout much of the new nation.

"'Medical,'" Phineas enunciated carefully, then paused as fifteen quills scratched the word onto the rough, thick pages of copybooks. Fortunately the temperature in the building had struggled far enough above freezing to thaw the ink in the inkwells.

"'Diadem,'" Phineas said once all the students had stopped writing. "'Alcoran'" was the next word he chose from the list of more than three hundred he'd directed this group of students to study at the beginning of the day. He followed that with "'abstinence.'"

"There's a word I don't ever plan to use," declared Silas Turner in a whisper intended to be heard by all in the room. He was a beefy, florid sixteen-year-old who over the summer had shot up six inches and begun to sprout stubble on his chin. Several of the older boys sniggered at the suggestive remark.

Phineas realized wearily that he needed to nip this rude juvenile swaggering in the bud before it disrupted the lesson. He laid his book down on the desk, and limped to where Silas sat, halfway down the long table in the middle of the room.

Phineas looked down at Silas's copybook. He had spelled "medical" correctly, but then completely botched "diadem," and had written only the first two letters of "alcoran" before giving up entirely and applying his quill to making lewd sketches.

"It doesn't look like you tried to master many of the assigned words," Phineas observed.

"Why should I?" Silas demanded with surly contempt. "When will the likes of me ever have need of such five-dollar words?" He opened his copy of the speller. "'Exigence,' 'symphony,'" he sneered, exaggeratedly mispronouncing the words as he played to the crowd of fellow students. "There won't be much call for such fancy talk when I'm a farmer like my father, spreading manure on my fields or butchering a hog. Some know-it-all from Yale just put them in this book to show how smart he is and to squeeze a few pennies out of people foolish enough to buy it."

"I don't think Mr. Webster wrote the speller to embarrass his readers," Phineas answered reasonably. "And there are many words you'll find useful when you become a man, Silas." Phineas ran his finger down the columns of words in Silas's book. "'Citizen,'" he read aloud. "'Currency,' 'family,' 'happiness,' 'honesty,' 'patriot.'"

"Don't forget 'laziness,' Mr. Lyman," called out Peter Ward, setting off an outburst of giggles.

"Or 'ruffian'!" suggested Asa Lucas.

"'Arrogant'!" a third boy shouted.

"'Flatulence'!" called out another youth. The entire class was convulsed with laughter, sharing the speakers' delight in the chance to needle Silas, whose bullying had left him with few friends among the students.

Phineas looked down at the floor for a moment while he pressed his lips together hard to suppress a smile. All the words the boys had suggested were, indeed, on the assigned list.

Composing his features into a stern expression, Phineas raised his head and glanced around the room at the culprits. He fixed each with a sharp look, both reprimand and warning against further disruption, perfected by years of supervising eight younger siblings.

Turning back, Phineas saw an angry Silas getting to his feet. He obviously intended to take physical revenge on the students who'd called out words he had no doubt were meant as insults, even if he didn't know the exact meaning of each.

"Sit down, Silas," Phineas said in a tone of firm authority that contained a hint of sympathy. Flushed with humiliation and anger, the boy glared at Phineas and growled, "Make me."

Phineas extended his arm to place a conciliatory hand on Silas's shoulder. Thinking Phineas meant to force him down onto his seat, Silas roughly shook off Phineas's hand. Thrown off balance by the unexpected move, Phineas unthinkingly shifted his weight onto his left leg to steady himself. His ailing knee buckled, and he stumbled forward, catching himself with both hands on the edge of the table.

Phineas waited for the agonizing pain in his knee to recede, then started to slowly push himself back up. Silas, who had focused on the teacher as the source of his humiliation, stuck a foot behind Phineas's left leg, placed a hand on his chest, and shoved. Phineas fell backwards and hit the wooden floor with a grunt of pain.

Silas took a step toward Phineas, bent on hurting him further – when a strong hand suddenly grabbed his queue of hair and yanked him backwards, slamming his head on the table. Billy Lyman, half a head shorter and twenty pounds lighter than Silas, released his grip on Silas's hair. Before the stunned youth could react, Billy leaped up onto the table and down onto the same side as Silas. He forced his forearm against Silas's throat, pinning him to the table.

"Leave my brother alone – understand?" Billy commanded in a low voice slurred with fury. When Silas didn't answer, Billy realized he was pressing so hard on Silas's throat that he couldn't speak or even move his head.

Easing up a bit with his arm, Billy repeated his question, and this time Silas nodded in surrender. Billy let him up and waited, breathing heavily with exertion and emotion, until Silas took his seat, where he sat rubbing his throat.

Billy turned to see that Phineas had gotten back on his feet. Billy walked around the table to his own assigned seat on a bench facing the wall. He sat back down next to his brother Alanson, who sank back on the bench from which he'd sprung up in anticipation of the need to back up Billy.

All the girls and most of the boys were visibly upset by the violent incident. Some of the smaller ones, including little Urania Lyman, were close to tears. Clearly no more learning would take place this day, and since it was well into the afternoon Phineas said tersely, "School is dismissed."

The students gathered up their books, slates, and quills and, except for the five Lyman children, all filed thankfully out the door. "Are you all right?" Esther asked Phineas gently.

Phineas forced a wan smile, and nodded to his sister. "You all go on home. I'll be along shortly." Esther studied Phineas worriedly, but at last turned away and began shepherding her siblings home.

Phineas set about banking the fire, breaking up the logs with a poker so the flames would die down and go out, reducing the risk of an accidental fire during the night. With a shovel he piled some of the coals together and covered them with ashes to keep them alive until the next morning, when he'd use them to kindle a new blaze.

Suddenly Phineas sensed someone behind him. Turning cautiously, he saw not Silas Turner, as he'd feared, but Billy.

"That temper of yours will land you in jail, or worse," Phineas scolded, purposely taking the offensive to cover his embarrassment at having had control of the school wrested from him so easily.

"You can't keep this up, Phineas," Billy said bluntly, ignoring his brother's warning. "You can't keep hiding from Papa how bad your knee has gotten. You have to tell him you can't teach school any longer. If you don't, I will," he added, surprising himself. He hadn't expected to have the nerve to issue an ultimatum to the big brother he'd always looked up to.

Phineas turned his attention back to the fire for a moment, scraping a few more coals onto the pile before facing his brother again. Billy was a handsome fellow, with well-balanced features that included a strong, square chin, a broad, high forehead, and intense blue eyes under gracefully arched brows. On Billy's face the long Lyman nose the brothers had in common looked aristocratic.

Their mother had made the jacket Billy wore not three months ago. But in that short time his shoulders had grown so much broader that they strained the jacket at the seams, while the sleeves were now a good two inches above his wrists.

"I've already let Papa down so dreadfully," Phineas said miserably, collapsing on a bench and running his hand back over his hair. "He set it up for me to go to Vermont to run the iron furnace he started in Woodford, but had to put it off when this swelling started in my knee."

"You've never wanted to leave Middlefield any more than I have," Billy replied. "You love farming. Why don't you suggest Papa send David to Woodford? He hates plowing, sowing, harvesting, and everything in between. When we're in bed at night he goes on so long about how many neighbors are pulling up stakes and taking off for New Connecticut or New York or Vermont that I have to tell him to shut up so I can get some sleep."

"I can't tell Papa I have no heart for this opportunity he's arranged for me," Phineas said, shaking his head. "He wouldn't be angry, but he would be disappointed – and I dread that more than anything in the world. When my knee is better I'll go to Vermont."

Billy stepped closer to Phineas, fastening the top button on his jacket as the building grew increasingly colder without the fire. The most pious of Sarah and David's children, Phineas took particularly seriously the commandment to "Honor thy father and mother." Billy knew if Phineas considered going to Vermont a duty he owed their father, there was no use trying to talk him out of it.

"But whatever possessed you to teach school while you're waiting for your knee to heal?" Billy demanded. "You were a student in this very building until five years ago. You deviled the schoolmaster often enough yourself. You know being able to keep Silas Turner and other–."

"Ruffians," Phineas interjected wryly in an attempt to deflect Billy's concern.

"Ruffians," Billy repeated, refusing to be diverted from his point, "under control is just as important for a teacher as book learning. It was only a matter of time until something like this happened. How did you think you were going to handle it?"

"I felt so useless!" Phineas cried out in despair. "I couldn't even be much help bringing in the harvest. I thought at least by teaching I could earn some kind of a living until my leg heals. When I took the job in October, I could still thrash the likes of Silas Turner if need be. It's not like I haven't done it before," he said with a faint, wry smile that faded as quickly as it came. "I didn't count on my leg getting so much worse in just a couple of weeks."

Phineas swallowed hard, then gnawed nervously on his lower lip. "I'm scared, Billy," he said at last, looking at his brother with haunted gray eyes. "Scared my leg won't get better, that I'll end up a cripple at the mercy of the Silas Turners of the world."

"I know," Billy replied with compassion and no hint of surprise at Phineas's confession.

Phineas's eyes widened with a dawning realization, then narrowed as he shook a forefinger accusingly at Billy. "That's why you asked Papa to come back to school – to protect me!" He studied his brother with a mixture of affection and exasperation. "You can't be mother hen to everyone you know, Billy, try as you might."

Billy blushed at being found out. "Doesn't the Bible say 'Blessed are the peacemakers'?" he countered.

"Is that what you did to Silas Turner?" asked Phineas, amused in spite of himself.

Billy gave a quick, tight-lipped smile, then returned relentlessly to his point. "It will happen again, Phineas. You know it will. And much as I enjoyed giving Silas Turner a taste of his own medicine, it's not something I want to do every day. I've seen how much pain you're in getting around, how you've tried to hide it from everyone."

Billy's perceptiveness and persistence touched Phineas. "I know this affliction, whether it is rheumatism as the doctors say or something else, is God's will," Phineas said slowly. "I pray for the strength to endure it, to play a man's part in the world in some way, especially for Papa's sake. But both the flesh and the spirit are weak," he said despairingly.

Billy desperately cast about for another argument. "Do you honestly think Papa wants you to endure such agony to please him?" he demanded. "Are you sure you aren't making yourself a martyr to your own pride?"

Billy saw instantly that the accusation caught Phineas unawares. He forged ahead. "Maybe this is God's way of teaching you humility." Billy didn't believe his own words, but he was willing to use any argument that would convince Phineas to stop putting himself through such mental and physical torture.

Phineas stared at Billy, mulling over his brother's words. "I never considered that," he said at last, and Billy could tell he was more than half-convinced of the truth of what Billy had said.

"Will you give up teaching school?" Billy asked hopefully. Phineas dropped his head and nodded in resignation, sending a surge of relief through Billy. "You'll tell Papa tonight?" Again Phineas nodded. Then he looked up and asked Billy, "Will you take the job?"

The question caught Billy off guard. Was this what it would take to get the stubbornly responsible Phineas to truly quit teaching? he thought despondently.

Before Billy could answer, Phineas broke into a mischievous grin. Billy rolled his eyes at how easily his brother had tricked him. He gripped Phineas's hand and helped him get carefully to his feet.

While Phineas finished closing up the schoolhouse, Billy went outside. When Phineas left the building he discovered Billy had cut a sturdy branch for him to lean on as they walked the mile home. He accepted it gratefully, and the two brothers started off side-by-side, Billy slowing his pace to match Phineas's.

The sight of the Lyman house on its gentle rise was a welcome and inviting sight to the cold and tired youths – until they saw the horse tied to the post in front of it. Both recognized the animal as belonging to Lot Benton. Only a crisis, they knew, could make Uncle Lot ride five miles on a raw November afternoon to reach their house just as darkness fell.

Chapter Fifty-One

November, 1798
North Guilford

At last – at long last – it was her turn. So many of those she cherished had gone before her, many of their lives cut short for reasons known only to the Lord. Her father. Her mother. Her two baby boys, the memory of whose deaths more than half a century ago still caused her heart to constrict in pain. Esther. Phineas. Hannah. Elihu. Elihu's two babies, her grandsons. And, above all, John.

Now Hope knew she wouldn't live to see another sunrise. And that knowledge filled her with joy.

Her health had begun to decline toward the middle of September, shortly after her seventy-ninth birthday. By the end of October she was unable to rise from bed, and it became clear this would be her last illness.

Catharine came every day to watch over her mother. She was relieved at night by Daniel, assisted by friends and neighbors. Mr. Bray, still pastor of the North Guilford church, had visited regularly.

Hope's dearest grandson Lyman, lately licensed to preach and called to the pulpit of a parish on Long Island, had come to see his Granny Fowler for what both knew would be their last visit. Catharine had sent word to David that their mother was not well. But Hope, fearing she might linger for weeks, had forbidden Catharine from summoning him to North Guilford only to hover uselessly to no good purpose.

But around noon on this day, Catharine had pleaded to be allowed to send for David. Sensing deep inside that her ties to the land of the living were fraying quickly, Hope had agreed.

Hope closed her eyes wearily as she listened to Lot's horse gallop off. She had but two regrets about dying: she would never see the son and daughter born to Elihu in Georgia, and she would leave Daniel Fowler bereft of a beloved wife for a second time. The latter was tempered by her expectation that Daniel would likely marry again. The prospect inspired no jealousy in Hope, just the comfort of knowing this good man would have the companionship he deserved.

She hoped David would arrive in time for one last word, one last look. But if he didn't, it would be no cause for regret, Hope thought as she drifted off. Their painful clashes of will, their distressing struggles for control were many years in the past. Any lingering resentments had been smoothed away by their separate happy marriages, their shared satisfaction in David's great success, and their mutual joy in the fine family he and Sarah had created. That she loved him and was proud of him, Hope was certain David knew – just as she knew he loved her.

When Hope opened her eyes again, the room was dark save for the glow of two candles. In the uncertain light she perceived a face that at first she thought was John. But as her eyes adjusted she realized it was David, still greatly resembling his father despite the graying hair, wrinkles, and slight middle-aged spread that John hadn't lived long enough to acquire.

Catharine started to rise to give David the chair next to the bed. But he motioned to her to stay seated. He knelt on the floor and took Hope's hand between his own two strong ones, stroking a thumb gently over the gnarled knuckles and prominent blue veins. Tears gathered in his eyes.

"Don't mourn for me," Hope whispered. Her eyelids drooped as her lips curved up slightly into a smile. "I go to meet your father, your brothers, your sisters. They wait for me in Heaven, as Mr. Whitefield promised."

David nodded in acknowledgement, even though Hope's eyes were closed again. He closed his own eyes and began to pray aloud the Twenty-Third Psalm, which bespoke the triumph of faith of this remarkable woman who was about to leave the world into which she'd brought him.

"'The Lord is my shepherd; I shall not want,'" David began. He held tight to Hope's hand as he recited the short psalm, arriving at the final sentence, "'Surely goodness and mercy shall follow me all the days of my life–.'"

David broke off abruptly and opened his eyes as he felt Hope's fingers go limp between his hands. There was a short, harsh noise deep in her throat. David put two fingers against the side of her neck, and felt no pulse.

David gazed for a long moment at his mother's face, then spoke the psalm's final words that described what he was confident awaited Hope Hawley Lyman Fowler: "'And I will dwell in the house of the Lord forever.'"

Chapter Fifty-Two

February, 1799
Middlefield

David watched nervously as the surgeon unpacked his knives and saws. He glanced involuntarily down at the grotesquely swollen leg. When at last the surgeon nodded slightly to indicate his readiness to begin, David clamped his hands firmly around the patient's arms and looked down into a pair of terrified eyes.

It was usually at this point that David awoke from the nightmare that only rarely troubled his sleep now. His racing heart would begin to slow with the relieved realization that it had been just an ugly dream. He would reach out in the darkness and gratefully embrace his sleeping Sarah, drawing comfort from her presence as he had on the morning of the first anniversary of his brother Phineas's death.

This time there would be no such reprieve. This wasn't an unwelcome memory of a tragic day in 1776, but events taking place on a February day in 1799. The young man lying on the table wasn't David's brother Phineas, but the son named in his memory.

As autumn had faded into winter, Phineas's leg had grown increasingly worse. He'd been forced to take to a bed set up on the first floor of the house to make it easier to meet his needs.

David had retained the most eminent physicians and surgeons in Middletown. They'd tried every remedy known to them, including the metallic tractors recently invented by Dr. Elisha Perkins of Preston, Connecticut. The tractors – two metallic rods resembling horseshoe nails – were drawn across the surface of the afflicted body part, on the theory that they produced an electrical charge with healing powers. Although thousands across the new nation claimed the amazing tractors had cured everything from cancer to broken bones, they hadn't helped Phineas. The evil-looking thing on his knee – the physicians called it a "white swelling" – had continued to grow.

At the beginning of February Phineas had developed a fever that also defied all the doctor's treatments. Yesterday the surgeons had concluded that the only hope of resolving the crisis was amputation.

Both David and Sarah, haunted by their dreadful memories, had resisted the recommendation. But the physicians had at last convinced them that the goal no longer was to heal Phineas's leg, but to save his life.

After six months of excruciating pain, Phineas himself agreed that losing a leg was an acceptable price to pay for relief. David lamented more than ever Middlefield's continuing lack of a permanent pastor who could offer sustained comfort for Phineas and his family and friends in this dark hour.

They hadn't even been able to turn to Durham for spiritual aid. Elizur Goodrich had died a year ago, and had yet to be replaced. A candidate, the Reverend David Smith, had just begun preaching in Durham on a trial basis. David and Sarah had arranged for the young minister to spend an hour with Phineas after one of his afternoon services. Fortunately, Phineas had a bedrock of religious conviction upon which Sarah had helped him build a shelter of faith that provided some sanctuary from fear and pain.

There would be one important difference between this operation and the one more than twenty years ago that still haunted David's dreams. Dr. Ebenezer Tracy, who'd been on the case since January, had given Phineas forty drops of laudanum to reduce his anxiety and take some of the edge off the anguish of the actual amputation. Additional doses would provide some relief as the stump healed following the surgery, which David refused to believe Phineas wouldn't survive.

Laudanum itself could pose a danger, Dr. Tracy had explained. A patient might be poisoned by an overdose or become dependent upon the drug and unable to quit using it once the medical need was gone. But David and Sarah agreed those were risks worth taking if they could spare their son the suffering they'd watched David's brother endure that long-ago morning in Norwalk.

Thus Dr. Tracy had cautiously administered enough laudanum to dull Phineas's senses but not to render him unconscious. David was holding Phineas's arms, not so much to keep him from thrashing violently in agony, but to suppress any unexpected movement should the pain penetrate his drug-dulled senses.

Sarah wasn't in the room. She wasn't even in the house. She'd wanted desperately to be with Phineas during his ordeal. She and David had had their worst argument ever, which ended when David, in a rare exercise of his absolute authority as head of the family, had forbidden her to be present. Strong as he knew his wife to be, this was no young stranger about to be mangled, but a child born of her body and nursed at her breast. He was determined to spare her from witnessing that horror.

David also suspected Sarah's presence might upset Phineas as much as comfort him. He'd arranged for Polly and David to take Sarah and the other children to Isaac Miller's house until the operation was over.

At the opposite end of the table from David, on the other side of Dr. Tracy and his apprentice, stood Billy. His face was chalk-white with fear, but he was holding Phineas's legs firmly.

With Phineas incapacitated, David had turned more and more to his third son for help. Billy, although just fifteen, had shown himself to be more conscientious and reliable than his older brother David.

Billy also possessed unusual compassion, as David had discovered once Phineas was confined to bed. Family and friends had taken turns sitting with Phineas around the clock, as was customary with the seriously ill. But nearly every night David, waking to use the chamber pot, had heard Billy's voice resonating up through the floorboards. He was talking to Phineas for hours on end about anything and everything to help distract his brother from the constant pain that made sleep impossible.

David had agreed when Billy asked to help out with the amputation. Now, David thought as he studied Billy with a flicker of grim compassion, he was about to learn if raw courage was also part of the teenager's make-up.

The new tall clock in the parlor struck the hour with a cheerful chime that mocked the gruesome scene about to unfold. Dr. Tracy glanced at David, then nodded to indicate his readiness to begin. He did the same to Billy, who was so afraid to move a muscle that he only blinked his eyes to signal his understanding.

Phineas moaned and shivered as the pain of the physician cutting successively through skin, flesh, sinew, nerves and finally bone pressed aggressively against the thin protective barrier created by the laudanum. David held Phineas firmly, staring down into his slightly glazed eyes.

"P– Pray, Papa!" Phineas pleaded in a thick voice. David began reciting the Lord's Prayer in a soothing tone. Phineas focused on the words, mumbling in unison with David. When a stab of pain made him made him gasp sharply, David raised his voice and continued to pray, never taking his eyes from Phineas's face. He assumed Billy was standing firmly at his post.

After a few minutes that seemed an eternity, David saw out of the corner of his eye Dr. Tracy straightening up, his hands dripping blood, in an attitude of completion. As Dr. Tracy began to bandage the stump, Phineas's head rolled to one side, and his eyes fell shut. Panicked, David leaned over, then closed his own eyes in a prayer of thanks as he heard Phineas's breathing – hot, shallow, but steady.

"He's a brave young man," Dr. Tracy praised Phineas, the words rolling off his tongue with the fluid lilt of his native Ireland. "Laudanum can help only so much. If his fever can be brought down, there's reason to hope he'll recover his health."

Heartened by the doctor's optimism, David gently released his hold on Phineas's arms and straightened up a bit unsteadily. His relief turned to alarm when he got a good look at Billy: the teenager's face, hands, and shirt were splattered with blood. His eyes were glazed with horror as he stared at his brother's inert body.

Suddenly Billy turned and stumbled out the hall door. David followed, and found him only a few steps past the doorsill.

Billy was standing with his back plastered flat against the clapboards of the house. His eyes were squeezed tightly shut, and his head was tilted back so the light needle-like sleet could hit him full in the face. His Adam's apple bulged as he swallowed forcefully to keep from vomiting.

Sensing his father's presence, Billy opened haunted blue eyes. He began to tremble, as much from shock as from the bitter wind.

Of all people, David could understand what Billy was going through. The man in the teenager had courageously performed a terrible duty that would have daunted most adults. But the part of him that was still a child suddenly burst into tears of fear and grief. Billy gratefully stepped into the familiar comfort of his father's outstretched arms, unaware of how much support David himself was drawing from their embrace.

Chapter Fifty-Three

June, 1799
Middlefield

A cock's crow pierced Sarah's slumber. Eyes still closed, she rolled from her side onto her back. She wriggled her shoulder blades to stretch her stiff muscles – then froze, as the memory flooded her brain like a monstrous icy wave: her child was dead.

Sarah lay motionless, waiting for the fresh anguish to recede, leaving behind the lump of dull, heavy sorrow into which her grief over Phineas's death had congealed. He'd died nearly two months ago, on April 5, less than six weeks after the amputation of his leg.

Somehow the fact that Phineas was dead seeped from her memory every night while she slept, only to return with heart-shredding pain during the first moments after she awoke. It was like re-living his death over and over.

All that kept Sarah from surrendering completely to the black despair that engulfed her each morning was the knowledge that her other children needed her, now more than ever. She waged a daily struggle to follow the advice she'd given to David more than twenty years ago, to love the living who were left to her. But it was so very, very hard.

Sarah at last opened her eyes, to see that David was up and almost finished dressing. Today, she remembered, he was going to Durham to talk to John Johnson the carver about making a tombstone for Phineas's grave in the Middlefield burying ground.

With an effort Sarah forced herself to sit up and swing her legs over the side of the bed. David came over to sit down beside her. He withdrew a folded piece of paper from inside his coat.

"I've composed an inscription for the gravestone," he said nervously as he unfolded the sheet. "Tell me what you think." He read aloud:

> Behold a youth who late in healthy bloom
> Appeared far distant from the silent tomb
> Withered like grass before the scorching sun,
> Now sleeps in death – which none can ever shun.

David stopped to clear his throat. His hands shook as if he had the palsy.

Tears blurred Sarah's vision at the four lines that sketched the swift, awful trajectory of the tragedy. Little more than a year ago Phineas had been whole, strong, the champion of a flock of ten fine children. In a matter of a few months he'd been felled by an agonizing ailment, then subjected to the gruesome amputation that had resulted not in healing, but in weeks of raging fever that ravaged Phineas's body and mind until death mercifully released him.

David tried to resume speaking, but his voice failed. Sarah reached over to take the paper from him. She wiped her eyes with the sleeve of her nightgown, then read the remaining two lines aloud:

> Trust not in life, in limbs, nor aught you have,
> But trust in God, for He alone can save.

Sarah leaned her head against David's shoulder. They sat for a long time without speaking, listening to the sounds of the rest of their family starting the day.

At last David spoke in a low voice. "As I prayed to God for the strength to accept my child's death as His will, I remembered how during his last days Phineas found solace in the hope that his suffering and death could inspire others to have faith in God." He gestured at the paper in Sarah's hands. "I tried to put that into words."

Sarah sat up, turned to look at David, and to his enormous relief, nodded in approval. She reached out a hand to stroke his cheek. "Your lines on Phineas's tombstone will give his life and death meaning long after all who knew him have passed away."

Chapter Fifty-Four

September, 1799
Guilford, Connecticut

If ever an occasion was truly bittersweet, this was it, David thought. Rain pattered on the roof as the Reverend Thomas Bray concluded the service uniting Lyman Beecher and Roxana Foote in marriage. It was the latest in a series of joyous events over the last three months, including Lyman's ordination as a Congregational minister, and his selection as pastor of a church on Long Island.

Roxana's mother and sisters surged forward to embrace the newlyweds. Happy as he was, David knew Lyman was grieving that his Aunt Benton wasn't here to share in the celebration. She had died in early July, after a short illness, just fifty-seven years old. Lyman's sorrow was all the deeper because he hadn't been with his aunt in her last hours.

Uncle Lot was here for Lyman today, though, struggling bravely to prevent his still-raw grief from tarnishing his pleasure in the wedding. David watched as Lyman extracted himself from the gaggle of females. He quickly paid his respects to David Beecher and his stepmother, then headed over to Lot Benton, standing with David.

Lot seemed lost without his beloved companion. David knew Lyman was glad Lot lived in the center of Guilford rather than in the isolated North Guilford farmhouse in which Lyman had grown up.

"This rain puts me in mind of your Aunt Benton," Lot mused with a tinge of melancholy, as Lyman came up to him. "You know what a one she was for crying when she was happy. This is about how weepy she'd be to see the blessings God has bestowed on you."

Lyman studied his foster father with open affection. "I count you high among those blessings, Uncle," he said. The pleased Lot broke into one of his rare smiles. It vanished as quickly as it came, as Lot retreated behind a discussion of practicalities to shield his feelings.

"I've paid for a small sloop to take you and Roxana across the Sound to your new home," Lot said offhandedly.

Lyman shook his head in bemused gratitude. "You still take care of me like I was a stripling of fifteen."

"Well, you're book smart, but you've got much to learn about life in the real world," Lot replied gruffly. "I have cash for you as well."

When Lyman opened his mouth to protest this excessive generosity, Lot held up a large, calloused palm to cut him off. "I'll take it as a sign of disrespect if you refuse," he said solemnly.

Lyman nodded in acceptance, not trusting himself to speak. Not for the first time he was humbled by Lot's generosity. How fortunate that Aunt Benton had seen Lot for what he truly was and wed him, an act that had shaped the course of Lyman's entire life.

Lyman turned to David. Sarah had joined the females around Roxana. The void created by Catharine's absence made Lyman all the more thankful that David and Sarah had made it through the inclement weather in time for the ceremony.

"It means more than I can express to have you here today," Lyman said to David. "I bled from the very heart when I heard Aunt Benton had died. Not even my Roxana is dearer to me than she was." The young man's voice shook slightly, and he paused to regain control. "You're all I have left in this world of my mother."

David couldn't tell whether Lyman was referring to Esther or Catharine. Probably both, he decided.

"And you're all that remains to me of my sisters," David said. "No woman could hope to have a finer son as her legacy."

Lyman's dark eyes warmed at his uncle's heartfelt praise. Before he could reply, they were interrupted by the women summoning him back to his bride. He smiled at David, shrugging his shoulders as if to say he had no choice but to obey, then returned to Roxana's side.

David was struggling to come to terms with the loss of the last of his siblings. His thoughts flew back to Hannah's wedding nearly thirty years ago. It was one of the last times all six of them had been together. None of them could have imagined the turbulent future that lay ahead for them personally and for their world. David was now the last survivor of those decades. The thought made him feel lonely, like the last apple left hanging on a tree.

Chapter Fifty-Five

July, 1801
Middletown

"The Fourth of July, 1776 – the Jubilee of the United States!" tavern keeper Ephraim Fenno cried with gusto. David Lyman, Elisha Coe, and several dozen men gathered at Fenno's Middletown establishment raised glasses of wine or mugs of cider or rum and cheered their agreement.

"George Washington – first in war, first in peace, and first in the hearts of his countrymen!" Fenno proclaimed the second toast, sparking an even more enthusiastic chorus of support.

"The President of the United States," Fenno said in a monotone. Glasses remained still, throats silent. Every face wore an expression of disgust, as if a skunk had sprayed its stench in their midst. At last each man took a small sip to toast Thomas Jefferson, whose inauguration as president four months ago most present considered a national calamity, for New England in particular.

Jefferson was widely believed to be an atheist, a Virginia libertine, and an enemy of the Federal Constitution. But respect for the principle of majority rule demanded that the Chief Executive, the people's choice, be included among the Independence Day toasts.

"Who would have believed the events of a single year could so deeply divide a community and a country," Elisha Coe said ruefully. "Last year all Middletown citizens were united in celebrating the anniversary of our independence. Today the Democrats won't even share the same building with us Federalists, but insist on holding their own celebration at Thaddeus Nichols's tavern." "Democrat" was the name the new president's supporters chose to distinguish themselves from the Federalists who'd controlled the national government during the terms of Washington and John Adams – and who still dominated Connecticut politics.

"There won't be a reading of the Declaration of Independence at our celebration today," said Fenno as he refilled each of the men's glasses from the bottle of Madeira he carried.

Both David and Elisha Coe looked at Fenno in sharp surprise, eyebrows raised questioningly. A public reading of the Declaration was an almost sacred tradition of Independence Day observances.

"Many here loathe Jefferson so deeply that they won't stand for hearing any of his words, even the document that expresses what we're celebrating," Fenno explained with an unhappy sigh. "The newspapers warn that with Jefferson as president, murder, robbery, rape, adultery, and incest will be openly taught and practiced. They say the Holy Bible itself will be banned."

That ominous prediction made David think of Joshua Stow, whose anti-religious agitation had contributed toward the ultimate disbandment of the Ethosian Society. Stow, not surprisingly, was a fanatical Democrat. But David made no comment, for Elisha Coe remained inexplicably loyal to his incendiary friend.

"I put no stock in such hysterics," Elisha said dismissively. "I don't believe Thomas Jefferson is the anti-Christ, nor that he's a tyrant who will suppress all that's decent."

"I pray you're right," Fenno said. He hurried off to fill an empty wine glass another patron was holding up to catch his attention.

"I admire your new house every time I pass it on the way into the city," David said to Elisha, eager to turn the conversation toward something positive.

"I was forced to build a bigger house – just as you were," Elisha replied in mock self-defense. "In sixteen years of marriage my dear Elizabeth has presented me with eight children, and she just told me she's expecting another! My family has outgrown the house we constructed as newlyweds the same year you built your house. We thought about adding on to it. But with my new responsibilities as a selectman, it made sense to build a home closer to the city."

"Which you could afford to do," David observed, meaning it as a compliment. Since his marriage, Elisha Coe had applied his energy and intelligence so effectively that he'd become, as anyone who inspected the tax lists would discover, the second-richest man in Middlefield. Only one person had a larger estate: David Lyman.

Coe had other ambitions as well. He'd been elected a selectman the previous December, which pleased David. Since David had decided not to stand again for selectman, Elisha's election meant Middlefield's interests would still be represented in the Middletown selectmen's meetings, the governing body of the town, where the wishes of outlying residents could all-too-easily be overlooked.

There had been rumblings about Middlefield joining the Westfield society of Middletown to form a new independent town. Nothing had come of it, but to David it was another indication of the challenges to long-established institutions that were remaking their world – sometimes for good, others for ill.

David was more certain every day that stepping down from public office had been the right thing to do. Phineas's death and the departure of David, Jr., to his father's lands in Woodford, Vermont, more than a hundred miles to the north had left the elder David with more demands than ever on his time.

"How does your David in Vermont?" Elisha asked, almost as if he could read the older man's mind.

"Well enough," David replied. "It was hard to send him so far away, to a barely settled area. But I needed someone to begin making those lands profitable."

David smiled in bemusement. "Fortunately, the boy was itching to go. I admit I had doubts, for at home David often needed a boot applied to his backside to keep him at his chores. But being his own master in Vermont seems to have worked a change, made him much more responsible, for all that he's only twenty.

"In fact," David went on, "we're thinking of sending Polly to Bennington for a stay. It's a thriving town, yet close enough to Woodford for her to afford some company for her brother."

David fell silent for a moment, turning the stem of his wineglass thoughtfully between his thumb and fingers. "So many young men have been driven from Connecticut by expensive land and burdensome taxes, there are precious few eligible bachelors left."

Elisha nodded in commiseration. "Middlefield is being bled dry of its young people."

"I've accepted that some of my sons will have to leave Connecticut to find land," David said. "But I never thought my daughters would need to look beyond Connecticut for husbands! Sending Polly to Bennington will be hard, but we have to do what's best for her. She's twenty-three, with no marriage prospects."

Elisha nodded sympathetically. For Polly to go to Vermont likely meant she would marry and make her home there, several days' journey from Middlefield. That David and Sarah were willing to risk that unpleasant prospect revealed how desperate they believed their eldest daughter's situation to be. Elisha understood all too well; he had four daughters for whom he would soon be seeking husbands.

"Will Billy be joining David in Vermont?" Elisha asked.

"No," David answered, the furrows in his brow disappearing. "I hope Billy will be the son I can rely on here at home, now and in years to come. He's sharp as a tack, a quick study, and dependable. He loves the land and has a feel for it."

David broke off in embarrassment at his boasting. But Elisha Coe wasn't at all bored with the subject of Billy Lyman.

"Have you given any thought to a wife for him?" Elisha asked.

"No!" David blurted out in surprise. His eyes narrowed. "What's on your mind, Elisha?" he demanded bluntly.

Elisha smiled, a trifle embarrassed, as if he'd been caught with his hand in another man's pocket. "My Alma is fifteen, and Sina is thirteen. Both are growing into fine young women. Each would make an excellent wife. From what you've said – and from what I've heard elsewhere – Billy has the makings of a good husband."

David was intrigued by the idea of a marriage uniting Middlefield's two most prosperous and prestigious families. And he was freshly impressed by Elisha Coe's ambition. This wasn't a spur of the moment idea; he'd clearly been making inquiries about Billy.

"But they're all too young to wed," David pointed out at last. "Billy won't turn eighteen until next month."

"Yet not too young to fall in love," Elisha observed. "Elizabeth and I weren't even Billy's age when our mutual affection began." He took a sip of wine. "Has Billy formed an attachment to any female?"

"No," David said quickly. "At least not that I know," he amended frankly after a moment's reflection. Elisha couldn't hide his relief.

"I want my children to marry spouses not just of suitable fortune and family, but for whom they care," Elisha said. "I take it you feel the same."

David nodded, and Elisha continued. "I'm anxious to keep my daughters from entangling themselves with shiftless youths with no prospects. It's not too early to start taking steps toward that end."

"Did you have a particular daughter in mind for Billy?" David asked, still a bit overwhelmed by Elisha's proposal.

"Either one," Elisha shrugged. "They're quite close, even for sisters, but very different in temperament."

"I'm not suggesting Billy begin courting one of them," Elisha added hastily. "All I propose is that you encourage him to begin seeing Alma and Sina as the young women they're becoming, not the girls he grew up with. What do you think?"

David was intrigued, but cautious. Sarah, he knew, might look differently on any attempt to arrange their children's personal lives.

"It's an interesting possibility," David said. "I must discuss it with Mrs. Lyman before I can say more." David had no reservations about admitting he sought his wife's opinion in many matters.

"Fair enough," said Elisha, satisfied that his seed of an idea had fallen on fertile ground. "For now, let us drink to possibilities," he said, raising his glass in a salute that David returned.

Riding home to Middlefield that afternoon, David mulled over Elisha Coe's proposal. Events of the past three years had combined to drive David's spirits to their lowest point since the war. Hope, Phineas, and Catharine had died within a span of seven months; Middlefield's spiritual stagnation continued in the absence of a pastor. The departure to Vermont of David, Jr., and soon of Polly, would fracture their family circle forever. The election of Thomas Jefferson had split the community in an ugly way reminiscent of the division between Tories and patriots during the Revolution.

But Elisha Coe's forward-looking proposition had sparked fresh optimism in David. He thought proudly of how far he'd come since that day, nearly forty years past, when he stood in the parlor of the old house, and watched his dying father dictate a will bequeathing a pitiful twenty shillings to each of his children – an inheritance that was worthless even as John made it. David had fulfilled the promise that frightened teenage boy had made to John on his deathbed.

And David was confident he'd be able to fulfill the vow he'd made to himself after John's estate auction. He was well on his way to realizing the level of prosperity that would guarantee that his dear Sarah would never find herself in the desperate straits Hope had faced following John's death. That would ensure his large flock of children wanted for nothing. That would mean his sons wouldn't have to postpone taking a wife and starting a family for lack of resources. With God's blessing, he would complete his goal in the new century.

Chapter Fifty-Six

July, 1801
Middlefield

"That would be a terrible mistake," Sarah objected, with a vehemence that stunned David. He'd expected her to have questions and concerns about Elisha Coe's proposal that Billy be encouraged to consider Alma or Sina Coe as a possible wife. But he hadn't envisioned anything like this automatic, adamant rejection.

"Don't you like Alma or Sina?" David asked, grasping for some explanation for Sarah's opposition.

"No, it has nothing to do with them," Sarah said. "What I don't like is a father dictating his children's personal lives."

"Elisha isn't proposing that I 'dictate' anything," David protested. "He only suggested that I point out to Billy that Alma and Sina are becoming young women he might consider courting when he's ready."

It was clear from Sarah's expression that she was unconvinced. "Billy doesn't need any help seeing that Alma and Sina are maturing," she snapped.

Sarah's sharp reaction perplexed David. "Why does this upset you so?" he asked, stepping closer to wrap his arms affectionately around his wife's waist. He looked down into her gray eyes, now dark as storm clouds. "What is it?" he demanded anxiously.

David could see that Sarah was debating whether or not to say something. At last she took a deep breath, and said, "If you do this, won't you be playing on Billy's sense of duty to achieve your goals – just as your mother did with you?"

David was dumbstruck. He owed so much to Sarah's keen insight, to the courage she'd shown when helping him face and conquer his painful inner demons. But these candid words cut him as never before.

"How can you think that of me?" David demanded, unable to keep the hurt from his voice. "I'll never forget the years of frustration I suffered under my mother's thumb. And I would never inflict that on one of our children." His face was flushed with anger at being judged so unfairly.

David's reaction shook Sarah. This was one of the sharpest disagreement they'd had since they'd married. She hastened to reassure him.

"I know you would never deliberately do such a thing. But with Billy the result could be the same. Don't you realize how much he wants to please you – even more since Phineas died?" she asked. "He'll consider any 'suggestion' from you as a command, and he'll try to fulfill it, whether or not it's what he truly wants."

David opened his mouth to protest, then stopped. Would Billy truly feel obligated to do whatever he asked? In his enthusiasm for Elisha Coe's proposal, the possibility hadn't occurred to him. But he trusted Sarah's understanding of their children.

Encouraged by David's hesitation, Sarah went on. "Billy still has a boy's heart. At least postpone any such 'suggestion' until he turns twenty-one," she half-pleaded, half-proposed. "By then he'll better know his own mind and heart, and should have the confidence to comply with or turn down your 'suggestion' as he sees fit."

David sighed deeply, letting the anger drain from him, to be replaced by disappointment. He nodded in acceptance of Sarah's wisdom. "I'll tell Elisha the time is not yet ripe for his plan."

Chapter Fifty-Seven

August, 1804
Middlefield

Alma Coe raced up the stairs and into the chamber, closed the door behind her, then with a deep sigh dropped down onto the feather bed she and her sister Sina shared. Sina, at sixteen two years younger than Alma, didn't immediately look up from the shift she was sewing. She finished a stitch tiny enough to meet the standard of twenty to an inch she'd been taught by her mother, then glanced up to see that Alma's face was flushed with agitation.

Alma had blossomed into full womanhood during the past year. Elizabeth and Elisha Coe's firstborn took after her father in physique, with large bones and a sturdy, well-developed figure that her above-average height allowed her to carry with grace and poise. She had her mother's thick, lustrous chestnut hair, which she wore parted in the middle.

Alma's deep blue eyes – dark now with whatever was upsetting her – were set in a face with a broad, smooth forehead, high cheekbones, and flawless skin. She had a long, straight nose, and a square, jutting chin which, while they gave her face a distinctively bold character, were prominent enough to keep her from being considered beautiful by popular standards.

Sina, by contrast, was slender, with light blue eyes and wavy auburn hair. Her features were more regular and delicate than Alma's.

"What's wrong?" Sina asked. Although less than two years separated the sisters, they weren't squabbling rivals as siblings so close in age often were, but close companions and confidants. The tranquil nature of their relationship owed much to Alma's even temperament, for Sina tended to be flighty and impulsive.

"Esther and Billy Lyman were just here," Alma said. "Esther is leaving tomorrow to go back to the Female Academy in Litchfield."

"I know how much you'll miss her," Sina commiserated. Esther Lyman, an attractive, vivacious girl just turned seventeen, was Alma's closest friend outside their family.

Alma herself yearned for the advanced education in topics such as geography, Latin, and astronomy offered at Miss Sarah Pierce's elite private school, which attracted girls from across the country. But Elisha Coe, prospering as he was, wasn't in a position financially to do without the services of his oldest child.

Sina herself hadn't picked up any book other than the Bible since she'd stopped attending common school. But she knew of Alma's longing, and sympathized with it, even if she didn't share it.

"And Billy asked me to a picnic Saturday at Crank Spring!" Alma blurted out, then startled Sina by throwing herself backward dramatically onto the bed, arms spread to the side. She stared up at the ceiling.

Sina tossed the shift onto a table. She bounded over to the bed, landing next to Alma on the feather mattress.

"That's wonderful!" Sina cried. Her enthusiasm was genuine, with no hint of envy. Touched, Alma rolled her head sideways and smiled wanly at her little sister.

"Billy's invitation upsets you?" Sina asked in bewilderment. "But why?" she demanded. "This is a wish come true. You've fancied him for months, and now it seems he wants to court you."

Alma sighed again, and resumed studying the ceiling. "Of course Billy's invitation excites me," she admitted. "But I can't help wonder why all of a sudden he wants to court me. Does he find me more attractive than any of the other girls he knows in Middlefield and Durham? If that was the case, Esther would know, and she would have told me before she left."

Alma frowned as she turned to look at Sina. "Or has Billy's father commanded him to court me – because the marriage of David Lyman's son to Elisha Coe's daughter would constitute a financially advantageous match for both families!" Alma bit off each of the last six words with brittle cynicism.

"What difference does it make?" Sina demanded. "You're very fond of Billy. He's handsome, with wonderful manners, comes from a good family, and has a rich father who will settle considerable property on him. What more could you want in a husband?"

Alma shook her head with the fierce stubbornness of a small child. "I won't marry a man who does not want me for myself first and foremost, with all my virtues and my faults. I will not be beguiled by a suitor who would consider our marriage as much a business arrangement as the union of two minds and hearts." Alma's chin began to tremble. "I can't imagine the Billy Lyman I know could be so calculating. But I must be sure."

"You think too much, Alma," Sina said bluntly. "Maybe it's from all that reading you do – fixing books to the spindle of your wool wheel so you can read while you spin! Among all that poetry is there no plain common sense like 'Don't look a gift horse in the mouth'?" Sina's pale blue eyes glittered with annoyance at her sister's insistence on complicating this stroke of luck.

The measure of Alma's distress was evident in her failure to take offense at her sister's criticism. Sina's irritation faded, and she said more kindly, "Be careful not to calculate yourself out of a piece of great good fortune. Plenty of girls will gladly trade places with you, and not care one whit why Billy Lyman is interested in them."

Chapter Fifty-Eight

August, 1804
Middlefield

Early on the last Saturday morning in August, Alma set out alone on horseback to make the three-mile journey to meet Billy at the Lyman homestead. She had accepted his invitation to a picnic, for which the weather – a bright sun in a clear sky and low humidity – was perfect.

Alma wore a full chemise of white cotton muslin that fell to the ground from a wide scooped neckline gathered with a drawstring. A wide sash of pale blue encircled her waist. The gown's loose elbow-length sleeves were gathered tight at two points to divide them into puffy thirds. A narrow white headband secured with a large-looped bow at the nape of her neck was nearly hidden beneath her full, thick tresses.

Alma guided her horse west along the road that skirted the edge of the Coginchaug Swamp, then crossed the river of the same name via a crude plank bridge, before dead-ending in front of the Lyman house. Small patches of orange, red, gold, or bronze had started to appear on a few trees, the earliest harbingers of autumn.

The road was bordered on each side by a riot of colorful wildflowers, many of which had medicinal properties every capable housewife would be expected to know. Joe-pye weed, with its broad lavender flowering heads, was used to treat gout. The stem of the delicate yellow-orange jewelweed blossoms, shaped like a mouth with a large lower jutting jaw, contained a juice that helped relieve the rash from poison ivy. The jaunty cascades of goldenrod, when dried and brewed into a tea, acted to produce urine. The seed pods of the cardinal flower, with its splashy spiky scarlet blossoms, when ingested induced vomiting. The roots of the tall brown cattails rising up from the damper spots were used to make a tea to treat kidney stones.

As she rode up to the Lyman house, Alma caught sight of Sarah and Sally walking from the chicken coop to the kitchen, each carrying a basket of freshly gathered eggs. They smiled and waved to Alma, who returned their greeting in kind, then continued on toward the house.

Billy appeared in the hall doorway, hastily pulling on a coat of indigo blue with a high fold-over collar. It was trimmed down the left side and on the turned-back cuffs with round, flat pewter buttons. The coat began to cut away at the waist, then fell straight to the knees.

At several inches over six feet, Billy had to stoop to step through the doorway. His broad shoulders and ramrod-straight posture made him appear even taller than he was. And he might not yet be done growing, for he was just twenty-one, having marked his birthday a few days earlier.

Billy wore a blue square-bottomed vest over a bleached linen shirt with ruffles at the chest and wrists. His matching blue breeches ended at the knee, below which tight-fitting white linen stockings revealed muscular, finely shaped calves.

Billy wore his thin light brown hair in a fashionable collar-length cut with short bangs falling onto his forehead. The effect was spoiled a bit by Billy's enormous ears, which Alma considered his only physical flaw, protruding through his hair.

Billy's wide, narrow lips turned up in a smile that conveyed both welcome and a slight apology for not being ready when she arrived. Suddenly he stopped short, held up one finger, then dashed back into the house. He re-appeared a moment later with a black, round-brimmed hat in his hand. His haste and forgetfulness were the only signs Alma could detect that Billy might be feeling some of the same nervousness that had her own stomach constricted into a knot.

"You look very pretty," Billy told Alma, as he grasped her horse's bridle near the bit to steady the animal. He stroked the horse's neck, casually studying Alma while trying to keep his gaze from resting upon any particular part of her anatomy. Billy found it strange to feel awkward with Alma, whom he'd known as long as he could remember.

"You put me in mind of Queen Anne's lace – all bright white with just a spot of color in the middle," Billy said. He wondered even as he spoke from where this poetic compliment had sprung.

"Thank you," Alma murmured, blushing fiercely. Comparing her to a blossom was hardly original, but Billy's choice of the lacy wildflower rather than a conventional rose or lily – and the appreciative expression on his face – told her his words were sincere.

This was going to be even harder than she'd expected, Alma realized, her anxiety rising to near panic. She would have to take the earliest opportunity to divine Billy's real motives before his good looks and easy charm – and her own attraction to him – overcame her determination to ferret out and face the truth, no matter the consequences.

Billy headed into the barn. He reappeared a moment later with his white horse, "Captain." Strapped firmly behind the saddle was a woven splint basket containing a picnic lunch.

Billy swung himself up into the saddle with admirable grace. "Ready?" he asked Alma with a smile. When she nodded, he swung the horse around and cantered off.

Despite her delicate chemise and side saddle, Alma had no difficulty keeping up with Billy as they rode toward Crank Spring, located on a corner of the Lyman property. They followed a road that snaked up the east side of Powder Ridge through the Lyman orchards. On either side were apple trees, their branches heavy with red fruit.

They rode side-by-side at a pace slow enough to allow them to chat. Alma kept the conversation going, as she had been taught a well-bred woman should. She asked Billy about safe topics, such as whether they'd received any word from Esther at school, or what the doctor in New Haven had said about his sister Sally's poor eyesight. She deliberately avoided inquiring about David and Polly Lyman up in Vermont. Both were now married.

Reaching the crest of Powder Ridge, they turned south and rode for a distance before leaving the road. They carefully descended the west slope into a bucolic valley formed by Powder Ridge to the east and the even higher and steeper Beseck Mountain to the west.

Crank Spring emerged from the ground not far from where Billy and Alma stopped, and flowed along the bottom of the valley formed by the two hills. The stream was narrow enough for long-legged Billy to leap across it with ease. Rain from the previous night caused it to run swifter and higher than usual, making a soothing rippling sound as it flowed over and around the many rocks in its bed

Most of the land around the spring had long since been cleared of trees cut for lumber or firewood or to create pasture for cattle and sheep. But several spots along the spring's banks were shaded by graceful willow trees. These created cool, inviting glens in which to spread a blanket and enjoy a delicious repast on a hot summer day.

Billy dismounted and tethered Captain and Alma's horse to a stout sapling. Without thinking he reached up and grasped Alma firmly around the waist, lifted her up from her side saddle, and set her on the ground, just as he did routinely with his sisters. However, the physical contact flustered Alma – and Billy as well, she noted. The arrival of two more couples from Middletown rescued them from the awkward moment.

"Are you thirsty?" Billy asked. Alma nodded, and he unstrapped the basket, taking out a pewter mug. He filled it with the pure, fresh water for which Crank Spring was known.

"Thank you," Alma said as she took the mug from Billy, noticing that his hand was unusually large, with long, powerful-looking fingers. His neatly trimmed nails were perfectly clean, something she knew required considerable time and effort to achieve for a farmer like Billy, who spent his days handling dirt and manure.

"Are we ready to climb to the top of the mountain?" Alma's eighteen-year-old cousin Joseph Coe demanded of the group. A chorus of voices enthusiastically agreed, and the remains of the picnic lunches – cold roast beef and mutton, wheat bread spread with butter and strawberry or raspberry preserves, and gingerbread – were hastily wrapped up and returned to the baskets.

The young men helped their female companions to their feet. Joseph had brought seventeen-year-old Eunice Ward, one of several girls Alma knew he'd been keeping company with of late.

The walk was a favorite among courting couples. The path was well-trodden, but steep. It provided a young man wearing sensible leather boots an excuse to take a young woman's hand or slip an arm tightly around her waist as he helped her walk the uneven ground in the thin shoes with slippery soles that were in fashion.

Those who reached the top of Beseck Mountain were rewarded with a spectacular vista. On a day as sparkling clear as this it was possible to see Long Island Sound fifteen miles to the south, to catch glimpses to the northeast of the shimmering blue Connecticut River, and to discern the outline of Mount Tom in Massachusetts more than fifty miles to the north.

Billy stood up along with the others. But Alma remained seated on the blanket. "Could we stay here?" she asked. "I'm still fatigued from the ride."

Billy's eyebrows rose in surprise. Alma was the most robust young woman he'd ever known, as accustomed as any man to riding horseback. Until her brother Asher had grown big enough, Alma had delivered the grain from her father's fields to the mill, and brought the flour ground from it back home.

But Billy was willing to humor Alma. He waved to the others to go ahead without them, ignoring the knowing looks some of the young men cast at him.

Billy sat back down next to Alma, then scanned the puffy, towering clouds that had started to develop since they'd arrived at Crank Spring. Like any good farmer, he was trying to divine signs of impending changes in the weather.

"Billy," Alma began, then almost lost her nerve as he turned from examining the sky to look at her. She plunged ahead, feeling as if she were leaping from Beseck Mountain, hoping that by some miracle she would land not on hard rock but on a feather bed. "Was it your idea to invite me here today, or did your father tell you to?"

The surprised, slightly sheepish look on Billy's face made Alma feel as if her heart had sunk into the pit of her stomach. Her cheeks burned crimson with humiliation and disappointment.

Alma quickly looked away to stare sightlessly at a butterfly fluttering from wildflower to wildflower. She pressed her thin lips together so tightly that the upper one nearly vanished from sight, as it did when she was tense or nervous.

Alma fought back tears as she waited for Billy to say something. Would he be annoyed that she'd guessed the truth? Offended that she'd dared pose the question instead of simply being grateful for his interest in her? Or, worst of all, relieved she'd given him the opportunity to tell her his invitation had been the act of a dutiful son, and nothing more?

"I like you, Alma!" Billy exclaimed at last. Her question had caught him unawares, and made him feel vaguely self-conscious. But one look at her strained and flushed profile gave him a good idea of what was going through her mind, and he hastened to reassure her.

"My father didn't tell me to do anything," Billy said. "It's true he spoke to me about you," he admitted, discreetly omitting the fact that David Lyman and Elisha Coe had gone so far as to discuss marriage between them. "He pointed out your many fine qualities and suggested I get to know you better." He felt a pang of sympathy when Alma winced at his last words.

"But I've never followed one of my father's proposals as willingly as this one," Billy went on quickly. Alma's only response was to shift her gaze from the butterfly to her hands, which were nervously twisting folds of her muslin chemise.

Billy gently placed his hands on Alma's shoulders and turned her toward him. "I like *you*, Alma," he repeated firmly. At last she looked up to meet his gaze, and saw sincerity in his clear blue eyes.

"You're pretty and smart and good-natured and, and–," Billy paused, searching for the right word, "forthright," he finished. That hint of teasing caused a timorous smile to play around Alma's lips.

"There's no girl I care for more than you," Billy continued. "I'm more than happy to court you – that is, if you want me to," he amended uneasily, wondering suddenly if Alma had questioned his motive because the situation was not to her liking.

Something like alarm came over Alma's face. "Of course I do!" she said, nodding emphatically.

Billy studied Alma's face until he was satisfied they truly understood each other. "If we come to love each other, and want to wed, that it pleases our fathers will be an added blessing," he said. "And if we don't, we can part as friends, wishing each other well in the search for a spouse to share life's journey. And our fathers will have to deal with their disappointment," he finished firmly.

At last Alma allowed the relief that had been building up to flood through her. It was followed by an intense happiness that she had done the right, if difficult, thing – and been amply rewarded.

"Now do you have energy enough to climb up Beseck Mountain?" Billy asked mischievously. He stood without waiting for her answer. Alma simply laughed and held out her hands for Billy to help her to her feet.

Chapter Fifty-Nine

September, 1806
Middlefield

"Religious revivals are like summer thunderstorms," Joshua Stow declared scornfully. "They roll in quickly, inspire some to examine the heavens with awe, send others scurrying in terror – and are forgotten as soon as they pass and the sun comes out. How many lasting conversions of faith do you think really result from such episodes of hysteria?"

Alma shifted uncomfortably, wishing her parents would get back from their visit to the home of her Uncle Joseph Coe, where they'd gone to see her father's brother Curtis, down from his parish in New Hampshire for a visit. Not long after they'd departed, Joshua Stow had unexpectedly appeared at the Coe house to discuss a business matter with Elisha. Good manners had left Alma no choice but to invite him to stay and join Alma and Sina where they were sitting in the yard behind the house, to await their parents' return.

Despite Joshua's insistent spreading of his increasingly unorthodox opinions, Elisha Coe remained his friend. When Alma asked her father how he could tolerate Stow's outrageous pronouncements on faith and religion, Elisha had replied that every man had a right to honestly question any authority, and to speak those doubts publicly. Hospitality aside, Joshua Stow was married to Elisha's cousin Ruth Coe, which made him distant family.

"I mean no disrespect, Mr. Stow, but I must disagree," Alma said reluctantly. She knew from unpleasant experience that contradicting this man would merely encourage him to press his arguments more forcefully. But Alma felt it would be wrong to let a statement go unchallenged, tacitly implying that she agreed with it.

"If a religious revival inspires only one person to lead a more holy life, is that not sufficient reason for it to have taken place?" Alma asked. "Don't the Scriptures command a shepherd to leave the ninety and nine sheep in his flock to search for the one lost lamb?"

Stow snorted condescendingly. He opened his mouth to provide what Alma expected to be a witheringly sarcastic reply, only to be distracted by the sound of a horse approaching. Alma and Sina, who hadn't said a word since Stow had shown up, were distinctly relieved – and Stow was clearly irritated – when they recognized Billy's voice inside the house asking the servant girl where to find Alma.

The sound of footsteps through the hall of the house was followed by Billy's appearance at the back door. He went directly to Alma, bestowing a discreet kiss on a cheek he noticed was brightly flushed. He greeted Sina with a warm smile, then turned to acknowledge Joshua Stow's presence with a polite, stiff nod. The servant's forewarning that Stow was in the backyard had saved Billy from an unpleasant surprise.

"Let's hear your young man's thoughts on this subject, Alma," Stow said. "I've been trying to open Alma's and Sina's eyes to the fact that the religious awakenings cropping up around Connecticut lately are nothing more than opportunities for pathetic people to experience excessively emotional 'conversions' and attract attention they otherwise couldn't hope for," he said to Billy. "What do you think? Have you witnessed any of these revivals? Maybe you've had your own eternal salvation assured at one," Stow sneered.

Billy remained silent for a long moment. He studied Stow with a blank expression that concealed his loathing for this man who delighted in agitating people's minds and hearts to no purpose. Billy found even Stow's face repellent; its extraordinarily high, broad forehead, close-set eyes, and broad nose reminded him of the bulbous death's heads found on many gravestones.

Refusing to reply wouldn't do, Billy knew. Stow would continue to prod until Billy answered. Failing that, he would return to tormenting Alma.

Billy sat down on the stone wall surrounding the Coe homelot before replying. He framed his words carefully. He was determined to speak as a grown man entitled to his own opinions, yet with respect for someone who was his elder and well regarded by many members of the community – although why Billy couldn't begin to fathom.

"I've never experienced the blessings of a revival," Billy began slowly. "But I recall my Granny Fowler describing the time she and my Grandfather Lyman heard George Whitefield preach in Middletown. She said his words kindled in both their hearts a faith that carried them through trials to rival those of Job. She was committed to leading a righteous life, and believed deeply in the wisdom and goodness of the Lord. In her I saw evidence that religious awakenings can inspire genuine renewals of the soul."

Stow harrumphed skeptically, thinking that the Hope Lyman Billy had known, the wise grandmother of advanced years and comfortable means, was a different woman from the domineering matriarch she'd been before Billy's birth. He considered goading Billy with this contradiction, but decided instead to attack the Bible.

"Alma was quoting Scripture to me just before you came," Stow said. "I was about to say that the validity of Scripture carries no weight in any rational argument, for the Bible frequently contradicts itself and is often literally fabulous. Do you truly believe the dead will be resurrected, their bodies to rise up from their graves?"

"I do," said Billy. He thought of Phineas, of the great comfort his brother had taken in that promise of life beyond death, where he would once more be whole and meet the loved ones he'd found it so painful to part with on earth.

Stow erupted into a harsh, mocking laugh that felt to Billy like a slap on the face. "That makes as much sense as believing that a turkey will rise up with its feathers on and gobble, after having been gnawed on by half a dozen hungry men," he said, enjoying the horrified gasps that his blasphemy forced from both Alma and Sina.

Billy stared in contempt at Stow. He struggled to suppress the rage that rose up in him at this man's despicable rantings, like water heated to just short of boiling. Out of the corner of his eye he saw that Sina was close to tears.

"I will concede that the Bible is good for something," Stow said with a grin that seemed literally diabolical to Billy. "After it's worn out, it will do to use at the little house!" Stow jerked his thumb toward the outhouse at the back of the homelot and cackled with pleasure at his own vulgar witticism.

Billy shot suddenly to his feet. His face was drained white, and his tall frame literally shook with fury. The veins at his temples were bulging, and his enormous hands were clenched into fists.

"You're a damned son of a bitch, Stow!" Billy snarled, taking a threatening step toward the older, shorter man before he was able to stop himself with a great effort. "When you mock the Scriptures in such a vile manner, you shit on the memories of my grandmother and brother. By following the teachings on the pages you desecrate, they accomplished more good in their lives than you could hope to do, should you live to be a thousand years old!"

Stow had shrunk back in his seat in reaction to Billy's unexpected menacing move in his direction. Much as he delighted in riling people, he realized he'd pushed too hard, gone too far this time. He was distinctly relieved when Billy came no closer.

Billy was disgusted with himself for letting Stow prod him into such a vulgar display of anger, not only in another man's home but in front of the woman he loved. He glanced at Alma – and his blazing anger changed instantly to ice-cold fear. In his mind he heard Phineas's warning from that day years ago in the schoolhouse: "Your temper will land you in jail – or worse!" Billy saw that "worse" on Alma's face: fear not of Joshua Stow's crude blasphemy, but of Billy's outburst of fury.

"I think it best to take my leave now," Stow said hastily when he found his tongue. When neither Billy nor Alma responded, he picked up his hat and scurried into the house, headed for the front, where his horse was tethered.

After a quick troubled glance at her sister and Billy, Sina went inside as well. Billy's anger had frightened her, too. She had no wish to witness whatever was about to happen between him and Alma.

The fear slowly faded from Alma's face. It was replaced by an uneasy wariness that made Billy's chalk-white cheeks flush bright red with shame.

"I'm sorry, Alma," Billy said, miserably repentant. "I know Joshua Stow lives to provoke people, and losing my temper just gave him what he wanted. But his last foul blasphemy was more than I could bear."

"What if I should 'provoke' you one day, Billy? Or one of our children?" Alma asked in a shaking voice. "Might it be more than you can bear? Will you be able to master your anger? Or will there be times when it will master you?"

Billy's mouth dropped open in shock at what Alma was implying. "I would never hurt you, Alma!" he protested with indignation so vehement that, he saw with dismay, only fed Alma's concern. He stared at her for a long moment, then looked down and forced himself to try to imagine what was going through her mind.

Many people thought it acceptable for a husband to strike his wife as part of maintaining order in his household. A woman had no legal recourse against a husband who beat her. Even the most vicious treatment was not grounds for divorce, which could be obtained only for adultery, desertion, or fraudulent contract.

This meant that, once married, a woman was truly at her husband's mercy. If he proved abusive she could expect to be rescued only by death – his or hers – or by deserting him, in which case custody of any children would be awarded to him.

No wonder Alma found his flare-up so frightening, Billy thought. He looked into her eyes, but before he could try again to reassure her, Alma spoke.

"It's not just the possibility that you would raise a hand against me," Alma said in a strained voice. "I won't live on pins and needles with a hot-tempered husband who might lash out with sharp words that would cut my heart."

Billy was appalled at the prospect of losing Alma. During two years of courting he had come to cherish her more than he ever could have imagined.

"I will prove to you I can control my temper, Alma," he said, tears gathering in his eyes. "I swear it. I would do anything for you," he finished in a tortured whisper.

"I pray God you can," Alma replied in a trembling voice. She had never seen Billy so upset, nor felt so shaken herself.

Billy held out his arms with a tentativeness Alma found heartbreaking. She stepped into them and allowed herself to be enveloped in the powerful embrace that had become so familiar and comforting. She laid her cheek against his chest as he rested his chin lightly atop her soft hair.

During their courtship, Alma had learned that Billy Lyman was a man of extraordinarily strong emotions – loving, loyal, protective, kind, and brave. She realized she shouldn't be surprised that his temper could ignite more quickly and burn hotter than most.

But all Billy's good qualities taken together would not, in Alma's opinion, compensate for living in daily fear of being hurt, physically or emotionally, by a husband to whom she'd committed herself body and soul. As on that fateful day at Crank Spring, Alma knew she had to follow the more difficult path of candor. And she would pray, as she'd never prayed before, for God to give Billy the strength to fulfill his promise. For she could no longer imagine life without him.

Chapter Sixty

April, 1807
Middlefield

As her room began to brighten in the hour before dawn, Alma gave up trying to sleep. She pulled back the sheet so as not to awaken Sina, slumbering soundly next to her, and slid her bare feet onto the floor. She walked over to a small table and poured water into a basin. She scooped cool water in her cupped palms and applied it to her face in the hope it would refresh her.

Billy had left for New York on business for his father at the beginning of the week. Alma missed him desperately – which was foolish, she chided herself. He'd been gone for several days at a time before. But always before, he'd been back in Middlefield by the Sabbath, and managed to spend Sunday evening with her. Even when foul weather left the roads seemingly impassable, Billy had always appeared, thanks to the strength and spirit of Captain, a worthy mount for as natural a horseman as he was.

But last night had been Sunday – the first Alma hadn't spent with Billy since they'd begun courting. Knowing he was farther from home than ever before, vulnerable to the perils such a long trip posed, made his absence even more trying for Alma, who studied her face, haggard from lack of sleep, in the looking-glass.

The evening had been empty and lonely; even the best efforts of her brothers and sisters had failed to cheer her up. She hoped Billy would return before the next Sabbath, as was expected. She dreaded the thought of another without him.

The intensity with which she ached for Billy was sometimes unsettling, Alma thought as she dried her face on a linen towel. She feared it would weaken her determination to be absolutely certain Billy had conquered his hot temper before they proceeded with any discussion of marriage – for which they both yearned.

They had been a bit reserved and restrained with each other for a few days following the terrible afternoon of Billy's explosion at Joshua Stow, but their relationship had soon regained an even balance. They hadn't spoken since of the intangible obstacle to their marriage, for both understood that talk counted for nothing. Action on Billy's part was all that mattered.

Alma hadn't seen or heard of Billy behaving with anything remotely like the fury he'd directed at Joshua Stow. But that wasn't sufficient. She was waiting for some sign – exactly what she didn't know – that she could wed Billy without reservation.

Alma blew out her frustration with a breath that made her lips vibrate. Determined to quit moping and get on with the day, she walked quietly to the window to check the weather. She slowly raised the lower sash, then leaned slightly out over the sill.

A whitish fog was swirling slightly as it dissipated in the morning's rising warmth. Out of the corner of her eye Alma noticed movement in front of the house. She blinked rapidly, as if that would somehow help her see through the mist, stared hard – and suddenly broke into laughter so loud Sina woke and sat bolt upright in bed.

Sina scrambled to get out of bed. But in her drowsy befuddlement her feet got tangled in the sheets; she rolled onto the floor with a loud thump.

By the time Sina freed herself and reached the window, Alma was pulling her head inside, laughing so hard tears trickled down her cheeks. Mystified, Sina stuck her own head out the window.

"It's Captain!" she cried in astonishment, bringing her head back in to look at Alma questioningly. Billy's horse, with no bridle or saddle, was standing next to the hitching post where he customarily waited each Sunday evening while Billy visited with Alma.

Alma wiped the tears from her cheeks with a forefinger as she managed to stop laughing and catch her breath. "Captain must have sensed it was Sabbath evening, time for Billy's regular visit," she said. "When Billy didn't show up, Captain made the trip anyway."

"He must have thought the courting unusually interesting for it to have kept him waiting here all night," Sina observed with a suggestive lift of her eyebrows that set them both to giggling.

"I'll take him home as soon as I get dressed," Alma said. "Billy asked Andrew to take care of Captain while he was gone. When

Andrew finds the horse missing, he'll scour the countryside from New Haven to Hartford."

Twelve-year-old Andrew Lyman was indeed beside himself when he found Captain missing. He was trotting down Miller Road on his brother Alanson's mount, peering through the fog that was rapidly burning off, desperately hoping to spy the stray animal. When he spotted Alma approaching on horseback, leading Captain behind her, he nearly burst into tears of relief. Andrew spurred his horse forward, hoping his eyes weren't playing tricks on him.

"Where did you find him?" Andrew demanded as he reigned in his horse next to Alma's. He was so relieved he forgot to offer even the briefest of polite greetings.

"At the hitching post at my house at first light," Alma replied, allowing Andrew's lapse of manners to pass. "I don't know how long he'd been there – maybe all night. I knew you'd want to know he was safe as soon as possible."

Alma had been impressed by Billy's thoughtfulness in deciding to entrust Captain to Andrew. Thin and somewhat short for his age, the sandy-haired boy tended to get lost in the shuffle of so many brothers and sisters. Billy had decided to risk having Andrew care for his prized horse while he was away in the hope that the responsibility would give his little brother a boost of confidence.

"Thank you, Alma," Andrew said, seizing Captain's lead from her. "When I found Captain's stall empty this morning, I panicked. This horse means more to Billy than anything in the world."

At another time Alma might have teased Andrew for implying Captain outranked her in Billy's affections. But his response prompted her to ask, as casually as she could manage, "Would Billy really have been so angry?"

"Angry?" Andrew repeated in surprise. He shook his head thoughtfully. "No. Billy hasn't lost his temper for some time now. It might have something to do with religion. He's been reading the Bible, and he and Mama talk a lot about it. No, I was afraid of letting him down."

The boy's answer lifted Alma's spirits. As self-controlled as Billy had been in her presence, she couldn't help but wonder if he exercised the same restraint when she wasn't around. Andrew's innocent, honest words gave her hope, made her care even more for Billy, who loved her enough to try to change his very nature if that was what it took to make her his wife.

Chapter Sixty-One

June, 1807
Middlefield

David stopped to listen as he washed the dirt from a day's worth of haying off his hands. Above the dull thud of Sarah working the butter churn in the kitchen below, he thought he had heard a rapping. As he dried his hands he heard the sound again – unmistakably a knocking on the kitchen door.

When the pounding of the churn continued, David realized that Sarah hadn't heard it. She had lost some sharpness in her hearing when she passed her fiftieth birthday. Shaking his head in slight exasperation, David hurried down the stairs with energy remarkable for a man of sixty who'd just spent ten hours laboring in the sun.

Sarah stopped churning when she saw David stride purposefully into the kitchen. Before she could speak, he opened the door to reveal Alma Coe standing on the stone stoop.

"Colonel Lyman!" exclaimed Alma. She'd expected Sarah or one of the children to answer the door. David was still addressed by his militia title, although he hadn't been active in the ranks for years.

"Come in, Alma," David said. His annoyance vanished at the sight of Billy's intended.

"You're early," Sarah said, chagrined to realize she'd left Alma waiting outside.

"I thought I might help prepare supper," Alma said, stepping into the kitchen. She was indeed dressed suitably for work, in a dress of brown checked homespun linen with a high waist formed by a drawstring, sturdy leather shoes, and a straw bonnet. But Sarah had no doubt the young woman's arrival a good two hours before the evening meal had more to do with the possibility of spending time with Billy, who'd been busy with haying from dawn to sunset every day for the past week.

David had no patience with such feminine pretenses. "Billy should be back in an hour or so," he told Alma, as he poured himself an earthenware mug of cider. "I just sent him with Alanson and Alfred and the hired man to bring in the sheep from pasture."

"What can I do while I wait?" a disappointed Alma asked Sarah.

"You can pick strawberries," Sarah replied. "There were a great many this morning that looked almost ripe. They should be ready by now. Take that basket."

Alma picked up the woven splint basket Sarah indicated. With a smile and a respectful nod toward David she went out the kitchen door, which he closed behind her.

"Do you think those two will ever marry, Sally?" David asked Sarah with a perplexed sigh, watching Alma through the window as she walked toward the strawberry patch at the end of the kitchen garden. Waiting until Billy turned twenty-one before suggesting he consider the Coe sisters as candidates for marriage had been trying for both David and Elisha Coe. But Sarah had been right. By the time David raised the issue, Billy had developed a strong interest in Alma on his own, although he hadn't made his feelings known to her. Alma, fortunately, had been most receptive.

"It's been nearly three years they've been courting!" David exclaimed. "I thought they would have wed and given us a grandchild by now. They know their marriage would please our families. Elisha and I have agreed on a marriage portion. I've promised Billy to help them settle in a house of their own. What's holding them back?"

David shook his head in bafflement. "I would have gone mad if I'd been required to wait half as long as they have to wed you," he said, looking at Sarah, who smiled at the compliment. He walked away from the window toward his wife. "Have their feelings for each other cooled?" he asked in helpless frustration.

Sarah eyed David as if he'd spouted gibberish. "If you can't see that Billy and Alma are in love, then you wasted the money you spent on those new spectacles," she teased, then went on seriously.

"As far as I can tell, their characters are well-suited, and both have been experiencing a deepening of faith." Sarah made the last comment with relief. She worried about the spiritual lives of all her children. More than twenty years after Abner Benedict's departure, the Middlefield parish still had no permanent minister, no foundation of organized religious guidance.

"I've wondered myself what's holding them back," Sarah admitted. "I've asked Elizabeth, but neither she nor Elisha know why they haven't set a wedding date. It's almost like–," Sarah paused, searching for a way to put her intuition into words, "like one stitch has been dropped halfway down a knitted stocking that's nearly finished. It's a small flaw, but if not fixed, with time and pressure the stocking will unravel."

David smiled at Sarah's homely comparison, expecting she'd come close to the heart of the matter. He took one of her work-roughened hands in his. He looked into her face with warm affection for a long moment, then his eyes went opaque with distraction.

Sarah studied her husband of almost thirty years. He still had a full head of hair, but it now was entirely the color of burnished pewter. Sarah thought it made David look dignified, but it was also an unmistakable sign, along with increasingly frequent joint pains, that he was entering the winter of life.

With advancing age, David had increased his efforts toward achieving his goal of creating a sound financial legacy for Sarah and their children. That had led him to take the biggest gamble of his financial career.

David had spent thousands of dollars to buy a number of Merino sheep bred from a flock of one hundred that Colonel David Humphreys of Derby, Connecticut, had brought back from Spain in 1802. The wool of the Merino was far finer, their fleeces much thicker than those of domestic sheep. Cloth woven in America from Merino wool was fine enough to compete with foreign imports, yet could be sold for a lower price that would still bring a handsome profit. Toward that end, David had also purchased a loom, and hired an experienced weaver to operate it.

The potential of the fledgling woolen industry seemed so great that David had mortgaged their homelot and the roof over their heads to obtain as much cash as possible to invest. Risking their home worried Sarah, but she'd kept her fears to herself. Thankfully, recent events made David's actions seem particularly shrewd.

The previous year, Colonel Humphreys had established a woolen factory in Derby, and the cloth it produced was finding a good market. An embargo against trade with England and France instituted by President Jefferson, although cursed by New Englanders as the "Dambargo" for the damage it inflicted upon the region's shipping, had also cut off the supply of imported fabric, greatly increasing demand for cloth made domestically.

David's great hope for seeing his various ventures, including this golden opportunity, come to fruition was Billy. Phineas was gone. David, Jr., was settled in Vermont. Alanson lacked the perseverance such an enterprise required. Andrew seemed unlikely to be strong enough to work the land for a living. Elihu at ten was too young for his potential to be clear. There was only Billy. That realization fueled David's urgency for Billy to marry and settle down in Middlefield.

"If you're worried Billy will go to Vermont or New York, you can put your mind at ease," Sarah said, standing up. David focused his gaze on her, no longer amazed that she could read his mind. "He's rooted as deeply in this farm as you are," she reassured him.

"That's not to say I don't share your frustration over a courtship as slow as molasses in January," Sarah went on. "David and Polly's babies are very dear, and I treasure every minute with them. But it's so hard to go months at a time without seeing them." Polly Lyman in 1802 had married Aaron Robinson of Bennington, a widower ten years her senior with four children, and now had two of her own. The same year David, Jr., had married a young woman named Sophia Park, and they had two children as well.

"It would be such a joy to have grandchildren nearby," Sarah said wistfully. "Little ones we could delight in every day."

"Well, if something doesn't light a fire under Billy and Alma, Elihu might give us a grandchild before they do," David grumped.

David slipped both arms around Sarah's waist, and smiled down at her with deep contentment. Bearing ten children had added more than a few pounds to Sarah's already ample figure, but David still found her enticing. Her hair was as much pearly silver as it was its original ripe wheat color. Crow's feet, worry lines etched into her brow, and her partial loss of hearing were other signs that, even though she was younger than David, the years were advancing on Sarah as well. But her gray eyes, even with the shadow of sorrow left by Phineas's death, were as loving and understanding as ever.

"If they knew what they were missing, Billy and Alma wouldn't be dragging their feet," David said. "After they've wed, they'll look back with regret on the time together they've lost."

The strawberry patch was fragrant with the aroma of berries crushed accidentally underfoot by children picking in the morning then baked in the sun all day. The trees and the house cast long shadows separated by swatches of butter-colored sunlight.

Alma crouched down and with both hands carefully brushed aside the leaves on the low plants, looking for the red, heart-shaped berries. The prickly leaves made her skin itch faintly – a small price to pay for uncovering one, or sometimes a cluster, of the berries concealed by the leaves or the straw placed on the ground from which the plant took its name.

The first dozen or so berries went right into the basket. But then temptation triumphed, and Alma plopped into her mouth a perfectly ripe berry, pleasantly warm from the sunshine that had transformed it from light orange to deep red in a single day. A uniquely refreshing sweetness flooded her mouth – the first true taste of summer.

Alma continued picking, treating herself to a berry every few minutes. Picking strawberries was a treasure hunt that quickly became a greedy compulsion to pluck as many berries as possible, to seize as much of their fresh goodness during the all-too-brief period Nature made them available.

At last the basket – and Alma – were full. She picked a couple more berries that caught her eye, then stood to brush the straw from her skirt. She looked toward the declining sun and saw Billy striding down the hillside. He, his brother Alanson, their cousin Alfred, and the hired man were carefully guiding four Merino rams. Each animal was worth $1,000 – a small fortune.

Alfred Lyman, Elihu and Esther's son, now in his late teens, had been working on the farm for the past several months. Phineas Miller had been of great assistance to Esther after Elihu's death, as Isaac Miller had predicted. Phineas himself had done well in Georgia, at long last wedding the widowed Catherine Greene in 1796. But in 1804 Phineas, only forty, had died from lockjaw.

After that Esther Lyman had brought her son and daughter back to Middlefield. They'd settled into a small house left to Esther by her father, and got along on what Esther received from Elihu's Georgia estate. Esther had politely refused David's offers of financial assistance, apparently feeling that would reflect unfavorably on Elihu's decision to seek his fortune outside Connecticut.

As for Alfred, he agreeably performed any assigned chore, but he was devoid of initiative. He couldn't have been more different from his daring, ambitious, inquisitive father. William told Alma that David attributed his nephew's lack of enterprise to spending his formative years in the indolent atmosphere of Georgia, as opposed to the bracing, invigorating environment of Connecticut.

As the four men descended the hillside, one of the rams suddenly bolted. The hired man ran after the animal so fast his hat blew off. But as he caught up with the runaway, he tripped over a rock and stumbled forward, falling so heavily upon the animal that Alma could hear it bleat.

Billy ran over to where man and animal lay. Alma held her breath, waiting to see if Billy would explode in anger at the man's clumsiness, which may have injured an animal worth as much as the farmhand earned in three years.

Billy helped the humiliated and frightened farmhand to his feet. Then he picked up the man's hat and planted it with good-natured firmness on his head. Only then did Billy kneel down to examine the ram which, after a long moment, scrambled to its feet, apparently unhurt, and scampered back to its companions. Alanson, Alfred, and the farm hand herded the sheep toward the barn, while Billy turned off toward the house.

Billy's eyes lit up at the unexpected sight of Alma waiting for him by the stone wall surrounding the homelot. Her red-stained lips betrayed her failure to resist temptation, and he leaned over to tease her about it.

To Billy's surprise, Alma reached up and, ignoring the sweat and dirt and faint sheep smell that clung to him, threw her arms around his neck. She pulled his face down and, in a startlingly public display of affection, kissed him full and hard on the mouth. Her straw bonnet fall back off her head.

For a moment Billy was too surprised to respond. But he recovered with admirable speed, throwing himself wholeheartedly into the embrace and the kiss. The lingering sweetness of the berries on Alma's lips made the kiss particularly pleasant.

At last Alma gently pulled away. Before Billy could ask what had sparked this delightfully passionate greeting, she looked him square in the eye and said with bold certainty, "I want to get married."

"Are you sure?" Billy managed to stammer, wondering what had so unexpectedly resolved her one great reservation about their union. But before he could say more, Alma pressed her lips to his again with a warmth and intensity that conveyed complete certainty.

"Does that answer your question?" she murmured into his ear. This time Billy replied with a kiss of his own, so full of relief and love and longing that it left Alma breathless.

Chapter Sixty-Two

October, 1807
Middlefield

From the intensity of the ardor with which Billy embraced and kissed Alma during their lengthy courtship, she had every reason to expect he would consummate their marriage with powerful urgency. The prospect made her more than a little anxious, but she took reassurance from the tenderness Billy had always shown toward her, and in the stirrings of her own flesh when they were together that she would at long last be free to explore.

Alma was a virgin, but she didn't know about Billy's sexual experience. He hadn't dallied with any other girl in Middlefield or the surrounding towns since their first trip to Crank Spring, of that she was as certain as possible. But he was a man of twenty-four, and Alma couldn't dismiss the possibility that during his trips to New York or New Jersey he had slaked the lust that all men felt.

Alma was alone now with Billy, in a chamber in her parents' house, directly above the parlor in which their wedding had been performed and celebrated on this evening, October 20, 1807. She felt more self-conscious with him than she ever had before.

Alma turned her back to her husband. She took off her floor-length wedding gown of sheer white muslin over a sky-blue underdress. Delicate white embroidery adorned the lower part of the muslin. The square neck was low, the sleeves elbow-length, and the gathered waistline high in the style of a classic Greek gown.

Alma could hear Billy undressing as well. She reached for the linen nightgown hanging from a peg on the wall, but Billy's hand came over her shoulder and closed gently over hers.

"You won't need that," he said in a low, husky voice. Taking her hand in his, he led her to the large featherbed.

Alma averted her eyes until Billy slid under the sheets up to his waist. She got in on the other side of the bed, and automatically started to pull up the sheets and coverlet. Billy again stopped her hand, then pushed the bedclothes down until she lay entirely naked before him in the flickering light of two candles.

Alma waited tensely for Billy to seize and claim her with the fierceness of lust denied satisfaction for more years than most men would consider reasonable to endure. She felt flickers of carnal passion, but they were banked by trepidation of the unknown.

To Alma's surprise Billy lay quietly on his side, his head propped upon his left hand. He made no move to touch Alma, but his eyes roamed her body with an expression that, when she at last looked into his eyes, made her heart begin to pound.

At last Billy began to caress her breasts, lightly and tenderly, with something like reverence that Alma found more arousing than any aggressive manipulation. Her anxiety drained away, and she was able to relax and close her eyes to better concentrate on the erotic sensations Billy's touch sent surging through her.

Billy's fondling at last raised Alma to such a fever pitch that her body began to make slight, involuntary movements, instinctively seeking satisfaction of the lust he'd conjured up. Billy's lips brushed his wife's cheek, then found her mouth. He gave her a full, penetrating kiss, and Alma brought her arm up to caress his neck and press his lips harder against hers. Billy slowly moved his hand from Alma's breasts, down over her stomach, then lower still, to the spot where she now yearned desperately for his touch.

Alma heard a soft rustle as Billy pushed down the sheet that had covered him to the waist. She felt him shift so that his body was poised over hers. When she sensed his hesitation, Alma slid a hand down to the small of his back, where she pressed firmly as a signal for him to continue. As he gently lowered himself, Alma wrapped her arms tightly around Billy's neck and abandoned herself to the exquisite sensations of two people becoming one flesh.

"I think I'll call you 'William' from now on," Alma said in the early morning darkness. She was snuggled with her back against her husband's chest, his arms around her breasts, one of his long, powerful legs lying possessively over hers. Their hearts had stopped racing from a second joining even more satisfying than the first.

"It's the woman who changes her name when she weds," Billy teased in a drowsy, contented voice.

"'Billy' is a boy's name," Alma said. "For a long time I haven't thought it suited you – and now I'm sure of it." The compliment made Billy smile to himself. "'William' is a more fitting name for a husband," Alma went on.

"I'm agreeable," said Billy, pleased by Alma's proposal. He'd grown tired of being called by a juvenile nickname, for the reason Alma noted. "I just wish you luck getting my family to give up 'Billy.'"

Chapter Sixty-Three

November, 1810
Middlefield

"Alma, let it be!" Sina snapped. "Can't I come to see the babies without you harping on me and Alanson?"

"I can't stay silent while you make a mistake you'll regret for the rest of your life," Alma replied with equal heat.

Alma glanced automatically out the window to check on two-year-old Phineas, born five days before she and William celebrated their first wedding anniversary, and named for the older brother William still missed. Little Phineas's doting Grandmother Lyman had come this morning to visit the boy and his eight-month-old baby sister, Adeline. When Sina arrived around noon, Sarah had taken the energetic Phineas outside into the tepid November sunshine to let the sisters talk without interruption.

William and Alma had lived with his parents in the first months after their marriage. In May of 1808, David Lyman made good on his promise to help the newlyweds acquire their own home by providing part of the funds to buy the house they occupied today.

The structure, located conveniently midway between the Lyman and Coe homesteads, was nearly a century old. With two rooms below, two chambers above, and a lean-to kitchen across the back, it wasn't even half the size of David Lyman or Elisha Coe's homes. It also retained some of the inconvenient features of homes built in the early 1700s, like the dangerously steep, sharply angled staircase.

Despite its drawbacks, Alma loved the house. It afforded her the opportunity, rare for a new wife, to raise her children, run her household, and work out her marriage with little daily interference from her in-laws. Sarah, having had the experience of sharing a household with the formidable Hope, had been a considerate mother-in-law while William and Alma lived under her roof. She'd rarely offered advice, but provided it generously when asked.

But Alma suspected once the grandchildren began arriving, Sarah would find it hard to continue her admirable restraint if they were occupying the same house. William had been as eager as Alma to separate their daily lives from those of his parents and siblings.

"Alanson loves me, and I love him," Sina was saying slowly to Alma, as if explaining a simple fact to a stubborn child. "We've been courting for three years – and I'm older than you were when you wed. Our families will be doubly connected by our union." Sina's tone lost its defensiveness. "Papa and Colonel Lyman have discussed a marriage portion. Maybe Papa will give us a set of chairs as he did to you," Sina said, enviously studying the spindle-backed, rush-seated maple chair on which Alma sat, nursing the baby.

"But the scales of affection between you and Alanson are dangerously unbalanced," Alma said. "You care far more for him than he does for you." It wasn't the first – or even the fifth – time Alma had confronted Sina with this harsh assessment. She couldn't hide her exasperation at her sister's pig-headedness.

Sina pursed her pretty mouth and waved a delicate hand in an airy gesture of dismissal. "Affection is never equal between a man and woman. When you began courting you were fonder of William than he was of you. I'm sure Alanson's love for me will deepen after we're married – particularly once I bear him a fine baby like this sweetheart," she said, reaching out to take little Adeline.

Sina laid the infant on her shoulder, and with the skill learned from years of caring for a gaggle of younger brothers and sisters, firmly rubbed the baby's back to produce a satisfactory burp. Once Alma rearranged her bodice, Sina reluctantly handed Adeline back.

"Besides," Sina went on, "this disagreement which has soured our every meeting of late will soon be pointless. Alanson right now is arranging for the banns to be posted so that we can wed on Thanksgiving," she announced on a note of triumph.

"Don't do it!" Alma cried, as if Sina were about to take arsenic.

Hurt and anger flooded Sina's blue eyes. "I would never have believed you could be so petty, to want to deny me the happiness you have! I won't listen to another word against our marriage!"

Sina leaped from her chair and stormed out the hall door, brushing past Sarah, who was bringing Phineas inside. It was an indication of how very upset Sina was that the normally well-mannered young woman didn't murmur even a token apology for nearly colliding with her prospective mother-in-law.

"Is she right, Mother Lyman?" Alma miserably asked Sarah, who had obviously heard the tail-end of the sisters' argument. "Am I petty to think Sina's marriage to Alanson is ill-advised?"

Sarah set Phineas on the chair his aunt had vacated, and began mashing up boiled turnips for his meal. She shook her head sadly.

"No, Alma, I think you're right," Sarah said, then went on with reluctance, "As much as it pains me to admit it, I agree with you."

Alma's look of surprise amused Sarah for a brief moment. "A mother's love doesn't necessarily blind her to a child's faults," she observed. She began feeding Phineas spoonfuls of mashed turnips.

"Alanson is handsome, and has charm most women find irresistible," Sarah went on. "I don't wonder Sina is in love. I think Alanson cares for her as much as he has for any girl."

Sarah sighed before continuing. "But Alanson is – inconstant," she said. "His intentions and enthusiasms are strong, but they don't last, especially when he runs into problems – like a brook that runs high in springtime but dries up under the summer sun. Courting Sina has been a pleasure, and by doing so Alanson has pleased his father, which is rare for him. But I fear he'll find the work of being a husband and father less to his liking," Sarah predicted gloomily.

"Even William doesn't understand my doubts about this union," Alma fretted. "He insists it's just the melancholy side of my nature which makes me examine any piece of good fortune for flaws."

"William has a good heart," Sarah said with a smile, wiping little Phineas's face. After three years, she no longer called her son "Billy," although David and the other children still sometimes slipped.

"Sometimes too good a heart," Sarah added with a frown. "He can be indulgent to a fault of those for whom he cares, his family most of all." Alma thought of William's willingness to master his temper in order to win Alma for his wife, when most men would have walked away from a woman who expected so much.

"Sina only wants what William and I have. Is that so much to ask?" Alma said plaintively.

Sarah suddenly looked weary. "Sad as it may be, I think what you and William have is more than most can expect from marriage."

"What can I do?" Alma asked despairingly. Although she didn't truly expect an answer, Sarah had one for her: "Love your sister, pray we are wrong – and be there to comfort her if we are right."

Chapter Sixty-Four

August, 1811
Middlefield

David stared at his signature on the neatly written document in his hand, then folded it carefully in thirds. He placed it in the bottom drawer of his bookcase and desk, which he locked. He set his spectacles on the desk's drop leaf, then rubbed his face wearily.

Later he would tell Sarah and William where to find the last will and testament he'd had drawn up. He should have done so long ago; he was, after all, sixty-five years old. But he never seemed to find the time, until unexpected tragedy forced him to make it a priority.

David Lyman, Jr., had died the previous March, short of his thirtieth birthday. In Vermont he'd matured from an inconstant youth into an exceptional man. He'd earned respect and affection as a friend, husband, parent, businessman, Christian, and public servant, having represented Woodford in the state legislature.

The family in Middlefield had had no warning of the impending sorrow. Looking back, David recalled that David, Jr., had seemed a bit under the weather when he, his wife, and their three children had come to Connecticut the previous November to celebrate Thanksgiving and attend Alanson's wedding to Sina Coe.

Once back in Vermont, David's health had deteriorated rapidly. He'd begun to display the unmistakable symptoms of consumption, the hellish disease that had robbed the elder David of his father and sister Esther. Not wanting to alarm his parents, the young man's letters to Connecticut had made no mention of his condition.

In a desperate search for a cure, David had traveled more than fifty miles to the town of Montague, Massachusetts, to consult with a physician who specialized in consumption cases. There he had died, without friends or family to offer comfort in his final hours.

When the terrible news reached Middlefield, David dispatched William to bring his brother's body home – to Connecticut. He sent Alanson to Vermont to escort David's widow and their now-fatherless children to Middlefield.

Middlefield still had no settled pastor. In 1808 David had been one of a handful of residents who organized themselves into a congregation, the first step toward reviving the church. But they were years away from hiring a minister. David had asked the Reverend David Smith, pastor of the Durham Congregational Church, to preach a funeral sermon before David, Jr., was laid to rest in the Middlefield burying ground next to his brother Phineas.

David put his spectacles back on, then picked up a copy of Mr. Smith's sermon that he'd arranged to have published. He riffled through it until he found Mr. Smith's candid words of consolation:

> And what shall I say to the parents of the deceased? My Christian friends, as your age increases, your trials multiply. You are called to follow another beloved son to the narrow house. The branches wither while the stock remains. May the hand which afflicts grant you the consolations of the gospel. May your trials be sanctified, and cause your graces to shine. Out of this furnace of affliction may you come forth as gold purified in the fire.

As always, Sarah responded to the death of a loved one by affirming life. She'd devoted herself to her family, in particular her bereaved daughter-in-law and fatherless grandchildren. After they returned to Vermont, she'd lavished attention on William and Alma's children. She'd spent time with Sina, whose marriage to Alanson was already beginning to fracture as she and Alma had feared.

David had found some distraction from his grief in the task of making provision for the security, after his own death, of his family. Without consulting anyone, he'd composed a will detailing his wishes, then had an attorney in Middletown cast it in legal language and arrange for David to sign it in the presence of three witnesses.

David had provided first of all for his beloved Sarah, leaving her the customary widow's thirds of his real estate and personal property, which would allow her to live comfortably should she survive him. He made two special bequests. To his daughter Sally, whose eyesight was extremely poor, he left $300. And he'd bequeathed $500 to William, identified with painful accuracy as "my oldest son," to "pay him for his services in doing business for me up to this time." William, who at this very moment was in Vermont acting as administrator of his brother's estate.

David had designated William and Alanson executors of his estate. Although he doubted Alanson would perform an equal share of the process, he hoped he would be of some help to William.

What would they do without William? David mused somberly. Time and again the family looked to him to shoulder a burden. He'd always accepted the responsibility, and never failed to fulfill it.

David had also provided for his fatherless grandchildren, directing that his surviving sons pay David, Jr.'s, son, Alanson, $400 when he turned twenty-one, and each of David, Jr.'s, two daughters, Sophia Emiline and Sina, $100 when she turned twenty-one, or upon her marriage if she wed before reaching that age.

The remainder of his estate David had divided among his four sons – William, Alanson, Andrew, and Elihu – and four daughters – Polly, Esther, Sally, and Urania – in the proportion of "one son to three daughters, that is to say William my oldest son three shares and Polly my oldest daughter one share." Anything he'd given a child before his death was to be counted toward their share of the estate.

David didn't worry that his daughters would resent their brothers' advantage in the distribution of his property. Polly and Esther had received generous enough marriage portions that anything they received under the terms of his will would be unexpected largesse. The formula would provide ample marriage portions for Urania and Sally as well.

David, Jr.'s, sad decline and lonely death had reinforced David's determination to do everything he could to keep his remaining sons in Connecticut. They would need as much as he could provide to set themselves up respectably here at home.

David continued to be the wealthiest man in Middlefield – and that was without counting the acres he'd purchased in Vermont, New York, and Pennsylvania, with the intention of selling them at a profit to new settlers. The Merino sheep had been a wise gamble, and would prove even more profitable if war erupted as many feared, increasing demand for woolen cloth as foreign supplies dried up.

Were David to die tomorrow, all would be well for the loved ones he left behind. Only Sarah knew how much it meant to him to know that his legacy to his family would be so different from that of his father.

Chapter Sixty-Five

July, 1812
Middlefield

It was late afternoon before Alma had a chance to sit down in the small parlor of her house and treat herself to the only tonic for what ailed her: letters from William. It was late July, nearly six weeks since he'd gone to Vermont to continue settling his brother David's estate and to tend to his father's land interests there.

From the pile of a dozen letters Alma selected the most recent, which her father-in-law had picked up from the postmaster in Durham and delivered to her three days ago. She began to read it for what was probably the tenth time.

As always, Alma was cheered to read in William's own hand that he was in good health and spirits. Her heart was warmed by the fact that he went to the considerable trouble and expense of writing often to her during a relatively brief separation simply because he knew his letters lightened her mood. Most husbands would consider one or two letters over the course of a six-week absence adequate, unless they contained urgent news, which William's hadn't.

Alma had written just as faithfully to William in Bennington, Vermont, keeping him up to date on everything of interest among their family and friends, particularly their children. She described how Phineas, nearly four, was able to sound out a few words in books. She assured William that the scratches and bruises Adeline had sustained in a fall from a stone wall had healed completely. Although Adeline was only two, William encouraged her to be as adventurous as her big brother. He'd delighted her by letting her walk along the top of a stone wall while holding his hand. But when

Adeline tried to do the same on her own, she'd tumbled off into her mother's thorny rose bushes.

At the moment Phineas and Adeline were playing together outside, where Alma could see and hear them through the window. Her thoughts turned to the new baby she was carrying; as if the child could read her mind, it started moving so vigorously that Alma felt like she had two puppies tussling inside her. The birth wasn't expected for another month at least; Alma refused to entertain the possibility that William might not be back from Vermont by then.

In his latest letter, dated eight days earlier from Bennington, William had tried to soothe Alma's troubled heart. As reluctant as she was to add to the burdens William already carried, she'd been unable to refrain from pouring out her worries in her letters to him. Foremost among these was Sina's health.

Four days after William left for Vermont, Sina, five months pregnant, had suffered her second miscarriage. The loss had left her dangerously weak in body and low in spirits.

The three younger Coe sisters – Sophia, eighteen; Delia, thirteen; and Lucia, ten – had spent almost all their free time with Sina. Alma had encouraged them to do so, for she thought their company might contribute toward Sina's recovery. But that meant that Alma, who'd been counting on her sisters' companionship while William was away, found herself alone most of the time, and missing her husband even more.

A much larger threat loomed over these personal concerns. It was bluntly announced by a headline in the July 25 issue of the *Middlesex Gazette* newspaper that lay atop the pile of newspapers Alma was saving for William to read when he returned.

"WAR! WAR! WAR!" the newspaper screamed. There followed an account of the U.S. Congress's declaration of war on Great Britain – and a blistering condemnation of that declaration as foolish and entirely unnecessary.

The Federalists who were still a majority in Connecticut considered war with Britain the bitter fruit of misguided Democratic-Republicans, as the Jeffersonians were now called, who still dominated the national government. In Federalist eyes this was a fight from which the United States – or at least New England – had nothing to gain and everything to lose.

News of war had fueled Alma's worries over William in Bennington, so close to British-controlled Canada. She closed her eyes and rested her head against the back of the chair. At least, she thought thankfully, William wouldn't be sent off to fight. Connecticut Governor Roger Griswold had refused the United States War Department's request to mobilize his state's militia under the authority of the federal government for defense of the Atlantic coast. Governor Griswold had declared that the U.S. Constitution didn't justify such action.

But still this misbegotten war had wreaked havoc on Alma's life. Her father had grown increasingly uncomfortable with the conservative principles of the Federalist Party, which in Connecticut was connected tight as a tick to the Congregational church. Elisha Coe at last had joined the Democratic-Republicans.

Elisha condemned Governor Griswold's refusal to mobilize the militia as requested by the federal government as dangerous and tantamount to treason. It could contribute to an eventual American defeat. The British would come swarming into Connecticut, and its people would have no one to blame but themselves.

Elisha Coe had shown his support of the conflict by permitting his son Linus, just twenty, to enter military service. Linus's unit had marched for Canada just a few weeks ago. Alma feared for her brother's physical safety, and also fretted that army life would corrupt his morals.

In this time of upheaval and uncertainty, when every earthly source of security seemed unreliable, Alma turned to God for support. She was deeply grateful for the re-establishment, however humble, of the Middlefield Congregational Church, even if the small flock still lacked a settled pastor.

Alma sorrowed that neither her parents nor her siblings had become involved with the church. Elisha Coe was a deeply religious man, but details of doctrine and formalities of worship services held no meaning for him. He had never even had his children baptized, something Alma intended to rectify for herself in the near future.

Alma's eyes flew open in alarm when Phineas and Adeline both suddenly shrieked. She hastily got to her feet to look out the window. What she saw caused her heart to skip a beat, for the children were being lifted up in their father's powerful arms. Tears of joy sprang to Alma's eyes as she hurried to the door as quickly as her ungainly figure permitted. She pulled it open just as William reached the stone stoop, Adeline in the crook of one arm, Phineas in the other.

A special light came into William's eyes at the longed-for sight of his wife. He freed himself from the clinging children by means of a favorite game in which he held them securely under the arms while allowing them to slide down his legs, until they landed giggling on the ground. When he straightened up he wrapped his arms carefully around Alma, kissing her hard and tightening his embrace – until the child in her womb kicked so powerfully he felt it against his own abdomen. He looked down in surprise, then a grin crossed his dusty face. "It seems our newest child doesn't want to be left out."

The sun had just slipped behind the ridgeline of Beseck Mountain, and the western sky was alight with a fiery pink and orange glow, by the time Alma was able to join William in the hall. While he'd gone about checking the corn crop and the sheep, which he'd hired a man to care for during his absence, and washing off the dust and dirt of the road, Alma had struggled with getting Phineas and Adeline, nearly hysterical with excitement at their father's homecoming, fed, into bed, and finally asleep.

William was lying on an outdated sofa, its fabric worn near threadbare from years of use. His head was propped up against one scrolled sofa arm, and his long legs dangled over the other. He was reading the *Middlesex Gazettes* Alma had put aside for him.

As Alma came into the room, William took a last drink of apple brandy from a stoneware mug, then set it and the newspapers on the floor. He pushed himself up on his elbows and hitched his body farther down on the sofa to make room for Alma. Then he lay back down, resting his head gently against her swelling abdomen.

"Someday I'll have enough money to order a sofa made especially long enough for my body," William declared, shifting his frame to a more comfortable position. Alma began to stroke his brow, and he closed his eyes in weary contentment.

"I can't thank you enough for your letters," Alma said. William acknowledged her words with a smile. Without opening his eyes, he reached up with his left hand to take her right one and intertwine her fingers with his.

"I can't think of many husbands who would go to such trouble to ensure a wife's peace of mine," Alma went on. "You give me so many reasons to thank God for uniting us, and that our affection remains strong – unlike that of others of our acquaintance." The specter of another not-so-happy couple hung between them.

They sat in silence as the light in the room slowly faded. "I saw Alanson in Fenno's tavern when I stopped in Middletown around noon," William said at last. He felt Alma stiffen at the statement.

"After I left Middletown I stopped by his house for a few minutes," William continued. "Lucia was with Sina, who looked better than I'd expected from your last letter." He hesitated, then went on, "Lucia said Alanson hasn't been home for two days."

Alma knew of Alanson's neglect of his wife, but hadn't mentioned it in her letters to William. She chose her words carefully.

"Alanson has little patience with weakness and illness," she said at last. "He told Sophia he finds the sickroom atmosphere in his house too irritating to bear for more than a few hours at a time."

"Whether it's to his liking or not is unimportant," William snapped with an annoyance Alma knew wasn't directed at her. "His wife is ailing, from trying to give him the son he so covets, and her own heart is heavy from her loss. His duty is to care for and comfort her as best he can."

William's sternness startled Alma. But she realized that however inclined William might be to overlook the faults of those he loved, Alanson had committed the one sin William couldn't abide: shirking a responsibility. It wasn't even one that had been thrust upon Alanson, but that he had eagerly embraced.

"I thought much about this while I was away," said William, as he absent-mindedly played tenderly with Alma's fingers. "Our father did Alanson no favor by allowing him and Sina to move right after their wedding into their own house on Papa's land, without requiring Alanson to even pay rent," he said solemnly.

"Papa's so afraid Alanson will leave Connecticut he'll do anything to entice him to stay," William went on worriedly. "He signed over forty acres to the two of us, so Alanson would own sufficient property to become a freeman." William shifted his head slightly back and forth. "But he gave it to us jointly because he feared if he gave it to Alanson alone, Alanson might sell it and take off. By handing him so much without expecting anything in return, Papa has denied Alanson the need to work for what he wants, to make himself an independent man."

Alma rarely spoke to William about their siblings' troubled marriage. There was, after all, nothing he could do about it, and criticizing his brother to no purpose would only hurt his feelings. And she suspected he might feel a bit guilty about not heeding her reservations about the marriage. But his unexpected candor made her feel free to share her own warring emotions.

"I'm so sad they haven't found happiness in marriage," Alma began in a thoughtful voice. "Alanson obviously finds being a husband much less amusing than being a suitor. Sina is desperately clinging to the hope that a child will bring them together, and she counts the pain and danger she's gone through small price to pay for that dream. But Alanson has done a poor job of concealing how these two miscarriages have disappointed him, and Sina feels she has failed him. Trying to have the baby Sina hopes will heal their marriage is driving them further apart."

Alma fell silent, and remained so for such a long time that William thought she was finished speaking. But then she added in a quiet voice of confession, "And my sister's loss makes me feel guilty in my blessed abundance."

William opened his eyes and twisted his head around sharply to look up at his wife's face, barely visible now in the twilight. "Don't do that to yourself, Alma!" he commanded. "If we are called upon to accept sorrow as God's will when it befalls us, we should be no less willing to embrace joy when that is His will."

Alma leaned over and kissed William gently on the mouth. She was grateful for his more optimistic character, which so often acted as a welcome counterweight to her tendency to melancholy. But his words reminded her of another concern, prompting her to ask teasingly, "And how many more times would you like us to be called upon to embrace this particular 'joy'?"

William was not fooled by her light tone. "Three babies in five years – and you not yet twenty-eight," he mused. "We seem to be well on the way to having as many children as our parents did. Yet I wouldn't like to have so large a family."

Alma squeezed his hand gently in agreement, for the room was now almost completely dark. They could make out only each other's silhouettes.

"I don't know any man who cherishes his sons and daughters more than my father does," William went on. "But his determination" – William had almost said "obsession" – "to accumulate enough wealth to set up ten children with a substantial stake in the world has driven him to take risks I wouldn't have." He was clearly uncomfortably criticizing David.

"Far better to have a smaller family," William said with absolute certainty. "I don't want our children to have to move to some distant frontier in order to make a decent life for themselves." Alma knew he was thinking not only of his brother David, sister Polly, and sister Esther, who had also found a husband in Vermont, but of his Uncle Elihu's tragic fate.

"Nor do I want to ever have to move myself in order to provide for my family," William went on. "Two years ago my cousin Lyman Beecher left his Long Island parish to become pastor in Litchfield in northwest Connecticut because he needed a larger salary to support his growing family. My father says his wife Roxana has borne seven children in just thirteen years."

William recalled how touched David had been when Lyman Beecher named his first child, a daughter, Catharine Esther, for the woman who bore him and the woman who raised him. "If Lyman's family continues to grow like that, he'll likely be forced to move again in search of an income that can support them.

"God willing, I want to know the men and women our children become. I want to watch our grandchildren grow up on land that has nurtured four generations of their blood. I want them to know the security of having kin nearby, not scattered over hundreds of miles."

"I agree with everything you say," Alma said. "But what can we do about it?" she asked despairingly.

The only reliable method of controlling the number of children Alma would bear was abstinence. Sitting in the warm summer darkness, savoring the intimacy both had missed so desperately these past weeks, William and Alma's thoughts were the same: to live together day after day, to lie next to each other night after night, and deny themselves for months or even years the gratification of the physical passion to which the holy covenant of marriage entitled them was unimaginable.

Alma didn't expect William to reply; he had no answer to their dilemma. Alma shook her head to banish these worries, which could wait until a later time, and addressed a more immediate concern. "When will you be going back to Vermont?"

"I won't be leaving again until after our baby is born," William replied reassuringly. "I stayed away these extra weeks to complete as much business as possible so that I wouldn't have to head north again until spring."

Alma resumed stroking his forehead. After a few minutes his eyelids drooped, and a bit later his steady breathing told her he was asleep. She gazed out the window at a patch of star-studded sky, thinking how wonderful it would be if time could be frozen forever at this instant of complete contentment.

Chapter Sixty-Six

January, 1814
Middlefield

It was good they hadn't tarried the previous afternoon when Alanson sent word that Sina's travail had begun, William reflected. He was sitting by the fire in the hall of the house David had provided Alanson and Sina. Nightfall had brought a storm of snow, sleet, and freezing rain that would coat everything with ice, making travel difficult or even impossible.

William shifted gingerly to take the weight off his left hip, painfully bruised in a spill he'd taken on the slippery ground while walking back from bedding down the horses in the barn.

William had first brought Alma and sixteen-month-old Elizabeth Coe Lyman, nicknamed "Lizzy" to distinguish her from the grandmother for whom she was named, here to Alanson's house. Lizzy needed to remain with Alma because she wasn't yet completely weaned. Then William had taken Phineas and Adeline to his parents' house for his sisters Sally and Urania to tend. Finally he had escorted Sarah back to Alanson's house, where they found that Elizabeth Coe had also arrived to be by her daughter's side.

For the past several hours Sarah, Alma, Elizabeth Coe, a midwife, and several neighbor women had been in a chamber with the laboring Sina. The shriek of the wind and the rattling of ice and sleet against the clapboards and windows obscured the voices of the women assisting a new soul into the world.

Alanson had no clock or watch, but William estimated it must be well past midnight, into the early hours of January 6, 1814.

William had agreed to sit up and keep Alanson company, for the father-to-be was too nervous to sleep.

William had finished reading the *Middlesex Gazette* he'd brought with him. Now he was leafing through his Bible, praying silently for the safety of Sina and her long-awaited baby.

Alanson was whittling a piece of wood, but his mind wasn't on his work. His hand slipped and the sharp knife sheared off a bit of his thumbnail, luckily not taking any skin or flesh with it.

William regarded his brother with amused sympathy. "Settle down, Lanson," he said, unable to resist using the boyhood nickname even as he tried not to sound patronizing. "This baby is coming right on time, and there's every reason to believe it will be fine, God willing." Alanson smiled self-consciously in appreciation for William's reassurance, then gave up his futile attempt at productive activity.

"I'm glad you laid in a good supply of Isaac Miller's apple brandy," William said, holding out his empty earthenware mug for Alanson to refill. "We would have a hard time making it through this bitter night without it."

Alanson picked up the bottle and tipped it over William's mug. Only a few droplets dribbled out. "This was half-full at supper time," he said, faintly surprised. "But there's plenty more where that came from. I'll fetch a fresh bottle from the cellar." Alanson pushed himself up out of his chair and started for the stairway, remembering to step quietly so as not to waken Lizzy, sound asleep in a cradle close to the hearth.

Both brothers had been dozing, for how long they didn't know, when a full-lunged squall awakened them like the striking of a hammer on iron. Another cry followed, and then another.

Alanson sat motionless, as if encased in the ice that covered everything visible through the windows in the pre-dawn light. He turned at the sound of feet descending the stairs. Alma appeared in the doorway to the room, tired, disheveled, her face aglow.

"Your wife and son are doing well, Brother," she announced. Alma waited to see the understanding of what she'd said light up Alanson's face, then hurried back upstairs.

Alanson looked at William as if he needed his older brother to confirm Alma's news. Amused by Alanson's stunned reaction, William stepped forward to embrace him in a hearty, back-slapping hug. Both men began to laugh with fatigue and relief and joy.

William pulled away and picked up his mug of brandy. He raised it toward Alanson in a salute, exclaiming, "A son! There's no finer way to start the year." Alanson simply beamed, still speechless

They hadn't heard their mother making her way slowly down the stairs. Sarah crossed the room to hug Alanson, then stepped back to hold him away from her at arms' length. "Well, don't you want to see my new grandson?" she asked in a tone of mock scolding. Alanson grinned, and at last went into motion, rushing over to the stairs and sprinting up them two at a time.

Sarah sat down heavily in the chair Alanson had vacated. She gratefully accepted the mug of apple brandy William poured for her. She took a drink, then closed her eyes and rested her head against the back of the chair, a smile of weary contentment on her lips. "God has at last blessed them with the most precious of His gifts," she said, her lower lip quivering with emotion.

"Have they chosen a name?" William asked.

"Roswell, for Sina's favorite brother," Sarah answered, "and David for your father – and your brother," she finished, a single tear sliding down each cheek.

Alma laid little Roswell Lyman in his cradle very carefully, so as not to waken him, then tucked a blanket tightly around to keep him warm. A wet nurse had just finished feeding the week-old baby – for his mother could not.

Three days after giving birth, Sina had developed childbed fever, which quickly raged out of control, despite the best efforts of several midwives and Dr. Tracy's various treatments and medicines. For the past twenty-four hours Sina had been intermittently delirious. It was now clear that the price for the son Sina had so yearned to bear would be her own life.

They might have been maintaining a death watch for little Roswell, too. But Alma had nursed him along with Lizzy for the days after Sina fell ill that it took to find a wet nurse. To all appearances, the baby was doing well.

Every morning William left Alanson's house to tend his own livestock, and then to visit Phineas and Adeline. They were being well cared for, even spoiled a bit, by their Aunt Sally and Aunt Urania, but they desperately missed their mother, who longed for them as well. Each night William returned to help with the essential chores at Alanson's house – and, it soon came to pass, deal with the problem of Alanson himself. When Alanson was first informed that

Sina might be in mortal danger, he'd refused to believe that God, having just blessed him with a son, would wound him so grievously. He'd sought escape in the brandy bottle, drinking heavily to numb his anger and feeling of helplessness.

William – exhausted, saddened by the unfolding tragedy, and worried about the toll the situation was taking on Alma – had come dangerously close to literally beating his younger brother into facing the crisis like a man. Most infuriating to William was that Alanson's pity for himself seemed to outweigh his grief for his dying wife.

When David Lyman arrived to help stand watch at his dying daughter-in-law's bedside, he'd relieved William of the responsibility of supervising Alanson. David had kept Alanson away from all spirits for the past twenty-four hours, grimly determined that his son should be sober and at his wife's side when the end came.

The final hour was near. William stood at the doorway of the death chamber. Despite the frigid temperature, the room was uncomfortably warm from the heat of all the bodies crowded into it. Lizzy was snuggled half-asleep on William's shoulder. Everyone was praying, including Elisha and Elizabeth Coe, whose faith in God seemed strong despite their lack of formal religious connections.

Alanson sat on a chair next to his wife's bed, his head hung low, clasping Sina's hot, limp hand between his two trembling ones. Elizabeth Coe sat on the opposite side, holding her daughter's other hand. She stroked Sina's brow soothingly, even though the dying woman almost certainly wasn't aware of her touch.

Sina's incoherent mutterings grew fainter, then stopped. Elizabeth Coe was the first to realize that Sina's soul had slipped away. She bit her lower lip as tears ran freely down her cheeks. She leaned over to kiss Sina tenderly on the forehead.

Alanson lifted his head. Looking from Sina to her mother and back again, he realized that his wife was gone. But he seemed unable to absorb the fact, just as a week earlier he'd been slow to process the reality of the birth of his son.

Alma, her heart and body drained empty by a nightmarish four days helping to care for her dying sister, nursing and caring for the newborn Roswell, comforting her distraught parents – and trying not to hate Alanson – could stand no more. She turned quickly to bury her face against William's chest. She began sobbing bitterly for the dead mother and wife, the motherless child, the grieving parents – and the cruel fulfillment of her foreboding about the marriage of her little sister to William's little brother.

Chapter Sixty-Seven

February, 1815
Middletown

The three sleighs glided over hard-packed snow as dawn broke, spilling brilliant sunlight across the countryside. In the rear of the lead sleigh Urania Lyman, twenty-three, gasped in surprise when the not-too-distant boom of a cannon shattered the morning calm.

Seated in front of Urania and her sister Sally, David chuckled at his youngest daughter's skittishness. He exchanged an amused smile with Sarah, who was seated next to him, then slapped the reins to urge the mare pulling the sleigh to increase her pace.

Their destination was the center of Middletown. A minute later the cannon boomed again, then continued to do so every minute, for a total of eighteen times. As the last echoes of the artillery fire faded away, they could hear the joyous clamor of church bells.

"Are your brothers keeping up?" David called back, never taking his eyes from the road. Urania knew the question was for her; Sally had been so nearsighted from birth that anything more than ten feet away from her was a blur.

Urania twisted around to look behind them. About a quarter of a mile back she saw the second sleigh, driven by William, with Alma next to him and their six-year-old Phineas bundled securely between them. Adeline and Lizzy had been left home, their parents deciding that the cold weather would be too brutal for their constitutions.

Urania spied the third sleigh perhaps half a mile further back. It was driven by Andrew, twenty, with his brothers Alanson and Elihu, now eighteen, as passengers. All three sleighs belonged to David, undeniable evidence of his significant prosperity.

"Yes, Papa!" Urania shouted as loudly as she could into the stiff wind created by the sleigh's swift movement. David nodded to indicate he'd heard. Urania wriggled back down under the heavy quilt that was keeping her and Sally warm on this exceptionally frigid Washington's birthday morning

Sarah, Urania, and Sally wore dresses of fine wool spun from fleece from David's prized flock of Merino sheep. Sarah's was a deep blue, made from yarn dyed by Cuff Boston, a free Middlefield Negro who specialized in the use of expensive indigo to produce the popular color.

Much more than the anniversary of the first president's birth was being celebrated on this February 22. The war with Great Britain was over. Most of Middletown was gathering to celebrate the end of three years of fighting that had inflicted great hardship on their nation, and in particular on New England, Connecticut, and the port of Middletown.

News that Great Britain and the United States had signed a treaty of peace in Europe in December had reached Connecticut only a couple weeks ago. Combined with the thrilling report that in early January American troops commanded by General Andrew Jackson had inflicted a devastating defeat on British forces at New Orleans, it had given a powerful lift to everyone's spirits. That Jackson's victory had occurred after the signing of the treaty in Europe, but before news of the peace agreement reached America – and thus had actually taken place after the war was over – didn't dim its luster in the least.

As the sleighs approached Middletown, Sarah thought of how difficult the atmosphere of rejoicing must be for Elizabeth and Elisha Coe, and for Alma. All of them wore mourning – but not for Sina, dead more than thirteen months now.

The year that had begun sorrowfully with Sina's death had ended in a double tragedy for the Coe family. Alma's sister Sophia, twenty, and her brother Roswell, eighteen, had both died of measles not six weeks apart.

In a period of less than twelve months, Elizabeth and Elisha Coe had buried a third of their children – an exceedingly heavy cross to bear. Sarah tried to view the deaths of youths like Sophia, Roswell – and her own Phineas – as the Lord gathering to Himself the freshest, loveliest, purest souls before they could be corrupted by the evils of the world.

Following Sina's death, Sarah had comforted Alma with the advice she'd given David when his brother Phineas had died – near forty years ago, so long past it seemed to belong to another lifetime – to love the living, not knowing how long they might be spared to her, or her to them. Alma had immediately taken her mother-in-law's words to heart, for which she would be forever in Sarah's debt. When Sophia and Roswell died suddenly and unexpectedly, Alma's grief at least had not been compounded by regret that she'd never voiced or shown her love for them.

And there was little Roswell, Alma's living link to her beloved sister. William and David had made it clear to Alanson after Sina's funeral that his infant son was one responsibility he wouldn't be allowed to shirk.

Fortunately, in his motherless child Alanson seemed at last to have found something he placed above his own selfish desires. Alanson and Roswell had been living with Sarah and David, but for how much longer was a question. Alanson had recently begun courting a young woman from nearby Wallingford, Lydia Bartholomew.

After much prayer and soul-searching, Alma had succeeded in forgiving Alanson in her heart for his callous treatment of Sina during their marriage. But she hadn't yet been able to let go of her bitterness that Alanson had discovered his sense of duty too late to do her little sister any good.

Both sides of Middletown's main street were lined three deep with people who'd flocked in from the surrounding countryside to watch the procession celebrating the re-establishment of peace. It was the largest parade ever staged in Middletown. Space was made in the front row for the ten members of the Lyman family.

At the head of the procession was Captain John Pratt, a hefty, double-chinned veteran of the Revolution. Captain Pratt had squeezed into his old uniform to serve as marshal for this special day. On his breast was pinned the bald-eagle medal of the Society of the Cincinnati. Seeing the badge triggered in David memories of his brother Elihu, of his enormous pride in belonging to that military fraternity.

Behind Captain Pratt came eighteen youths, one for each state of the Union, walking two by two, sporting white scarves and carrying palm branches. They were followed by a band, military companies, local officials, and a contingent of Revolutionary War veterans, whose numbers were shrinking as death finally claimed men who had cheated it while serving in the ranks more than three decades earlier.

"There's Grampa Coe!" shouted little Phineas excitedly from his perch on William's shoulders. It was easy to spot Elisha Coe in the procession, for in his role as lieutenant colonel of the militia he was wearing a black beaver half-moon officer's hat, which added a good six inches to his height. It was decorated with a silk cockade and gold cord, topped by a jaunty black ostrich plume.

Elizabeth Coe was still too bereft to bring herself to attend the celebration. But Elisha had felt duty-bound to take part in this public commemoration of the end of the war that he had considered necessary and justified. Alma watched her father with pride and compassion as he marched by. Head held high, shoulders square, eyes focused straight ahead, he betrayed no sign of the attacks of black melancholy she knew he'd suffered in the wake of his triple tragedy.

The formal celebrations concluded with music and more cannon fire, after which the Lymans gratefully made their way to the warmth of the Washington Hotel. The Madeira drunk for each of the eighteen toasts thawed the frozen innards of men and women who'd endured several hours in the brutal cold.

The last toast was to "The Fair of the United States – While they joyfully entwine the Olive with the Laurel, their smiles will reward the brave." William interrupted his conversation with several men, including his father and father-in-law, to turn and hold up his glass in a gallant salute to Alma, who blushed with pleasure at the flattering gesture.

"What do you have to say now about those wrongheaded fools from across New England who attended that convention in December in Hartford?" Elisha Coe was demanding of Captain Pratt, when William turned back to the discussion. "Meeting in the State House in secret sessions to plot treason, even as a treaty of peace was being concluded!" Elisha sneered.

"Connecticut's representatives to the Hartford Convention were men of integrity – the chief justice of the state supreme court and the lieutenant governor among them," Captain Pratt countered, his face florid with indignation. "They sought assurances that the national government would defend New England against the enemy, that the voices of all the people are heard by the national government, not just those of our 'friends' from Virginia."

Before Elisha could launch a rebuttal, David Lyman cut in. "Stop it!" he commanded both men in a hard, low voice. "We're here to celebrate peace, not perpetuate the political war."

A Federalist himself, David shared Captain Pratt's opinions on the Hartford Convention's purpose. Federalist New Englanders had become increasingly disturbed by the power of a national government that for the past fourteen years had been led by a president who was a Democratic-Republican from Virginia. That federal government had refused to help pay the cost of Connecticut and Massachusetts militia defending their coasts against the British. Although the war had been an ongoing economic disaster for New England shipping, Congress had passed new legislation that crippled maritime trade even further.

The Convention had been called to seek resolutions to these and other complaints. It had recommended amendments to the United States Constitution to ease what many New Englanders considered the Southern states' stranglehold on the federal government. Elisha Coe's charge of treason was based on rumors that the delegates discussed secession of New England from the Union, or the region negotiating a separate peace with Great Britain.

When news of the peace treaty with Britain arrived barely a month after the Convention, Federalists were acutely embarrassed. The delegates looked like a bunch of hysterical old women. The Federalist Party's prestige had been seriously damaged, clearing, some feared, the path to power in Connecticut for Democratic-Republicans like Elisha Coe – or his apostate friend Joshua Stow.

David had had a reason besides political harmony for intervening in the squabble between Elisha Coe and Captain Pratt. Elisha wasn't typically one to gloat. David suspected his uncharacteristic goading of Captain Pratt sprang from inner pain, from the need for a personal victory, however small, to help offset his many losses.

"We need to concern ourselves with what peace will bring," David pointed out, guiding the discussion into calmer waters. "With the war's end, trade with foreign countries will resume. We must work to retain our countrymen's attachment to the products of industries established here during the past half dozen years. If they go right back to buying imported goods, our nation once again will be dependent on foreign powers – and our fledgling domestic manufactories will be gravely damaged."

After a long, tense moment Captain Pratt made the smallest nod that could pass for polite, and withdrew from the group. A look of frustration, irritation – and, David thought, a bit of embarrassment – appeared on Elisha's face as he watched Captain Pratt's retreating back.

"Is your work in Vermont finished, William?" asked Alma's brother Asher, as eager as David to avoid dissension. Both Asher and Elisha were pleased when William nodded in the affirmative, for they knew how difficult William's long absences were for Alma.

"David's estate is finally settled, and Andrew will be moving to Vermont to handle our father's interests there. I'll at last be able to focus on my own affairs," William said with obvious satisfaction.

David was looking forward to having William in Middlefield permanently. William would help David take advantage of opportunities that would arise for the wool business, assist him with running the farm, and provide informed advice on how to manage his lands in Vermont and New York.

Andrew Lyman, now twenty-one, had displayed enough initiative and responsibility for David to entrust him with his Vermont investments. Thankfully, the youth's once frail constitution had toughened as he'd grown. David and Sarah's youngest son, Elihu, who would turn eighteen in but a few days, would learn by working with his father and William.

That the years ahead were fraught with uncertainty, David understood all too well. Still, he mused, he'd known nothing but uncertainty since his youth. He'd learned not to let the future's unpredictability paralyze him, but instead to keep a sharp eye out for the opportunities created by change, and to take advantage of them.

Chapter Sixty-Eight

February, 1815
Middlefield

For Sarah, these hours had long ago become her favorite part of the day – or, more correctly, the night. Early in her marriage she'd learned that if a wife and mother wanted time to herself – to write, to read, or simply to think – it would have to be late at night, after everyone else was in bed. So long as anyone, even David, remained up, Sarah couldn't concentrate fully on any mental task, for part of her brain was always attuned to others, anticipating an interruption at any moment to respond to a request, a demand, a need.

So once the entire household had retired, she typically settled down for several hours of enjoyable solitude. With her dulled hearing, Sarah wasn't distracted by the crackling of a small blaze in the parlor fireplace, the chiming of the tall clock, the scurrying and scratching of mice in the walls, or, on this blustery February night, the rattling of window sashes assaulted by howling gusts of wind.

Sarah found a special contentment in the thought of her husband, all their children still at home – Andrew, Sally, Urania, Elihu, Alanson – and their grandson Roswell, tucked safely into their beds for another night. She'd spent this evening, the last but one in February, at David's desk, writing to Polly and Esther and David, Jr.'s, widow, Sophia, in Vermont. She described the victory celebration five days ago, updated them on the health of everyone back home in Connecticut, provided details of the advances made by little Phineas, Adeline, Lizzy, and Roswell, and filled them in on other news.

Sarah wrote letters until after the tall clock chimed midnight. Now she moved from David's desk to the rocking chair they'd bought last year. Warm and cozy in a nightgown made of wool from David's Merino sheep, of which he now had more than four hundred, Sarah was reading the Bible she'd owned since before her marriage.

The tall clock had just chimed one when Sarah felt eyes on her. She looked up to see Sally on the stairs, clutching the banister, her face a study in unhappiness. Sally padded in bare feet down the remaining few steps, then across the expensive carpet that was David's most recent addition to the parlor furnishings. She pulled over the chair from her father's desk and sat down in front of her mother. Sarah planted her feet on the floor to stop the rocking chair.

"Mama, you must convince Papa to let me marry Abner," Sally pleaded. "With the war over, Abner's father will start making serious plans to leave Connecticut and go to New York. He wants Abner to go with him – and Abner is willing. If I don't marry Abner before he leaves, I'll lose him forever!" she finished on a note of panic.

Sarah closed her Bible and let out a troubled sigh. Sally and David had quarreled several times about her wish to wed Abner Miller. Sarah so far had deferred to David's authority. But Sally was right; time had run out, and Sarah would have to take a stand.

"Your father wants only what is best for you, Sally," Sarah began. "He knows Abner intends to leave Connecticut, and he fears for your welfare, with your weak eyes, on some raw frontier."

"Does he think life as a spinster in Connecticut would be a better fate?" Sally cried. "Living on sufferance in one of my brothers' homes, little better than a servant!" She shivered with revulsion.

Sally went on in a trembling voice, "I can't hold a candle to a shining beauty like Urania." She shook her head firmly to forestall Sarah's instinctive protest to hearing a beloved child speak with such brutal candor about the way God had made her.

"There's no denying the truth," Sally went on doggedly. "I'm as ungainly as an ox, my hair is like dry straw, and often I can't see any better than a bat caught in sunlight. And I'll be soon be twenty-seven! Not the most desirable matrimonial prize," she said harshly.

"There are so few available men in Connecticut, and so many girls far prettier and wittier than me looking for husbands. I've known since I was old enough to think about such things that my chances of finding a husband were slim, even with the marriage portion everyone knows Papa will provide." Sarah's eyes filled with tears at her daughter's unflinching, yet accurate, assessment.

"But then, somehow, Abner came to care for me – to want to make me his wife!" Sally exclaimed, as if that were no less a miracle than Moses' parting of the Red Sea. "This will likely be my only chance to have a husband and family. Papa must let us marry!" Sally sank down on her knees and reached out to take Sarah's hands between hers in a desperate appeal for help.

Sarah studied the hands that had seized hers. They were square, with stubby fingers and rough nails – not attractive in any way. But they were strong, skilled, caring hands that could make a happy home and deserved a chance to do so – with the right man.

"I believe Abner cares for you," Sarah began, choosing her words carefully as she stroked her thumbs over Sally's hands with soothing affection. "He's been patient with your father's opposition to your marriage, has remained constant to you when many another young man might have given up and looked elsewhere for a wife."

Sarah raised her head and looked straight into Sally's gray eyes. "But what of you? Do you truly care for Abner? Or is your terror of spinsterhood so great you'll snatch at any offer of marriage?"

Sally sat bolt upright, taken aback by her mother's candid question. "Of course I love Abner!" she insisted indignantly after a moment's hesitation that she realized undercut her sincerity.

"At first I cared for Abner because he was the only man interested in courting me," Sally admitted reluctantly. "I wasn't sure if I could be happy with him, for he's unlike Papa. Abner lacks Papa's confidence, his ability to take charge of a situation." Sarah kept a straight face even as she smiled inwardly at the memory of the David Lyman she'd met on that September day nearly forty years ago, so very different from the man his admiring daughter knew.

"But I've come to appreciate the qualities Abner does possess: protectiveness, loyalty, affection – sweetness." Sally blushed as she spoke this last characteristic, not one of the standard features sought in a man. "But I knew I truly loved him when he marched off with the militia after the British bombarded Stonington. I felt my own life would end if he didn't return safely."

"That's good to hear," Sarah said, more than a little relieved. "I've kept my peace until now, for the war made any plans to remove to the west impractical. But I will talk to your father. I'll tell him I believe a marriage between you and Abner would be a good thing – although it will take you farther from home than any of your brothers and sisters." Sarah's voice cracked, and she stroked the cheek of this most vulnerable of her children.

"Thank you, Mama," Sally said with a tremulous smile. She stood up, then leaned over to kiss Sarah on the forehead before tripping silently up the staircase, leaving her mother to ponder the implications of her promise.

Sally's marriage and removal from Connecticut would further rend the already shredded fabric of the Lyman family. Phineas and David, Jr., were dead. Polly, Esther, and Andrew were all lost to Vermont. Alanson's future was uncertain.

True, William would never leave Middlefield. Sarah and David intended to do everything they could to see that Elihu would have the resources to establish himself in Middlefield.

Urania would be Sarah's last chance to have a daughter marry and settle close by. There was more than a little truth in the old rhyme, "A son is a son 'til he takes a wife, but a daughter's a daughter for all of her life."

At twenty-three Urania was a delicate, elegant blonde with her share of suitors, none serious as yet. Sarah clung to the hope that Urania would choose a husband from among the young men who would make their home in Middlefield or a neighboring community, usually because they were first-born sons who had received the lion's share of their father's land.

Sarah mulled over the situation until the fire had died down to glowing embers. She picked up the candle to light her way up the stairs. The wind had grown fiercer in the past three hours, promising a bitter cold day to come. If March came in like a lion, it would go out like a lamb, according to the old saying. Sarah hoped it would prove true, as she thought longingly of the soft warmth of spring.

Sarah opened the door to their chamber carefully, so as not to awaken David. She set the candlestick atop the chest, then smothered the flame with the cup of the long-handled brass candle-snuffer. A thread of smoke rose from the wick.

Sarah pushed aside the blue-checked window curtains to look out at the moonlight shining on pristine snow. Then she parted the heavy drapes hanging from rods connecting the top posts of their bedstead that kept in the heat during long, cold winter nights like this one. Perhaps, she thought as she fluffed up her feather pillow, she would broach the subject of Abner and Sally marrying with David in the morning, while they were still abed. It would be cruel to keep Sally in suspense any longer than necessary.

Sarah slid under the linen sheet and the heavy quilt. Bedtime was one of the rare occasions when she was thankful for her diminished hearing, since it kept her from being disturbed by the soft snoring David had developed with age.

Sarah rolled over to snuggle up against David's warm backside – only to recoil the moment she made contact. After an endless moment she reached out to touch his arm, his cheek. It was pitch-dark inside the closed bed curtains, but Sarah had no need of sight to verify what her fingers told her: David was stone cold, dead, taken by the Lord in his sleep.

Sarah squeezed her eyes shut and huddled herself up tightly under the covers, as far as possible from the empty shell from which the soul of her beloved husband had flown. She was too shocked for tears.

As the terrible truth slowly penetrated the wall of denial her mind had instinctively thrown up, Sarah began to pray silently for David. She asked the Lord to forgive David's sins and to reward his stout faith and many virtues, to grant him entry to Heaven, where he would once again see the loved ones, too many to count, who'd proceeded him to the realm beyond the grave.

And then Sarah begged the Lord to take her, too, this very minute, to reunite her on the other side of the veil with the man whose love and goodness had brought her so much joy.

Chapter Sixty-Nine

March, 1815
Middlefield

"Are . . . are you sure?" Sarah stammered. She stared at her son, seated at his father's prized desk and bookcase.

"I am, Mama," William replied reluctantly.

The Lord hadn't seen fit to take Sarah to Him as she'd prayed after discovering her dear David dead in their bed on that night a month ago. It was God's will that she, not yet even sixty, endure the sorrow of life without her husband – now deepened by William's revelation.

"I suspected it from the start, but didn't want to say anything until I went over Papa's records," William went on, watching his mother's reaction carefully. "There's no mistake. Papa's estate is insolvent."

Sarah shifted her gaze out the window at a March afternoon that mirrored the bleakness of her mood. Naked tree branches reached up toward a low cloud cover so smooth and solid it seemed the color of the sky had changed from blue to whitish-gray. A damp chill penetrated her black mourning garments to the very marrow of her bones.

Sarah had no doubt William's grim assessment was correct. David had never involved her in his business dealings, and like most wives she'd been content with that arrangement. But William had been helping his father manage his many and varied business activities for several years. He was familiar enough with David's financial affairs to determine in short order the state of his father's accounts at the time of his death.

Sarah continued to stare out at the drab countryside. At last William said, with gentle reassurance, "You needn't worry about being taken care of, Mama. You'll receive your widow's thirds–." William stopped in mid-sentence, as Sarah shook her head slowly from side to side. Had the grim term "widow" upset her? he wondered anxiously.

Sarah turned back to face her son. The gentle warmth of her gray eyes had dulled to the drabness of weathered stone.

"I don't have any concerns about my well-being, William," she said. "I require very little, and I know you and your brothers and sisters will see all my needs are met. What distresses me is regret for your father."

"Regret, Mama? For what?" William asked.

"Your father's family was well-off when he was a boy," Sarah said. "But then your Grandfather Lyman was sick for many years with consumption. His medical treatment was very expensive. He couldn't work, and most of the children were still too young to help. Your father, just seventeen, was the oldest son. Your Grandfather Lyman died deeply in debt, his estate insolvent."

William remained silent. He'd known vaguely that his Granny Fowler, his father, and his aunts and uncles had some lean times after the death of the Lyman grandfather he'd never known. But he'd had no idea their situation had been so desperate.

"Most of the family's movables were sold at public auction to settle the estate," Sarah went on, then found it necessary to pause. Even now, the memory of David's anguish when he told her of that terrible day caused her heart to constrict with sympathy. She continued with difficulty. "The humiliation of that auction, and the fear and embarrassment of being near destitute after his father's death, made your father vow to himself to do whatever was necessary to make sure his own wife and children wouldn't suffer a similar fate. His family's security was the legacy that mattered most to him."

Troubled by his mother's disclosure, William tried to imagine his father as a frightened, embarrassed, overwhelmed teenager. But it was impossible. He'd never known David as anything but strong and confident. Yet his mother's revelation did help explain David's compulsive, relentless pursuit of prosperity – and public respect.

"What you tell me makes me thank God that your father died in his sleep, without any warning," Sarah continued after a moment. "He died not knowing he failed to keep his vow."

"Papa didn't fail!" William protested. He leaned forward to take his mother's hands in his, lowered his head so he could look up into her eyes.

"He just . . . ran out of time," William went on. "He knew we would take care of you no matter what. He'd already provided for Polly and Esther and David and Alanson. True, he was nearing seventy, but he was never sick. I think he believed God would bless with him with as long a life as Granny Fowler, would allow him time to complete the plans that would let him provide for the rest of us." His blue eyes pleaded with her to believe his words.

Sarah knew William was speaking honestly. When David had written his will four years earlier, he'd assured Sarah there would be ample resources left after his estate was settled to fill the bequests to her, his children, and even his grandchildren. But since then David apparently had taken financial risks he calculated would allow him to provide even more substantial bequests, while choosing to ignore, whether out of hubris, ambition, or misguided faith, the inescapable reality that his life could end at a moment's notice, before his investments came to fruition.

Sarah studied her tall, handsome son with exasperated affection. William certainly knew the details of whatever David had done to create this crisis. But loyalty to the father he loved wouldn't allow William to fault David for the misjudgment that left him with the daunting responsibility of salvaging what he could from David's tangled, far-flung business ventures.

Sarah slipped her hand from William's, and stroked his cheek tenderly. "One thing I know for sure," she said with a trembling smile, as a single tear slipped down her cheek. "With you, your father most certainly succeeded."

Chapter Seventy

June, 1816
Middletown

"I knew a great many people would turn out today – but I never imagined this!" William exclaimed. Alma and his brother Elihu nodded in agreement. Men, women, and children were arriving to jam themselves around the courthouse in Middletown. They reminded William of the teeming shad that had just finished their annual spring migration up the Connecticut River.

"There must be ten thousand people here!" said Elihu. Now nineteen, he was a wiry bachelor, a head shorter than William, with black hair, and hazel eyes. He was deceptively strong, a diligent worker with an instinct for the land, and an amiable personality. William had been able to devote himself largely to the task of settling their father's estate, which required extensive traveling, because Elihu was tending the crops and livestock back in Middlefield.

Elihu had welcomed the chance to prove his competence. Sarah had doted on him, the youngest of her ten children. Entering his teens, Elihu had begun to chafe at being tied so tightly to his mother's apron strings, but was too respectful to rebel openly.

Elihu's liberation had come six months earlier, when William moved his family into the homestead. Sarah now had three grandchildren under her roof upon which to lavish affection and attention. His mother was slowly clawing her way out of the mental abyss into which she'd been cast by David's passing – and by the death soon after of her daughter Esther, thirty-one, in childbirth.

Elihu's eagerness to involve himself in the farm's operation pleased William for another reason. Since the start of the year, their sister Sally had married Abner Miller, their brother Andrew had wed Ann Hall of Wallingford, and Alanson had taken Lydia Bartholomew as his wife. All three sets of newlyweds were in various stages of planning their removal from Connecticut. Andrew and Ann were destined for Vermont, while the other four intended to strike out for the region around Whitestown, New York, where David Lyman had invested in land. Alanson would take his son Roswell with him.

The couples' departure would leave just three of David and Sarah Lyman's ten children in Middlefield: William, Elihu, and Urania. And now it appeared they might lose Urania to the west.

At an Election Day ball in Hartford the previous month, Urania, now twenty-four, had met David Buttolph of Norwich, New York. Buttolph was a graduate of Williams College with a well-established law practice in his new hometown in western New York.

Buttolph was entranced by the blonde, petite Urania. David Lyman had once told William that she reminded him of Sarah's little sister Hannah when he met her at the Comstock house in 1776.

Urania in turn had found Buttolph very appealing. Although at thirty-six he was half again as old as Urania, the age difference worked to his advantage. He was more mature and sophisticated than any of the men of Urania's own age who came courting. And he was a bachelor, having been too occupied with his studies and legal work to find a wife. This, too, was in his favor; any woman he wed wouldn't have to contend with the memory of a deceased first wife.

Urania and Buttolph had managed to meet several times before he had to return to New York, and they'd agreed to write to each other. William had tried to convince a distressed Sarah that it was premature to fret that this sudden flurry of socializing and corresponding would lead to marriage and Urania's removal to New York. In that William wasn't successful, for who knew better than Sarah that from a few days spent together and an exchange of letters could grow a love for which a woman would leave family and scenes of her youth for a new, distant home among strangers?

His siblings' exodus from Connecticut distressed William, too. He now better understood why his father had taken such extreme measures to keep Alanson from emigrating. But while William was eager for Elihu, who at thirteen years his junior was more like a son than a brother, to settle in Middlefield, he was determined not to take any action toward that end that wasn't in Elihu's best interest.

Scanning the throng assembled at the courthouse, William suspected Elihu's estimate of numbers might be conservative. The crowd was at least twice as large as the one that had celebrated the end of the war with Great Britain last year.

A murmur started at the crowd's edge, then rippled across it, from person to person: "He's coming!" From their vantage point on the courthouse steps, William, Elihu, and Alma saw a middle-aged man, wearing a white gown and cap, flanked by two militiamen, ascend the steps to a platform constructed for the occasion.

The man's demeanor was composed, his expression almost cheerful. Immediately behind came the Reverend David Dudley Field of the neighboring town of Haddam.

Mr. Field paused for a long moment, both to allow the crowd to quiet down and for dramatic effect. Then he intoned a passage from the Old Testament: "'Ye shall take no satisfaction for the life of a murderer, which is guilty of death; but he shall surely be put to death – for blood it defileth the land; and the land cannot be cleansed of the blood that is shed therein, but by the blood of him that shed it.'" The minister paused to let the Lord's harsh command sink in, then proceeded to preach the last sermon that the man in white, Peter Lung, would ever hear.

"'Take heed to yourselves lest at any time your hearts be overcharged with surfeiting and drunkenness, and cares of this life,'" Mr. Field continued. These words from the New Testament would serve as the theme for his sermon to those assembled to witness the hanging of Peter Lung for the murder of his wife – a killing Lung couldn't recall having committed, so drunk had he been at the time.

Peter Lung had spent an unsettled youth in Middlefield. He and his wife, Mary, had moved into the city of Middletown, where their family grew to include nine children.

The violent quarrels that erupted between Mary and Peter Lung when both were drunk became a staple of local gossip. Then came four days in the summer of 1815, during which Mary and Peter, both intoxicated, had carried on a vicious, jealous, foul-mouthed argument, during which Lung shoved and kicked his wife.

Then one morning Peter Lung awoke to find his wife dead. He claimed to have no memory of hurting her in any way that would have been fatal. Nor did he recall suspicious actions family members and acquaintances testified he'd done the night before his wife's death. He'd been convicted of murder, and sentenced to hang.

Executions were held in public both as a demonstration of justice fulfilled and a grim warning of the punishment awaiting anyone who committed so heinous a crime. People flocked to them to witness the majesty of the law being enforced – and for the excitement a hanging provided in an otherwise humdrum existence.

For weeks people had been eagerly anticipating this hanging, the first ever in Middletown. Spectators had begun arriving before dawn from throughout Middletown and surrounding towns. They jockeyed for the best vantage points from which to watch the event, chatting as animatedly as if awaiting the start of a performance by a slack-wire walker or some other itinerant entertainer.

Many people had brought young children, William saw. Death was common enough that seeing a corpse was unlikely to frighten most youngsters. Many parents reasoned that a child old enough to understand what was happening could benefit from the words of the minister and the condemned man, and from the hanging itself.

William and Alma had firmly denied little Phineas's pleas to accompany them to what the boy was sure would be the most thrilling event ever to occur in Middletown. They'd left the disappointed eight-year-old and his sisters with their Grandmother Lyman, who had no interest in witnessing the tragic end of a man she'd known as a sad youth with little stability to his life.

But most of Middlefield was here today for the same reasons as the other spectators. William, however, had a secret purpose for coming, one he hadn't shared even with Alma.

The sixteen months since his father's death had been full of struggle and aggravation for William, with no end in sight. He'd been away from home more often than not on long, tedious trips to Vermont and New York, hundreds of miles from Middlefield.

William had worked almost nonstop to sort out his father's complicated estate, trying to verify and settle claims against it while still holding on to something for the heirs. His charge had been rendered even more difficult by an economic depression that hit New England following the end of the war with Great Britain. The value of land and other property, including sheep, had plummeted.

Many a night this past year William had found himself alone in a crude, isolated inn, desperately missing Alma and the children, bedeviled by doubts that he could ever straighten out the tangled mess of his father's possessions and debts. He feared he'd prove unequal to the responsibility of seeing his father's life-work result in a tangible legacy for those he loved. And he harbored a guilty resentment toward David for dying and leaving him with this duty that he worried was slowly but surely crushing him.

On nights when the combination of weariness, worry, shame, and loneliness threatened to overwhelm him, William had indulged himself with an extra mug or glass – or two, or more – of cider, brandy, beer, wine, rum, whiskey, or whatever the innkeeper had on hand. He'd thought nothing of it, for spirits were as basic as bread to every person's diet, and known for their restorative powers. He'd seen in Alanson the shameful result of trying to drown problems in alcohol, but he knew himself to be a stronger man than his brother.

Then had come the nights when, for whatever reason, spirits weren't available to William in the quantity he desired, or sometimes not at all. And he'd found that no matter what he tried – reading, writing, sleeping, praying – his thoughts returned, like a stubbornly rebellious child, to what had become a craving for spirits.

More alarming still had been the rare cherished days at home in Middlefield, when he had determined to drink no more than had formerly been his practice, only to find himself yearning for more spirits. The longing never completely left him, even – to his intense shame – during his most intimate moments with Alma.

William had asked God's help conquering this lust – there was no other word for it. At times he felt the Lord's strength in him, enabling him to refuse a glass of wine or a mug of rum, to focus on something other than the desire for alcohol. But there'd been other occasions, imbued with sheer terror, when even God's help hadn't been enough for William to resist the temptation of spirits.

This weakness had driven William to make certain he arrived back home yesterday from his latest trip to Vermont, even though that meant he'd reached Middlefield long after dark. He was determined to be in Middletown on this day, in the desperate hope that witnessing the terrible end to which spirits could bring a man would give him the strength to break their stranglehold on him.

"Did you know old Mrs. Lung died last week, right after you left for Vermont?" Elihu whispered to William.

"No," said William, startled, looking down at his brother.

"They say grief over her son's crime sent her to her grave," Elihu said. The minister resumed speaking, saving William from having to comment on this appalling news. His mind reeled in horror at the thought of being the instrument of death not just for a wife he had vowed to cherish but for the woman who had given him life itself.

"None become suddenly confirmed drunkards," Mr. Field was declaring. "Intoxicating liquors are taken first in small quantities, in conformity with existing customs or at the solicitation of supposed friends, under notions that they contribute to health and usefulness. As a desire rises for them, they're used more freely, till at last an appetite is created which never saith enough. The only remedy against this evil is to avoid all approximations to this vice."

Throughout the crowd people shifted uneasily. It seemed Mr. Field's words were striking home in more hearts than William's.

"Believe not the unsupported doctrine that men cannot labor and perform the duties of life without ardent spirits," Mr. Field called out. "Strict temperance will render you fairer and fitter for every service than those who partake even of royal banquets, purer than snow, more ruddy in body than rubies."

Mr. Field then stepped back so the wretched Peter Lung could speak his last words to those gathered to see him sent into eternity.

"I was a man of violent passions," Lung said, in a weak but steady voice. "When misfortunes came upon me, I got into the habit of making too free a use of ardent spirits." A shiver of fear ran through William, for Lung could easily be describing him.

"I have two things to console me as I prepare to present myself for judgement," Lung continued. "My faith, come to me recently, in the pardoning mercy of my Redeemer, and hope that my example might deter you here today from following the path of drunkenness."

William's eyes blurred with tears – of compassion for a wretched sinner and of terror for his own imperiled soul. He swallowed a lump of fear and forced himself to take deep, regular breaths, desperate not to reveal how profoundly the scene was affecting him.

The sheriff moved forward. He tied Lung's hands behind his back, then rolled the brim of the cap down over the murderer's face. The sheriff slipped the thick noose dangling from the gallows over Lung's head and tightened it around his neck. The silent crowd seemed to be holding its breath as the sheriff stepped back. The platform fell from beneath Lung's feet. William heard the sickening snap of Lung's neck, followed by a low gasp from the crowd.

The body swayed back and forth briefly, then hung motionless in the sunshine. The throng began to talk in excited voices.

There but for the grace of God go I, William told himself with brutal honesty. He studied the scene, burning it into his memory. To his own dying day William intended to harbor the memory of the corpse of Peter Lung, condemned for the murder of his own wife, dangling from a rope before a horde of gawking townspeople. It would be his talisman against the ardent spirits that, with their power to poison him body and soul, were truly the Devil's spittle.

Chapter Seventy-One

May, 1818
Middlefield

The tattoo of a drum split the soft May air, drawing everyone's attention to a lanky man in front of the Lyman house. William pulled the watch from his vest pocket to check it; one o'clock, right on time.

"By order of the honorable Court of Probate for the district of Middletown," the man cried, "I will now commence the public vendue of so much of the real and personal estate of Colonel David Lyman, late of Middletown deceased, as will raise the sum of five thousand, one hundred dollars, and ninety-nine cents."

The Lyman house front yard was alternately in sunshine and shadow as large puffy clouds dappling the afternoon sky floated past the sun. The crowd, which William guessed exceeded two hundred, congregated eagerly around the auctioneer. Many were strangers to William, drawn by the auction notices he had published in the *Middlesex Gazette*, as required by law.

William had already sold nearly half of his father's Connecticut acres, as well as all the Merino sheep. But prices for both had declined so drastically that he'd been able to realize only about half the value at which they'd originally been appraised. It wasn't nearly enough to pay his father's debts. To satisfy as many outstanding claims against the estate as possible, William had resorted to auctioning off the assets – including the house and homelot.

A few of those present had come out of curiosity, eager to get a close look at some of the elegant possessions of the man who had once been the wealthiest in Middlefield. But William hoped most had come to buy. He would find out soon enough.

Several people who knew William glanced surreptitiously at him, no doubt feeling pity, or embarrassment, for a man reduced to selling off his family's home and many of its fine furnishings. But William didn't care what others thought. He was at peace with himself over what he was doing this day. In his heart he knew he'd done his best to fulfill a challenge that had nearly destroyed him.

William had achieved this state of acceptance with his mother's support. He'd always assumed Sarah drew her strength from David, and feared his death would leave her a broken reed – as indeed it seemed to for a time. But Sarah had slowly rallied from her despondency to help her family move beyond their devastating loss. In particular she did all she could to make sure William wasn't scarred by the great burden that had descended upon him – the way his father had been by a similar, if far more desperate, situation.

William didn't know if his mother had perceived his struggle with alcohol. If she had, she'd never said anything. But she had gently counseled her son against reproaching himself for not accomplishing the impossible in settling his father's estate. She lovingly told him when she detected indications that the difficulties, disappointments, and outright dishonesty he encountered in his dealings seemed to be turning him cynical and callous. Most important, she had never let him despair, reminding him they were all in the hands of a loving and all-wise God whose will must be accepted, even if His purposes were not always clear to His servants.

Thus William was reconciled to this auction. But he wouldn't relax until the first items to come on the block – the house and homelot – were disposed of.

Sarah's dower rights in the property, confirmed earlier in the month, entitled her to fifty acres that included the homelot, the south half of the house, a barn, half of the woodhouse, and use of the well. Whoever purchased the property this day would have to allow Sarah to occupy the south half of the house and enjoy use of the fifty acres for the rest of her life, an arrangement that considerably reduced its appeal for most bidders.

The auctioneer opened bidding at $4,500, roughly the combined total of the values most recently assigned to Sarah's dower and the north half of the house. It was less than two-thirds of what the property had been appraised for four months after David's death.

William jammed his hands deep into the pockets of his fawn-colored cotton trousers. They'd belonged to David, which meant they'd needed much altering by Alma to fit William's taller frame.

After a prolonged silence a man toward the front of the crowd called out, "One thousand dollars!" A red flush raced up William's neck to stain his cheeks. Not only was it an insultingly paltry opening bid, but he recognized the voice as belonging to Joshua Stow. As sure as the sun would set that day, William knew he would never allow Stow to own the house his father had built. Now he was truly glad he'd persuaded Sarah not to attend the auction, but to go with Alma and the children to Alma's parents' house.

"One thousand dollars from Joshua Stow," the auctioneer repeated in a stricken voice, then quickly sought to coax a higher bid from the crowd. "Do I hear fifteen hundred?"

"Fifteen hundred dollars," Elisha Coe said in a loud, firm voice.

"Fifteen hundred and fifty," called out John Birdsey. The young man had recently come into possession of the land immediately south of the Lyman house, with the final settlement, after more than fifteen years of bickering, of his namesake grandfather's estate.

Joshua Stow wasn't heard from again. Under other circumstances William suspected Stow might have kept bidding for the perverse pleasure of upsetting William. But he'd apparently chosen not to antagonize his friend Elisha Coe by running up the price of the property.

John Birdsey continued his bidding duel with Elisha Coe. The men increased the price at $50 increments, until it stood at an offer of $ 1,950 from Birdsey.

"Two thousand dollars!" Elisha Coe called out in a voice ringing with the finality of a gate clanging shut. William nervously pulled his hands from his pockets and crossed his arms over his chest while the auctioneer sought doggedly to cajole a higher bid. But neither John Birdsey nor anyone else had missed the message in Colonel Coe's tone: he would brook no further interference with his intention to acquire this property. Continuing to bid against the wealthiest resident of Middlefield who, all knew, had a personal interest in the property, was sure to earn the influential man's enmity.

"Sold to Colonel Elisha Coe, Esquire, for two thousand dollars!" the auctioneer declared at last, banging his gavel on a barrel head. Elisha Coe turned to catch his son-in-law's eye, and the two exchanged a slight, conspiratorial nod.

"If anyone else but Colonel Coe bought the house and homelot for that price, it would be outright stealing," observed Elihu, who'd been standing silently by William's side since the bidding started.

There was no anger in the younger man's voice, for he knew about the agreement between Elisha Coe and William.

Elisha had purchased the house and homelot with the understanding that William would buy them back for the same price when he was able to. In the meantime William, Alma, their children, Elihu, and Sarah as specified by her widow's rights, could continue living in the house and improving the land.

William shrugged. "What matters is we can stay in our home – Mama in particular. She's got little enough left since Papa's death, especially with Urania gone to New York as the new Mrs. Buttolph."

William turned back to watch the auctioneer. "I should probably count myself lucky we got what we did," he observed philosophically. "The summer before last scared people like never before. It was bad enough here in Connecticut, with frost in every month during the summer, stunting or killing the Indian corn, leaving barely enough seed to sow a decent crop the next spring. But in Vermont the summer was even colder. I saw cattle dying for lack of fodder there, people near perishing from starvation–." He broke off, still haunted by the memory of desperate hunger and privation of the kind he'd never imagined could afflict America, a land of limitless bounty.

"People are calling 1816 'the year without a summer,'" said Elihu uneasily. "They think New England is becoming a frigid zone."

"That unnatural weather was the last straw for many folks already itching to leave New England for other reasons," William said, shaking his head regretfully. "I've heard of people packing up and heading west with no particular destination in mind, so long as it's out of New England, as if the entire region were cursed."

William put the bleak memories out of his mind, and turned his thoughts to the future. In proposing the arrangement concerning the homestead, Elisha Coe had been characteristically both practical and compassionate. It meant his daughter and grandchildren wouldn't be evicted from their home – a development that would have pained Coe personally and embarrassed him publicly. It rescued Sarah Lyman from the awkwardness of sharing the house of which she had been mistress for more than thirty years with strangers or acquaintances who might prove less than congenial.

William was genuinely grateful to Elisha Coe for his help. But no man could rest easy being beholden to his father-in-law for the roof over his family's head – especially William, about to turn thirty-five, married for more than a decade, father of three. He intended to buy back the house and homelot at the earliest opportunity.

That the property had sold for far less than the appraised value was a mixed blessing. While it meant the opportunity to regain title would come sooner than William had expected, it also meant more of the other property would have to be sold to satisfy David's debts.

William watched impassively as the auctioneer moved on to selling personal possessions his parents had accumulated during nearly forty years of marriage. William was interested in the price each bought. But he felt no sense of loss when the two chaises were sold to strangers. He harbored no resentment toward John Birdsey for purchasing the painted carpet and looking-glass to help furnish the eight-room house he and his young wife, Esther, had built several hundred feet south of the Lyman home.

Sarah was entitled to items of personal property as part of her widow's dower. Included in her share were the few objects that held any meaning for William: the cherry desk and bookcase at which he remembered his father working each day, as now he himself did, and the half dozen or so books on religion and history that comprised David's small library. These William would have use of during Sarah's lifetime, and they would pass to him upon her death. Sarah had designated other possessions as heirlooms for William's brothers and sisters: David's pistols for Alanson, his musket for Andrew, his tall clock for Elihu, the best feather bed for Sally, the best quilt for Polly, silver teaspoons for Urania.

"Have you ever thought of putting Connecticut behind you, starting over someplace new?" Elihu asked out of the blue.

"No!" William exclaimed, staring at Elihu as if he'd asked if William had considered moving to the moon. "Alma and I – are rooted here," he said haltingly, trying to articulate his life-long feeling of being as much a part of this particular patch of God's earth as the streams that meandered through it or the soil he tilled. "Besides," he went on, a touch cynically, "I've been to the 'promised lands' to which so many are flocking. I didn't find them an improvement on what we have here."

William heaved a sigh of resignation before continuing. "Even this auction won't settle Papa's estate. I need to make several more trips to Vermont, and another to New York. But I hope to have everything squared away in a year or two. Then I'll gladly stay settled in Middlefield. I want to get to know my children as well as you do," he said with self-recrimination, for Elihu had often filled in as a combination father/big brother during William's absences.

"Maybe I can give them another brother or sister before Alma's time is past," William went on. "I haven't slept enough nights in my own bed these six years to get my wife with child even once." He recalled with bitter irony how he and Alma had once worried over how they would limit the size of their family.

William was suddenly embarrassed by this out-pouring of self-pity, even into the understanding ear of his brother. As his emotions simmered down, it occurred to him that his own reaction might have blinded him to another meaning behind Elihu's question.

"Are you thinking of emigrating?" William asked. The prospect of Elihu departing Middlefield, leaving William the last of David and Sarah's children in Connecticut, filled him with apprehension.

Before Elihu could answer, William rushed on, "Even after Papa's debts are paid, there should be sufficient land, oxen, cattle, and horses to provide a decent living for two families."

"Don't fret, Brother," Elihu said reassuringly, with a hint of amusement. "The frontier doesn't call me." He was touched by the profound relief that swept across William's face.

"Then you'll probably soon be looking for a wife," William said genially. Elihu opened his mouth to make a light-hearted reply, but William stunned him by asking, "Have you considered Alma's sisters?"

Elihu took several moments to recover from his shock, then delayed as long as politeness would allow before answering. He cleared his throat uncomfortably. "I think Colonel Coe will be looking for something finer than me in a husband for Delia and Lucia. Why else is he sending them to that fancy girls' school in Litchfield that Esther went to? He's probably hoping they'll marry students from the law school up there. I doubt he – or Delia or Lucia – would consider a simple farmer who owns next to nothing and isn't even yet a freeman to be a matrimonial prize."

William pursed his lips thoughtfully as he studied Elihu. What his brother said was likely true, for Alma's father was cut from the same ambitious cloth as David Lyman had been. He most likely had someone better educated, more refined, and richer than Elihu Lyman in mind for his two remaining unwed daughters.

But Elihu's self-effacing answer revealed nothing of his personal feelings about Alma's sisters – which William was reasonably confident he knew. Fine education and substantial marriage portions notwithstanding, Elisha Coe might not easily find husbands for Delia and Lucia.

Delia, nineteen, had a body that put William in mind of a lump of dough in need of considerable kneading. She was intelligent, kind, and usually thoughtful of others.

But Delia shared Alma's tendency toward melancholy, although in Delia's case it was deeper and lasted longer. Delia's melancholy alternated with periods of excessively high spirits, making her unpredictably and unsettlingly moody. The deaths of her siblings had left Delia inordinately attached to her parents. It would take an uncommonly patient, even-tempered – "long-suffering" came to William's mind – man to make a good marriage with Delia Coe.

Sixteen-year-old Lucia Coe had a high opinion of herself, which she expected men to reinforce with lavish compliments. She had a bright, but brittle personality that, when contrasted with Delia's frequent morbid spirits, seemed more appealing than it otherwise might have. And she possessed a juvenile yearning for a more exciting, sophisticated way of life than Middlefield could offer.

William agreed that neither Delia nor Lucia would make a good match for Elihu. But the deaths of two brothers and two sisters had clouded Alma's perceptions of them. At the same time she'd gotten to know Elihu Lyman better, and to appreciate the unassuming bachelor's true worth. It was but a short step in Alma's mind to the idea of a marriage between William's brother and one of her sisters.

At Alma's urging William had reluctantly agreed to broach the idea with Elihu. He was grateful his brother had disposed of the matter so tactfully. To report to Alma that Elihu felt unworthy of her sisters was one thing; to tell her he found them unattractive for whatever reason was quite another. "I understand," William said, then added, "But don't sell yourself short, Brother."

The bidding on a set of wine glasses was getting off to a lively start as two of David's old friends, Ichabod Miller and Deacon Prosper Augur, joined Elihu and William.

"The cider and beer you provided today are first-rate, William," said Miller, "but investing in some powerful West Indies rum for this crowd would have paid for itself." Miller, who William knew was near four score years old, spoke in a tone of friendly advice. "Folks are more likely to get caught up in the spirit of the bidding, drive prices higher when they've got a mug or two of rum in their bellies."

William shook his head in respectful, but firm, disagreement. "Fermented beverages like beer and cider are known to be wholesome, but there's much evidence that ardent spirits such as rum and whiskey are harmful and addictive. I can't in good conscience ply people with something I know to be bad for them just to pull in a few extra dollars."

"I've been hearing that claptrap for more than thirty years," the old man told William with condescending indulgence for his naïveté. "I know one thing for certain. There hasn't been a day since I was a boy that I didn't drink at least one mug of rum, usually more, and it's done me a world of good. I'll be eighty my next birthday," he concluded triumphantly, wagging a gnarled finger in William's face.

Elihu shifted uncomfortably at Miller's aggressive attitude. But William remained unperturbed. "My cousin Lyman Beecher has attracted much attention with his preaching from his Litchfield pulpit against intemperance."

"Not everyone has your iron stomach, Ichabod – or perhaps it's your head," jibed Deacon Augur, a short, round man in his early sixties. He went on seriously, "We've all seen enough men brought to ruin by ardent spirits to justify encouraging temperance. I think William should be commended for his decision not to offer rum or whiskey today. For many they are as poisonous as snake venom."

William shot the deacon a look of appreciation for his support. During his struggle to free himself from the stranglehold of liquor, William had come upon the pamphlet *An Inquiry into the Effects of Ardent Spirits Upon the Human Mind and Body*, first published in 1784 by Dr. Benjamin Rush, the most celebrated physician of his day and a signer of the Declaration of Independence. The eminent doctor had called for complete abstention from distilled beverages such as rum and whiskey, while promoting as healthful fermented beverages such as beer and hard cider.

William had followed Dr. Rush's recommendations. But he'd been dismayed to find that for him cider and beer were as addictive and debilitating as ardent spirits. With great effort he'd sworn those beverages off as well, and now drank only coffee or tea, or molasses or vinegar mixed with water. His cousin Beecher's pronouncements against intemperance had helped bolster William's resolve.

Having had his say on a subject, Ichabod Miller felt no need to repeat himself; if his listeners were foolish enough to ignore his sage advice, that was their loss. He went off on a different tangent.

"I remember when they auctioned off your grandfather's goods to settle his estate, long before the war," Miller said to William. He drew his wrinkled features together in an expression of sincere sympathy. "It was a dark day for the Lymans, but your grandmother and father didn't lose heart. They built the family's fortunes back up beyond anything your grandfather ever achieved. I have no doubt you'll do the same." He gave William a hearty clap on the arm.

"I'm honored by your confidence," William replied sincerely. He knew Miller meant to console and encourage him on what the elderly man considered a low point in William's life. "But I'm not the man my father was. I doubt I could accomplish all he did even if I were to pursue it with the same zeal – which I have no intention of doing."

Miller studied William with a blank expression, as if the younger man had spoken in a language Miller didn't know.

"Our Lord Jesus said, 'Lay up not for yourselves treasures upon earth, where moth and rust doth corrupt, and where thieves break through and steal; But lay up for yourselves treasures in heaven. For where your treasure is, there will be your heart also,'" William went on quietly. "I've spent too many years tending to my brother's and father's worldly possessions. Everything they owned taken together couldn't compensate me for that time I lost, and can never get back. Time I could have spent being a better husband and father, a better man and Christian."

Ichabod Miller's toothless jaw fell open in astonishment. He looked so much like a schoolboy struggling to work out in his head a difficult mathematical problem that William couldn't help but chuckle.

"I haven't lost my senses," William reassured him. "Just because I don't aspire to the riches and positions of power my father relished doesn't mean I intend to beggar my family. You don't see me giving away my father's property today, do you?"

Miller's expression changed to skepticism. William's words were heresy to all he'd held as gospel since boyhood – that a man should labor and save, plan and bargain shrewdly, spend frugally, to increase his estate, for prosperity on earth was one measure of the Lord's approval. He shook his head, wondering how William had come to be so misguided.

Miller clapped William again on the arm, this time as if in condolence, and turned to walk away. After a polite nod and smile to Elihu and William, Deacon Augur caught up with Miller, matching his pace to the old man's in case he became unsteady on his feet.

Augur was impressed by William's attitude, by how he hadn't let the past decade's trials embitter him or drive him to frenzied acquisitiveness. All William had endured seemed to have hammered his character into something Augur suspected was almost unbreakable.

Chapter Seventy-Two

October, 1818
Middletown

"Are you going to vote to gut the faith of our ancestors?" Prosper Augur demanded. They were the first words out of the old deacon's mouth after he fell in with William on the road to Middletown.

"The secrecy of the ballot box is guaranteed," William began. "Nonetheless, I will tell you that I intend to vote to approve the new state constitution."

Augur sucked in air sharply through his teeth, then expelled a blustery sigh of dismay. "Connecticut has governed itself well for more than one hundred and fifty years under the Royal Charter granted by King Charles. To replace it with a misguided constitution cobbled together at a convention is madness!"

"The Charter denied many good men the vote only because they didn't own a certain amount of property," William responded.

"The General Assembly eliminated the property requirement in May," Augur shot back, in a tone of disapproval. "Any man who pays taxes or serves in the militia can become a freeman. Last month, eighty-seven new freemen were accepted in Middletown, where before there had been perhaps just two hundred and fifty!" Augur's voice was dry with disgust. "How can men who own no property to speak of be trusted to cast their votes as conscientiously as we, who have so much at stake in our community?"

"They pay taxes," William said shortly. "If they're denied the vote, it's 'taxation without representation' – the same injustice that sparked the war for independence from Great Britain."

Prosper Augur shifted agitatedly in his saddle; he had no good rejoinder to William's comment. Instead, he raised the issue that disturbed him most of all.

"What of the greater evil at the heart of this new constitution?" the deacon demanded. "The end of Congregationalism as the established church of Connecticut. This connection with the government has existed since our very founding. Your own cousin Beecher up in Litchfield has preached strongly against this, calling its supporters 'drunkards' and 'adulterers.'"

Lyman Beecher had certainly been making a name for himself, William thought, with his sermons against intemperance, and now his opposition to the disestablishment of the Congregational church in Connecticut. Since Lyman had moved to Litchfield, William had seen him only when he visited Guilford to see Lot Benton. Uncle Lot had died four years ago, leaving Lyman Beecher with no reason to visit Guilford.

Lyman, so William had heard, had his hands more than full with his own family cares. His wife Roxana had died two years ago, barely forty years old, leaving him with nine children. Lyman had remarried, and his new wife had already presented him with a son.

Even with these heavy personal responsibilities, Lyman Beecher somehow managed to be a phenomenal whirlwind of energy and conviction, throwing himself passionately into vigorous campaigns against what he perceived as evil. While William had drawn strength from his cousin's advocacy of temperance, he disagreed with him on the proposed constitution. The predictions of the triumph of depravity if the constitution were approved reminded him of the ominous – and ultimately baseless – warnings made after Thomas Jefferson's election as president.

"Times have changed," William said. "Congregationalists no longer constitute the great majority of Connecticut's people. There are many Baptists and Episcopalians and Methodists who are faithful followers of Christ. It's reasonable for them to expect 'no preference shall be given by law to any Christian sect or mode of worship,' as the proposed constitution states."

"But what will become of the Congregational church when it no longer enjoys the state's special favor?" Augur demanded, with a tremor of genuine fear in his voice. Augur had been a key supporter of the revival of the Middlefield church. He was its first – and still only – deacon. Since the church still lacked a permanent pastor,

Augur sometimes presided over Sabbath services and conducted funerals.

William shook his head. "If Congregationalism can't survive without the crutch of many of the state's people being forced by law to pay taxes towards its support, without its catechism being taught in the common schools, then we should beg God's forgiveness for the shallowness of our faith."

Deacon Augur was chastened by William's words, but only for a moment. "We know who crafted that 'religious freedom' clause," he said darkly. "Joshua Stow!" He spat out the name like an insect that had flown into his mouth. "The man who said in the convention that government had no more right to provide by law for worship of the Supreme Being than for the worship of the Devil!" Augur was now shaking with fury. "The infidel who once called the Virgin Mary a whore and Jesus a bastard!"

William managed to maintain an impassive expression. Joshua Stow's key role in crafting the provision establishing religious equality was the hardest thing about the new constitution for him to swallow.

They rode in silence for a minute. "It is possible," William said slowly, "that Joshua Stow is an instrument of the Lord's will."

Augur guffawed loudly at this outrageous suggestion, but William continued. "Perhaps God has placed him among us, like an irritating stone in a shoe, to keep us from becoming complacent in our faith."

This was too fine an interpretation for the old deacon. "If I can't make you see reason, maybe I can convince your brother. Elihu is a freeman, isn't he?" Augur asked.

"He is," William confirmed, "as of March, when he turned twenty-one. But he won't be voting," he added with a mixture of disapproval and disappointment. "He loathes squabbling, has no interest in politics or elections. The only constitution Elihu finds interesting is Cornelia Geer's," he said, smiling at his own feeble pun.

"Cornelia's father is making noises about moving to Vermont," William went on, glad to steer the conversation away from Joshua Stow. "Elihu is anxious to win a promise of marriage from her before the family picks up and goes." And William was on pins and needles waiting for the outcome – and whether Elihu could convince his bride to stay in Middlefield, or if she would insist they join her family in Vermont.

Chapter Seventy-Three

October, 1820
Middlefield

A sense of well-being such as he hadn't experienced in nearly a decade came over William as he rode home through the autumn afternoon. The sun warm on his shoulders, he held the reins loosely between his fingers, and half-closed his eyes as he let the horse jog leisurely along Miller Road.

Many things, great and small, taken together accounted for William's contentment. Two months earlier the Probate Court had accepted his final report on the administration of David's estate. That signaled the end of nearly a decade spent settling the affairs of first his brother, then his father, during which he'd neglected his wife and children, sacrificed his comfort and happiness, and, most frightening, only narrowly escaped being enslaved to alcohol.

Now William was enjoying focusing all his attention on the affairs of his own hearth, where the future was bright. It had taken him more than a year, but last August he had bought back the house and homelot from Elisha Coe. It now housed Sarah, William and Alma and their three children, and Elihu and his bride, twenty-one-year-old Cornelia Geer.

William had been thrilled and relieved by his brother's marriage. Cornelia was pretty and congenial – and deeply devoted to her new husband. Her entire family – parents, brothers, and sisters – had moved to Vermont shortly after she and Elihu wed. But Cornelia hadn't pressed Elihu to go with them, accepting without question that they would remain in Middlefield.

William's forecast that once their father's estate was settled there would be enough acres in Middlefield to support two families had proven correct, although it would be some time before Elihu could afford to buy or build his own house. But William was confident Elihu was in Connecticut to stay. The thought of having his brother near at hand, sharing what the years would bring, was a heartening prospect.

William had spent the day pursuing the mundane pleasure of errands. He'd stopped at Asa Kimball's house to pick up new shoes he'd ordered for Phineas, now twelve; Adeline, ten; and Lizzy, eight. All three had outgrown their old shoes over the summer. Then he'd proceeded to the home of his cousin Esther Maria Lyman, to take delivery of new shirts she'd sewn for Phineas, and the dresses, one in a blue plaid, the other in a red, she'd made for the two girls.

Esther Maria had to be past thirty by now, William reflected, but showed no inclination to marry. She seemed content to live with her mother, his Aunt Esther, and with Aunt Esther's spinster sister, Anna Camp, on a small plot of land inherited from their father. Esther Maria's brother, Alfred, had married in January and moved from his mother's house into one of his own. William had been glad to see Alfred, now thirty, display even this much initiative and independence.

Esther Maria, her mother, and her aunt were all faithful members of the revived Middlefield Congregational church, which was making slow but encouraging progress. In a surprising but gratifying turn of events, the new state constitution, approved by a narrow margin, had proven not to be the downfall of Congregationalism, but actually a blessing.

The wheat had been separated from the chaff, as people who claimed Congregational membership only to satisfy the law, or for the prestige of belonging to the established religion, left the church, leaving behind a core of sincere believers. At the same time, others who'd been offended by the aura of elitism attached to Congregationalism because of its special status were now more receptive to its spiritual message. The Middlefield church itself had grown strong enough to engage the services of a part-time pastor – the first since Abner Benedict's departure thirty-five years earlier.

William smiled, savoring the irony of Joshua Stow, through his work on the state constitution, unwittingly aiding the Congregational church in Connecticut. He'd been more right than he knew when he told Prosper Augur that Stow might be an instrument of God.

William had been pleasantly astonished when Lyman Beecher, having fiercely opposed the new constitution, experienced an almost immediate change of heart once it was adopted. His cousin now urged all denominations to collaborate on activities to advance Christian morals. Lyman was busy inspiring religious revivals across New England. While cynics noted that Lyman Beecher's radical change of principle was conveniently building him an even greater audience, William was willing to accept that his cousin was truly following his conscience.

William turned his thoughts from politics and religion to what awaited him at home. He and Alma had marked their thirteenth wedding anniversary yesterday, but cause for even greater joy was the fact that Alma was expecting a baby any day. It was the first child she'd conceived since Lizzy's birth more than eight years ago.

Phineas had hoped the baby would be born on his own birthday, October 15, but that date came and went. Both Adeline and Lizzy had been good about helping Sarah run the household since Alma had taken to her bed two months ago after experiencing unfamiliar – and unsettling – pains. All three were children to be proud of, for which, William acknowledged with humility, Alma deserved the lion's share of credit.

As he rounded the last bend in the road and his home came into view, William spied two figures standing atop the stone wall surrounding the homelot. He sat up straighter in the saddle, and squinted.

One of the figures was Phineas, wearing a blue-and-white checked shirt, trousers held up by suspenders, and a broad-brimmed straw hat. Phineas was shooting up so fast that he remained rail thin, despite the astonishing amounts of food he consumed as fast as the women could set it on the table. With his gangly arms and legs and unruly shock of hair, blonde courtesy of his Grandmother Lyman, Phineas put William in mind of a stalk of Indian corn growing under the most favorable conditions.

William couldn't tell if the other figure was Adeline or Lizzy, so similar were the sisters in coloring and in height, despite the two years separating them. But when the girl began to jump up and down and wave excitedly with one arm, William knew it was Lizzy. Adeline at ten would consider such antic behavior too childish for the young lady she fancied herself to be.

Phineas leaped down from the wall and began running as fast as he could down the dusty road toward his father. He had to clamp his hand on his straw hat to keep it from flying off his head.

William's heart skipped a beat at the boy's almost frantic haste, for his first thought was that something was amiss with Alma. But when Phineas got close enough for William to see his face, he knew it was not trouble propelling him.

"I have a brother!" Phineas yelled, taking off his hat and waving it in celebration. A wide grin split William's face; he was both overjoyed at the news and amused by Phineas's view of the baby's birth as first and foremost a personal boon for him.

"Then I guess that means I have another son," William said in a teasing tone that was completely lost on the excited Phineas. William reached down to grip his son's forearm, and with one powerful pull brought him up to land with a hard thump behind him on the rump of the horse, which William spurred to a gallop.

As they approached the stone wall, Lizzy held out her arms in excited anticipation. Without slowing the horse, William extended his left arm and grabbed Lizzy securely around the waist as they sped by, lifting her in one motion off the wall and depositing her giggling onto the saddle in front of him.

It was a game William had played for years with all three children. Alma fretted about such risky, boisterous stunts, particularly where the girls were concerned, but she hadn't objected. She knew William wanted all his children, daughters included, to grow up as fearless as possible.

William reined in the horse at the side of the house. He lifted Lizzy down onto the ground, then waited for Phineas to slide down from behind before swinging his long leg over the horse's rump to dismount. He tossed the reins to Phineas.

Sarah appeared in the doorway, her face aglow with a joy William had seen only rarely since his father's death. She reached out to take William's arm and usher him in for his first look at the baby that he and Alma had agreed, if it were a boy, would be named David.

Chapter Seventy-Four

June, 1824
Durham

"I won't rest easy until I hear of your safe arrival at your father's," Elihu said. "You must send word as soon as you get there."

Cornelia nodded in almost childlike obedience. They were standing inside the door of John Swathel's inn at the intersection in Durham of Crooked Lane and the New Haven Turnpike, as the main street was also known. They were awaiting the stagecoach that would take Cornelia to her parents' house in Vermont. Outside a warm June rain fell steadily.

"You know I'd come with you if I could," Elihu said. "But we'll need every man once haying starts. Even with Phineas now able to do a man's work, and William hiring John Gale's son to come down from Vermont, I still can't be spared."

Cornelia nodded again. "I'm sorry to leave–," she started to say, but Elihu shook his head and quickly placed his fingertips against her lips. "There's nothing to apologize for," he said firmly. "I know how much you miss your family in Vermont. I've never begrudged your trips to see them. I've seen how much it means to my mother when Polly or Urania or Sally comes home to visit."

But this journey to Vermont was different from any Cornelia had made before, a fact that weighed heavily upon both of them. When she'd traveled north the past two years she'd taken their little daughter, also named Cornelia, with her to show to her family. But Cornelia, barely two, had died in her mother's arms three weeks ago of a raging fever that had raced through the community's children.

The fever had carried off Alfred Lyman's infant son, the second child he and his wife had buried. Little Sarah Comstock Lyman, the daughter Alma had borne a year ago this February, had contracted the disease, but had survived and was now on the mend.

Cornelia's need for the balm of her own mother's love had grown so desperate it at last outweighed the guilt she felt over leaving Elihu, whose grief was deep. But he would be in good hands, with Sarah, Alma, and William doing everything they could to help him deal with his sorrow. And from now until the beginning of August Elihu and every other available man would be working from dawn to dusk on harvesting the hay crop. The exhausting labor would leave him little time or energy to do much else but eat and sleep.

They turned toward the rain-splattered window as a horn heralded the stagecoach's approach. Cornelia threw her arms around the startled Elihu's neck. "I love you," she whispered in a quivering voice into his ear.

"I love you," Elihu replied, putting his powerful arms around her in a protective embrace. They clung tightly to each other until the rumble and splash of wheels on the muddy, puddle-filled road, followed by the squeal of wet wooden brakes, announced the stagecoach's arrival.

With a great effort Cornelia released her hold on Elihu and stepped back, straightening her traveling outfit. Elihu picked up her baggage and carried it out to the driver, who lashed it to the back of the coach. Elihu stepped to the vehicle's door, and Cornelia walked as quickly and carefully as she could from the tavern doorway to Elihu, who took her hand and helped her inside.

"I'll be counting the days until September," he said longingly. Cornelia mustered up a brave smile, hoping Elihu didn't notice the tears mingling with the raindrops on her cheeks. Elihu stepped back to allow the driver to close the door, after which the man hoisted himself up into his seat. With a snap of a whip the coach jolted off.

Elihu remained standing in the soaking rain, watching the stagecoach rumble north toward Middletown, until it disappeared from view. He always worried about Cornelia when they were apart, but his fears were now greater; the death of their little daughter had rendered his wife that much more precious to him.

Elihu's spirits were so low that he toyed with the idea of going back into Swathel's tavern for a mug of rum. But he thought better of it, and climbed resolutely into the chaise and set out for home.

Chapter Seventy-Five

July, 1824
Middlefield

Although he'd been laboring nonstop since before sunrise, and it was now nearly noon, Phineas pushed himself to maintain the speed with which he swung the two-handed wooden scythe. With rhythmic strokes he mowed down stalks of grass that would become hay to feed the cattle and horses for the coming year.

All but the most essential tasks had been set aside so that William, Elihu, Phineas, and hired men John Gale and Negro brothers Jesse and Chester Caples, could devote themselves to haying. The work had to be performed during these few weeks, for it was seriously vulnerable to the weather. The men kept an eye on the sky constantly. If clouds began to build in the west, they would leave off mowing and cover the cut grass, or roll it into large cylindrical haycocks to protect it from the rain that would cause it to rot.

Phineas, three months shy of sixteen, was determined that this year he would keep up with the grueling pace of work set by the men. He'd stopped getting taller, at least for the moment, making him slightly shorter than his Uncle Elihu. That slowing of his growth had given him a chance to add some flesh, most of it muscle, to his frame. His strength and stamina had increased as well.

Phineas's red cotton shirt was plastered to his back and chest with sweat, which ran in rivulets down both sides of his face. But he willed himself not to slacken, to earn respect from those with whom he toiled for doing a grown man's work.

"Dinner!" William called out. Phineas cut one last swathe before stopping with a relief he hoped wasn't obvious.

"I'll go get more water for the afternoon," William said. "After we're done eating, we'll rake out what we mowed this morning." He started walking to the Lyman house, and the five workers drifted toward the shade of one of the few mature trees in the field.

"This is the first year you haven't gotten your ankles nicked by one of our blades coming up behind you, Phineas," teased Jesse Caples. In his early thirties, Caples had skin the color of coffee. He had a lean, powerful body that he held ramrod straight in the military manner taught him by his father, also named Jesse, who'd learned it serving in the army during the Revolution. The elder Jesse Caples, now more than eighty years old, was one of the last surviving veterans of the war for independence in Middlefield.

Phineas allowed himself a small smile and a short nod of acknowledgement for the older man's praise. But he was thrilled that his effort had been noticed.

"Water!" snorted John Gale, dropping wearily to the ground. "You might as well expect a man to work without air as without rum or brandy – or at least beer or cider! If I'd known how strict a temperance man your brother was, Elihu, I would've asked for double pay for these months of work," he said.

Elihu sat down beside Gale in the welcome shade. Gale, just twenty-two, had voiced this same complaint without fail every day since the beginning of haying. Elihu himself had been taken aback by William's decision last year to ban not just ardent spirits, but beer and cider as well from his household. Even their mother had been surprised at such an extreme measure, especially when William insisted he wouldn't serve alcoholic beverages to guests.

That they'd all been putting in a full day of hard work week after week without alcohol failed to convince Gale that water was sufficient to sustain laboring men. But Elihu endured his grousing, for Gale never used this galling deprivation as an excuse to shirk his share of work.

Jesse and Chester Caples had accepted William's unorthodox conditions as well. Not every man would hire Negroes; they appreciated the work and respected William, who paid them fairly.

"I've had the gripes for two nights past," Gale complained. "And I've got them again," he said in a strangled voice. He scrambled to his feet and hurried off to find a place to relieve himself.

"Don't I know it," Elihu said dryly, watching Gale's retreating figure. "He visited the outhouse four times last night, and woke me up each time. That's one more reason I'll be glad to have him out of my bed and my wife back in it come September," he added longingly.

"William says your wife is expecting a baby," Jesse said. He was sharpening the blade of his scythe on a whetstone between bites of Indian cornbread, cheese, and salted beef.

Elihu beamed. "She is," he said. "I learned of it only yesterday in a letter from Cornelia. We didn't know she was with child when she left in June. We expect it will be born sometime after the new year."

Elihu noticed that Phineas was looking intently across the mown field toward the road. He turned and saw that the object of his nephew's interest was a dark-haired teenaged girl in a red plaid dress, holding a little boy by the hand as they walked past the Lyman house. Squinting hard, Elihu recognized the girl as Ann Birdsey, daughter of Samuel Birdsey. He couldn't tell which of her three little brothers she had in tow as they turned onto the road that led to the home of her cousin John Birdsey, the Lymans' neighbor.

"I thought it was Betsy Ward you fancied," Elihu said loudly enough to break Phineas's concentration. "But that was last month," he said as the youth looked around and his cheeks, already flushed by heat and exertion, grew redder at his uncle's teasing.

"And who was it before Betsy?" Elihu went on, making a comically exaggerated show of searching his memory. "Lucy Coles? But Ann Birdsey!" Elihu gave a long, low whistle. "Lymans have neighbored and argued and bargained with Birdseys as long as our families have been in Middlefield, but we've never courted them."

"I'm not courting anyone," Phineas insisted quickly. "At least not yet," he amended with a suggestive grin that caused Elihu to stop and take a good hard look at his brother's eldest son.

Phineas's physical maturity obviously involved more than the ability to swing a scythe. Elihu had noticed how much he enjoyed flirting with just about any girl. He suspected his good-looking nephew was going to find it more difficult than most to control the lustful urges that occupied a good portion of a young man's thoughts while awake and his dreams while asleep.

Suddenly Elihu grimaced, grunted, and got to his feet. "It seems John's not the only one with the gripes," he said, as he stumbled off into tall grass, hunched over by a cramping in his belly.

Phineas watched his uncle with a sympathetic frown. When he turned back toward the road, he was disappointed to discover that Ann Birdsey had disappeared from view.

Chapter Seventy-Six

September, 1824
Middlefield

"Cornelia wants to come back to Middlefield," William told Alma, looking up in surprise from the letter in his hand.

"I was sure she'd stay in Vermont with her parents," said Alma.

William glanced back down at the paper. "She says this is where she and Elihu were husband and wife, and she wants to give birth to his child here. She'll be back by the middle of September, as they originally planned." He studied the letter for a long moment before handing it to Alma. "She's far braver than I gave her credit for," he admitted, sitting down wearily in a Windsor chair.

Three weeks ago, on August 10, Elihu Lyman had died from a savage case of dysentery. The disease had reduced him in less than a fortnight from a robust man to an emaciated one unable to lift his head from the pillow. His suffering had been so terrible, and the physicians' treatments so ineffective, that William had actually thanked God that the illness had progressed so swiftly.

Elihu had forbidden William from summoning Cornelia back to Middlefield from Vermont, at first because he expected to recover. But as it became clear that the disease would prove fatal, he didn't want his wife's last memories of him to be as a befouled near-skeleton wracked with constant pain. He also feared the effect of such trauma on their unborn child.

On his last lucid day, Elihu had dictated to William a letter for Cornelia, telling her of his impending death and of his decision not to call her back to Connecticut. He had assured her of his love, and commended her and their baby to God's care. After Elihu was gone,

William had added some words about his brother's final hours, then mailed the letter.

John Hale had succumbed to the same disease two weeks after Elihu. The intense August heat and the nature of his illness had made transporting his body home to Vermont for burial out of the question. He'd had been laid to rest with Elihu in the Middlefield burying ground.

William was still numb from the shock of Elihu's sudden death. But whenever he was tempted to indulge in self-pity, he had only to look at his seventy-year-old mother. For a time Sarah had reeled from this blow, but with God's help as always, she was steadily, if slowly, emerging from her sorrow. She possessed that 'faith which passeth all understanding' for which every Christian strove, William thought with admiration – and a touch of envy.

Still, in the days following Elihu's death, William had several times caught his mother studying him anxiously, as if he, her last child left in Middlefield, might suddenly be snatched away. William himself had begun to feel like the tall maple tree in the middle of his hayfield, a solitary survivor left standing after all around him had been uprooted or mown down by death.

William reminded himself that the Lymans still had ample reason to be grateful to God. None of his and Alma's five children had been stricken with dysentery. Cornelia's decision to bear and raise Elihu's child in Middlefield would mean that Elihu would live on among them. And Alma had just learned that she was expecting another baby.

Chapter Seventy-Seven

July, 1825
Middlefield

"Betsy Miller died yesterday," William announced tonelessly to Alma and Sarah as he sat down stiffly on a straight-backed chair in the kitchen. "Dr. Cone told me when I saw him in the city."

Both women had to suppress panic at the news of the death of the neighbor who until two weeks ago had been as hearty as any middle-aged woman. For Betsy Miller had died of the same disease with which Phineas, Adeline, Lizzy, and Cornelia all lay seriously ill.

The physicians disagreed on the exact nature of the sickness, the primary symptom of which was a dark-red bumpy rash over much of a patient's body. Old Dr. Tracy, who'd been caring for Lymans for more than twenty-five years, diagnosed it as common typhus. Others, including Dr. Thomas Miner and Dr. Ebenezer Cone, were convinced it was sinking typhus, a relatively new disease that had swept through the center of Middletown two years ago. Whatever it was, this time the pestilence had targeted Middlefield.

Cornelia had been the first of the family to fall ill, after having helped nurse Betsy Miller. Although Cornelia had miscarried her child a month after returning to Middlefield, she had stayed on with Elihu's family. The three Lyman children had begun to exhibit symptoms a day or two after their aunt did.

"I purchased the opium and arsenic Dr. Miner prescribed at Southmayd and Boardman's," William said, holding out small paper packages he'd bought at the Middletown apothecary. "And I bought a bottle of wine at Swathel's inn." This last act had been a great concession on William's part, but Dr. Miner had insisted that opium, arsenic, and alcohol were all essential to treating the disease.

"I'll dose them as soon as they're alert enough to swallow," Alma said, taking the packages and bottle from William. "We blistered their foreheads with hot bricks as Dr. Miner instructed. I can't tell if it's done them any good," she said in a discouraged voice.

Both Alma and Sarah were worn to a nub from endless days of caring for four gravely ill people, applying the different treatments prescribed by the physicians, and constantly worrying and praying. There was no help to be had from other families, since just about every household had been stricken.

"Dr. Cone said he'd try to come by tonight, but he couldn't promise," William went on, so overcome by weariness he had to work to drag the words out one by one. "Phineas Augur and his mother are down with the disease, as are old Captain David Birdsey, and his nephews Benjamin and Seth," he reported. He reached up under his rolled-up linen shirt sleeve to absent-mindedly scratch a louse bite.

Vermin had been more annoying this year than anyone could ever remember. Hardly any rain had fallen since the first week of June, two full months ago, threatening crops and causing some wells to go dry. The available water was used for cooking and drinking, with any extra being used to wash the small garments of the littlest children and help keep them as cool as possible in the intense summer heat. So far the adults' efforts and prayers had been answered. None of the little children had exhibited signs of typhus.

Those youngest ones included David Lyman, four; Sarah Lyman, two; and five-month-old Elihu Elisha Lyman. Alma had wanted to name their latest baby for her father. But she and William had decided to honor his late uncle as well. That decision seemed preordained when the baby arrived on what would have been Elihu's twenty-eighth birthday.

"I'm so thankful Lucia left Middlefield when she did," Alma said. Her youngest sister had moved to Hartford at the end of June, following her wedding to Charles Bliss of that city. William had been privately amused when Lucia Coe had foiled her own carefully laid plans – and those of her father – for a splendid marriage to a lawyer or merchant by falling in love with Bliss, who was a tanner.

Alma dipped a tin cup into the bucket of water she'd lugged in from the well, and handed it to William. He took it from her, but it slipped from his fingers and hit the wooden floor with a dull "clank," spilling its precious contents. Alma took a startled step backwards as a fierce spasm of shivering shook William's entire frame, as if a winter blast had suddenly blown in through the window.

Alma placed a palm on her husband's forehead, then pulled it back reflexively when she felt its great heat. She stared in speechless horror at William, who was now among those infected with typhus.

William struggled to open his eyes. It took several tries, for his lids felt as heavy as anvils. As his vision came into focus, he realized he was flat on his back in his own bed. Natural light dimly illuminated the chamber, but he couldn't tell if it was early morning or late evening. He had no idea what day it was.

Slowly fragments of memories began to coalesce. He recalled Sarah and Alma helping him to his bed, then lying here in the stifling heat, watching the tell-tale typhus rash erupt first on his chest, then spread over the rest of his body except for his face. He remembered slipping in and out of a bottomless darkness, the taste of wine and of other unidentifiable substances.

Voices had seemed alternately close by and at a great distance, and there had been a searing heat on his forehead, his temples, and the crown of his head. He had prayed, sometimes incoherently, sometimes lucidly. During his moments of clear-headedness he had placed himself in God's hands with the words of ultimate Christian submission, "Thy will be done."

The chamber door opened, and Sarah entered with a cup in each hand. Her shoulders sagged, and her step was slow. Her hair and clothing were disheveled as William had never seen them.

It took a moment for the fact that William was conscious to register with Sarah. Her eyes opened wide and then overflowed with tears of joyous relief. She placed the cups on a small bed-side table, sat down on the feather mattress, and took William's hand.

"You've been out of your head for nearly a week," Sarah said. "Thank God for His mercy in sparing you."

William's tongue and lips were so swollen and dry he couldn't form words. His mother held a cup of water to his lips to moisten them, and he swallowed a few sips. Still unable to speak, his eyes searched Sarah's haggard face, clearly asking about the family.

"Everyone is well," Sarah assured him. "You mustn't think of anything else but getting better." William nodded slightly, then closed his eyes, having exhausted what little strength he possessed. But as he slid back into unconsciousness, one disturbing impression remained: his mother was lying.

Chapter Seventy-Eight

October, 1827
Middlefield

William lifted the iron latch, swung open the gate in the whitewashed wooden picket fence, then fastened it behind him to keep the sheep from escaping. He walked up the slope toward the back of the Middlefield burying ground.

Halfway up the gradual incline, its grass close-cropped by the grazing sheep, William passed the brownstone tombstone for his great-grandmother Hope Hawley. A short distance beyond was the one for his brother Phineas, dead twenty-eight years, with the epitaph their father had composed chiseled into it. William knew his Grandfather Lyman was here somewhere, but no stone marked his grave. His Granny Fowler had been laid to rest in North Guilford.

Many new gravestones among the weathered ones testified to the wide swathe death had cut through Middlefield during the summer and autumn of 1825, which people had taken to calling with grim simplicity the "sickly year." Seventeen residents of Middlefield had died in the typhus epidemic; from August through December scarcely a week had passed without a funeral.

William spied the marker for Prosper Augur's wife. Augur had been struck by typhus, but the tough old deacon had survived to live on, bereft of his wife, as well as of his only son. There were stones for David, Seth, and Benjamin Birdsey, who'd perished in a span of just two months. Another marked the grave of nine-year-old Sally Miller, the last Middlefield resident to die of typhus.

Next to the gravestone William had erected for his brother Elihu stood one for his wife. Cornelia Lyman had died of typhus on August

14, 1825, having survived her husband by barely more than a year. It was the death of Cornelia, the only Lyman family member to perish in the pestilence, that Sarah had been concealing from William when he first emerged from the delirium of typhus.

The nightmarish epidemic had seemed like a Biblical plague. In their houses of worship and in their hearts, those who had lived through it struggled to understand why God had so afflicted their community, and why they had been spared while so many good people had gone to their graves.

A few more steps up the gentle incline brought William within sight of an irregular cluster of white granite stones that he'd ordered several years back from a carver in Vermont for the graves of his relatives by blood or marriage, including his father, his brother David, and his sister-in-law Sina. In the shade of a tall maple tree, its leaves a vibrant yellow, stood two more rectangular white stones that had been set in place just last week.

The new stones were carved with the classical urn and weeping willows that at the start of the century had replaced winged angel's heads as the prevailing motifs for gravestones. There William spotted what he'd come looking for.

Alma was sitting on the grass in front of the new markers. She wore a high-necked, long-sleeved dress of plain olive green wool, with a pink sash tied just beneath her breasts and a crisp white double ruffle around her throat. She'd removed her white bonnet; sunshine filtering through the leaves glinted off her glossy hair. Despite her forty-two years and her multiple sorrows, there wasn't a single strand of white or gray in her chestnut tresses.

Something seemed not quite right to William as he studied his wife. Then he realized it was her dress; it was the first time he'd seen her out of the black mourning clothes that a succession of tragedies had kept the entire Lyman family wearing for three solid years.

Not wanting to startle Alma, William deliberately stepped on some dry leaves so their rustling would alert her to his approach. When she stirred slightly, he knew she'd heard him coming, but she didn't turn to face him.

William stood for a long moment by his wife's side. At last he sat down next to her on the grass, his long legs bent in front of him.

"Lizzy told me where you were," William said. Alma smiled faintly. "Sometimes I wonder who's the mother – me, or Lizzy," she said. "She wouldn't let me leave without telling her where I was going."

There was a long silence, as William and Alma studied the newest additions to the forest of gravestones. The inscription on the stone to the left read, "Phineas Lyman, son of William & Alma Lyman, died February 13, 1826." Its companion on the right read "Adeline Lyman, daughter of William & Alma Lyman, died Aug. 6, 1826, AE 16."

William and Alma had thanked God when their oldest son and daughter survived their bout with typhus – only to be plunged into grief before a year had passed. The disease had weakened Phineas and Adeline's constitutions, leaving them vulnerable to new infections. Phineas had succumbed to a lung ailment he contracted during the winter. Adeline had died of measles the following August.

None of the deaths they'd experienced had prepared William and Alma for the heart-rending agony of having a child die. They'd clung to each other, and together to God, like survivors of a shipwreck, fighting to keep from being overwhelmed by the surging anger, sorrow, guilt, and helplessness that battered them mercilessly.

William plucked a long blade of grass the grazing sheep had somehow missed. Holding it in his left hand, he ran it repeatedly between the thumb and finger of his right, thinking. He and Alma had been here last week, when the stones had been set in place. Always before they'd come to the graveyard together. He was concerned that she'd felt a need to come alone, without telling him.

"I know they're not here," Alma said, sounding so like a lost child that William's heart constricted. "I haven't lost faith in our Redeemer's promise of life everlasting. I'm sure they're in His loving arms. But I feel closer to them here, especially with the gravestones in place." She didn't look at William, but continued staring at the granite markers.

"I miss them so terribly!" Alma burst out. She blinked hard; tears collected on the ends of her long eyelashes, then fell to the grass where they clung to the blades like glistening drops of dew.

"I miss everything about them," she went on in anguish. "Phineas's grin, the way he shook the whole house when he pounded down the stairs in the morning, how he would tease David to the point of tears, then have him giggling a minute later. I miss how excited Adeline would get picking out cloth for a new dress, how she could never get enough pumpkin pie, even her squawking when I combed the snarls from her hair in the morning."

Alma stopped to catch her breath, sniffled and swallowed, then said through quivering lips, "I'm afraid I won't be able to hold their dear countenances in my mind, that their faces will fade from my memory." She stopped, gulping down a sob, then turned to look at William for the first time since he'd arrived.

"This pain will always be with us," William said, placing his hands gently on Alma's shoulders. "But never forget, it is our pain, not theirs. They're beyond all unhappiness, all sorrow, all suffering."

William hoped he sounded convincing. He believed what he said. But he'd had his own dark moments when that knowledge provided no balm for the searing memories of his children's anguished last days, for the loneliness created by their absence, for the regret for all they would never have a chance to do, to become.

A shadow of a sad smile came to his lips. "And don't torment yourself about recalling their every feature," he said consolingly. "You'll know them when we all meet in heaven,"

Alma turned from William to gaze at the new gravestones. Then she turned back to face him, meeting his eyes with a look of fear. "I'm going to have a baby," she said in barely more than a whisper.

William became as still as the surrounding stones – except for his hands, which tightened reflexively on Alma's shoulders. Although Alma hadn't yet gone through a woman's "change," it had been more than two and a half years since Elihu Elisha's birth. William and Alma had come to assume he would be their last child.

Every other time Alma had spoken these words to him, William had rejoiced. But now that news was shadowed by anxiety.

A new life would be a welcome blessing, an antidote to the many, many recent deaths. But Alma would be forty-three when the baby was born; what if – his mind recoiled almost instantly from the unbearable thought – she should die bearing this child? Was that the source of the torment in her eyes?

"Does the prospect of giving birth frighten you?" he asked gently.

Alma shook her head. "What I fear is that I won't be able to love this new baby as I have our others, knowing as I do now the agony of burying a child." Guilt and shame had joined the pain in her glistening blue eyes.

William shifted to his knees and gathered Alma tenderly in his arms. "There are few things in this world of which I am absolutely certain," he said with conviction. "One of them is your limitless capacity to love." He was relieved to see the fear and guilt begin to recede from Alma's eyes, and hugged her tightly to his chest.

Chapter Seventy-Nine

December, 1829
Middlefield

The scraping and scuffling of little children dressing quickly on the frosty morning soon changed to nervous, excited whispers and giggles. The youngsters gathered at the top of the stairs, then descended as a group with a great clattering of shoes.

"Do you think he really came, Lizzy?" William, Alma, and Sarah heard six-year-old Sally, as Sarah was called to avoid confusion with her grandmother, ask her sister as the children approached the kitchen,

"I certainly hope so, Sally," Lizzy, seventeen, replied seriously. "We'll know in a minute."

When they entered the kitchen, awed amazement lit up the faces of Sally, her four-year-old brother Elihu, and their cousins, David Buttolph, seven, and Jane Buttolph, three. Eighteen-month-old Adeline Urania Lyman was too young to understand what was transpiring, but she'd sensed the excited anticipation pervading the household since the previous night

William watched with delight as the children stopped momentarily in their tracks. The four little ones suddenly made a bee-line toward the fireplace, from which dangled stockings bulging with treats Saint Nicholas had stuffed into them while they slept.

William stood and cleared his throat, bringing the near-stampede to an abrupt halt. The first order of business every day in the Lyman household was the coming together of the family for prayers. Lizzy, David, and their cousin David took turns reading a passage from the large family Bible aloud. Then everyone except

Sarah, whose joints were painfully stiffened by arthritis, followed William's lead in kneeling on the wooden floor and bowing their heads as he prayed aloud.

The little ones' muscles were twitching impatiently, but even William's "Amen" didn't release them. He opened his eyes, lifted his head, and nodded in their direction. The children jumped to their feet and scampered to the fireplace.

William had first learned of the custom of a magical elfin figure delivering presents to children on Christmas Eve in an anonymous poem titled "A Visit from Saint Nicholas" in a Troy, New York, newspaper in 1823. Three years later he'd introduced the custom into his own family. He'd done so partly to provide for David, then six, and Sally, two, a bright break in the somberness that engulfed the family following the deaths of Adeline and Phineas – and partly just because he enjoyed indulging his children.

Sarah Lyman had been scandalized by this observance of Christmas – let alone a frivolous deception that involved a Popish saint! When she was a girl Congregationalists had deliberately avoided any acknowledgement of Christmas, treating it like any other day of the year. She was convinced this was just one more symptom of the breakdown in traditional religious values that had begun with the dislocations of the Revolution and culminated in the disestablishment of the Congregational Church.

There had been so many changes that Sarah sometimes felt like a foreigner in the land of her birth. At times even William seemed a stranger, with his unorthodox new ideas about religion, politics, and temperance that often contrasted sharply with the principles her generation had grown up with.

William had listened respectfully to Sarah's warnings that this foolishness of a gift-bearing saint constituted a serious breach of his Puritan ancestors' rejection of the pagan excesses of the Romish church. But he assured her of his conviction that children who were receiving a proper Congregationalist upbringing wouldn't have their immortal souls imperiled by being treated to an innocent fantasy that they would soon outgrow.

In an unprecedented display of recalcitrance, Sarah had kept to her chamber the first Christmas Saint Nicholas visited the Lyman house. The following year, conceding that while the silly custom served no good purpose, it didn't seem to have harmed the children, she had relented and rejoined the family on Christmas morning.

However, she still retired to her chamber on Christmas Eve before William read "A Visit from Saint Nicholas" aloud to the children.

Seven hand-knitted woolen stockings, one for each of the five younger children as well as for David, now nine, and Lizzy, were nailed to the board above the kitchen fireplace. They'd been stretched hopelessly out of shape by six years of use for this purpose.

David Lyman, a dark-haired, round-faced version of his father, had during the past year confirmed his suspicions about the authenticity of Saint Nicholas. But rather than shatter his siblings' illusions, he'd joined in making this small piece of magic for them.

The younger children danced with impatience as Lizzy and David carefully removed the stockings and handed them to their owners. They plopped down onto the brownstone hearth in front of the warm fire to explore their contents.

"Saint Nicholas must be quite the nimble fellow," William observed with a straight face as he settled back into a chair to watch the activity. "Imagine being able to come straight down the chimney carrying a heavy pack of toys and manage not to get stuck in the ash hole or have all those presents fall out of his sack into the dish kettle."

The children pulled from the stockings treasures that sparked excited exclamations and occasional squeals of delight. Each child found an assortment of rock candy and cinnamon comfits. Sally received a set of ivory combs for her hair, and little Jane Buttolph a set made from horn. Both girls, and Adeline Urania, discovered a soft, hand-sewn stuffed doll with button eyes and nose that Alma had stitched late at night after they were asleep.

For Elihu there was a wooden top and a copy of *Peter Parley's Juvenile Tales,* with hand-colored engraved illustrations. He was turning out to be such a bright little fellow that William knew it wouldn't be long before he would be able to sound out the words in the book for himself. David Buttolph discovered a small Bible in his stocking, for William and Alma had learned that he was an unusually pious boy.

Into the toe of each stocking was tucked a fat, fragrant orange. William and Alma had purchased all the presents, except for the top and dolls, on a visit to Charles and Lucia Bliss in Hartford at the end of November. Lucia was the mother of a three-year-old son and was expecting another baby around the beginning of the new year.

Alma had been eager to see her younger sister in case bad weather made it too hazardous to travel to Hartford for her confinement.

Clutching her new doll tightly in one hand, Adeline Urania toddled over to her grandmother and held out her arms. William lifted the child gently onto her grandmother's lap, where she nestled down and began an inspection of her toy that included some thoughtful chewing on a soft arm.

Sarah wrapped her arms protectively around this granddaughter. Born in May of 1828, Adeline Urania had been named in memory of the sister who died before she was born, and of her Aunt Urania. Urania Lyman Buttolph had died in 1827, only thirty-five years old, three months after delivering her fourth child. The cause had been bleeding at the lungs, resulting from consumption that had taken root in her constitution a year earlier.

David Buttolph, left with four children under eight, had soon remarried to a widow whose age that made it unlikely she would bear him any children. In response to William and Alma's request, he'd sent little David and Jane to spend the autumn and winter with their mother's family in Middlefield. He kept his other two daughters, both of delicate health, at home in Norwich, New York.

Having these grandchildren with her, even for a short time, meant a great deal to Sarah, especially since Urania wasn't the only child whose recent loss she mourned. At the beginning of the current year, Andrew Lyman, also just thirty-five, had come home from Vermont to die. He'd breathed his last in May, and been buried in the new graveyard near the meetinghouse. Sarah had now outlived half of her children.

Andrew's widow had returned with her three children to her family in Wallingford. Sarah had seen those grandchildren only rarely in the ensuing months.

"Aren't you going to look to see what Saint Nicholas brought for you?" Elihu asked Lizzy. Lizzy, who'd been enjoying watching the smaller children thrill to their presents, obligingly picked up her own stocking. She reached in, prepared to feign surprise at the small items she'd placed in it to maintain the fantasy of Saint Nicholas bringing gifts for all the children, but her expression became puzzled when her hand touched something unexpected. She pulled from the stocking a brand-new book handsomely bound in glossy dark-brown leather with gold stamping around the edges of the covers.

Lizzy opened the book carefully and, after reading the title page, broke into a smile of delight as broad as that of any of the youngsters. She cast a knowing glance of gratitude at William, who wore an expression of exaggerated innocence.

Lizzy stopped herself just in time from blurting out her thanks to her father. "How do you think Saint Nicholas knew I would like to find a copy of Dr. Johnson's *Rasellas* in my stocking?" she asked him instead.

William jutted out his lower lip and tilted his head thoughtfully. "Maybe he heard your health has so improved that you'll be returning to Miss Beecher's seminary, and will need the book for class," he offered disingenuously.

"Maybe," was all Lizzy said. At Elihu's urging, she emptied her stocking, which revealed no further surprises.

If there really were a Saint Nicholas who granted wishes, William thought, he could have given Alma and him no greater gift than the return of the vibrant rose color to Lizzy's cheeks and the rekindling of the sparkle in her sky-blue eyes. Lizzy was a genuine beauty who, despite frequent bouts with illness, usually radiated vitality. She had her mother's thick, wavy hair, but Lizzy's was the color of rich honey, with a texture as smooth as that sweet liquid flowing from a jar. Several inches taller than Alma, Lizzy was also much slenderer than Alma had ever been, putting William in mind of her willowy Aunt Lucia.

Lizzy's character matched the loveliness of her appearance. She was an extraordinary combination of qualities: her parents' keen intelligence, William's optimism, Alma's firmness, her Grandmother Lyman's sensitive intuition, and her Grandfather Coe's generosity. She had a strong backbone, but not a mean bone in her body.

Lizzy's departure to attend school in Hartford had created a great void in their family circle. William was beginning to dread the day when she exchanged the role of daughter for that of wife and left their house for good. That led him to ponder whether a man worthy of her could ever be found – or even existed.

Lizzy possessed such extraordinary promise that William and Alma hadn't hesitated to grant her request to attend the Hartford Female Seminary, established six years earlier by Lyman Beecher's eldest daughter, Catharine Esther Beecher. The Seminary was a new kind of school for girls, offering young ladies an education equal to that provided to boys in private academies, including study of the same subjects, among them algebra, Latin, geometry, composition, history, and French.

Sending Lizzy to the Female Seminary had required financial sacrifice. Tuition was $12 per term, and board cost $2.50 per week. The total cost of a year at the Seminary was $134 – enough to pay for the lumber to build a small house.

This enormous outlay had provided further ammunition for friends and relatives who'd expressed to William and Alma their doubts about the wisdom of schooling a daughter in subjects that would be of no use to her as a wife and mother. Some had reminded them of the generally accepted fact that the female mind was fragile, warning that tackling such demanding intellectual work could injure Lizzy's brain.

William had scoffed at this last observation. The women closest to him in his life – his Granny Fowler, his mother, his wife – had minds every bit as sharp and strong as his. The notion that their brains would collapse under rigorous mental activity was absurd. If God had given a woman a fine mind, she ought to improve it to the best of her ability.

For Alma, sending Lizzy to the Hartford Female Seminary was a personal victory. She still regretted that she'd been born too soon to be favored with the education her younger sisters had received at Miss Pierce's School. To provide her own daughter with not just an education, but the best available to a woman anywhere in the country, gave Alma enormous satisfaction. It was worth whatever scrimping and saving they had to make.

They'd taken Lizzy to Hartford in May to enroll in the Seminary. Catharine Beecher's sister, Harriet, just a year older than Lizzy, was already a teacher there. Once the sharp pangs of homesickness passed, Lizzy reveled in the pursuit of knowledge and the exercising of her intellect at the Seminary. She enjoyed immensely the company of other young women who shared her passion for learning.

But after only three months had passed, Lizzy fell seriously ill at school with scarlet fever. William had hastened to Hartford to bring her home to Middlefield. For several days they had feared for her life. She'd at last rallied around the time of her seventeenth birthday in early September, and began to make a slow, steady recovery that had restored her to full health by the beginning of December.

Lizzy planned to return to the Seminary for the beginning of the summer session in mid-May. That would put her on track to finish her course of study in 1833. That year David would be twelve, old enough to start attending one of the many private academies springing up across Connecticut in response to increased dissatisfaction with the abysmal quality of instruction offered in the common schools.

While intelligent and inquisitive, David didn't share Lizzy's thirst for knowledge for its own sake. He was practical, through and through, and already displayed energy and determination such as William had seen in few mature men.

Moses might have been a better name for this son, William mused, for when David set a goal, he pursued it doggedly, no matter how long it took or how many obstacles he encountered. Frustrated by the haphazard instruction in the common school, he'd taught himself the fundamentals of arithmetic by studying old schoolbooks at home so late into the night that his eyesight had suffered.

The self-control William had had to fight so hard to achieve seemed to come naturally to David. The tremendous patience that was key to his perseverance David displayed in his dealings with others, particularly his little brother.

William watched David help Elihu try again and again to set his new top spinning on the floor. After fully ten minutes of repeated failures, Elihu wanted to give up in despair. But under David's calm encouragement, the little boy at last got the hang of how to set the toy whirling properly. Elihu flashed a triumphant grin at David.

Save for occasional bouts of rheumatism, David was a strong fellow. He had a genuine interest in working the land and caring for the animals, but it was the farm's business dealings that truly fired his interest. Just recently William had surrendered to his son's polite, yet relentless, requests to be allowed to help maintain accounts, to calculate values and expenses and profits and losses.

Proud as they were of David's precociousness, both William and Alma at times wished he would display as much zeal for spiritual matters as for business ones. The boy's religious convictions were sincere, and he participated in all the usual church activities. But watching David happily lose himself in numbers and calculations raised in William disquieting memories of his own father's obsession with money and prosperity. William resolved to help guide David toward applying his talents to worthier goals.

Chapter Eighty

May, 1831
Middlefield

Hauling, sawing, and hammering heavy timbers had William sweating underneath the wool coat he'd donned that morning. This late May day held a raw dampness that felt more like early March. But removing the coat would risk catching a dangerous chill, so he stopped working for a few moments to let his body cool down,

Leaning on one hand against a stud he'd just nailed into place, William surveyed with satisfaction this piece of God's work he was supervising. More than two dozen men of the Middlefield Congregational Church were raising the frame of a parsonage. After more than forty years – two full generations, almost William's entire lifetime – Middlefield Congregationalists again had a permanent, full-time pastor.

The Reverend James Noyes had been ordained four years ago. Having found their new pastor suitable, the congregation had taken up a subscription to build a parsonage.

William had been selected to oversee the project. That decision was an acknowledgement that the Lymans were among the largest contributors to the building, and also testimony to the trust William had earned. As soon as the earth had thawed sufficiently, a cellar hole had been dug on land not far from the meetinghouse.

William had hired Jesse Caples to haul heavy brownstone blocks from a small quarry on Powder Hill to the site. The stones had been assembled piecemeal into a foundation over the past weeks whenever men found a few hours to work on it.

At last it was time to come together as a group to erect the frame. While the men labored, their families were at the nearby home of Obed Stow. The women were preparing the food for which the workers would be ravenous by noontime.

"How fares your father-in-law, William?" asked Obed, who had also stopped to catch his breath. At sixty-four, Obed was five years younger than his notorious brother, Joshua. It would be hard to find two brothers more different in character, William thought. Obed Stow was a stolid, deeply pious man, one of the faithful who'd helped revive the Middlefield church back in 1808.

William shook his head sorrowfully. "Elisha's doing poorly, Obed. I wouldn't be surprised if he lies over there before another year passes." William gestured with his chin toward the new burying ground just visible to the east.

William hesitated, then made a decision. "Linus took Elisha to the Retreat in Hartford last week," he said.

Obed's mouth dropped open in shock, as William had expected. As if unsure his old ears had heard correctly, Obed asked in a low voice, "The Retreat for the Insane?" William nodded.

"Why, William?" It was as much a challenge as a question. "I know Elisha has been dispirited of late, that his reason has been affected. But such afflictions are often temporary. You know I myself was distracted for some weeks years ago, yet recovered. Couldn't Elisha have been kept at home, to spare Elizabeth and the rest of the family the–," he faltered, searching for a tactful word.

"'Shame' is the word you want," William said to Stow, but with no anger. "No, Obed, we can't continue to hide deranged relatives away – even cage them up like poor Phoebe Swathel." Everyone knew the tragic story of Durham innkeeper John Swathel's wife. She'd become so violently and dangerously insane that her husband for years had had to keep her chained up, first in the attic of his tavern, later in a little building erected specially for the purpose.

"Elisha has experienced spells of melancholy for years," William went on. He wanted Stow, an old friend of Elisha's, to understand what had led to this unpleasant step. "Each has been longer than the last, but he's always come out of them. But these past months he was overcome by a darkness that didn't lift. He claimed a black cloud had descended upon him. He wouldn't eat, wouldn't even rise from bed."

William stopped speaking abruptly. Stow could see in the tightness of his features, the unconscious clenching of his jaw, how much strain the situation was putting on the younger man.

"The doctors tried everything – bleeding, purges, emetics, plasters," William went on. "Mr. Noyes came to speak and pray with Elisha. He listened, but the pastor could have been speaking Chinese for all that Elisha seemed to understand. Nothing helped.

"In recent weeks he began complaining of an emptiness of the soul so painful only death could provide relief," William said with difficulty. "My mother-in-law was terrified he'd take his own life."

"I had no idea," the stunned Stow said quietly, now understanding why Elisha Coe's family had taken such drastic action. Suicide, or "self-murder" as it had been called until recently, carried a great stigma. Members of the older generation could remember a time when suicides were buried in unmarked graves.

"When I took Lizzy back to school in Hartford I rode out to consult with Dr. Eli Todd at the Retreat for the Insane," William said. He was speaking as much to himself as to Stow. "He believes insanity is an illness that can be treated with diet, activity, and medical procedures provided with kindness and respect by skilled physicians and assistants. In the seven years since he opened the Retreat, Dr. Todd said he has seen enough patients improve to offer cautious hope that Elisha may benefit from their treatment. Rather than being ashamed of taking him there, we thank God one of the few hospitals of this kind in the country is located so near."

William didn't mention the considerable cost of having Elisha cared for at the Retreat, which was a private facility. Elisha's own financial resources had been so depleted that the expense had to be borne by his two surviving sons – Asher, who'd long since moved to Ohio, and Linus – and his son-in-law William.

No help could be expected from Elisha's daughters. Delia remained at home, unmarried. She herself sometimes showed signs of mental imbalance, although nothing as extreme as her father.

Lucia Bliss had died in March of 1830, of complications from the birth of her second baby. The bereaved Charles Bliss had all he could do to run his tannery and provide for his two small sons. He had, however, promised to visit Elisha at the Retreat, just two miles from his home in Hartford, at every opportunity.

With William paying for Lizzy's schooling at the Hartford Female Seminary, contributing toward the cost of Elisha's stay at the Retreat for the Insane stretched his finances almost to the breaking point. But William was determined to be there for Elisha Coe in his hour of need – just as Elisha had been there for the Lyman family when they'd been threatened with the loss of their home after David's death.

"I suspect my brother bears the lion's share of the blame for this sorry state of affairs," Obed said grimly. There was also a hint of apology in the older man's voice, for no matter how far Obed might distance himself from Joshua, they were still flesh and blood.

The pause from labor having cooled William's body, he pulled his coat tightly around him. He didn't bother making even a perfunctory denial of Obed's statement, which was the simple truth.

"Losing his house and farm as the result of being betrayed by two men he believed honorable – one a friend for sixty years – would drive almost any man mad, let alone a proud one like Elisha," William said. He couldn't keep the bitterness from his words.

Obed shook his head. "I've long grieved that Joshua is an infidel," he said. "Yet I still believed he had a sense of loyalty and decency. He showed me to be a wrongheaded fool!" Obed spat the words out with contempt for both his brother and his own gullibility.

"Sometimes I wonder if he didn't succeed in conjuring up Satan that night so long ago, and sold his soul to him," Obed mused. "What else could explain his immoral and unethical conduct?" Both men stood in silence, mulling over the sordid tale of deception that stretched back over more than a decade.

In 1817 Joshua Stow had convinced Elisha Coe to join him and two others in signing a bond for $50,000 guaranteeing Middletown manufacturer Arthur Magill's faithful performance as cashier of the Middletown branch of the Bank of the United States. Three years later, examination of the bank's records revealed that Magill had fraudulently mismanaged his position by allowing a number of individuals – Joshua Stow among them – to illegally overdraw substantial sums from their accounts. It was revealed that Joshua had cooperated with Magill in his underhanded activities and helped him cover up the corruption.

Years of expensive litigation had followed, with Elisha Coe ultimately being held liable, as one of the signers of the bond, for more than $17,000. The case had gone all the way to the United States Supreme Court, where Elisha lost.

In 1827 Elisha had turned over his well-cultivated two-hundred-and-twenty-acre farm, his house, and his barn, to the

Bank of the United States, which sold them. Alma's father had been ruined financially, his reputation left in tatters.

Magill had gone to jail, after which, bankrupt, he'd gone to western New York. The Bank had also confiscated Joshua Stow's land.

"Still, for all the pain he's caused, I pity my brother," Obed said.

"So do I," William said at once, to Obed's surprise. "Losing a child is a terrible blow, to lose an only son an even greater tragedy. And Albert was a fine young man any father would be proud of."

"He took after his mother," Obed observed cynically. "It's been two years since Joshua took Albert to Ohio hoping to cure his consumption, only to leave him in a grave there. Yet my brother still mourns for Albert as if he'd died yesterday."

William said nothing more, recalling with shameful guilt how his sincere sadness upon learning of young Albert Stow's death had been followed by a spurt of malicious satisfaction that Joshua Stow, who'd caused pain to so many, had been grievously wounded. William had immediately been disgusted with himself. Only a pitiful excuse for a Christian would take pleasure in the suffering of any man, even one who for thirty years had been a thorn in William's side – as well as a source of grief for Alma and others he loved, which William considered a much greater offense.

As he spoke with Obed, out of the corner of his eye William saw Horace Skinner, a short, skinny farmer in his mid-forties, walking over to the barrel set up for the men to refresh themselves. Skinner raised the wooden stopper in the tap in the end of the barrel. He filled one of the tin cups provided for the men's use, replaced the stopper, then took a draught so large his cheeks bulged. A puzzled expression came over his sweaty, flushed face, followed by one of distasteful recognition. He swallowed the liquid with an effort.

"This is sweet cider!" Skinner exclaimed in an indignant voice that caught the attention of every other worker. "Is this your idea of a joke?" he demanded, rounding on William. "If so, it's not funny. We'll need plenty of rum to see us through this house-raising, especially on such a lowery day as this."

William had expected such a reaction, and answered in an even and reasonable tone. "The notion that laboring men require spirits to keep up their strength is false, Horace. I can testify to it personally. Sweet cider or cool water from the well will quench our thirsts."

"But we've always had spirits at house and barn-raisings," Elijah Crowell, a spare, balding man in his late fifties pointed out plaintively. "I can't recall one without them. What was good enough for my father and grandfather is good enough for me – and you."

"Your father and grandfather were subjects of the British Crown, but did that stop them from casting off political tyranny when their eyes were opened to its evils?" William replied mildly. "It's the same with alcohol – more and more we realize the toll it takes on men's bodies and souls. If we are to have any hope of achieving the perfection that our faith tells us will help hasten the Lord's second coming, we must liberate ourselves from the scourge of alcohol."

"You have the right to be a temperance man if it suits you, William," fired back Edward Turner, a burly man of about William's own age known for his quick temper. "But it's wrong to force your convictions on us by failing to supply the spirits that are as much a tool of a house-raising as hammers and saws." Most of the men had gravitated toward the escalating confrontation. The majority murmured and nodded in agreement with Turner.

William marveled at the power tradition exerted over men. They were determined to cling to the familiar practice, no matter how evil it had been shown to be.

"I prayed over this since the congregation charged me with building the parsonage," William said patiently. "I concluded it would be wrong for me to supply spirits for the house-raising. To do so would make me, and the church itself, party to the poisoning of the bodies and souls of my fellow men."

"You concluded!" snapped Turner. "This is a congregation, not a kingdom. You could at least have put it to a vote."

"A man doesn't decide matters of conscience by a vote," William answered evenly.

"How much harm can a mug of hard cider or rum do?" Elijah Crowell whined. "The men here aren't sots who beat their wives in drunken rages. They don't squander their money on liquor, or loiter at taverns. They don't neglect their livelihoods or let their families fall into poverty. It's a good old custom. Why take it away?" Crowell's voice began to quiver, and William was appalled to see tears in the older man's eyes, as if he were pleading for a friend's life.

"If we partake of alcohol, others who can't handle liquor will point to us and ask how great an evil can alcohol truly be, if the church-going drink it?" William answered earnestly. "When Satan works his evil through even so time-honored a practice, we must do away with it."

"You're risking the health of every man here, and casting doubt on his character, with your mulish insistence on total abstinence," Horace Skinner said, clearly disgusted with William's rhetoric. "If you're not going to provide rum, or at least hard cider, I'm done."

William responded with a steadfast gaze that he hoped conveyed principled commitment, with no suggestion of defiance or challenge.

After a full minute had passed, Skinner gathered up his tools and stalked off toward Obed Stow's house, where the women and children, their attention attracted by the sudden cessation of hammering and sawing, were watching uneasily. One by one the others followed Skinner. At last only four men were left standing with the dumbfounded William by the barely started house frame.

"You did the right thing," a voice said from behind William. It belonged to Deacon Prosper Augur, who stepped up beside him.

"I expected some would be unhappy," William said, trying to make sense of what had just happened. "I thought a few men might insist on fetching rum or hard cider from their homes. But I never imagined they would abandon almost to a man an enterprise undertaken for the good of the congregation."

"If the misery caused by alcohol were the result of a disease, people would be clamoring for all drinkers to be quarantined," Augur said. "No man would permit a small amount of spirits in his house any more than he would permit a small amount of smallpox. But this evil wears so pleasant and familiar a guise that they can't recognize it until it's too late – if ever." The old deacon sought to buck up William with a solid slap to his back, then set about picking up his tools.

"That was an inspiring stand for a principle," said Marvin Thomas, a relative newcomer to Middlefield. William shrugged dispiritedly, unwilling to accept praise for what he considered a complete failure on his part. He squatted down to begin collecting his own tools.

When Thomas remained standing next to William, he glanced up curiously at him. A head shorter and probably twenty years younger than William, Marvin Thomas was originally from the town of Haddam on the other side of Durham. He'd come to Middlefield seven years ago to marry Lucretia Miller Hubbard, a widow in her late forties. The new Mrs. Thomas had inherited the homestead of her father, Isaac Miller, when he died not long after the auction of David Lyman's estate.

The great difference in their ages, and the fact that control over the Miller property came to Marvin Thomas as a result of the marriage, had inevitably led to cynical speculation about his motives. But he'd proven himself an honorable man, a fond husband, and a solid member of the church. He was a recent convert to temperance.

"You know I share your conviction that alcohol is an evil that must be eradicated," Thomas said. William turned back to packing up his tools, but nodded to indicate he was listening; Thomas clearly had something on his mind.

"But a sickness of the spirit more vicious than intemperance eats at the soul of our entire nation: the abomination of slavery," Thomas said fervently.

William stopped abruptly and cocked his head to cast a sharp glance up at the younger man. He straightened up to give Marvin Thomas his full attention.

"Millions of our fellow men are held in chattel slavery, bought and sold like cattle. They are subjected to the most inhumane treatment, for no other reason than that their skins are of a darker hue than our own." The words tumbled forth from Thomas, as if he couldn't get them out fast enough.

"Slavery shames every American. As Christians we are doubly shamed, for many slaves are denied knowledge of our Savior, are denied the chance to seek their immortal soul's salvation. And this is done to them by men who claim to be followers of Jesus."

Thomas continued without giving William a chance to speak. "So long as Americans with black skins remain in chains, none of us can truly be free, nor rest easy in our consciences." Thomas almost seemed to grow taller as he made his impassioned plea. "Today you took a stand to free men from the invisible bondage of intemperance. I implore you to apply that same conviction to liberating millions of men, women, and children from an evil system that shackles their bodies and keeps their minds and souls in darkness." Thomas at last fell silent. He searched William's face closely for his reaction.

William's lower jaw jutted out slightly, and he ground his back teeth together while thoughtfully studying Thomas. The young man's eyes glowed with a combination of fervent conviction and moral outrage, with a hint of desperate pleading.

William had given little attention to the issue of slavery, for it was a dead letter in Connecticut. Slavery had been practiced in Connecticut since the earliest settlements, but the number of slaves had always been small. Connecticut's soil and climate weren't suited to crops like cotton or rice, which required huge numbers of hands to cultivate.

The few slaves with whom William had come into contact during his lifetime had worked as house servants or side-by-side in the fields with their owners. Now almost every Negro in the state was free, usually due to legislation providing for gradual manumission of slaves passed after the Revolution.

On the national level, the Missouri Compromise of 1820 had seemed to resolve the issue of slavery for the foreseeable future. Maine had been admitted to the Union as a free state, and Missouri as a slave one, thus keeping the number of free and slave states equal. The Compromise also banned slavery from any new states formed out of unsettled territory north of latitude 36 degrees, 30 minutes.

But William was aware that a small, yet slowly increasing number of people were deeply troubled by the continued existence of slavery in the United States. William knew as much as the average Northerner – which admittedly was not a great deal – about slavery in the South. It was unjust and harsh, but also was essential to the region's farming economy.

For more than a decade William had been consumed with fighting the intemperance that was damaging and destroying lives right in his own community. Now this idealistic young man was challenging him to lift his eyes, to join the crusade against an evil that, while it was taking place hundreds of miles from Connecticut and didn't touch William personally, was a far more monstrous work of the Devil than intemperance.

Watching William's eyes, Thomas felt confident that the seed he'd dropped had landed on fertile ground. "Here," he said, pulling a creased and dog-eared newspaper from inside his coat and holding it out to William. "Take this home and read it. It opened my mind and heart to the need for the people of Connecticut to actively concern ourselves with the wretched plight of slaves in the South. I hope it will do the same for you."

William silently took the paper, which he tucked inside his own coat with nothing more than a nod of acknowledgement. Today he'd tried to help fellow Christians accept a great truth that seemed as obvious to William as anything he'd ever known – only to be scorned and spurned by those he hoped to help. How could he refuse to at least hear out a man who sought to do the same for him?

Chapter Eighty-One

May, 1831
Middlefield

The evening was so chilly that William kindled a fire in the cast-iron stove he'd installed on the brownstone hearth of the fireplace in the parlor. The heat from the stove radiated out from its iron sides into the room, warming nearly the entire parlor with a much smaller amount of wood than would have been needed to keep a roaring blaze going in the fireplace. Two centuries of clearing trees to make land for crops and to supply fuel to heat homes and cook food had depleted Connecticut's forests, making wood increasingly expensive.

The family circle was nearly complete this evening. Absent were Lizzy, studying at the Hartford Female Seminary, and Sarah, now seventy-five, who'd retired to her chamber when dusk fell. Sarah's eyesight had deteriorated, so she now had difficulty reading in full daylight, and couldn't do so at all by the illumination of the whale-oil lamp on which William and Alma had splurged for the parlor.

Sometimes Sarah would sit up past sunset and have someone read to her from the Bible. Other times she sat knitting; after decades of practice she could deftly work the yarn around the needles to produce rows of perfect stitches almost without thinking, let alone seeing. Although she couldn't hear or see her family well, knowing that they surrounded her was a source of contentment.

Tonight the unseasonable chill and dampness had set Sarah's joints aching. With David's help she had slowly, painfully climbed the stairs to her chamber. William missed her powerful presence in the room. He admired his mother for the courage with which she uncomplainingly adjusted to the afflictions of advancing age.

Alma sat in a chair beside the small round table on which the whale-oil lamp stood. She was reading her well-worn Bible, searching, William suspected, for words to help her endure the misfortunes that had befallen her family.

It had been terrible enough for Alma to watch her father deteriorate from a confident, proud, successful man into a broken mind within a fragile shell of a body that didn't seem long for this earth. But Alma was also assailed by guilt for agreeing to have Elisha Coe removed from his home and cared for by strangers at the Retreat for the Insane, even though she knew it was best for him and for his family. Alma also struggled mightily to forgive the man she held most responsible for this tragedy: Joshua Stow.

Eight-year-old Sally was sitting cross-legged on the floor in front of the stove, teaching four-year-old Adeline to work simple stitches on a pair of their grandmother's knitting needles. David, now ten, was sitting beside them, helping six-year-old Elihu sound out words of multiple syllables from a lesson in Webster's blue-backed speller, the same copy Phineas had with him that day in the schoolhouse when William had forced him to face up to the affliction that would ultimately kill him.

Little Elihu came down so frequently with colds, earaches, and other ailments that William had decided against sending him to the common school. But having David work with him on reading and with numbers, which Elihu also loved, would serve him just as well.

William was stretched out full-length on the oversize settle he'd had specially made to comfortably accommodate his tall frame, as he'd told Alma so many years ago that he one day would, The spectacles he'd recently begun to use for reading – small oval pieces of glass in a steel frame perched on his nose – would have been the casual observer's only hint that William was edging past middle age, for otherwise he looked a decade younger than his forty-seven years.

William unfolded the newspaper Marvin Thomas had thrust upon him that morning. He saw without surprise that it was a copy of *The Liberator*, a weekly that had begun publication at the start of the year in Boston, edited by William Lloyd Garrison. William had met Garrison briefly two years earlier in Bennington, where he was editing what proved to be a short-lived newspaper dedicated to the temperance cause and the gradual emancipation of all slaves.

William recalled Garrison as a thin, be-spectacled man who looked older than his twenty-four years due to a hairline that had receded to the crown of his head. During a chat about their mutual interest in temperance Garrison had displayed an intense conviction that made William think of a bowstring pulled as taut as possible.

William heard later that Garrison had spent time in jail somewhere, Baltimore perhaps, for libeling a slave trader in another newspaper he was editing. Thus it had come as no surprise when he heard Garrison was in Boston putting out yet one more publication.

From the masthead William saw he held the first issue of *The Liberator*, published January 1, 1831. He began reading Garrison's address to the public, in which he railed against Northerners' apathy, even hostility, to the cause of ending Southern slavery:

> During my recent tour for the purpose of exciting the minds of the people by a series of discourses on the subject of slavery, every place that I visited gave fresh evidence of the fact, that a greater revolution in public sentiment was to be effected in the free states – and particularly in New-England – than at the south. I found contempt more bitter, opposition more active, detraction more relentless, prejudice more stubborn, and apathy more frozen, than among slave owners themselves.

William almost squirmed in embarrassment at the all-too-accurate description of the attitude of most in the land of his birth. Reading on, he learned that Garrison now endorsed the immediate abolition of slavery. This was a profound change from his previous position that emancipation should be a gradual process. Garrison's apology for that error in judgment was followed by a ringing personal declaration of war upon slavery that took William's breath away:

> On this subject, I do not wish to think, or speak, or write with moderation. No! No! Tell a man whose house is on fire, to give a moderate alarm; tell him to moderately rescue his wife from the hands of the ravisher; tell the mother to gradually extricate her babe from the fire into which it has fallen: – but urge me not to use moderation in a cause like the present. I am in earnest – I will not equivocate – I will not excuse – I will not retreat a single inch – AND I WILL BE HEARD.

Here in black-and-white was the challenge Marvin Thomas had put to William that day: to acknowledge an evil even greater than intemperance that, although taking place far from Connecticut, he as a Christian and an American had a moral obligation to combat. In Garrison William recognized a kindred spirit, a man who would never be satisfied with half-measures, who would let nothing short of death prevent him from pursuing a cause he believed to be righteous. William knew at that moment that conscience and faith and patriotism required him to answer Garrison's call, to join the fight to eliminate slavery throughout the United States – and to be willing to accept the consequences, whatever they might be.

Chapter Eighty-Two

September, 1831
Hartford, Connecticut

By the time Miss Harriet Beecher finished teaching the composition lesson, Lizzy's stomach was growling, for it was almost noon. Lizzy closed her textbook, stood up, and exited the classroom in the Hartford Female Seminary's fine two-story building. The structure had been erected four years ago on Pearl Street through Catharine Beecher's phenomenal drive and determination.

Lizzy's fellow students came from throughout New England and far beyond. They included her cousin Katy Brush of Burlington, Vermont, the daughter of Lizzy's late Aunt Esther, and Anna Bliss, sister of her late Aunt Lucia's husband Charles. The presence of these relatives, along with her second cousin Harriet Beecher, meant the Hartford Female Seminary was almost a family outpost for Lizzy.

Lizzy passed through the school doors into the mellow sunshine of a September afternoon. She wore a dress of red-and-white striped cotton, with a full skirt that fell from a wide waistband to within a couple inches of the ground. The "leg-of-mutton" sleeves were large and puffy from shoulder to wrist, where they ended in a tight band.

Around her neck Lizzy wore a lace-edged kerchief fastened with a cameo brooch. Her golden hair was parted in the middle, and curled into large, soft rolls on each side of her face above her ears. Two wide rows of white, lace-edged ruffle trim on the white day cap tied under her chin formed a delicate frame for Lizzy's face.

Lizzy lifted her skirt with one hand to avoid tripping as she descended the half dozen brownstone steps. She waited by the gate in the wooden fence that surrounded the building for Miss Beecher, who'd stopped to speak with another student.

After a morning spent in the classroom, Lizzy was looking forward to the brisk walk to her lodgings at Mrs. Strong's house on Main Street. There a hearty dinner would be waiting for her and the other young ladies who boarded there, including her cousin Hattie, as Miss Harriet Beecher became to Lizzy the moment they were outside of school. Only a year apart in age, Hattie and Lizzy had become as close as sisters in the year and a half since Lizzy had returned to the Seminary in the spring of 1830.

Hattie finally emerged from the building. "At last!" Lizzy groused good-naturedly. "I was going to start gnawing the bark off that tree!"

The two young women strolled east on Pearl Street. Hattie was shorter than Lizzy, with a softer version of the Lyman nose, high cheekbones, small eyes, and a full mouth. Her dress was similar to Lizzy's, but of a chocolate color that accented her glossy brown hair.

Hattie wasn't particularly pretty, but she had a pert quality, a special brightness and quickness of mind. After making his young cousin's acquaintance, William Lyman had likened Hattie affectionately to a chickadee – a small but lively and curious bird with handsome black and white plumage. The comparison had delighted Hattie, who insisted that if she were a chickadee, then Lizzy was a swan. Lizzy did glide with a natural grace as they reached Hartford's busy Main Street, which ran parallel to the Connecticut River, visible a few hundred yards away.

Almost directly in front of the young women, across Main Street, stood Hartford's impressive four-story brick-and-brownstone State House. It was crowned with a white cupola, topped with a gold-leafed dome supporting a gilded statue of the figure of Justice.

Hartford was a prosperous, progressive, even visionary city, home to several other pioneering institutions besides the Hartford Female Seminary. These included Washington College, only the second institution of higher learning in Connecticut; the Asylum for the Deaf and Dumb, the first school in the nation for the education of children who couldn't hear; and the Retreat for the Insane, where Elisha Coe was still a patient, three months after being admitted.

As they came within view of the Strong house, Lizzy stopped abruptly in her tracks at the unexpected sight of her parents in front of her lodgings. William and Alma were standing with their backs to the street, next to the horses from which they'd just dismounted.

Once the moment of surprise passed, Lizzy broke into a smile of pure joy. Hiking up her skirts she ran across Main Street, dashing between two carriages, deaf to Hattie's warning to beware of traffic.

Alma turned first and saw Lizzy running toward them so fast that her bonnet was in danger of flying off her head. Alma touched William's elbow, and he turned around just in time to brace himself for the impact of the ecstatic Lizzy throwing her arms around his neck as if she were a girl of ten instead of a young lady of nineteen.

Lizzy hugged and kissed Alma, stooping slightly just as she had stood on tip-toe to embrace William. Her parents made a handsome couple, Lizzy thought, especially dressed in their best clothes for this visit to the city. William was dignified in a black cutaway coat. Alma's dress was a deep burgundy, her simple white bonnet trimmed with a row of ruffles. A stranger would have been surprised to learn that Alma, with her still-smooth skin, had marked her forty-sixth birthday, or that broad-shouldered William was near fifty.

"What are you doing–," Lizzy started to ask. She stopped talking when a young man jumped down from the seat of a covered chaise.

"Cousin Charles!" Lizzy exclaimed in delight as the young man made a bee-line for her. Charles Mills was also second cousin to Lizzy, but on the Coe side of her family.

Lizzy and Charles exchanged decorous kisses on the cheek. But the intimacy with which they gazed into each other's eyes, and the manner in which Charles seized Lizzy's hand, left no doubt they felt something stronger than the usual affection between cousins.

Hattie by now had caught up with Lizzy at the Strong house. She'd never before seen this tall, spare young man with the narrow face and coarse brown hair. But she'd heard enough from Lizzy to realize this was her dear Cousin Charles. Hattie also knew from Lizzy how the cousins had met and become so close.

Charles Mills was the grandson of Alma Lyman's Uncle Ebenezer Coe, who'd moved to New Jersey during the Revolution. Lizzy had met Charles, about the same age as she, when he'd come to Connecticut this past spring to inspect Yale College, with an eye toward possibly enrolling as part of his plan to become a minister.

During his visit, Charles, who didn't enjoy robust health, developed a debilitating fever. His Cousin Alma's family had taken him in for what proved to be an unexpectedly lengthy illness. Lizzy, home from the Seminary during much of Charles's convalescence, had taken responsibility for nursing him back to health.

The cousins had spent hours in stimulating conversation, discussing history, literature, astronomy, religion, and politics. Lizzy was delighted to discover that, unlike most young men she knew, Charles wasn't daunted by her advanced education, but found it greatly appealing. That Charles was already family, if distantly related, somehow made Lizzy more at ease in his presence.

Charles had enjoyed being the object of Lizzy's ministrations. And Lizzy had found great satisfaction in her ability to alleviate Charles's physical pain and to raise his spirits.

The experience had kindled a romantic spark that had become a warm, steady glow of affection by the time Lizzy returned to the Seminary. Charles had gone home to New Jersey, where he'd enrolled in Princeton, despite preferring Yale's proximity to his beautiful, accomplished, affectionate Connecticut cousin.

Charles and Lizzy hadn't seen each other since, but they'd exchanged a flurry of letters. Now, as if by magic, here he was, right in front of Lizzy, gazing at her with near-adoration.

The moment was shattered when from the chaise a scratchy, quavering voice called out, "Charles!" Charles released Lizzy's hand and hurried to the chaise. She watched him help down an elderly man, clearly once tall but now bowed by arthritis. The aged stranger's close resemblance to her Grandfather Coe left no doubt in Lizzy's mind that this was Elisha Coe's older brother Ebenezer.

"Grandfather, permit me to present to you my dear cousin, Elizabeth Coe Lyman," Charles said, emphasizing Lizzy's middle name. Ebenezer leaned on a walking stick with one gnarled hand, but extended the other to take Lizzy's in his. Lizzy bent over to give the old gentleman a warm kiss on the cheek. "Welcome home, Uncle," she said with a brightness that pleased Ebenezer.

"It's high time I came back to the land of my birth," Ebenezer responded, dispensing with meaningless amenities to cut to the heart of his concern as the very old often do. "My generation has all but passed away – I lost two brothers in the last three years alone. I reckoned I'd better make the trip now if I wanted to once more see my sister Hannah, who I found unwell, and my little brother Elisha."

Ebenezer placed a shaky hand on his grandson's arm. "Young Charles here was good enough to make the sacrifice of leaving his studies at Princeton to bring me," he said. He spoke the last without a trace of irony, so that Lizzy couldn't tell if he was aware of the special affection she shared with Charles.

Lizzy felt uneasy at Ebenezer's mention of her grandfather, but she realized he must be aware of Elisha's mental state. William and Alma would never have brought him here without having frankly informed him about his brother's condition.

Hattie was hanging back uncertainly, not wanting to intrude on this reunion of Coe relatives. When William spied her, he called out, "Cousin Hattie! Come join us and round out the other side of the family circle!" He walked over to escort Hattie to the group.

William formally introduced Hattie to Charles and Ebenezer. He made a point to the latter of the fact that Hattie was the daughter of the esteemed Reverend Lyman Beecher, and also a teacher at the Hartford Female Seminary. Both facts clearly impressed Ebenezer.

"I don't know about you, Uncle Ebenezer, but I feel humble in the presence of such knowledge and accomplishment," William said, beaming with pride at Lizzy, Hattie, and Charles. "Who would've thought Lymans and Coes would produce such fine scholars?"

William's praise sparked an unexpected pang of envy in Hattie. He clearly considered the young women's intellectual achievements as valuable as those of Charles Mills. Hattie couldn't help but compare William's attitude to her father's. On more than one occasion, when Hattie had done something exceedingly well, Lyman Beecher's response had been to lament that she hadn't been born a boy. Hattie doubted William Lyman had ever wished Lizzy was a boy.

"We'll be staying at your Uncle Bliss's house tonight," William told Lizzy. "Can you join us for supper?" When she nodded her acceptance, Charles Mills glowed with pleasure.

Lizzy sat beside Charles that night as a total of fourteen Bliss, Coe, and Lyman family members gathered in the parlor of Charles Bliss's home. The red house, with a lean-to addition on the back, had been built before the Revolution by Charles Bliss's grandfather. It was shaded by towering maple trees as old as the house. Dwellings like it were disappearing from Hartford, as the city sprawled ever farther west, causing old structures to be razed to make room for new ones.

The Bliss house was located close to Main Street, with a view of the stone buildings of Washington College on a rise to the south. The site would have been most pleasant, had it not been near the meandering Hog River – so named because it was heavily polluted by generations of tradesmen like tanner Charles Bliss and his father before him dumping the refuse from their livelihoods into it. The Lymans, Charles Mills, and Ebenezer Coe politely refrained from commenting on the stench rising from the river. The others around the table had long ago become oblivious to the smell, just as farmers became so used to the odor of manure they no longer noticed it.

The Bliss family members included Charles, his parents, a bachelor brother and two spinster sisters, and Charles's sons: his namesake, Charles, now four, and Henry, not yet two. Looking at the boys, Lizzy couldn't help but think of her Aunt Lucia's grief at leaving them to grow up without her, knowing they would have no memory of her, and that however deeply her husband mourned her, a new wife would eventually fill her place in his bed and at his table.

"How goes the work on the parsonage?" Charles Bliss asked. William shook his head slowly to signal a negative response until he finished swallowing a bite of oyster pie and could speak. "A couple members of the congregation agreed to return to work on it without any alcohol, but the rest remain mulishly stubborn," William said. "I've had to pay out of my own pocket to get most of the work done. And still it won't be finished this year," he concluded resignedly.

"How is my father?" Alma asked her brother-in-law. Charles made regular visits to Ebenezer at the Retreat for the Insane.

Charles shook his head sadly. "No better, no worse, when I saw him two weeks ago. The doctors and nurses treat him with great kindness and patience and respect. They do all they can to get him up and walking about the grounds, to interest him in eating, in reading, or in joining some of the other patients in light diversions. But despite their ministrations, he's shown little improvement." Charles was uncomfortable making his report, but those going to the Retreat tomorrow needed to know what to expect.

"He lies abed for hours in silence, his eyes open but unseeing, his mind shrouded in darkness," Charles continued with difficulty. "When I've been able to induce him to converse, he talks over and over about his multiple misfortunes and sorrows, about the deaths of so many of his children, of the loss of the fortune and reputation he spent his life building, of the betrayal of a friend he trusted."

Alma's features twitched as she fought to control her emotions. Watching her mother, Lizzy made up her mind about something she'd been considering since she learned the reason for her parents' visit. She placed a hand gently atop her mother's. "I want to go with you to see Grandfather tomorrow," she said.

Alma didn't object, as Lizzy had expected, out of a desire to spare her daughter the difficult experience. Instead she turned her hand palm upwards to squeeze Lizzy's tightly in gratitude.

Chapter Eighty-Three

September, 1831
Hartford

The next morning Lizzy joined Charles and Ebenezer in the chaise for the trip to the Retreat for the Insane, located in a pleasant rural neighborhood of farms, cultivated fields, and meadows in the south end of Hartford. The Retreat itself was an enormous structure atop a hillside. The three-story center building was flanked by two-story wings, each of which terminated in an identical three-story structure, creating a pleasing sense of order and symmetry. The plain stone exterior had been coated with brilliant white cement, which created an airy, almost cheerful atmosphere.

The grounds were attractively landscaped with fruit and ornamental trees and gardens. The area around the building bustled with activity, as patients who were permitted to do so walked about or rode out on horseback or in carriages.

Not a word was spoken during the entire trip to the Retreat. But as Charles reined in the horse, he turned to Ebenezer and blurted out, "Grandfather, I wish I could persuade you to change your mind about this visit. Wouldn't you prefer to remember your brother Elisha as he was when you last saw him, rather than as he's become, through no fault of his own?"

Ebenezer studied his grandson for a long moment, then, having apparently made up his mind about something, spoke. "I was younger than you when Redcoats captured me during the Battle of Long Island – with your father's Uncle Elihu, God rest his soul," Ebenezer said the last with a nod to Lizzy.

"They put me in one of those hellish ships they had the gall to call a prison," the old veteran continued in a level voice. "I saw men and boys subjected to the tortures of the damned – crowded together in frigid weather with no heat and nothing but rags to cover their bodies, starved to skeletons, forced to lie in their own filth and vomit, covered with vermin, ravaged by smallpox and the flux and camp fever without any medical care, taunted and tormented by the Hessian scum assigned to guard them."

Ebenezer paused for a moment, wrestling with memories he'd struggled for more than half a century to suppress. "I watched some escape into madness – and I envied them," he said. "I likely would have followed them, if I hadn't been one of the lucky few who were paroled after a few months. I think I can endure the sight of my brother, whatever his state of mind."

Lizzy and Charles were silent, appalled by Ebenezer's horrific revelation. Charles had sometimes heard his grandfather describe the terror of going into battle. Never until now had Ebenezer mentioned the nightmare of captivity.

Charles nodded in surrender, and got out of the carriage. He helped first Lizzy, then his grandfather, down to the ground.

Following directions provided by one of the matrons, the visitors found Elisha Coe, but not in his room as they'd expected. He was sitting on a bench in a courtyard, nicely laid out with flowering gardens and surrounded, for security, by a high brick wall. A nurse hovered watchfully at a discreet distance.

Lizzy and Charles Bliss were slightly ahead of the others, and so it was they Elisha first saw when he turned at the sound of approaching footsteps. As he got slowly to his feet, Lizzy observed sadly that, while her grandfather still stood straight, months of inactivity and poor eating had turned his once well-developed muscles into slack flab. But her dispiriting first impression vanished when Elisha flashed a broad smile of greeting, shook Charles's hand, then proceeded to hug Lizzy warmly.

"It's so good to see you!" Elisha exclaimed, his voice weaker than Lizzy remembered it, but his enthusiasm genuine. Lizzy was perplexed; this wasn't what her Uncle Bliss had prepared them to expect.

"But where are the boys?" Elisha asked. Lizzy opened her mouth to explain that David and Elihu were ill with chickenpox. But before she could speak, her grandfather chastised her gently, "I know Henry is but a month old, but you might have brought Charles."

Cold goose flesh rose up on Lizzy's arms as she realized her grandfather had taken her for her Aunt Lucia, his daughter now dead more than a year. She was speechless, paralyzed with shock – as was Charles.

William and Alma approached. "Daughter!" Elisha cried with delight, enfolding Alma in a hug. Alma's features registered astonishment at her father's recognition, then crumpled into an expression of equal parts joy and pain. Tears escaped from her tightly closed eyes.

Releasing Alma, Elisha looked her up and down for a moment with approval. He turned to heartily shake hands with William, who was as stunned as everyone else.

"I'm so glad you've come today," Elisha said to his son-in-law. "Could you help Linus supervise the sowing of the wheat while I'm away at the General Assembly?"

William's open mouth moved slightly, but he couldn't make a sound. Elisha was referring to a time more than a decade in the past. William glanced at Alma, whose happiness at her father's recognition of her was fading as she absorbed the import of Elisha's words.

"I . . . I . . . ," William stuttered, as Elisha waited for an answer. He was saved from concocting a reply when Elisha's gaze strayed to focus on something behind him. William turned, and saw that Ebenezer, walking slowly and leaning heavily on his grandson Charles's arm, had at last caught up with the rest of them.

"Ebenezer!" Elisha cried, his voice cracking with joy. Tears began to stream down his cheeks as he stepped forward to embrace his older brother so tightly that Ebenezer's joints hurt. But Ebenezer ignored the pain, so thrilled was he at being reunited with the little brother he hadn't seen in more than twenty years. The two stood locked together for nearly a minute, both weeping unashamedly.

At last Elisha stepped back. He swiped away tears, and beamed with happiness as he examined Ebenezer. "I feared never to see you alive again in this world," Elisha said. "But you're so thin, and bowed! Did the damned Redcoats do this to you? How did you manage to escape? How long have you been back in Connecticut?"

Ebenezer turned so pale at his brother's question that William feared the old man would have an apopletic fit. But Ebenezer recovered almost immediately from his shock, and simply shook his head. "I'll tell you about it some other time," he said. "For now I want only to savor being reunited with you after so long apart."

Ebenezer sat down on the bench, and gestured for Elisha to join him. The brothers proceeded to chat about friends and family long dead as if they were alive and well.

Unaccustomed to so much physical, mental, and emotional stimulation, Elisha quickly tired. After no more than twenty minutes the nurse who'd observed the reunion noticed his fatigue and came over to escort Elisha to his room to rest. He bade everyone farewell casually, as if he would see them again later in the day.

Once Elisha was gone, his visitors stood in silence, drained by the bizarre experience of interacting with Elisha as he'd slipped from one period in his past to another. The episode had been disturbing, yet oddly comforting, for Elisha had been his old affectionate, confident self.

Alma clung to William's arm, wanting to cry but somehow unable to. Ebenezer, who'd come expecting nothing, had derived genuine pleasure from reliving his youth with his brother, if only for a few moments. Lizzy, once she recovered from the trauma of being mistaken for her dead aunt, had responded with deep compassion. She'd willingly entered into her grandfather's delusion, assuring Elisha all was well with her and his grandsons.

At last Charles Bliss broke the silence. "I had no idea his condition had changed so radically," he said with a hint of apology. "Perhaps Dr. Todd can explain it."

Half an hour later they all sat in the Retreat's main hall, waiting for Dr. Eli Todd, the hospital's founder and superintendent. A handsome man in his sixties approached them with the brisk stride of someone needed in three places at once, yet still exuding compassion.

The physician seized a straight-backed chair from against a far wall. He placed it firmly in front of Elisha's family, then sat down facing them.

Charles Bliss introduced Lizzy, Charles Mills, and Ebenezer, then asked directly, "Doctor, when I visited my father-in-law a fortnight ago he was in a black despair, scarcely speaking. Today he was a different man, almost the father and brother we once knew, yet – deluded about people's identities and even what year it is."

Dr. Todd nodded understandingly. "Colonel Coe began to emerge from his deep melancholy about three days ago. Why, we can't say, but it became evident from his conversation that he's retreated in his mind to times of greater contentment in his life. Despite his delusions, I consider this a sign of improvement. I'm hopeful we'll be able to persuade him to eat better, to assume a regimen that will give him a sense of order and control. In time perhaps his mind may heal sufficiently to cope with his present situation."

"Has he been bled?" Ebenezer demanded bluntly. Everyone knew bleeding was a sovereign remedy for afflictions of the brain.

"Indeed he has been, Mr. Coe," Dr. Todd assured him patiently. "We use other traditional methods as well, including emetics and herbs. But we put our greatest hope in 'moral treatment.' We believe deranged individuals are not depraved, but suffer from an illness of the brain that can often be improved and sometimes even cured. In the tranquil setting of the Retreat, we care for them with dignity and respect, encourage them to participate in physical and mental activities to the extent they can."

"Do you think my father might recover sufficiently to come home?" Alma asked eagerly. William frowned, but said nothing. Alma's mother herself wasn't in good health, worn down by the constant work and worry of months of caring for Elisha at home. And Elizabeth Coe had her hands full with Alma's sister Delia, whose moods were so extreme they at times seemed like seizures. It was becoming increasingly clear that Delia was mentally ill as well.

Elisha would have to make a complete recovery before there could be any discussion of bringing him home – on that point William knew he'd have to be adamant. Although keeping Elisha in the Retreat was putting a severe financial strain on his relatives, William believed it was worth the sacrifice to have him cared for by compassionate professionals in the forefront of the treatment of mental disease.

Dr. Todd studied Alma with sympathetic understanding; he'd heard the same question countless times during the more than a decade since he'd helped establish the Retreat. He got to his feet, clearly needing to move on to his next stop.

"I can't promise Colonel Coe will continue to improve, let alone recover fully," he said gently, speaking to the entire family. "But I can promise we'll do everything in our power to help him make as much progress as possible."

It wasn't the answer Alma, or any of them wanted to hear, but they knew it was an honest one. "We're very grateful," William said for all of them. Dr. Todd nodded in acknowledgement, then turned and headed out the door, leaving Elisha Coe's family to make what sense they could of the day's unexpected, unsettling events.

Chapter Eighty-Four

March, 1833
Middlefield

It was usually Alma who wrote to far-flung family members about what was occurring back home – for to many who'd left, no matter how far they'd traveled, no matter how many years had passed, Connecticut would always be home. But this was one letter William had to compose himself.

"Dear Sister Sally," he wrote with one of the steel nib pens that had replaced quills. The sheet of paper rested on the drop leaf of the desk at which he and his father before him had penned mundane accounts and vital communications for a total of nearly fifty years. "Although it can come as no surprise, I know you'll nonetheless be deeply grieved to learn that our cherished mother has exchanged this mortal world for the brighter one promised by our Redeemer. She died on February 28."

William dipped the nib into an inkwell, marveling at the coincidence of Sarah dying on the eighteenth anniversary of David's death in 1815. His mother's health had been failing steadily since early winter, but she'd retained her reason to the very end.

In her last hours on the morning of February 28, Sarah had found a fitting symmetry in the idea of sharing with David the same date of death, just as they had shared so much in life. As she lingered into the evening, she made a small joke about hastening her departure so as not to miss what she said was clearly the "appointed" date for her passing.

Several neighbors who'd come to take turns sitting with Sarah had been nonplussed by her candor about her imminent death. But

Sarah, who all her life had deftly read the hearts and minds of others and helped them plumb the depths of their thoughts and emotions, wasn't about to dissemble about her own feelings as she lay on her deathbed. She was ready to answer the Lord's summons – indeed, William knew in his heart that despite the blessings and joy his mother had given and received since David's death, she'd been ready every day for the past eighteen years.

William briefly recounted the details of their mother's final days, knowing Alma would write soon with a fuller account. "Polly arrived in time to be with Mama at the end," he wrote. "You were much in her thoughts and prayers in her last hours. It was her fondest wish to see you once more and assure you of her love. But she understood that the great distance and deep snows would prevent your arrival before her passing."

Sarah had been buried beside David, in what was now called the North Burying Ground, to distinguish it from the graveyard opened not long ago near the Middlefield meetinghouse. One of the first to be interred in the new cemetery had been Elisha Coe.

Elisha had died on December 1, 1831, in the Retreat for the Insane. He'd never returned home, despite the prayers of family and friends and the Retreat staff's compassionate treatment.

Alma's brother Linus had put a notice in the *Middlesex Gazette* stating that Colonel Elisha Coe had died "at the Retreat in Hartford." The same words were included in the inscription on Elisha's gravestone. William had approved of Linus's candor, which declared that Elisha Coe's family wasn't embarrassed by his affliction or ashamed of having sought care for him at the Retreat.

Elisha's epitaph also named five children who'd preceded him in death, three within a single year. "Frank, kind & benevolent, he was a friend to man," it read, followed by verses that conveyed the anguish of his last years:

> To feeling minds no pangs so keen
> Oh God my King as mental pain
> Drop then a tear thou passing friend
> Calm be your days, soon here to end.

Alma found comfort in having her mother still alive in the world. But he, William thought suddenly, was now an orphan. Not a term ordinarily applied to a man near fifty, it nonetheless expressed his feelings in the days immediately following his mother's death.

Sarah had been a living reminder of the time when William was a member of a large, loving, energetic, occasionally overwhelming family, well cared for, as secure as a child could be in a world fraught with uncertainty. With his mother gone, William felt as he had when, as a boy, he stood knee-deep in the waters of Long Island Sound in Guilford. A wave had washed in and retreated, sucking the sand from beneath his bare feet without warning, throwing him off balance. Sarah's death had removed part of the foundation of his life, and it would take time for him to regain his equilibrium.

William had wept at his mother's passing, but as he told Alma that day when they sat before the gravestones of Phineas and Adeline, he was crying for himself, for his pain, for his loss. There was nothing in the life, the death, or the eternal happiness beyond the grave that William was certain Sarah Comstock Lyman now enjoyed, over which to shed tears.

Now there remained alive just three members of the Lyman family that at its largest had numbered a dozen: David and Sarah's first-born, Polly Robinson, up in Vermont; Sally Miller out in New York; and William. Alanson, they'd heard, had died the previous summer, in Ontario in Canada, where he'd moved after spending less than a decade in New York.

William roused himself from his morbid musings. He signed the letter and waited for his signature to dry. He folded the paper down into a rectangle the size of his palm. After sealing it closed with a dollop of hot wax, he turned it over and addressed it to "Mrs. Abner Miller, Westmoreland, New York."

Chapter Eighty-Five

June, 1834
Middlefield

Although exhausted from twelve hours working in the fields under a brutal late June sun, William couldn't fall asleep. The night was oppressively hot and sticky, even though he was naked in bed, covered from the waist down by only a light cotton sheet. One or more of the fierce mosquitoes that bred prolifically in the Coginchaug swamp seemed always to be buzzing annoyingly in William's ear or inflicting sharp bites that kept him scratching fitfully.

After tossing and turning for what the chiming of the tall clock downstairs told him was at least three hours, William dozed off – only to be awakened within what seemed a matter of minutes by the need to urinate. With a soft sigh of exasperation he untangled his legs from the sheet, then rose quietly so as not to awaken Alma, who somehow had managed to at last fall asleep.

In the dark William felt for the trousers he'd laid across the back of a chair beside the bed. He slipped them on, pulling the suspenders attached to them up over his bare shoulders. He fumbled around on the floor until he located his shoes, which he carried to the top of the stairs, where he sat down to put them on.

The night was moonless, but William had no difficulty finding his way down the staircase and through the rooms in the darkness. He opened the kitchen door carefully so as not awaken anyone else in the house who might have had the good fortune to somehow fall asleep, leaving it slightly ajar after he stepped into the yard.

It was no cooler outside than in. William was perspiring heavily, but the air was so laden with moisture that the sweat couldn't evaporate, leaving his skin feeling slightly slimy. The sky was clear, but the atmosphere was so humid that it dulled the luster of the stars, which were outshone by hundreds of fireflies flashing their yellow lights in the trees and bushes. Crickets chirped with almost manic cheeriness.

William paused for a second to let his eyes adjust to the slightly greater amount of light before starting down the well-worn path to the outhouse just inside the stone wall that enclosed the homelot. The privy was situated at one end of a long, deep copse of towering lilacs; when the bushes were in bloom, the scent of the cascading lavender and white blossoms helped mask the stench.

William had taken just a few steps when his stomach instinctively tightened. The outline of what might be a man's head and shoulders appeared just below eye level toward the back of the yard, about ten feet to the side of the outhouse. For a moment William thought his sleep-starved senses were playing tricks on him. Then he heard a soft rustling of lilac branches, a sound he ordinarily would have dismissed as caused by a breeze blowing through them – except the night air was still as death.

"Who's there?" William challenged in a voice loud enough to carry to the end of the yard but that he hoped wouldn't disturb anyone in the house. When there was no response, he assumed he'd surprised a sneak thief who would take to his heels as soon as William moved closer.

Suddenly out of the darkness, a male voice, tentative with uncertainty and fear, said in a hushed tone, "We come from de stone house wit de heart an' de diamond." There was the sound of feet rustling through the grass, and then William, peering hard into the darkness, could discern the approach of a man a few inches shorter than himself. The stranger's skin was the color of ebony, which explained why he'd been nearly invisible at a distance on this inky black night.

William inhaled sharply in surprise and held it as his brain processed this unexpected development. Clearly this man, who looked to be in his mid-twenties, was a slave fleeing his Southern owner via the "Underground Railroad," as the network of safe houses staffed by "conductors" had come to be called.

Those involved in the illegal and unpopular work of helping fugitive slaves revealed their names, even to those they aided, only when unavoidable. The conductor who sent this fugitive had managed to identify himself to William without giving his name. In the nearby town of Wallingford stood a brownstone house distinctive for the spade, heart, club, and diamond cut into the outside of a wall. The carvings were the mischievous retaliation of some Irish stonemasons for the owner's disapproval of their card playing while building the structure. The fugitive's reference to the odd features told William he'd been sent by Nathan Hall. William knew Hall was an abolitionist, but until this moment he hadn't realized he aided runaways.

William had remained silent so long that he saw the wariness in the black man's eyes threatening to turn into panic. "You're safe here," William reassured him hastily. The man's body sagged with relief.

Suddenly William caught in his mind the echo of the fugitive's words – he'd said "we". Before William could ask, a woman of about the same age as the man, considerably shorter and with skin the color of chocolate, emerged from the darkness behind the unexpected visitor. She fixed William with a look of weary yet forthright appeal.

William stared at the couple, thinking of how he'd come to this moment. Since the day Marvin Thomas handed him the first issue of *The Liberator*, events hundreds of miles away had impressed upon William the urgent necessity of emancipation. The first occurred in the summer of 1831, just months after Garrison started *The Liberator*. A Virginia slave named Nat Turner had led an uprising of more than seventy slaves and free Negroes who killed nearly sixty white men, women, and children before their rebellion was crushed. Turner had been captured and executed.

The grisly episode had traumatized the nation. The South saw it as a wake-up call to enact more oppressive restrictions on slaves and free blacks alike. Abolitionists viewed it as incontrovertible evidence of the bloody fate awaiting a country that continued to allow the sin of human bondage within its borders.

Shameful incidents in Connecticut had testified to Garrison's characterization of New Englanders as indifferent to the evils of slavery and bigoted against free Negroes in their midst. In 1831 a proposal to establish in New Haven a "Negro college" to instruct free black youths in both academic and manual skills had been rejected by the city's voters, with seven hundred against, only four in favor.

In 1833, Quaker teacher Prudence Crandall had admitted a black student to her private girl's school in the town of Canterbury. When local residents protested, Miss Crandall responded by turning her school into one for black girls only. Miss Crandall's neighbors had retaliated by polluting her well, barring her students from attending church, refusing to sell her food, and vandalizing the building. The Connecticut General Assembly had passed legislation to close the school. Miss Crandall had been jailed, and put on trial for violating the "Black Law."

That same year an incident of disgraceful bigotry had occurred right in Middletown. Amos Beman, son of the pastor of Middletown's black church, had been denied admission to the city's new Wesleyan University because of his race. Determined to secure an education, young Beman had been privately tutored by a white student with abolitionist sympathies. That arrangement had lasted only six months, until Amos Beman received a letter from a dozen anonymous Wesleyan students threatening to harm him if he didn't give up his studies.

William was sure the racism that besmirched the good name of the Connecticut he loved was strengthened by the fact that elsewhere in much of America, Negroes were considered subhuman creatures fit only to be slaves. In fact, while nearly every Negro in Connecticut was free, slavery was still technically legal in the state. A tiny handful of blacks remained in bondage, most too old to have been liberated by the gradual emancipation legislation or too feeble to support themselves if manumitted.

These events and facts, taken together with many others, had moved William to speak out publicly and privately against slavery. Then a year ago he'd been approached by a young Middletown merchant, Jesse Baldwin, who'd been converted to abolitionism after witnessing the horrors of slavery while traveling through the South as a peddler.

Baldwin had discreetly asked William if he would be willing to take what Baldwin euphemistically called "a more active role" in the anti-slavery cause. That, William understood, meant sheltering fugitive slaves and conducting them to their next stop on the road to freedom.

William had hesitated at taking this dangerous step. Then a final drop of outrage caused his rising moral indignation to overflow and sweep him toward violating the law. It was produced by the book *A Picture of Slavery in the United States of America*, by a man named George Bourne, published in Middletown in 1834.

William had read the book's more than two hundred pages in a single sitting. When he finished he felt wrung out. His emotions had run the gamut from shame to disgust to anger to horror at the author's depiction of a Southern society steeped in unimaginable sin, brutality, and depravity. There were accounts, illustrated with painfully explicit engravings, of slaves being auctioned off or bartered like brute animals, parents separated from children, husbands from wives; of lustful slave owners forcing themselves upon helpless black women who subsequently bore children who were the property of their white fathers; of slaves being tortured and even murdered on the whim of a master or mistress who incurred no legal penalty for taking a human life.

William had discussed Baldwin's proposal with Alma. It wouldn't be right for him to decide on his own to become involved in an activity that, as a violation of federal law, could land him in jail and ruin their family financially. Alma had also read *A Picture of Slavery*, and unequivocally supported William in accepting Jesse Baldwin's offer. She had pointed that his conscience – their conscience – would be an empty vessel if he spoke out against the institution of slavery, yet refused to help victims who had journeyed hundreds of desperate miles to reach Connecticut.

William had joined Jesse Baldwin, and since then had twice helped fugitive slaves. Each time the runaway had been brought to the Lyman farm under cover of night and in deepest secrecy, by a man William knew and trusted. William had hidden the runaways, fed them, then escorted them the next night to Jesse Baldwin's house.

But both these times William had been notified in advance of the impending arrival of a "package," as runaways were referred to, giving him time to make the necessary preparations. And both times it had been only a single man he had harbored. He'd had no warning that any fugitives would be coming to his house this night – let alone two of them, and one a woman!

With a determined effort William shook off his shock and began to think about what needed to be done. The first order of business was to get his surprise visitors out of sight; for all he knew they were being pursued by slave catchers, which could explain their unexpected, unannounced arrival.

William gestured for the couple to follow him. He led them to the hatchway into the cellar, and opened the doors as quietly as possible.

Once safely in the damp cellar, with the hatchway closed and barred from inside, William felt his way up the stairs. He returned a couple minutes later with a whale oil lamp, which provided enough light for the three to see each other's faces.

"I apologize for my behavior earlier," William began. "I wasn't expecting you. Why did you come alone?"

"De man in de stone house – his wife an' children come down sudden wit de summer complaint," the black man began. "We were hidin' in de basement. Folks started comin' to help care for de sick ones, and de man got afraid someone gonna find us, or dat we gonna get sick. Soon as de sun went down, he sent us here. His children were so sick, he was afraid to leave 'em to come wit us."

William had to concentrate to be sure he understood the man. The Negroes William knew in Connecticut by and large spoke like the average white person. But this man spoke with a thick accent not always easy to comprehend.

"De man tole me what roads to follow to get here, tole us what de house look like, and dat you was a great big tall man," the Negro continued. "Soon as it got dark enough, we started walkin'."

William marveled at the sense of direction that had enabled the fugitives to find this house, and at the stamina both must possess. It was a good five miles from Nathan Hall's house to here.

William nodded, studying the couple more carefully. Their garments had probably been supplied by abolitionists earlier in their flight, both to replace the rags they'd set out in and to foil any description of their clothing included in advertisements for their capture. They looked well nourished, but fatigued, not just from tonight's trek but from weeks or even months of being on the run.

William started at the sound of the door at the top of the stairs opening. Terror sprang into the eyes of both the man and woman.

"Are you down there, William?" Alma called in a low, uncertain voice.

"Yes," he replied, his voice barely more than a whisper, then turned to nod reassuringly to the couple. They watched the ghostly outline of Alma's white cotton nightgown descend the steps with only a slight scraping sound on the wooden risers created by her bare feet. She crossed the cellar's dirt floor toward William's lamp.

"Is anyone else up?" William asked.

"I don't think so," Alma replied. "I woke and found you gone from bed. When you didn't return after a few minutes, I started to worry and searched the house. The cellar was the last place I thought to check before waking Lizzy and David to help–." Alma stopped abruptly in mid-sentence as she realized other people were present in the dark cellar. She immediately grasped the situation. "Did you know they were coming?"

"No," William said, unable to keep his concern out of his voice. "I ran into them on the way to the privy. In fact, I think I'd better complete my original mission," he said. He handed Alma the lamp and started up the stairs into the house. "Stay with them until I get back, and then I'll decide what to do."

Alma nodded, but William was uneasy. He'd been determined not to involve any of his family in the actual work of helping fugitive slaves, but this unforeseen development had foiled that plan.

As William disappeared up the stairs, the black man put his arm around the woman in a protective gesture that made clear they were husband and wife. Gauging their fatigue, Alma gestured to the man to pull up two hogsheads that had been emptied of their contents of dried apples, for him and the woman to sit on.

"Where did you come from?" Alma asked. The black man cast her a wary look, as if she might be trying to trick him into revealing the name of their previous helper. She rephrased her question. "I mean, where did you come from to begin with?"

The Negro pondered this for a moment, then apparently decided it would be safe enough to provide a simple answer. "We're from Virginny."

"How long ago did you leave?"

"It's been five weeks dat we been followin' de North Star."

Alma was appalled. She'd assumed they'd stowed away on some coastal vessel that docked in New Haven or perhaps even Essex on the Connecticut River, and walked from there. Five weeks on foot! She couldn't stop herself from pressing further.

"It's dangerous for a black man alone to run for freedom," she began, "How . . . why . . . did two of you–?" She stopped when the man shook his head slowly to indicate that they'd had no choice.

"Lucy and me, we belong to Massa Gray ever since we was children. We both worked in de fields. We jumped de broom four summers past. Massa Gray ain't never sold husband from wife – or children from der parents." His voice had thickened with emotion, and a quick sob caught in his wife's throat.

By the sputtering lamplight Alma could see tears in the man's eyes. "Right after Christmas, Massa Gray died. He had just the one son, who inherited de whole plantation. Folks started comin' in, lookin' at everythin' – de house, de fields, de cattle, de slaves –

writin' stuff down." Again the man stopped talking, then took a deep breath before continuing with a quaver in his voice.

"Lucy and me – we had us a li'l girl, just turned two last spring, name o' Lottie. At first Lucy brung her to de fields while we worked. But after she was weaned she stayed behind wit de other children in de slave quarter while we went to work. One day, we come back to find–." He stopped, too overwhelmed by emotion to continue. Alma's heart constricted with compassion for a father still too distraught by the sudden death of a beloved child to actually speak the terrible words.

"Dey sold her away!" Lucy finished for him in a voice raw with anguish and fury. Alma went ice cold with horror.

"Dey took her away from her mama and papa dat love her," Lucy went on, tears streaming down her face. "Just a li'l baby! Sent her off where she won't have no one to dry her tears or sing her songs or comfort her when she sick or hurt. Sent her off to be brought up like some calf until she old enough to be put to work."

Lucy choked for a moment on her tears, then went on. "And me, lyin' ev'ry night for de rest of my life, wondrin' where she be, if someone hurtin' her, if she sad, or lonely, or tired – wondrin' if she cryin' for me, not understandin' why her mama don't come for her."

Lucy's eyes locked onto Alma's, one mother to another. "I ain't never gonna see my baby, my Lottie, again," she said in a dead voice, then buried her face in her husband's chest.

The man gently stroked his wife's hair, then spoke slowly. "Eben den, we might not've run. But den Lucy tol' me she gonna have another baby. An' we knew we'd rather die runnin', 'cause dyin' couldn't hurt as bad as havin' another child stole away. So we ran."

This anguished testimony to pure evil sickened Alma physically. She'd been certain there was no greater pain than to bury a child. But here she'd been confronted with something even more agonizing: for a mother to have a child taken from her forever, not by the will of God, but by the greed of man.

Alma at least had the small comfort of knowing Phineas and Adeline were no longer suffering, as well as her faith's assurance that they had gone to a better place. Lucy and her husband didn't have even that. They would never know if their daughter was being treated decently or brutalized, if she was alive or dead. They would bear the torment of realizing that Lottie had been taken so young she might not even remember that she once had parents who loved her. Lucy's mother's heart would bleed for this lost child until she drew her own last breath.

Alma felt embarrassingly naïve. She'd read accounts of slave children sold away from their parent in *A Picture of Slavery* and in *The Liberator*. But that heartless crime was now more than words on paper; its victims stood before her in flesh and blood. She swallowed hard to push down the bile rising in her throat.

The sound of shoes on the steps signaled William's return from the privy. He walked over to Lucy and her husband. "We'll bring down some blankets for you to sleep on, and food as well," he said. "Tomorrow is the Sabbath, so the family will be away most of the day. I'll try to move you to the next stop tomorrow night." He frowned with worry. "It won't be safe to leave you here alone all day Sunday. I'll have to stay home from meeting."

"I'll stay with them, William," Alma said. When he began to protest, she continued quickly. "It will arouse less suspicion if I'm absent. If anyone asks after me, tell them I am sick – and it will be no lie. For I am truly sick at heart that people who call themselves Christians and Americans treat fellow human beings like this man and woman in a manner that would shame the heathen barbarian."

Chapter Eighty-Six

June, 1834
Middlefield

William waited until it was completely dark before setting out for Middletown with his two charges three days after they'd shown up. He'd originally planned to escort them to Jesse Baldwin's home. But on the Monday after their arrival he'd sent David, now almost fourteen, to Middletown to alert Baldwin to expect two "packages." When David came back with the news that Baldwin was out of town, the date of his return uncertain, William had to scotch that plan.

Each day increased the chance that the fugitives would be detected by some unsympathetic person. Their presence was kept secret from the younger children as well, lest one of them make an innocent slip of the tongue that could reach unfriendly ears. Only David knew of his parents' Underground Railroad work. But Jesse Baldwin was the only other conductor William knew farther along the line.

As the situation grew more tense, David had come up with a solution. Lucy and her husband, whose name was Ben, would be guided to the house of the Reverend Jehiel Beman, until recently pastor of Middletown's African Methodist Episcopal Zion Church.

William had made Beman's acquaintance through their shared interest in the temperance and abolitionist movements, and had read the minister's contributions to *The Liberator*. Although he had no knowledge that Beman was a conductor on the Underground Railroad, William was certain he would take these fugitives in.

Jehiel Beman himself was the son of a slave named Caesar who had earned his freedom by fighting in the American Revolution.

Upon achieving his liberty, Caesar had chosen a surname for himself – "Beman" – short for "be a man" – to declare his free status.

David had insisted on coming along. William resisted until David convinced him he understood that this wasn't an adventurous lark, but a serious, possibly perilous, mission.

David had his father's fine straight brown hair, and the distinctive Lyman nose, set in a round face. His smooth cheeks had yet to sprout peach fuzz, making him look younger than he was.

In deciding when to make the trip, William had consulted the current almanac. The moon was only a thin crescent, meaning the night would be very dark. The almanac predicted dry, hot weather.

They'd decided to make the six-mile trip on foot. Although it would take longer than on horseback, they'd be less likely to attract attention, and would be able to hide quickly in the fields, woods, or swamps along the road if necessary.

The chorus of buzzing cicadas and chirping crickets was loud enough to cover the sound of their feet on the hard-packed dirt road. Although all the houses they passed were dark, everyone gone to bed with the sun in anticipation of an early start to another hard day of work, William's heart beat faster each time they approached one. He could only guess at the anxiety Lucy and Ben were feeling.

They were a bit more than halfway to their destination when they heard the first rumble of thunder off to the west, beyond Beseck Mountain. The noise quickly grew louder and more frequent, until it sounded like the growl of a demon at their heels. Suddenly a jagged bolt of lightning split the night sky, illuminating the entire countryside, followed a few seconds later by a crack of thunder so sharp and loud it made all four of them jump.

The speed with which the storm had come up, and the danger it posed – underscored by another brilliant flash of lightning followed even more quickly by a crack and roll of thunder – made finding shelter imperative. Their options were few; William wasn't confident enough in the sympathies of the occupants of the houses closest to their position to risk seeking sanctuary with them. That left a barn, or a grove of trees tall enough to protect them yet broad enough not to act as a lightning rod – if either could be found quickly.

David spoke in the darkness. "On my way back from Middletown I saw that Ezekiel Wilcox has mown his hayfield. If we leave the road and cut across it, we can reach the old Fairchild place before the storm breaks."

William was grateful for David's quick thinking. The Fairchild house was still empty a year after its owners had gone to Ohio, unable to find a buyer for the worn-out acres on which it stood. "Let's hurry," was all he said by way of accepting David's plan.

David led the way across the freshly mown field, the others following with little difficulty, for he was visible for a split-second every time a flash of lightning lit up the surrounding countryside. William held Lucy's arm firmly to keep her from stumbling as they ran across the uneven ground. The first fat raindrops were starting to fall when the four reached the abandoned Fairchild homestead. William silently cursed the almanac's inept weather prognosticator.

William had to throw his considerable weight against the kitchen door four times before it crashed open. He realized with a wry twist that he felt more guilt about breaking into an empty house than he did about violating the federal fugitive slave law.

The four travelers huddled gratefully inside the dusty, musty house as the storm's full fury broke. The heavy downpour made it impossible to see more than a few inches beyond the windows. For a time it seemed the lightning bolts were striking in the front yard, followed immediately by thunder that shook the house's frame.

The storm raged for half an hour before sweeping swiftly east toward the Connecticut River. William, David, Lucy, and Ben resumed their journey. The storm had brought cooler, drier, fresher air; walking would be easier than in the oppressively humid, enervating atmosphere of just an hour earlier.

They were perhaps a quarter of a mile from Jehiel Beman's house when they glimpsed the faintest brightening of the eastern sky behind the hills on the opposite side of the Connecticut River. They summoned up what little energy the nerve-wracking night had left them to walk with a briskness that would make them look like early risers getting a head start on the day, not exhausted travelers desperate to reach their destination.

They approached a tiny house next to the simple African Methodist Episcopal Zion Church, not far from the Wesleyan University which had denied Jehiel Beman's son Amos admission because of his race. They stopped briefly while William scanned their surroundings. When he was as certain as he could be that they weren't being watched, William motioned for the other three to follow him as he slipped around to the back of the house.

William rapped softly on the door. He waited a few nervous seconds, then prepared to knock more loudly in order to wake the household, all of whom he assumed were still asleep.

"Who's there?" Jehiel Beman's wary voice asked from behind the closed door before William could knock again. William was startled, but after a moment's weary reflection he realized he should have expected Mr. Beman to be sleeping lightly these days.

Jehiel Beman was one of the founders of the new Middletown Anti-Slavery Society, the members of which had been physically assaulted by anti-abolitionists at their first meeting this past spring. Similar anti-slavery gatherings and lectures had been disrupted by violence in communities across Connecticut. A Negro who openly espoused the unpopular cause of emancipating all slaves would be a fool not to be prepared and on guard for a personal visit by men vehemently opposed to his principles and activities.

"It's William Lyman, Mr. Beman," William said in a low voice he hoped would carry through the door. "I have two friends with me who need your help."

William heard the door being unlatched, after which it swung open to reveal Jehiel Beman dressed in clothes so wrinkled he'd obviously slept in them. For a moment the minister studied with amazement the four bedraggled travelers on his back door step. Then he quickly motioned for them to come inside, closing the door quietly behind them.

Jehiel Beman was a slender man in his mid-forties, with a narrow face, high cheekbones, broad forehead, and tightly curling hair that he wore cropped short. His skin was the color of light coffee. Heavy bags beneath his piercing black eyes bore testimony to too much strain and not enough sleep.

Next to Mr. Beman stood his eldest son, Leverett, a young man in his early twenties. Leverett was clearly on edge and ready to step in if their unexpected pre-dawn visitors should provoke trouble. From behind them appeared Mr. Beman's wife, Nancy, a woman about the same age as her husband.

When Nancy Beman spied the exhausted and obviously pregnant Lucy, she walked over to the young woman and enfolded her in a motherly embrace. Lucy laid her cheek on Mrs. Beman's shoulder and closed her eyes in inexpressible relief. Ben also was visibly buoyed by the sight of people of their own race. William thought of how very hard it must have been for this couple to place their trust in a series of strangers of the white race, which until the day they'd run away had meant only oppression to them.

"I apologize for coming with no warning," William began, but Mr. Beman shook his head. He seized William's hand in a powerful grip developed from years of work as a shoemaker to supplement the small pastoral stipend that didn't begin to support seven children. "A man never needs to apologize for doing God's work."

William smiled in appreciation, but still felt he owed Mr. Beman an explanation for their unheralded arrival on his doorstep. "I had planned to bring this couple to another–."

"But he is out of town," Mr. Beman finished for him, confirming that he was indeed a participant in the network that spirited fugitives to freedom. Still, neither man spoke Jesse Baldwin's name, for even between two active agents of the clandestine undertaking, the less hard information shared the better.

"You must be starved," said Nancy Beman as she gently released Lucy. "I'll cook up some breakfast and then you can get some sleep until it's dark again."

William started to protest that he and David had to return home at once, then realized the wisdom of Mrs. Beman's words. Both father and son were physically and mentally spent, and looked like something the cat had dragged in. For them to be seen leaving the Beman house in their condition would certainly arouse suspicions.

If they did get away from the Beman home without attracting attention, the walk to Middlefield would be an ordeal for them, hungry and exhausted as they were. There was also the chance they would run into someone of their acquaintance who, even if he didn't divine their true mission, might understandably conclude the two were returning from a night of carousing in Middletown – and wouldn't that set tongues wagging!

So David and William sat down to breakfast with Lucy and Ben and the Beman family, then collapsed gratefully onto the beds Mrs. Beman offered. The straw mattresses were uncomfortably lumpy, but all four quickly fell asleep.

Before surrendering to his fatigue, William considered that, while he'd known Negroes all his life, had employed them, eaten at the same table with them, and boarded them in his house, this was the first time he'd ever spent more than a few moments under one of their roofs. It was, he reflected before the welcome oblivion of sleep overcame him, an indication of how very far all Americans had to travel before the two races could live in harmony and true equality.

Chapter Eighty-Seven

September, 1834
Middlefield

"You can't!"

Charles's vehemence unnerved Lizzy. He was excitable, sometimes impulsive – as when he left Princeton to enroll in Yale in order to be closer to her in Middlefield. But in the three years she'd known him, she'd never seen him this agitated.

Lizzy was glad they'd chosen to walk abroad to savor the mellow warmth of this September evening, nine days shy of her twenty-second birthday. They were alone on the road around the swamp pasture, out of earshot of the Lyman house. No one else heard the outburst Charles regretted the moment the words left his lips.

"I love you," Charles went on, in a low, urgent voice. "How can you leave me?" he asked miserably.

Lizzy studied Charles with affection – and exasperation. They'd had this same conversation a dozen times or more over the past two months. But this would be the last, for tomorrow Lizzy would start her journey – which accounted for Charles's wretchedness.

"You know I love you," Lizzy said patiently. "I'll miss you greatly. But I believe God calls me to this work. I won't be gone forever."

"Why can't you keep teaching at the Seminary?" Charles demanded. Upon graduation from the Hartford Female Seminary two years ago, Lizzy had joined the faculty. She found teaching fulfilling, and had taken satisfaction in no longer being a financial drain on William and Alma, who'd sacrificed to pay for her elite education. "Why go to a cesspool of disease like Cincinnati?" Charles pressed.

Stifling a sigh of irritation, Lizzy proceeded to once more explain her decision, not because she expected that this time Charles would understand, but out of respect for his dogged devotion.

"You know Mr. Beecher believes America's destiny will be decided in the West, which is filling rapidly with foreign immigrants who have little or no education. Their ignorance makes them easy prey to sin and vice and religious infidelity, and unprepared to take part in government by the people."

Charles, bless him, was listening, Lizzy noticed, although he knew as much as she did about Lyman Beecher's crusade to educate and evangelize the West's ignorant masses. He'd grown greatly in influence on the nation's religious scene, leaving Litchfield in 1826 to become pastor of Boston's Hanover Street Church.

Beecher had become convinced of the need to save the West through education and evangelism. Two years ago he'd moved most of his family more than eight hundred miles to Cincinnati. There he became president of the new Lane Theological Seminary, established to train ministers to spread the Protestant gospel through the West.

Having resigned from the Hartford Female Seminary, Catharine Beecher had accompanied her father to Cincinnati. There she'd founded the Western Female Institute to train young women as teachers to educate immigrants to be responsible Americans. Hattie had also gone to Cincinnati to teach at the Institute.

"As an assistant principal at the Western Female Institute I'll prepare teachers to rescue minds from the darkness of ignorance," Lizzy went on passionately. "I'll help strengthen our nation, and perhaps save some souls. Cincinnati is where I'm needed."

Charles's anguished dilemma was plain on his face. As a future minister committed to spreading God's word, he couldn't fault Lizzy's desire to go where she felt she could do the most good. But he was distressed that her calling would take her so far away from him for so long before circumstances would allow them to reach an understanding about what future they might have together.

Lizzy and Charles had grown increasingly close after he'd enrolled at Yale. But there'd been no talk of marriage between them. Charles was in no position to broach the subject; he had another year of study at Yale, after which he would need additional training before he could be ordained. Even then he would need to secure an appointment as a pastor before he could think of taking a wife.

For her part, Lizzy hoped her face didn't betray the fact that, while everything she'd told Charles was the truth, it wasn't the whole truth. She had another reason, one that would wound Charles if he knew it, for going to Cincinnati.

Lizzy didn't doubt that as soon as it was possible and proper, Charles would ask her to be his wife. But she did have doubts about what her answer would be.

Lizzy loved Charles, respected him, enjoyed his company, and shared his deep religious beliefs. But she felt a nagging uncertainty about whether what they felt for each other was sufficient foundation for a successful union of heart, mind, body, and soul.

Lizzy couldn't sort out her feelings for Charles when they were so much together. He visited her often in Hartford or Middlefield. He'd become as much a part of the family circle as her brothers.

Then Catharine Beecher's letter had arrived, asking Lizzy to join Hattie and another Hartford Female Seminary graduate, Mary Dutton, in running her school in Cincinnati. Lizzy considered the job a chance to be involved in the inspiring purpose of the Western Female Institute – and a welcome opportunity to gain some perspective on her relationship with Charles. The trip to Cincinnati would also be an adventure of the kind that would be impossible once Lizzy was a wife, especially after she became a mother.

So Lizzy had accepted Catharine's offer. Her decision pained not just Charles. William and Alma's first reaction had been to oppose Lizzy moving to a frontier hundreds of miles away, exposing her to the dangers of the road and of the tumultuous western river port. But Lizzy had convinced them the same way she had Charles, by comparing work at the Western Female Institute to that of a missionary, bringing education to people who desperately needed it, thus advancing the causes of religion and of democracy.

William had even presented Lizzy with the $150 that, as an assistant principal, she was required to invest in the school. It was a sum Lizzy knew William could ill afford. His gesture meant a great deal, as evidence of his confidence in her judgement and ability.

Lizzy would set off on the morrow with Hattie and her brother Henry Ward Beecher, to whom Hattie was particularly close. Hattie alone of all the Beechers had made the long journey back from Cincinnati to attend the graduation from Andover College of this brother, just two years younger than she. They would travel to Cincinnati by canal boat, lake steamer, stagecoach, and horseback.

When she saw that Charles was about to speak, Lizzy put her fingers gently against his lips. "Let's not waste the last few minutes we'll share for many months by quarreling," she said tenderly.

Although she was relieved when he nodded in agreement, it still hurt to see the flicker of forlorn hope in his eyes snuffed out.

"It's such a fine evening – let's walk up Powder Hill, so I can take in the view to last until I return," Lizzy suggested. She slipped her aim coaxingly around Charles's elbow, and after a moment he patted it affectionately, and they strolled off.

From a chamber window, William watched the young couple. He was pondering the challenge upon which Lizzy was about to embark.

The journey would be tiring, uncomfortable, and probably dangerous. That it would end in Cincinnati was cause for concern. William envisioned Cincinnati as a barely tamed city, teeming chaotically like a disturbed ant hill. Last he'd heard, Cincinnati was in the grip of an epidemic of cholera, a new disease that since its appearance in America a couple years ago had killed thousands..

William was so lost in thought that he didn't hear the chamber door open. He started when Alma touched him on the shoulder. He put an arm around her and pulled her tightly against his side.

Together they watched Lizzy and Charles as they walked toward the foot of Powder Hill. The hillside was covered with apple trees, bearing an abundance of fruit just a week or two away from harvest – which Lizzy wouldn't be there to see, William thought gloomily.

"I'm not eavesdropping," William said to Alma, then admitted with an abashed shrug, "they're too far away to hear anything. But I can tell Charles is trying one last time to persuade Lizzy not to go." He paused, then confessed quietly, "And I'm hoping he'll succeed.

Alma laid her head consoling against William's arm. "I worry too – the steamboat trip on Lake Erie, cholera in Cincinnati. But we can't stand in the way of Lizzy using the talents God gave her to advance His truth. If David or Elihu wanted to become a missionary, we'd gladly send them. We should rejoice that Lizzy will be serving God's holy mission for a time, even if it takes her far from home."

"You're right," William sighed. "There's much to do in the West." He frowned. "But I don't share my Cousin Beecher's belief that the greatest enemy they face is the Roman Catholic Church. He's terrified that the Catholic Church has a secret plot to set up a religious despotism in America by sending to the West thousands of Catholic immigrants who will vote as their priests tell them."

They stood in silence, watching Lizzy and Charles wend their way toward Powder Ridge. "God forgive me my weakness," William whispered almost to himself, "But I wish she wouldn't go."

Chapter Eighty-Eight

November, 1834
Cincinnati, Ohio

The most unpleasant part of Lizzy's journey to Cincinnati had been the hours spent crammed with two dozen other women into the crudely furnished passenger quarters of a boat on the Erie Canal. But she found herself shaking with laughter at the description of that experience Judge James Hall had just finished reading to the Semi-Colon Club, a group of men and women who met weekly to read and discuss literary works written by its members.

The group enthusiastically applauded the writer's skill in turning the details of an irritating, mundane experience into an amusing tale. With a small, gallant flourish, Judge Hall handed the manuscript to its author, Hattie Beecher. She took it with a self-conscious smile, her eyes downcast, her cheeks blushing at the attention.

Lizzy knew Hattie had a sharp intellect. But during the past year she'd discovered that her cousin was an extraordinarily talented writer. In April Hattie's story "A New England Sketch" had been published in the *Western Monthly Magazine*, edited by Judge Hall. It was a colorful, highly amusing description of Lot Benton as Hattie had heard him described by Lyman Beecher. After reading it William Lyman declared Hattie had perfectly captured his uncle's quirky character.

Lizzy had begun attending Semi-Colon Club meetings as soon as she arrived in Cincinnati. Most of the members were transplanted New Englanders. The pleasant social occasions helped Lizzy cope with the homesickness that had been particularly sharp of late, as she spent her first Thanksgiving ever apart from her family.

They were meeting this evening in the parlor of the newly constructed mansion of Samuel Foote. Foote was the brother of Hattie and Catharine Beecher's late mother, Roxana Foote. He was a tall, open-hearted and open-handed man whose features bore indelible witness to the seafaring life he'd pursued for many years.

Samuel Foote had given up the ocean to come to Cincinnati, where he'd grown wealthy and built this fine new house at the corner of Vine and Third streets, with a vista of the Ohio River and Kentucky on its opposite bank. He and his wife had the ability to bring total strangers together in an atmosphere of casual warmth that quickly put them at ease with each other. The Footes had taken an instant liking to Lizzy, bringing her into their family fold as if she were a long-lost relative.

Noticeably absent tonight was Catharine Beecher. A piece by Catharine, titled "Castle Ward, the Residence of My Ancestors on My Mother's Side," had been read at the first Semi-Colon Club meeting Lizzy attended. Lizzy had been surprised to hear Catharine describe her grandparents' house in Guilford as a grand home on an expansive estate, when in fact it was much like the Lyman homestead.

Lizzy and Hattie had refrained from pointing out the exaggerations in Catharine's piece. But Samuel Foote had good-naturedly chided his niece for "making a silk purse out of a sow's ear."

Catharine's inflated description of her family home was just one example of her willingness to embellish the truth to impress Westerners with her eastern sophistication and culture. Lizzy, Hattie, and Mary Dutton were running the Western Female Institute almost entirely by themselves, while Catharine traveled to various towns making social connections and speaking on her philosophy of education. Catharine excused her frequent absences by claiming the mere affiliation of her name with the school was enough of a contribution on her part toward its success.

The irony, Lizzy had perceived, was that Westerners were suspicious, even offended, rather than awed by the condescending attitude of "Yankees" like Catharine Beecher and her father. Judge Hall himself had published an article mocking Lyman Beecher's terror, which Catharine shared, of Roman Catholics. Far from making her a social and intellectual leader, Catharine's pretensions had alienated many of Cincinnati's influential residents.

Lizzy, seated next to Hattie, noticed that her cousin seemed to be waiting for something. Hattie flashed a quick glance at the Reverend Calvin Stowe, whose face beamed with approval. In a heartbeat Hattie's gaze was once more directed demurely down, but her nervous smile relaxed into one of happiness. Lizzy raised her eyebrows as the truth dawned on her.

Calvin Stowe was a young professor of Biblical literature at Lane Seminary. He was mourning his wife, Eliza, who had died of cholera in August. Eliza had been one of Hattie's close friends.

Calvin Stowe had been invited to live for a time in the Beecher home, rather than deal with his sorrow alone in an empty house. He and Hattie had spent much time together, consoling each over the loss of the woman they had both loved.

But not until now, when Lizzy detected in that quick glance Hattie's eagerness for Calvin Stowe's approval, had she suspected new love might be rising like a phoenix from the ashes of grief of Eliza Stowe's untimely death. The possibility made Lizzy very happy for her cousin.

Thoughts of romance between Hattie and Mr. Stowe naturally brought Charles Mills to Lizzy's mind. During three months apart Lizzy hadn't pined passionately for him. But she did miss Charles in less dramatic, yet telling, ways.

While it was exciting to be plunged into a circle of strangers, some from backgrounds far different from Lizzy's, it was also stressful. With men she had to conduct herself with the reserved propriety required of a young unmarried woman. She found herself yearning for the pleasant hours she'd spent with Charles, completely at ease, with no need to be anything more or less than what she was.

Apart from comfortable familiarity, Lizzy realized she also missed the satisfaction she received from her power to make Charles happy. Perhaps her most important discovery had been that none of the charming, sophisticated, well-educated young men she'd met since coming to Cincinnati had sparked in her emotions any more compelling than what she felt for Charles.

After some universally complimentary discussion of "The Canal Boat" story, the young men and women helped themselves to refreshments. Lizzy found herself seated next to young Robert

Stanton, which meant the topic of conversation would be the upheaval at Lane Seminary.

Lizzy and her traveling companions had arrived in Cincinnati to find Lyman Beecher's theological school engulfed in a firestorm of controversy over abolition. During the winter of 1834, a number of Lane students had held debates on controversial issues, including whether the South should immediately abolish slavery. Some Lane students had gone beyond talk, making the two-mile trip from the Seminary into the heart of Cincinnati to provide assistance to the city's black residents.

Although geography placed Cincinnati in Ohio, the slave state of Kentucky was just across the river. The city was largely pro-Southern in sentiment. The open discussion of the incendiary subject of abolition and the sight of Lane students mingling with the humble people of color had infuriated much of its citizenry.

This public reaction had been so hostile that the Seminary's trustees and faculty had voted to ban all anti-slavery activities and discussions at the school – in private as well as in public. When the fall term began in October, most of the Lane students had asked to be dismissed, and had left Cincinnati.

The exodus of students from Lane was a national sensation, and the anti-slavery press exploited it to the fullest. Lyman Beecher had been unavailable to deal with this crisis, which broke out while he was in the East soliciting funds for the Seminary.

Robert Stanton was one of the Lane "rebels," as the students who had withdrawn from the school were called. But his presence at the Semi-Colon Club gave credence to the rumor Lizzy had heard that he hadn't written off Lane.

"Is it true you're returning to the Seminary, Mr. Stanton?" Lizzy asked. Stanton was caught off-guard, with his mouth full of cake. He held his right index finger up in a signal to wait, chewed energetically, then swallowed forcefully.

"Yes, I am, Miss Lyman," Stanton answered when at last he could speak.

"I'm delighted to hear that!" a voice said from behind them. They both turned to see Calvin Stowe, who pulled up a chair and sat down.

"This doesn't mean I've changed my mind about the trustees' and faculty's oppressive actions," Stanton declared firmly. "Abolishing slavery should be of paramount interest to all Christians. I understand why many of my fellow students chose to leave Lane rather than suffer the suppression of their consciences and of their right to free speech."

"What do you think, Miss Lyman?" Calvin Stowe fixed his dark eyes on Lizzy in a forthright, but not challenging, gaze. The question didn't fluster Lizzy. She'd been intrigued by how the abolitionist cause, an incendiary topic in Connecticut, had ignited a firestorm in Cincinnati.

"I agree with Mr. Stanton that the abolition of slavery is one of the great moral challenges confronting Christians," she began. "The reaction of the trustees and faculty was too extreme, and clearly made the situation worse." She paused for a second before adding diplomatically, "Yet I can concede that they believed they were acting in the best interest of the Seminary's greater mission."

Calvin Stowe nodded in agreement. "The disaffected students fail to understand that their anti-slavery actions, however noble, are undermining the more important purpose of Lane Seminary, to bring all the West into Christ's fold."

"That's the conclusion I reached," said Stanton. Even now the strain of that difficult decision was evident in his voice. "First I must complete my theological studies, so that I may be the best instrument possible for the Lord's use. But I will make abolition one of the pillars of my ministry."

Calvin Stowe clapped the young man encouragingly on the back, then observed sardonically. "You'll enjoy a singular advantage when you return to Lane: the nearly undivided attention of the faculty. Until new students are enrolled, we'll have perhaps a dozen scholars under the instruction of a faculty meant to teach one hundred or more."

That observation elicited only a faint smile from Stanton, who clearly wasn't entirely at peace with a decision some might consider a betrayal of his fellow Lane rebels. Lizzy sympathized with his dilemma. She knew her father wouldn't have given the Lane administration the benefit of the doubt she had. He would have condemned as cowardly their surrender to anti-abolition and anti-Negro sentiment.

Chapter Eighty-Nine

September, 1835
Middlefield

Alma worked her way slowly through her cherished flower garden, plucking faded, wilted blossoms from the pinks, asters, marigolds, chrysanthemums, and other flowers blooming in mid-September. She stooped to pull weeds that had invaded her sanctuary.

The trilling of a flute floated through the open parlor window. Ten-year-old Elihu was playing with a verve that made up for the occasional wrong notes. The music soon stopped, and a few minutes later Alma heard someone else rustling through the garden. It was Elihu, searching so intently he was oblivious to his mother's presence. He carefully cut leaves from plants, picked up a blue jay feather, trapped a green fly in a bottle, and coaxed a lady bug from a stalk onto his finger.

Nodding to himself in satisfaction, Elihu took his samples of flora and fauna back into the house. There, Alma knew, each one would be carefully examined under the microscope William had purchased for Elihu late last year, not long after Lizzy's departure for Cincinnati.

Their youngest son had a keen mind and an interest in everything imaginable, from music to natural science to politics. He was also deeply pious, which naturally pleased his parents.

A spindly, delicate boy, Elihu was already taller than his older brother David, but weighed less. He had a long, oval face, with an unusually narrow, sharp version of the signature Lyman nose, and a small, tight mouth. He had long, slender, sensitive fingers, which could nimbly play the flute or carefully prepare a specimen for scrutiny under his microscope.

Chronic poor health had left Elihu too frail to attend a private academy as David did, and he'd quickly mastered everything the common school had to teach him. William and Alma had recruited the entire family to provide the bright boy with as extensive an education as possible right at home.

Books on various academic subjects had been secured for Elihu, and singing and music lessons arranged as well. His sister Adeline Urania, now eight, shared his passion for music, which had created a special bond between them.

The microscope was the most recent addition to Elihu's educational arsenal. He spent hours looking at magnified items, carefully sketching the tiny world visible through the eyepiece. The substantial sum William paid for the instrument had been money well spent, given Elihu's continued delight in using it to explore the natural world.

Alma was in a fine mood, for William and David were expected back tonight from a trip to Massachusetts. They'd gone there to purchase mules to drive back to Connecticut. They would sell the mules to the New Haven trading firm of Alsop and Trowbridge, which would ship the animals to the West Indies islands, where they would be used to power equipment that squeezed the juice from sugar cane.

David and William hated the long days on the road dealing with the difficult animals, the nights spent in uncomfortable taverns. But the pay was good, and the money welcome.

William was still in debt for the $150 he'd given Lizzy to invest in the Western Female Institute. The bills for her attendance at the Hartford Female Seminary soon had been replaced by ones for David's studies at Lee's Academy in the town of Madison on Long Island Sound. Books and equipment to satisfy Elihu's inquisitive mind didn't come cheap.

There was no way the farm could produce enough to pay for such expensive extras; hence the mule-buying arrangement with Alsop and Trowbridge. Still, William would have refused the work if slavery hadn't been abolished in the British colonies in the West Indies the previous year. Now he knew the mules they supplied didn't help strengthen an economy that rested on the backs of slaves.

This would be the last trip they would make until next spring, for which Alma was deeply grateful. The past months had been particularly difficult ones for her. Lizzy's absence was still felt keenly by the entire family. Then in June, Alma's mother had died suddenly at the age of seventy-three.

Elizabeth Coe's death had plunged Delia, a spinster now in her mid-thirties who lived with her mother, into an abyss of grief so deep her relatives had feared for a time to leave her alone. Delia had spent the months immediately following her mother's death at William and Alma's house, then had gone to live for a time with her brother Linus.

It was impossible to deny that Delia suffered from some disease of the brain, as their father had. She disrupted any household in which she lived.

Delia would become wildly excited about some idea, such as visiting their brother Asher in Ohio, talking incessantly about plans and making preparations. Within a day or two the project would be forgotten. Delia would sit for hours staring at a mourning picture she'd made at Miss Pierce's Academy to record the early deaths of so many of her brothers and sisters.

Alma was startled out of her brooding by the sound of a horse approaching. Coming down the road from Durham she saw their neighbor John Birdsey.

The Birdseys remained, as they always had been, a cantankerous clan who had little contact with the Lymans save in times of crisis. They were as tight with a penny as with a dollar, rarely willing to do a favor for others but bold as brass about borrowing items they somehow never found time to return. So Alma was surprised when John Birdsey didn't ride on by to his own house, but instead reined in his horse outside the stone wall surrounding the Lyman homelot.

Alma picked her way carefully between the thorny rose bushes to the wall. With typical Birdsey parsimony John, who was about the same age as Alma and William, wasted no words on purposeless pleasantries. He reached inside his coat and pulled out a letter. "I was at the postmaster's in Durham Center. He asked me to bring this to you," Birdsey said laconically. "He thought you'd want to get it straightaway, seeing as how it's postmarked from Cincinnati."

Birdsey's last word sent a thrill through Alma. She snatched the letter with an abruptness that bordered on rudeness.

It had been more than a month since they'd received a letter from Lizzy. Alma had begun to feel a bit hurt by this prolonged silence. She'd speculated to William that perhaps Lizzy was enjoying her new school and her new friends so much she couldn't find time to write to her family back in Connecticut. Charles Mills hadn't heard from Lizzy in weeks either; William had found him in a black despair when he stopped at Yale during a visit to New Haven.

But Alma's hopes were dashed by the handwriting in which the letter was addressed. It wasn't Lizzy's, nor that of Hattie Beecher or Mary Dutton or Catharine Beecher, all of which Alma would have recognized.

After a moment Alma recovered from her disappointment to remember to thank John Birdsey. "What do I owe you for the postage?" she asked, for the cost of mailing a letter was paid by the recipient, not the sender.

Birdsey shook his head. "Postmaster said William could pay it next time he's in Durham," he said. He slapped the reins and clicked his tongue to urge his horse down the road to his own house.

Alma studied the letter, turning it over, wondering if it contained some message for William about the Underground Railroad. Cincinnati, located in the free state of Ohio right across the Ohio River from the slave state of Kentucky, was a destination for many runaways. If William had any connection to the network that far west, Alma wasn't aware of it. Her involvement with the fugitives Lucy and Ben last summer had been accidental. William kept her in the dark as much as possible about his activities; the fewer people who knew anything, Alma included, the less chance there was for a slip-up.

Alma left her garden's vibrant color and went into the parlor. She put the letter into a pigeonhole of William's desk, with others that had arrived during his absence. She proceeded into the kitchen to see how Adeline and Sarah and the hired girls were progressing with preparing the supper of roast chicken, squash, turnip soup, and Indian pudding that she hoped William and David would reach home in time to eat.

Alma's wish was granted; William and David, now a month shy of fifteen, rode in around sunset from New Haven, where they'd delivered the mules to Alsop and Trowbridge. David dragged himself up to bed as soon as the meal was finished. An excited Elihu followed, peppering his big brother with questions about what he'd seen on his trip. Alma put Sally and Adeline to work husking and shelling Indian corn.

William put his hands on his hips, and arched his back in an effort to ease muscles grown sore from days on horseback and nights in lumpy tavern beds. Alma read in his eyes the yearning to follow David upstairs to bed, but it was immediately replaced by disciplined resolve. He sat down at his desk and began to go through the packet of papers he'd brought home from the trip, entering expenses and income in his account books.

William was still at his desk when Alma joined him an hour later, having sent Sally and Adeline off to bed. She settled herself down on his settee and began to darn socks, savoring the contentment she so missed when William was away.

"Dear God, no!" William said suddenly under his breath. It was a prayer, not an exclamation.

Alma's head snapped up, and she saw he was reading the letter John Birdsey had brought. Her first thought was that it contained news of some disaster related to the abolition movement. But William's expression of panicked terror, as if some wild beast had him by the throat, told her the letter could be about only one thing.

"Lizzy," Alma said flatly, a statement, not a question. William nodded. "Is . . . Is she–?" Alma stammered, unable to make herself ask the dreaded question.

"No, she's not dead," William said, but there was no reassurance in his voice. "The letter's from Samuel Foote, written three weeks ago. Lizzy is at his house, very sick. The doctors agree she must leave the climate of Cincinnati as soon as possible if there's to be any hope of her recovery."

Alma made a small choking sound; anything could have happened to Lizzy since that letter had been posted. "Is it cholera?" she asked fearfully.

William shook his head, still staring at the letter. "Samuel doesn't say. Just that someone must come fetch her at once."

William convulsively clenched his fist, crumpling the letter into a tiny ball, as if by crushing it he could obliterate the dreadful news it brought. "I'll leave at dawn," he said, his voice grim. When he looked up, Alma saw in his eyes not just fear but, to her alarm, a flicker of the ferocious temper that, while always vigilantly banked, had never been extinguished. "I pray God I'm not too late," he whispered.

Chapter Ninety

September, 1835
Cleveland, Ohio

William staggered among the people on the dock like a drunkard who'd sucked down a quart of rum in a single sitting. He'd been horribly seasick during the twenty-three-hour steamboat trip from Buffalo to Cleveland on Lake Erie. A stiff, steady wind had raised high waves that tossed the vessel about like a cork. To make matters worse – if that were possible – the ship had been crammed, dangerously so, with several hundred passengers, many as sick as William.

Within an hour of leaving Buffalo, William had vomited up his entire breakfast over the side of the steamship. But the nausea had persisted, and he'd continued to retch and gag in misery such as he'd never experienced.

It had been a week since William had set out from Middlefield to bring Lizzy home. He'd followed much the same route as she had to Cincinnati, riding first to Albany, taking the Erie Canal from there west to Niagara, then riding to Buffalo, where he boarded the steamboat for Cleveland.

Now all William wanted to do was find a hotel and lie down long enough to allow the queasiness to recede and his strength to return before starting the final leg of his journey. He'd had the good sense to ask a stranger on the steamboat to recommend a decent place to lodge in Cleveland. The man had suggested the Cleveland Hotel on the Public Square, easily reached by walking straight up Ontario Street from the lake shore.

As he trudged along, William received through the fog of his misery the vague impression that Cleveland, although founded perhaps forty years earlier, was already as large as Middletown and growing by the day. The smell of fresh-cut lumber and the sounds of hammers and saws at work testified to a crop of new buildings sprouting up. Many of his fellow passengers on the steamboat were newcomers bound for Cleveland.

At last William reached the broad, rectangular Public Square, and wearily crossed to the three-story Cleveland Hotel. He secured a room from a desk clerk who eyed him with slightly amused sympathy; William wasn't the first lodger to arrive at the hotel looking as gray and limp as a wrung-out scrub rag from seasickness. William requested a pitcher of water and a glass, which he carried as he painfully climbed to the second floor, one step at a time. He was enormously grateful to find that his room was the first one at the top of the stairs.

Once in his room, William fell fully clothed onto the bed, and surrendered to the relief of unconsciousness. When he awoke it was dusk, meaning he'd slept a good eight hours.

The nausea was gone, but in its place were sharp abdominal cramps. William jumped up and barely made it in time to the chamber pot, where he experienced an agonizing bout of diarrhea. He staggered to the bedside table on which he'd set the glass and pitcher of water, and drank thirstily of the tepid liquid. He lay back down on the bed with his eyes closed, his entire body trembling. Within five minutes he vomited up the water along with some bile, followed immediately by another attack of diarrhea.

Panting for breath and drained by the violent spasms of bowel and stomach, William supported himself on the floor on his hands and knees. His arms and legs, he suddenly realized, were ice-cold, and the skin on the back of his hands was puckered. This was something other than seasickness, of that he was sure. During one of the brief periods between attacks of vomiting and diarrhea that started up again, when he was able to think clearly, the terrible word appeared in his mind: cholera.

Although cholera had reportedly disappeared from America last year, William knew his symptoms were nonetheless those of the dreaded disease that killed up to half of its victims. Some died within a few hours of the onset of symptoms. What chance of survival did he have, William thought, fighting off panic – alone in a strange city, barely able to stand to summon assistance that might not be provided, for fear of contracting the disease from him?

William leaned his forehead against the bedpost and prayed. He asked God to spare him, not for his own sake, but for all who depended upon him – Alma, their children, Lizzy most urgently of all. He tormented himself with the thought that at this very moment Lizzy might be looking for him, waiting for him to rescue her from death's door.

Suddenly a gleam of hope pierced William's despair. Asher Coe, Alma's brother. He lived in Olmsted Township, which William knew wasn't far from Cleveland. Surely someone at the hotel would be able to locate him and deliver a message from William.

William pulled himself to his feet, but that simple effort sapped so much of his energy that he realized he had no hope of finding paper and pencil, let alone composing a note. He staggered over to the door, which he yanked open, slamming it loudly against the wall. He had to try three times before he could make his parched lips and raw, swollen throat produce a sound strong enough to reach the ears of the desk clerk at the bottom of the stairs.

When the clerk appeared, holding an oil lamp, his horrified expression upon beholding William confirmed William's worst fears. The man took an involuntary step backward, repelled by the stench emanating from the room.

Gathering all his strength, William rasped out, "Asher Coe, Olmsted Township - send - message - I'm here - sick - come."

William gripped the door sill with both hands to support himself as he stared at the clerk with desperate entreaty. At last the clerk nodded and repeated, "Asher Coe, Olmsted Township." He took a couple of halting steps backward, then turned and hurried down the stairs.

William sagged against the doorpost, then pushed himself away and closed the door. He fell to the floor and began to retch, even as he felt his bowels loosen again. He crawled over to the bed, pulled himself up on it, and lost consciousness.

Chapter Ninety-One

November, 1835
Cincinnati

The driver cursed as he waited impatiently for a herd of hogs clogging the road to be moved aside to let his stagecoach pass. William leaned out the window of the vehicle in an anxious attempt to calculate how long they'd be delayed by the milling swine. The animals were being driven to one of the many slaughterhouses that had earned the nickname of "Porkopolis" for Cincinnati – which William discovered had at last come into view in the distance.

When the stagecoach finally made its way into the city, William was struck by an atmosphere of raw, exotic vitality, due he suspected in large part to the immigrants whose souls his cousin Lyman Beecher was so dedicated to saving. At the same time he was surprised to realize Cincinnati was no primitive frontier community, but a city far larger than Hartford, the streets lined with handsome new churches, public buildings, and private homes.

William's favorable impression diminished when he observed with distaste several hogs running loose, rooting through mounds of garbage smack in the middle of the road. It wasn't hard to see why Cincinnati had proven unhealthy for so many people.

Three days ago William had left Olmsted Township. Alma's brother had brought him there, dehydrated and half-delirious, from Cleveland, after receiving news of his desperate situation. William had spent four days flat on his back in bed, barely able to keep liquids on his stomach, tended by a doctor and Asher's wife.

On the fifth day William had been able to sit up and take solid nourishment. On the sixth he'd managed to stand. And on the seventh he'd insisted, despite his brother-in-law's protests, on continuing his journey to Cincinnati. He'd lost a precious week in his rescue mission, and could ill afford to lose an hour more.

When it had become clear William would survive, Asher had dispatched a letter to Alma, telling her of her husband's illness. William hated to add to Alma's burden of worries, but he realized prolonged silence from him would cause her even greater anguish. He'd insisted Asher play down the seriousness of his sickness, and had forbidden him to use the word "cholera."

William had been riding in a series of stagecoaches almost constantly since leaving Asher's house. Unwilling to waste an entire night sleeping at an inn, he'd stayed at such establishments only until the next stage to Cincinnati was ready to leave.

William had an appetite, and knew he needed to eat to regain the weight lost during his illness, but he could keep only small amounts of the wretched tavern food on his stomach. He tried to sleep in the stagecoach, but the bouncing and jostling as it rumbled along made it almost impossible. His sacrifices had paid off, however, for he'd made the trip from Cleveland to Cincinnati in three days, rather than the four that was typical.

After disembarking from the stagecoach, William set out to find Samuel Foote's house. He had to inquire of three strangers on the crowded, busy sidewalks before he found one who spoke English. The man's directions brought him to the corner of Vine and Third streets, in front of a handsome new two-story mansion in the fashionable Greek Revival style. The facade was crowned by a triangular pediment supported by four massive columns.

With one final prayer to God for the strength to endure whatever awaited him inside this house, William knocked on the door. The serving maid who answered looked at him askance, and he could hardly blame her. He was gaunt, pallid, disheveled, bleary-eyed, and dirty, with a three-days' growth of beard.

"I'm Lizzy Lyman's father," William said, studying the girl's face for her reaction to his words. He saw surprise, and disbelief, but nothing to confirm his greatest fear, that he'd arrived too late.

"Is Lizzy here?" William asked. When the girl nodded warily, it was only with great effort that William kept from breaking into tears. "I'll get Mr. Foote," the girl said uneasily, and scampered away.

William barely had time to cross the threshold into the elegant entrance hall before Samuel Foote hurried in. "William?" he asked uncertainly, appalled by his unexpected visitor's appearance.

William nodded weakly, and Samuel looked him up and down with undisguised concern. "You look like you've been through Hell and back! I doubt I would have recognized you had Annie not told me your identity. Whatever happened–."

"Where's Lizzy?" William asked.

Foote took no offense at being interrupted so curtly, understanding William's desperate concern. "Come with me," he replied, gesturing for William to follow.

"I must prepare you," Foote said as they climbed the stairs. "Lizzy has improved since I wrote you, and the doctors no longer despair for her life, but she's still very ill. You mustn't show any distress at her appearance, lest it shock her frail constitution."

William hardly heard Foote's words. By the time they reached the landing, his heart was in his throat. Foote rapped gently on the door of a chamber at the left of the stairs. A weak voice William barely recognized called, "Come in."

Foote opened the door, then stood aside to let William enter the chamber. Lizzy was seated by a window, in a patch of weak November sunshine. William's reaction at seeing her was two-fold: exhilaration that she was alive and shock at how her illness had reduced her to a pale shadow of herself. He felt as Samuel Foote had upon beholding him a few minutes earlier; had he not been told this was Lizzy, William might not have recognized her. Tears of joy and anguish streamed down his cheeks, and he found he couldn't speak.

Lizzy turned her gaze from the window to the door. At first she seemed not to know William. But after a long moment her beautiful blue eyes, dulled by illness, blazed with the joy of recognition. "Father!" she cried. Never had a word sounded sweeter to him.

Lizzy held out arms that were alarmingly thin. William walked over, knelt down, and gathered her carefully into a protective embrace. He could feel the heat of lingering fever from her soft cheek pressed against his rough, stubbly one. "God be praised," he said.

Reluctantly letting Lizzy go, William took a close look at her. Her eyes were sunken in a face that had lost so much flesh it seemed the cheekbones might break through the skin. She was as pallid as the November sunshine, her hair limp and lusterless. She was weeping for joy, but her tears became ones of pain and sorrow as William's distressing condition became clear to her. She began to understand what he must have endured to reach her.

"I'm taking you home," William said to Lizzy, hugging her even tighter.

"You can't be serious, William'" Samuel Foote exclaimed. "Your illness must have addled your brain."

William was politely adamant. "Lizzy and I will leave for Connecticut in the morning."

"But you've not been here an hour!" Foote protested. "Lizzy can scarcely walk and you look like death itself. I don't know how you got to Cincinnati alive. The journey back to Connecticut could kill you both. I beg you – spend a few days here, regain your strength and allow Lizzy to do the same."

William knew Samuel was speaking common sense. But he was determined that he and Lizzy escape this living nightmare as soon as possible. He shook his head like a stubborn child.

"There's nothing in Cincinnati but suffering and death for both of us," he said. "Our only hope is to flee this accursed city at once. Fool that I was to have countenanced this scheme in the first place." The last sentence was spoken softly in self-recrimination.

"Catharine Beecher has much to answer for," William continued in a cold, hard voice, speaking mostly to himself. "She lured Lizzy away from those who love her to a city ridden with pestilence and unrest. Then she abandoned all responsibility for her school, leaving the work to Lizzy and Hattie and Mary, taking the credit for herself."

Samuel Foote opened his mouth to speak, whether to defend his niece or to try again to persuade William to delay his departure William never knew. He held up his hand palm outward to silence Samuel. "However great the perils of the road, they'll be nothing compared to the pernicious influence the atmosphere of Cincinnati has had on Lizzy. I can't believe the Lord has preserved us both so miraculously through our separate trials and reunited us only to let us die on the journey home. But if that is His will, so be it."

Foote searched William's face for any chink in his determination. He shrugged in surrender to this irrational decision.

William was relieved there would be no more well-intentioned opposition, for he didn't want to waste precious energy on useless bickering. And he was thankful Foote hadn't picked up from his indiscreet remarks about Catharine Beecher the other reason he was anxious to leave Cincinnati as soon as possible. Should Catharine Beecher appear, William didn't trust himself to control his fury at this woman, blood relation or not, who'd nearly sacrificed Lizzy to her selfish ambition.

Chapter Ninety-Two

November, 1835
Middlefield

The haunting sound reached David's ears in the field where he'd just finished digging up enough potatoes to make a bushel. Sighing, he started lugging the basket across the rutted field to the barn.

As the Lyman house came into view, David saw his mother standing on the stone step outside the hall door. She put a large conch shell to her lips and blew a second time to summon David and the hired men in from the fields for supper.

As the sound faded, Alma peered hopefully down the road toward Durham. After a long minute her shoulders slumped in disappointment. She returned the conch shell to its spot beside the door, and went inside. At that moment David reached a decision about the dilemma he'd been turning over in his mind all day.

David carried the heavy basket into the barn, and thankfully dropped it to the ground. His sister Sally was milking the cows. Three years younger than fifteen-year-old David, she was transforming into womanhood, and had recently decided she preferred to be called the more dignified "Sarah" instead of "Sally."

Sarah was nearly as tall as her brother, and filled out a green print work dress handed down from Lizzy. The silky, straight blond hair inherited from her namesake Grandmother Lyman was parted in the middle and pulled severely back from her pretty face. When she looked up past the brim of her bonnet to see who'd come in, David saw she wore a troubled expression.

Sarah placed the pail of warm milk at a safe distance from the cow's hooves and tail, then put the milking stool in a corner. She brushed straw and hay from the hem of her skirt and the long blue apron she wore over it, then straightened up and faced her brother.

"David, do you think Father and Lizzy are ever coming home?" Sarah asked bluntly. William had been gone for more than five weeks, during which they'd received no word other than their Uncle Asher's disturbing letter ten days ago.

"I don't know," David answered with painful honesty. He hesitated before declaring, "If they aren't back in two days, I'm going to find them."

"No, David!" Sarah cried in panic. "The West will swallow you up, too!" She spoke of the West as if it were some horrible monster.

"I have to do something!" David burst out in frustration. "I can't stand just waiting." Melancholy filled his blue eyes. "You should have seen Mother calling us in for supper. She stared down the road for the longest time. I know she was looking for Lizzy and Father, as if the sound of the conch shell might summon them home."

"Do you really think you could find them?" Sarah asked.

"If God wills it," was the best answer David could give. "But I won't ever give up until I find out what's become of them. I couldn't bear for them to vanish without a trace."

"Promise you won't go until after Thanksgiving," Sarah pleaded.

David hated the thought of five more days of uncertainty and inaction. "Please," Sarah persisted, tears glistening in her blue eyes.

"I promise," David said after a long silence. He was rewarded with his little sister's tremulous smile of relief.

"We'd better get inside," David went on briskly. "There's not much time to get everything done before Sabbath starts at sunset."

Connecticut's laws against secular pursuits on the Sabbath weren't commonly observed these days, and rarely enforced. But the Lymans continued to keep it as a day consecrated to God, on which only essential labor was performed.

Sarah nodded, brushing away the tears that would betray her distress to her mother. She picked up the bucket of milk and started for the house. David stared after her, trying, and failing, to share her hope that a few days' delay would truly make any difference.

It was still dark enough when Alma rose from bed that she needed a candle to find her clothes and get dressed. She never slept well without William by her side. His prolonged absence had transformed their bed from a warm haven of intimacy and security into a cold, lonely place where Alma spent as little time as possible.

As days of anxious waiting added up to weeks, then a month, now stretching into a second, Alma had descended into the deepest despair of her life. Her brother Asher's letter had been upsetting. She suspected he hadn't told her the whole truth about William's illness, but knew he wouldn't hide it if William were truly in danger.

There'd been no word since that one letter. The silence spawned countless fears. Had William fallen ill between Asher's house and Cincinnati? Was he lying helpless, or dead, somewhere along the road? If William had reached Cincinnati, why hadn't he sent her news of his arrival and of Lizzy's condition? Had he gotten to Cincinnati to find Lizzy consigned to the grave, and was on his way home to tell her, not wanting to put such terrible news in a letter? Or had William and Lizzy started back to Connecticut, only to meet with some misfortune? Had they been aboard one of the steamboats that reports said went down in Lake Erie with alarming frequency?

Alma thought of the fugitive slave Lucy's grief over never knowing what had become of the daughter who'd been sold away. Was something similar to be her fate? Alma wondered. Would she spend the rest of her life at the edge of a yawning abyss of ignorance about William and Lizzy – wondering, hoping, waiting – in vain?

Alma had no close family with whom to share her fears and worries. Of the Coes there remained in Middlefield only her sister Delia, whose increasing irrationality ruled her out as a confidant, and her brother Linus, who had his hands full dealing with Delia under his roof along with two small children and a new wife.

David had proven a rock of dependability. He hadn't returned to Lee's Academy as had been planned, but instead assumed responsibility for the farm. He'd overseen much of the harvest and supervised the slaughter of hogs for meat. He'd accomplished this with the help of several hired men. Their number included Edward Boston, a Negro youth of David's age. William had taken Edward under his wing after the death of his father, Cuff Boston, who'd done the indigo dyeing of Merino wool from the Lyman flock.

Alma had turned to the Lord for support in fending off the demons that assailed her. Conversations with Mr. Noyes, pastor of the Middlefield church, had provided some solace. When, after a month, hope for William and Lizzy's safe return began to fade, Alma had tried to put herself entirely in God's hands. Although bedeviled by worry and fear, in the Lord's promise of eternal life beyond the grave Alma could at times find refuge from the agonizing possibility that she might never again see Lizzy or William in this world.

Alma had just finished dressing when she heard a slow clopping of hooves. Only an emergency could bring a rider out before dawn on this frigid morning. It was likely a doctor called to treat a patient – or, judging from the horse's weary pace, returning from a visit. But maybe, fear whispered, it was a reluctant bearer of bad news.

The hoof beats stopped in front of the house. Alma reached out a trembling hand to part the curtain and peer out.

In the slight glow from the sun below the horizon Alma could make out only the vague outline of a horse, and the oddly shaped, indistinct form of a large rider. Suddenly that form split into two, and the bigger one dismounted awkwardly.

Alma's heart began to race as she recognized William's tall, long-limbed silhouette. She raced out of the chamber and clattered down the stairs. David, Elihu, Sarah, and Adeline opened the doors to their chambers, bleary-eyed, curious about the commotion.

Alma reached the gate in the homelot's stone wall just as William lifted the second rider off the horse. Alma's head spun with the shock and joy of recognizing Lizzy.

As soon as William had set Lizzy safely on the ground, Alma flung herself into his arms. She erupted into a crying jag as William pulled her to him fiercely.

Through Alma's mind flashed the realization that she could feel William's ribs through his heavy coat. But that unsettling impression was forgotten in the ecstasy of the moment. Lizzy and William were alive. They were home. Nothing else mattered.

Alma took a deep, sobbing breath to bring herself under control. She stepped from William's embrace, and turned to clutch Lizzy to her. Lizzy, alarmingly thin, clung to Alma like a small child, weeping.

David and Elihu burst out the hall door, followed by Sarah and Adeline. Their clothes were askew, having been thrown on in haste. They surrounded their parents and sister with a jubilant clamor.

At last the near-hysteria burned itself out. As she got her first good look at William and Lizzy, Alma saw both were near collapse. "You must get inside out of this cold and into bed," she admonished.

William sketched a slight nod, so weary that just moving his head took a great effort. "We've been riding all night."

At that moment the rising sun's rays reached the Lyman house, bathing it and the family in golden light. The sight, and the realization that their ordeal was truly ended, overwhelmed William. Tears coursed down his thin cheeks, as he choked out, "No family will have greater reason for Thanksgiving than we."

Chapter Ninety-Three

October, 1836
Durham

William snapped the reins sharply to urge the horse drawing the wagon to a greater effort as it began the ascent to the Durham green. He had come to Durham on this autumn Saturday to pick up mail at the post office and purchase goods at the general store.

William had regained most of the flesh he'd lost on his harrowing mission to Cincinnati a year ago. He attributed his restoration to health to following much of the regimen of diet, exercise, and hygiene recommended by temperance-lecturer-turned-health-reformer Sylvester Graham.

The Graham system, based on the belief that overstimulation was the source of disease, was all the rage. Graham advocated giving up not only alcohol but tobacco, coffee, pepper, mustard, tea, salt, and even meat. He prescribed consumption of fruits and vegetables, and in particular "Graham bread" made from coarsely ground flour and allowed to stand at least twelve hours after baking to ensure all heat had dissipated from the loaf.

Graham's recommendations of vigorous exercise had been easy for William to fulfill. Three seasons of work in the fields had put muscle back on his frame. His forearms and hands were deeply tanned, but the hat he wore in the fields had spared his face the same exposure. He again looked a decade younger than his fifty-three years.

William had, however, eschewed the third pillar of Graham's program: abstinence from sexual activity, which Graham considered – even within the bonds of marriage – a major source of nervous excitement that could seriously damage a person's health. William was willing to entertain new, often radical ideas, but he judged them critically rather than embracing them unquestioningly. And simple common sense, not to mention more than thirty years of marriage, told him sex between a loving husband and wife was a healthy thing.

Riding in the bed of the wagon were David and Edward Boston. More than a month away at Lee's Academy, from which he was home on a brief break, had faded the tan David had acquired working outdoors alongside his father. Edward was short but powerfully built, his skin the deep rich brown of molasses.

Next to William on the wagon bench was seven-year-old Adeline. William alternated taking her and Sarah with him on his excursions into Durham. Although not as exciting as a trip to Middletown, a visit to Durham provided a welcome break in the routine of rural life.

William stole a glance at Adeline, recalling Alma's fear that the pain of burying a son and daughter would leave her unable to love this child. He smiled to himself at those baseless worries. This last of their children was a source of great joy for the entire family.

Adeline Urania Lyman, called by her first name, was an enchanting, contradictory combination of little girl one moment, grown-up-lady-in-the-making the next. She had adopted the latter attitude today, sitting regally erect beside her father. Her wide-brimmed bonnet shielded delicate features that included a turned-up nose – she had been spared the signature Lyman one, never an asset to a feminine face – and a cleft chin. She had pale blue eyes and blonde hair, and faint rose tinged her alabaster cheeks.

Adeline showed promise of being every bit as intelligent and talented as Lizzy. She could read as well as most adults, and would pick up a book whenever she had a free moment. She delighted in spending hours with Elihu on his scientific studies, singing or playing instruments together.

They would need to provide Adeline with an education worthy of her abilities, a thought that plunged William into a familiar quandary. Apart from the cost of private school, he and Alma were reluctant to send her to board with strangers a day's ride or more away.

William gladly dismissed this as one concern with which he didn't have to deal immediately. The Durham green came into view, dominated by the new clapboard Congregational Church built just last year. Designed in the fashionable Greek Revival style, with four massive pillars and a soaring three-tiered steeple, it had replaced the century-old meetinghouse in which William's grandparents John and Hope Lyman and great-grandparents Ebenezer and Experience Lyman had worshiped for years.

William had been sad to see the old structure come down. It had symbolized an ancient family connection to Durham that still held meaning for him, and explained why he always had a pleasant sensation of coming home when he visited here

Patches of leaves on trees at the edge of the green had turned vivid orange, vibrant yellow, rich red, or deep bronze, forming an erratic pattern of brilliant, sun-lit colors against a rapidly diminishing background of green. The Durham green and the roads around it were busy with people running errands or visiting taverns where news and gossip were exchanged, business deals struck and – despite the existence of flourishing temperance societies in Durham – rum, whiskey, and other spirits sold and consumed.

The Lymans' first stop was the post office in the house of Asher Robinson, a few doors south and across the road from the green. The children waited in the wagon while William went inside to collect the mail that had accumulated since his last visit. He patiently stood behind several other men, until it was his turn. Robinson handed him two letters and the most recent issues of the weekly *Liberator*.

William thrust the newspapers under his arm, and eagerly examined the letters. The first was for Alma from his sister Sally in New York. Unfortunately, Abner Miller hadn't prospered as he'd envisioned in his new homeland. William hoped this letter contained news of an improvement in their fortunes.

William frowned when he saw the second letter was postmarked from Cincinnati and addressed in Mary Dutton's hand. Mary had written twice begging Lizzy to return to Cincinnati to help run the Western Female Institute. Hattie Beecher had married Calvin Stowe not long after Lizzy's departure, and last month had given birth to twin daughters. Hattie had given up entirely her involvement in the Institute, leaving Mary to handle it all alone.

Lizzy didn't share William's opinion that Catharine Beecher had exploited the young women unconscionably. But she did agree with William's frank opinion that for her to return to the Western Female Institute would be suicidal. She felt that her work in Cincinnati was finished, and she had mostly wonderful memories of the time she'd spent there.

The polite letter of refusal Lizzy had mailed to Mary Dutton in response to her latest plea had gone out four days ago. It couldn't have reached Cincinnati yet, so the missive in William's hand was most likely another even more urgent appeal for Lizzy to come west.

Just the thought of Lizzy returning to that city caused the blood to pound in William's temples. He resisted the urge to tear up the letter. Lizzy was a grown woman with the right to make her own decisions. He'd been encouraged by the good sense she'd displayed in her handling of Charles Mills.

Charles had been so thrilled by Lizzy's return from Cincinnati that he'd impetuously asked her to marry him, even though he still had to complete divinity school. It would have been easy for Lizzy to accept Charles's premature proposal. She'd told him she would be happy to become his wife – once he'd finished his studies and secured a position. Crestfallen, Charles had agreed.

Lizzy had told her parents how while in Cincinnati she'd come more and more to value the relationship she and Charles had for the warm, rewarding thing it was, rather than fretting that it wasn't a passionate romance like those idealized in novels. Their connection had remained steady during the year since Lizzy's return.

William liked and respected Charles Mills, but wasn't convinced he was the right husband for Lizzy – although he had to admit that the man who possessed all the sterling qualities he believed his daughter deserved in a spouse probably didn't exist. He couldn't shake off a nagging concern that Charles's intense temperament, his occasional tendencies toward emotional excess, might not meld easily with Lizzy's sunnier, less volatile personality.

For once Alma's outlook on the situation was the more optimistic. She'd chided William for his misgivings about a devout young man who was pursuing the highest of callings, and had proven his deep, steadfast love for Lizzy. William resolved to accept Alma's judgement, knowing his own could be clouded where their children were concerned.

Deep in his musings, William failed to notice three men standing outside Asher Robinson's house share disgusted glances when they saw *The Liberator* issues tucked under his arm. They watched William hand the mail to David, then climb up onto the wagon seat and drive around the green to the general store.

The disapproving trio drifted over to a group of five men conversing at the south end of the green. "We just saw William Lyman picking up copies of *The Liberator* at the postmaster's," said Benjamin Seward, a bespectacled farmer in his forties, as they joined the larger group. The news was greeted with murmurs of exasperation and even contempt.

"I'm not surprised he subscribes to that abolitionist rag," said Seth Baldwin, a husky young shoemaker. "He was at the meeting in Hartford winter before last to start the Connecticut Anti-Slavery Society. Had his name published on a broadside bold as brass."

"What I can't understand is why respectable men like Lyman get mixed up in such a dirty business as abolitionism," said Noah Strong, an elderly blacksmith, shaking his head.

"It's none of our business what Southerners do with their slaves," Benjamin Seward said emphatically. The other men nodded their vigorous agreement. "If the abolitionists are allowed to continue their reckless agitation, it's going to cause real trouble. Southerners might just get fed up with holier-than-thou Northern abolitionists meddling in their affairs, and decide to leave the Union and go their own way. This needs to be stopped before it goes too far."

"It's not like folks haven't tried," Noah Strong said. "Remember that first abolitionist meeting in Middletown two years ago? People dumped pails of water on them, threw eggs and stones at them. A couple got roughed up pretty badly. But they keep holding meetings. It makes you wonder if they're in their right minds."

"William Lyman is always coming up with new ideas about what's best for other people," observed Seth Baldwin sourly. "He was behind the temperance activity over in Middlefield early on. He got a lot of folks there to swear off spirits – even hard cider and beer!"

"There's some sense to advocating temperance like our societies here in Durham do," Seward pointed out. "We all know men whose fondness for spirits has run their families into poverty and misery. Then the town has to take care of them."

A look of bafflement came over Seward's face. "But this abolitionism is pure nonsense. Everyone knows Negroes aren't equal to white men. You can see it in most of the ones right here in Connecticut. I wager the ones down South are even worse."

"Slavery's probably the best condition for Southern Negroes," chimed in young Baldwin. "They likely couldn't take care of themselves if they were free. Why the abolitionists are so fired up about liberating them is beyond me."

By now half a dozen more men had drifted over, drawn by curiosity about what the knot of men was discussing so animatedly.

"There's one of those abolitionist troublemakers," said one of the newcomers, pointing to William, who was coming out of the general store. "Maybe it's time for someone to set him straight."

William noticed the small crowd, with most of whom he had at least a slight acquaintance, as he started over to the wagon. He placed a small keg of salt and a new shovel in the wagon bed, then turned to take a closer look at the group. An uneasy feeling crept over him when he saw they were staring – glaring – right at him. When a moment later the men began to walk slowly and deliberately in his direction, William knew what was on their minds.

Abolitionists in New England had been the targets of scorn, intimidation, and physical violence in recent years. William Lloyd Garrison had only narrowly escaped being lynched by a Boston mob.

William hadn't allowed the increasing hostility toward abolitionists to inhibit his anti-slavery activity. If anything he'd become more outspoken on the subject. He assumed it was only a matter of time before he would be confronted by unhappy anti-abolitionists, and he was prepared to handle it. But he didn't want the children mixed up in what could turn into an ugly situation.

"David," William called to his son, who was on the threshold of the store, Edward and Adeline right behind him. "You and Edward take your sister over to Mr. Smith's house and wait there for me."

As William spoke he kept his eyes on the approaching mob, which he calculated numbered perhaps fifteen men. William knew the children would be safe in the house of Durham's retired pastor, a short distance off the green.

The strained urgency in his father's voice perplexed David, until he, too, caught sight of the mob moving with insidious steadiness toward William. It wasn't difficult to discern the crowd's intent.

David exchanged glances with Edward, who'd sized up the situation as well. Adeline stood between them, not understanding why the two youths were suddenly so tense.

"No, sir," David replied with as much firmness as he could muster. "We'll stay with you."

William swung around to stare in astonishment at David, the most obedient of sons. In the two teenaged boys' faces he saw loyalty and courage that touched his heart. But he couldn't permit them to be caught up in whatever was about to happen.

"I know these men," William said in a low voice. "They just want to talk." He saw disbelief plain in both boys' eyes.

"I know you mean well," William said with rising urgency, glancing quickly to his left to keep track of the mob's progress. "If there's trouble I can take care of myself. But I don't want to have to worry about you – especially Adeline." When the children still didn't move, William said to David, not as a father ordering a child but as one man to another, "I'm asking you to go to Mr. Smith's."

David still hesitated, torn between fidelity to his father and the common sense of William's request. Finally he took Adeline by the hand and started to walk reluctantly to the minister's house.

Edward Boston didn't move. His lips were pressed firmly together in determination, his eyes riveted on William's face.

"Please, Edward," William pleaded softly. "It's not safe here for you, especially." William expected that while the mob might bully him, he probably wasn't in danger of serious injury. Far greater was his fear that the throng would see the Negro youth as a more legitimate – and vulnerable – target for its anger. In that case, Edward could be hurt badly – or worse.

Another long moment passed, as Edward pondered William's request. Then with a tormented expression on his face, he gave a single, short nod before turning to follow David and Adeline. As Edward reached the doorstep of the minister's house, he looked back to see William standing alone, his back to the wagon, facing the crowd that was now almost upon him.

With calculated casualness William slipped off the wool coat Alma had made for him and draped it over the wagon seat. He forced a smile to his face, concealing churning emotions that included apprehension mixed with exasperation. Why, he wondered, were men who were decent and sensible in most respects so threatened by efforts to free other people whose only offense was to have dark skin? And why, he thought in a surge of illogical annoyance, must they mar so glorious an autumn day with their ugly intolerance?

The mob came to a halt about ten feet from William. "We'd like to have a word with you William," began Benjamin Seward, who'd assumed leadership of the group by unspoken consensus.

"Of course," William replied genially, his heart pounding hard.

"We've been talking among ourselves, and we agree this abolitionist nonsense you've been spreading could cause a lot of trouble. We want you to stop it."

"I can't do that," William replied politely, as if Seward had asked him to do the impossible, like pick up the meetinghouse.

"What business is it of yours if Southerners want to keep slaves," Seth Baldwin demanded. "They don't try to tell us how to run our lives."

"It's my business and your business, and the business of every Christian American, because for one man to hold another in slavery is a vile sin against God," William answered reasonably in a forceful voice meant to be heard by the entire crowd. "We can't consider ourselves truly free so long as other Americans are held in chains."

"Don't be so high and mighty, Lyman," sneered Baldwin. "You're not going to ram this abolitionist shit down people's throats!"

Benjamin Seward winced in embarrassment at Baldwin's vulgar language, which was met with murmurs and shouts of agreement from several men. Determined to keep the encounter civil, Seward twisted his head around to try to silence the group with a disapproving glare – just in time to see a man at the back of the mob pick up a horse dropping and fling it hard at William.

The missile of manure struck the startled William square in the chest. Most of the men in the crowd laughed, but several older ones shifted uneasily. They remembered the young Billy Lyman of more than thirty years past, and his quick, ferocious temper.

Seward turned back to see William staring down at the brown stain on his white shirtfront. Seward was annoyed by the crude gesture – but then how did William expect people to respond to his abolitionist troublemaking?"

"Negroes aren't men like you and I, William," Seward began again. The face William raised to Seward was flushed, but wore an impassive expression.

"The Constitution considers blacks property, and even the Bible condones slavery," Seward went on reasonably.

"We didn't come to debate," cut in Baldwin, elbowing Seward aside to stand face-to-face with William. "Just to warn you that you're asking for trouble if you keep up this anti-slavery agitation. You know what's happened to your kind in other towns."

"Is that a threat?" William asked in a deceptively calm voice.

"Let's call it friendly advice," replied Baldwin sarcastically. Stepping closer, he said in a voice intended only for William's ears, "And here's more. If we can't convince you to change your ways, the law can. Word is you help runaways from down South. There's a $500 fine for helping fugitive slaves. That's a lot of money – enough to cause a man to lose his farm."

William's gut turned to ice, and his face went pale at the churlish young shoemaker's words. William had been careful to keep every detail of his work with the fugitive slaves a secret. Had Baldwin just made a lucky guess, or did he really know something? Had William or someone else along the line made a slip? Or, worst of all to contemplate, had someone betrayed them?

"I see that put a good scare into you," Baldwin said with malicious satisfaction, certain he'd succeeded in cowing William. "You'll do as we say, if you know what's good for you – and your family." To drive his point home, Baldwin grabbed the front of William's shirt with both hands and shoved him backwards hard against the side of the wagon.

Baldwin's threat against his family and the pain that shot through his back when he struck the wagon unleashed the fury William had been fighting to keep in check. Pushing himself off the wagon with both hands, he lunged forward and backhanded Baldwin across the face with his right hand, knocking the shoemaker to the ground. When another man stepped forward to grab him, William jammed his left elbow hard into his attacker's gut, then swung his right fist around to punch him in the jaw, painfully bruising his own knuckles.

The rest of the mob, who'd likewise mistaken William's self-control for weakness, were momentarily dumbfounded by their prey's unexpected violent resistance. William took advantage of their hesitation to grab from the wagon a shovel to use as a makeshift weapon. Gripping its handle tightly, he turned to confront the mob, mentally cursing himself for losing control of his temper.

The silence was broken only by the coughing of the man William had elbowed in the stomach. But the mob quickly recovered from its shock, and stared at William with new resentment, that of a bully for the victim who dared to fight back. Half a dozen men began to advance towards William, who brandished the shovel in a menacing gesture he knew was meaningless against such overwhelming odds. This must be what it felt like to be a fugitive slave about to be captured, the thought flashed through his mind – alone, afraid, desperate, outnumbered, with no hope of escape.

"For shame!" The powerful shout came from behind William. Startled, the men stopped, and heads turned toward the source of the voice: a short, white-haired man standing on the northwest corner of the green. Behind him stood David, Edward, and Adeline.

The crowd waited as the Reverend David Smith, pastor of the Durham Congregational church for more than thirty years until his retirement four years ago, made his way slowly toward them.

"Just a year ago many of you helped raise that new house of God," the minister said, pointing to the Congregational meetinghouse. "Now you stand in its very shadow and violate the blessed Jesus' message of peace and love that you hear there every Sabbath. And you call yourselves Christians!" Mr. Smith said contemptuously. The chagrin, and shame on the faces of most of the men made it clear the minister's words had hit their mark.

"But pastor," began Seth Baldwin, who'd been helped to his feet. "Lyman here is a dangerous man. His abolitionist activities–."

"I don't care what your grievance is with Mr. Lyman," Mr. Smith cut off the young man dismissively. "Ganging up on him and brawling like schoolboys is no way to settle it. Now go about your business, all of you!"

The mob broke up as its members made their way sheepishly in ones and twos off the green. William relaxed his grip on the shovel and let it slip from his sweaty hands. He sagged back against the wagon as the tension drained out of him.

The children came running up behind Mr. Smith. David was agog; he'd never seen his father raise his voice to another human being, let alone strike one. Edward was studying William with a mixture of admiration and gratitude.

But William felt a sharp twist of remorse at Adeline's expression. Clearly disturbed by William's violent outburst, she was eyeing her father warily, as though he were a stranger.

"Are you all right, Father?" David managed to ask at last.

"I'm fine, Son," William answered, straightening up and forcing a reassuring smile. "Thanks to Mr. Smith," he added, turning and nodding at the minister.

"I regret you were subjected to such inexcusable behavior, William," Mr. Smith said apologetically. "I was working in the fields beyond the house when your son came to get me. I would have gotten here sooner, but I'm not as spry as I once was," he explained with a wry smile that was quickly replaced with a sober expression.

"You must admit you bear part of the blame for this incident, William," Mr. Smith admonished. "These were not shiftless ruffians who confronted you, but respectable citizens. Your abolitionist activities offend and frighten many good men."

William sighed deeply with frustration. He stared down the length of the green for a moment before bringing his gaze back to meet the minister's. "I can't let the fact that some people are blind to evil stop me from following my conscience," he said resolutely.

Mr. Smith heaved his own sigh of exasperation. "I've known you since you were no older than these two," he said, gesturing toward David and Edward. "I know better than to expect you to compromise your principles to please anyone. But I just saw you lose your temper in a way you haven't done in decades. And this won't be the last or even the worst of it. I stopped it this time, but there may be other mobs, who will take out their anger on not only you, but perhaps on your family as well. Think about it," he pleaded.

"Don't you think I have?" William snapped, instantly regretting his sharpness. "Alma and I have lost many a night's sleep worrying about what evil our abolitionist work might bring down on us. But she agrees it's a risk we must take. We were put here on earth to do what we believe is God's will, to love and help one another, no matter the color of our skins."

Mr. Smith regarded William with a mix of admiration and dismay: admiration for his commitment to his beliefs, even ones Mr. Smith considered unrealistic and misguided, and dismay for the ruin that misplaced commitment might bring down on his family.

"Then I can only pray God will protect you," said the minister

"Thank you, sir," said William. "I trust He will as He did today."

William turned to the children. "Let's head home. You all get in the wagon."

As they started down the hill from the Durham green, Adeline asked tentatively, "Should we tell Mother what happened, Father? Won't it just cause her to fret?"

"Of course we'll tell your mother," answered William gently. "I keep no secrets from her. Even if we didn't, she's sure to learn about it from someone else sooner or later. Better she hear the truth from us. Besides," he said in a lighter tone, "she'll certainly want an explanation for this smelly stain on my shirt."

William's reassuring words for Adeline concealed how badly the incident had shaken him. Knowing many people despised abolitionists was one thing; being accosted by men of his acquaintance, some of whom he would have called friends, and being physically assaulted was another. The dark experience cast an even more sinister light on the path William knew he nonetheless had to continue traveling, no matter what.

Chapter Ninety-Four

November, 1839
Middlefield

The infant smiled up at David, who shot the baby's mother a cocky smile. "See, this little fry and I get along fine," he said.

No sooner had David spoken than the child, for no discernible reason, twisted his tiny features into a grimace, grew red in the face, and erupted into a piercing, warbling wail. The now-chagrined David hastily handed the baby to Lizzy.

Lizzy laid her son against her left shoulder, and rubbed his back in small, comforting circles. Little Lyman McKee Mills stopped crying, then struggled to lift his head with neck muscles not yet strong enough to do the job. The seven-week-old infant at last settled for resting his left cheek on his mother's breast and gazing around with bright eyes at his surroundings.

"It will come to you naturally when you have your own," Lizzy assured David. She instinctively swayed her body slightly from side to side to create a slight motion that soothed the baby.

David emitted a startled snort. He certainly expected to someday have a family. But at just nineteen years old, fatherhood was relegated to a far-distance, indistinct future.

"I think I'd like a dozen children!" David said, primarily for the fun of seeing Lizzy's shocked reaction. But he was surprised to realize his statement wasn't that great an exaggeration. Growing up within the secure embrace of a large, loving family had been a rare and precious gift, and he would want no less for his own children.

Lizzy sputtered with laughter at David's outrageous statement. "I hope you intend to warn any woman you court about this, this–,"

Lizzy searched for the appropriate words, "this great ambition," she finished. "Not every woman will be enthusiastic about striving to achieve such a goal."

"That would be fair," David conceded with a wry smile that quickly faded. "But I'll not likely be dealing with that any time soon. Weeks on the road hundreds of miles from home in the company of mules doesn't leave much time for charming the fair sex."

Lizzy drew her eyebrows together in concern. The financial panic that had swept the nation in 1837, the year of her marriage to Charles Mills, had hit the Lymans as hard as anyone in Connecticut. David had withdrawn permanently from Lee's Academy. This premature ending to his formal education hadn't distressed David nearly as much as it would have Lizzy.

David now was primarily occupied making trips to the West and South to purchase mules for the Trowbridge firm. These had become increasingly important as a source of income for the Lymans.

David made the trips alone. William had to remain at home, to work the farm to its maximum profitability, and assist any fugitive slaves conducted to him – an increasingly dangerous activity.

The backlash against abolitionists in the North had intensified as their crusade gained attention and attracted supporters. Two years past, in 1837, an anti-abolitionist mob in Illinois had brutally murdered Elijah Lovejoy, editor of an anti-slavery newspaper.

"It must be a great trial for you," Lizzy said sympathetically. "Especially traveling through dark lands of slavery such as Virginia and Kentucky, where human life is held so cheap."

David sketched a shrug of acceptance. "The work needs to be done. And I'm prudent enough to keep my convictions on certain subjects to myself. But the days – and the nights – can be lonely."

Lizzy's frown caused David to regret giving in to self-pity. "That's not to say I don't find satisfaction in the work," he amended. "Mr. Trowbridge entrusts me with large sums of money, and I enjoy the challenge of finding the finest animals, negotiating the best prices. And it means much to know I'm helping make ends meet at home."

"If you say so," Lizzy said skeptically. She decided not to pry any further. She knew David truly did relish handling complicated financial matters, for which he'd displayed a natural talent. He was extremely conscientious, yet also affable, a combination that served him well when making a deal. Young as he was, he'd impressed a hard-headed businessman like Trowbridge with his honesty and his commitment to fulfilling any responsibility he accepted.

But David also displayed an enterprising streak. He was willing to take a gamble – although never impulsively or recklessly – on a fresh idea, or project, or vision that he thought had a good chance of success. In this, William had told Lizzy, David reminded him of his own father. Lizzy sensed that the resemblance troubled William.

Lizzy and David turned their heads as Alma emerged from the kitchen, where she'd been closeted since before daybreak, supervising preparation of Thanksgiving dinner. The mouth-watering aroma of roast turkey wafted into the hall.

"Everything should be on the table in about an hour," Alma announced confidently. "Sarah and Adeline made all the pies by themselves – including your favorite Marlborough pie, Lizzy. It was devilishly difficult to secure sufficient sugar produced by free labor." William and Alma had sworn off purchasing sugar from slave-holding areas, which accounted for most of what was available.

"I decided to steal a few minutes away from the hearth to spend with my grandson," said Alma. Lizzy lifted the dozing baby from her shoulder and carefully placed him in her mother's arms. Alma studied her first grandchild with adoration.

"Can you believe it, David?" she whispered in wonderment, not taking her eyes from the infant. "This sweet baby makes five generations of Lymans who have lived on this land."

"Let's go see your grandfather, Lyman," Alma said softly to the sleeping baby. She turned away a step, then stopped and looked at Lizzy for her consent. Since the Mills family's arrival Alma had tried not to usurp her daughter's authority as a first-time mother.

Lizzy nodded. With careful, measured steps, so as not to awaken the baby, Alma walked to the adjacent room where William had been in deep conversation with Charles for more than an hour.

"How much has changed in four years," David mused as he sat on William's oversized settle, where Lizzy joined him. "Thanksgiving of 1835 saw just the seven of us rejoicing over the miracle of you and Father returning from Ohio. Today twice as many will gather here to feast and thank the Lord for blessings too numerous to count."

"A week on the road from Indiana was an ordeal for all of us – Charles with his weak constitution most of all," said Lizzy. "But it was worth it to spend my first Thanksgiving as a mother with my family, to see Mother and Father's joy in their first grandchild."

"Did you know Cousin Esther and Cousin Alfred and his wife and daughter are coming today?" David asked.

Lizzy shook her head. "Everything's been such a hubbub since we arrived yesterday, I've barely been able to catch my breath."

"Since Aunt Esther died, Father's been trying to bring them closer into the family fold," David added. "Annis must be close to sixteen now," he mused about Alfred Lyman's daughter who, if he calculated correctly, was their second cousin.

"Speaking of cousins, how are Charles and Henry faring?" Lizzy asked. "Charles is eleven now, and Henry must be nearly nine."

"They haven't had it easy," David said. "You know their stepmother wasn't very fond of them, especially after she had her own baby. When the doctors told Uncle Charles he wouldn't ever recover from the sickness he got from working as a tanner, he asked Father and Uncle Linus to be guardians for Charles and Henry. The lion's share of their care has fallen to Papa. They live mostly with their Grandfather Bliss in Hartford, but Father says he's near eighty and getting too old to handle a couple of bumptious boys. They spend a little time at Uncle Linus's house, but more here."

The mention of her Uncle Linus brought another relative to Lizzy's mind. "What about Aunt Delia? Is she at all improved?"

"No. She's worse, in fact," David said with sad candor. "I haven't witnessed much myself, being away. But Elihu says when she's here they're careful not to leave her alone. The smallest mishap can cause her to plunge into a sudden melancholy so black I know Mother fears she'll harm herself. Then just as suddenly something will spark her to a frenzy of excitement. She'll tear about the house, refusing to brook any opposition to her plans, however ludicrous."

Her aunt's plight left Lizzy numb with sorrow – and fear. "I know God must have some purpose in afflicting Aunt Delia so, but I can't fathom it," she admitted. "When she's in her right mind she is so intelligent, so congenial. She was such a faithful, delightful correspondent when I was in Cincinnati."

"It hurts to watch her be tormented by irrational delusions, and not be able to help her," David said with frustration. "It's worst for Mother. It raises disturbing memories of Grandfather Coe's last years." David didn't have to add that insanity in father and daughter raised the specter of it surfacing in other family members as well.

Lizzy shook her head slowly. "I hope Charles can find a permanent settlement in New England," she said with fervent longing. "I yearn to be closer to all our loved ones, to share our joys and support each other in our trials."

Lizzy paused for a moment before confiding, "It was a hard blow for Charles when the Indianapolis congregation didn't ask him to stay on permanently once his year as an evangelist ended." She went on in a confessional tone. "But I was relieved. The people of Indianapolis are good folk, but the town is small and rough and provincial next to Hartford or even Middletown. I tried to embrace Indiana as my home, but it could never be my beloved 'Yankeeland.'"

David nodded his agreement. "I've been everywhere from Vermont to Virginia to Ohio to Kentucky. And like you and Father, I've yet to see a place I prefer to Connecticut."

He fell silent for a moment, debating whether to reveal something to Lizzy. "I wouldn't raise your hopes," he said at last. "But Father is talking to Charles right now about whether he has any interest in filling the vacancy in Durham created by Mr. Gleeson's death in August."

Lizzy eyes blazed with joyous hope at David's revelation. But she immediately reined in her emotions. "I thought William Fowler had received a call from the Durham church," she said cautiously.

"He did, in late October," David confirmed. "But Father learned he'd declined it two weeks ago, just about when your letter arrived telling us Charles wasn't called by the Indianapolis church. Father has made some discreet inquiries about the status of the Durham search. They're now considering issuing a call to James McDonald."

"Oh," Lizzy replied, struggling to conceal her disappointment.

"But that's not necessarily the end of the story," David went on. "The Durham congregation is a fractious one–."

"It couldn't possibly be more so than Middlefield," Lizzy interjected. David acknowledged the truth of her remark with a rueful smile.

"There is more than a small chance that Mr. McDonald won't accept the call," David went on. "Father wanted to talk to Charles at the first chance to learn if he had any other prospects, or if the Durham pulpit would interest him."

"It would be bliss to come home," Lizzy sighed. "I will pray it be God's will for Charles to minister to the people of Durham. But I won't plan on it, will go with Charles wherever the Lord sends him."

The sound of the baby fussing snapped Lizzy out of her reverie. She got to her feet as Alma re-appeared with her grandson. Lizzy knew what her son wanted; her uncomfortably full breasts told her it was past time for his feeding. She took him from Alma and carried him upstairs to nurse in the privacy of a chamber.

Alma smiled at David, then bustled back into the kitchen. David lay his head back against the settee, and pondered Lizzy's situation.

The Indianapolis rejection hadn't been Charles's first. Shortly after he and Lizzy wed, Charles had been called to serve as a supply minister to a Presbyterian church in South Hanover, Indiana. They'd returned east when that hadn't resulted in an offer to become the congregation's permanent pastor.

Lizzy and Charles had been in Connecticut barely long enough for Charles to be ordained as an evangelist before heading west again. This time their destination was Indianapolis, which had also failed to extend him an invitation to a permanent post.

Charles was a man of profound faith, a gifted orator, and he possessed a crusader's zeal. But word had it that as the spiritual shepherd of a congregation, Charles was easily frustrated when members of his flock didn't all follow him obediently on the path to salvation. He grew impatient with any who strayed or dawdled and had to be coaxed onto what Charles judged the right course.

William Lyman wasn't willing to consign his daughter to what was looking more and more like the life of a peripatetic preacher's wife. Thus when William learned, almost simultaneously, that Charles hadn't been offered the Indianapolis pulpit, and that the candidate for the Durham pastorate had declined the offer, he sprang into action. He'd asked discreetly among his acquaintances in the Durham congregation about the next step in their search, and had alluded to Charles's availability. But William had had to wait until he could speak with Charles face-to-face to assess – and if necessary, stoke – his son-in-law's interest in the plan, and secure his enthusiastic cooperation in pursuing the Durham pastorate.

Ordinarily William would have resisted the temptation to meddle in the life of a child of his who was a grown woman, a wife, and a mother. But three times in the past five years he and Alma had bidden Lizzy goodbye, and watched as she vanished into the void of the West, not knowing when, if ever, she would return. If there was a way to see her securely settled in Connecticut, William would do whatever he could to make it come to pass.

William had admitted to David reservations about trying to manipulate a situation as important as the selection of a minister to suit his own personal wishes. Then yesterday David had seen any lingering doubts William harbored about his course of action vanish in an instant – when he laid eyes for the first time on his first grandchild.

Chapter Ninety-Five

April, 1841
Durham

William stood with his back to the wall surveying the crowd that packed the second-floor ballroom of Lemuel Camp's tavern on Durham's main street. Occasionally he caught a glimpse of Lizzy or Charles through a breach in the wall of well-wishers around the couple waiting a turn to congratulate Charles on his ordination this Sabbath morning as pastor of the Durham Congregational Church.

Charles was dignified and solemn to the point of stiffness as he accepted the kind words of parishioners, friends, and relatives. The collar of his black dress coat, rigidly starched and sharp-edged, reached so close to his jaw line in the current style that it seemed as if it could cut his throat if he turned his head too quickly.

Lizzy was a striking contrast to Charles in appearance and demeanor. She was the personification of spring in a gown of dandelion-colored silk. Layers of ruffles encircled the bottom half of her skirt and the long, fitted sleeves, and trimmed a neckline low enough to reveal her slender neck and her shoulders. A bonnet of deep brown, with a wide brim that extended out beyond her face was tied at her throat with a broad silk bow. It concealed her honey blonde tresses, save for two small rolls at each temple.

Lizzy leaned forward to greet each person with unpretentious warmth. There were faint shadows of fatigue under her eyes – not surprising, since this day marked her first public appearance since the birth in February of the couple's second son.

The two-month-old infant had obliged everyone by sleeping through the morning ordination service. Afterward Lizzy had nursed him, then turned him over to Alma. That freed Lizzy to devote her full attention to the first of the social responsibilities that were the job of a pastor's wife.

Alma was proudly showing off her new grandson to a clutch of admiring matrons. Alma was dressed far more conservatively than Lizzy, as befitting a woman of more than fifty. Her dress was a deep indigo with a ruffle of layers of snow-white lace surrounding her throat. Her bonnet was the same color, and hugged her head, tied with a small bow at her throat. Deep lines on either side of her nose, her taut, almost pursed mouth, and a hint of wariness in her eyes were subtle, yet to William readily detectable, signs of the toll the events of the last two years had taken on his wife.

Still, Alma retained the blooming complexion of her youth, and her forehead was unwrinkled. The hair that current fashion permitted to peek out from beneath her bonnet was still a rich, glossy chestnut, with not a single strand of gray, in contrast to William's hair, which by now was as much silver as it was brown.

Slow, erratic movement caught William's eye. Sixteen-year-old Elihu, tall, thin, seemingly all angles and joints beneath the cloth of his Sunday suit, was threading his way through the crowd. In the unusually large hands he'd inherited from William he was balancing a plate heaped with macaroons and slices of sponge cake, and two glasses of lemonade. His eyes were fixed with a frown of concern on his destination, his sister Adeline. In the moments he'd been away securing refreshments she'd been approached by three young men who were vying for her attention.

William smiled in amusement. The closeness between brother and sister, just three years apart in age, that had existed since childhood had taken on a new dimension of protectiveness on Elihu's part as Adeline, who would turn thirteen next month, began to emerge into womanhood.

The attention Adeline attracted from young men told William that his assessment of her beauty and charm were not a fond father's wishful thinking. Adeline wore a dress of cranberry red, ruffled, although not as heavily as Lizzy's. Her blonde hair wasn't covered by a bonnet, but adorned with a caplet of lace and flowers.

Adeline enjoyed the attention she'd recently started receiving from the opposite sex. Her fierce attachment to Elihu had kept her from chafing under his big-brother protectiveness – so far.

Search as he might, William couldn't locate eighteen-year-old Sarah in the crush of people, although she'd been at the ordination.

Her absence saddened, but didn't surprise William. Sarah had grown into a very pretty young woman, sweetly gentle in character and with a formidable intellect. But the outgoing personality that had characterized her at thirteen had changed since the accident.

Sarah had been shutting the pair of ten-foot-tall barn doors after finishing the last of the day's milking, something she'd done countless times. But one evening her right hand had gotten caught between the two heavy doors as they swung closed. Her hand had been crushed.

The damage was so extensive that despite the best medical care available, the bones knit together poorly. Sarah's fingers were twisted in an awkward manner that had reduced her once clear, elegant script to a scrawl.

Although a person meeting Sarah for the first time couldn't help but notice the disfigured hand, it was by no means repulsive, and quickly forgotten in the brightness of Sarah's beauty and warmth. But Sarah had grown increasingly self-conscious about her mangled hand. She'd developed a habit of casually holding it at her side, concealed in the folds of her skirt, when in the presence of anyone but family. And she'd become more reserved, spending her time with books rather than socializing with men and women her own age.

Alma fretted continually about her middle daughter, and William was concerned as well. He took some consolation in the fact that Sarah's passion for books was genuine, and her dedication to reading was honing her natural intelligence into a first-rate mind. She alone of William and Alma's children had a touch of wanderlust, yearned to travel not just in America but to foreign lands. She'd been carrying a slim volume when they left the house that morning, and William suspected she'd slipped away to read alone for a while.

David probably could have persuaded Sarah to attend the reception, William mused. But David, too, was absent, somewhere in Kentucky on the first mule-buying trip of the season.

Charles Mills's ordination was due in no small part to William's personal connections – and to the contentiousness of the Durham congregation. After the second minister to whom they offered the position turned it down, the committee charged with finding a pastor had been relieved to have a new candidate materialize almost miraculously – even one who'd been rejected for a permanent position by two congregations in as many years.

Charles Mills had sterling educational credentials and was married to the daughter of a family with roots a century deep in adjacent Middlefield. While William's abolitionist activities had earned him the dislike of some, most still considered him a respectable citizen whose enthusiastic advocacy for his son-in-law for the Durham pastorate carried considerable weight.

So many people had crowded into the tavern room that it had become oppressive. William slipped down the stairs and out the door, emerging in front of the building. He'd barely stepped outside when a stagecoach rumbled past, churning up a thick cloud of dust from the dry roadbed.

As the dust settled, William saw across the street a short, trim, man of about thirty, wearing steel-rimmed glasses that enhanced his scholarly demeanor. With weary irritation, Dr. Seth Childs slapped at the coat and pants of his Sunday suit, trying with little success to remove as much dust as he could as he crossed to the tavern.

William smiled in rueful amusement at the younger man's futile attempt to spruce himself up. As Dr. Childs reached his side, William inhaled the spring air deeply through his nose, evaluating its subtle qualities as he once might have those of a wine.

"I smell rain," William stated. "It will put down the dust. But I calculate it won't arrive before nightfall."

Dr. Childs squinted up at the cloudless, sparkling blue sky. "It looks like fair weather to me, William," he began dubiously. "Still, I can count on the fingers of one hand the number of times in the three years I've known you that your sense about anything related to farming has proven wrong."

William smiled graciously at the compliment. "But if your prediction comes true," the physician continued, "it will be a mixed blessing. I'll just have to slog my way to my patients through mud instead of choking on dust as I did earlier."

William was silent for a moment, then said reflectively, "Forty years ago a stagecoach running on Sunday in Connecticut would have been as unthinkable as a sea serpent swimming up the Connecticut River. The new state law permitting transport of the federal mails on the Sabbath is one of the last nails in the coffin of the Sabbath I prized as a boy, a day of rest consecrated to the Lord."

Dr. Childs studied William with surprise. His first contact with William Lyman after arriving in Durham three years ago had been to subscribe to the abolitionist newspaper *The Christian Freeman,* for which William was an agent. There had developed between the two men a trust strong enough that William had sought the young physician's assistance in treating a fugitive slave who'd been injured in the course of his flight.

"You're the last man I'd expect to have regrets about change – having labored to bring about so much of it," Dr. Childs said.

William's mouth twisted into a wry smile. "I plead guilty to having been an agent of multiple changes, to the distress of a great many people. But in my nearly sixty years I've seen enough to understand that not all change is progress. Sometimes I fear we are throwing the baby out with the bath water. Who had need of your services this morning?" he asked abruptly, changing the subject.

"Amos Randall came at dawn to fetch me," said Dr. Childs. "His father took a bad fall down the stairs. I rode out to their place and found he'd broken his leg. Setting the bones was – difficult."

William understood the meaning behind the doctor's last word. Azariah Randall was notoriously irascible under normal circumstances, and consumption of spirits made him even more so. William expected he'd been intoxicated when he fell down the stairs.

"It's a pity you missed the service this morning," William said. "Your prescription worked wonders for Charles. His voice from the pulpit was as strong and clear as a bell. No one would suspect that just three days ago his throat was so sore he could barely speak."

The young physician shrugged modestly. "I think my instructions to stay in bed for a day and utter not a word had as much to do with his improvement as the medicine I prescribed. The man was simply talked out by all those relatives this past week."

Dr. Childs glanced up at the ballroom window, through which the chatter and clatter of the reception could be heard, then looked back at William sympathetically. "I suspect you've had your fill of them by now as well."

It was William's turn to shrug, but in stoic resignation. The Lyman house had for the past week been inundated by Charles's relatives who had traveled great distances to see his elevation to the Durham pulpit. Charles's father, mother, brother, and three of his seven sisters had come from New Jersey, while his uncle Dr. Isaac Coe and his cousin Henry, who at fifteen had his own ambitions for the ministry, had come from Indianapolis. Some of these relatives William and Alma hadn't laid eyes on since they'd traveled to New Jersey shortly after their wedding thirty-four years ago; several of the younger ones they were meeting for the first time. Truth be told, although they were blood kin, most were in fact strangers

"It has meant a great deal to Charles – and to Alma – to have them here, which is why I declined her brother Linus's offer to take a few of them in," William said. "But unfortunately once you forbade Charles to speak, Alma's relatives turned their attentions upon me. I was severely chastised for having Delia admitted to the Retreat." An uncharacteristic note of bitterness crept into William's voice as he gazed unseeing at the houses and fields across the road.

"Did you tell them how desperate her condition had become?" Dr. Childs asked, indignant on William's behalf. "About her delusion of being invited to the wedding of Queen Victoria and Prince Albert, and how she became violent when thwarted in her desire to go to New York to board a ship for England?"

When William made no reply, the physician continued with unshakeable certainty, "It was but a matter of time until Miss Coe harmed herself or someone else. Yet in her very few rational moments I observed during the three years she was my patient I perceived how she suffered from knowing what a weighty cross her affliction was for those she loved and who tried to help her."

Concerned when the older man remained silent, Dr. Childs stepped squarely in front of William. He spoke in the deliberate, earnest tone he used when delivering a diagnosis or prescribing a remedy. "Admitting Miss Coe to the Retreat wasn't an act of cruelty, but of love. If hope for her improvement exists anywhere, it's there. I'll gladly tell Alma's relatives all I know and saw of her condition."

William at last looked down at the doctor, a good foot shorter than he. He managed a wan smile of gratitude, even as he shook his head slowly to refuse the offer.

"It wouldn't change their minds. They still haven't forgiven us – me – for admitting my father-in-law to the Retreat ten years ago. They'd prefer we imprison Delia in a chamber in one of our houses rather than endure the 'embarrassment' of sending her to the one place she might find help. It was a most difficult decision," William paused, "especially for Alma. But I'm at peace with what I did," he said, adding a heartbeat later, almost to himself, "in that case."

Dr. Childs was certain he knew what lay behind William's qualification. "Charles has the makings of a good pastor," he observed. The startled William stared at Dr. Childs as if he'd read his mind. "He was a great source of comfort to me and my wife when we lost our little Henry to the spotted fever two Christmases past."

William's expression turned haggard at the doctor's reference to the epidemic that had visited Middlefield and Durham the year before last. "Alma and I learned that terrible winter that the well of sorrow is bottomless," he said. "We had not only to mourn the death of the grandson, whose sweet smiles had just begun to gladden our hearts, only a month after we'd welcomed him home, but watch our daughter grieve as only a mother bereft of a beloved child can.

"After little Lyman died," William went on, "I became obsessed with keeping Charles and Lizzy in Connecticut – especially after we learned Lizzy was expecting another child. I would have found Charles a position close to Middlefield if I had to start my own congregation and pay his salary out of my pocket."

William glanced guiltily at the physician before continuing. "I did all in my power to secure him the call to the Durham pulpit. I never considered whether what I labored so hard for was truly God's will, or the best thing for Charles and Lizzy or for the people of Durham. I didn't care. I thought only of my own wishes and needs, of those of my wife. My faith in the Lord's wisdom crumbled," he finished, looking away, his face mottled with wretched self-contempt.

Dr. Childs studied William for a long moment. "You overestimate yourself, my friend," he observed at last. William looked at him curiously. "The Durham congregation selected Charles for many reasons. Your unflagging support for his candidacy was an important one, but just one. This day's events may very well be God's will, and you are simply too blinded by your passions as a father and a husband to accept that you may have been an instrument of it."

"I pray you're right," William replied in a flat voice.

"He is foremost a God of love," Dr. Childs reminded him gently. "He sent me and my Julia our daughter to help soothe the sorrow of Henry's death. And he blessed Lizzy and Charles with their fine little son."

"Another Lyman Mills," William said, remembering how touched he and Alma had been when Charles and Lizzy told them they wanted to give this second son the same first name as the child they had lost. He raised his head and looked Seth Childs squarely in the eye. "I never knew that your talents including ministering to the soul as well as the body," he said sincerely. "Thank you for helping me see the light, my young friend." He extended his hand and the doctor took it in a firm grip.

"Out of the mouths of babes," Dr. Childs said self-effacingly with a crooked grin, to which William responded with a hearty laugh.

Chapter Ninety-Six

June, 1843
Middlefield

A tug on the line made Elihu sit up. He pulled his fishing pole up until the hook emerged from the water, and he saw the bait was still attached. He cast the line again into the placid waters of the Coginchaug River, then leaned against a sturdy tree trunk, grateful for the protection of its leaves against the merciless sun.

William was sitting a few feet away, his back braced against a tree, his own line in the river. The day had started with William, Elihu, Edward Boston, and two hired men spreading ash on a cornfield for fertilizer. By noon the temperature was so high, and the humidity so oppressive, that William decided it would be dangerous to keep working. He'd given Edward and the other men the rest of the day off. And he'd surprised Elihu by suggesting they go fishing.

Ignoring the bills and letters on his desk to go fishing made William feel like a schoolboy playing hooky. But he'd always tried, with varying degrees of success, to carve out from his mountain of obligations time to spend with each of his children – if only an hour of angling. Two recent events had caused him to redouble his effort.

In early March Lizzy had given birth to her third baby, a daughter she and Charles named Elizabeth. But the infant had lived less than two months. This death of a second grandchild seemed to William like the fraying of an already fragile connection to the future. William and Alma had thanked God Lizzy and Charles were so near, allowing them all to support each other in their grief.

Just weeks after the infant's death, Alfred Lyman had died of an apoplexy. In recent years, William, sensing his generation was disappearing, had made an effort to get to know his cousin better. They'd spoken mostly of their fathers, the two long-dead brothers whose lives had diverged so dramatically, with profound consequences for their sons. They'd begun to build an emotional bond to go with the blood one they shared. Then suddenly Alfred was gone. William felt like a line to his past had been cut.

Elihu and William were seated on large tree roots exposed as the result of erosion by the repeated rising and falling of the river. They were just a few feet downstream from the bridge of wooden planks over which ran the road between Benjamin Miller's house and that of the Lymans. At this point the Coginchaug was perhaps fifty feet wide, and could more accurately be described as a brook than a river. Today it could be mistaken for a pond, as only the slightest languid movement in the center gave evidence of a current.

The sunlight penetrating the canopy of leaves made patterns on the water's surface. Delicate yet fierce-looking dragonflies darted in zig-zag patterns just above the stream. Cardinals, blue jays, and robins, as well as several types of water birds, flitted among the branches of the towering trees.

The heat was slightly less brutal in the shaded glen formed by the trees. A few gusts of breeze had kicked up as the afternoon progressed. Although the moving air was very warm, it helped cool them by drying out their sweat-drenched shirts.

"I wonder where David is," Elihu said, keeping his eyes on the spot where his line entered the water.

"The letter that came yesterday was posted from Wheeling on the Ohio River," said William. "So I calculate he's in Kentucky by now." David had left a week ago on a mule-buying trip for Trowbridge & Alsop.

"It's too bad he can't be here with us," Elihu said.

William snorted skeptically. "You know if David were home he'd be anywhere but here. He must always be moving, doing – accomplishing something! Dangling a hook in the water, not caring whether a fish bites, would–." William faltered; he'd been about to say "drive him mad," and madness was something he no longer joked about. "Be torture for him," he finished.

The two anglers fell into a long silence, undisturbed by any nibbles on their hooks. Perhaps it was too hot for the fish to bite. William lapsed into a pleasant drowsiness.

"Father," Elihu said at last. William murmured to indicate he was listening, but when Elihu said nothing further he glanced curiously at his son. The trepidation on Elihu's face concerned him, but before he could say anything, Elihu continued.

"Mr. Trowbridge is leaving later this month for Cincinnati on business. I want to go with him and join David on the road."

The words shattered the afternoon's serenity for William. "Why?"

"Any hired man can do my work here on the farm – do more of it faster and better, for that matter," Elihu said with painful candor. William couldn't deny the truth of that statement.

"But no one else can fill David's need for a totally trustworthy companion on the road as I can," Elihu went on. "And a man must do something to get his living," he finished with surprising fervor. William recognized the last remark as the true heart of the matter.

William looked away from his son to stare at the river. He toyed absent-mindedly with his fishing pole as he weighed Elihu's words.

Elihu had turned eighteen in March, the same month David had achieved the honor of being accepted as a freeman of Middletown. William realized Elihu had been wrestling with the need to establish himself as an adult pulling his full weight in the family.

But that weight was so slight, William thought with a pang. Elihu's constitution had always been worrisomely weak. How could he possibly withstand the hardships of a mule-buying trip? William's instinctive reaction was to oppose this idea, to encourage Elihu to remain safely in the bosom of his family, to whom his warm heart and sharp mind more than compensated for his physical frailties.

But then William remembered his brother Alanson. His manhood had been stunted by their father's well-intentioned but misguided efforts to keep him in Connecticut. It would be just as wrong, William realized, to let his fears for Elihu's health thwart his son's effort to become a self-sufficient man.

William turned to face Elihu, who was holding his breath in suspense. He said in as matter-of-fact voice as he could manage, "You're a man, Elihu. The decision is yours." He turned back to stare at the river before Elihu could see the tears pooling in his eyes.

It was Elihu's turn to be stunned. He'd expected opposition from William. Once he resumed breathing, he said, "Mr. Trowbridge plans to leave New Haven on June 28. If I send a letter to Maysville today telling David I'm coming, he should get it in time to expect me."

William nodded his agreement as casually as if Elihu were outlining plans for picking the bean crop. That simple gesture cost him more than Elihu could ever know.

Chapter Ninety-Seven

July, 1843
Kentucky

"Husa! I never would have recognized you!"

David finished pulling on his boot, then twisted around, wondering to whom Elihu was speaking. David knew no one with the peculiar name of "Husa." He assumed some acquaintance Elihu made on the trip from Connecticut had tracked them down at this tavern in the misnamed Kentucky town of Paris, where they'd just spent a thoroughly uncomfortable night.

But David saw only his brother studying his reflection in a small, cracked, fly-specked looking-glass on the dingy wall. There was no one else in the tiny chamber.

"Who were you talking to?" David demanded as he stood up and walked around the end of the lumpy straw mattress on which he'd been sitting. "Who's 'Husa'?"

Elihu grinned. "I am." He chuckled at David's blank expression. "Trying to say 'Uncle Elihu Elisha' tangled our little nephew Lyman's tongue," he explained. "The best he could manage before I left home was 'Husa.' And having just gotten a good look at myself in a mirror for the first time since coming to Kentucky, I see I have a new face to go with my new name."

"You certainly don't resemble the man who got off the steamboat at Maysville a fortnight ago, I'll grant you that," David agreed. Elihu's face was deeply tanned from two weeks of riding in the brutal July sun. Although he'd scrubbed it energetically, it still looked dirty from the road dust that seemed to grind itself permanently into their pores. A three-day growth of beard sprouted on his cheeks. Bed bugs and mosquitoes had tormented the brothers overnight, inflicting red blotches on their bodies and faces.

"I suspect if you turned up at home unannounced even Mother and Father might have to look twice before they would claim you as their own," David added, only half in jest.

More striking than the change in Elihu's appearance, David thought, was the improvement in health he'd experienced in his short time in the West. He'd added several pounds to his thin frame – a minor miracle considering the unpalatable meals served at nearly every inn at which they'd stopped between Maysville and Lexington. Best of all, Elihu's throat and chest troubled him less.

"Well, Uncle Husa," David teased, "will you be starting a fresh life in the West to go with your new face and name? Maybe you could become a card sharp on an Ohio River steamboat?" David couldn't help but laugh at his own question; no man could be more ill-equipped for such a career than his scrupulously honest brother.

To David's surprise, Elihu immediately grew serious. "There's no chance of that happening," he assured him. "The life he left back in Connecticut suits Husa just fine."

David used a handkerchief to wipe away the stinging sweat that trickled down into his eyes, then stuffed the cloth back into a pocket as he squinted up at the sun almost directly overhead. Six hours, he calculated, since he and Elihu had left Paris, but the herd of sixty mules they were shepherding along the dusty, cratered Limestone Road moved so maddeningly slow that they'd abandoned any hope of covering the fifteen miles to Lexington before sunset. That meant another night at a crude roadside tavern, David thought wearily.

It wasn't that Kentucky lacked large, comfortable inns of the first quality, known as "stage-stands" or "tavern-stands," patronized by those who traveled by stagecoach. But the brothers had to keep their expenses to a minimum, if these long months away from home were to result in any profit. Thus they chose the cheapest lodgings they could find, the taverns called "drovers-stands" that catered to those who drove herds of cattle, swine, sheep, mules, and other livestock. These establishments offered only the most rudimentary accommodations and food. Most lodgers at drover-stands were heavy drinkers of the cheap whiskey served by the proprietors.

David heard Elihu riding up from behind, leaving his post at the rear of the herd to join him to break the monotony with a few minutes of conversation. David noticed that his brother shifted his buttocks gingerly. "Saddle sores still plaguing you?" he asked.

Elihu nodded, visibly uncomfortable. "Boils, too," he reported with a grimace.

"Twelve hours straight on horseback will do that," David observed. Both he and Elihu had ridden back in Connecticut, but neither had spent long, uninterrupted stretches of time in the saddle as was now required. Although he was somewhat hardened to the saddle, David, too, had developed a few raw, sensitive abrasions.

"Can you imagine how Father would admire our horses?" Elihu asked.

"'Envy' would be more accurate – if it weren't a sin," David replied wryly. The mounts they'd purchased in Maysville were finer specimens of horseflesh than any William Lyman had ever owned. "The reputation of this part of Kentucky for superior livestock, especially horses, is certainly justified," he went on. "The farmers credit the bluegrass."

Elihu twisted in the saddle to check on the herd. After determining that none of the mules had strayed or straggled, he turned back to face David, wincing slightly.

"Why do they call it 'bluegrass'?" he asked, looking across the fields and rolling hills covered with the long, broad-bladed grass that grew so lushly in north-central Kentucky. "It looks green to me."

"I wondered that myself," answered David, "until last year, when I came out early, in April. In spring the grass has blue flowers."

"I'd like to see that," Elihu said thoughtfully. "What do you think it is about bluegrass that's so beneficial to livestock? Do you know if anyone has tried growing it outside Kentucky? We should ask about obtaining some seed to experiment with in Connecticut."

"Always the scientist," David said, shaking his head with mock ruefulness. But in truth he'd always been impressed by Elihu's insatiable curiosity, and admired his desire to learn as much as he could about any aspect of nature.

Elihu turned again to check the mules, this time remembering to lift himself up a bit from the saddle so as not to irritate his sores. He frowned. "That mule that got into the skunk cabbage is still dragging. I'd best take a look at him."

David watched Elihu ride back to the rear of the herd, and bring his horse up alongside the ailing mule. Never had he been so grateful for his brother's conscientiousness as during these past two weeks. Elihu had taken it upon himself to check the physical condition of each animal every night. Two days ago he'd discovered that one had consumed some skunk cabbage, which had induced a painful, dangerous case of colic. On his own initiative Elihu had stayed up an entire night tending to the sick mule.

They plodded along for several minutes under the broiling sun. Suddenly David heard the clanking of metal from behind a stand of trees that blocked an intersecting road from view. The noise grew steadily louder, until, as they reached the crossroads, its source came into sight: a coffle of five black men, each with his hands cuffed behind his back. They were bound together single file by a long chain to which the cuffs of each were connected by a shorter chain. They looked to be between fifteen and twenty-five years old.

Walking beside the shackled men was a white man of about fifty, with a vigilant expression on his face and a rifle cradled in the crook of his left arm. A coiled whip hung at his belt.

On the other side of the coffle walked another white man, about David's age, armed with a three-foot-long stick as big around as a man's forearm. He so closely resembled the first man that there could be no question but that they were father and son.

The older man's face brightened when saw David. He scanned the herd of animals with an appraising eye. "Those are first-rate mules," he said appreciatively to David, in the slight drawl of the bluegrass region. "Did you buy them hereabouts?"

David nodded in the affirmative, but said nothing.

"I thought so," the man replied sagely. "There's no better place than Kentucky bluegrass country to pick up prime stock – whether it be mules or mulattoes," he said gesturing at the men on the coffle. He put exaggerated emphasis on the first syllable of the term for individuals of mixed racial background to underscore its similarity to the word "mule," as if to indicate the animals were on a par with the men. He chuckled at his own cleverness.

David was insulted by the man's assumption that they were kindred entrepreneurs. Glancing at the shackled men, he saw that all of them did indeed have skin light enough to leave no doubt they had white blood in their veins.

Although the slaves' faces were partially obscured by their broad-brimmed hats, David could see that all five kept their eyes fixed straight ahead, and maintained impassive, unreadable expressions. He also detected in the tautness of their neck muscles, the manner in which they clenched and unclenched their hands behind their backs, indications of the anger, fear, and humiliation the men felt, but had learned to master in order to survive.

"We're taking these prime bucks to Lexington, to Hughes and Downing," the man went on genially. "Maybe you've heard of them. They're just starting in the trade, and they're looking for healthy Negroes for their first shipment to the slave market in Natchez. They need to make a good first impression on the cotton planters. They engaged me to bring in some stock," the man said proudly.

"I paid $300 apiece for each of these Negroes, except for the big one in the middle," the man rattled on. "I had to give $500 for him, as he's got training as a blacksmith. All told I laid out $1,700 for the five – a smart sum, but Hughes and Downing promised me no less than $400 for every one, and I won't part with the blacksmith for less than $600. That's at least $500 profit for a month's work! It would me take three years working on someone else's farm to earn that kind of money!"

The man shook his head from side to side, as if he still could not believe the enormity of his good fortune. "Enough trips like this one and maybe I'll be building myself a fancy mansion like the one you passed a couple miles back." David assumed the man was referring to a large, stately brick house, fronted by enormous white classical columns that they'd glimpsed at the end of a long tree-lined drive not far outside Paris.

"Mule trading is all well and good," the man ran on in an avuncular tone, "but a young fellow like you looking to set himself up in style would do far better to turn to trading Negroes."

David was caught off guard by a surge of loathing for the loutish, loquacious slave trader. He gripped the pommel of his saddle until his knuckles turned white as he grappled with anger and outrage. He instinctively glanced back to make sure Elihu was still at the rear of the herd.

"Are you planning to sell all those mules in Lexington?" the trader asked. David shook his head in the negative. "You're taking them to market in Louisville, then?" Again David shook his head.

Annoyed by David's silence, the man demanded, "Well, where are you taking them?

"Connecticut," answered David. He'd hoped the man would continue on his way without requiring him to speak, but that was not to be. And there was no point in lying about his destination; his accent would betray him as a New Englander.

"Connecticut!" the slave trader exclaimed, as the reason for David's reticence became clear to him. "The very bowels of Yankeeland," he added with sarcastic heartiness.

"You know what comes from Connecticut, don't you, Aaron?" The slave trader addressed the question to his son, but kept his now suspicious eyes on David. "All those slick Yankee peddlers. Sharpers always looking to talk some soft solder to a lonely farmwife like your mother, selling them wooden nutmegs and the like."

David remained silent. He'd heard the tales of Yankee peddlers passing off nutmegs whittled from wood as the real item. He doubted there was any truth to them. But he suspected many of the hundreds of peddlers who fanned out across the country to sell tin ware, clocks, pins, buttons, and other products of Connecticut factories deserved their reputation for sweet-talking isolated inhabitants of the back roads and frontiers into buying not only goods they didn't need but goods they didn't really want.

"And when they're not cheating our women out of a few pennies, some of them are looking to steal more valuable property," the slave trader snarled. He no longer pretended to be speaking to his son.

"Hughes and Downing commissioned me to bring them six young and likely Negroes, and two days ago I had that many," the man went on, his face growing redder with anger. "I bought one from a widow in Claysville. The Negro had become insolent toward her since her husband's death, and she was eager to be shed of him. I paid just $150 for him, a real bargain. But he got wind of the sale and took off during the night. I'm pretty sure he disappeared into that damn Underground Road the Yankee abolitionists run. Now I'm out the $150 I paid for him, not to mention the profit I would have made selling him to Hughes and Downing."

"Well, Pa, we're back home in Bourbon County, where they know how to deal with abolitionists." The son spoke for the first time, in a menacing tone. "If a man lets it be known he's one of their black persuasion, he'll soon wear a coat of tar and chicken feathers."

"And if that doesn't set him straight, the fool will end up swinging from a length of hemp," added his father, his voice thick with hatred. He shifted the rifle in his arms.

The blood began to pound in David's temples, threatening to drown out the voice of prudence. He forced himself to recall his sister Sarah's last letter. "I fear you'll make imprudent remarks upon some subject," she'd written, the "subject" unquestionably being slavery. "You must not open your lips," she'd cautioned.

David took a deep breath, then another, and then a third, each one slowing his racing pulse a bit more. He managed to do nothing other than match the slave trader's menacing glare with his own steady, scornful stare.

When the slave trader realized his poisonous barbs weren't going to provoke David into a rash fury as he'd hoped, the man broke off eye contact. He uncoiled his lash and cracked it over the heads of the five black men, who broke into a trot.

David watched the tragic little group head down the road. They disappeared from view just as Elihu rode up. He'd caught the tail end of the exchange. "What did you say to him?" he asked anxiously.

"Just one word," David replied, still seething. "'Connecticut.' With the slave trade growing ever more profitable here in Kentucky, that's all it takes to light the fuse of an anti-abolitionist hot-head."

David was suddenly seized with fear for his brother, still naïve in so many ways. "It was bitter as gall to bear that slave trader's threats and insults in silence," he said. "I felt like a cowardly hypocrite. But tangling with those two would have exposed us to danger, and interfered with our fulfillment of our commitment to Father and Mr. Trowbridge. It wouldn't have helped those five Negroes. And it wouldn't have advanced the cause of abolition! It would have been like–," David paused, trying to think of an apt comparison – "like trying to cut the rattle off a rattlesnake, risking death to do something that causes no real damage to the serpent."

David paused to collect himself, then went on in a low, urgent voice, desperate for Elihu to understand the ugly reality. "In a few days you'll set out on your own to buy mules. You can't let yourself be goaded into an imprudent comment. It could mean the difference between life and death."

David fell silent, waiting for Elihu's reaction. He was afraid not only that his idealistic younger brother would reject his advice, but would be contemptuous of David for his expedient attitude.

"'To every thing there is a season, and a time to every purpose under the heaven,'" Elihu quoted from the Biblical Book of Ecclesiastes. "'A time to keep silence, and a time to speak.' However difficult, this is the time for us to keep silent. But the time to speak will come," he went on, "and then we'll be heard loud and strong."

David had underestimated his brother's maturity. "What you say is God's truth," he said. "And still," he said sadly, staring down the road toward Lexington, "I can't help but wonder when, if ever, those five poor souls will have their time to speak."

Chapter Ninety-Eight

April, 1844
Durham

"That's him! The one half a head taller than the others," Adeline whispered urgently to Catherine Hart. From her seat in a pew four rows from the front of Durham's Congregational meetinghouse, Catherine craned her neck to get a look at Elihu Lyman. He was one of four young men stepping onto a temporary stage erected in front of the pulpit.

The girls had met two months ago when Adeline, sixteen, enrolled in the Durham Academy, where Catherine, seventeen, had been a student since its opening a year ago. Both boarded at the home of Charles and Lizzy Mills. They'd quickly become fast friends.

Catherine had heard a great deal about her new friend's favorite brother. When Adeline discovered that Catherine shared Elihu's interest in singing, instrumental music, and science, she decided the two had to meet.

Catherine's first impression of Elihu Lyman left her doubting Adeline's description of him as a young man with a warm, winning personality that endeared him to both family and a close circle of friends. He was good-looking in a broodingly romantic way. He had deep-set brown eyes in a long, lean face. His straight brown hair, long enough to cover the back of his collar, was worn brushed back from his forehead.

But Elihu was not only almost as thin as a poker, he held himself as rigidly as one. In his somber expression, which made him look considerably older than nineteen, Catherine thought she detected a hint of aloofness.

"Don't let his manner deceive you," said Adeline knowingly in a low voice. Catherine cast a startled look at her friend, who'd read her thoughts so easily.

"Elihu is always a sobersides in company," Adeline said. "But with family and friends he unbends, and you couldn't find a more delightful companion," she added reassuringly.

"Who are the others?" Catherine asked.

"You know my 'strictly confidential friend,' with the sandy hair and sea-green eyes," Adeline said in a deliciously conspiratorial whisper. The "friend" was Judson Carpenter, a seventeen-year-old farmer's son from Branford. In the six months since Judson had entered the Durham Academy, an affair of the heart had blossomed between him and Adeline. They'd kept their romance secret from all but a few trusted confidantes, which included Adeline's sister Sarah and, just recently, Catherine Hart.

"The fleshy young fellow with mouse-brown hair is our cousin Charles Bliss, who's thirteen," Adeline went on. "He's visiting from Hartford, where he attends the public high school. The last is my brother David," she concluded hastily, for it was clear the four men were ready to begin their presentation.

The girls fell into an expectant silence along with the rest of the audience packed into the meetinghouse on this raw spring afternoon for a program of rhetorical and musical presentations. According to the printed program, Elihu, David, Charles, and Judson were to present the vignette *The Death of Captain Nathan Hale.*

The four youths wore ordinary street clothes for their performance. Admission to the day's entertainment was free. Both factors were essential to avoid violating the Connecticut law prohibiting the performance of "theatricals" for pay.

Every member of the audience knew the story of Connecticut's own courageous patriot Nathan Hale, whose hanging by the British as a spy had transformed him into a martyr of the American Revolution. But none had ever before seen his tale brought to life.

Elihu and Charles stepped to the front of the stage. Elihu, identified in the program as portraying General George Washington, addressed Charles and Judson, playing Continental Army officers.

"Soon will the radiance of the bright gem that is our darling Hale be hidden in the night of death," Elihu intoned sorrowfully. "But Hale shall not die," he said with a flare of resolution. "In your heart he'll live; he will in mine; in future times fathers will tell his virtues to their children, and bid them emulate him."

"Many a noble youth, reading Hale's history, will feel his soul enkindle with a generous fire of patriotic love," Judson said.

"I trust we ever shall feel ourselves spurred on to nobler efforts in the same good cause by his example," said Charles, nervously rushing through his line.

The three youths moved back on the platform. David, in the role of the condemned Captain Hale, stepped forward to stand alone. He clasped his hands together behind his back, creating the effect of a prisoner whose arms had been bound in preparation for the gallows. He gazed out over the heads of the audience for a long moment before speaking.

"'Tis the last morning I shall spend below the skies," he began. His tone was gently pensive, but his strong voice was audible at the very back of the meetinghouse.

"Eyes, look your last on this fair land, whose every mountain, dell and stream, whose every forest, rock, and shore, shares my warm love." He turned his head slowly from left to right, as if scanning a vista. "O my loved country. Is it reality or do I dream that I must leave thee," he said despairingly.

Catherine leaned forward, intrigued to detect in David's words affection for his native soil that owed nothing to the actor's artifice. Searching her memory for the few details Adeline had shared about David, she recalled only a passing mention that he was several years older than Elihu. Catherine wasn't sure of even that, for with his smooth, rosy cheeks, short, neatly trimmed hair, and bright blue eyes David appeared younger than Elihu. Something else Adeline had told her came back to Catherine: of the five Lyman siblings, only Lizzy was married.

David lowered his gaze, and for the first time addressed the audience. "That I can no more help this bleeding land, nor prop its failing fortunes – this is my bitter grief," he said, as if confessing a sin. As he scanned the gathering his eyes briefly met those of several individuals, including Catherine, to whom they looked dark with real regret.

David once again gazed out over the audience's heads, as if seeing something in the far distance visible only to him. "To my brethren now struggling in the field," he declared, his voice gaining strength and power, "to the unborn millions who, free themselves, shall think of those who made them so, these parting words I leave for legacy." He paused for a heartbeat. "Would that I had another life to give to thee."

Silence reigned for a long moment, then the fragile spell David's performance had cast over the audience burst like a bubble, and they broke into enthusiastic clapping. David was startled out of his characterization by the sudden applause. After a moment he acknowledged the audience with a short, self-conscious nod and a brief smile. The speakers filed off the platform and made their way toward a table of refreshments along a side wall of the meetinghouse.

"Come meet him," Adeline said excitedly, grabbing Catherine's hand and almost dragging her from the pew. When they came up behind the four men Adeline loudly cleared her throat to get their attention. They turned around and Adeline blushed deeply, so flustered by Judson's admiring gaze that it was a moment before she could proceed with her introductions.

"Elihu, David, Charles, I would like you to meet Miss Catherine Hart of Guilford," Adeline said formally. "She's a student at the Academy."

The three young men murmured polite greetings, each taking Catherine's physical measure as best he could within the bounds of good manners. Miss Hart was a bit shorter than average, with dramatic dark eyes. No bonnet covered her glossy chestnut tresses, which she wore parted down the middle then gathered and fastened above each ear into a bundle of bouncy "sausage" curls that hung to her shoulders. Sharp, high cheekbones set widely apart gave her face a diamond shape. Her strong, almost masculine chin was balanced by a wide, sensuous mouth.

Catherine wore a red plaid dress with a modest scoop neck that revealed smooth, white shoulders. The dress had short, full sleeves with deep ruffles, matched by a wide flounce around the bottom of the floor-length skirt. Although her torso was tightly corseted into the standard narrow waist, Catherine had softly rounded arms and square hands with short fingers.

"You were splendid!" Adeline exclaimed, her compliment ostensibly meant for all four men, but intended for Elihu. Elihu responded to his sister's praise with a wide smile that illuminated his long, sallow face, giving Catherine her first glimpse of the man Adeline insisted existed behind the sober facade.

"Your judgment, as always, dear sister, is perfect and undeniable," Elihu replied. He spoke with exaggerated humility calculated to let the men accept the compliment without appearing vain.

"But the true praise this day belongs to the five men, our honored Mr. Mills among them, who had the vision to establish this Academy," Elihu continued, growing serious. "It not only offers young men and women an education superior to that of the common schools, but it is a cultural center where the people of Durham and Middlefield can improve their minds and refresh their spirits with musical and literary presentations."

"Did you see the new Academy building on Main Street, Charles?" Adeline asked her cousin, who nodded shyly. "Mr. Mills says it will be finished by summer's end, with classes to start this autumn," she went on excitedly. "Then we'll be able to hold concerts and rhetorical exercises there, instead of in the meetinghouse."

Elihu glanced over the two young women's heads at something that had caught his attention. He set his empty cup on the table. "They're summoning us for the musical performance," he informed Adeline and Judson. "Please excuse us, Miss Hart," he said as he began to make his way toward the stage. Adeline and Judson followed him.

Charles mumbled something about needing some fresh air, and suddenly Catherine found herself alone with David. They stood side-by-side for a moment watching the musical performers assemble on stage.

Catherine looked up at David, who topped her by several inches. "You made a most noble patriot," she said. When he glanced down in surprise, her curiosity got the better of Catherine. "A man who can speak so convincingly of commitment certainly must possess that virtue." Catherine lifted an eyebrow inquiringly.

David was nonplussed. This wasn't chit-chat to fill an awkward silence between strangers, but a true compliment – and a question. When he found his tongue he opted for a light-hearted response to these bold comments from a young woman he'd met just five minutes earlier.

"I've spent the better part of the last four years as much in the company of mules as of people," he began with a self-deprecating smile Catherine found appealing. "It would be no surprise if some of their stubbornness rubbed off on me."

"The mules or the people?" Catherine asked archly.

David uttered a short, appreciative laugh. "Your point is well made. People often do behave in ways that make mules seem cooperative by comparison."

"And yet, under the right circumstances stubbornness can be a virtue," Catherine replied.

David studied this forthright young woman appraisingly. Misinterpreting his scrutiny, Catherine began to fret that David found her directness on first acquaintance unbecoming behavior.

"It's a pity performing theatricals for money is illegal in our state," Catherine said airily. Caught off guard by the abrupt change of tone and topic, David stared at her quizzically.

"With your thespian talents you would never want for employment as an actor," she explained. It took David a split second to realize Catherine was teasing.

"I think not," he said, amused at the preposterous thought of making his living trodding the boards. "Actors are vagabonds, traveling from town to town in search of fresh audiences. And I've had my fill of weeks on end apart from family, friends, and home." The last he said as much to himself as to Catherine, who knew from Adeline about David's mule-buying expeditions to the South and West.

"Then perhaps the bar or the pulpit?," said Catherine, hoping to lift the melancholy that had crept into David's voice. "Have you ever considered becoming an attorney or a minister? Your oratorical talents would serve you well in either profession."

David shook his head slowly, then he answered thoughtfully. "I've seen enough of courts to know the wheels of justice grind with maddening slowness, and even when finished there's no guarantee that right will prevail. And I lack the profound faith required to assume the awesome responsibility of leading others on the path to Heaven."

David stopped abruptly in astonishment at himself. Although he'd long ago dismissed law or religion as his life's work, he'd never articulated his reasons – until now in conversation with a woman who half an hour earlier had been a total stranger to him.

"What of cultivating the soil – the 'fair land' of which you spoke with such affection?" Catherine asked. David was taken aback by how Catherine had sensed true emotion in his delivery of the play's dialogue. He thought for a moment, and then his lips turned up slightly in a smile Catherine found heartening.

"I cherish the fields that have sustained four generations of my family for a century," David confirmed. "I hope always to make my home on these acres. I draw strength from them just as the trees do." Catherine had never heard a New Englander speak so romantically of the region's stone-pocked soil.

"And still," David hesitated briefly before plunging ahead, "I couldn't be content with farming alone as my life's work. I require something more – although what I don't know." His cheeks reddened, and he glanced away from Catherine. He regretted blurting out this vague yearning, which she undoubtedly would deem better suited to a stripling than a man of twenty-four.

The light touch of her hand on his arm made David turn back slowly to look at Catherine.

"It sounds like searching the heavens for a single star that you alone will recognize," she said sympathetically, responding to the despair she'd heard in his voice. "But it is there, and you must not give up the quest," she continued with absolute certainty. "Think of how satisfying it will be when you at last find it, and how fulfilling it will be to embrace it!" she said, her voice rising, her brown eyes shining with excitement at the prospect.

For a moment David wondered if he had heard correctly. Catherine hadn't dismissed his dilemma, hadn't mocked him for it. Her encouragement validated his need for something to which he couldn't even put a name.

Catherine Hart was unlike any girl David had ever known. She was certainly different from his sisters – Lizzy the brilliant dreamer, spright-like Adeline, and shy, gentle Sarah. However unlikely it seemed for a teenage girl, she was coolly perceptive and warmly supportive. David was suddenly eager to share with her the many observations and experiences, good and bad, at the heart of his conviction that his purpose in life included more than crops and livestock.

"Might we interrupt your tête-à-tête?" A startled David turned and came face-to-face with his father, who had approached unnoticed from behind.

"Vous parlez le français, Monsieur?" Catherine asked William brightly. She didn't know what to think when William responded by throwing his head back in a hearty laugh.

"'Tête-à-tête' is one of at most a dozen French words I've learned from my daughters that make up everything I know of the language," he said, shaking his head in rueful amusement. "This learned assemblage seemed the perfect opportunity to trot out one of those fancy phrases, but I should have known I would be immediately exposed as a fraud." Alma, standing beside her husband, rolled her eyes slightly in exasperation.

Catherine responded to William's smile with one of her own. She was relieved she hadn't embarrassed this good-natured stranger with a remark made in all innocence.

"I hope you can find it in your heart to forgive an old farmer's pretensions to culture, Miss– ?" he asked, then looked to David for his companion's name.

"Miss Hart, may I present my parents, Mr. and Mrs. William Lyman," David said formally. "Mother, Father, this is Miss Catherine Hart of Guilford, a schoolmate of Adeline's at the Academy."

William's eyes narrowed with curiosity at Catherine's name. "Are you any relation to Colonel William Hart, who maintains the inn at Guilford Point?" he asked.

"He is my father, sir," Catherine replied.

"A man of rare courage and conscience," William said forcefully. "When next you see him please tell him that William Lyman of Middlefield sends his respectful regards – as well as congratulations on being blessed with such a lovely and well-educated daughter."

"I will be sure to do so," Catherine replied, blushing at William's gallantry.

"David, do you know where Sarah is?" Alma asked abruptly. "We haven't seen her since we arrived."

"No, I'm sorry, Mother," David replied. Alma shook her head slightly in concern and irritation.

"Maybe she walked down to visit Lizzy," David suggested. Seven months pregnant with her fourth child, Lizzy hadn't felt well enough to attend the day's events. She'd remained in the house Charles had purchased two years ago just a few steps south of the Durham green. Charles had solicitously foregone the day's events to keep his disappointed wife company and three-year-old Lyman Mills occupied.

That possibility had already occurred to Alma. "It was a pleasure meeting you, Miss Hart," she said, a bit distractedly, then started toward the back of the meetinghouse. William exchanged a look of amused resignation with David over his mother's dogged pursuit of her elusive daughter, then hastened to catch up with Alma.

"I'm impressed," David said, turning back to Catherine. "My father doesn't bestow such praise lightly. Might I ask what your father has done to earn his esteem?"

Catherine's expression grew so troubled that David regretted posing the question. But before he could assure her she didn't need to answer, she began to speak.

"From his earliest days my father was a member of Guilford's First Church, as were his father and grandfather before him. He poured his heart and soul, his sweat and his coin into it. Before opening his inn he worked as a carpenter, and I recall as a little girl watching him help build with his own hands the splendid meetinghouse on the green. He was a leader in starting the first Sunday school, which I attended."

Catherine's features had softened as she described what was clearly a happy time in her father's life. But they quickly grew somber again as she continued her story.

"Four years ago our dear pastor, Mr. Dutton, began to speak from the pulpit about the evils of slavery and the duty of Christians to take action against it," she said. "My father wholeheartedly supported him. However, many members of the congregation disagreed with Mr. Dutton's position. So great was their opposition to his support of abolitionism that they eventually dismissed this faithful shepherd from the pulpit he'd filled with love and wisdom for thirty years."

Catherine stopped speaking for a moment, her thoughts snagged on this outrageous injustice. David nodded slightly to encourage her to continue. "My father wrote me something about this when I was in Kentucky."

"This unworthy action greatly distressed my father," Catherine went on. "Still he held to his belief that good Christians would come to see the light – until last spring when the Society refused even to allow the meetinghouse to be used for gatherings of the anti-slavery society. Father couldn't countenance such mulishness." Catherine smiled fleetingly at David at her instinctive use of the word, then continued, "Such deliberate blindness to evil, as if not talking about slavery made it not exist. He could no longer tolerate the hypocrisy of so-called Christians who send missionaries to convert the heathen on the other side of the globe while insisting that the vilest transgressions of God's law in their own country not a day's journey from Connecticut is none of their concern."

Catherine stopped to take a breath, dismissing the hypocrites she'd described with an indignant toss of her head that set her curls dancing – an effect that with her flashing eyes and heightened color David found most attractive.

Warmed by David's rapt attention and admiring smile, Catherine continued. "Finally, last November, Father and several other like-minded men led more than one hundred parishioners in withdrawing from the First Church and forming their own congregation, the Third. His stand cost him more than a few friendships, and strained relations with several family members. It earned him the scorn and even the hatred of many people he knew. But once he decided it was the right thing to do, he didn't hesitate."

Catherine looked down at her hands, then back up at David with a strained expression. "That's why when I turned seventeen last spring, and it came time for me to own the covenant, I didn't make my profession of faith in the church of my ancestors. Instead I united with the Durham church which I've attended since enrolling at the Academy."

David hoped his face didn't betray the onslaught of emotions Miss Hart was inspiring in him: admiration, gratitude, respect. He also felt a physical attraction that was manifesting itself in an almost overpowering desire to kiss her – irrational in the midst of a conversation about the moral crisis of slavery. He was still struggling with how to convey these feelings to her, when Elihu, Judson, Adeline, and another man began their performance, singing in four-part harmony "The Old Granite State," a song made popular the previous year by the Hutchinson Family Singers.

"I assumed Sarah came to see David and Elihu take part in the exercises," Alma said to William as they reached the entrance of the meetinghouse. "I fear she lost her resolve and fled."

William and Alma stepped into the vestibule, from which a set of double doors led outside onto the Durham green. William pushed open the left door, then stood aside to allow Alma to pass through first. He automatically made to follow her, only to stumble against his wife, who had stopped on the doorsill.

William's annoyance vanished when he saw Alma's stunned expression. He looked up anxiously to determine what sight had halted her dead in her tracks. When he located it, he, too, was thunderstruck.

Four massive fluted white pillars, each ten feet around, supported the two-story portico at the front of the meetinghouse. At the far southern end of the portico, leaning against one of the columns, stood Sarah. She was talking animatedly with the Reverend James Dickinson, a Congregational minister in his late thirties who'd taken up residence in Middlefield late last year. As William and Alma watched, their daughter emphasized whatever she was saying with sweeping gestures of her hands – both hands.

Glancing down, William saw Alma's chin quivering slightly, as her eyes filled with tears. William swallowed the lump of emotion that rose in his throat, even as he cautioned himself not to read too much into a single conversation, however extraordinary Sarah's behavior might be.

A cloud drifted in front of the sun. Sarah's dress of dark green checked linen flattered her complexion and figure, but its wide scoop neck and short sleeves left her shoulders and arms exposed. She instinctively reacted to the loss of what little warmth the feeble early spring rays had provided by crossing her arms tightly across her chest.

James Dickinson immediately removed his coat and draped it with tender gallantry around Sarah's shoulders. She lifted her chin so that he could fasten the top button to secure the coat in place. When he was finished their eyes met and lingered in an intimate gaze.

William recovered sufficiently from his astonishment to run over in his mind what he knew about this man with whom Sarah lost the self-consciousness about her deformed hand that had shackled her spirit for the past eight years. He and Alma had first met the minister more than a decade ago, when Dickinson, fresh out of Yale, had briefly supplied the Middlefield pulpit.

Soon after that visit, Dickinson had accepted the pastorate of the Second Congregational Church in Norwich, Connecticut. Less than two years later, shattered by the death of his nineteen-year-old bride, Dickinson resigned the post.

The grieving widower had sought solace in missionary service. Under the auspices of the American Board of Commissioners for Foreign Missions, Dickinson spent nearly a decade in the Far East, most of it in Singapore.

Dickinson had returned to the United States last year. An inheritance sufficient to meet his needs and desires allowed him to retire to devote himself to theological writing. Recalling with pleasure his short sojourn in Middlefield at the beginning of his career, he had chosen to make his home here.

William and Alma had welcomed this well-educated man of God and world traveler into their home for many an evening of illuminating, entertaining conversation. Dickinson was of medium height, with the lean, almost ascetic look of a man who, if required to choose between life with books but only bread and water to eat, or no books but all the delicious delicacies the world could offer, would have unhesitatingly selected the former. He was eager to share what he discovered in his extensive readings, to listen to the reactions and thoughts of others, and to learn from them in turn.

The younger Lymans, including Sarah, usually took part in these discussions. William recalled that Sarah, who took second place to no one in her passion for reading, had been impressed by the breadth and depth of Mr. Dickinson's intellect and education. She, who voraciously devoured books on foreign travel, had been enthralled by the minister's vivid accounts of experiences in exotic lands, and by his command of the Chinese and Malay languages. But William hadn't picked up a clue that the heart of his twenty-one-year-old spinster daughter was becoming entwined with that of the widowed clergyman nearly twice her age.

Alma was first to recover from their shock. She tugged on William's sleeve. "We're intruding," she whispered, when he glanced down. Nodding, he turned to follow her back into the meetinghouse. He allowed himself one quick glance over his shoulder, and saw the smiling Sarah hugging Dickinson's coat around her tightly, clearly wishing it were his arms.

William closed the door quietly. He looked down at Alma and used his thumb to gently wipe a tear from her cheek.

Alma shook her head in wonderment. "How greatly we love our children, yet how little do we truly know about them."

Chapter Ninety-Nine

July, 1844
Durham

William could tell something was wrong the moment he stepped out of the carriage in front of the Mills house. Lizzy and Alma were sitting on the porch, obviously waiting for him. But neither extended the warm welcome he'd expected, especially after more than a month's separation. Their posture was unnaturally stiff, and it seemed to William that both self-consciously avoided meeting his eyes.

At least it wasn't one of the children, William told himself with relief as he secured the horse's reins to the hitching post. One-month-old Catherine Elizabeth Mills – "Kitty," as Charles had already nicknamed her – was snuggled on her mother's shoulder, somehow sleeping in the oppressive early July heat. Through the balusters of the porch railing William could see three-year-old Lyman sitting cross-legged on the floor beside Alma's chair. He was doggedly trying to spin the wooden top Elihu had given him – the same one Saint Nicholas had brought more than a decade earlier.

William pushed the broad brim of his hat back off his forehead as he racked his memory for anything he'd said or done – or forgotten to say or do – that could account for this restrained reception. He couldn't think of any offense he'd committed – although after more than thirty-five years of marriage he knew that didn't necessarily mean he hadn't done so, unconsciously or unintentionally.

Maybe mother and daughter had clashed over some domestic matter, William speculated. Alma had arrived at the Mills house the day after Kitty's birth on June 4 to help care for Lizzy, her new granddaughter, and little Lyman. She'd planned to stay for three weeks, but before that time was up she'd sent William word of the need to extend her visit an additional two weeks.

Charles had decided at the last minute to attend a conference in New York City on missionary work. Her husband's abrupt departure less than a month after Kitty's birth had so upset Lizzy, Alma explained in her note, that she was reluctant to leave her alone to cope with two children. Although Alma longed for her own home and fretted over how Sarah and Adeline were managing the housework in her absence, she'd decided to remain in Durham until Charles returned. Two vexed women pining for their absent husbands, spending two sweltering weeks with a newborn baby, and a rambunctious three-year-old, was a recipe for spats and squabbles, William realized, even between a mother and daughter as close and normally even-tempered as his Alma and Lizzy.

Since Charles had assured Lizzy he would be gone no more than a fortnight, William calculated his son-in-law should have arrived back in Durham by yesterday at the latest. William had set out before noon to fetch home his wife, whom he had sorely missed. It appeared he'd arrived none too soon.

Lyman Mills glanced up at the sound of William's boot striking the first of the porch steps. The boy's eyes lit up with excitement. "Grandpa!" he squealed with delight as he scrambled to his feet and raced heedlessly across the porch. The baby on Lizzy's shoulder started at her brother's sharp cry, but didn't waken.

Lyman stumbled when he reached the top of the steps. He would have plunged head-first down the stairs onto the hard-packed dirt had not William's reflexes still been quick enough for him to catch his grandson in mid-fall.

"Always in such a hurry," William admonished the boy. But the sting of the mild scolding was neutralized by the grin his grandson's energetic exuberance brought to William's face. He lifted the little boy high into the air, then playfully slung him over his left shoulder like a sack of grain, so that the child's upper torso dangled down behind him. Lyman giggled as William, holding him securely around the knees, affectionately swatted the boy's wriggling bottom while simultaneously mounting the steps to the porch.

William's grin faded as he got a close look at his wife and daughter. Emotions far sharper than domestic disharmony had etched deep grooves into both their faces, which were pale despite the heat. He was disturbed to see in Lizzy's expression an emotion he'd never before seen there and never expected to: humiliation.

William was about to break the awkward silence, when Alma spoke. "Charles didn't come home yesterday," she said. William's first thought was that some evil had befallen Charles during his journey, much as it had him on the road to Cincinnati. He dismissed that assumption when Alma added, in a flat, matter-of-fact tone that contained no fear or sorrow, "He won't be returning for some time."

Alma turned her gaze on Lizzy in a tacit signal that it was her daughter's place to explain more fully. The young mother's lips were pulled in so tightly they they'd all but disappeared. Although her eyes remained downcast, when William cocked his head to one side he could see she was blinking fast to hold back tears.

"What is it, Lizzy?" William asked gently.

With obvious effort Lizzy raised her eyes to meet her father's. "This morning the postmaster stopped by with a letter for me that arrived on yesterday's mail stage. It was from Charles. He sent it from New York four days ago–." Lizzy stopped to try to steady herself with a deep breath. "Just before he sailed for England."

"England?" William could only stupidly parrot the word, for it made as much sense as if Lizzy had announced Charles had set off for Mars. He waited patiently for his daughter to explain this baffling revelation, but her nerve failed her. She turned her head away to stare sightlessly out toward the road, as tears trickled down her cheeks.

William pulled little Lyman upright on his shoulder and set him down on the porch. The child had confidently expected his all-powerful grandfather would fix whatever problem had been upsetting his mother and grandmother all morning. But William's arrival seemed to have made things worse. Bewildered and troubled, Lyman scampered into the house to escape the unhappy, upset grown-ups.

William turned to look beseechingly at Alma. He held his hands open before him, palms upward, in a desperate appeal for enlightenment. Alma heaved a great sigh as she shot Lizzy a glance largely of compassion, but tinged, William noticed, with exasperation.

"Charles wrote he'd been summoned unexpectedly to England on missionary work," Alma began. "He said the call was so sudden and urgent he couldn't spare the time to return to Durham before sailing. He didn't indicate when Lizzy could expect him back."

"That's all he wrote?" William asked, struggling to absorb this bizarre turn of events. "What of his family and his congregation? What arrangements did he make for their care while he was away?"

Alma shook her head. "He didn't mention any." Lizzy sniffled, and swallowed hard, but continued gazing out toward the road.

Alma kept her eyes fixed on William apprehensively. His face turned chalk white with shock as he absorbed the news, then instantaneously flushed crimson with fury as the full import of Charles's action became clear

"I marvel he bothered to write before he left, that he didn't just wait until he landed in England," he said, choking on his anger. A vein along the side of his forehead throbbed ominously. His right hand clenched convulsively into a fist, which he slammed against the house with such violent force it split a clapboard. Lizzy's head snapped around at the sharp report, which woke little Kitty, who began to wail.

Alma got quickly to her feet and stepped over to William's side. The rage flooding his brain so distorted his vision, that for a moment he saw the alarm on Alma's face as if through a pane of wavy window glass.

Alma laid a firm yet tender hand on William's arm. Her touch, and her expression of deep concern, had the hoped-for effect of banking William's rage. But what extinguished it was the flood of shame that coursed through him when he saw on Lizzy's face another emotion he'd never seen there and never expected to: fear. His daughter was cringing in stunned terror.

Heartsick, but still not entirely in command of himself, William released his arm from Alma's grasp with a shaking hand, strode across the porch, and leaped down the stairs. He walked quickly and determinedly to the back of the house in search of privacy in which to regain control of himself.

Lizzy broke down into sobs that were punctuated by the baby's cries. Alma turned from watching William's retreating back to crouch down in front of her daughter. "He's not angry with you," she assured Lizzy.

William stopped at the western edge of the Mills homelot. He grasped the lowest limb of a stout maple tree with his left hand, gripping it hard in an attempt to still his trembling body. He gazed out across the expanse of the Coginchaug swamp, lifted his eyes to the orchard-dotted ridge of Powder Hill.

"William?" It was Alma's voice close behind him, cool and steady.

"Is Lizzy all right?" he asked, still facing westward.

"I think she understands your anger isn't directed at her," was all Alma was willing to offer by way of reassurance. But her words had the unintended effect of reminding William of the true culprit in this outrageous affair. He swung around, his fury rekindled.

"I entrusted our daughter to that man!" he raged. "I did everything in my power to secure him this pastorate! And what of Lyman and Kitty? How could he abandon them all to traipse off across the ocean on what had to have been nothing more than a whim? Has he lost his mind?" he cried.

William frightened himself when he realized he meant his last words literally. Charles's impulsive, erratic, irresponsible behavior, together with the tragedy of Elisha and Delia Coe's derangement, raised the specter of mental illness running in the Coe blood.

Embarrassed by his ranting, hoping Alma had read nothing more than bewildered frustration into his last words, William stared at the ground. For a full minute they stood in silence, which Alma finally broke. "The man said, Lord, I will follow thee; but let me first go bid them farewell, which are at home at my house. And Jesus said unto him, No man, having put his hand to the plow, and looking back, is fit for the kingdom of God,'" she quoted from the Biblical Book of Luke.

At last William looked up at Alma, chastened in part by the Scriptural command to place God ahead of all worldly concerns, including family. Angry as she herself undoubtedly must be with Charles, she was doing her best to try to understand how genuine zeal might be at the heart of his actions.

"One of the first lessons I learned at my Granny Fowler's knee was that we must stand ready to part with everything, when God shall require it," William said slowly. Although it had been more than fifty years since he'd heard Hope's account of George Whitefield's soul-shaking visit to Middletown a century ago, the passionate conviction with which she recounted the great evangelist's message had impressed it permanently on his memory.

"But Charles has God's work to do here in Durham – dozens of souls in need of his spiritual guidance," William said stubbornly. "He has a holy responsibility to them, and I can't believe it would be God's will for him to abandon them."

"Only Charles knows the answer to that question," Alma replied. "We must wait until his return to learn it. In the meantime–."

"We'll take Lizzy and the children home with us," William finished for her. Alma nodded her agreement, then continued gazing steadily at him.

William's face flushed, this time with shame. "I ask your forgiveness for my loss of temper," he said in a low voice. "And I must ask for Lizzy's as well, although I don't know how I can. The fear on her face–." He winced at the memory, then went on in self-disgust. "I not only failed her in her hour of need, I added to her pain."

Alma studied her husband compassionately, but made no attempt to lighten his shame or guilt. She'd discovered during their long marriage that William could, with great effort, maintain his composure in the face of the most outrageous behavior directed toward him. Only a threat, an attack, or an injury to someone he loved could make him lose his grip on his temper.

Much as Alma admired William's selflessness, she couldn't allow him – or her – to consider it an excuse for an outburst of anger. He could have so easily been injured or killed – or wounded someone else – during the confrontation with the anti-abolitionist mob on the Durham green. Today he'd blindly lashed out with his fist, if only at the house. Worst of all, witnessing her adored father change in an instant into a violent stranger had devastated Lizzy, who was beginning to wonder if there was anyone upon whom she could rely.

Alma extended her hand. William, looking as miserable as a man headed for the gallows, took it gratefully, and together they walked slowly toward the house.

Chapter One Hundred

November, 1844
Durham

Eighteen adults were packed tight as shad in a barrel around the table in Charles and Lizzy's parlor on Thanksgiving Day. Charles, in the seat of honor at the head of the table, folded his hands and bowed his head. Everyone followed suit, except three-year-old Lyman Mills, who couldn't resist staring at the mouth-watering feast spread upon the table.

The loud growling of her little son's stomach caused Lizzy to discreetly glance over at him. Without a word she deftly tightened her right arm around six-month-old Kitty, swaying drowsily on her mother's lap, and with her left hand reached over to gently but firmly push down on Lyman's head until it was bowed properly.

"We thank You, Lord, for our families, our friends, and our neighbors, and for the health, peace, and plenty you have bestowed upon us," Charles intoned. "We thank You for everything, large and small, that we take for granted each day: our homes, the clothes upon our backs, the beds in which we take our weary rest at day's end, for our cattle, sheep, swine and other creatures, for the grains and fruits and vegetables that spring from our fields. And may we never forget that all we have and enjoy in this world comes to us through Your endless bounty. Amen."

Eighteen faces looked up simultaneously. There immediately followed much bumping of elbows and exchanging of apologies as serving platters heaped with slices of roast turkey, roast goose, home-made cheese, and fresh-baked bread, and bowls filled with potatoes, pickles, dates, prunes, home-churned butter, preserves, puddings, and nuts were passed from one diner to the next in the cramped seating arrangements.

Alma hid her exasperation at the thought of how much more comfortable the diners would have been in the larger Lyman hall, where she and William had hosted Thanksgiving every year since David's death in 1815. They would have done so this year as well, were it not for their son-in-law's unpredictable behavior.

Charles had returned from London in October to a congregation understandably infuriated by his abrupt desertion of his post for four months. After hearing Charles out, however, many parishioners had accepted that, no matter how unhappy they might be, Charles himself had honestly believed he was responding to an urgent call from God when he sailed to England. With Christian forgiveness they decided not to discipline Charles, and allowed him to resume his pastoral duties.

Lizzy, desperately eager to expunge the humiliation of Charles's impulsive abandonment of his parish and his family, had pleaded with William and Alma to allow her the privilege of hosting the family Thanksgiving dinner. This most cherished of family gatherings would consecrate the Mills house as a true home, as well as underscore Charles's role as a reliable provider and stable householder.

It had been no easy thing for William and Alma to relinquish their leading roles in this holiday. But after discussing and praying on it, they'd concluded that Lizzy's need outweighed their own pride.

The original guest list had included Alma and William; Charles and Lizzy; David, Adeline, Elihu, and Sarah; Lyman and Kitty Mills; and Alma's nephews Charles Bliss, seventeen, and Henry Bliss, fourteen, both down from Hartford. Ten adults and two children would be a snug, but not too tight, fit around Lizzy's table.

Then Alma received a letter from William's sister Sally Miller in New York, accepting the invitation Alma extended every year for Sally, her husband Abner, and their three daughters, Mary, twelve; Urania, fourteen; and Esther, sixteen, to return to Middlefield for Thanksgiving. Then William persuaded his nephew David Buttolph, now a student at Williams College in Massachusetts, to join the family celebration instead of spending the holiday in his rooms. And Sarah had asked that James Dickinson, with whom her romance was no longer a secret, be invited to the Lyman gathering.

Instead of ten adult dinner guests there were now eighteen, more than the room could comfortably accommodate. But the prospect of hosting the traditional feast had so lifted Lizzy's spirits from the depths into which they'd plummeted after Charles's departure for London that Alma didn't have the heart to suggest moving the meal back to the Lyman house.

Lizzy had gladly accepted all offers of assistance in preparation for the holiday. Alma, Sarah, and Adeline had cooked the greater part of the day's bounty, most of which had come from the Lyman farm. But during the past week Lizzy had made time to bake most of the pies that crammed the sideboard to its edges, including pumpkin, apple, mince-meat, and Marlborough-pudding.

Soon the babble and confusion of dishes being passed around was replaced by the clinking of cutlery against porcelain and the satisfied sounds of food prepared by experienced cooks being savored. When everyone had eaten enough to dull the sharp edge of hunger, the conversation picked up.

William closed his eyes to savor his first spoonful of a dish, only to open them immediately in astonished recognition. "Mama's special quaking plum pudding!" he exclaimed. "It's been years since I tasted it!"

William turned a knowing look on his sister. "Only you could have made it, Sally," he said, with a grin. "No one else could reproduce Mama's recipe so perfectly."

Sally confirmed William's speculation with a nod and a smile of delight. Such praise was particularly sweet coming from her big brother, for that was what William would always be to her, even if, at fifty-seven and sixty-one, the four years separating them were now insignificant.

"Sally's always been a fine cook," Abner said proudly. "You need only look at me to see the truth of that."

A ripple of amusement ran around the table, for Abner Miller was indeed stout as a barrel. However, most of his bulk was muscle, for at fifty-six he still worked his farm almost single-handedly. Sally had borne him half a dozen daughters, but no sons.

"She's had a much easier time of it the past two years, since I bought a stove for her," Abner continued. "She made that quaking pudding in it at least half a dozen times to be sure she had the recipe down right for this visit."

"You delivered a fine Thanksgiving sermon," Abner said to Charles, who nodded in appreciation of the compliment. "The meetinghouse is handsome, a much finer structure than the one that stood when we left for New York."

"It was completed in 1835," Charles confirmed. "It's the pride and ornament of our town."

"I hope you won't take offense if I tell you it was fearsome cold inside the building," said David. There were murmurs of agreement from around the table.

Charles shook his head, half-annoyed, half-amused, at his brother-in-law's observation. "Thrift is among my sexton's many virtues, but one to which he sometimes adheres too zealously. He decided that since there would be only a morning meeting, it was wasteful to light the stove in the meetinghouse. I tried to persuade him otherwise, only to get a sharp lecture about how when he was a boy they did without stoves or any kind of heat in the meetinghouse at all. I was informed that any minister worth his salt could preach with sufficient ardor to warm his congregation's spirits so that they would forget the cold."

Everyone chuckled, save for little Lyman, whose expression was one of puzzled amazement. "Did people really sit through meeting without any heat?" he asked his grandfather.

William nodded. "Indeed they did – and not all that long ago. I remember spending many a frigid Sabbath in the meetinghouse. The minister would preach in his coat and mittens. We could see our breath while sitting in our pews. Sometimes the bread would freeze solid in the communion plate."

"One Sabbath I was so miserably cold that the minister's description of the flames of Hell sounded appealing," Abner chimed in.

"When stoves became available, you would have thought people would have welcomed them in the meetinghouse," said Alma. "But that wasn't the case. Many considered stoves a sign of spiritual weakening, of softness. It took quite a bit of persuading to win over those who objected."

The shelf clock on the mantle struck one. "That looks like the same clock we have in our house in Westmoreland," Abner observed of the two-foot-tall timepiece. "A peddler had it in his stock, and the girls took a fancy to the painting of Mount Vernon on the glass."

"When I was a girl, only the very rich could afford a clock," Sally recalled. "Back then the only ones to be had were like the one Papa owned, that's now in William's parlor – taller than a man, with the brass works hand-made by one craftsman and the case by another."

"We have Eli Terry of Plymouth to thank for changing that," said David, always eager to talk about mechanical innovations, especially those originating in Connecticut. "He invented machinery that makes wooden parts for a clock mechanism so nearly identical they can be changed one for another. Then he set up a factory powered by a river to make huge numbers of parts, which are assembled into shelf clocks by the thousands. They cost so much less to make than tall clocks that a person doesn't have to be rich to afford one. And they're so much shorter that peddlers can carry them as part of their stock."

Before David could continue his enthusiastic description of clock manufacturing, which William suspected some of the guests might not find as fascinating as his son did, William turned to David Buttolph. "What do you plan on doing with that fine education you're receiving, Nephew?" William asked. "Will it be the law for you, like your father?"

Young Buttolph shook his head thoughtfully. "I'm inclined toward the ministry, but I'm not yet sure I have a true calling," he replied seriously. Then his expression brightened. "I've been offered a position as an instructor in a girls' seminary in Charleston, South Carolina, after I graduate next year. It would provide me with an income while I seek to determine God's will regarding my future."

David and Elihu exchanged alarmed glances at their cousin's news. If they had encountered virulent hatred in Kentucky simply because they hailed from the North, what hostility would await David Buttolph in Charleston, the chief jewel of South Carolina, the bastion of the slaveocracy?

Others around the table had similar thoughts. However, Thanksgiving dinner wasn't the proper place to raise such troublesome issues. David resolved to speak to his cousin Buttolph about what he could expect to encounter in the South before he left to go back to college.

"I have plans," James Dickinson said, "although of a different nature." He looked across the table at Sarah with such affection that she blushed and looked down at her hands. "Sarah has done me the great honor of agreeing to become my wife. We hope to wed in May." Dickinson's second sentence was almost drowned out by the chorus of congratulations for this welcome, if not exactly unexpected, news.

David joined wholeheartedly in wishing the engaged couple well. But at the same time he felt strangely hollow. He was able to conceal his melancholy from the others – save for Lizzy. His sister recognized in David's eyes the loneliness of a lover witnessing another couple's joy while pining for the absent object of his own affections.

Since their serendipitous introduction six months ago, David and Catherine Hart had fallen in love. They exchanged letters when David was away, and when he was home spent as much time together as possible, often at the Mills house.

Adeline had been briefly disappointed at the failure of her scheme to make a match between Catherine and Elihu. But she'd quickly refocused her energies on fostering a romance between David and Catherine.

Whether this love would lead to marriage, Lizzy wouldn't hazard a guess. Although David was relentless once he fixed upon a goal, he was never impulsive in selecting that goal. She knew he wouldn't commit himself to taking a wife until he felt the circumstances were right – and spending five months of the year away from home certainly didn't qualify. There was no chance of Elihu taking over the mule-buying expeditions. Despite its encouraging start, the trip he'd made with David had left Elihu so exhausted that he'd had to spend several weeks in bed to recover.

"Fire! *FIRE!*"

The cry from outside shattered the camaraderie in the Mills parlor. The men instinctively pushed themselves away from the table. Urgent footsteps pounded across the front porch followed by hammering on the door and a youth's voice yelling "Mr. Mills! Mr. Mills! The meetinghouse is on fire!"

Charles leaped to his feet, knocking his chair backwards onto the floor. He grabbed the handle of the leather fire bucket kept behind the front door, raced outside, and started sprinting the quarter mile to the snow-covered green. Close on his heels were William, David, Elihu, James, Abner, David Buttolph, and the Bliss brothers.

Lizzy stood up, hugging Kitty tightly to her breast. Adeline darted out the door after Lyman. The little boy had raced after the men and gotten as far as the end of the porch before his aunt caught up with him. Lizzy stepped out onto the porch, with Alma, Sarah, Sally, and Sally's three daughters behind her, all heedless of the sharp cold.

Through the branches of trees stripped of their leaves they could see the meetinghouse. Thick smoke was rising from the tops of the columns on the northeast corner of the roof. From every direction men were rushing toward it like moths drawn to a flame.

Lizzy inhaled sharply in terror when she saw Charles reach the front door of the building, pull it open, and plunge inside. She thrust

Kitty into Alma's arms, and ran toward the green as fast as her long skirt would permit, her mother's frightened warning ringing in her ears.

The interior of the meetinghouse was still, although the smell of burning wood was strong and a crackling sound was audible from far off. Charles raced to the long rope dangling from the belfry. He grasped the rope with both hands, praying that enough men would respond to the ringing of the bell in time to save the building.

Charles yanked down hard on the rope – only to pitch forward, thrown off balance when there was no resistance from the heavy bell on the other end. He stumbled, caught himself with both hands, then regained his footing.

He turned to see the rope fall into a tangled coil on the floor. The end close to the bell had burned through. This made no sense, for the flames Charles had seen as he rushed toward the building were located far from the steeple. Peering up into the belfry Charles saw that the small length of rope still attached to the bell was burning. Beyond that he saw a square of slate-colored sky where the trap door leading from the roof into the belfry stood open.

Charles heard footsteps behind him and turned to see his brother-in-law David. David glanced at the bell rope on the floor, then said in a voice of command that sliced through Charles's confusion, "Let's save as many of the moveables as we can."

Charles hurried up the aisle of the sanctuary, which was beginning to fill with smoke. From the altar he grabbed the Bible and the silver communion service. Coughing from the thickening smoke, he made his way back to the door. David meantime had moved several of the lighter pieces of furniture outside onto the green, where David Buttolph was removing them a safe distance from the burning building.

Charles handed the Bible and silver to David Buttolph, then turned and went back into the building to salvage more objects. His brother-in-law gripped his arm to stop him. Charles turned toward David, who shook his head and shouted, "We've got to get out now!" When Charles hesitated, David literally pulled him through the doors and down the steps into the fresh air of the green.

Charles doubled over in a choking cough. After catching his breath he straightened up and saw to his horror that in the short time he'd been inside the meetinghouse the fire had spread over the entire roof. Flames were beginning to lick up the sides of the steeple.

Two human chains had been formed from the meetinghouse down the hill to Allyn Brook. William Lyman was at the head of one chain, comprised entirely of men, along which leather buckets filled with water from the stream were being passed from hand to hand to be thrown on the blaze. The lighter empty buckets were passed back down by the line of women and children, which included Sarah, Adeline, and Sally Miller and her three daughters, to be refilled.

But the fire had started at the top of the structure, and spread rapidly across the roof, out of reach of the water buckets. There was no hope of saving the meetinghouse. The bucket brigades were working to contain the blaze and prevent it from spreading to nearby structures, including the schoolhouse and the Reverend David Smith's home. Fortunately it was a calm day, with no wind to blow sparks and embers onto other buildings.

Charles was transfixed by the awful spectacle. He couldn't tear his eyes away even when Lizzy came up behind him and slipped her warm, trembling hand into his cold one. The slender steeple was fully engulfed in flames, like a gigantic beacon fire, then collapsed straight down. Through the roar of the inferno came the sound of windows being blown out by the intense heat.

A few minutes more and the walls began to collapse inward. At last the massive wooden pillars came crashing down one by one. An hour after the alarm had first been sounded, all that remained of the Durham meetinghouse was a blackened, smoking heap of rubble.

Chapter One Hundred and One

May, 1847
Bark Isabella
Atlantic Ocean off Virginia

"Land ho!"

The trio standing on the deck of the bark *Isabella*, twelve days out from the West Indies island of St. Croix, reacted to the look-out's cry by peering eagerly westward across the expanse of gray, choppy water. One by one they spotted on the horizon, highlighted by shafts of morning sun piercing the leaden clouds, a dark thin sliver of wooded land – the first they'd seen since setting sail on April 25.

"That would be Virginia, probably Cape Henry," Captain Alexander McKee, commander of the *Isabella*, informed Elihu Lyman and their female companion, Miss Emily Finlay. The pretty nineteen-year-old blonde had the clear, milk-white complexion that bespoke a genteel lady, for it was testimony that she'd never had to work under the sun of her native West Indies.

"How long do you make it before we reach New York?" Elihu asked.

"Three, maybe four days," Captain McKee answered, then hastened to qualify his prediction. "That depends, of course, upon the winds. We made no progress at all during this last day and a half of storm."

Elihu's lower lip jutted out slightly in a worried frown. "I wrote my family to expect me home around the first of May, and today is the sixth," he said, more to himself than the others. "I'm sure they're beginning to grow anxious over my failure to appear."

Elihu had sailed to the West Indies at the start of the year with two goals. The first was to transport a shipment of mules to St. Croix for sale. The second was to see if the mild Caribbean climate would help ease whatever malady afflicted his lungs, which had steadily worsened over the past year.

Suddenly a stiff gust of icy wind raked the ship's deck, setting the heavy canvas sails flapping loudly. Miss Finlay shivered and pulled the collar of her coat tightly together under her chin.

"It's so fearsomely cold I can scarce believe it's May," she complained through chattering teeth. "Still, this is better than endless hours trapped below decks in a cramped cabin during a terrifying storm. It shook the ship so hard I could scarce keep from falling out of my bunk."

Miss Finlay didn't suffer even small discomforts in silence, Elihu had discovered, but this particular complaint was entirely justified. The *Isabella* was a cargo ship, designed to carry livestock and barrels and boxes of produce. Two tiny cabins had been constructed below decks, near the captain's cabin and the crew's sleeping quarters, to accommodate a passenger or two. The passenger cabins were uncomfortable in the best of conditions.

"That was a great blow," Captain McKee acknowledged almost with relish, tactfully ignoring the whining of a female landlubber. "The *Isabella* withstood a fierce battering," he said proudly, as if boasting of an accomplished child. "But that was nothing like what we endured on the voyage out, eh, Mr. Lyman?" he said to Elihu.

Elihu nodded, as he reflexively clutched the ship's railing and shifted his feet to keep his balance on the deck, which had begun to roll and heave. "We set sail from New York on January 2," he began explaining matter-of-factly to Miss Finlay. "Two days out we were caught in a storm that lasted two weeks. The gales were so contrary that at one point Captain McKee was steering for Nova Scotia, and at another for England. Monstrous waves tossed the *Isabella* about like a cork. More than once I feared we would be sent to a watery grave. It took us twenty-eight days to reach St. Croix."

Miss Finlay's eyes grew wide. She glanced for confirmation of this frightening story to Captain McKee, who nodded in agreement. "Mr. Lyman is not exaggerating. That was by far the worst of the dozens of voyages I've made between New York and the West Indies over the past eight years."

During that nightmarish trip, Captain McKee had had ample opportunity to measure the mettle of Elihu Lyman. Upon first acquaintance he'd dismissed the young man as a sickly, stiff-necked, priggish fellow. That impression had been reinforced when Elihu suffered an especially violent bout of seasickness as soon as they reached open water. But during the prolonged tempest Elihu had pitched in to help however he could, displaying a courage and steadfastness that won Captain McKee's respect.

The wind increased in intensity. Elihu hunched up his shoulders and turned so his back faced the wind.

"Already you miss the sun-kissed isles of the West Indies," Captain McKee observed with sympathetic amusement. Miss Finlay nodded vigorously, but Elihu surprised them by shaking his head in emphatic disagreement.

"How can you not long for the Caribbean shores, Mr. Lyman?" Miss Finlay asked in disbelief. "They're paradise on earth. The climate is always gentle, the land verdant year round. The Indies have none of the extremes of weather I endured in Philadelphia three years ago," she said, the memory clearly not a pleasant one. "There's no harsh winter that turns the world bleak for months, no unpredictable extremes of heat and humidity."

Elihu turned his head to answer, keeping his back to the stiff breeze. "I found paradise can grow monotonous after a time. I recall a lovely night on St. Croix, when the air was soft and warm as a baby's breath. The atmosphere was so clear the full moon seemed to shine more brilliantly than ever I remembered in Connecticut. Yet I found myself yearning for one of the magnificent storms that on hot, humid summer days can sweep without warning through my native Yankeeland."

He paused, and when he spoke again it was with lyrical nostalgia. "I longed to see black clouds gathering into majestic mounds, to feel the wind blowing the storm in from the west. I pined to hear a sharp crack of thunder that would shake the ground, to see lightning bolts streak across the firmament, to watch the rain fall, slowly at first, then faster and harder still – and, when it was over, to savor the freshness of the atmosphere cooled and cleansed by the storm."

Elihu's eyes had brightened as he described the displays of the power of God and Nature that never failed to awe him. Miss Finlay grimaced as if he were a lunatic. Wrapping her coat even tighter around herself, the young lady walked unsteadily to the opposite side of the deck.

Captain McKee watched her go, shaking his head in amused exasperation. He'd given Elihu a perfect opportunity to impress the pretty girl with a dramatic account of his bravery during their harrowing voyage from New York to St. Croix. Instead, he'd squandered it in favor of rhapsodizing about the violent weather of his native land.

"I can think of more appealing topics than the climate upon which to converse with so attractive a female," Captain McKee observed, not unkindly.

"I hope she didn't find me rude – I didn't mean to be," Elihu said earnestly. Still, it was clear to the captain that Elihu didn't regret the lost opportunity.

Elihu had completed his business dealings soon after arriving on St. Croix. He'd then accepted the invitation of a transplanted Connecticut family by the name of Armstrong to spend two months as a guest at their delightful plantation, Lebanon Hill.

Elihu at first had been enchanted by the exotic lushness of the tropical island. But not long after arriving at Lebanon Hill, the Caribbean's charm had begun to fade. His host and his family were the soul of warm hospitality, but their conversation was inconsequential, consisting of little beyond local gossip and discussion of Mr. Armstrong's business affairs.

There wasn't much beyond horseback riding in the way of diversions at Lebanon Hill – no instrumental or vocal groups to join, no lectures or debates to attend. There'd been so little reading material in the Armstrong house, and none of any value to be had for purchase, that Elihu had been reduced to browsing through old newspapers. With no meaningful work, social activities, or intellectual pursuits to occupy him, time began to hang heavy on Elihu's hands.

The consistently superb weather, in which he could have pursued so many pleasant and productive purposes in Middlefield, seemed to mock Elihu's enforced idleness. He'd become increasingly bored and homesick.

These festering emotions had come to a head on March 2, Elihu's twenty-second birthday. He sank into a mental morass of self-pity, and of self-recrimination over his inability to shoulder his share of the farm work over the past year. He despaired over his failure to establish himself as a self-sufficient man.

When he surfaced from his depression, Elihu concluded that the unchanging, undemanding climate, landscape, and society of the

West Indies instilled a lethargy in those who, like him, were accustomed to more variable and challenging climes and cultures. Still he'd stayed on, turning down an earlier opportunity to return home on the *Isabella*, hoping the tropical climate would, if not cure, at least improve his chronic lung and throat problems. His health had seesawed, until at last it became clear he wasn't reaping any benefit.

"Miss Finlay reminds me of the West Indies," Elihu observed to Captain McKee.

"It doesn't sound as if you mean that as a compliment," Captain McKee replied.

"Miss Finlay's face and form are lovely," Elihu continued. "But there's about her a languid quality, a shallowness of intellect and personality for which her physical beauty cannot compensate. She can't hold a candle to the sturdy, sharp-witted females in Connecticut – nor could any girl I met in the West Indies."

Captain McKee sighed in surrender. Himself a New Yorker, he never ceased to be amazed by the intense, to him sometimes irrational, passion of New Englanders for their native land. To them, nothing anywhere, not just the weather and the women, was as good as it was in New England.

Perversely, New Englanders were always ready to bend a man's ear with laments about the unpredictability of the weather, about the stones their fields produced in greater abundance than any crop. But get them away from the land of their birth for any length of time and they grew homesick for those very same features.

Captain McKee clapped Elihu twice on the back. Then he strode toward the ship's bow, leaving Elihu to his thoughts.

Elihu forgot the sting of the icy wind, the eternal shipboard dampness that penetrated to his very marrow, as he imagined the delights of home and family waiting for him in Middlefield just a few days hence. He hoped he would arrive while the apple trees were still so thick with delicately fragrant blossoms that from a distance they looked like gauzy pink and white clouds. His mouth watered in anticipation of the delicacies that could be savored only in the springtime – shad straight from the Connecticut River served with asparagus fresh out of the garden, pies warm from the oven filled with a mixture of rhubarb and strawberries picked just hours earlier. The exotic mangoes, bananas, and coconuts of the tropics, although certainly tasty, simply couldn't compare.

Best of all, amidst the glory and bounty of spring he would be reunited with his family – his parents; Sarah and James Dickinson; David, doubtless spending as much time as he could in the company of Catherine Hart; and Adeline. He would revel in the simple pleasures of home: attending church with his family, browsing through James's library, singing duets with Adeline.

Lizzy, Lyman, and Kitty would be there to greet him as well, although probably not Charles. The burning of the meetinghouse on Thanksgiving had been the catalyst for the Durham congregation, so long plagued by disagreements, to formally split into two distinct religious societies.

It had been made plain to Charles that neither of the new churches would want him as its minister. He'd lost the confidence of his flock by failing to heal the long-standing rift in the Society, by impulsively abandoning his duties to run off to England, and then, after being taken back by the congregation, by trying their patience by devoting much time to missionary work at the expense of his pastoral duties.

Charles had requested and received his dismissal from the pastorate at the end of 1845. Poor health was his official reason, and there was some truth to it.

Charles embarked on the missionary work he so enjoyed. Since he was away for long stretches of time, he sold his Durham house and arranged for his family to board with William and Alma. That had tempered William's vexation at his son-in-law's departure from the position he'd worked so hard to secure for him. The presence of Lizzy and the grandchildren had also provided some balm for Alma when her sister Delia died last summer, little improved by the time she'd spent at the Retreat for the Insane.

Fat, cold raindrops started to spatter the *Isabella's* deck, then to pelt down faster and faster. Elihu reluctantly headed for the hatchway that led down to his cabin. Captain McKee, studying the sails with concern, spotted him and called out above the wind, "Don't hold me to that estimate of four days to New York."

Elihu lay on his back on the short, narrow bunk in his cabin. He'd felt increasingly unwell since leaving the deck several hours earlier. His attempts to sleep had been futile, resulting only in much frustrating tossing and turning.

Suddenly, without warning, Elihu was seized by a fit of coughing. It grew worse the longer he coughed. He felt a sharp pain deep inside his chest, on the left side.

Elihu swung his long legs over the side of his bunk and sat up. The hacking continued uncontrollably; at one point the spasms compressed his diaphragm so forcefully he nearly vomited. He hastily pressed a handkerchief against his month in case that should happen. But he brought up only phlegm that he spat into the handkerchief.

With that the coughing eased, and then ceased. Elihu sat for a full minute, panting heavily, until he regained his breath. He was perspiring heavily in the close cabin. He lowered the handkerchief, thinking to fold it over and use the clean side to wipe the sweat from his face.

But before he could do so, he noticed a dark splotch on the cloth. He leaned closer to the swinging oil lamp that was the cabin's only illumination to examine the handkerchief more closely.

What Elihu saw rendered him cold with terror, as if the frigid waters of the Atlantic suddenly coursed through his veins. The stain was bright crimson. For the first time in all the years he'd been plagued by afflictions of the lungs and throat, Elihu had coughed up blood – the telltale symptom of consumption.

Chapter One Hundred and Two

May, 1847
Middlefield

"I'll be back to collect the eggs when they're gone," William whispered conspiratorially to Adeline before swinging himself up into the saddle. It was an old joke between them, but one that always made Adeline grin. For the chattering of the ladies Alma was entertaining in the parlor this afternoon did sound, as William had often teased his wife and daughters, like the cackling of hens.

Innately hospitable, William had welcomed each of the women to his home – then had gratefully made his exit. While he enjoyed the conversation of intelligent women, the chit-chat that would be exchanged this day held no interest for him. And besides, what woman wanted her husband at a tea party?

William cantered off westward, to inspect the progress of the apple blossoms that were in full bloom this perfect spring day, the tenth of May. Adeline hurried back into the parlor. A dozen middle-aged matrons, dressed stylishly but comfortably, were seated in chairs around the parlor, knitting or sewing as they chatted. Fresh-cut flowers from Alma's gardens brightened the room.

"Any word from Mr. and Mrs. Mills?" inquired Lydia Hale.

"A letter came last week," Alma replied. "They seem content with Ashland."

Three months earlier, Charles, who was now temporarily filling pulpits in eastern Massachusetts, had moved his family to the town of Ashland, about thirty miles outside Boston. After two idyllic years of having Lizzy, Lyman, and Kitty living with them, William and Alma had been heartbroken to have the Mills family move away. But

Ashland, not even a hundred miles from Middlefield, was far more accessible than Indiana.

"We hope they'll be able to come down sometime this summer," Alma went on, "and we plan to visit them in the autumn."

"Did they ever determine what caused the meetinghouse fire?" asked Abigail Cornwell.

"No," Alma replied, "although there's reason to believe it was the work of an arsonist," she added uneasily. Alma's distress was shared by every woman in the room. For someone to set fire to any building was disturbing enough. To deliberately burn down a meetinghouse was appalling. Worse still was the unthinkable yet unavoidable possibility, given the prolonged discord in the Durham congregation, that the arsonist was a disgruntled parishioner.

Each of the two new religious societies had decided to build its own meetinghouse. The North Congregational Church had just finished its new house of worship, near the intersection of Main Street and the Wallingford Road. The location was less than a mile from the site of the meetinghouse consumed by flames, where the South Congregational Church planned to build its meetinghouse.

"Lucinda Cornwell was delivered of a girl day before yesterday," reported Almira Skinner, dispelling the grim thoughts and prompting pleased nodding of heads and murmurs all around.

"That's good news," said Lydia Hale. "After four boys I know she was hoping for a daughter." She paused to glance up from her needlework at Alma. "Any signs of a baby for Mr. and Mrs. Dickinson?"

Alma shook her head. "They've been married just two years," Alma replied. "And Sarah's only twenty-four. They have plenty of time to start a family."

"When do you expect Elihu home from the Indies?" asked Clarissa Hubbard. She strove to sound casual, and failed. When the eldest of her three daughters had reached marriageable age four years ago, the ambitious Mrs. Hubbard had targeted David Lyman, one of Middlefield's most eligible bachelors, as prime husband material for any one of the trio.

David, however, had dashed Mrs. Hubbard's dreams by inconsiderately falling in love with Catherine Hart. Although there'd been no announcement of an engagement, it was widely understood that David Lyman was off the marriage market.

Rallying from this setback, the determined matron had focused on Elihu. Although as the younger brother and a man of chronically slim health he was a lesser catch than David, Elihu had much to recommend him as husband material. The two brothers would share the farm when William, now in his mid-sixties, died. Elihu was intelligent, well-mannered, and devout. His uncertain health might even prove an asset, making it highly unlikely he would spirit a wife away to some far-off frontier as so many ambitious young men had.

Alma frowned and glanced at Elihu's portrait on the parlor wall. "In his last letter he said to expect him around the first of May."

Although all the women knew unpredictable delays were a given when traveling on the ocean, for Elihu to be ten days late was long enough to give cause for unease. Clarissa Hubbard wanted to ask if Elihu had written anything about the young women of the Indies, if he'd spent much time socializing with them, if he'd formed an attachment to any one in particular. But in light of Alma's troubling news of Elihu's long-overdue homecoming, she decided against it.

Alma excused herself to the kitchen to check on the food. Adeline followed to make sure the table in the hall was completely set with her mother's best china.

Alma returned a moment later. "Dinner is ready, ladies," she announced. The women displayed a remarkable degree of energy and agility as they laid aside their needlework, hefted themselves out of the chairs, and bustled into the hall.

It was a perfect mid-day meal for an increasingly warm afternoon in May. Laid out in generous helpings on the table were cold biscuits, dried beef, and cheese. There was bread, raspberry preserves, and doughnuts, and coffee, tea, and water to drink.

Adeline helped herself to a slice of cheese and a donut, then slipped out of the hall. She detoured to retrieve a pencil and paper, then retreated to the porch. Although Alma had requested her daughter's assistance with preparing and serving the meal, she'd promised Adeline could leave after those duties were fulfilled, understanding that an afternoon with middle-aged matrons exchanging news, domestic advice, and gossip would be torture to a lively young woman not yet twenty.

Adeline was relieved to have escaped before one of the women interrogated her about her own matrimonial prospects. Adeline was still smarting from the unhappy ending two months ago of her romance with Judson, who, she'd learned from Catherine, had wasted no time taking up with a girl in Guilford, She had no desire to answer questions about something she herself didn't understand.

Adeline sat down on the top step of the porch, and set her plate of food next to her. Although she'd intended to compose a letter to David, who'd left five days ago on his first mule-buying trip of the season, the paper and pencil remained untouched in her lap. She hesitated to write to him until she could include the news she knew he was most anxious to receive: that Elihu was home safe.

Instead, Adeline nibbled at her cheese, surveying the lush spring landscape before her. She closed her eyes, enjoying the warmth of the strong sunshine tempered by a refreshing breeze.

Adeline's eyelids fluttered open at the sound of a deep voice coming from the direction of the dirt road that skirted the swamp before curving toward the Lyman house. It was a man urging on a team of two horses drawing a wagon that from Adeline's vantage point looked empty. She watched its progress with idle curiosity.

When the wagon drew near enough for her to hear the creaking of the wheels and the clanking of the horses' harness, she could make out the driver's face. She'd seen him before, but didn't know his name. She could also see something in the wagon bed. She squinted to see better; a sudden suspicion chilled her to the marrow.

Another hundred feet closer and the wagon's cargo was unmistakable: a long, rectangular wooden box. A coffin.

Adeline's eyes remained riveted on the approaching wagon. She prayed that the driver wouldn't come to their house, would instead turn off and head east toward Durham.

But her waking nightmare continued as the man drove his wagon right up to the gate in the stone wall surrounding the Lyman homelot. He beckoned Adeline toward him, as if he were the Grim Reaper. Adeline, frozen with dread, couldn't answer the summons.

Finally the driver, annoyed by Adeline's rude ignoring of his gesture, stood up. He cupped his hands around his mouth, and called out, "Tell your folks old Mrs. Pickett's dead. The funeral is at two o'clock tomorrow. I'm taking the coffin down for her now."

When Adeline didn't respond, the driver shook his head in bewilderment. He sat back down and slapped the reins to direct the team down the road to Durham.

Mrs. Pickett. The name echoed through Adeline's brain. The widow Ruth Pickett, near ninety years old, stricken by an attack of apoplexy last month. Mrs. Pickettt was dead – not Elihu! Relief surged through Adeline, thawing her terror.

Adeline jumped to her feet, pen and paper sliding to the ground. She could barely see for the tears blurring her vision. Yanking open the front door, she nearly tripped over the sill. She raced into the hall, where all eyes were on her, drawn by the racket of her most unladylike approach.

"Old Mrs. Pickett's dead," Adeline blurted out to the astonished women. "And I'm glad of it!" she added with an edge of hysteria. Even Alma was so shocked by this bizarre behavior that she simply stared at her daughter, her mouth hanging open in amazement that changed to consternation when Adeline burst into tears.

Chapter One Hundred and Three

December, 1848
Guilford, Connecticut

Catherine heard the faint jingling of bells, and peered anxiously out the front window of her chamber as she'd done half a dozen times during the past hour. This time her vigilance was rewarded by the sight of a sleigh drawn by a single horse approaching from the direction of the Guilford green. The driver, she could be sure after a moment, was David Lyman.

Catherine scrambled away from the window and raced down the stairs to the front door as fast as her long skirts would allow. "David has come, Mother," she called out as she threw a heavy woolen cloak around her shoulders.

David had barely brought the sleigh to a full stop before Catherine was out the door and standing next to the conveyance. He leaned across to extend his hand, which she gripped to steady herself as she got into the sleigh.

"I apologize for my tardiness," he said. She shook her head to indicate his lateness was of no moment, although in truth she'd been on pins and needles once the appointed hour of his arrival had passed. Now that he was here, that no longer mattered.

David snapped the reins, and the horse set off at a trot. The sleigh glided smoothly along on hard-packed snow between drifts as high as their heads.

Catherine let herself luxuriate in the simple fact of David's presence. Heavy snows had clogged the roads for a week, and she'd heard nothing from him until the arrival of a brief note the previous evening announcing that he would call for her on Friday at 2 p.m.

"How is Adeline?" Catherine asked. David shook his head slowly and sadly, without taking his eyes from the road. "My father took her to a specialist in New York, the same one Elihu consulted, last week just before the snowstorm hit. The physician has no doubt it is consumption. Knowing of Elihu's case, and seeing how rapidly her symptoms have advanced, he doesn't think she'll live another year."

Catherine sucked in her breath sharply. David's revelation left her heartsick. She had allowed herself to hope that the lung problems afflicting her friend for the past three months would turn out to be something other than this dreaded disease.

"I'm so sorry, David," she said at last, slipping her arm gently around his. He acknowledged her sympathy with a short nod and a quick grateful glance. He didn't look for very long into her eyes, for fear that the sorrow and compassion he would see would make it impossible for him to keep his composure.

The bleakness of the frozen landscape, which met with a leaden sky at the horizon, matched David's mood. Death and loss had plagued the year now drawing to a close for the Lyman family.

It had actually begun the previous May. Three days after Adeline's fright over the coffin meant for the deceased Mrs. Pickett, Elihu had arrived home alive – but far from well.

The blood Elihu spat up on the *Isabella* was a harbinger of doom. It was soon obvious that consumption had taken root in his lungs. He declined so rapidly that by October all hope of recovery was abandoned.

Riddled with grief, William had helped his son confront his looming mortality with an exercise in Yankee practicality. He'd worked with Elihu to settle his financial accounts. It turned out Elihu had a modest estate, and he took great satisfaction in leaving half of it to his cherished sister Adeline. He directed that part of the bequest be used to purchase for her a piano, something for which she'd long yearned. It was his legacy to her, a tribute to the many delightful hours they'd shared making music.

His earthly concerns in order, Elihu devoted his remaining time to making his peace with God. He lingered longer than anyone had expected, growing weaker by the day. Death at long last released him on April 26, 1848. He was only twenty-three.

That blow of Elihu's death had been followed by the news that Charles Mills had accepted an assignment to supply the pulpit for a year at the First Presbyterian Church in Indianapolis. He intended to take his family with him. William and Alma had been devastated by the prospect of Lizzy once again heading for the west from which nothing good had ever come to her.

Then in the autumn Adeline, grieving deeply for her favorite brother, had developed a respiratory ailment. Her health had declined quickly. Although there was little question in anyone's mind that it was consumption, no one had been able to bring themselves to acknowledge it openly until the New York doctor confirmed the diagnosis.

David had given up the mule trade after Elihu's death. His presence at home was needed far more than was any income from his trips.

Catherine had watched with compassion and admiration as David absorbed his family's repeated tragedies, all the while providing support of every kind. His qualities had proven to be as fine as she'd sensed the first time they met – trustworthiness, honesty, gentleness, persistence, and above all a loving dedication to home and family.

Catherine had assumed that, once David returned to Middlefield for good, they would begin making plans for a life together. But he had yet to raise the subject. For Catherine disappointment had given way to dismay, then to doubt, and, just recently, to resentment that would simmer only so long before it boiled over into anger.

"Catherine," David said suddenly. He hesitated, then stumbled on. "I don't–," he said, then stopped again. He hadn't taken his eyes off the road.

Catherine's heart sank. She'd never known David to be tongue-tied. It could only mean he had something so unpleasant to say he had trouble forcing the words out.

David's cheeks flushed brightly. He abruptly yanked the reins, bringing the sleigh to a lurching stop; Catherine tightened her hold on David's arm and gripped the seat with her other hand to keep from pitching forward. He turned to her and blurted out, "Will you be my wife?"

Hearing the opposite of what she'd expected so flustered Catherine that for a moment she could only gape at David. Brief as her moment of shock was, David found it unnerving. He rushed on, almost like a little boy explaining why he was late to school.

"I would have asked you in the spring," he said, "but Elihu's death, and Lizzy's plans to leave, and now the terrible news about Adeline have so laden me with responsibilities that I doubted my capacity to take on the sacred one of marriage. But I can't wait any longer. I know whatever chance I have for happiness in this world depends upon you."

Listening to David plead his case so anxiously snapped Catherine out of her shock. "Yes, David, yes!" she cried. "You don't have to convince me," she said gently. They stared at each other, then broke into nervous laughter at the awkward, convoluted course the conversation had taken.

Catherine swiped tears of happiness from her eyes, then composed herself. "I would be honored to marry you, David."

She was touched by the joy her acceptance brought to David's face. How could he have ever doubted what her answer would be? But he quickly grew serious. "I doubt I'll be able to offer you the life you deserve," he began, then stopped as Catherine shook her head vehemently.

"Don't say that, David. You offer me your loving and constant heart, and acceptance into a family of warmth and faith. That is all any woman can ask for from a marriage, and much more than many receive."

David pulled her into his arms, and they sealed their bargain with a kiss. Catherine wondered why, even if he'd felt unable to propose marriage, he'd neglected to regularly reassure her that his desire to make her his wife hadn't wavered. And then it came to her. David was truly steadfast. Having declared his love for her, it never occurred to him that she could think his intention had changed.

At last their lips parted reluctantly, although David still held her close, looking deep into her eyes. Suddenly his lips twitched in a mischievous smile at the memory of how he'd shocked Lizzy with his claim of a plan for a dozen children.

"What?" Catherine demanded suspiciously.

"Nothing," David said, then kissed her again with an ardor that seemed to heat the frigid air around them.

Chapter One Hundred and Four

March, 1849
Middlefield

James and David trailed William as he paced off with long, measured strides the perimeter of a large rectangle in the northwestern corner of the Lyman homelot. When he reached the point from which he'd started William stopped. "The door will go here," he proclaimed.

Sarah and Lizzy, huddled against the back of the Lyman house, could hear William's firm pronouncement clearly over both the stiff, cold breeze rattling bare branches on this first day of spring and the strains of popular new composer Stephen Collins Foster's "Autumn Waltz" being played with admirable skill on the piano in the parlor. The sisters exchanged knowing glances, and Sarah's lips twisted into a smile of rueful affection when she saw James nod in dutiful agreement.

The location William had chosen for the front door of the house he was planning to build for James and Sarah didn't face the road, as one would expect, but the kitchen door of the Lyman house. That unusual orientation would establish an immediate intimacy between the two dwellings. William's decision was no surprise, given a condition in the deed, witnessed that day by David and Lizzy, recording William's sale of the land to James. It stipulated that James couldn't sell or rent the lot to another party without William's consent.

If James resented his father-in-law's presumptuousness about the design and legal control of the Dickinsons' future home, he didn't show it. James understood that desperation, not domination, was driving William to demand a degree of authority so out of character for him.

The fabric of the Lyman family was being mercilessly rent, and William was fighting to hold the precious remnants together. The urgency of his struggle was poignantly underscored when the piano playing inside the house abruptly stopped, replaced by a spasm of coughing and choking that lasted two full minutes before at last subsiding into ragged wheezing.

Lizzy and Sarah looked at each other again, this time their expressions grim. "It's not been even a year since Husa left us," Sarah said, shaking her head in sorrowful disbelief.

"I still wish I could have seen him one last time before he answered Heaven's call," Lizzy said, her voice heavy with regret at being in Ashland when Elihu died.

Sarah reached out to touch Lizzy's arm. "You did the right thing by not coming down," she reassured her. "The excitement of so many people, and the ruckus raised by the children only would have agitated him," she said, knowing Lizzy wouldn't take offense at the simple truth about the normal rambunctiousness of a boy of seven and a girl of four.

"Your letters were of great solace," Sarah went on sincerely. "When Charles wrote we are closest to the threshold of Heaven immediately after a loved one recently among us in the flesh has passed into Paradise, it helped lighten a bit the black pall that had descended upon us." Elihu's drawn-out suffering and death had left Alma, Adeline, and even William so numb with grief that it had fallen to Sarah to write to Lizzy and Charles and other relatives about Elihu's passing.

"We're nearing that threshold again," Lizzy said bleakly. Adeline's consumption had proven so virulent it was expected it would kill her before summer's end.

"I shall miss you so desperately!" Sarah blurted out suddenly. "It's been so wonderful to have both my sisters so close all these years – and now to lose you both within the space of a few months–." She stopped, overcome with emotion, surprising for the usually self-controlled Sarah.

"We'll only be gone to Indianapolis for a year," Lizzy said reassuringly. Where the Lord's work would take Charles after that, only He knew, but Lizzy was hopeful they would come back, at least for a time, to New England, if not Connecticut.

Charles had gone on ahead to Indianapolis. Lizzy had remained behind in Middlefield with Lyman and Kitty, to help tend Adeline in her last days and then to mourn with her family.

Out of distress over these tragedies and separations had come William's offer to build a house for Sarah and James in the corner of the homelot. The restrictions on James's disposal of the land had simply confirmed what everyone knew; this was a blatant strategy to bind the couple tight to Middlefield.

One joyous development had helped offset the long stretch of sorrow. David had married Catherine Hart two months earlier, in January of 1849. The newlyweds had settled in at the Lyman house.

The piano playing resumed, weakly, tentatively. Sarah and Lizzy listened with aching hearts.

"Charles and I have decided to leave Lyman here rather than take him with us to Indianapolis," Lizzy said suddenly, deliberately avoiding her sister's eyes.

Sarah simply stared at first; then a glimmer of understanding penetrated her surprise. "Why?" she asked gently.

Still Lizzy didn't look at Sarah. "Lyman flourishes here," she said. "He's become so very attached to Father, and to David."

Behind that simple statement hovered a truth so painful Lizzy couldn't speak it, not even to Sarah. During his two years of missionary work, and the two years in Ashland, Charles had largely abdicated his responsibility as a father to Lyman. He'd neglected his duty to guide the little boy on the difficult road toward manhood.

William, with assistance from David, James, and Elihu, had filled that void. The result was that at eight little Lyman Mills was a child to be proud of, and showed signs of becoming an extraordinary man. Lizzy found it bitterly bewildering that not only did Charles not resent being supplanted as the most important man in his son's life, he seemed, if anything, oblivious to the reality.

Putting her son's good ahead of the desperate yearning of a mother's heart, Lizzy had broached with Charles the idea of leaving Lyman behind in Middlefield when they moved to Indianapolis. She'd mustered such legitimate arguments as the superior education available to Lyman in New England, the benefits of the pure country air of Middlefield over that of Indianapolis, the solace their only grandson would provide William and Alma in their grief over Elihu and Adeline, even the joy Lyman could bring to Sarah and James, who after four years remained childless.

Lizzy wasn't surprised when Charles readily agreed. Lyman's reaction to the proposal had both relieved and distressed her. Although his reluctance to be parted from his parents and sister was obvious, it was clearly outweighed by his joy at the prospect of remaining in Middlefield.

But suddenly Lizzy had misgivings about this plan. She had envied Sarah's good fortune in being permanently settled near their parents and David and Catherine. With great effort she'd largely suppressed that unworthy, sinful emotion. But what if Alma and Sarah should come to replace her in Lyman's affections? That Lizzy couldn't bear.

At last Lizzy looked up to gauge Sarah's reaction. She read in her sister's intelligent blue eyes and compassionate expression understanding of the pain of the sacrifice Lizzy was making, and her fears about what might result.

"Mother and I will do everything we can for Lyman," Sarah said. "But you must promise not to fault us when we fall short, as we certainly will. For even the two of us together can't hope to fill the part of a child's heart that belongs to his mother alone."

Lizzy's features crumpled under the weight of conflicting emotions, and tears that would no longer be denied trickled down her cheeks. She held out her arms and embraced Sarah, thanking God for blessing her sister with such insight.

The men, deep in discussion about the proposed structure, were oblivious to the emotional exchange between Sarah and Lizzy. "I calculate it will have two floors with an attic," William said. "Three windows across the front – the side, that is," he corrected himself, for the front would be the gable end where he had put the door. "A good-sized bay window where Sarah can sit and read," William said, knowing his daughter. "And I'll have the carpenters install a fine fanlight over the door."

He looked at the two younger men for their reaction. James nodded his acceptance, for both he and Sarah had simple tastes. But to William's surprise David was frowning, as if something didn't quite meet with his approval.

"Would you do something differently?" William asked. He startled David, who hadn't realized his critical consideration showed on his face.

"It's really not my place to say," David began hesitantly, looking first at William, who was building the house, then at James who would live in it. He plunged ahead, "But what you propose seems rather plain. This is a chance to build a house of grace, even elegance, perhaps like Jesse Miller's, but smaller." William and James knew well the Miller house, which was noteworthy for its large three-part Palladian window.

Although his father and brother-in-law listened politely, David could see neither shared his vision. He shrugged in good-natured resignation. "It will be fine just as you have planned it, Father," he said. "I'll save my grand notions for when I build a house of my own."

David's offhand remark made William's heart skip a beat. David knew that, as the only surviving son, the Lyman house would one day be his. Why then this talk, even in passing, of building a house of his own – and a fancy one at that?

You're becoming a jumpy old man, reading hidden meanings into every casual comment, William chided himself. He gave David's words no further thought, and gladly turned his attention to planning the raising of James and Sarah's new home.

Chapter One Hundred and Five

September, 1850
Middlefield

"I'm sorry to interrupt, Mr. Lyman." The thin young woman standing in the parlor doorway spoke diffidently in the brogue of the Ireland she'd left less than a year ago. "Could you calculate the sum of what's been set aside from my wages?"

"Of course, Bridget," answered William, who was sitting in front of the drop leaf of his father's desk. He pulled down from the bookcase a tall, narrow leather-bound account book.

From one of the pigeonholes in the desk William removed a pair of oval, metal-framed spectacles that he required for reading. They were a recent acquisition, undeniable evidence of his advancing age. He was, after all, sixty-seven years old.

William perched the spectacles on his nose, then by the light of an oil lamp leafed through the account book until he found the facing pages with "Bridget Currance" written across the top of each. He ran his finger down the lists of debts and credits until he arrived at the number he sought.

"Fourteen dollars and thirty-seven cents," he reported, looking up. Bridget nodded with somber satisfaction. "Could you see to having $10 sent to my mother?" she asked. "Mary Currance, Killarney Parish, County Kerry, Ireland. I trust there will be enough left in my savings to pay the postage."

"The excess should be more than sufficient. I'll attend to it the next time I'm in Middletown," William assured her. This request explained why Bridget Currance practiced a frugality extreme even by New England standards of thrift. She'd spent only a few pennies of her wages of $5 a month, requesting that William deposit the lion's share in a bank account.

"When do you think that might be?" Bridget asked, an urgency underlying her hesitant question. William realized it wasn't impertinence, but anxiety that drove the girl to risk offending her employer by pressing him to be specific.

"I expect to be riding in on Tuesday," he replied. As Alma came into the room through another door, William plucked from among the papers on his desk an almanac for the year 1850. He found the calendar for September, then did a quick mental calculation.

"Tuesday will be September 24," William said, peering at Bridget over the top of the spectacles. "If I send it that day I would think it will reach your mother by the middle of October."

Bridget sighed with relief. "Could you also send another of my dollars for the relief of the Irish?"

"I'll do it at the same time," William replied. He'd have to make inquiries to determine a proper agency to receive such a donation.

"Thank you, sir," Bridget said with, at last, a faint smile. She turned to Alma, who had settled down on William's oversized couch with the weekly *Middletown Constitution* newspaper. "Have I permission to attend Mass this Sunday?" Bridget asked.

Alma looked up. "Of course. Only be back by four o'clock."

The smile grew wider, although still tight-lipped, as if too open a display of satisfaction would tempt fate. "I'll be sure to finish mending Mr. Lyman's shirts by then. And I'll study the speller," she promised. She then bobbed a small, respectful curtsy and turned to leave the room.

"Bridget, wait!" Alma called, setting the newspaper down as she got to her feet. The servant stopped abruptly, then turned to nervously face Alma.

"William, do you have–?" Before Alma could finish her question, William was searching among the documents on his desk.

It took him only a moment to find what he sought. Although William's desk was six inches deep with letters, receipts, documents, and newspaper clippings arranged in no discernible order, he knew where in the hodge-podge every item was located. He pulled out a single sheet of paper, about twelve by fourteen inches. He handed it to Alma with a small smile of triumph; his cluttered desk was a never-ending source of despair to her.

"I thought you might like to have this," Alma said, proffering the paper to Bridget, who stepped forward to accept it.

Bridget half-expected the sheet to be some Protestant religious tract, for during the reading lessons Mrs. Lyman gave she regularly sought to engage Bridget in conversation about matters of faith. But when Bridget looked at the paper, her mouth parted slightly in awe. Her eyes blazed with an adoration William found unsettling.

The paper was a lithograph depicting the legend of the Roman Catholic Saint Patrick banishing all snakes from Ireland. Produced by the Hartford firm of E.B. & E.G. Kellogg, it showed Ireland's patron saint in full bishop's costume, wearing a mitre and carrying a crozier. It had been hand-tinted with vibrant colors. St. Patrick's cape was crimson, billowy clouds of a soft blue-gray hue formed a halo around his head, and the coiled serpents writhing at his feet were a sickly yellowish-green.

"It's so very fine," Bridget whispered. "Is it mine – to keep?" she asked, raising her eyes to Alma, who nodded. William was touched, but also bewildered and somewhat discomfited by the young woman's intense emotional response to what was, after all, nothing more than ink and paint on cheap paper.

The Kellogg brothers turned out lithographs of hundreds of different subjects quickly, in huge numbers, and inexpensively. Kellogg prints cost so little that Alma had been able to afford half a dozen images of flowers and animals to brighten the parlor walls, and another half dozen depicting sentimental scenes of family, home, and hearth for their bedchamber.

The lithograph of Saint Patrick was a recent addition to the entrepreneurial Kellogg brothers' product line. Its market was the burgeoning number of Irish Catholic immigrants in the Northeast, most of them, like Bridget, refugees from the famine that had ravaged their homeland.

Alma had seen the St. Patrick image listed in a newspaper item of prints available from the Kellogg brothers, and asked William to purchase one on his next visit to Hartford. Bridget, twenty-five, was an impressively conscientious servant, doing her best at any task assigned to her. Alma had wanted to give her some small token of appreciation for her efforts.

"Thank you, ma'am," Bridget said quietly. She laid the print carefully against the bodice of her dress, folded her hands protectively over it, and started up the stairs to find a safe place for her new treasure.

Alma sat back down and picked up the newspaper. William shut the account book and slid it into its space on the shelf. He removed his spectacles, folded them up and returned them to their pigeonhole.

William stood up, put his hands on his hips, and arched his back to stretch a tight muscle. While he did so he affectionately studied Alma, who was absorbed in her newspaper. This would be the first night in nearly a week that they would share the same bed.

Five days earlier Alma had received an urgent early morning call to the bedside of a dangerously ill friend. The crisis had kept her away for two nights. She'd returned home on the third morning just in time to see William, David, and Catherine off to Guilford.

More than a year after their wedding, Catherine had at last conceived a child, which was expected around Thanksgiving. Catherine was anxious to visit her family once more before she was so far along in her pregnancy that it would be imprudent to travel. She and David had planned a stay of several days in Guilford. The ever-solicitous William – he suspected, and cared not, that both Catherine and David considered him overly solicitous – had insisted upon escorting them to William Hart's house, with the intention of being back in Middlefield by nightfall.

A dangerous storm of rain, wind, and lightning had forced William to spend the night in Guilford. When he arrived home the following morning, there was only enough time to share a quick breakfast with Alma, during which she asked him to purchase the Saint Patrick lithograph, before she hurried back to the bedside of her ailing friend, who'd taken a turn for the worse.

Within an hour of Alma's departure William had left on an overnight trip to Hartford to tend to business, personal, and legal matters. He marveled at how he and Alma, now both in their sixties, seemed to be as busy as ever.

During his grandparents' absence, Sarah and James Dickinson had watched over Lyman Mills. The couple, who still had no children, enjoyed acting as surrogate parents to the boy.

William had reached home late this afternoon, to discover that Alma herself had only just gotten back, with the welcome news that there was hope for her friend's recovery. They made do with a supper of cold chicken, Alma's home-made cheese, cornbread, and sweet apple cider. William dutifully reported to his desk to attack the mail he'd picked up in Durham and documents from his trip to Hartford.

William glanced up as rain began to drum soothingly on the roof. He resumed gazing at Alma, who at last feeling William's eyes on her, looked up with a smile of weary contentment. William covered the distance between them with two strides of his long legs. Taking Alma's hand gently in his, he asked, almost formally, "Would you join me on the porch?"

William's smile was one he reserved for Alma alone, one that could still make her heart skip a beat like that of a girl of sixteen, not a grandmother of three score and three years. He waited for her response tentatively, as if he were still courting her, still seeking to win the love that had been his alone for more than forty years. She studied his face, grown leaner with age that had sharpened his features, and now displaying its share of wrinkles. But to Alma these changes, along with his steel-gray hair and even his new spectacles, gave William an appearance of dignified maturity.

William's eyes lit up with delight when Alma accepted his offer. The years were beginning to show on her as well. She'd put on more than a few pounds, and there was nearly as much silver as chestnut in her hair. But William saw the bloom on her cheeks, the warmth that still glowed in bright blue eyes that had seen so much pain.

On the porch they settled into two wooden rocking chairs painted bright yellow, the headrests stenciled with vividly colored depictions of flowers and fruit. Thirty years ago William couldn't have afforded such fancy chairs, each of which would have had to be made by hand by a skilled artisan. These had been created in a factory in Barkhamsted, Connecticut, established by a clever fellow named Lambert Hitchcock, which mass-produced fifteen thousand chairs a year. The cost of making them was so low they could be sold for a fraction of the price of a handcrafted chair. No one but an expert joiner could easily tell the difference.

Chairs, clocks, and lithographs were just three stars in a galaxy of consumer goods, some once affordable only by the rich, others only recently invented, that were now widely available at prices the average farmer or mechanic could pay. This unprecedented abundance was the result of an explosion of ingenuity in manufacturing and marketing centered in Connecticut. In just a few decades, everything from pistols to rubber boots, sleigh bells to cotton and silk thread, axes to brass buttons, had become everyday possessions.

William would be the first to admit that these innovations helped lighten the drudgery, and improve the comfort, of men and women alike. Items unimagined a generation earlier now made daily existence more pleasant. But William also had been dismayed to see how quickly individuals came to take the new goods for granted, and how acquiring the latest affordable product stoked the flames of avarice in many people.

William resolutely banished that nagging apprehension. The late September night air was invigoratingly cool, but without the nip of autumn. Light from the oil lamp on the table next to William's desk inside spilled through a window onto the porch, providing enough illumination for husband and wife to see other's features.

They sat in intimate silence for several minutes. William reached over to place his hand atop Alma's, stroking it tenderly with his thumb. Alma laid her head back against the chair's headrest. She let her lids droop shut, lulled by the sibilant sound of the steady rain that she imagined as a curtain rung down by Nature to temporarily shield them from the vexations of the outside world.

"When next you go into Middletown, I must go with you to buy cloth for new trousers for Lyman," Alma said. "He grew three inches over the summer."

William smiled in amusement. "I noticed. His trousers are so short it looks like he's expecting a flood."

"I've written Lizzy about what a balm to our hearts it is to have Lyman here with us," Alma said. Adeline had succumbed to her consumption a little more than a year ago, less than four months after construction of Sarah and James Dickinson's house began. Caring for their grandson had helped both Alma and William carry on in the wake of Adeline's painful death, and keep their sights focused on the future.

William and Alma had been surprised and disappointed when Charles and Lizzy decided to remain for another year in Indianapolis after Charles's temporary pastorate there ended. But they'd also been immensely grateful for their decision to leave Lyman with his grandparents in Middlefield. And Lizzy had assured them that she had made it clear to Charles that, come hell or high water, she and Kitty at least would return to Connecticut this coming summer for a long visit.

William and Alma fell again into a comfortable silence that William abruptly broke with a rueful chuckle.

"Papists celebrating Mass openly in Connecticut, building their own church in Middletown, sleeping under this very roof," he said, shaking his head in amazement. "You making a present of a saint's image! I never thought such a day would come in Connecticut – certainly not in my lifetime!" He shook his head in amusement. "My parents would be appalled – especially my dear mother, who feared innocent Christmas celebrations could lead to the infiltration of Popery."

Alma nodded. "During my reading lessons with Bridget I've sought to draw her out about her religion. What little she's told me seems so rigid. There's so much superstition and secrecy, so much complicated ceremony, so many glittering images and trappings in Roman Catholicism. For me these would be barriers to a personal connection to Our Lord."

Alma fell silent for a long moment, thinking. "But however alien Bridget's faith is to us, it carried her through a plague as horrible as any described in the Bible. She told me the famine in Ireland is so devastating that starving orphans wander the roads dressed in filthy rags." Alma paused for another long moment. She gripped William's hand tightly, then resumed speaking with obvious difficulty.

"Bridget watched her father and two little brothers slowly die of starvation. She and her mother dug graves for them with their own hands – and they thanked God they were able to do it. She says the Irish countryside is littered with maggoty corpses of famine victims left to rot where they died, for no one has the strength to bury them."

Alma took a deep breath to steady herself before continuing. "If the faith of Rome can sustain a people through such afflictions, give them the fortitude to start life anew in a foreign land, and inspire them, even as they struggle in poverty, to make the sacrifice to glorify God with a church, it can't be the scarlet whore we've always been told it is," she said, and with more than a hint of defiance.

"I've seen the plans a New York architect drew up for the church in Middletown," William said. "It will be of brownstone, grander than any house of worship Middletown has ever seen." He paused thoughtfully before continuing. "The Irish will make their mark on Connecticut, by sheer numbers alone. According to this year's census, more than six hundred of Middletown City's four thousand residents are Irish. Most came to America within the past five years."

William fell quiet, pondering these and other profound changes recent decades had brought to their community and to hundreds across the state. "Our children's children will live in a Connecticut far different from the one we've known," he said at last.

"I wonder what Joshua Stow would say about this latest result of the religious toleration he helped bring about," William said. Their old nemesis had died in 1842, at the age of eighty. Most of his substantial estate had ultimately been confiscated by the state, leaving his widow Ruth with little more than their furniture.

Alma refused to waste any time thinking about Joshua Stow. "I wonder what Mr. Beecher thinks of all this," she said.

"No doubt my Cousin Lyman is horrified," William said with weary cynicism. "I never completely shared his views, and we've grown even farther apart over the years as his principles have hardened. He has done great damage."

William stared into the rainy darkness. He brought his rocking chair to a stop. "If a man with Lyman Beecher's national eminence had publicly condemned slavery as an affront to God that cannot end soon enough, and called for acceptance of all Negroes as our brothers and sisters in Christ, he would have greatly advanced the cause of abolition. Instead Lyman supports the unjust, unworkable idea of transporting freed slaves to Africa," he said with sharp scorn.

"Establishing Lane Seminary was a worthy evangelical enterprise," William went on. "But Lyman's terror of Catholic immigrants has rendered him unable to accept that there can be many paths to God besides Protestantism, that good men can honestly worship the same Lord and Savior in different ways."

William resumed rocking. "Now young Henry is another matter altogether," he said approvingly of Lyman Beecher's son, who appeared on the way to eclipsing his famous father as America's most prominent Protestant divine. After a number of difficult years spent in pastorates in the West, Henry three years ago had landed the plum position of pastor of the newly established Plymouth Church in prosperous, fashionable Brooklyn, New York. He was making a name for himself as a charismatic minister and had come out openly against slavery. Although William doubted Henry Ward Beecher felt warmly toward the Church of Rome, he did seem to be free of Lyman Beecher's fear of immigrants.

"I read the other day that Henry was asked about the claim that Irish immigrants would overwhelm the country and transform it into a colony of the Vatican," William said. "He dismissed the idea with plain common sense, saying that, 'When I eat chicken, I don't become chicken, chicken becomes me'!" Alma laughed in appreciation of the home-spun wisdom.

William abruptly planted both feet on the porch floor to stop the rocker, sat bolt upright, and released Alma's hand. He cocked his head and drew his eyebrows together in concern, listening for something that, while still out of earshot, a sixth sense told him was approaching in the darkness.

When the rain let up briefly, Alma could hear the sucking sound of a horse's hooves in the thick mud on the road. The horse stopped at the gate to the stone wall surrounding the Lyman homelot, and within seconds they heard boots splashing hastily up the stone walk.

"Who's there?" William called out cautiously, getting to his feet.

"It's Marvin Thomas, William," the reply came back from the darkness. A moment later Thomas appeared, rain cascading off his broad-brimmed hat as he walked up onto the porch.

"What brings you out on such a foul night?" William asked, suspecting – and dreading – the answer.

"It's done, and it's even worse than we feared," Thomas said grimly as he removed his hat and shook it over the side of the porch railing. There was no need to explain what "it" was. William and Alma knew it could only be the new law concerning fugitive slaves that Congress had been wrestling with for several months.

"President Filmore signed it into law on September 18, the day before yesterday. I was down to New Haven this morning and saw a New York newspaper reporting the particulars." He pulled the folded paper from inside his coat, but had no need to consult it; the evil details had etched themselves into his memory after a single reading, like a corrosive acid.

"The new law directs United States marshals to seize alleged runaways, and empowers any citizen to have an alleged fugitive seized without a warrant. Fugitive slave cases are to be brought before special federal commissioners, and accused runaways won't be permitted to testify in their own defense. If the commissioner finds in favor of the alleged fugitive, he'll receive $5 for his services; but if he finds in favor of the alleged owner, he'll receive $10! There will be no penalty imposed upon someone who falsely claims a free Negro to be a slave."

Outrage began to burn in William's belly. "This law slaveholders claim is essential to preserve the Constitution in reality guts it of some of its most sacred principles!" he fumed. "And for good measure they throw in a cash bribe that will guarantee free men are dragooned into slavery." His upper lip curled with contempt.

"There's more," Thomas said quietly. "The law directs all citizens 'to aid and assist in the prompt and efficient execution of the law.'

And it provides a fine of $1,000 and up to six months in prison for every instance of helping a fugitive slave."

William was stunned. Alma quickly stood up to stand beside her husband, whose face had turned ashen. Such a penalty would ruin most men, William included. He'd helped a dozen runaways on the road to freedom this year alone. If he were to be convicted of aiding only eight of them, the combined fines would strip him of every one of the four hundred acres he owned. Six months behind bars would cripple, or more likely kill, a man of William's age. Yet even as William and Alma pondered these harsh facts, the possibility of deserting the crusade to abolish slavery never entered either of their minds.

"Wouldn't the morning have served for delivering such distressing news?" asked a heartsick William. "Why travel through the dark and pouring rain to reach us with it tonight?"

Alma knew the answer. "Sam Burton." A year ago fugitive slaves Sam and Kate Burton had arrived at the Lyman house, having run away from their owner in Delaware. The couple hadn't continued on north, however. They'd left three children in bondage back in Delaware, and couldn't bear to go to certain freedom in Canada without them.

Before Sam could make plans to go back to bring them out, a letter from a friend in Delaware had arrived for them, addressed care of William. Their owner had died, and the Burton children were in danger of being sold as part of the settlement of the estate. William had advanced the desperate Sam enough money to purchase the children's freedom. James Dickinson had gone to Delaware to execute the sale and bring the children to their parents in Middlefield.

The Underground Railroad had spirited Kate, who was still a fugitive slave, and the three now-free children to Canada. But Sam had insisted on staying at the Lyman farm to work until William's loan was repaid before joining his family in Canada.

Thomas nodded in grim confirmation of Alma's words. "At a tavern in North Haven I overheard men talking about the new law, of how they could jump the gun and pick up a few dollars by seizing local Negroes they suspected to be fugitives and carrying them before a magistrate. I set out at once, stopped first in Wallingford to warn our conductor there in case he was harboring any fugitives, then came directly here."

"Would you tell Bridget to find Sam and have him come out here?" William asked Alma. "Edward, too," he added.

'Take a seat, Marvin," William offered, belatedly remembering his manners.

Thomas shook his head to refuse the offer; although weary to the bone he preferred standing after so many hours in the saddle. William walked slowly to the far end of the porch, almost disappearing into the darkness. Balling both his hands into tight fists, he planted them shoulders' width apart on the porch railing and leaned his weight on them. For a long moment he hung his head, then raised it to stare out into the black night.

"How long has it been since you pressed that copy of *The Liberator* on me, Marvin?" William asked.

"Eighteen years, best I can recall," Thomas said after a moment's thought, not sure if William really expected an answer.

William shook his head back and forth wearily. "Eighteen years we've argued with, pleaded with, reasoned with, prayed for, cajoled, and coddled our Southern brethren, seeking to open their eyes to one of the most monstrous evils in history. We've tried to help them turn away from the sin that makes a mockery of our nation and imperils their immortal souls. When desperate, courageous men and women have appeared among us, fleeing the South's 'peculiar institution,' we've risked 'our lives, our fortunes, and our sacred honor'" – William quoted the Declaration of Independence with dark irony – "to help them claim freedom that is every American's birthright.

"But what have we accomplished?" William went on, in a defeated voice. "The South has not only gone blind and deaf to our entreaties, they now insist we violate God's commandments and prostitute our consciences to appease them. We are not only to cease aiding the brave wretches who reach us in their quest for freedom, but are commanded to actively assist in hunting down fugitives and sending them back to slavery, or face our own ruin and that of our families."

"The race is not to the swift, William," Thomas said, unnerved by William's despair. "Thousands once in chains sleep tonight in freedom because of what you and I and countless others have done, one or two people at a time. I count that a victory, no matter how small. We can't lose faith in God's larger plan."

William nodded reluctantly, then straightened up and turned to look at Thomas. "Perhaps that's what frightens me most. God certainly will bring about an end to slavery, but I begin to fear He'll extract from our hypocritical nation a far greater price than we have anticipated."

William resumed staring into the darkness, as if straining to see something. He chewed nervously on his lower lip.

William stepped back into the dim lamplight as Alma came out the door, followed by Sam Burton. The black man had dressed hastily, and his eyes were full of anxiety.

"There's no easy way to say this," William began. "We've just learned that Congress approved a new law to encourage the capture of fugitive slaves. Every citizen is commanded to help return runaways to their owners. Those who do so will be rewarded; those who don't will be punished. You're in greater danger than ever of being seized and dragged back into bondage, and that danger will grow with every hour you remain in Connecticut. Getting to Canada is your only hope. You must leave at first light."

The obviously shaken Sam spoke. "But I still owe you–."

William shook his head as if to chase away an annoying insect. "I know you're an honest man who wants to pay his debt. But you can't earn money if you're returned to slavery. Once you're settled in Canada, do what you can to honor the obligation. That's enough for me."

William fell silent, but it was obvious he had something else to say. He struggled for a moment, then looked directly at Sam with eyes brimming with tears.

"I apologize to you for my country – for our country," William amended quickly. "I'm ashamed that men, women, and children who ask for nothing more than freedom must flee America to secure it. Forgive us for failing to right so hideous an injustice."

Sam was stunned by this apology from a man who'd done more than any other white individual to help him and his family escape slavery. Before he could fashion an answer, Edward Boston appeared in the doorway, hastily buttoning his shirt.

William addressed Edward with crisp efficiency. "Edward, a new federal law commands all citizens to assist in returning fugitive slaves to their masters." Edward's face registered shock, but he waited for William to finish.

"This place is no longer safe for Sam. Will you see him to Canada?"

"Of course," Edward replied. But he was puzzled. It would make much more sense, and greatly increase the chances of success, to send Sam to Canada under the escort of James Dickinson. His status as a white clergyman would help protect his black companion from interrogation. And unlike Edward, Dickinson wasn't a worker whose labor was sorely needed to finish bringing in the harvest.

The plan seemed so illogical that Edward opened his mouth to question William. He was stunned into silence when the older man said quietly, "Perhaps you should remain in Canada, rather than return to Connecticut."

"But Mr. Lyman–," Edward started to object. William cut off his protest with uncharacteristic abruptness. "This vile law threatens not just fugitive slaves but free Negroes like yourself," he said in desperation. "You'll be at the mercy of any unscrupulous individual willing to perjure himself before a commissioner and swear you are a runaway bondsman. The law allows accused fugitives no trial, not even the right to speak in their own defense. It is an open invitation to kidnapping!"

Alma's heart ached as she watched the young black man, who had spent much of his life under their roof, absorbing the implications of William's words. "Mr. Lyman is speaking wisely, Edward," she said compassionately. "You have no wife or children to uproot, you could start life anew in a country that practices freedom, doesn't merely pay hypocritical lip service to it."

"I know you both mean well," Edward said. He was touched by their concern for his well-being, yet also a little indignant that they would think he would so easily turn tail and run. "But Connecticut is my home; the United States is my country," he continued, almost defiantly. "I was born here. The dust of my parents, and my grandparents, and theirs before them lies here. To make my life here is my birthright, and nothing can frighten me into abandoning it."

William wanted to admire the young man's courage and pride and patriotism. But his fear that they could result in his being sucked into the maw of the slaveocracy was too great for that. Yet Edward Boston was a free man, thirty years old, entitled to make his own decisions, however dangerous or ill-advised others might consider them to be.

"As you wish," William replied, then turned to Sam Burton. "There's a great deal to be done before dawn. Let's get to it."

Chapter One Hundred and Six

October, 1850
New Haven

"We know of no higher law as a rule for political action than the Constitution of the United States, and we have no sympathy with men who encourage forcible resistance to the constituted authorities of the country!" Ralph Ingersoll, former United States Congressman, basked in the cheers his impassioned statement brought forth from the two thousand men packed into New Haven's Brewster Hall.

Ingersoll stretched his arms before him, palms down, to quiet the crowd. They immediately fell silent to hear his climactic declaration.

"As for those who claim to be too conscientious" – Ingersoll infused the word with sarcastic contempt – "to yield their obedience to the laws of the land, they should remove themselves to some other country whose institutions they prefer!" He swept his right arm toward the door in a slashing gesture of dismissal, like a vengeful God casting Adam and Eve from the Garden of Eden.

The roar of approval literally shook the building's floor and walls. Men thrust their fists skyward in pugnacious triumph; some tossed their hats into the air. Others stamped their feet, clapped furiously, even whistled. Ingersoll was one of the last in a succession of speakers who over the past hour had whipped the crowd into a near-frenzy.

At the edge of the roiling sea of emotions was a tiny island of dead calm. William Lyman, David Lyman, and James Dickinson stood with their backs against a side wall, arms folded across their chests, expressions grim. Under other circumstances William might have found Ingersoll's pompous posturing amusing. But there was nothing remotely funny about this night's gathering.

William had heard that more than eighteen hundred New Haven citizens had signed the call to hold a "Great Union Meeting" to express support for the Fugitive Slave Law on the evening of October 24. He'd decided to attend the meeting, hoping the alarming report of a groundswell of approval for this evil legislation had been greatly exaggerated.

Alma, David, Sarah, and James had argued vehemently against William going. When they failed to change his mind, David and James had insisted on accompanying him.

To the horror and disgust of all three, the reality they were witnessing was worse than the advance reports. Not only was the throng larger than predicted, but the men here included the cream of the city's wealthy and powerful.

With the crowd's cheers still filling his ears, Ingersoll stepped down from the podium, and took a seat next to Henry Trowbridge. William was disappointed, but not surprised, to find the Lymans' erstwhile partner in the mule trade numbered among the meeting's thirty-one "vice presidents."

Many New Haven merchants and manufacturers, and the clerks and mechanics they employed, had common cause in placating the South, which was a prime market for the city's products. Just one of many affected industries was the production of carriages, which more than four dozen New Haven firms manufactured for sale mostly to Southern customers. Anything that threatened to upset Southern consumers endangered these men's livelihoods.

The next of the meeting's "vice presidents" ascended the platform: a slender, distinguished figure in his sixties. Dr. Nathaniel Taylor was a renowned minister who for more than a quarter of a century had been professor of didactic theology in Yale's Divinity School. James Dickinson had studied under him.

James wasn't surprised to see his former teacher among the speakers. For years Dr. Taylor had been indoctrinating his divinity students in the principles that the national good justified the continuation of slavery, and that it was wrong to aid fugitive slaves.

"Why should not the slaves at the South submit to the condition, which Providence has assigned them?" Dr. Taylor posed the clearly rhetorical question in the voice of authority perfected during decades in the pulpit and classroom. "Their condition is a thousand fold better than it would have been, in the pagan midnight and savageism of their native land," he reasoned calmly. "Why should they not be grateful for its blessings, and submissive to its evils, till by some practicable change, it can be made better instead of immeasurably worse?" A general buzz of agreement rose up from the crowd.

To hear Dr. Taylor, endowed with the authority of both a minister of God and a Yale faculty member, declare Negroes should be thankful for being held in dehumanizing bondage disgusted James. He instinctively started to raise his hand to attract Dr. Taylor's attention to make a rebuttal – but a vise-like grip on his wrist stopped him. He struggled against it for a moment until he realized the hand holding him back belonged to his father-in-law.

William's resolute gaze and barely perceptible shake of his head conveyed to James the absolute necessity for restraint. David was studying him with alarm, James saw. David pointedly surveyed the men around them. James followed his gaze, and saw that half a dozen men who clearly recognized the trio from Middlefield were watching him intently, like keen-eyed hawks waiting for a rabbit to break cover and expose itself to attack. James slowly lowered his arm.

"I have another question to ask," continued Dr. Taylor, who hadn't noticed James's interrupted gesture. "What right to protection do fugitive slaves acquire at the North?" he demanded indignantly. "What right have they to come here, and claim our protection, when by affording it, we violate a lawful compact, and endanger the existence of such a nation as this? Am I bound to receive into my family, and to protect and support every man or woman whose condition would thereby be improved, be the consequences to the well-being of my family what they may?"

The crowd rumbled an even stronger approval of the minister's words. This time it was William who reacted. His nostrils flared and his eyes blazed with contempt. Dr. Taylor was callously equating a fugitive slave seeking sanctuary, in mortal fear for his life, with an ill-mannered beggar asking for an inconvenient favor.

Still William held his tongue. As a prominent – some would say notorious – abolitionist, many suspected he participated in the Underground Railroad. Yet he'd never yet spoken specifically in support of aiding fugitive slaves. To do so, he feared, might compromise his ability to help runaways.

David, equally incensed, thought of what the Bible said Jesus would say on Judgement Day to righteous men who would inherit the kingdom of Heaven by virtue of having fed, or clothed, or sheltered the Savior they'd never met in life: "Inasmuch as ye have done it unto one of the least of these my brethren, ye have done it unto me." To offer aid to a stranger was to help the Savior. Those who failed to do so, Scripture went on, would be condemned to everlasting fire. How Dr. Taylor could spurn fugitives who "claim our protection" – refuse to take in a stranger – and not fear eternal damnation, David couldn't fathom.

Former New Haven mayor Dennis Kimberly, president of the meeting, rose to meet Dr. Taylor as he descended from the platform. He shook the minister's hand in hearty congratulation before stepping up to address the assemblage. The enthusiastic applause quickly died down, and into the silence Kimberly called out, "I propose that this meeting adopt the following resolutions:

"Resolved, that the Constitution of the United States is the supreme law of the land, which every citizen is bound to regard.

"Resolved, that the requirements in the Constitution, that 'persons held to service or labor in one State, under the laws thereof escaping into another State, shall be delivered up on claim of the party to whom such service or labor may be due,' is of no less binding force than the other parts of that sacred instrument.

"Resolved, that the recent act of Congress regarding fugitives should be truly and faithfully sustained by every friend of our glorious Union, in furtherance of the sentiment." Kimberly paused for a moment, then shouted as if a battle cry, "Liberty and Union, now and forever, one and inseparable!"

Thunderous applause again shook the building. Kimberly could barely be heard as he yelled at the top of his lungs, "All in favor of the resolutions, say aye." Two thousand throats roared their assent. As the din died down, Kimberly asked, almost as an afterthought, "All opposed, say nay."

Many pairs of hostile eyes focused challengingly on William, James, and David. All three maintained impassive expressions.

"I think it's accurate to record that the resolutions passed unanimously," Kimberly said wryly, sending a ripple of satisfied laughter through the crowd. Pleased with their evening's work, the hordes of men gratefully spilled out of the hot, stuffy hall into the bracingly chill night air. Enthusiastically congratulating themselves and each other, they quickly dispersed, some in carriages, others on horseback, most on foot.

William, David, and James held back until the hall was largely empty. After exiting the building William walked a short distance and stopped. He craned his neck back and looked directly overhead, studying the stars glittering against the pure solid black of the clear night sky, seeking a moment of peace in which to compose himself.

"How can so many New Englanders not just endorse the enslavement and persecution of other human beings, but do it ardently?" he heard David say in angry confusion.

William shook his head sorrowfully, his eyes focused on the glory of God's firmament.

"Fear fuels them," he said. "Fear of the Union being rent in two, fear of losing their jobs and being unable to feed their families, fear of the lies they've been told about the Negro–."

"Father!" William's head snapped down at David's cry of alarm. Following David's gaze, he recognized Dr. Taylor strolling home alone – and James advancing on him, clearly intent on a confrontation.

William and David hastily wove their way through the remaining members of the crowd. But they didn't reach James before he planted himself directly in the professor's path.

"Dr. Taylor, you should remember me," James said in a challenging tone. "I'm James Dickinson, one of your ministerial students."

Dr. Taylor responded at first with a smile of vague acknowledgement. Although the man before him was familiar, he couldn't place him among the hundreds of pupils he'd instructed over the years.

"You preached the sermon at my ordination in Norwich," James prompted impatiently. Dr. Taylor's eyes lit up with recognition. "Norwich, of course!" he exclaimed. "That was near twenty years ago. I heard you spent but a short time there before becoming a missionary." Pleased with his sharp memory, the minister waited politely for his former student to add to the praise that had been showered upon him from the moment he took the platform.

"Sir, your words tonight shamed yourself, and all true Christians," James said harshly. Dr. Taylor's smug satisfaction collapsed into confusion at the unexpected criticism.

"How can you say slaves should meekly submit to the horrors of bondage?" James demanded, thin face taught with fury. He spoke in a low voice that carried greater weight than a shrill rant – for which David and William were thankful, since a handful of those who had attended the meeting still lingered close by.

"What in the Hell of life in chains could you possibly consider a blessing for the Negro?" James went on, unaware of David and William's presence. "Would you meekly stand by and let fellow Christians deny the sanctity of your marriage, rape your wife or your daughter or your mother, sell your children away, never to be seen again?"

James's voice was growing louder as his outrage flared. William stepped forward to lay a restraining hand on James's shoulder, but the younger man shrugged it off, not seeming to even recognize his father-in-law.

"You know you would not, sir!" James pressed Dr. Taylor. "You would resist, you would fight, you would die if necessary! You might try to escape, trusting true Christians to inconvenience themselves to help you secure the liberty that would offer your only hope of achieving salvation. For how can a slave denied the free exercise of his will hope to live the righteous life required to enter the kingdom of Heaven?"

James stopped to catch his breath and to allow Dr. Taylor the chance to respond to his blistering indictment. But the only sound was the harsh rasp of James's breathing.

The dismayed confusion Dr. Taylor had displayed throughout James's barrage of accusations vanished – but not to be replaced by shame, contrition, or even the anger James had expected. Instead Dr. Taylor studied James with the smug, condescending smile of an egotistical man confident of his power to envision the larger picture that a lesser mortal such as this erstwhile student lacked. Without a word, he stepped carefully around James as if he were a puddle in the street, and continued serenely on his way.

The flabbergasted James turned and stared at the minister's retreating back. He started to follow Dr. Taylor, determined to hector him into a response, until William stepped in to block his path. His surge of anger spent, James's head drooped in despair.

"Father, we can't remain silent on this abomination dressed up as a law," David said. "We must make our opposition known."

William turned to study his son, managing to conceal his surprise. David abhorred slavery, and during the few times the need had arisen during his months at home between mule-buying trips he had unhesitatingly helped spirit several fugitive slaves from the Lyman house to the next stop on their pilgrimage to freedom.

But David hadn't involved himself in the abolitionist crusade with his parents' all-consuming fervor. William wondered why now, just five days past his thirtieth birthday, with his wife heavy with their first child, David felt compelled to step into the maw of the nation's monstrous moral and political crisis. Perhaps marriage and impending fatherhood had made him more acutely sensitive to the barbarity of a system that rendered a husband powerless to protect his wife and child from the most heinous cruelties.

William resisted the temptation to question David about his motive. His son was a solid, sensible, honorable man in whose decisions William had complete confidence.

"I agree," William said wearily. "No amount of pleading and persuasion will result in the repeal of this law. Let's go home and get what little sleep we can. In the morning we'll call on some of our like-minded neighbors to ask if they'll join us in taking a stand."

The trio trudged towards the stable where they'd left their horses. James cast David a quizzical look, wondering many the same things William had. David let James assume he hadn't seen his questioning expression in the darkness. He had no wish to explain the militant declaration he knew had surprised both William and James.

During the moment in the hall after Kimberly had called for negative votes, and a dozen openly hostile men waited for the three abolitionists to do anything that would provide an excuse to assault them, David had held his tongue – and burned with shame and humiliation. It was the confrontation with the slave trader on the road in Kentucky all over again.

That day, six years ago, Elihu had consoled him with the Bible's assurance that there would be a time for them to speak out against slavery. For David that time had arrived. It was a debt long overdue both to his own conscience and to the memory of the beloved brother who had given him the gift of compassionate understanding when he desperately needed it.

Chapter One Hundred and Seven

October, 1850
Middletown

William Starr's eyebrows shot up, and his eyes widened, as he read the paper William Lyman had handed him. The printer thoughtfully stroked his chin with an ink-stained thumb and forefinger. When he finished reading he looked dubiously at William.

"Are you certain you want to publish this in the *Sentinel and Witness*?" Starr raised his voice slightly to be heard over the clanging and thumping of the printing press being operated by a young apprentice in Starr's tiny shop on Middletown's Main Street.

"That's what I said," William replied firmly.

"Isn't it better suited for the *Constitution*?" Starr asked, although he suspected what he held in his hands might be too strong even for readers of Middletown's other newspaper. The *Constitution* was the editorial voice of the Whig Party, whose principles were closer to William Lyman's than those of the *Sentinel and Witness*.

"I've arranged for it to run in the *Constitution* when it next appears on Wednesday," William replied. "But that's preaching to the converted. We want to make our sentiments known to those likely to support enforcement of the Fugitive Slave Law. That means it must run in the *Sentinel and Witness*, since it's the journalistic organ of the Democratic Party in these parts."

"You've been an abolitionist for as long as I've been editor of this newspaper," Starr said, like a father giving advice, even though William was twenty years his senior. "I've seen you endure much abuse for your actions in support of your convictions. I've respected your fidelity to your beliefs, even when I didn't agree with you –

which was most of the time. But this–." Starr held the paper out at arm's length, as if it might suddenly burst into flames.

"Here in the North we still have freedom of speech and of the press – at least until the South demands those rights be stripped from us as part of their ongoing extortion of Congress," William replied stonily. "Even Democrats can't deny the hypocrisy of this law," he added. "Southerners yelp when any outside authority seeks to interfere with a 'state's right' to sanction slavery within its borders, but they're content to have the federal government meddle with the laws of a free state if it will help them get their human property back," he went on. "They want to force every American to take part personally in their crime against humanity."

William paused for a moment, then asked, "Will you publish it?"

"Yes," Starr replied with a weary sigh. "Every man has the right to be heard," he agreed – even, he thought, one dangerously blinded to reality by the intense glow of an impossible ideal.

"I knew you were a man of principle and courage," William said. Both realized many citizens would be incensed by publication in the *Sentinel and Witness* of what they considered treasonous material.

"Let me read this aloud to you – to be sure I understand your handwriting clearly," Starr said. "God forbid a word of type be set wrong on this item," he added grimly.

"For the *Sentinel and Witness*," Starr began.

> The undersigned are friends of Law. Law comes from the bosom of God, and is sacred. Even an imperfect law we will respect and bear with, till we can obtain its modification or repeal. But when iniquity forms itself into law, the sacredness of law is gone. When an enactment, falsely calling itself law, is imposed upon us, which disgraces our country, which invades our conscience, which dishonors our religion, which is an outrage upon our sense of justice, we take our stand against the imposition. The Fugitive Slave Law commands all good citizens to be slave catchers; good citizens cannot be slave-catchers, any more than light can be darkness.

Pausing for a breath, Starr reflected that this last sentence had the best chance of striking a receptive chord among his paper's readers. Many Northerners supported the South's right to practice slavery in principle. But he suspected few could stomach being forced to personally participate in capturing and returning a fugitive.

"You tell us, the Union will be endangered if we oppose the law," Starr read on.

> We reply, that greater things than the Union will be endangered if we submit to it: Conscience, Humanity, Self-Respect all greater than the Union, and these must be preserved at all hazards. This pretended law commands us to withhold food and raiment and shelter from the most needy – we cannot obey.

Starr glanced up at William, as if he might have a last-minute change of heart about announcing in print his intention to break the law. William nodded for Starr to continue.

> When our sense of decency is clean gone forever, we will turn slave catchers; till then, never. You tell us, that great men made the law; if great men choose to disgrace themselves, choose to plunge into dishonor, it does not follow, that small men should do so too. We farmers and working men tell you, we are not ready to give ourselves to all manner of villainy. Be the consequences what they may, come fines, come imprisonment, and what will, this thing you call law, we will not obey.

The last four words were underscored with three bold slashes of the pen. The document was signed not only by William, but by David Lyman, James Dickinson, Marvin Thomas, and kinsmen Russell and Alfred Bailey, the latter owner of a Middlefield button factory.

"William, reconsider," Starr said urgently. "This could cost you everything your family has." A shadow crossed William's face as he recalled the discussion he and the other signers had had about the grave consequences of publishing the statement they'd spent a long, grueling day composing. James had settled the issue for them with the Scripture passage that William quoted now in response to Starr.

"'What shall it profit a man, if he shall gain the whole world, and lose his own soul'?" William gave the printer a steady look. "I'll settle the bill when I'm next in Middletown. And I'll look for that in Tuesday's *Sentinel and Witness.*" He rapped the counter with the knuckles of his right hand to signal the sealing of the deal, then turned to leave. As the door closed behind him, he heard Starr calling his apprentice to come take the document for setting in type.

Chapter One Hundred and Eight

July, 1851
Indianapolis, Indiana

"I've known Hattie has a gift for writing since we taught together in Cincinnati," Lizzy said thoughtfully. "I've enjoyed the stories she's published in magazines since. But I never imagined that something this–." Lizzy stopped, searching for the right word. "Potent, could come from her pen." She shook her head in wondering admiration as she carefully folded over the June 26, 1851, issue of the weekly *National Era*, an abolitionist publication.

"If future installments of "Uncle Tom's Cabin" in the *National Era* measure up to the first four, your cousin will deal slavery a devastating blow," Charles observed.

"It can't help but change people's opinions," Lizzy agreed. She unfolded the four-page newspaper, and searched the front page until she found the passage she sought.

"Listen to Hattie's description of Uncle Tom's grief at the prospect of being sold away from his children," she said, then read, "'Sobs, heavy, hoarse and loud, shook the chair, and great tears fell through his fingers on the floor; just such tears, sir, as you dropped into the coffin where lay your first-born son; such tears, woman, as you shed when you heard the cries of your dying babe.'"

Lizzy knew Hattie wrote from agonizing experience; she'd lost a little son to cholera two years past. She looked up to meet Charles's eyes in shared heartache, for the passage summoned up memories of the deaths of their own two babies. "Only a heart of stone could be unmoved by those words," Lizzy said with quiet certitude.

Lizzy re-folded the newspaper with sharp, decisive creases. "Hattie always had such a keen eye and ear, picked up little details others never noticed," she said proudly. "It seems she stored up in her memory everything she saw or heard of slavery during her years in Cincinnati."

Charles nodded thoughtfully. "Perhaps we could visit Mr. and Mrs. Stowe at Bowdoin when we're back in New England," he suggested. After nearly two decades in Cincinnati, Calvin Stowe last year had joined the faculty at Bowdoin College in Maine.

"Oh, Charles, I would like that very much!" Lizzy replied with a delighted smile, then immediately amended herself, "but not until after Thanksgiving." Ever since they'd decided in May to return to Middlefield, she'd been dreaming of long, uninterrupted hours with her parents, with David and Catherine, with Sarah and James, and above all, with her son. She hadn't laid eyes on any of them in nearly two years.

Lizzy placed the folded newspaper into a woven straw basket next to her chair. "I'm saving these for James and Sarah. They'll want to read the entire series when they return."

"When will that be?" Charles asked.

"In Sarah's last letter from London she wrote they expect to be back in time for Thanksgiving."

"Then they will have been away . . ." Charles started calculating in his head, but Lizzy saved him the trouble.

"Nine months," she said, adding dryly, "A long time, but I understand there is much to see and do in Europe. She and James spent two days touring the exhibition of industry at the Crystal Palace in London. Sarah says James was especially excited by the display of American inventions – the electric telegraph, a sewing machine, even the revolving gun made in Colonel Samuel Colt's Hartford factory." Lizzy had to fill in Charles on the accounts Sarah sent back of their experiences, for he couldn't decipher the scrawl Sarah produced with her crippled right hand.

Charles nodded distractedly in response, but his mind had moved on to other concerns. He got to his feet and pulled on his coat. "If we're to leave by month's end, I must finish arranging for shipment of our furniture and my books. I'll be back before supper."

Lizzy stared thoughtfully at the door for a long moment after Charles closed it behind him. The past two years in Indianapolis had been a time of unexpected happiness and satisfaction for Charles, Lizzy, and Kitty. Indianapolis had changed dramatically from the crude village she'd known in 1839, thanks to the arrival of the railroad in 1847. Its population had burgeoned until it now exceeded eight thousand, making it nearly as large as Middletown.

Indianapolis had also enjoyed greater prosperity and a refinement of its cultural life. Several private girls' schools had been established, and soon after arriving Lizzy had accepted a position at one. She'd been overjoyed at this unexpected opportunity to resume the teaching she loved, and grateful that Kitty had been able to enroll in the school.

When Charles didn't immediately receive a fresh assignment upon completion of his duties at the First Presbyterian Church, the parents of Lizzy's students had pleaded with her to continue teaching. Charles had joined the school's faculty as well.

Even after Charles received a summons to return east to discuss his next assignment, friends and colleagues had done their utmost to persuade Lizzy and Charles to send for Lyman and make Indianapolis their home. But serving God was Charles's calling, and Lizzy knew deep in her heart that home would always be Connecticut. It was the wellspring to which she had to return regularly to replenish her spirit. And so they'd made plans to go back to Middlefield, where Lizzy and the children would remain for an unknown length of time before following Charles to his next post.

Lizzy's happiness in Indianapolis had helped temper the envy that, to her shame, she'd felt upon receiving in January Sarah's letter with the news of the Dickinsons' planned European tour. Lizzy suspected this magnificent trip had been inspired by more than just James's desire to experience the wonders of Europe with his beloved wife. By taking William's cherished daughter farther from home than any of his children had ever before traveled, James was making a tacit yet firm declaration that neither his affectionate respect for his in-laws nor his acceptance of William's restrictions on the home he and Sarah had occupied for the past year would compromise his independence as a man or a husband.

Lizzy had waited anxiously for news of William's reaction to the European journey. She'd been relieved when his letters, and those from Alma, David, Catherine, and Sarah, proved him to be enthusiastically in favor of the tour.

Reading between the lines of everyone's letters, Lizzy could tell William was refusing to let his own fears prevent Sarah from seeing so many of the far-away places she'd read about during her years spent immersed in books, a semi-recluse. And he knew it would be wrong – and futile – to try to impose his will on James, whose tender, patient, perceptive love had drawn Sarah out of her self-imposed shell. Still, Lizzy could imagine how much anguish it cost William and Alma to have one of the three children left to them cross an ocean and travel through foreign lands.

William and Alma had Lyman to keep them occupied, as well as another new member of the family. In December Catherine had presented David with their first child, a girl they'd named Mary Elizabeth. Perhaps, it occurred to Lizzy, James had planned this European trip in part to distract Sarah from brooding on the fact that, after five years of marriage, there was no sign of children.

Lizzy suddenly recalled with amusement David's declaration more than ten years ago that he wanted a dozen children. Had he ever had the courage to repeat that outrageous statement to Catherine? she wondered. Lizzy mischievously considered sharing it with her sister-in-law when she saw her again in Middlefield.

Lizzy had never wanted twelve children, but she had hoped to have a large family. The likelihood of that happening was fast fading. There'd been little chance to become pregnant during the years after Kitty's birth, with Charles so often away from home. But she hadn't conceived once during the years at Ashland nor here in Indianapolis. She fought her disappointment by rejoicing in the two fine children God had entrusted to her and Charles. And she hadn't abandoned all hope; she was just thirty-eight; women older than she, including her mother, had borne children.

Lizzy resolutely shook off the mild melancholy that had descended upon her, rose from her chair, and started up the stairs to continue packing their winter clothing and small personal belongings. When she reached the landing she heard Kitty talking in her bedroom.

The little girl was speaking to Arabella, a rag doll Alma had made for her just before she and Lizzy had left for Indianapolis. The doll was simplicity itself: two pieces of scrap cloth cut out in a rough outline of a human figure, then sewn together and stuffed with duck down. Arabella had buttons for the eyes and nose, a smiling mouth stitched out of red yarn, and strands of yellow yarn for hair.

Lizzy smiled; Kitty was reassuring Arabella about the upcoming move by parroting with impressive accuracy what Lizzy had told her the previous evening.

"I know you'll be sad to leave your friends and home here in Indianapolis, but it will be wonderful in Connecticut," Kitty was telling Arabella in a grave voice. "There are beautiful green hills, and big white houses, and stone walls . . ."

Kitty stopped for a moment, perplexed. She had no idea why stone walls were wonderful, but her mother spoke of them with such warm affection that there had to be something special about them.

"There will be a new baby cousin to play with!" Kitty continued excitedly; like most seven-year-old girls, she adored babies. "And brother Lyman will there, too," she added, with less enthusiasm.

Lizzy's heart constricted at Kitty's mention of Lyman almost as an afterthought. She had never for a minute regretted leaving Lyman in Connecticut – for his sake. He was by all accounts growing into a fine young man under the guidance and example of his grandfather and uncles. William reported he was making arrangements for Lyman to begin attending the Durham Academy. Alma wrote that he was growing like a weed, and was already nearly as tall as his grandmother!

But Lizzy fretted over the impact the long separation would have on Lyman's relationship with his parents and sister. He'd spent one-fifth of his life apart from them. And a child changed so very much between eight and ten! He would look far different; in her worst moments Lizzy feared she might not recognize her own son. Any memories Kitty had of her big brother would be blurred fragments at best. He would be as much a stranger to her as her newborn cousin.

Lizzy peeked into the bedroom, where Kitty was sitting cross-legged on her bed. The little girl hugged Arabella tightly to her, and Lizzy could just barely hear her whisper, "There's nothing to be afraid of. Mother and Father will be there to make everything all right."

Chapter One Hundred and Nine

August, 1851
Middlefield

"There's a carriage coming down the road, Mrs. Lyman," Bridget called from the hall. Alma hurried in from the kitchen, drying her hands on a towel. She peered out the window, and her expression told Bridget that the carriage's occupants were the visitors for whom the family had looked anxiously each day for the past week.

Alma nervously crumpled the towel into a ball, then let it fall to the floor unheeded. By the time she reached the front door of the house and stepped out onto the porch, the carriage had stopped at the open gate in the stone wall. Charles Mills waited for the August road dust stirred up by the vehicle to settle before stepping out. He turned to lift a child from her seat in the carriage and set her down on the path to the house. He proceeded to supervise the unloading of luggage and to settle accounts with the hackman he'd hired to drive them from Middletown, where they'd arrived by train.

Alma hastened down the sandstone pathway, stopping a few steps from the little girl. She swallowed hard and fought back the tears that welled up at her first sight in two years of her granddaughter Kitty. The child was a delicate miniature of Lizzy.

Alma crouched down, ignoring the aching protests of her arthritic knees, so that she didn't tower intimidatingly over Kitty, but was almost on the same eye level. The hack driver drove off. Alma glanced up briefly at Charles, who was thinner than when she'd last seen him, with an unhealthy pallor and dull eyes.

Alma returned her attention to Kitty. The little girl's lovely light blue eyes were as clear and bright as semi-precious gems – which made the fearful confusion in her gaze all the more painful to see.

Alma knew Lizzy often spoke to Kitty with nostalgic affection of the Lyman family and homestead back in Connecticut. But the child's actual memories could only consist of random fragments. She was essentially coming to a strange place inhabited by people she didn't know. Accepting that hard truth, Alma had resisted rushing out to scoop Kitty up in her arms, knowing that was as likely to frighten the child as make her feel welcome.

Alma wracked her brain for a means to gently bridge the gulf of time and distance. Then her eyes fell on the stuffed rag doll Kitty clutched tight to her chest with both hands.

The doll's lumpy shape was proof of how well it was loved. Little arms had hugged it around the waist for hundreds of nights until most of the stuffing had been squeezed to the bottom or top, leaving it alarmingly thin in the middle. A fluff of duck down poked out from a split seam, and one button eye dangled by just two threads.

"Is that Arabella, Kitty?" Alma asked. Kitty's eyes widened with wonder that this woman – who must be her Grandmother Lyman, for it was to her grandparents' house in Connecticut that Father had said they were going – should know her doll's name. She nodded.

"I made Arabella for you — do you remember?" Alma asked with a smile. The memory of that day two years ago shortly before Kitty and Lizzy left for Indianapolis was bittersweet. "You picked the cloth from my bag of scraps – it was left over from the dress I'm wearing now." Kitty looked from Arabella to her grandmother's dress, then looked up at Alma, who thought she saw a glimmer of recognition.

"We sat on the porch while you watched me sew Arabella," Alma continued. "You decided she should have yellow hair like yours."

Alma watched Kitty intently. She saw her gently leading questions fan the flicker in Kitty's eyes into a glow of remembrance.

"It looks like Arabella could use fixing," Alma went on gently. "Would you like me to mend her?" She held out her arms.

After a long moment, Kitty nodded solemnly. She handed Arabella to Alma, then thrust herself forward into Alma's arms.

Alma enfolded Kitty in a loving embrace as firmly as Kitty had clutched Arabella. And Kitty felt safe for the first time since the day a few weeks past when her father told her that her mother, who'd been sick with something the grownups called "cholera," had gone to Heaven to be with God forever.

Chapter One Hundred and Ten

July, 1854
Hartford

Several thousand men, women, and children gathered in Colonel Samuel Colt's meadow along the Connecticut River in Hartford slowly lifted their faces skyward in unison, as if they'd rehearsed the movement. All eyes were fixed on two enormous balloons, rising slowly and majestically into the sky. From each was suspended a large woven basket, one occupied by aeronaut Silas Brooks, the other by Brooks's associate, William Paullin.

Some spectators held their breath in suspense, others inhaled sharply in amazement, still others exhaled in astonishment. The phenomenon of seeing men ascend into the heavens so mesmerized them they scarcely noticed the blaring accompaniment of the Hartford Brass Band.

When the second balloon had risen to about five hundred feet, its passenger unfurled an American flag. The sight of the national banner fluttering so proudly broke the spell. The crowd erupted into cheers for the brave balloonists and for the Fourth of July, 1854.

As the balloons continued to rise, upper air currents wafted them eastward, over the Connecticut River, congested with tall-masted sailing ships, large paddle-wheeled steamboats, smaller craft, and ferries. The spectators watched until the balloons were tiny dots against the clear afternoon sky. They chatted excitedly about the extraordinary occurrence they'd witnessed.

The young man standing to William's left turned and said excitedly, "That's a sight I'll never forget, Uncle. It was well worth making the trip up from Middletown in this infernal heat to see it."

He spoke with the slight drawl that had crept into his speech during ten years' residence in the South.

William smiled in agreement. He thought again, as he had a week ago upon seeing his sister Urania's son for the first time since the ill-fated Thanksgiving at the Mills home in Durham, how uncanny a resemblance David Lyman Buttolph bore to his late cousin Elihu. He had Elihu's long face, high forehead, and prominent nose. Like Elihu, David Buttolph was tall and lean, but this was his natural physique, not due to chronic illness.

A difference between the cousins was that while Elihu had been reserved with strangers, David Buttolph was at ease among people he didn't know. William and Alma had been instinctively drawn to this nephew who so reminded them of the son they'd lost.

William had been deeply moved to see that David still carried the Bible "Saint Nicholas" had left in his stocking that Christmas two decades ago. The well-worn cover testified to its frequent use.

Now thirty-one, David Buttolph had chosen religion for his life's work. After graduating from the Columbia Theological Seminary in South Carolina, he'd been ordained a Presbyterian minister, then served as assistant pastor at a Charleston church. He'd made this journey north to visit his father, stepmother, and sister in New York, and his aunts, uncles, and cousins in New England, before becoming pastor of the Midway Congregational Church in Georgia.

The Midway church had been established a century earlier by emigrants from New England, making David Buttolph's selection to lead it particularly fitting. David informed his Northern relatives with pardonable pride that the Midway congregation was recognized throughout the South as a community of exceptional piety, intellectual and social refinement, and wealth.

"This intense heat must make you feel like you're back in Charleston, Mr. Buttolph," observed a young woman to whom David had been introduced upon their arrival in Hartford that morning. She tipped back the parasol she held to protect her skin against the sun's fierce rays just far enough to look up into David's eyes. "I hear the thermometer reached one hundred degrees at noon today."

David smiled indulgently. The girl's unoriginal opening gambit to conversation was of the kind he'd heard half a dozen times since arriving in the North. In addition to being a young, handsome, charming, college-educated, ordained minister about to assume the pulpit of his own congregation, David Buttolph was unmarried.

Word of this highly desirable bachelor's arrival had spread like wildfire among available young ladies and their mothers. That the woman who became his wife would have to move hundreds of miles away to Georgia was a drawback, but a minor one. After all, David Buttolph had been born and bred in the North. He was one of them.

"Even in South Carolina temperatures this extreme are rare," David corrected the woman politely. "But our summers are indeed typically much hotter than those of Connecticut."

William came to his nephew's rescue. "We'd best head to the dock," he said. "We don't want to miss the steamboat to Middletown." William didn't say it was two hours until the boat left.

Kitty Mills raced over to William. Sarah and James Dickinson followed more slowly in the heat. "Weren't they wonderful, Grandfather?" Kitty exclaimed breathlessly, her eyes sparkling with excitement. "It was like magic – or a miracle!"

William nodded, thinking what an unpredictable being a ten-year-old girl was, on the cusp of childhood and womanhood. Kitty had agonized for half an hour this morning over which dress and bonnet to wear to the Independence Day festivities. She'd comported herself with lady-like reserve on the steamboat from Middletown.

But the novelty of the balloon launch had swept away Kitty's pretensions of maturity, turning her back into a little girl. Tomorrow William knew Kitty would again be the thrill-seeking tomboy, standing on the stone wall around the homelot, her arms outstretched, waiting for William to gallop by on his horse and scoop her up in his embrace, as he'd done with her mother so long ago.

"As soon as I get home I'm going to write down everything in a letter to Lyman," Kitty went on. "I'll wager he's never seen such a sight!" she declared, pleased at besting her big brother in something.

William, politely maintaining the fiction that they had a boat to catch, started walking northward along Main Street. Kitty, David, Sarah, and James followed.

"I feel bad Uncle David had to miss seeing the balloons," Kitty said. "He was telling me that someday people might travel by air, fly over mountains and rivers like birds! Imagine Father and Lyman floating from Cincinnati to Connecticut, instead of spending days on a smelly, noisy, bumpy train!" As if on cue, they heard the shrieking whistle of a train approaching Union Station about half a mile away.

William studied Kitty thoughtfully. He and Alma had worried when last fall Charles Mills decided to take Lyman, then twelve, when he and his new wife went to Cincinnati, where Charles had been assigned a pulpit. Lyman had been thrilled that his father wanted him along, even as he struggled with parting from the people who'd been his family for as long as he could remember.

The prospect of being separated from the brother to whom she'd grown close in the three years since Charles brought her to live with her grandparents upset Kitty. But William had detected no resentment that Charles wasn't taking her with him as well.

"Your Uncle David has more than enough to keep him busy without fantasies about flying," James Dickinson said wryly. David Lyman, eager to find another source of income besides farming their own land, had become an officer of the newly established Farmers' Milling Company. The firm planned to purchase grain from local farmers, grind it, and market it in large quantities. The company had sold shares of stock to raise money to build a grist mill on a stream about two miles from the Lyman house. Among the two dozen investors were David himself, William, and James.

The mill had to be completed by month's end to take advantage of the season's crop of Indian corn. When word had come yesterday afternoon of a problem at the site, David had decided to forego the junket to Hartford and work on resolving the difficulty.

"You'll have to describe everything to your Uncle David as well as to your brother," David Buttolph said to Kitty.

"And to Grandmother and Aunt Catherine," added Sarah. The idea of being the one to report such doings pleased Kitty greatly.

Neither Alma nor Catherine had accompanied them to Hartford. Two months earlier Catherine had presented David with their first son, named William for both grandfathers. Catherine was recovering from her third birth in fewer than four years. Alma had stayed home to help with the baby and to keep his sisters, Mary Elizabeth, three, and Harriet Augusta, twenty-two months, out of mischief.

As they came within sight of the gold dome of the State House at the head of State Street, which ran down to the steamboat wharves, William thought of how everyone in the family had enjoyed David Buttolph's week-long visit – and how relieved he would be when his nephew left tomorrow for Georgia. By tacit mutual agreement, there'd been no talk of slavery or politics in the Lyman house during David Buttolph's visit. Recent events had made this no easy feat.

At the end of May Congress had passed the Kansas-Nebraska Act. President Franklin Pierce signed the legislation repealing the Missouri Compromise of 1820, which had prohibited slavery above 36 degrees, 30 minutes north latitude. In its place was established the principle of "popular sovereignty," which left the decision about whether a territory would be admitted to the Union as a slave or free state up to its voters. At one stroke millions of western acres that would have been free states under the Missouri Compromise became potential slave states. The development horrified abolitionists.

William, unsure of how David Buttolph, after a decade in the deep South, felt about abolitionism, had erred on the side of caution. He'd sent word that no fugitives be sent to him during David's visit.

As they reached Central Row, which ran along the southern side of the State House, a commotion to the left drew everyone's attention. A respectably dressed, yet sweaty and disheveled fellow, surrounded by a knot of excited men, was struggling to make his way down Pearl Street to Main. He disappeared into the State House, reappearing a minute later between the massive pillars on the building's second-story portico facing the river.

William didn't recognize the man, who obviously had something urgent to report. William wondered uneasily if one of the balloons had met with an accident after disappearing from sight.

The man's face was flushed crimson with heat and exertion. He was sweating so profusely that his hair was as soaked as if he'd just gone for a swim. He slipped off his coat, then leaned on the black wrought iron railing surrounding the portico to catch his breath.

A curious crowd was gathering on the State House's eastern lawn, trampling grass already scorched brown by the heat. They speculated among themselves about this mysterious development until the man stood upright, indicating his readiness to speak.

Although hoarse with strain, the man's voice could be heard at the far reaches of the growing throng. "I've just come on the train from Framingham," he began.

William's stomach clenched. The Massachusetts Anti-Slavery Society was meeting that day in Framingham, outside of Boston.

"A gathering of abolitionists, more than two thousand, was held there today," the speaker continued. "William Lloyd Garrison addressed the group in a most provocative manner. He condemned Congress for passing the Kansas-Nebraska Act. He called our federal constitution 'a compact with the devil,' because it allows slavery."

William glanced around him, seeing reactions that ran the gamut from shock to anger to grim approval. He turned his attention back to the man on the portico.

"Mr. Garrison concluded his presentation by burning a copy of the federal constitution!" the speaker cried out. "I saw it myself!"

The crowd gasped in shock at this heinous insult to the sacred document. "As the flames consumed the paper," the man continued, "Mr. Garrison declared 'so perish all compromises with tyranny.'" He staggered back to lean against the brick wall of the building.

Consternation swept through the crowd. People broke into agitated, mostly angry, discussion of such an outrageous act. A few women wept in fear.

William felt sick to his stomach as he contemplated the calamitous implications of Garrison's fanatical act. But at the same time he understood the absolute commitment to freedom for all men and the frustration at recent events that had driven Garrison to it.

Kitty looked up at William, troubled. "Did this Mr. Garrison do something wrong, Grandfather?" she asked. But it was David Buttolph who answered her.

"William Lloyd Garrison committed an act of treason, for which he deserves to pay with his life," he said with cold fury.

William couldn't allow that statement to go unchallenged. Kitty was forgotten as he addressed his nephew.

"In his zeal Mr. Garrison perhaps exceeded the bounds of respectable public discourse," William acknowledged. He continued in an even voice, "But it's not treason to condemn a government that from its conception has perverted the principles of freedom upon which it was founded, and that continues to compound the original sin with acts that allow slavery to flourish and spread."

"If Garrison and his followers aren't traitors, then who is?" David said angrily. "I'm aware of your abolitionist sympathies, Uncle, and I've forborne to discuss them out of respect for you and for the sake of a harmonious visit with those with whom I share ties of blood and affection. But this latest sacrilege is intolerable!"

"And what would you call the recent misbegotten legislation by Congress?" William shot back irritably.

Sarah and James, who'd been standing a way off, quietly came up behind Kitty, who was on the verge of tears. Sarah put her arms comfortingly around Kitty's shoulders and gently pulled her several steps back from the arguing men, who'd completely forgotten her.

Noticing that the confrontation was drawing curious looks from people on the State House lawn, James shepherded William and David around the corner of the building's foundation. There their argument was less likely to attract attention.

"The North prostituted its principles and its conscience and its honor and its very soul when it accepted the Fugitive Slave Law,"

William went on, "with the understanding that this final, obscene appeasement would satisfy the South."

David broke in before William could continue. "The North has given nothing but lip service to compliance with the Fugitive Slave Law," he shot back scornfully. "If anything, the illegal theft of Southerners' rightful property has increased in the past four years."

William maintained an impassive expression, unsure if David knew or suspected his uncle assisted fugitive slaves. He continued as if his nephew had made no mention of the Underground Railroad.

"Not content to force Northerners to be accomplices in their sin, the South extorted this new legislation, breaking the agreement, however imperfect, that held slavery in check for more than thirty years. The South's hunger for power is insatiable!" William said.

William abruptly clamped his mouth shut, and looked away from his nephew. He was as close as he'd come to losing his temper since the day he'd learned of Charles's abandonment of Lizzy. He couldn't risk repeating that shameful behavior.

Sarah had stepped up to put a calming hand on William's arm. She was alarmed by his face, mottled with heat and anger. He was past seventy now, and she feared what the strain might do to him.

James stepped in to carry on William's point. "This thing they call 'popular sovereignty' might as correctly be called 'popular tyranny,'" he said to David. "If the people of a territory can vote to permit slavery within their borders when it becomes a state, why could not an existing state do the same? The South will never be content until they've made slavery legal throughout the land."

"That's not true, Cousin," David argued. "But the people of the South won't be fenced in. If they're restricted, their way of life will wither and die." William resisted saying that the demise of a society rooted in slavery was a thing greatly to be desired.

"Cousin, you can't deny that slavery permits and even condones the cruelest, most degrading treatment of those in bondage." Sarah said in a tone of reason.

David Buttolph's face grew even redder with anger at Sarah's observation. "I'm not surprised to find you've read that pack of lies written by our cousin Mrs. Stowe," he said, spitting out the name. Since its publication in book form in 1852, *Uncle Tom's Cabin* had sold more than half a million copies. Hattie had become an international celebrity – and was only slightly less reviled than Satan in the South.

"There are no doubt slaveowners who are cruel and abusive," David conceded quickly. "But there are husbands who are cruel and abusive – yet we don't outlaw marriage. The 'solution' would create far more evil than the problem."

When Sarah opened her mouth to speak David held up his hand to forestall her. He'd kept much pent-up during his visit to the North, and couldn't resist taking advantage of this opportunity to vent his views.

"You say slavery denies Negroes their humanity – I say it saves their immortal souls," David declared. "They're instructed in the tenets of Christianity, made aware of God's love, and shown the path to achieve eternal life. My own flock in Midway is known far and wide for their commitment to the religious education of their servants. Local slaveowners employ a minister to devote himself full-time to the salvation of the Negroes under their care."

David paused briefly to catch a breath of the hot, humid air. "The Holy Bible itself condones slavery," he went on. "The Apostle Paul said 'Servants, be obedient to them that are your masters according to the flesh, with fear and trembling, in singleness of your heart, as unto Christ.'" He at last fell silent, as if the Scripture quote had settled the question.

William was heartsick at the thought that from the Bible he'd given his nephew the young man had extracted such poisonous error. And at that moment he lost all hope that his beloved country could cleanse itself of the abomination of slavery without wholesale destruction and death.

David Lyman Buttolph was an intelligent, compassionate, gifted young man who'd received the finest education his country had to offer. He'd grown to manhood in New York and Massachusetts, states from which slavery had long been banished. His calling to God's work was unquestionably genuine, his faith sincere.

If such a man as his nephew could be seduced by slavery's siren song, William thought despairingly, what chance was there that Southern whites, born into a society based on the exploitation and dehumanization of Negroes – what they euphemistically called their "peculiar institution" – could be brought to see the error of their ways without violence? Thomas Jefferson's prophecy about slavery in America echoed in William's mind: "I tremble for my country when I reflect that God is just; that his justice cannot sleep forever."

Chapter One Hundred and Eleven

May, 1857
Middlefield

Alma, Sarah, and Catherine skeptically eyed the contraption David had just finished setting up in the kitchen. It consisted of a round wooden tub, about two feet high and two feet in diameter, mounted on a rectangular wooden base. From each end of the base projected at about a sixty-degree angle a thin, slightly curved slat of wood, about six feet long, that tapered to a point.

The tip of each slat was connected by a long, narrow spring to a wooden shaft centered over the tub. A wooden handle extended out from each side of the shaft about halfway down its three-foot length. The shaft terminated about a foot above the tub, in a flat, circular piece of wood. From that piece of wood were suspended, at regular intervals, sixteen pestle-like pieces of wood about six inches long. To Sarah they looked like the teats of some bizarre milk cow.

"How does it work?" Alma asked dubiously.

David stepped forward to demonstrate with the proud excitement of a child showing off a new toy.

"You fill the tub with hot water, then add the clothes and the soap," he began.

"Then you grasp the handles," he went on, gripping one of the handles in each hand, "and push down. This presses the wooden pestles onto the laundry, which pounds the dirt out of it." He proceeded to do as he described, the downward motion of the shaft causing the springs that connected its top to the slats to become tauter.

All three women stepped forward to peer down into the tub. "You see," David said, "that there's a strong spiral brass spring atop each of the pestles, which are compressed by depressing the shaft. This gives the downward thrust greater force, and together with the pull of the springs at the top of the pounder makes the shaft return to its original position with little effort on the user's part." He released his pressure on the shaft, and it rebounded to its original position, startling his mother, wife, and sister into hastily stepping back.

"With this machine you can do a week's worth of laundry with much less effort and in a far shorter time!" David exclaimed. He studied the three women's expressions with concealed anxiety – and was delighted to see their skepticism give way to dawning excitement as the contraption's potential became clear to them.

"It doesn't damage the clothing?" Alma asked.

David shook his head. "No more than a washboard," he said confidently. All three women were silent at the prospect of having one of the most detested household chores significantly lightened.

"Try it!" David urged. Sarah stepped forward and repeated David's motions. After several determined plunges of the shaft, she nodded her head at her mother and sister-in-law. "It certainly is an improvement over bending over a scrub board scraping clothes in hot soapy water with bare hands." Sarah studied her brother with keen appreciation. "If this machine lives up to your claims, housewives will erect a statue in your honor."

David grinned with pleasure, even as he held up his hands with palms outward to deflect the praise. "I had no hand in inventing this machine," he said. "The credit for that belongs to others far more ingenious than I. But I plan to establish a factory to produce them so that every woman in America can have one – for a reasonable price." He spoke rapidly with mounting excitement.

"It will be called the Metropolitan Manufacturing Company. I expect we'll begin producing them by summer's end, as soon as the factory buildings we purchased on the Beseck River can be outfitted properly."

Alma shook her head in bemusement. "Machines that sew clothes, machines that wash them – what will they think of next?" she said.

"A machine that dries them would be wonderful," Sarah replied, only half in jest. In her thirty-five years of life alone, there had been a succession of inventions that a short time ago would have been only figments of fantasy. "You just need to make the wind blow where and when you want it to," she said to David with a disingenuous brightness that made him laugh.

"We can't let our dirty laundry pile up while we wait for David's new company to start making machines," Alma said briskly. "I'll help you carry yours over here," she said to Sarah." I'll get Bridget to help, and we'll start right in." The two women left for Sarah's house.

David looked at Catherine. "You haven't said anything yet."

"I've listened to you describe it and looked at the drawings for months, yet it still seems a wonder to me," Catherine replied. "Can you truly make enough of them to succeed in business?"

David nodded. "Absolutely," he declared with the confidence that was key to his character. "It could be extremely profitable."

Catherine stepped closer to her husband. "Could we get one of your wonderful washing machines before the year is out?" she asked, then continued without giving him a chance to answer, "Five children produce a mountain of dirty laundry."

David at first looked puzzled, then his eyes widened with understanding. His expression became one composed of equal parts sheepishness, happiness, and concern.

"Again already?" he asked. It was Catherine's turn to nod and reply, in good-natured imitation of her husband, "Absolutely."

David pursed his lips and blew out silently, still slightly in shock. Their fourth child, Henry, had just marked his first birthday. Their eldest, Mary, wouldn't turn seven until December, by which time the new baby Catherine had just announced would have arrived. Five children in less than seven years.

They stood for a long moment in silence, looking into each other's eyes, their thoughts traveling the same path. After their wedding, David had discovered that Catherine was hesitant, almost timid, about intercourse – even as she yearned for the completion of their love it would bring. With tender persistence David had slowly helped her shed the awkwardness, the embarrassment, and the fear of the unknown, beneath which her carnal instincts lay waiting to be aroused, like seeds atop the soil waiting for winter's snows to melt so they could germinate.

It had been almost spring before Catherine at last achieved that for which they'd both yearned. David would never forget that fresh, moon-lit April night when for the first time his wife's entire body had quivered with uncontrolled ecstasy, nor how, once she could speak, she'd murmured breathlessly into his ear, "At last I'm fully yours."

After that David had given his ardor full reign. Sometimes when they came together, Catherine wrapped herself around him, as if their combined passion were a flash flood that threatened to sweep them away, and her only hope of surviving the surge was to hold tightly to David with perfect trust.

It had taken an entire year before Catherine conceived their first child. Since then they'd come in rapid succession. Each pregnancy had been easy, each delivery uncomplicated, each baby – two boys and two girls – healthy.

Catherine recovered her strength and energy with reasonable speed after each birth – which had led them to this newest development. After the first baby, David had waited for Catherine to approach him about resuming intercourse. When she did, David was uncertain whether she was doing so out of a sense of wifely duty. He'd half-heartedly suggested it might be wiser to wait longer. She had dismissed that idea with the teasing observation that it would be cruel for him to withhold the fruit that he'd taught her to savor.

David's lips turned up in a smile of contentment. He put his hands gently atop his wife's head, and stroked them down over her shining hair along each side of her face, stopping to hold her cheeks tenderly between them. He kissed her on the forehead, and then softly on the lips.

Catherine's revelation stoked David's determination to make a financial success out of this new manufacturing project. Catherine was just thirty; if their family continued to grow at this pace, he realized the dozen children he'd jokingly once spoken about to Lizzy was a distinct possibility.

David was adamant that his sons and daughters would never be forced to spend months away from home to earn a living as he and Elihu had done, or leave Connecticut altogether as his aunts and uncles had. He'd concluded that the farm alone, no matter how many acres or how skillfully cultivated, couldn't return sufficient income to ensure his children would escape a similar fate.

David intended to resolve this financial dilemma by seizing the golden opportunity presented by the combination of Yankee ingenuity with innovative manufacturing technology. With God's help, he would establish a profitable new industry that would not only secure the Lyman family's future, but benefit the people of Middlefield as well.

Chapter One Hundred and Twelve

January, 1863
Middletown

The sun shone with dazzling brightness in a vivid blue sky, but it had no effect on the brutal cold that had enveloped the Connecticut River valley for the past three days. William was relieved to reach the outskirts of the center of Middletown, for the clustered buildings acted as a buffer against the wind that had been slashing and howling since last night.

As he turned his horse onto Main Street, however, an icy blast struck him full in the face, and the shock momentarily stole his breath. He pulled the woolen muffler wrapped around his neck up to cover his mouth and nose for the brief remainder of his ride.

Main Street was relatively deserted on this first day of January, 1863, for anyone with a lick of common sense who didn't have a compelling reason to be outside was indoors close to a stove or fireplace. William began to think that perhaps making the long ride into Middletown on such a raw day had been an imprudent undertaking, as everyone had insisted. But around noon he'd been unable to stand the suspense any longer. He'd saddled up their strongest horse and set out for Middletown.

As he secured his mount's reins around the hitching post, William saw that his destination, the telegraph office, was filled with men. When he opened the door, the gust of wind that entered with him caused every man to turn around with a shiver.

William pulled the door closed quickly behind him. The small room was warm from the coal stove and the body heat of the crowd.

William unwound the muffler, took off his hat and gloves, and rubbed his hands together vigorously to get the blood circulating.

William thought of how many times over the past twenty months this office had been filled to overflowing with men and women awaiting the arrival, via the fastest method of communication possible, of news they alternately longed for or dreaded. William had been among their number more than once.

William had helped keep vigil after word spread on April 12 of 1861 that rebel forces had commenced bombarding the United States military post at Fort Sumter on an island in the harbor of Charleston, South Carolina, plunging the Union into civil war. He had grieved when news arrived of the fort's surrender two days later.

There had been a long stretch of days late this past July, when William had haunted the telegraph office, waiting for any scrap of news about the Vermont infantry regiment in which Charles Bliss had enlisted. The unit had been engaged in fierce fighting near Richmond, Virginia. Charles had corresponded regularly with his aunt and uncle since signing up. When weeks passed without a letter or message from him, they'd begun to fear the worst. Mercifully, Charles had come through the battle safe and whole.

William scanned the crowd for familiar faces. He spotted Jesse Baldwin and Samuel Griswold, two of the founders nearly twenty years earlier of the Middletown Anti-Slavery Society. Black faces scattered around the room included Leverett Beman, Isaac Truitt, and Amster Dingle, all residents of a tight-knit Negro neighborhood that had grown up not far from the Wesleyan University.

William spied the leonine profile of Benjamin Douglas. He edged through the crowd toward the smartly dressed factory owner.

"Has any news come across the wire?" William asked

"None," Douglas answered with the patient reserve that had made him so effective a conductor on the Underground Railroad. William nodded, and said nothing more as he removed his coat.

William had the greatest respect and admiration for Benjamin Douglas, who, in his mid-forties, was young enough to be William's son. He was a dramatically handsome man, with long, wavy black hair and a full, neatly trimmed beard and mustache, all streaked with gray. Craggy eyebrows jutted out over steel-gray eyes.

The youngest of eight children, Douglas had been just six years old when his father died. With just a smattering of schooling he'd indentured himself to a machinist when he was sixteen. Douglas and his brother had gone into business together in 1839, when

Douglas was twenty-three. Three years later the two had invented a revolving stand pump, which they'd made a fortune manufacturing at their factory in Middletown.

Douglas had also been, for as long as William had known him, a foe of slavery, which he loathed. Like William, he'd attacked the evil openly, for which he'd been stoned by an anti-abolitionist mob, and clandestinely as a conductor on the Underground Railroad.

Douglas had enjoyed success as a businessman and, despite his abolitionist principles, in politics, serving five years as mayor of Middletown. He'd been one of the first in Connecticut to join the new Republican Party, which had abolition as its core creed, and to which William and David Lyman also belonged. Douglas had just completed a term as lieutenant governor of Connecticut under Republican Governor William Buckingham.

Buckingham was one of the staunchest supporters of Republican Abraham Lincoln, whose election as president in 1860 had been the straw that broke the camel's back for Southerners. South Carolina had seceded from the Union in December of 1860, followed over the next five months by ten more Southern states.

Everyone gave a small start as the clacking of the telegraph key broke the silence. They waited breathlessly as the operator wrote down the short message. He clicked back a brief acknowledgement, then looked up. "President Lincoln signed the Emancipation Proclamation this afternoon at the White House," he said solemnly.

The reactions were mixed and intense. Many men cheered triumphantly, pounding each other on the back heartily. Others laughed in sheer delight. Some embraced. A few, William among them, were moved to quiet tears of joy and exultation.

Everyone fell silent when the telegraph key started clicking again. "The text of the proclamation will be sent later this evening," the operator reported.

A murmur ran through the crowd; the document's wording was of great interest. In his preliminary proclamation of September 22, 1862, President Lincoln had declared that on January 1, 1863, "all persons held as slaves within any States or designated part of a State the people whereof shall then be in rebellion against the United States shall be then, thenceforward, and forever free."

The January 1 proclamation would "designate the States and parts of States, if any, in which the people thereof, respectively, shall then be in rebellion against the United States." Just how powerful a blow the document would deal to slavery wouldn't be clear until it was known what areas were to be declared still in rebellion.

"The telegraph operator will send me a copy of the proclamation text as soon as it's received," Benjamin Douglas said to William. "I'd be gratified if you would join me at my house to await its arrival."

"I would be pleased," William replied.

Most of the men spilled out of the telegraph office and, hunched against the bitter cold, dispersed in all directions, headed for the welcome warmth of their home hearths. Beman, Truitt, and Dingle hurried together up Court Street, doubtless to deliver the great news to the members of the A.M.E. Zion Church.

William untethered his horse and led the animal along as he and Douglas strode briskly south on Main Street. They crossed to the opposite side which brought them in front of a handsome brick residence. It was the home of Brigadier General Joseph Mansfield, who had taken a fatal bullet through the lung four months earlier at the Battle of Antietam in Maryland.

"Joseph Mansfield wasn't the only man Middletown lost at Antietam," Douglas said. "I've learned that George Brown and Robert Hubbard also fell there. When the casualties from both Union and Rebel sides are tallied up, they're expected to amount to six thousand killed and seventeen thousand wounded on just that one day," he added grimly. "It's hard to believe."

"Have you seen Matthew Brady's photographs of the battlefield?" William asked. Douglas shook his head. "Corpses stacked like cordwood," William said tersely. "The slaughter must have been unimaginable."

"Yet Antietam was enough of a Union victory for Lincoln to issue the preliminary emancipation proclamation," Douglas reminded him. "Those who suffered and died there helped advance the cause of human freedom."

The walked in silence for a minute, and then William spoke. "Alma and I had long since accepted that blood would have to be shed to cleanse this land of slavery. But we didn't expect the awful cataclysm to happen in our lifetimes. After the Kansas-Nebraska Act was passed, events became like a giant snowball rolling downhill, growing larger and gathering speed, crushing everything in its path."

Following the Kansas-Nebraska Act, pro-slavery and anti-slavery supporters had poured into the Kansas Territory, each determined to control its destiny as a state. They'd set up rival, equally illegitimate, governments. Civil authority had proven impotent to enforce the law, and anarchy was the result.

Henry Ward Beecher had helped inflame the situation by declaring, "You might just as well read the Bible to buffaloes" as to the supporters of slavery. He advocated supplying fighters for a free Kansas with rifles that came to be popularly known as "Beecher's Bibles." Deadly clashes between the opposing factions had coined a new phrase: "Bloody Kansas," epitomized by the brutal murder of five pro-slavery men in the town of Osawatomie by a small band of abolitionists led by the fanatical John Brown.

The next blow had fallen in 1857, with an entirely unexpected decision by the United States Supreme Court on the case of a slave, Dred Scott, who had sued for his freedom. The Court decreed that Congress had no authority to prohibit slavery in territories, and then declared that Negroes, in the words of the chief justice, had "no rights that white men were bound to respect."

Late in 1859 the long-festering infection began to rapidly come to a head. John Brown led nineteen followers in an assault on the federal armory at Harper's Ferry, Virginia, with the irrational expectation of sparking an uprising of slaves who would be supplied with weapons from the armory. Seventeen lives had been lost before federal troops took Brown and his surviving followers into custody.

Brown was convicted of treason, and hanged on December 2, 1859. While the South considered him a traitor, many in the North elevated him to the status of a martyr.

When war had finally broken out in April of 1861, many exuberant Northerners had predicted the fighting would be over in ninety days. William knew differently, and soon those foolish optimists did as well. With the war dragging into its third year, there was no end in sight to the carnage.

William emerged from his musings to see they'd arrived at Douglas's house, a massive, two-story brick structure on a slight rise near the South Green. Douglas had renovated the originally plain building into a stylish home befitting a man of wealth and influence. A two-story entrance porch to the front was crowned by a triangular pediment. Each level of the porch was supported by two symmetrically arranged pairs of classic columns.

Douglas had remodeled the interior as well, including the installation of marble fireplaces, and furnished it lavishly in the most modern fashion. Here he lived with his wife of twenty-five years and their four sons.

Thirty minutes later William was comfortably settled into a plush armchair in Douglas's drawing room. The men were sipping fresh coffee served by a young Irish servant girl, who had turned up the gas lights in the room to their brightest, for darkness had fallen.

"I understand David's factory is a great success," Douglas observed. William nodded, setting his cup back onto its saucer before answering.

"It is," he confirmed. "The washing machines have sold extremely well from the beginning. Last year he added clothes wringers to his list of products, and they've proven equally popular."

Douglas nodded. "I purchased both a washing machine and a wringer for my household this autumn. My servant girls cannot sing their praises too highly," he said.

"Managing a manufacturing enterprise consumes nearly all of David's time, as I'm sure you understand," William said. "That's left running the farm almost entirely to me." He frowned uncertainly. "I don't know how much longer I can continue to do so. I'll mark my eightieth birthday this year. James helps, but he's near sixty himself, and his constitution has never been strong."

Douglas looked sharply at William, and did detect small signs that the years were beginning to take their toll on the old man. William had always been thin, but now, Douglas thought, he looked almost frail. There was the slightest bend in his characteristically ramrod-straight posture, and he moved more slowly as his joints stiffened with age. In previous conversations he'd mentioned a serious inflammation in one eye.

"What of your grandsons?" Douglas asked. "Lyman has reached his majority, hasn't he? And if there's one thing David doesn't lack, it's children. How many has his wife presented him with now – six?"

"Seven," William corrected him good-naturedly. "Lyman has joined his uncle in running the manufactory," he went on. "As for David's sons, William, the eldest, is but nine."

"Then you have no choice but to live to be ninety," Douglas said lightly. William's mouth twisted into a wry smile of skepticism.

Douglas's expression grew thoughtful as he sipped his coffee. "The Metropolitan Washing Machine Company has been a tremendous boon for Middlefield," he said. "But it can't reach its full potential until transportation is improved. The same problem retards my pump business. A railroad through the center of Connecticut, including Middlefield and Middletown, connecting to New York at one end and Boston at the other, would be a great advantage."

William said nothing, but he had little hope for the realization of Douglas's vision, which David shared. Plans to erect a railroad through Middletown and across the Connecticut River had been floating around for nearly twenty years, with little success. But this was not the occasion to puncture a seemingly impossible dream.

"I assume it's only a matter of time before Middlefield decides it must be a town unto itself," Douglas observed cagily. "Have you heard anything along those lines?"

William shrugged non-committally. For Middlefield to become a separate town would have an unknown, but unquestionably significant, impact on Middletown taxpayers like Douglas. It was, in fact, a topic of increasing discussion among Middlefield leaders, including David Lyman. "Middlefield people have been talking about setting upon on their own since I was a boy," was all William said.

Douglas started to reply, only to be interrupted by a sharp knock on the door. The servant girl hurried to open it, and took an envelope from a messenger. She brought it in to Douglas, who held the cold envelope for a moment before opening it and extracting the handwritten document.

William could barely contain his curiosity as Douglas scanned the paper. As his eyes reached the middle of the page there appeared on his face a smile that grew broader as he read on. When he was finished he looked up at William, his countenance glowing. "It's all we hoped for – and more!"

Unable to wait any longer, William stepped forward to take the document from his host's hands. He fumbled in his pocket for his reading glasses, put them on, and eagerly perused the short proclamation.

"He frees forever the slaves in all the states that have seceded, save for those parts of Louisiana and Virginia under control of the Union Army," William said approvingly, "and commits the power of the United States to defending their freedom. And–." William stopped to adjust his spectacles, so he could be absolutely sure of what he was reading. "He opens the door for Negroes to enlist in the armed services of the United States."

The power for good in this short document suddenly overwhelmed William. His hands began to tremble. Douglas quickly placed a steadying hand on the older man's shoulder.

"The chains struck from three million men, women, and children," William whispered wonderingly. "We have worked and waited more than thirty years for this moment. Praise God that He allowed me to live to see Him work this miracle."

Both men sat back down, feeling weak in the face of the enormity of what they had just learned.

"This is no longer a war for the sole purpose of preserving the Union," William said. "It's now a fight for human liberty. Its moral purpose will make powers such as Great Britain think twice before they offer recognition or assistance to the Confederacy."

Douglas roused his thoughts to focus his sharp mind on the next steps to be taken. "There's much more to be done," he said resolutely. "For the Emancipation Proclamation to become a reality the Union Army must conquer the states still in rebellion. And the Proclamation says nothing about freedom for the million slaves in border states such as Maryland and Kentucky. We must move heaven and earth to ensure their liberty as well," he said fervently.

"Not everyone will welcome this new goal," Douglas cautioned. "Since news of the impending proclamation was announced in September, I've heard rumblings from both civilians and men in uniform who resent this new purpose to the war. Some soldiers have written home from camp to complain that they enlisted to save the Union, not to free the Negroes," he said ominously.

Douglas's comment raised a troubling issue in both men's minds. Even before the proclamation, some in the North had bitterly pointed out that the abolitionists had agitated against slavery, but when the war broke out many of them let others do the fighting and dying. There was enough truth to the charge to make it sting.

Benjamin Douglas had worked hard to recruit volunteers for the Union Army. But none of his sons, the eldest of whom was now twenty-four, had enlisted. Neither had Lyman Mills, who had been twenty when the war broke out.

Lyman hadn't discussed with William whether to join the army. Since he was fast becoming his uncle's right-hand man in the running of the washing machine factory, William thought perhaps David required his nephew's assistance to ensure the continued operation of the business upon which dozens of local households depended for their livelihood. On top of those responsibilities, David had to be prepared to assume running the farm when William could no longer do so. Given his advanced age, that day couldn't be far off.

Ultimately, William had accepted that Lyman was a grown man who acted according to his conscience. He didn't owe his grandfather an explanation for the decisions he made.

"The proclamation has already ignited a fury in the South," William said, continuing Douglas's train of thought about negative reaction to the document. "It was denounced in September as a criminal act, as an infamous step calculated to incite slaves to at the very least flee their owners, at the worst to rape and kill them."

Douglas could guess at what was going through William's mind. "What news have you had of your nephew in Georgia?" he asked.

"Just smatterings and rumors," William replied glumly. David Buttolph had come north to New York in 1856 with his new bride to see his father, who'd written to William about the visit. David's marriage had made him joint owner with his wife and widowed mother-in-law of more than three dozen slaves, who, William was discouraged to learn, David continued to hold in bondage.

"I heard that toward the end of the year he relocated his family farther inland, away from the coast for their safety," William continued. "He moved his slaves as well, to make it more difficult for them to attempt a flight to freedom."

William was both angered and sorrowed that David Buttolph should embrace so tenaciously the evil of slavery. Yet he was still family, and William would never cease praying for his safety and that he be brought to see the error of his ways.

William sat his coffee cup on a table, and got stiffly to his feet. "I'm reluctant to leave your warm hospitality, but it's time for me to return home, to share this good news with my family."

William turned up the collar on his coat and wound the muffler around his neck before he opened the door of the Douglas house. Night had fallen while they waited. Thankfully the wind had died down, although the still air was bitterly cold.

William paused on the threshold. "I can't help but think of those who labored as faithfully as we, yet didn't live to rejoice in this sweet day of jubilee," he said to Douglas. "Marvin Thomas, to whom I will forever be indebted for opening my eyes to the need to fight slavery. Jehiel Beman, the son of a slave, who risked much more than we ever did when he helped found the Middletown Anti-Slavery Society and guided fugitives on their journey to liberty."

Douglas looked up, and from the countless sparkling points of light in the black night sky picked out the North Star, the beacon for thousands of runaway slaves seeking their freedom. "They know," he said, his voice thick with emotion. "They know."

Chapter One Hundred and Thirteen

April, 1864
Middlefield

On the site where, in 1785, David Lyman constructed a fine new house to shelter his expanding family and demonstrate his prosperity, the grandson who bore his name had done the same thing nearly eighty years later. But the handsome house in which the first David had taken such pride was a wren's cottage compared to the grand mansion that had risen in its place.

The ungainly washing machine David had demonstrated in the kitchen that day seven years ago had proven even more widely popular among the nation's housewives than he'd anticipated. The press had hailed it as a "great labor-saving device, destined to become a household blessing throughout the land." David and several business partners had developed the firm into an extremely successful manufacturing enterprise that marketed washing machines, as well as clothes wringers, throughout the Northeast and beyond. And David Lyman found himself, at just forty-four, a rich man.

With David and Catherine and their seven children, William and Alma, and, more often than not, Kitty and Lyman Mills, there was usually a baker's dozen of family members living in the house. Most of the time a couple of servant girls and hired farm laborers were also in residence.

David and William had initially attempted to deal with the crowding caused by David's growing family in 1859 by adding wings to the back and the south side of the original house. But as his family continued to expand, David had decided a new house was called for. William had concurred.

David considered building a new home somewhere else on the farm. But he was deeply attached to the rise on which the house in which he'd been born stood

It meant much to David that this site was part of the original parcel of land his great-grandfather John had purchased in 1741. He loved the view of the fields in all seasons. He enjoyed the proximity to James and Sarah's house. That arrangement had proven congenial for all involved in the fifteen years since William had built it for them.

But neither William nor David could bear to contemplate razing the house that had sheltered Lymans for more than seventy years. The solution had been to relocate the old building. It had been removed from its foundation, then dragged by oxen over logs that acted as rollers to a site half a mile to the west, close to the old Isaac Miller house.

David had engaged renowned architect Rufus G. Russell of New Haven to design a comfortable, spacious, fashionable, but not ostentatious dwelling that bespoke the success of its owner. The finished product was like nothing ever before seen in Middlefield.

David took a few minutes on the morning of this April day on which the family would move into the house to study the architectural masterpiece that now crowned the rise. He stood across the road, near the long-abandoned well that had belonged to the house Hope and John had purchased in 1741. The sun, about an hour above the horizon, felt pleasantly warm on his back, and reflected brightly off the new dwelling's fresh white paint.

Like the house it replaced, the new structure was two-and-a-half stories high, and five bays, or windows, across the front. It was built of clapboards painted white, with shutters at each window. But there any similarity between the old and the new ceased.

David had gotten an education in architectural terminology during the course of consulting with Rufus Russell on the design and construction of his new home. Russell had drawn upon the popular *Architecture of Country Houses,* published in 1850 by acclaimed architect Andrew Jackson Downing. He'd chosen to use primarily the Italian Villa style.

A single-story wooden portico ran the width of the house. It was supported by simple wooden pillars, and decorated with ornate trim cut with a scroll saw.

The eye was drawn upward to a gabled dormer that projected out through the roof of the top floor directly above the main entryway. A pair of round-arched windows was set in the center of the dormer, which also featured decorative wood trim.

The house was crowned at the ridgeline by a cupola, tall enough for a person to stand upright inside, with a bellcast roof. Each of the cupola's four sides featured a pair of round-arched windows from which beautiful views of the surrounding countryside could be enjoyed.

The total effect was a house that was grand but not overbearing, sophisticated but not excessively ornate. The interior was equally stylish.

David walked onto the portico, and turning the knob on the imposing front door, crossed the threshold into a spacious foyer which had a ten-foot-high ceiling, as did all the first-floor rooms. Straight ahead was a handsome, narrow staircase with turned spindles and a wide banister of polished dark wood that terminated in a conch-like curl. To the left was a hallway with a polished hardwood floor that ran the length of the new house, into the dining room, and then into the kitchen of the 1859 addition, which had been left intact when the original house was moved.

David stepped into the room to the immediate left. Sunshine flooded in through two east-facing sash windows, each eight feet tall and three feet wide with six-over-six panes of glass.

David ran his hand appreciatively over the cool, silk-smooth surface of the white marble mantelpiece and fireplace surround. Fashionable gas-light fixtures of iron had been installed in both the ceilings and walls. Looking upward, David admired the cornice moldings, fashioned in leafy grapevine patterns. The room managed to feel both cozy and spacious at the same time. The other three downstairs rooms were much the same, save for the northwest one, which had a bay window to serve as a reading nook.

The four bedrooms upstairs had lower ceilings, and were simpler in detail, save for the master bedroom, directly above where David stood, which also had a marble mantelpiece. More, smaller rooms were on the third floor, where a door gave access to the narrow, tightly spiraled staircase into the cupola. Taken together with the two wings added to the old house in 1859, which had been left in place and connected to the new structure, there was a total of twenty-four rooms in the house.

The house had cost the breath-taking sum of $18,000 to construct – as much as an ordinary laborer might earn in a lifetime. David – or rather, the females of the family – had spent an additional $11,000 on decorating and furnishing the home in the latest fashions.

Catherine had selected the furniture, with assistance from Sarah, whose European tour had refined her taste, and sometimes from Mary, Harriet, and Kitty. They'd chosen the popular "antique French" style, inspired by the royal French court of the 1700s.

The furniture featured lavish, intricate ornamental carving of handsome rosewood or mahogany, often in motifs drawn from nature, such as leaves and grapevines. Armchairs, settees, and sofas were upholstered in silk, brocade, or plush velvet in rich, vibrant yellows, oranges, and reds. Tables were topped with polished slabs of marble.

Most of the furnishings for the first-floor rooms had been purchased from one of the leading makers in New York. Brussells carpets covered the polished floors.

David climbed into the cupola to look out at the countryside, the new foliage emerging in many different shades of green. He allowed himself a brief moment of satisfaction at what he'd achieved.

It wasn't in his nature, however, to rest on his laurels. After a minute he clambered back down the staircase and headed outside to check on the status of several outbuildings under construction. These included a brick gashouse to supply the lamps in the residence, and a carriage house over which there would be a schoolroom where Kitty, now twenty, could teach her younger cousins.

As David was exiting the rear of the house, the rest of his family was arriving at the front with their belongings. William and Alma had been reluctant to leave the old house in which they'd lived as husband and wife for more than half a century. But David had persuaded them, arguing in part that the new house was as much William's as his. William's continued management of the farm, even as he passed his eightieth birthday, had freed David to pursue the manufacturing venture upon which he'd built his fortune.

Alma, Kitty, and Mary were directing the unloading and disposition of clothing, books, and dishes, and making sure the children kept at the task. William had gladly volunteered to keep an eye on his grandsons, three-year-old John and one-year-old James, while the transfer of possessions was underway. He stood with his arms crossed in the passageway connecting the new house to the rear addition, watching the brothers play contentedly, at least for the moment, with a cast-iron toy train David had bought for them.

Hearing footsteps behind him, William turned to see Catherine. He smiled warmly at his daughter-in-law, who he'd only just learned was four months pregnant with her eighth child.

"How do you like your new home?" Catherine asked.

William put on a doubtful face, pursed his lips in thought. "I fear it's too fancy a house for an old farmer."

Catherine laughed at his echo of their first conversation two decades ago. "I confess, I feel it's too grand for a simple innkeeper's daughter," she told William in a conspiratorial whisper.

"Nothing could be farther from the truth," William said with a sincerity that made Catherine blush. "A loyal, loving wife and mother deserves the finest things her husband can provide for her. Nobody knows that better than my son. You'll make this grand house a warm home."

"Thank you," Catherine managed to reply to this unexpected praise. She patted William affectionately on the arm and turned quickly to resume her work.

Chapter One Hundred and Fourteen

April, 1865
Middletown

William handed the stationery store owner several bills to pay for the new textbooks Kitty had requested. She was instructing ten-year-old William, nine-year-old Henry, and seven-year-old Charles in the classroom above the carriage house at the Lyman home.

"Have the shad started to run?" William asked the shopkeeper.

"I had my first of the season last night," the man replied contentedly.

"We should buy some while we're in town," William said to Alma. He was particularly fond of the dark, oily fish that could be enjoyed fresh only during the few weeks in the spring when they swam up the Connecticut River by the millions to spawn.

"So long as it's been boned," Alma replied. Shad's drawback for dining was the many needle-fine bones that had to be removed. It was so difficult that there were individuals who specialized in boning shad.

Alma gathered up the books, and husband and wife stepped out onto the sidewalk on the western side of Middletown's Main Street. "At least we can be sure there'll be a call for these books in the years to come," William observed wryly. Catherine and David now had eight children. The youngest, a girl named Adeline but nicknamed Addie, was seven months old. If the couple continued their pace, there would likely be two or three more, for Catherine was only thirty-eight. But as yet there were no indications of another baby on the way – at least so far as William and Alma knew.

"And Kitty will be sure of work as a teacher for another decade," Alma added.

"Do you think that's why David and Catherine continue having babies – to keep Kitty employed?" William asked with false naïveté. Alma shot him a look of good-natured exasperation .

The book purchase was the first of half a dozen errands – now increased by the stop to buy shad – that had brought them to Middletown on this Saturday morning, April 15, 1865. The day was cool, the sky overcast with slate-colored clouds that threatened to release a sudden shower. But William and Alma were awash in a sense of well-being that nothing short of a hurricane could have disturbed. At last, after four gruesome years, the war was over.

The extended Lyman family had suffered its share of sorrow. James Thrall, husband of Alfred Lyman's daughter Annis, had returned from the service to Connecticut on a disability discharge at the end of 1863. He'd died less than a month later, leaving his widow with several children, including a five-year-old. General William Tecumseh Sherman's march of deliberate devastation during the last two months of 1864, intended, as he proclaimed bluntly, "to make Georgia howl," boded ill for David Buttolph and his family. But their fate remained unknown.

William and Alma hadn't expected to live to see the war end. Long after it was evident the Confederacy had no hope of achieving victory, Southerners had continued to fight, seemingly willing to prolong the carnage indefinitely.

When the Confederacy could no longer recruit and support an army, it had been feared that small forces, supplied and concealed by the civilian population, might continue to carry out swift, bloody raids. These guerrilla bands could target Union troops, Union sympathizers, and free Negroes. They might even strike into the North, as Confederate General John Morgan had done in a daring raid deep into Ohio in 1863. The war would be transformed into a blood-feud, passed down from one generation to the next.

In the address at his second inauguration the previous month, President Abraham Lincoln had reminded people that God had given "to both North and South this terrible war as the woe due to those by whom the offense came," the offense being slavery. Lincoln had expressed his fervent hope that the war would soon end, but had also acknowledged it might be God's will for it to rage "until all the wealth piled by the bondmen in two hundred and fifty years of unrequited toil shall be sunk, and until every drop of blood drawn with the lash shall be paid by another drawn with the sword."

But the events of early April had offered hope that God might deem the deaths of upwards of half a million soldiers and an unknown number of civilians, the wounds and diseases suffered by countless others, the devastation of much of the South, and the misery inflicted by the war upon almost every person on either side of the conflict, to be sufficient atonement. The Confederate capital of Richmond, Virginia, had fallen to the Union Army on April 2. One week later, Confederate General Robert E. Lee had surrendered his army to Union General Ulysses Grant at Appomattox Court House in Virginia. There was strong reason to believe that the conflict wouldn't continue on in endless skirmishing and suffering.

The news had flashed across the continent – the war was over, the Union had been preserved. The three million slaves liberated in principle by the Emancipation Proclamation were now free in fact. Everyone was sure that it was only a matter of time until those in the border states were emancipated as well.

Alma and William had gotten their usual early start on the day. It was only a few minutes past eight o'clock as they strolled down Main Street, past a series of impressive buildings that included the McDonough House hotel, the brownstone custom house, the Congregational meetinghouse, the brick Baptist church, and the court house with its massive pillars. The streets bustled with vehicles and pedestrians.

"Tomorrow will be an Easter like no other," William said happily to Alma. "Distributing the elements of communion on this first Sabbath of peace in four years will be the most meaningful of any of the times I've done it in my decades as a deacon."

Off to their right, a bell suddenly began to ring. "It's the workers' bell at the Douglas Pump Company," William told Alma. Benjamin Douglas's factory stood at the corner of Broad and Williams streets, a block west of Main.

Puzzled, William pulled out his pocket watch. It read 8:22 – not a regular time for a factory bell. The ringing continued with frantic urgency. Maybe there was an emergency, William thought, possibly an accident on the production floor, or perhaps a fire – although no smoke was visible rising from behind the buildings on Main Street.

William and Alma walked faster, then turned right onto Williams Street, as did many other people, some already abroad, others emerging curiously from their homes or shops. William forced himself to keep pace with the slower Alma.

The ringing stopped abruptly, then after a long silence started up again – now tolling mournfully. They were nearing the pump factory when William saw something that made his blood run ice-cold. The American flags Douglas flew proudly at his place of business began to slowly descend, then stopped halfway down on their poles.

Alma clutched William's arm at the sight of the flags flying at half-staff. Neither could imagine what calamity could account for this. All William could think was that, impossible as it seemed, perhaps the surrendered Confederacy had somehow treacherously resumed fighting.

A crowd of curious, agitated men and women had collected six deep around the door to the factory's office. As William and Alma approached its fringe, they began to catch words and phrases – "the President." "Lincoln." "At the theater." And then "dead." "Assassin."

William stopped in his tracks, suddenly not wanting to know whatever terrible news awaited. He felt like a child who believes if he ignores something unpleasant it doesn't exist.

The crowd fell silent as Benjamin Douglas appeared at the door. His face was ashen, his eyes were red and swollen from weeping. He composed himself with obvious effort, then began to speak in a voice that threatened to break and crack at each syllable.

"News has been received by telegraph, and confirmed, that President Abraham Lincoln died earlier this morning in Washington. He was murdered by an assassin who has not yet been caught."

For a moment it appeared Douglas would say more, but he dropped his head and waved his hand in a vague gesture of dismissal before retreating into his office. The crowd became a chaos of intense emotions – fury, fear, sorrow, panic, disbelief.

Alma felt as if a black pall had suddenly been draped over her mind. She looked up at William, whose head was bowed, eyes closed, teeth clenched, and features twisted in anguished grief. Tears began to course down his cheeks. She leaned her head against his trembling shoulder and began to weep as well, as the bell continued to toll for Lincoln the president, the emancipator, the peacemaker – and now the martyr.

Chapter One Hundred and Fifteen

July, 1867
Hartford

"A nefarious purpose cowers behind this railroad's request for permission to build a drawbridge across the Connecticut River at Middletown," warned the orator standing at his desk in the Connecticut House of Representatives. "David Lyman intends this bridge to be an obstacle to navigation that will prevent most vessels from proceeding up to Hartford. If his plan is approved, Middletown will replace Hartford as the northernmost point ships can reach on the Connecticut. Middletown will steal from Hartford the maritime commerce that for centuries has been its lifeblood!"

The ridiculous accusation caused David to shift slightly in annoyance in his aisle seat in the last row of the House chamber's visitors' section. But he had to endure Representative William Eaton's bombastic slander in silence. David wasn't a member of the House and thus not entitled to enter into its debates.

Joseph Coe of Middletown was a member, however, and with an agility remarkable for a man of eighty rose from behind his desk to defend David. "The gentleman from Hartford misrepresents Mr. Lyman's intention," Coe countered firmly.

Eaton scoffed at Coe's objection. "The massive piers to be built in the river to support the bridge will be a major hazard to steamboats and sailing vessels alike, particularly in darkness or in bad weather, and especially in winter when ice builds up around them. Many vessels will be too large to pass through the opening when the bridge is drawn up. The loss of river traffic to Hartford will cripple one of the state's great cities!"

Legislators and spectators alike glanced at David to gauge his reaction to the exchange. David was president of the newly chartered New Haven, Middletown, and Willimantic Railroad. The company sought to build a rail line first proposed by others more than twenty years earlier and bitterly opposed for much of that time.

The rail line would consist of fifty miles of track that would run through more than a dozen towns, including Middlefield and Middletown. The line would cut across the state in a diagonal so direct it had been nicknamed the "Air Line" railroad. At its terminal points the Air Line would connect with existing railroads to New York and Boston. Towns along the route would have greatly improved rail access to larger markets for their products – such as washing machines and wringers.

Lyman Mills, seated next to David, was impressed by his uncle's ability to maintain an impassive expression under such scrutiny, much of it hostile. David was forty-six years old, and for the first time in his life actually looked his age – by design.

David had decided his naturally youthful appearance would be a disadvantage in his new role as president of a major transportation enterprise. In preparation for negotiating with investors, contractors, and politicians, he'd grown a beard and mustache. While a few strands of gray had appeared in his straight brown hair, which had begun to recede slightly after he turned forty, everyone had been surprised when his full beard and mustache came in completely silver. The facial hair, which he kept neatly trimmed, had the desired effect of making him look much more mature.

Representative William Minor of Stamford, another advocate of expanded rail service, spoke without bothering to rise from his seat. "Mr. Eaton is mistaken. The purpose of this bridge is to carry the railroad over the Connecticut River. There is no sinister motive behind Mr. Lyman's proposal," he finished with obvious impatience.

"My duty is to the people I represent," thundered back Eaton. "To that end I must urge this body to reject this infamous design for severely damaging the immense business interests involved in the navigation of the river to accommodate minor railroad interests — nay, in this case, nonexistent, chimerical interests."

David couldn't suppress an exasperated sigh. He got to his feet and quietly pushed open one of the enormous doors to the House chamber. Lyman Mills hesitated, as many heads turned to watch his uncle's departure, then followed David out of the room.

David stood for a moment in the center of the large, high-ceilinged space that separated the House chamber from that of the Senate. It had gleaming wood floors, white plastered walls, and finely detailed woodwork. Three enormous Palladian windows that extended from the floor almost to the ceiling opened on hinges to allow access to the small second-story balcony on the eastern side of the State House.

David stepped out onto the balcony. After several hours in the hot, stuffy House chamber, its air hazy with cigar smoke, he was tempted to remove his coat. But that might subtly convey an air of fatigue or even defeat to anyone who saw him, which was to be avoided at any cost. He contented himself with unbuttoning his coat of rich black cloth and slightly loosening his wide black cravat.

David placed a palm flat against one of the massive brownstone columns that supported the portico's roof and leaned stiff-armed against it. He glanced around at the sound of a door opening, and saw Lyman Mills joining him on the balcony. David hadn't realized his nephew had followed him out of the House chamber, although he should have expected it.

Lyman Mills, now twenty-six, was more like a son or a much younger brother to David than a nephew. He and Kitty had lived on a more or less permanent basis with William and Alma since Lizzy's death. Charles Mills had never summoned Lyman and Kitty to live with him permanently. He'd been content to leave them with his late wife's parents, arranging for them to make sporadic visits of different lengths.

Charles's behavior toward his son and daughter could have devastated Lyman and Kitty. Their salvation had been the warm, unconditional, understanding love of William and Alma, aided by James and Sarah and David and Catherine.

David wished Lizzy could have seen what a fine young man her son had become. He was handsome, with a grave demeanor better suited to someone much older. He wore a beard even fuller than his Uncle David's – and, of course, much darker. He was intelligent, and able, and utterly devoted to his mother's family. And soon, presumably, he would have a family of his own; last June he'd wed Jane Andrews of New Britain.

During the past year, as railroad matters had increasingly occupied his time and attention, David had entrusted more and more responsibility for running the washing machine company to

Lyman. His nephew had shown himself to be a most effective, efficient manager, upon whom David could rely completely.

"I know how the vote will go," David said by way of explaining his departure from the House chamber. "I don't need to watch the casting of ballots against it, like stones thrown at a mad dog."

"But they approved the charter for the railroad yesterday," Lyman said optimistically.

David snorted scornfully. "Only because they know the charter is worthless without permission to build the drawbridge," he said. "The suspension bridge at the Narrows that the charter authorizes is prohibitively expensive. And it would be two miles down the river from the center of traffic and commerce."

David stepped away from the column and locking his fingers together leaned on his wrists against the waist-high black wrought-iron fence that ran around the balcony. "You need look no further than that," he gestured straight ahead with his chin, "to realize the enormous power of our opponents. The State House was built seventy years ago facing the river, with State Street running from it in a straight shot down to the water, almost as if in homage. Many a fortune has been built and still rests upon the activity of the steamboats, sailing ships, barges, and fishing boats you see crowding the river before us. Many thousands of people work on those vessels, on the wharves, in the warehouses, or in the stores that sell the goods they bring in." David heaved a sigh of frustration.

"The slightest suggestion that something might alter this system is enough to frighten anyone who depends upon the river, wealthy and working man alike," David continued. "Mr. Eaton knows that when the Middletown drawbridge is opened the largest vessels will be able to pass through, but rather than convince his constituents of this truth he instead lies to block the bridge and appease their fears."

The doors of the House chamber suddenly flew open, and men poured out. Several were in a hurry – probably reporters for one of the three daily newspapers published in Hartford or for the one in Middletown, anxious to file their stories. David remained quietly on the balcony until they disappeared down the wide staircase to the ground floor of the State House.

The expressions of his supporters and opponents alike confirmed David's assumption that the bridge had been defeated. He straightened up, squared his shoulders, pulled down the points of his black vest to straighten it, adjusted his black cravat, and buttoned his coat. His posture bespoke a near-martial self-discipline.

David opened the door into the space separating the chambers, and without hesitation walked over to William Eaton. He held out his hand in a gesture of good sportsmanship.

Immensely pleased with himself, Eaton shook the offered hand. He exuded the condescending air of one who could afford to be magnanimous in victory. But David Lyman's demeanor disturbed him, for he didn't appear properly chastened by his defeat.

"How long will you persist in this hopeless case?" Eaton asked. His attitude was a combination of scorn and pity for a man who wouldn't realize when he was beaten.

David broke into a broad grin of delight, as if Eaton's words had reminded him of the location of a valuable treasure. "Until the end of my life," he replied confidently, "which I have reason to believe will be a very long one, since both my parents are past eighty and still with us. Then I will leave it as a legacy to my remotest descendants, whose numbers should be more than sufficient for the task, as my wife last month presented me with my ninth child."

Eaton's startled expression crusted into a scowl, for there was no bluff or bravado in David's declaration. The man was completely serious.

Eaton knew David Lyman had spearheaded the successful effort last year to separate Middlefield from Middletown and have it incorporated as a separate town. Lyman would be back, Eaton realized with annoyance and dismay, and he would have to be prepared to deal with him.

Chapter One Hundred and Sixteen

January, 1869
Middlefield

William's eyelids fluttered open, and he found himself staring up at the ceiling of his bedroom. He blinked rapidly to bring his vision into focus. Then he gazed around the room, at first uncomprehendingly, then with a puzzled expression.

At last Alma's face came into his field of vision. William managed a smile that, although faint, was the one he kept for her alone. He saw not her wrinkles, her graying hair, or the jowls she'd developed with age, but recognized in her still-bright blue eyes the forthright young woman who had captured his heart, and for whose love he'd made himself a better man.

"Wife, I did not last night expect to see you again," he said in a weak, bemused voice. "I thought the river should be between us. But the boatman did not come."

Alma immediately understood his meaning. Their favorite Sunday school hymn was "Waiting by the River," a joyous song of anticipation of crossing the Jordan River to Paradise on the other shore.

"The lung plaster Sarah applied to my chest last night has given me some relief," William observed just as David appeared in the door to check on his father's condition before deciding whether to go to the railroad office today. "Perhaps I'll get well after all," he said.

Alma and David looked at each other, allowing themselves some guarded hope. When William had marked his eighty-fifth birthday in August, he was still taking a role in supervising the farm. But as the year had progressed, he'd increasingly had the sense that his time on earth was winding down.

Still, William had been in reasonably good health until the past Sunday night, three days ago, when symptoms of weakness, chest pain, and difficulty of breathing had come on suddenly. Dr. Rufus Mathewson had diagnosed it as fever in the right lung, dangerous to an individual of any age, but extremely so for an "old man," as William cheerfully insisted upon referring to himself. The physician had ordered William confined to bed.

That Sunday night William had felt so unwell he doubted he would survive until dawn. Since then his condition had swung from one extreme to the other.

Tuesday morning William was much improved, greeting David with the wry observation that, "I am here yet!" He had briefly enjoyed visits from his littlest grandchildren and inquired about affairs at the barn. But before the day was out it became evident that his left lung had become affected as well.

Despite that worrisome new development, William had spent Wednesday comfortably. But in the middle of the previous night his breathing had become rapid and shallow, giving cause to fear the worst. Again, he'd predicted he might not live to see the dawn. Yet the morning had brought improvement.

"Are you more comfortable, Father?" David asked, crossing the room to the bed.

"As comfortable as a man can be in this world," William answered good-naturedly.

"Sarah will be up shortly with some porridge and brandy," David reported. It had taken considerable persuading to get William to take the dose of brandy prescribed by Dr. Mathewson, for the old temperance crusader was highly skeptical that there were any genuine health benefits to be obtained from alcoholic beverages. However, the brandy had indeed seemed to ease some of his symptoms, and so he no longer resisted taking it, although his conscience was still clearly not at ease.

"I'll try to come back at dinnertime to see how you're faring," David said, then started for the door. "If you need anything, don't hesitate to have me summoned," he said firmly. A moment later they heard his footsteps rapidly descending the stairs.

"Is Sarah all right?" William asked Alma.

"Yes," she replied. William's prediction that he wouldn't survive the night had so upset Sarah she had broken down crying.

"What I told her was true," William went on. "Death has no terrors for me. I feel as if I had done nothing in my life to offend."

William was speaking for Alma's benefit, even though he knew there was no need. Since his sickness had come upon him, they had prayed together at length, for her, for their children and grandchildren, and for their church. He had assured her his worldly affairs were settled, that she would have no worries once he was gone. He took great comfort in knowing she would have David and Sarah to depend upon.

Neither had felt the need to make a final declaration of love and devotion. Sixty-two years as husband wife, weathering life's tempests and celebrating its joys together, had forged a bond deeper than any words could express.

William drifted back to sleep, and Alma resumed reading her Bible. Around noon Sarah came quietly into the sickroom carrying a tray with a bowl of porridge and a small glass of brandy. Alma looked up from her Bible and smiled wearily.

William stirred at the sound of Sarah setting the tray on the bedside table. Sarah hesitated, unsure whether to let her father continue to sleep. But William opened his eyes and looked up at her.

"I brought porridge and brandy, Father," Sarah said. "Would you like some?" Encouraged by William's nod, Sarah continued to talk as she bent over the tray to stir the porridge to cool it enough to eat. "We want you to take all the nourishment you can," she said encouragingly.

"Yes," William agreed, "I rode and walked so far this morning I need a good meal."

Sarah abruptly stopped stirring. She glanced over at her father to see if he was joking. His expression was vaguely thoughtful. She looked uneasily at her mother, who seemed as baffled as Sarah.

Before either woman could say something, William spoke again. "Andrew, be sure to saddle Captain right after breakfast," he said. Sarah and Alma turned to stare at him. "I'll be riding over to call on Alma Coe. I want to take her to see David's grand new house," he went on.

Alarmed at this irrational rambling, Sarah looked to her mother. Alma was studying William with a tremulous, bittersweet smile.

Sarah sent a messenger to David, who arrived half an hour later. Coming hastily up the stairs, he encountered Sarah on the landing. "Catherine said Father has taken a turn for the worse," he said anxiously.

"His brain is now affected," Sarah confirmed.

"He's not raving," Sarah quickly assured her horrified brother. "He seems to think he's in the old house, and he wanders in his mind from one time to another, speaking affectionately of people long gone and times past."

"How is Mother?" David asked.

"She's wonderfully calm. I finally persuaded her to eat a little something, but she refuses to leave Father's side for even a few moments of rest."

David nodded somberly, and, after taking a deep breath, walked into the room. Alma was holding William's hand, listening attentively as he rambled, not entirely coherently, about Christmas, about his cousin Lyman Beecher, now six years dead, and about fishing with Elihu.

David squatted down beside his mother. "It cannot be long now before the boatman comes to carry him across the river," she said, sad but resigned.

David took her free hand in his and looked up into her eyes. "You must get some rest yourself," he insisted gently. "I'll sit with him while you sleep. I promise I will summon you if there is the slightest change in his condition."

Alma wanted to protest, but she was weary to the point of collapse. She allowed David to help her to her feet, and Sarah led her into an adjacent bedroom.

Twenty-four hours later the family still maintained their vigil. William had fallen into a stupor. Twice he'd roused into brief moments of lucidity, during which it was clear he understood the gravity of his condition.

Early on Friday morning William had lapsed into unconsciousness. Dr. Mathewson had stopped briefly and confirmed what everyone already knew, that William was on his death bed.

Alma had resumed her post at William's side, holding his bony, now gnarled hand firmly between hers. The sun was about to sink below the horizon on Friday, January 29, when, a peaceful expression on his face, William Lyman's great heart stopped beating.

Chapter One Hundred and Seventeen

January, 1871
Middlefield

The piercing shriek of the engine's whistle broke David's concentration on the New Haven newspaper he was reading. Peering out the coach window, he saw the train was rolling through Reed's Gap. The engineer had blown the whistle to warn anyone at the Wallingford Road crossing of the train's approach.

From his vest pocket David drew a heavy gold watch. He snapped it open and saw approvingly that the train was right on schedule. He closed the timepiece and tucked it back into place. He folded his newspaper, then sat back to study the passing countryside that, even in its dormant drabness under the slate-gray sky of an early January day, seemed incomparably beautiful to him.

Suddenly a chill that had nothing to do with the frigid winter weather shook David's body. The fit lasted for perhaps half a minute before subsiding.

The train chugged over a stone trestle that spanned Reed's Gap Road on the final leg of the trip to Middlefield. David scanned the horizon until he spotted the cupolas of his house and barn, two beacons welcoming a very weary traveler home.

The train began to slow as it approached the Middlefield depot, then with a great hissing of steam, lurched to a stop. David got to his feet and buttoned up his heavy coat. Toting a large valise, he stepped onto the platform of the brand-new depot that had been built to handle both passengers and freight shipments on the New Haven, Middletown, and Willimantic Railroad.

True to his promise to William Eaton, David in 1868 had succeeded in securing government approval to build the drawbridge that was critical to the railroad's success. Construction of the part of the line from New Haven to Middletown had been completed the previous year. It had required the labor of a thousand men to do the job. Many were immigrants from Ireland, several dozen of whom had settled in Middlefield.

The sight of Lyman Mills at the far end of the platform was a welcome surprise for David. He'd planned to walk the short distance from the depot to his nephew's house, and borrow a horse to ride the half mile home. But the fatigue that had dogged him for the past week had turned into an exhaustion so deep that the prospect of a walk to Lyman's house had become daunting. All of David's muscles ached, and the valise felt like it was filled with lead instead of clothing and business papers.

Approaching Lyman from behind, David saw he was supervising the unloading of crates from a box car. Lyman turned to give directions to a laborer, and spied David.

"Uncle David!" Lyman cried in surprise. "I didn't know you were arriving today. Welcome home."

Lyman still wasn't entirely accustomed to his uncle's newest look. David had allowed his beard, now snow-white, as was his hair, to grow out long and bushy, until it extended half-way down his chest. It was a style favored in the past few years by such powerful national figures as Secretary of the Navy Gideon Welles and Secretary of War Edwin Stanton.

The beard gave David a patriarchal look he considered desirable for a man who owned an expansive farm, and headed both a thriving manufacturing company and a railroad. But it also made him appear far older than his fifty years. His frenetic, non-stop work schedule had caused him to lose considerable weight and etched deep lines of fatigue into his gaunt face. And Lyman observed with unease that his uncle's skin had an unhealthy pallor. He might have been mistaken for a man of three score and ten.

"I was able to leave Pittsburgh a day earlier than I had planned," David said simply. "More rubber?" he asked, gesturing toward the crates.

Lyman nodded. "Enough to make five thousand rollers. When the train passes through on the return run this evening we'll load five hundred washing machines and as many wringers. It's so much more efficient and less expensive than carting supplies and products to and from a depot in Wallingford or Meriden," Lyman declared. "I finished preparing a preliminary report for you this morning. Last year the factory produced twelve thousand washing machines and forty thousand wringers."

"Well done, Nephew!" David said approvingly, flashing a smile. "You certainly have one of the finest heads for business I've ever encountered."

Lyman beamed at the praise. Since David had assumed the presidency of the railroad, he'd paid little attention to the affairs of the washing machine company. Management of the factories had been left to Lyman Mills. Although still a month shy of his thirtieth birthday, Lyman had proven himself perfectly suited to the challenge of supervising all aspects of an enterprise that employed more than one hundred workers. In that regard Lizzy's son reminded David of himself at the same age, a capable, determined young man who could be safely entrusted to see through to successful completion the most daunting of duties.

"My meetings with the officers of the Keystone Bridge Company in Pittsburgh were very encouraging," David said. "They gave me every reason to hope the drawbridge can be finished by the middle of next year. With God's blessing the entire line from New Haven to Boston should be open by the end of 1872, and we'll be able to ship machines from Boston as well as New York. There will be no limit on how large the enterprise can become." David's eyes glowed at the prospect of his two visions, the washing machine factory and the railroad, converging to such mutual benefit and tremendous success.

Lyman Mills's carriage rolled up the driveway of David's house. Night was falling rapidly, and the mellow glow of the gas lights inside the house was a comforting sight.

David got stiffly out of the vehicle, then stepped up onto the portico. He glanced across the road to check on the activity at the new barn. Two farmhands were bringing in hay to feed the cattle, after which they would milk them for the last time of the day.

Built just four years ago, the barn was a gigantic structure, with a central block three stories high and two wings each two stories high. It represented David's enduring commitment, no matter how many diverse enterprises he might undertake, to the land that his family had called home for one hundred and thirty years.

David thought as he often did of his father, gone two years now, who'd worked the farm for so many decades. Although everyone missed William, the peaceful passing of a man who'd accomplished so much good in his more than eighty years on earth had seemed as much a reason for giving thanks as for mourning.

David had retained Rufus Russell, the architect for his house, to design the barn. They'd worked closely together to develop a plan that would be the most practical, efficient, and economical. The completed structure had been so remarkable an innovation that the *American Agriculturist* newspaper had run a lengthy article on it.

David stepped inside his house, pulling the heavy door closed behind him. A large gas ceiling fixture bathed the foyer in soft light. With a great sigh of relief David let the valise drop from his hand. It hit the floor with a loud thud.

Overhead David heard feminine footsteps hurry from the front of the house toward the staircase. Mary, who had seen the carriage arrive from the windows at the front of the upstairs hall, came into view, leaning over the banister to make sure who had arrived.

"Father!" she cried happily, then descended the stairs so excitedly David feared for a moment she might trip on her long skirt. She wrapped him in a bear hug that brought a smile to his face.

At twenty, Mary was almost as tall as her father. She had her grandfather Lyman's lanky frame, and his sharp features that could appear severe on a woman's face. But she also had straight golden hair and soft gray eyes that reminded David of his grandmother Sarah.

Mary released David, who slowly removed his topcoat. She took it from him, then mischievously called upstairs and into the rooms on either side of the staircase, "Everyone, come greet our guest." David smiled sheepishly at what had become an ongoing joke in the family ever since his railroad responsibilities had required him to be frequently away from home for days or weeks at a time.

A moment later there came the clatter of heavy feet on the back stairs, and Charles Elihu, thirteen, appeared in the hallway. "How nice of you to pay us a visit, sir," he said with mock formality, approaching his father and extending his hand in greeting. "I regret I did not catch your name. You are–?"

David answered his son's sauciness by batting the proffered hand aside affectionately. Charles broke into a grin.

Catherine came hurrying down the hallway from the kitchen. Her face was alight with joyous anticipation that dimmed as she got close enough to perceive David's pallor and exhaustion. "A most welcome guest indeed," she said as cheerfully as she could, playing along with the children. "Will you be joining us for dinner, sir?"

"I accept your gracious invitation," David replied. "And I would very much like to spend the night – or perhaps the week. That is, if you have a bed available."

"I think we might have something you would find comfortable," Catherine replied with a smile, her contentment at the prospect of having her husband home outweighing for the moment her concern over his wan appearance. Unable to play-act any longer, she put her arms around David's neck, kissed him, and then hugged him tight. His arms rose up to embrace her. He closed his eyes and rested his head on her shoulder, a smile of pure bliss illuminating his face.

The door from the back porch into the kitchen flew open, and in rushed a tangle of arms and legs that quickly separated out into four children: John, ten; James, eight; Adeline, called Addie, six; and David, three.

Catherine and David hastily separated. The youngsters surrounded their father in noisy, exuberant welcome. After a moment they were followed into the house by an exasperated Kitty Mills, and eighteen-year-old Harriet.

"I apologize, Uncle David," began Kitty, blushing with embarrassment. "Once they realized you were home, there was no keeping them in their seats."

"No apology is necessary," David assured her. "I guess school is out for today. Where's Mother?" he asked Catherine, a look of concern crossing his face as he noticed Alma's absence.

"She's visiting Sarah and James," Catherine assured him.

"And William and Henry?" David asked.

"They returned to the Agricultural School in Amherst the day before yesterday," Catherine replied. "They delayed their departure as long as they could in hopes of seeing you, but at last they had to go or be late for the start of the term."

David nodded slowly in disappointed resignation. "Well, most present, and all accounted for," he said resolutely. "I would like to rest up a little. Call me when supper is ready. Charles, would you please bring my valise up to my room?"

Charles grabbed the leather handles and bounded up the stairs two at a time. David followed, each of the fifteen steps requiring a great effort.

It was approaching ten o'clock by the time Catherine found time to spend alone with David. She located him, as she knew she would, in the southeast front room, sorting through documents at the desk originally owned by his grandfather that had descended to him upon William's death.

Although he heard his wife approach David didn't immediately turn around. Catherine placed a hand on his forehead as she would with one of the children. He looked up, startled, then smiled at her gesture of maternal concern.

Catherine frowned at him worriedly. "How long have you had a fever?" she asked, removing her hand.

"Two days – perhaps three," David acknowledged. "A week here at home with you will restore me, as it always does."

Catherine balled her hands into fists and placed them on her hips, arms akimbo, in a no-nonsense stance. "One week may serve to clear up your fever, but it won't begin to provide you with the rest you need," she said, sitting down in the chair next to him. She took his hand in hers and looking earnestly into his eyes. "David, I'm afraid for you. You drive yourself mercilessly. You wouldn't work a mule with such cruelty. I implore you, take some time to rest, to recover your strength."

David shook his head as he patted Catherine's hand reassuringly, even as he sighed inwardly. This was an old bone of contention between them.

"Catherine, I can't afford to coddle myself," he began. "Thousands of people depend upon me. The city governments of Middletown and New Haven have invested more than $2 million in the railroad project. Hundreds of men rely upon their jobs constructing and maintaining the railroad to feed their families. Dozens of communities along the route, Middlefield among them, will prosper as never before when this railroad becomes a reality, or will remain stagnant if it doesn't. I can't let my personal ease and comfort prevent me from fulfilling my responsibilities to them."

Catherine stared at David, opened her mouth to protest, then thought better of it. Arguing with him on this subject would accomplish as much as talking to a stone, she thought resignedly.

"I haven't had the chance to tell you how much better you look than when I left," David said, eager to change the subject.

Catherine nodded. "The sudden spells of light-headedness have stopped, and the headaches aren't as frequent as they had been. But I still tire easily."

Whatever other problems his frequent lengthy absences from home had caused, they had at least helped speed Catherine's recovery of her health, thought David. God had blessed them with six sons and three daughters, all healthy and thriving – and all born within a span of just seventeen years. The repeated pregnancies, births, and periods of nursing, coming so close together they seemed to combine into a seamless whole, had finally proven too much of a drain on even Catherine's robust constitution.

After little David's birth in 1867, the doctor had warned that for Catherine to bear another baby anytime soon might leave her an invalid, even endanger her life. They had reluctantly accepted the necessity of suspending intercourse until her body could fully recover. David's increase in travel had reduced significantly the moments of temptation they both found so difficult to resist. At times they had succumbed, but so far there'd been no consequences – a minor miracle considering how easily Catherine conceived.

Catherine's recovery was taking far longer than anyone had expected. Bouts of influenza had twice set her back on the road to health. Small tasks often left her exhausted. Then she had begun to experience headaches, usually during David's absences, which were so agonizing that sleep was impossible.

For a time Catherine had no appetite, and had lost an alarming amount of weight. She had gained nearly all of it back, which accounted for her healthier appearance. But she was improving so slowly, and seemed so vulnerable to any setbacks, that they'd begun to consider the dismaying prospect that they'd have to abstain from intercourse until Catherine experienced a woman's "change of life," which, given that she was only forty-four, could be quite a few years.

"When will you come home to stay?" Catherine cried out suddenly, startling David. "When you are gone my heart is heavy as a stone, and yet it aches constantly. I feel every day the absence of your counsel and advice about the children God has entrusted to our care. You're becoming a stranger to your sons and daughters."

Upset by her pain and stung by her contention that he was shirking his duty as a father, David reached out to gather Catherine in close, her face half-buried against his chest. "Please try to understand," he began. "Never in my life have I failed to fulfill a commitment. Building this railroad is the work God has appointed me to do. He will give me the power to do His bidding. I must see it through to completion. But once it's finished, I promise you I'll remain at home contentedly with you and the children." Catherine remained still and silent.

"Do you believe me?" David asked.

Catherine nodded like an obedient child, but didn't look up. She knew he meant every word. But she feared the railroad was becoming David's Lorelei, luring him to his doom.

"I find it hard to believe I ever had a baby this small," Catherine whispered wonderingly, studying the sleeping infant in her sister Harriet's arms. She touched the tiny, perfect fingers, stroked the baby's soft cheek.

Catherine sat back down in her chair in the southeast parlor. A coal stove set up in the room and vented through the fireplace took the chill off the January night.

Catherine gave her little sister a warm, almost maternal smile. "I'm so glad you decided to come tonight, Hattie." Sixteen months ago Harriet Lavinia Hart, younger than Catherine by eleven years, had become the third wife of Middlefield's pastor, the Reverend Andrew Denison. Their first child, little Catherine Mabel Denison, had been born on December 8. This was Hattie's first venture out of the house with her new baby.

Andrew Denison breathed in deeply, closing his eyes the better to savor the mouth-watering aroma from the kitchen. "Your cook makes the best pork roast I've ever tasted," he said, opening his eyes.

"I know it's your favorite," Catherine said. "And David has several fine wines for you to choose from." David had adhered to temperance principles out of respect for his father, but since William's death he'd put in a supply of high-quality alcoholic beverages, mostly for his guests.

"Where is that brother-in-law of mine?" Denison demanded in mock impatience. "I haven't seen him since he got back last week."

As if on cue David appeared in the doorway. Catherine's greeting died in her throat when she saw his overcoat over his arm.

"Hattie, Andrew, please accept my apology," David said. "I won't be able to join you for supper tonight. I've been summoned to an emergency meeting about the railroad in Middletown."

"David, you mustn't," Catherine protested, getting quickly to her feet. "The fever left you just yesterday. Can't one meeting take place without you?"

David shook his head ruefully as he slipped his arms into his overcoat.

"Andrew, would you try to talk some sense into him," the agitated Catherine pleaded with her brother-in-law.

Ordinarily Denison would have refrained from being drawn into a disagreement between husband and wife, even among members of his own family. But he found David's pallor and the dark, heavy bags under his eyes worrisome.

"David, everyone knows you're the last man on earth who would shirk his duty in favor of personal ease or comfort," Denison began. "But exhaustion is written all over your face. The night is raw and cold and damp. I implore you to remain here with us in the warmth and affection of your home and family. Nourish your body, your mind, and your soul. Surely one meeting more or less can't affect the ultimate success of your enterprise."

David smiled, mulling over his response to Andrew's words, even as he pulled on his leather gloves. "Your concern is much appreciated. But what would you say, Andrew, if I were to encourage you to remain home on Sunday morning with the argument that one Sabbath sermon more or less can't possibly make a difference in your crusade to save souls? You would chide me, remind me that when you accepted the Lord's call to the ministry, you committed yourself to doing everything within your power to shepherd your congregation along the narrow, rocky path to salvation.

"I believe the Lord has made building this railroad my calling," David continued, with something like a crusader's fervor. "Its success or failure is no trivial matter. It can improve tens of thousands of lives. It will invigorate local industry, it will bring us closer together as a people and as a nation. It will open up opportunities for improving our hearts and minds. Just as you wouldn't neglect any part of your duty, neither can I."

Denison turned to Catherine and shrugged, holding his hands out to the side, palms up, in a posture of surrender. "You know better than anyone that when David's will is set on a goal, it would be as easy to change the course of a river, as to turn him from it."

David finished buttoning up his coat. "I beg you not to let unnecessary fretting spoil your evening," he said. "I have a constitution of iron."

He took a step toward Catherine, who was holding herself rigidly, half in anger, half in genuine concern. He leaned over to kiss his wife on the cheek. "Don't wait up for me."

Chapter One Hundred and Eighteen

January, 1871
Middlefield

"Typhoid."

It had taken Dr. Rufus Matthewson no time at all to make his diagnosis. The patient's symptoms were classic for the disease: fever, headache, acute tenderness in the intestinal area, diarrhea, lethargy, and exhaustion so extreme he had difficulty lifting his head.

"Unquestionably aggravated by overwork," Dr. Matthewson added sternly, staring down at his patient, whose face was the color of cold ashes. The physician spoke so severely that even David, who typically dismissed most ailments as annoying inconveniences to be ignored and endured until they ran their course, looked chastened.

"I'll leave some medicine, and directions for a diet to follow," the doctor went on. "But complete rest is essential if there's to be any hope of recovery. I know just how tall an order that will be to fill," he said in response to Catherine's expression of dismay. Dr. Matthewson had been the Lyman family's physician for enough years to know of David's relentless pace.

Dr. Matthewson glanced at David, then back at Catherine. "Tie him down, hide his clothes, lock the door – do whatever it takes to keep him in bed." There wasn't a trace of levity in his voice. "Otherwise I won't answer for his life."

"You're almost out of the woods," Dr. Matthewson announced on a morning just five days later. David was emaciated following nearly a week of intestinal inflammation that had made it difficult to eat and of diarrhea that flushed any food he could keep down through his digestive system before it could do him much good. But his eyes were clear and bright, the dullness of fever gone. The headache had left him as well as the bone-deep exhaustion, although he was still very weak. Once the abdominal symptoms had eased, he'd slept two days straight.

Catherine wouldn't have believed it possible, but David had obediently remained abed the entire time. With Sarah's help she'd even managed to keep him from doing any paperwork, and had barred any visitors but family. Clearly the severity of his illness and Dr. Matthewson's forbidding warning had brought David to his senses concerning his health, for which she fervently thanked God.

"A few more days of rest and you should be able to chance getting up and about," Dr. Matthewson said. "Once you regain the flesh you've lost, you can consider returning to work. Last I looked, the railroad was still there."

That night, Catherine was sleeping soundly in the room adjoining the bedroom into which she'd moved during David's illness. But a mother's innate sensitivity to the slightest indication of a child's distress brought her immediately awake. She sat up in the darkness, and listened carefully.

Catherine realized the sound that had roused her had come from David. It was the first night in a week that it had been thought unnecessary to have someone sit watch by his bedside.

Catherine threw aside the bedclothes and stood up. She walked toward the door between the two rooms, which she'd purposely left slightly ajar before retiring. As she placed her hand on the knob to pull it open, David exploded into a hoarse cough that sounded as if it had been torn from deep in his lungs. Alarmed, she turned up the gas light on the wall and hurried over to him.

David was on his side, propped up on one elbow, the other hand clutching his ribs in pain. He was sweating profusely, and his face was hotter with fever than it had been with typhoid.

James Dickinson's attention was caught by the sparkling dot in the eastern sky that was the planet Jupiter, outshining the brightest star. Somewhere in the house he heard a clock chime twelve times, signaling the beginning of a new day, January 24.

Dr. Matthewson had left an hour earlier, having been summoned frantically after David's new symptoms appeared. The physician had diagnosed lung fever, left two different medications, and promised to return late the next morning.

The uproar caused by this fresh crisis had finally receded, and James had volunteered to sit with David through the remainder of the night. The gas fixture on the wall was turned up enough for him to barely make out the words of the book he was reading.

James's attention was distracted from the sky outside the window by a change in David's breathing, a distinctive raspiness. He saw that David was awake.

"A little stimulant might help ease that congestion," James suggested. He picked up the decanter of red wine that stood on the marble top of a table next to the bed. He removed the stopper, and tipped the lip of the decanter over a small wine glass.

"No," James heard David say, in reference to what he didn't know. He filled the glass half full with wine.

"No," David repeated. "A dying man needs no stimulant."

James's hand jerked, spilling wine on the table. He hastily set the decanter down and turned to stare at his brother-in-law's face in the grayness of the lowered gas lights.

"Death is upon me," David said in the matter-of-fact tone he might have used to announce he was walking over to the barn to check on the dairy cattle.

When he recovered from his shock, James opened his mouth to protest. David forestalled him with a wave of his hand and a shake of his head. "I am mortally ill," he said. "Bolster me up, give me a pencil and paper, and summon my family."

Catherine and Sarah hurried into the room to find David propped up on four pillows James had put behind his back before leaving to get them. He was writing on a pad of paper.

Catherine hastened over and peered anxiously at her husband. She appeared relieved to find him alert. "James said–," she began, but stopped when David reached out and took her hand firmly in his.

"I am dying, Catherine," he said simply.

"That's not true!" Catherine cried, half in anger, half in fear. "This is some delusion brought on by the fever. Dr. Mathewson will be able to prescribe something to banish it."

Catherine started to straighten up, but David tightened his grip on her hand. "Do not trouble that good man any more on my account," he said firmly. "My hours left on earth are few, and I have too much to do to waste precious time denying it." Catherine stared at him, unable to accept this nightmarish turn of events.

"Send word to William and Henry to come home at once," David said. With that Catherine knew he truly believed he was dying. David would never call his sons away from their studies except for the direst of reasons.

David held Catherine's hand until she nodded in agreement. Then he turned his gaze to James. "I need to speak with Lyman."

One of Lyman Mills's earliest clear memories was of the day the terrible news came to their house in Ashland of his Uncle Husa's death. Just seven years old, Lyman had hidden behind a door, and sobbed as if his heart would break.

Three years later, when his grandfather had told him of his mother's death, Lyman had again sought privacy, this time in the garret of the old house. There he could cry until he had no more tears without worrying that he was adding to his beloved grandparents' already intolerable grief.

Lyman wanted nothing more in the world than to be alone to grapple with this fresh tragedy. But he was no longer a child. Lyman knew his Uncle James wouldn't exaggerate, that if he said his Uncle David was dying it must be true. He'd dressed hastily and arrived at his uncle's house a half hour after James had left to summon him.

Lyman thought he'd steeled himself for the scene that awaited him. But the sight of David, looking so small and frail and powerless in the bed, pushed him to the brink of tears. He stopped at the threshold to the sickroom to regain control of his emotions before walking over to the bed. Catherine was sitting on a chair beside it.

David managed a weak smile for Lyman. "Please tell your good wife I apologize for calling you away from your family in the middle of the night," he said. "But some things cannot wait until morning." Lyman could only nod in response.

"Your Uncle James informed you of my condition?" David asked. Again Lyman nodded. "I wish there were more time to prepare you," David continued, "but that is beyond my control. Nephew, I commit my family and my worldly interests to your care after I am gone."

Lyman was as stunned as if someone had dropped an anvil on his head. He looked at Catherine, but his aunt's face was a mask, as if she were trapped in a terrible dream.

"I know I'm asking much," David went on, studying his nephew with sympathy. "But I count it one of God's greatest blessings that I have a kinsman such as you to whom I can commit all that is dear to me. I have complete confidence in your affection, your honesty, your dedication, and your ability. Will you accept this sacred trust?"

"Of course, Uncle," Lyman managed to say. David smiled in relieved gratitude.

"I will put down on paper as much useful information as I can to help you," David said. His voice was becoming strained; he was finding it difficult to summon the energy to talk.

"I would like to speak with my wife in private," David said in a voice barely above a whisper. Lyman, James, and Sarah rose and left the room.

"I'm losing my power of speech," David said to Catherine when they were alone, "and there are things I must say to you before it is gone altogether." His heart ached at the torment on her face.

"Your guest must leave you yet again, to answer the summons from on high that cannot be put off," David said gently. "This separation will be longer than any we have so far endured. But we believe – we know – that we will be reunited to spend eternity together, in the company of all the dear ones who have gone ahead of us."

David was abruptly seized with a gagging, wheezing cough that left him gasping for air. With obvious effort, he forced the next words out. "Until that day, place your trust in Him who cares for the widow and the orphan. Of all the blessings God has showered upon me, I thank Him most for giving me you to be my loving companion."

Catherine's composure finally crumbled, and she burst into tears. David reached out to draw her to him. She lay her head on his bony chest and sobbed convulsively.

As David stroked his wife's hair tenderly, he suddenly found himself fighting back tears of his own, tears of regret for all he wouldn't live to see or do. He'd expected to grow old with Catherine, watching their children mature into fine men and women. He had planned to make improvements to the washing machine company, to pursue ways to make the farm more productive, to oversee the completion of the drawbridge and ultimately the entire railroad line.

With a fierce effort of will David forced those thoughts away. There was no point in sorrowing over the fate that was certainly God's will. He allowed himself a moment to make sure he'd regained control, then said to Catherine, "I would like to see my mother."

At nearly four score and five years of age, Alma had long since come to expect death to be a frequent visitor to her world, carrying off relatives, old friends, and acquaintances. But she'd never again expected to be called upon to endure that most terrible of sacrifices, the death of a child. It had been twenty years since Lizzy's death, and she'd thought herself safe at least from that particular agony.

As she approached David's bed, Alma could tell that the hand of death was indeed upon him. His voice was failing fast, but he managed to say "Mother" clearly.

Alma stroked her gnarled hand tenderly across David's damp brow. In her heart she saw not the emaciated, prematurely aged man on his deathbed, but the precious baby whose birth had so delighted his brother Phineas.

"Good bye, my son," Alma said. "I don't understand how it is that you should be taken and I left," she cried out in pained bewilderment. Then her features relaxed into a faint, calm smile. "But I shall join you soon," she added with a mother's reassurance that touched David's heart.

"Good-bye, Father," was all Mary could manage to say. His voice entirely gone now, David had resorted to writing brief notes of paternal affection on his note pad to each of the girls – Mary, Harriet, Addie, and Kitty, who was like a daughter – who'd come in together to bid him farewell. The three older ones were weeping, stunned by this seemingly impossible turn in their young lives. Six-year-old Addie realized that her father was once more leaving, but didn't understand the concept of death.

"It's time to go, Addie," Mary said, picking up her little sister and starting for the door. Addie twisted around in Mary's arms so suddenly and with such force that Mary nearly lost her balance.

Addie looked back expectantly at her father. Understanding, David pressed his right palm to his lips, then lay it flat in front of his mouth and "blew" the kiss to Addie, as he always did when leaving for a trip. Addie gently patted her right cheek where the "kiss" landed. She was smiling as Mary carried her from the room.

A minute later Charles, James, John, and David came in and approached David's bed hesitantly. Charles was distraught, wishing desperately that his elder brothers would arrive, still hoping a miracle would pull his father back from the brink of death.

David studied them with immense pride and deep sadness. They were all fine boys, for which so much of the credit had to go to Catherine, William, Alma, Sarah, and James. He had no doubt they would grow into splendid young men, who would honor and care for their mother. He realized with a sudden pang that little David probably would have no memories of him.

On the pad of paper David wrote "William? Henry?" Sarah read the words. "They telegraphed that they'll be on the very next train," she reassured her brother.

David nodded. He knew the older boys were unlikely to arrive from Massachusetts in time for him to see them one last time. He thoughtfully studied his four youngest sons, then wrote something else on the paper. With a trembling hand he carefully tore off the sheet and handed it to Charles.

Charles read aloud in a shaking voice, "Don't let a Lyman boy ever do a dishonest act.' We won't, Father," he managed to whisper, looking at David through a blur of tears.

The approaching dawn stained the eastern sky a vibrant pink. David had bidden farewell to all he loved, save for Henry and William. The whistle of the morning train kindled a faint expectant light in David's eyes, until he remembered that they wouldn't be on this one.

Lyman, who held in his hands a sheaf of pages upon which David had written instructions and advice about everything from his personal finances to railroad contacts to his funeral to the spring planting, watched incredulously as his uncle began to write yet another message. For the six hours since he'd become aware of the mortal nature of his illness, David had worked without pause. He'd dealt with his imminent death with the same relentless commitment and sense of responsibility he'd brought to every major challenge in his life.

"Don't you want to rest for a bit, Uncle David?" Lyman asked. David shook his head. "Want to die in the harness," he scrawled on the paper, which he tipped at a slight angle so that Catherine, Lyman, James, Sarah, and Alma could all read it.

David moved his hand down on the paper and began to compose another message. Suddenly his grip on the pencil loosened, and it fell from his lifeless fingers.

Epilogue

David Lyman was laid to rest in the Middlefield Cemetery. Lyman Mills spent fifteen years administering his uncle's estate, which was appraised at the equivalent of more than $5 million in modern dollars. Lyman Mills also managed the Metropolitan Washing Machine Company.

The railroad bridge over the Connecticut River that David Lyman had fought for so doggedly was finished in 1872. The Air Line Railroad between New Haven and Willimantic opened in 1873.

Alma Lyman survived David by four years. She crossed the river to join William in 1875, at the age of eighty-nine.

Catherine Lyman never re-married. She died in 1894, on her sixty-eighth birthday.

David and Catherine's sons Henry and John, and their daughter Addie, all died of illness in young adulthood. In 1878 their son William, an avid sportsman, started a firm to manufacture an improved gun sight he'd invented. It became a globally known company and was a major Middlefield employer for more than a century.

William Lyman died in 1896, at the age of forty-two. The ever-dependable Lyman Mills assumed operation of the Lyman Gun Sight Corporation. Lyman Mills went on to serve as lieutenant governor of Connecticut. He died in 1929 at the age of eighty-seven.

James Lyman graduated from Yale's Sheffield Scientific School in 1883, and became an electrical engineer in Illinois. He had one child, a son. James Lyman died in 1934 at the age of seventy-two.

David Lyman, Jr., graduated from the Sheffield Scientific School in 1889. He spent most of his life in Europe, dying in Switzerland in 1929 at the age of sixty-one.

David and Catherine's daughter Mary Elizabeth never married. She studied art and became an accomplished painter. Following

James Dickinson's death in 1884, Mary lived with her Aunt Sarah in the house William Lyman had built for her. Sarah Dickinson, the last of William and Alma's children, died in 1913, at the age of eighty-nine.

Mary Elizabeth Lyman lived in the Dickinson house after Sarah Dickinson's death. She was the longest-lived of David and Catherine's children, dying in 1938 at the age of eighty-eight. Their daughter Hattie died unmarried in 1927, at the age of seventy-five.

Kitty Mills married Elias Forsyth in 1876. They lived for many years in Indiana, eventually moving to Skaneateles, New York. Kitty had one child, a daughter named Elizabeth Lyman Forsyth. Kitty died in 1917 at the age of 73. Her daughter never married.

It was David and Catherine's son Charles Elihu Lyman, an 1886 graduate of the Massachusetts Agricultural School, who guided the Middlefield farm into the twentieth century. Charles Elihu expanded the farm, until by 1915 it included more than fourteen hundred acres. He introduced peaches as a crop; eventually more than five hundred acres of the Lyman farm were planted with peach trees, yielding as many as thirty-thousand baskets of fruit in a year.

Disaster struck the peach business during the winter of 1917-18. Temperatures that dropped as low as thirty-two degrees below zero killed all the trees. Charles Elihu replanted his orchards with apples, a hardier fruit than peaches.

Charles Elihu Lyman died in 1923, at the age of sixty-five. He left the farm to his six children. Management of the farm was taken over by John Lyman, the youngest of Charles Elihu's three sons and a Yale graduate.

In 1949 Charles Elihu Lyman's six children incorporated the farming operation as the Lyman Farm, Inc. which remains the controlling agency. John Lyman, Sr., was elected the first president of the Lyman Farm, Inc.

John Lyman, Sr.'s, son, John, Jr., known as Jack, served in the United States Army, then graduated from Yale in 1950. The day after commencement he was back helping his father run the farm, which now comprised more than eight hundred acres. Six thousand apple trees, forty-two hundred peach trees, and three hundred and fifty pear trees were under cultivation, with a herd of more than two hundred dairy cattle. In 1968 Jack took over the position of president of the Lyman Farm, Inc., from his father.

Farms were rapidly disappearing from Connecticut during the latter half of the twentieth century. The Lyman family was able to continue working the land by converting some of their acres into supplemental activities.

The cattle operation was phased out, and much of the pastureland was converted into two eighteen-hole golf courses. One designed by Robert Trent Jones opened in 1969, the second designed by Gary Player, opened in 1994. In 2012 the Golf Center and Apple Nine course, a learning and practice facility, opened.

The farm expanded its retail operation with the completion of construction in 1972 of the Apple Barrel store. The store proved so popular it had to be expanded in 1990 to nearly thirteen thousand square feet. The farm also established a wholesale pie operation in 1996.

John Lyman, Sr., died in 1982, at the age of eighty-six. His grandson, John Lyman, III, a graduate of Colby College, had joined the family operation in 1980.

Jack Lyman retired from the farm in the late 1990s. John Lyman III, Hope and John Lyman's great-great-great-great-great-grandson, is executive vice president of the Lyman Farm, Inc. Members of the next generation of Lymans, the ninth, are working for the company today.

The 1864 Lyman homestead is listed on the National Register of Historic Places. In 2000, after more than one hundred and thirty years as a home, it was made available for special event rentals, including weddings, corporate events, and meetings. The house David Lyman built in 1785 still stands. It is owned privately by a descendant.

Today the Lyman Farm, Inc. is an agricultural/recreational complex of approximately eleven hundred acres, three hundred and fifty of them devoted to growing fruit for pick-your-own, retail and wholesale, and use in Lyman products. As it marks its 275th year in 2016, the Lyman Farm is recognized as the twelfth oldest family-owned business in America. More than half a million people visit annually.

More about the modern Lyman Orchards operation can be found at www.lymanorchards.com.

Acknowledgements

More people than I can possibly name have contributed over the years in many and varied ways, large and small, to making this novel a reality. I'm tremendously grateful for the support, guidance, encouragement, suggestions, and advice each has provided.

I owe special thanks to:

Members of the Lyman family, especially

Dorothy Lyman Waller

Mike Waller

Dr. Margaret Lyman

Jack Lyman

John Lyman, III

The Lyman Farm, Inc.

Elizabeth Abbe

Nancy Smith

Jack A. McCain, Jr.

Diane Dahlke

Dione Longley

Diane Bray

Heather Schroder of Compass Talent

Leslie Wells of Leslie Wells Editorial

And my parents, Sarah Jane Ross and Louis Ross, Jr.,

for their unconditional love and support.

Institutions with important collections of documents include:

The Middlesex County Historical Society, Middletown, Connecticut

The Connecticut Historical Society, Hartford, Connecticut

The Connecticut State Library, Hartford, Connecticut

Made in the USA
Columbia, SC
12 May 2018